Pointers To Profession

An Astrological Exposition

Science of Light

Pointers To Profession

An Astrological Exposition

MRIDULA TRIVEDI
T.P.Trivedi • R. Asthana

Motilal Banarasi Dass

Second Revised Edition: Delhi, ***2016***

ISBN: 978-81-208-4076-8

MOTILAL BANARSIDASS
41 U.A. Bungalow Road, Jawahar Nagar, Delhi 110 007
8 Mahalaxmi Chamber, 22 Bhulabhai Desai Road, Mumbai 400 026
203 Royapettah High Road, Mylapore, Chennai 600 004
236, 9th Main III Block, Jayanagar, Bengaluru 560 011
8 Camac Street, Kolkata 700 017
Ashok Rajpath, Patna 800 004
Chowk, Varanasi 221 001

MLBD Cataloging-in-Publication Data
SCIENCE OF LIGHT – 1
POINTERS TO PROFESSION
An Astrological Exposition
MRIDULA TRIVEDI
T.P. TRIVEDI, R. ASTHANA
in *Science of Light Series*
ISBN : 978-81-208-4076-8

Printed in India
by Replika Press, India,
and published by Motilal Banarsidass Publishers (P) Ltd,
www.mlbd.com • mlbd@mlbd.com

Dedicated to our loving son-in-law

Rahul

whose simplicity and modesty, cheerful and acquiescent attitude, amenable and amiable disposition, cooperative and accommodating demeanor has always touched our heart.

May Goddess bless him with eternal bliss and all-round accomplishment.

Foreword

The authors who have been working in the field of astrology for over three decades have come up with books on almost all important topics of astrology. The present work on profession carries the fruit of their labour of years of the study and practice of astrology on the subject. Though there are some very good books covering the subject of profession, the present volume is different in that it deals exclusively with and is almost exhaustive in its treatment of the subject.

As all students of astrology know, the 10th house is the house of vocational life. But it is not limited to this house but entails a careful and deep study of several other houses and astrological factors which the authors have successfully identified and explored in their professional life as astrologers and which they place before the astrology enthusiast.

One's career and finance are intricately linked which none can dispute. Keeping this in mind , the authors have included houses related to finance in their examination of vocational choices. At the same time, no less important are the running Dasas and Bhuktis as also the transits of Saturn. The degree of vocational success is dependent on the 9th house or Bhagyastana as also Yogas which have been lucidly dealt with in these pages. The authors quote extensively from the classical works in support of their contentions making for an authoritative work on the subject.

It is hoped that the authors' research studies will explore further this subject in all its ramifications of specialization which is the trend today.

I wish the authors greater success in their efforts to share their understanding of astrology with the interested.

Bangalore

July 22, 2016

Gayatri Devi Vasudev

Editor: MODERN ASTROLOGY

या श्रीः स्वयं सुकृतिनां भवनेष्वलक्ष्मीः
पापात्मनां कृतधियां हृदयेषु बुद्धिः ।
श्रद्धा सतां कुलजनप्रभवस्य लज्जा
तां त्वां नताः स्म परिपालय देवि! विश्वम् ।।

We bow to Goddess Durga, who lives as Lakshmi with pious souls, as poverty with sinners, as intelligence in the heart of clear hearted, as devotion in holy people and as shyness in virtuous persons. May Goddess nurture the whole world.

Preface

'Pointers to Profession : An Astrological Exposition' is indubitably the most exhaustive and extraordinary treatise, among the works so far available in the astrological arena, on the judgement of fitting and appropriate vocation of the native. Every human being has to work to earn his livelihood, except, of course, the parasites. This work becomes his career and his identity as well. To be inquisitive about one's future career is, therefore, a natural corollary of a curious mind. However, it is a regrettable fact that no serious astrologer has ever made a sincere, honest, practical and research oriented endeavors to work on this vital aspect of astrology. 'Pointers To Profession : An Astrological Exposition' is the outcome of such abysmal absence of worthy literature on the aspect of one's career. A little, what is available, is a cursory repertoire of sketchy and generalized essentials. This all inspired us to bring forth an exhaustive work related to profession, covering its every aspect, as far as possible, on the basis of our research-based studies for the last many decades and taking the essential abstract from all the classical works, so far available to us, like Brahat Hora Parashar, Brahat Jatak, Saravali, Phaldeepika, Jatak Parijat, Man Sagri, Jyotish Tattwam, Vradh Yavan Jatak, Uttara Kalamitra, Purva Kalamitra, Jatak Deshmarg, Jatak Bhushan, Phalit Martand, Jatak Alankar, Hora ratnam,

Horasar, Shambhu Hora Prakash, Sarvarth Chintamani, Chamtkar Chintamani, Sanket Nidhi, Jatak Satyacharya, Laghu Parashari, Bhava Kotuhalam, Khet Kautukam, Bhava Manjari, Jatak Sardeep, Jatak Bharnam, Jatak Tattwam, and Satya Jatakam etc.

'Pointers To Profession : An Astrological Exposition' will certainly make the students, readers and scholars of astrology adept in finding out the apposite, exact and appropriate vocation of the native. Judgement of profession is indeed a tough exercise, which requires a vast experience and systematic analysis of all the houses and planetary setup of the birth chart, in addition to the ponderous and deep research and multifaceted study of the combinations of various vocations. This is not only the 10th house, which reveals the appropriate means of livelihood, though however the 10th house is the most important house for the judgement of future prospects of profession.

Planets owning and placed in the 10th house are the important significators for the right profession one is likely to go in. *Navamsa* occupied by the 10th lord mostly plays an important role in the study of direction of the place of work. Similarly, the 2nd, 11th and 9th houses are of no less consequence in the examination of the occupation of the native.

There will certainly be more than one planet which will indicate the occupation of the native, if the 2nd, 11th & 9th houses are taken into consideration, in addition to the 10th house. Proper blending of the results of the stronger planets, if made intelligently, will reveal one's most appropriate occupation. Almost all the classical works pronounce that the judgement of the 10th and other houses should be made form the ascendant, Moon or the Sun, which ever is stronger. But the strength of planets can not be compared with that of the ascendant because both have different units of measurement. We, therefore, opine that the 10th, 2nd, 11th and 9th houses should be examined from the ascendant only, and not from the Sun or Moon, to avoid ambiguity.

Some kind of change, better or worse, may happen at the time of change in the major or sub period of planets, depending upon the planetary configuration of the birth chart. Therefore, apart from the study of houses, having a control over one's occupation, *Dasa bhukti* under operation must also be examined carefully to reach at the right denouement, with regard to appropriate direction of one's profession, professional prosperity, progression and changes.

The lord of which house has an influence over the house of profession must be seriously looked. It is a fundamental principle that the lord of the house, which signifies the activities or working related to a particular occupation, will play a prominent role e.g. for police personnel, the 6th house and its lord should also influence the occupation because the 6th house governs crime, thieves, loan and litigation etc. Mars, Saturn and Jupiter are the main and supporting significators of police services. Similarly, the 5th house should also be examined, along with 10th and other houses, for legal profession because the profession of advocates and judges requires high argumentative skill and application of brain. All such professions, which include diplomacy, creativity, manipulation and the like, will have a role of the 5th house and its lord in the matters of occupation.

The 8th house is involved where a control over number of people or workers is a part of the job. In the horoscopes of IAS, engineers, MBA, politicians etc, the 8th house and its lord play a prominent role. This all has been illustrated by us quite vividly. Therefore, the 8th house should not be ignored during the examination of one's profession. If the 8th lord is posited in the 10th house or vice versa, one should think of IAS, MBA, or engineers. Analysis of other houses will reveal the appropriate line of occupation.

The 6th house must have influence over the occupation of the native, if service is indicated in lieu of self employment. Influence of either of the luminaries, Sun or Moon, on the 6th house or its lord will certainly be there, if government service is indicated viz. the 10th lord occupies the 6th house in Cancer or Leo, or otherwise 6th lord is placed in the 10th house and obtains the *navamsa* or constellation of the Sun or Moon. This all has been lucidly explained in detail, in various chapters of 'Pointers To Profession : An Astrological Exposition'.

Promotion, demotion, elevation, extension, suspension or termination, resignation, welcome or unwelcome transfers are all part & parcel of the profession. We have devoted a separate chapter and have explained all about these most scientifically and systematically.

A pertinent and natural anxiety among the querrists, as well as students of astrology, is regarding the type of work they will undertake. Whether it will be a government job or a private enterprise, an independent business or work in a business house? The question of service or business has been exclusively dealt with, in a proper manner, in a separate chapter. What kind of business is suitable or profitable to the native has also been explained in detail, with the help of a number of illustrations.

Navamsa chart must be taken in consideration before pronouncing the final outcome in respect of each and every aspect of life. It is, indeed, a great injustice to the native if due importance is not given to the *navamsa* chart. *Navamsa* lords of the 10th, 2nd and 11th houses will assist a lot in deciding the means of livelihood of the native.

Besides *navamsa*, the constellations are also quite vital in every study. Strongest planet among the lords of the 10th, 2nd, 11th and 9th, in addition to *Atmakaraka* planet, certainly helps a lot in finding out one's occupation. All the 27 constellations have their own significations with regard to vocational direction. These all should be blended with, intelligently, keeping in view the principles of judgement. These are the planetary pointers for an individual's career, job or occupation.

A thought provoking research oriented chapter on the secrets of the role of Saturn on one's occupation has also been included in this work 'Pointers to Profession : An Astrological Exposition'. How does Saturn's transit help in timing the events has also been explained and illustrated. To understand, the exact influence of Saturn on an individual, in different ways, requires vast practical experience apart from deep scientific study of the subject. Students will find valuable information and observations with regard to Saturn. Evil effects of Sade Sati of Saturn and certain other specific observations about the influence of Saturn add to the usefulness of this chapter.

Saturn is a planet of complications, hard work, tough exercise and secret activities. Saturn is a king maker at times, whereas a negative Saturn becomes a curse and brings never ending problems. Saturn, if posited in the 12th house, gives rise to prosecution and imprisonment in addition to various kind of adversities, hazards, disasters, disappointments, distress and despair, dejection, desolation, depression, demotion, termination or reversion. Saturn is a planet of paramount importance as it contains innumerable secrets in its influence on individuals. Therefore, this chapter has been titled as 'Secrets of Saturn'.

Finance and profession are parallel to each other in reference to prosperity. It is a popular saying that nothing succeeds like success. If the native is very well placed professionally but the houses ruling over his financial aspect are afflicted or weak, the native will not be called prosperous. Apart from the house of wealth and income, the ascendant, the 5th and the 9th houses must be examined thoroughly. The triangular houses from the 2nd and 11th may also be judged for further accuracy and sharpness. We have explained this research point in our most authoritative, thought provoking classical based observations on practical birth charts in our book entitled *'Samriddhi Sutra'* part 1 and 2. The chapters covering the financial prospects, prosperity, poverty, fortune and misfortune in the present work, have been captioned as 'Fate and Finance' and 'Pointers to Prosperity and Poverty'.

If the 9th and the 10th houses are well fortified, the house of education and brilliance should also be properly studied to know the kind and level of education indicated to the subject. This has been dealt with very systematically and scientifically in the chapter 'Houses and Significators of Education'

We believe that events can be predicted almost with cent per cent accuracy with the help of the birth chart but timing of an event is truly a tough exercise and needs lot of research work to obtain the desired and aspired accuracy. However, we have explained and explored the procedure of timing the events in relation to one's profession i.e. timing transfers, promotion, reversals or change of job etc in the chapters named 'Timing Promotion in Service' and 'Timing Occupation and results of the 10th house' and 'Timing Transfers and Change of Job'.

Moon is nearest to earth and has quite quick and powerful influence on the creatures of earth. Accurate predictions are not possible without understanding Moon properly and correctly. Fertility and activities of brain, in addition to creativity and level of intelligence & memory, depend on the exact position of Moon. We are confident to aver that the Moon is the battery of the birth chart. If the Moon is afflicted or weak or ill disposed, one's progress, prosperity, popularity and power, education and future will be adversely influenced. After completing almost all chapters of 'Pointers to Profession : An Astrological Exposition', we incorporated the chapter on 'Moon: Myths and facts' for the benefit of our readers. 'Moon is a planet of paramount importance' is quite distinct due to certain specific findings of the facts about the significant and vital role of Moon.

Some of the learned readers have some confusion about the *Badhaka Grahas* i.e. the planets creating obstacles and obstructions in the path of progress, prosperity, promotion and welcome change of job. A small chapter entitled *'Badhaka Grahas'* has been included in the book, along with preventive measures.

A customary question, which an astrologer has to face everyday, is about the profession of the prospective spouse. Since this work is devoted to the professional aspect of a native, how could we ignore to investigate the aspect of the profession of the prospective spouse? And therefore, the chapter named as 'Profession of the Prospective Spouse' is an added attraction of this book.

This work has been divided in 19 chapters covering almost all aspects of profession and prosperity etc. This is an unique and most useful work on the aspect of occupation, which carries our research oriented findings, based on various classical works, during the last 35 years. A few of such research findings have been widely and greatly appreciated by millions of readers of 'The Astrological Magazine', 'The Times of Astrology', Planets and Forecast', and the like, in which we contributed our observations from time to time since 1982. The most significant and utilitarian part of this work is the inclusion of about 123 practical illustrations, with lucid analysis, to show how to ferret out the precise results. Our astute and discerning readers, as well as scholars and students of astrology, will undoubtedly find 'Pointers To Profession : An Astrological Exposition' the most informative and enlightening dissertation on the subject of profession, so far.

Study of astrological combinations in relation to various aspects of profession would not be complete without the understanding of planetary set up for different professions. Being aware of it we have, after analysis of thousands of birth charts configurations responsible for specific professions. What are the combinations which make one a doctor, or an engineer, or a teacher, or a lawyer have all been worked out. We have been able to work out the combinations making one successful in IAS, IPS, IFS and the like. As this all would have added further volume to already voluminous "Pointers To Profession : An Astrological Exposition", we decided to encompass all this vital information in another book titled "**Astro Equations for Specific Professions**", which is, in true sense, a continuation of the present work. This book contains chapters like, 1. Planetary Configuration and Classification of Occupation, 2. Propensities for Administrative Services, 3. Determinants of Medical Profession, 4. Planetary Combination for Engineers, 5. Teaching : An Honourable Profession, 6. Third House and Journalism, 7. Planetary Proposition for Actors, 8. Stars Support Sports, 9. Pointers to Police Personnels, 10. Engagements in Banks and Planetary Equations, 11. Planets and Political Power, 12. Determinants of Legal Profession, 13. Engagement of Chartered Accountant, 14. Planets Manage the Management Course, 15. Astrological Science and Scientists, Discoverers or Inventors, 16. Astro Calculus for Experts in Calculations i.e. Mathematicians, 17. Entrepreneurship : A Vocation of Life and 18. Miscellany and Remedies.

Readers would find the descriptions in "Astro Equations for Specific Professions" very interesting and informative. This book is also being published by the illustrious publishers M/s. Motilal Banarasi Dass Publishers, Delhi.

Any research work of this magnitude requires inspiration from inside and affection from outside. Had such inspiration not come from someone, whose divine beauty is beyond any description, the work of mortal being would have never seen the light of the day. She was none but the Goddess of learning, who fired our imagination when after the days of hard work, body was fatigued and refused to obey the orders of mind, it was her blessings and motivation that infused new life.

Any organized work of this mammoth dimension would require the assistance of sincere co-workers. We thank all associates who have assisted in one or the other way during the process of research carried out in this work.

We offer our thanks to Mr. Sadashiv Tiwari for making flawless CRC of the book and also to Mr. Rajesh Tyagi for their assistance in typing and carrying out the enormous spade work, so essential to complete this comprehensive book.

M/s. Motilal Banarasi Dass Publishers, Delhi are renowned to be the largest, distinguished and the best publishers, not only in India but that of whole Asia. Mr. Rajeev Prakash Jain, who is a very worthy son of his worthy father, has expressed his valuable acceptance with regard to publication of **'Pointers To Profession: An Astrological Exposition'** and **'Astro Equations for Specific Professions'.** For this gracious gesture of his, we are extremely indebted to him and M/s. Motilal Banarasi Dass Publishers.

Last but not the least, this work does not pretend to be complete in any sense of term. What we have broached is the outcome of our experience after the study of thousands of birth charts. More and more research work is required to make the observations still more pin pointing. We are, more than anybody else, conscious of many defects and blemishes, which would have inadvertently crept in this book. For this, we shall be extremely grateful to accept any suggestion from our valuable readers.

Rakesh Asthana
C-43A, Sector-A
Mahanagar
Lucknow - 226 006
Tel: 0522-2323686

Mridula Trivedi & T.P. Trivedi
'Mridul Vatika', 24 Mahanagar Extn.
Opp. E-40, Corporation Quarters,
Pili Colony, Lucknow - 226 006
Tel: 0522-2326625

Dated: May 13th, 2016

Index

About the Book

'Pointers to Profession : An Astrological Exposition' is one of the most exhaustive and comprehensive works, among the books available so far, on the judgement of suitable occupation of the native. One of the important queries to an astrologer is about the profession and professional prospects of the native or his children. Absence of any authentic book, which covers all aspects of profession, led to the creation of this exhaustive work related to profession, covering its every aspect, as far as possible, on the basis of authors' research based studies for the last many decades, supported by the abstracts from all the classical works.

'Pointers to Profession' will certainly make the students, readers and scholars of astrology proficient in finding out the appropriate vocation of the native. Judgement of profession is indeed a tough exercise, which requires a vast experience and systematic analysis of all the houses and planetary setup of the birth chart, in addition to multifaceted study of the combinations of various vocations. This is not only the 10th house, which reveals the appropriate means of livelihood, though however the 10th house is the most important house for the judgement of future prospects of profession. Planets owning and placed in the 10th house are the important significators for the right profession one is likely to go in. Similarly, the 2nd, 11th and 9th houses are of no less consequence in the examination of the occupation of the native. What roles do the navamsa, constellation and Atmakaraka planet play in deciphering the prospects of profession has been vividly explained. Whether it will be a government job or a private enterprise? The question of service or business has been exclusively dealt with, in a proper manner. What kind of business is suitable or profitable to the native has also been explained in detail, with the help of a number of illustrations.

Secrets of the role of Saturn on one's occupation have also been included in this work. How does Saturn's transit help in timing the events has also been explained and illustrated. Evil effects of Saadhe Sati of Saturn and certain other specific observations about the influence of Saturn add to the usefulness of this book.

This book has been divided in 19 chapters covering almost all aspects of profession and prosperity etc. This is a unique and most useful work on the aspect of occupation.

The most significant and utilitarian part of this work is the inclusion of about 123 practical illustrations with lucid analysis to show how to ferret out the precise results. Astute and discerning readers, as well as scholars and students of astrology, will undoubtedly find **'Pointers to Profession : An Astrological Exposition'** the most informative and enlightening dissertation on the subjet of profession, so far.

Chapter-1

Specific Rules for the Judgement of Occupations

Before judging the profession, it is necessary to ascertain the mental, intellectual and physical abilities of the native by a careful examination of the strength or weakness of the Sun, the Moon and the *lagna* respectively. The position of Mercury is also equally important. For, though classical astrology has assigned the mental outlook of a person to the position of Moon, Mercury controls wisdom and intelligence. His auspicious disposition is equally important in order to measure one's mental make-up. When, either the Moon or Mercury, receives a series of evil aspects, particularly those of Rahu and Saturn, one lacks the strength of mind needed to face critical situations and would be unfit for professions involving responsibility and the ability to meet critical situations.

It would be reasonable to expect a planet in the tenth or ruling the tenth house to have more influence over the vocation than a planet of general prominence in any other part of the chart. This, however, is different from implying that the ruler of the tenth or a planet in the tenth house can be considered a fixed factor for any of the professions.

A planet in the tenth house, receiving a powerful aspect from a benefic, denotes that the individual is not lacking in the ability of the nature of the aspecting planet that he could make a success of it. If the Sun and Rahu are in the tenth house, aspected by Jupiter, the native may preside over political meetings and take interest in political activities; but politics will not be the native's profession. If the Sun and Mars are in the tenth house, with Mars fortified and in dignity, the native may be a medical man but would be interested in politics and even involved in it.

1.1 Classification of Profession in Groups

For the purpose of study, we may classify various occupations into six broad groups or categories, viz,

1) Intellectual avocations,
2) Economic avocations,
3) Aesthetic activities
4) Routine works,
5) Mechanical professions and
6) Trades.

This classification is too general because it is impossible to draw a line of distinction between the different categories. An author, whose main work is intellectual, may spend a part of his time in composing and printing or insurance business. In his occupation, therefore, both the intellectual and economic aspects come in. There are instances when people suddenly change their careers from teaching to business. This is explained by the fact that there is a special stimulus to certain qualities at certain ages, probably depending upon the nature of the directional influences (*Dasas* and *Bhuktis*) operating then.

Taking the first group- **Intellectual avocations**- historians, mathematicians, scientists, philosophers, doctors, astronomers, astrologers, psychologists, psycho-analysts, judges, lawyers etc., come under this group. To the **Economic group** may be assigned politicians, bank workers, insurance workers, actuaries, industrialists, mill-owners and manufacturers. Musicians, actors, singers, dancers, dramatists, cinema stars, artistes belong to the **Aesthetic group**. **Routine workers** include the large number- clerks, shop assistants, waiters and the general staff in offices, government and business organizations. Labourers, agriculturists, carpenters, artisans, mechanics, compositors, mill-workers etc. belong to the **fifth group**. **The sixth, viz. traders** include the rank and file of merchants, book-sellers, publishers, stationers, grocers, printers, journalists, manufacturing representatives, etc.

Each one of these avocations can be divided into a number of divisions. For instance, an artist may be a sculptor, photographer or etcher; a musician may be a violinist, vocalist, composer or flutist. An engineer may be an inventor, designer or a mechanic and so on. Hence, it would be impossible to make an entire catalogue of professions and group them to suit astrological factors.

Generally speaking, Jupiter and Mercury refer to intellectual avocations, Venus to aesthetic professions, the Sun, the Moon and Mars to economic occupations, Mercury to traders, Saturn to hard working jobs and Rahu and Ketu to routine workers.

Mercury is a very important planet for creative or fictional writing. Jupiter and Venus, influencing Mercury in the tenth house, may give rise to a poet. Mercury and Jupiter may make one shine as an author of spiritual, literary and religious subjects. Mercury's situation in the tenth is the best gift for an author. In the absence of such combinations, Mercury should occupy a quadrant, preferably the seventh house.

For all physical work and occupations, which require physical labour, the tenth house from ascendant should be taken into consideration. For the occupations, which require mental merits, deep thoughts, research and intelligence etc., the tenth house from Moon, should be analyzed to find out the appropriate occupation.

If the tenth house in any horoscope is occupied by one or more than one planets, the native is fortunate in respect of fame and prosperity with regard to one's career. If the planet, which is placed in the tenth house, is in exaltation, the progress and prosperity of profession will be beyond imagination.

However, if the planet placed in the tenth house is debilitated, one will even then progress, more than the other members of his family, but the progress and prosperity may not be smooth. If debilitated and exalted planets are there in the tenth house, such as Jupiter and Mars in the tenth house in Cancer, or the Sun and Saturn in Aries, or Mercury and Venus in Pisces or Virgo, the progress of the native will still be there but there will be occasions, when the native will suffer dishonor, disgrace or depression at times. It should be noted that if any planet is placed in the tenth house, either exalted or debilitated, or in own sign or in inimical sign, that will certainly enhance the professional prosperity of the native, particularly during its *Dasa-Bhukti*.

Many times, we find it difficult to ascertain as to which occupation will be most appropriate for the native. In that case, we should concentrate on *Atmakaraka* planet and its *navamsa* lord.

1.2 Main Significator of Occupation

Before reaching to any conclusion, with regard to particular profession and means of livelihood, we should try to find out the particular planet, which is the main significator of the profession of the native, and this could be:

1. Planets placed in the tenth house.
2. Lord of the tenth house.
3. *Navamsa* occupied by the tenth lord.
4. *Atmakaraka* planet.
5. Lord of the seventh house (Seventh house is tenth from tenth).
6. Planets placed in the Seventh house.
7. *Navamsa* occupied by the Seventh lord.
8. See, which planet falls in the constellation of the planet placed in the tenth house. That planet will help in deciding the exact occupation.

After finding out the *Karaka* planet for the profession, see that the planet is owner of which house and which aspects are governed by that house. The sixth house governs litigation, thefts, illness, loans etc. So, if the concerning planets own the sixth house, one may become a doctor, thief, advocate etc. Suppose the concerning planet rules over the fifth house, one may be a teacher, lawyer, financer, minister, journalist, writer, author, speculator and the like. Thereafter, examine the other planets, who are laying there influence over the concerning planet and the tenth house. This will help in finding out the exact profession of the native. We have given various combinations of planets, showing different professions. This requires high degree of skill and vast experience with deep study of the subject to select the right combination.

9. If Sun is tenanted in the tenth house, one earns by his own endeavors and is capable of doing independent work. The native gets property of his father or from those, who are related with father. If the Sun is exalted in the tenth house, and is well fortified and well aspected, one gets parental property and wealth very easily and quickly.
10. If Moon is posited in the tenth house, one earns through mother in one or the other way, apart from the articles for whom, Moon is the significator.
11. If Mars is placed in the tenth house, one earns through his brother.
12. Mercury in tenth gives money through friends or one secures job through his friends.
13. Jupiter in tenth, gives money through brother, cousin, teacher and books.
14. If Venus is placed in the tenth house, one gets money through any rich woman.
15. Saturn in tenth will result into earning through servants and low class people.

1.3 Various Planetary combinations and Specific Occupations

Here we will deal with certain specific planetary

combinations, which will help in the judgement of one's occupation. These factors should be taken as specific guidelines for various kinds of professions, but the results will be modified due to influence of various factors, such as aspect, conjunction with malefics or benefics, constellations occupied by the concerning planets and *navamsa* obtained by the lord of the respective houses. However, the combinations mentioned hereunder will be of immense benefit during the examination of the results of the tenth house with regard to the determination of the exact occupation of the subject.

16. The lord of the first in the tenth is a strong argument for enhancing the general prestige of the native and giving him success in his projects. If the lord of the tenth also occupies the first, the prospects will be still better.

17. Similarly, the lord of the tenth in the ninth, or the lord of the ninth in the tenth, is a very good reason for good luck and eminent position. If the lords of the ninth and the tenth are together in the ninth or the tenth, it is still better. Or if the lord of the tenth is in the ninth and the lord of the ninth in the tenth, the mutual exchange of houses, or if both the lords combine in any house, in an angle or trine, it is considered a good *Raja Yoga*.

18. The placement of the lord of the fifth in the tenth or the lord of the tenth in the fifth is very good. If they mutually exchange places, it is still better. So also, if both the lords are conjoined and together occupy any house, preferably an angle or trine; this is considered a very good *Raja Yoga*.

    We have referred to the conjunction or mutual exchange between (I) the lords of the ninth and the tenth, and (ii) the lords of the fifth and the tenth. In fact, any kind of relationship between the lords of an angle and that of a trine causes *Raja Yoga*.

19. If a benefic planet occupies the tenth house and the lord of the tenth is strong in his own house or his sign

of exaltation, in an angle or trine, the native occupies a high position and is long lived.

20. If the Sun or Mars occupy the tenth house, and the lord of the tenth house is well placed, the native commands great respect and is daring and pushing. He is also popular.

21. The Sun and Mars in the tenth will escalate the native's own position; though, however, they would curtail the father's longevity, particularly so if they are aspected by or conjoined with malefics.

22. Saturn in the tenth is not considered bad in Hindu astrology, though according to some leading Western astrologers it brings downfall after reaching apex.

23. Saturn in the tenth elevates the native very high and then his career crashes to the ground. In Hindu astrology, no such stigma or prejudice is attached to Saturn. On the other hand, the lord of the sixth, eighth or the twelfth in the tenth is considered a pulling down force for career and rise in life.

24. The lord of the eighth in the tenth is considered particularly evil, both in regard to curtailing longevity of the father and in respect of the native's career. For judging longevity of the father, consider also whether the Sun in strong and well placed or otherwise, because the Sun is *Karaka* for the father.

25. Since the tenth house also governs trade and commerce and business activities, and most businessman carry on trade and should be bestowed to the seventh house and its lord also. The natives who have malefics in the seventh or whose seventh lord tenants the sixth, eighth or the twelfth house, as counted from the ascendant, should not carry on partnership business. Either the partner will let him down or the partnership will be broken or there will be a financial loss.

26. *Karakas* : The four Karakas for the tenth house- the Sun, Mercury, Jupiter and Saturn- each represents one or more features.

    a. The Sun represents the self and health. If the self is strong physically and mentally, the native will be vigorous in pushing ahead and mentally alert.

    b. Mercury governs speech, nimbleness, activity, quick disposal, dealings with others, expression, and correspondence etc. Besides, it presides over nerves and a person has to be good in all these to achieve success in his efforts and be diplomatic in his dealing with others.

    c. Jupiter represents wealth and also wisdom. If our personal efforts are to result in an increasing bank balance, Jupiter has to be strong and well placed. Besides, a shallow mind may emit a flitting light but cannot be a permanent source of illumination. It is the deep seated wisdom of Jupiter, which is always necessary for arriving at sound judgement.

    d. And lastly, a good Saturn bestows the quality of patience and perseverance, hard work and laborious application to work. A rolling stone gathers no mass and a person who is impatient or does not have enough perseverance, leaves the task in hand incompleted. As the wise proverb goes, 'success is one per cent inspiration and ninety-nine per cent perspiration'. Saturn stands for hard and persistent application and those who lack in labour are unsuccessful.

We have emphasized the role of *Karakas* so that the readers, while judging the tenth house, may not overlook them. We have seen even some good astrologers devoting time and attention, exclusively to the tenth house and its lord, and ignoring the *Karakas* altogether, with the result their judgments miscarry. We wish to specify that one should not ignore Moon. We can consider the sign occupied by Moon, and the tenth house from it.

1.4 Planets placed in the tenth house

A planet in the tenth, from the ascendant or the Moon, gives an indication of the type of work a man is destined to do, in general. But overall judgement of the tenth house will reveal the most appropriate and suitable vocation. We will be dealing and discussing it quite distinctly, specifically and exhaustively, so that one may pin point one's profession, singly and correctly. This has been dealt exhaustively in Chapter No. 2.

1.5 Prominent Profession and Planetary Configuration

To find out, the most appropriate and best suitable means of livelihood, is extremely complicated and confusing exercise, though this is one of the most valuable and very common query. This is really a tough work to foretell accurate and appropriate occupation and concerning education of an individual. This requires vast experience in addition to wide knowledge and deep study of the aspect of profession and education.

The analysis and consideration of only the tenth house cannot help us, to find out the most suitable profession, unless other concerning houses are taken into account. The sixth, eighth, fifth, second, eleventh, ninth and third houses have a powerful concern, in addition to the tenth house. First of all, we should carefully examine the birth chart with utmost concentration to see as to which house and planet is going to control the profession of the subject. We cannot afford to leave any house or any planet, if we wish to arrive at the right result with regard to means of livelihood of the native. The students of astrology must know, before examination of a birth chart for appropriate profession of the native, that which profession is connected from which house and planet. The findings so arrived must synchronise with the indications of the tenth house along with the significator of that profession.

27. For administrative and civil services, examination of the sixth and eighth house is also essential in addition to the tenth and ninth. Luminaries and Karmic Control Planets do have a concern with the concerning houses in the birth charts of those, who will be successful in the competition of civil services etc. Similarly, the Sun, Mars and Jupiter are related with the professional aspect of Doctors, in addition to the sixth, eighth and twelfth house, apart from the tenth and second house. Journalists are usually controlled by Mars, Mercury and Jupiter along with the third and tenth house. All professions have specific combination in the birth chart. We will now study various combinations of planets for different occupations.

Certain observations have been given below, which have been experienced during our last 35 years of experience, study and practical horoscopy :

28. If the lord of the tenth house falls in the eleventh house with Mars, one will earn his livelihood through technical or scientific nature of occupation. However, if tenth lord is associated with Saturn in the eleventh house, one will earn through hard work and hard toil. He may be dealing in industry as well, if other indications support.

29. Lord of the tenth, if placed in the *lagna* or tenth house, brings greater prosperity and success with brilliance.

30. If the lord of the tenth house joins the ninth lord, in association with Ketu, one will earn through religious activities of various types.

31. If the lord of ninth and fourth are associated in the tenth house, and lord of the tenth occupies the second or the eleventh house, one earns through manufacturing goods. However, what kind of goods will be manufactured by the native will be decided by the examination of the tenth lord, its *navamsa* and *nakshatra* etc.

32. The third house should be examined for the occupation connected with journalism. Mercury and Mars are the primary significators, whereas Jupiter is the supporting significator for journalism. Mars and Mercury, if placed in the tenth or the third house, tend one to move to journalism. The sixth house may also be taken as the supporting house. However, Mercury and Mars must be strong and well placed, having an influence over the tenth, ascendant or the third house.

33. The position of Moon and sixth house should also be examined.

34. If the tenth lord is placed with the ninth lord, and either of Jupiter or Mercury influence, one earns through writing articles, books, script, poetry, or novels etc.

35. For judgement of profession, the ascendant should be examined with its *navamsa* position etc., as it indicates aptitude of the native.

36. For medical profession, the *Karaka* Sun and Mars, and *karaka* of healing Jupiter, should be examined in respect of the tenth house. Involvement of the sixth, eighth or twelfth house is also essential as all the *Trik* houses rule over some kind of ailment. Illnesses of all kinds have something to do with *Trik* houses. Therefore, the involvement of lord of these houses with Sun, Mars and Jupiter, having an influence over the tenth house indicates one's success in occupation connected with medicine, or surgery etc.

37. If the tenth lord and the lord of the sixth house are associated with each other, anywhere in the birth-chart, one is likely to earn through service. However, if Saturn's influence is also there, on either of these lords or on the sixth or the tenth house, service career will be strongly pronounced.

38. If the indications of service career are present in the birth chart and the influence of a luminary is also there, in one or the other way, one will earn his livelihood

through Government service. If the tenth lord or the lord of the sixth house, or the lord of the *lagna* obtains the *navamsa* of the Sun or Moon, government job will be secured. If the lord of the ascendant, the sixth or the tenth, fall in the constellation or sign of the Sun or Moon, or these are associated with the Sun or Moon, the government job will be the primary vocation of the life of the native.

39. Since, civil services come under the government service, therefore, involvement of the sixth house, along with the influence of the luminaries on the sixth and the tenth or the ascendant is essential. At least one of the Karmic Control Planets (dispositors of Rahu and Ketu) should have an influence over either of the concerning houses.

40. If a benefic is placed in the sixth house, one earns through service. If the *lagna* lord and lord of the tenth house occupy the sixth house, one will earn through service.

41. For civil and administrative services, eighth, ninth and tenth houses should be examined properly. If there is mutual exchange of ninth and tenth lords, one becomes successful in civil services provided one of the luminaries has an influence over any of these houses.

42. For the profession of law, Venus, Jupiter and Mercury should influence the fifth or the tenth house, in addition to the sixth house, the house of crime. The fifth house and Mercury govern intelligence and capability for argument. Libra sign indicates judgement. In fact, symbol of Libra is Scale (balance). Libra is ruled by Venus. Therefore, Venus, Libra and Aquarius have also a prominent role to play in the horoscope of advocate, judges, lawyers, magistrates etc.

43. Jupiter and Mercury must have a concern with the fifth and tenth house, if one has to select teaching profession as the career.

1.6 Combinations by aspect or conjunction, related to the Tenth Lord

The following combinations, by aspect or by conjunction, related to the tenth lord, give rise to specific means of livelihood.

Mercury and Venus	Writing of poetry, screen-play, drama; ambassadors, and representatives.
Mercury and Sun	Executive post, mercantile activities, export and import business.
Mercury and Saturn	Cartoon drawing, automobile driving, Buffoonery, Brokerage, Postal service, librarian, book trade, clay manufacturing.
Mercury and Moon	Cinema, exhibition.
Mercury and Jupiter	Research, religious and philosophical writings; corporation and councils.
Mercury and Mars	Service in Telephone Exchange, printing, drugs, surgery, auditing and accountancy.
Jupiter and Saturn	Occultism, hypnotism, clairvoyance, contractors, charitable work, poor homes.
Jupiter and Mercury	Technology, ministership.
Jupiter and Sun	Religious organizations, posts of power and authority.
Jupiter and Moon	Authorship, journalism.
Venus and Saturn	Sale of betel leaves, soap, musical instruments, cosmetics, inks, lime, shoes of good quality.
Venus and Moon	Shipping agency, hotel-keeping, sale of wine, scents, cosmetics and fancy goods.

Venus and Mars	Robbery, dacoity, automobile driving, menial jobs.
Venus and Mercury	Music teaching
Moon and Rahu	Air hostess
Mercury and Rahu	Radio-station, watch merchants, photography.
Mars and Rahu	Space travel and space science
Saturn and Rahu	Circus
Venus and Rahu	Radio artist.

These combinations get modified according to the benefic or malefic aspects they receive.

In addition to the above, the position of the lord of the tenth is worth considering, especially in its relation to the ascendant, or to another benefic aspecting it.

These are simply the guidelines for the judgement of vocation of the native. Various sages have given number of occupations on the basis of various combinations of planets. In modern times, these results, with regard to specific professions, hold good provided sincere and systematic analysis is made for finding out the most suitable occupation of the native. If two planets have an influence over the profession of the native, the native will enter into the occupations indicated by those planets. For example, if Mars is posited in the tenth house in Leo, the combined effect of Mars and the Sun will make the native a surgeon. However, if Mars in tenth is posited in Virgo, one may become a mechanical engineer because Mars and Mercury signify mechanical engineering. If Mars falls in Scorpio in the tenth house, one may become a police personnel or he may join defense services. This is again a guideline because the sign, *navamsa* and constellation lords of the tenth house, should also be taken into consideration. The ownership of the planet, occupying the tenth house, also helps in deciding a particular profession of the native.

1.7 Profession as per *Brihat Jataka*

Maharshi Varahamihira has specified certain professions on the basis of the joint effect of two planets on the profession of the native. In Chapter XIV of *Brihat Jataka*, following combinations and specific professions have been laid down by the great Varahamihira.

तिग्मांशुर्जनयत्युशेषसहितो यन्त्राश्मकारं नरं
भौमेनाधरतं बुधेन निपुणं धीकीर्तिसौख्यान्वितम् ।
क्रूरं वाक्पतिनान्यकार्यनिरतं शुक्रेणरङ्गायुधै
र्लब्धसवं रविजेन धातुकुशलं भाण्डप्रकारेषु वा ।।

(*Brihat Jatak,* Chap-14, Vers-1)

Sun-Moon	:	Mechanic, sculptor.
Sun-Mercury	:	Clever, expert, intelligent, happy.
Sun-Jupiter	:	Cruel, doing others' jobs.
Sun-Venus	:	Dying, use of weapons.
Sun-Saturn	:	Expert in metals, minerals and the manufacture of vessels.
Moon-Mars	:	Sale of drinks, pots etc.
Moon-Mercury	:	Eloquent in speech, expert in interpretation, astrologer.
Moon-Jupiter	:	Foremost in family, wealthy.
Moon-Venus	:	Expert in cloth work.
Mars-Mercury	:	Merchant, an athlete.
Mars-Jupiter	:	A king, a person in charge of a town.
Mars-Venus	:	Cowherd, athlete, clever, gambler.
Mars-Saturn	:	Sorrowful, liar, despised and lowly.
Mercury-Jupiter	:	Likes music, knows dance.

Mercury-Saturn	:	A cheat, disobedient.
Mercury-Venus	:	Clever in speech, a king, leader of a group.
Jupiter-Venus	:	Learned, having wealth, wife, and virtues.
Jupiter-Saturn	:	Barber, potter, or a cook.

1.8 Certain research oriented observations with regard to occupations

Some learned astrologers indicate the following professions for the planetary combinations thus:

Sun-Mars	:	Police, military, factory, able surgeon.
Sun-Mercury	:	Engineer, mathematician, inspector, astrologer.
Sun-Jupiter	:	A teacher, judge, good physician.
Sun-Jupiter-Mercury	:	Magistrate
Sun-Jupiter-Mars	:	Magistrate, bank agent, principal.
Sun-Venus	:	Transport, women's hospital.
Sun-Saturn	:	Geology, coal, mines, dentist.
Moon-Mars	:	Navy, employment in boiler and steam engines.
Moon-Mercury	:	Agent, engineering, cotton trade, textiles (Moon represents textiles, Mercury trade).
Moon-Jupiter	:	Auspicious Guru-Chandra yoga, minister, king, captain etc.
Moon-Venus	:	Petrol, scents, scented oil, milk, music, paints.
Moon-Saturn	:	Kerosene, digger of wells.

Moon-Rahu	:	Poisonous articles.
Mars-Mercury	:	Mechanical engineer, paper press, building construction, contractor.
Mars-Jupiter	:	(Jupiter indicates lawyer, Mars criminal), criminal lawyer, Judge, Bank agent, physician.
Mars-Venus	:	Music, musical instruments, tailor, leather trade, automobiles (Venus is *Vahanakaraka* and Mars denotes machines).
Mars-Saturn	:	Factory, chemist, operation, hardware, steel, slaughter house.
Sun-Moon-Mars	:	Mechanical engineer, a great officer, factory manager.
Sun-Moon-Mercury	:	Government press, (Sun-Government, Mars-Machine, Mercury-printing) government engineer, government contractor.
Mercury-Jupiter	:	Writer, mathematician, engineer, bank clerk, treasury manager. (Because Mercury indicates writing, mathematics; Jupiter indicates bank, treasury).
Mercury-Venus	:	Good artist, proficiency in literature, sanitary engineer, drama-writing etc.
Mercury-Saturn	:	Shorthand writer, engineer, stenographer, teacher.
Mercury-Rahu	:	Employment in jail (Here we have to consider the lord of the sign in which Rahu is placed, and decide the occupation).
Mercury-Ketu	:	Here also, we have to consider the lord of the sign in which Ketu is placed.

Jupiter-Venus	:	Teacher, musician in religious line, cine actor and a poet etc. (vary according to sign).
Jupiter-Saturn	:	Physician, broker, service in bank.
Venus-Saturn	:	Tailor, leather worker.
Mars-Jupiter	:	Police officer, or high officer in military.
Mars-Mercury	:	Mathematician, typewriter, press, engineer, technician.
Sun-Mercury	:	Advocate, lawyer, accountant.
Moon-Venus	:	Actor, dramatist, film director.
Mercury-Venus	:	Engineer, photographer.
Sun-Mercury-Venus	:	Artist, poet, writer.

In the above cases, it is not necessary that the planets should be combined together. What is intended is that they should be connected with each other by aspect, exchange of signs, or conjunction etc. These jobs are possible even when there is favourable aspect between the said planets. It is also important to note that the planets should not be subject to the influence of other planets, benefic or malefic. In that case, the profession will not remain the same. This should be taken as a guide to indication of profession of the native. Proper judgement and thorough examination of the birth-chart, *navamsa* chart and constellation occupied by the concerning planets will certainly help an astrologer to find out the most appropriate, suitable and profitable profession of an individual.

One might change one's job. If the tenth house is aspected by its own lord or benefics like Jupiter, Venus, Mercury & waxing Moon, and its lord is also placed in *Kendras* or *Konas*, it becomes strong. Benefics on either side of the tenth house would cause *Subhakartari Yoga* and render it strong.

Note, which planets are placed in the tenth house, or aspect it or its lord. This should be considered from *lagna* and *Chandra Lagna* both. Similarly, the planets, conjoined with the lord of the tenth house, should also be considered. They have definite influence on the profession. Certain combinations, as given below, may be of immense benefit in finding out the exact occupation of the natives.

1.9 Particular Profession and Planetary Conjunctions

1. Mars and Jupiter : Post in police.
2. Mars and Mercury : Mathematician.
3. Mercury and Venus : Engineer, photographer, artist.
4. Venus and Moon : Actor, dramatist, cinema director.
5. Moon and Jupiter : A very favourable yoga for much wealth.

(This is called *Guru chandra yoga*)

1.10 Results of planets in tenth house from *Chandra Lagna*

Saravali devotes a separate chapter (33rd) for discussing the results obtained, when different planets are placed in the tenth house, from *lagna* or *Chandra lagna*. This is summarized below:

1. Sun : Successful, wealthy, powerful, and healthy.
2. Mars : Brave, passionate, cruel, bad conduct.
3. Mercury : Learned, well-read, wealthy, famous, artist, wise.
4. Jupiter : Successful, virtuous, wealthy, noble conduct, a minister, famous.
5. Venus : Fortunate, handsome, wealthy, successful, respected by the king.
6. Saturn : Sickly, poor, sorrowful, issueless.

Thus, the effects of Saturn and Mars in the tenth house from the *lagna* or Moon are told as bad. But, placement of benefics in the tenth house from the *lagna* or Moon will give auspicious results. However, if malefics or benefics are *Yogakaraka*, *swa-kshetriya* (own house) or exalted, pleasant results should be expected in the professional sphere. Similarly, debilitated planets, malefic or benefic, or *Trik* lords or the affliction of the tenth house by malefics, in one or the other way, will produce inauspicious results with regard to professional prosperity, progress and promotions etc.

Nature of planets indicate nature of occupation. In astrology, the placement of a specific planet in the tenth house and a study of its ruler and the planet aspecting it also helps in determining a native's career or means of livelihood. Broadly speaking, different planets, considered in this way, give different clues to the source of earning:

1. **Sun** suggests earning through merchandise, dealing in food-stuffs, administrative post, good inheritance, auditing, accountancy, drugs and chemicals, woolen, mills, fertilizers, brokerage, wood or timber.

2. **Moon** refers to arts, crafts, textiles, horse racing, dairy-products, contracts, mercantile activities, navy, nursing, orchards, liquids, hotel-keeping, petrol & oil companies, salt, costly clothes, fish, hospitals, women welfare, ladies' garments, water works, irrigation, psychiatry, sea-products.

3. **Mars** indicates engineering, soldiers, liquor, military department, hunting, animal-training in circus, armed services, ambassador, collector, electrical engineering, atomic energy, postal services, match factory, kerosene oil, ammunition depots, jobs connected with punishment, lands, estates, surgery.

4. **Mercury** denotes salesmanship, writing, arts, teaching, poetry, crafts, preaching, public-speaking, weaving, selling of cloth, buying and selling, journalism, printing, book-trade, literary activities, designing and

architectural work, clerical services, diplomatic missions, auditing, postal department.

5. **Jupiter** points to commerce, trade, priest, craft, astrology, charitable or religious organization, spirituality, executive post, Revenue department, research guidance, treasuries, income-tax department, High Courts, ancient lore, temples, holy places.

6. **Venus** refers to artistic and musical pursuits, dance and acting, writing of poetry, dealing in gold, silver and gems, bars, fineries, perfumes, wealth-tax, hotels, restaurants, horse race, excise, pictures, flowers, dealings with fair sex.

7. **Saturn** indicates farming, medical service, insurance agency, cooperative business, *panchayats*, community development works, pharmaceutical works, cattle breeding, black-mailing, hardware and labour, trade unions, iron goods, engraving on woods, stone work, execution, shoe making, physical and hard work, theft, factories.

8. **Rahu** indicates radio, circus, space travel and spiritual healing, aviation.

9. **Ketu** refers to foreign trade, secret sciences, clairvoyance, mesmerism, palmistry.

1.11 Character of Signs and Nature of Profession

Character of signs indicates nature of various vocations. Again, a study of the nature of the sign, in which the tenth lord falls, is also a pointer to the natural leaning of the natives:

1. The airy signs are Gemini, Libra and Aquarius. They are intellectual signs and refer to thinking, planning, fluency of speech, intellectual pursuits, literary and artistic bent of mind.

2. The watery signs are Cancer, Scorpio and Pisces. They indicate liquids, salesmanship, hospitals, navigation,

dealings in textile goods and fabrics, brewers, druggists.

3. Aries, Leo and Sagittarius are fiery signs. They suggest employment in industrial concerns, hospitals, military departments, factories and mechanical and civil engineering.

4. Taurus, Virgo and Capricorn are earthy signs. They indicate agriculture, foodstuffs, stocks and shares, clothes, stationery, gardening, farming products and landed property.

The choice of career depends on one's personality or one's mental trait or on the necessity of entering service or on the capacity to pursue an independent profession.

For the judgement of profession, the nature of the ascendant and its lord, the position of the Moon and the strength of the sixth house of service, should also be taken into account. A benefic in the sixth, or lord of *lagna* or the tenth in sixth, usually indicates that the native is destined for service. For smooth service-career, lords of *lagna* and the tenth, should be on friendly terms with the lord of the sixth, otherwise due recognition of one's ability is not forthcoming, from one's boss or employer. Again, a planet in the tenth or the tenth lord receiving the aspect of a benefic, denotes uncommon ability for successful administration and management. Mercury rules intelligence and Jupiter intuitive insight. When these planets are well disposed in a horoscope, the native is intelligent and efficient.

1.12 *Navamsa* occupied by the Tenth Lord

If the lord of the *navamsa* occupied by the tenth lord is the **Sun**, the native earns through work connected with medicine, wool, grass, grain, gold, diplomacy and mediation and arbitration.

If this planet be the **Moon**, the native will deal in ships, pearls, sea-products, agriculture, horticulture, humour (cartoonist), women and clothes.

If **Mars** be the ruler of the *navamsa* occupied by the tenth lord, the native makes his living through metals, minerals, buildings, occupations involving fire, thieving, feats of valour, military occupations, butchering, driving, chemist-shops and doctoring.

If **Mercury** be the ruler, the native earns as a mathematician, poet, artist, sculptor, writer, journalist, astrologer, priest, whose services can be engaged, and similar callings.

Jupiter gives the occupations of a judge, teacher, counselor, lawyer, bankers, ministers, preachers, and similar callings.

If **Venus** is the lord, the native earns as a dealer in gold, precious stones, cattle, apparel and textiles, beautician, perfumes, elephants, horses, cars and other conveyances, hotelier and through the show-business such as cinema, dancing, dramas and the like.

Saturn makes one engage in humble professions such as craft, tilling, factory and mill-workers, labour of every kind, jailors, wardens, shoe-maker, miner, practitioner of witchcraft and similar occupations.

1.13 Role of Fixed, Movable and Cardinal (common) Signs in determining professions

All the twelve signs can be divided into three categories:

1. Fixed signs
2. Movable signs
3. Cardinal signs or dual signs or common signs.

Examine that how many planets are posited in the fixed sign or movable sign etc.

- If more planets, relevant for determining profession, viz.

lord of the tenth house, eleventh house, seventh house etc. occupy **movable** sign, one will earn his livelihood by an independent occupation. If so placed planets are strong and well disposed, the native will have high aspirations and make sincere endeavors to reach at the top.

- If the concerning planets fall in **fixed** signs and those are well disposed, one will earn his livelihood through service in most of the cases. He may earn money by medical profession, engineering or through bank services, in which patience and courage are required.
- If the **dual** signs are prominent in the birth-chart, one may earn by more than one profession, such as a teacher who may also engage himself in some other business. Many other time bound service personnel may do some part time jobs after the office hours.
    - ❖ The persons, who are engaged in the liaison work.
    - ❖ Natives, who do office works as well as side business.
    - ❖ Consultants and professionals like Chartered accountant, Doctors, Designers, Stenographer, Typist etc. also come under this group.

Find out the strongest planet in the birth chart and the 10th lord from the ascendant, along with the lord of *lagna*. Also find out the sign, occupied by the stronger planet and examine the character, element and strength of these planets and concerning signs.

(a) Fiery Element (Aries, Leo and Sagittarius) : If fiery element is strong, one will progress in a profession, where wisdom, intelligence, mental caliber and logics are required, such as astrologer, advocates, journalist, and authors etc.

(b) Earthy Element (Taurus, Virgo and Capricorn) : If earthy element is prominent, one will earn money by involving himself in jobs where physical labour is needed, such as labourer, carpenter, blacksmith, clerks etc.

(c) Watery Element (Cancer, Scorpio and Pisces) : If watery element is prominent in the chart, the native will always be changing his job from one to another. He may switchover from one occupation or business to another quickly.

(d) Airy Element (Gemini, Libra and Aquarius) : If airy signs play a vital role in the horoscope, one will earn through a different set up as a writer, philosopher, psychologist, poet, *pandit*, priest etc.

1.14 Examination of Various Houses for Profession

As a general rule, the 10th house is taken into account to determine the profession of a subject. But in practice, we find that people are not always engaged in professions as indicated by the 10th house. Any one or more, out of the 1st, 2nd, 6th, 7th, 9th or 11th houses may be directly responsible for determining the profession of a native.

Planets associated with these houses and their lords, particularly the planets posited close to the midpoint of the house, and planets placed in the constellations of the occupants, and the house lords, during their period and sub-period, may influence the selection of the profession. Also, the basic character and categories of the signs falling in these houses greatly tints the final outcome.

People do not necessarily follow one or the same profession throughout their life span. One may suddenly change to an altogether different profession. A person, who may have started his or her career with a service, may suddenly change to a business or the other way round. Some people follow more than one profession at a time. Some are engaged in part time work in order to supplement their income from the main occupation.

The *dasa* and *antardasa,* running between the ages of 15 to 30 years of a native, play an important role in the selection of the profession.

Let us discuss each of the above-mentioned houses in order to understand the logic behind their involvement.

The Ascendant or the 1st house:

The profession becomes the identity of a person. The 1st house indicates person's aptitude, outlook, personality; & physical and mental make up etc. All these features indicated by the 1st house have a say in selecting and prospering in a particular line of occupation.

The 2nd house or '*Dhan Sthan*':

The 2nd house indicates one's accumulated money or wealth. This house also signifies status. Both these factors are related to the occupation of a person. In fact, the 2nd house shows source of income and accumulation of wealth.

The 6th house:

The involvement of the 6th house is because of the following reasons:

Work undertaken by the native due to compulsion of circumstances, or work involving hard labour and difficulties, is represented by this house. The 3rd, 6th, 10th and 11th houses are categorized as *'Upchay sthan'* or progressive houses, therefore these contribute towards the progress of the native. The 6th house is 9th from the 10th house and the 10th from 9th house, and hence it may be considered as the *Bhagya sthan* for the 10th house, and decides the professional progression, promotion, prosperity and popularity.

The 7th house:

According to the principle of *'bhavet bhavam'*, the 10th from the 10th house, that is the 7th house, also indicates profession. The 7th house also indicates the business partner, in case one is involved in partnership pursuits.

The 8th house:

The 8th house is 10th from the 11th house and the 11th from the 10th house. Therefore, this indicates professional prosperity and masses working under the native. High ambitions and administrative positions, having wide fame and honour, come under the role of 8th house.

The 3rd, 6th, 10th and 11th houses are categorized as *'Upchay Sthans'* or progressive houses, therefore these contribute towards the progress of the native.

The 9th house:

The 9th house is the *Bhagya sthan* or the house of fortune. Whatever be the profession of the native, his or her luck plays a crucial role in it. Therefore, the role of this house is of paramount importance. Sometimes, this house is directly involved in determining the native's profession.

The 11th house:

This is the house of income or gains. The efforts put in by the native fructify through this house and income flows in. Therefore, in some cases this house may directly decide the profession of the native.

We have contributed different chapters on the above mentioned houses with regard to professional aspects of the native. This will be of immense benefit in the examination of proper, appropriate and suitable profession of the native.

Mostly the 10th house is taken into consideration for finding out one's most appropriate profession. Planet or planets placed in the 10th house should be endowed with maximum importance for suitable occupation. The lord of the *navamsa* occupied by the 10th lord is equally significant for the judgement of profession. Consideration of the *nakshatras* is also essential. Constellation lord of the planet or planets placed in the 10th house; planets, whose constellations have an ownership of the planets, who occupy the 10th house and planet, who is owner of the 10th house, all should be carefully judged.

Illustration : 1.1 (**KB**) *Horoscope No.: 1*

Date of birth : 09.06.1949 Time of birth : 14:10:00 hrs

Place of birth : Amritsar Lat 31:35:00 N Long 74:56:00E

Ayanamsa : 23:08:55 Sidereal Time : 6:49:17

Pln	**Degree**	**Rasi**	**Nakshatra**	**Pad**
Asc	17:26:44	Vir	Hasta	3
Sun	25:01:12	Tau	Mrigshira	1
Mon	4:37:31	Sco	Anuradha	1
Mar	6:21:57	Tau	Kritika	3
Mer (R/C)	17:02:16	Tau	Rohini	3
Jup (R)	8:24:52	Cap	Uttarasadha	4
Ven	9:11:32	Gem	Ardra	1
Sat	7:27:34	Leo	Magha	3
Rah (R)	1:21:21	Ari	Ashwini	1
Ket (R)	1:21:21	Lib	Chitra	3

Lagna Chart

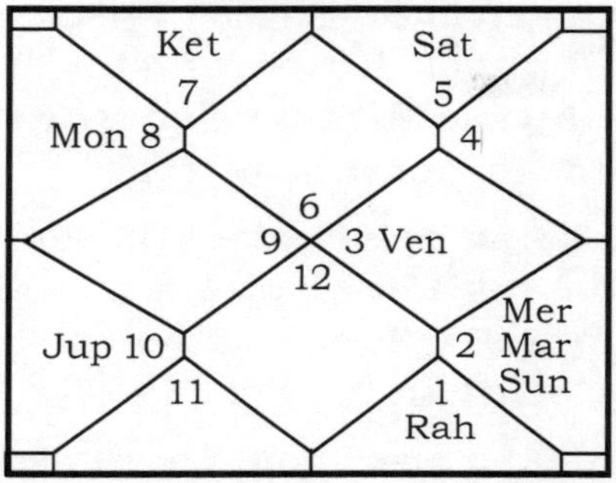

Navamsa Chart

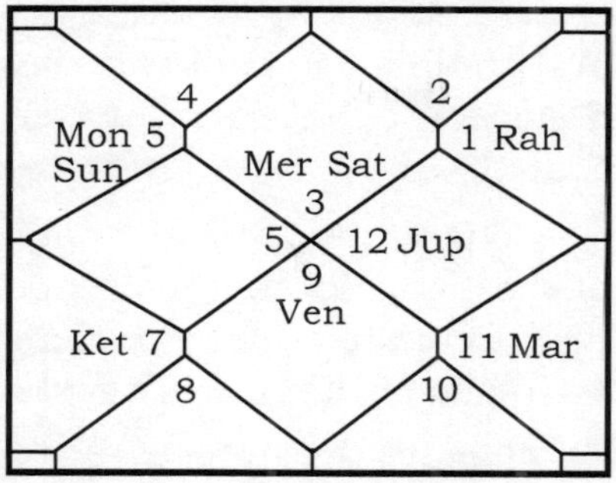

Balance of Vimsottari Dasa of **Sat 17Y 1M 28D**

In this case, Venus occupies the 10th house identical to sign Gemini. The first significator of profession is Venus and the second is the lord of the 10th house, Mercury. Now we see, whether any planet occupies the constellation of Venus. In this birth chart, there is no such planet. Then examine the *navamsa* occupied by the 10th lord Mercury, and *navamsa* of the planet placed in the 10th house i.e. Venus. Venus obtains Sagittarius *navamsa* and Mercury obtains own *navamsa* Gemini. This shows that the profession of the native may be connected with art, acting, dancing, singing or script writing.

Now examine the *Atmakaraka* planet, which is the Sun in this case. The Sun is posited in the 9th house in Taurus, in *Mrigshira* ruled by Mars i.e. the Sun falls in Mars' constellation *Mrigshira.* The Sun and Mars are the strongest planets in this birth chart. The Sun obtains 1.87 *Shadabalas* and acquires own *navamsa*. This shows success in administrative field i.e. I.P.S. Exchange of the 9th lord, Venus, and 10th lord, Mercury, confirms civil or administrative services. Mars and Sun are associated with the 10th lord, Mercury, in the 9th house and further suggest success in police service.

The third step is the analysis of the 2nd house, which is owned by Venus in this case, who falls in the 10th house.

Venus obtains *navamsa* of Jupiter and falls in Rahu's constellation *Ardra*. Rahu is tenanted in Aries ruled by Mars and obtains *vargottam navamsa*. It means that Venus is under the effects of Mercury, Jupiter, Rahu and Mars and that shows that the profession tends towards engineering or police.

Thereafter, the 11th house should be analyzed. The lord of the 11th, Moon, falls in Scorpio, ruled by Mars. Moon falls in the constellation *Anuradha,* ruled by Saturn and obtains *navamsa* of the Sun. This shows police services of high level.

Lastly, the judgement of the 9th house should be made. In this birth chart, the 9th house is occupied by Mercury, Mars and the Sun, which indicate police service and administration. There is mutual exchange of constellations between the Sun and Mars. The Sun falls in *Mrigshira* and Mars fall in *Kritika*, whereas Mercury falls in *Rohini*, whose ruler Moon occupies Scorpio. This also signifies police service of administrative level i.e. I.P.S. Mars obtains Saturn's *navamsa*; the Sun obtains own *navamsa* and Mercury obtains Gemini *navamsa*. The lord of the 9th house, Venus, falls in the 10th house and obtains *navamsa* of Jupiter and falls in *Ardra* constellation.

Thus, the Sun, Mars, Jupiter, Mercury and Venus have a profound concern with the occupation of the native. The strongest planet is the Sun, who obtains 1.87 *Shadabalas*. The 2nd strongest planet is Venus, who obtains 1.32 *Shadabalas* and 3rd strongest planet is Mars, who obtains 1.21 *Shadabalas* and then Jupiter obtains 1.1 *Shadabalas*. Mercury is weak as it obtains less than 0.1 *Shadabala*. Therefore, Mercury should be eliminated. Now the Sun, Venus, Mars and Jupiter will decide the occupation of the native. We have explained in length, in a different chapter, that for administrative services, Venus, Sun and Moon are the significators. In this horoscope, Venus occupies the 10th house; the Sun occupies the 9th house and the Moon aspects the Sun and 10th lord Mercury. Moreover, mutual exchange of the 9th lord Venus and the 3rd lord Mercury gives rise *Mahayoga* or *Maharaja Yoga*, which is one of the strongest planetary positions for administrative services. Overall, the horoscope strongly indicates Class-I administrative services.

Now, the remaining significators are the Sun, Mars and Jupiter, who are inter-related with each other as explained above. The influence of these planets strongly signifies police services. Now consider both i.e. administrative services and police services. Then, it will be quite clear that the native will be a successful, famous and strong I.P.S. officer. In fact, this is the birth chart of Mrs. Kiran Bedi, who has earned world wide reputation of a very strict I.P.S. officer.

This is the procedure and steps, which are to be followed to find out the most appropriate and exact occupation of the native.

●

CHAPTER-2

Placement of Planets in the 10th House

Each planet offers different outcomes in the tenth house for the same ascendant, and same planet has different actions in respect of one's occupation for different ascendants. For the exact judgement of results of any planet, one should consider the nature of that planet and that of the sign wherein that is placed. Lordship, conjunction, aspect and *yogas* are also equally important. Here, let us study the results of individual planets, if placed in tenth house, irrespective of other factors, which will modify the results accordingly.

2.1 Placement of Sun in the Tenth House

The native will be famous, learned, courageous, valorous and wealthy. He will be blessed with conveyances and servants and his merits will be recognized by one and all. He will be quite intelligent and will accomplish the significant tasks. His enemies will be routed. He lives at a place other than his birth place. The progress in profession is inevitable. He inherits fame, property and wealth. Such a native acquires a high position in the government and becomes famous for his outstanding performance.

If a strong and well-placed Sun is there in the tenth house, the native will have achievements and distinctions in the field of education before the age of 18. If three or more planets have an aspect over Sun, the native will receive favours from government, high officials, ministers, relatives and friends etc. If the Sun is exalted or placed in own sign Leo, the native will have immense popularity due to his good deeds, qualities and achievements. If Mars is also well placed in *Kendra*, along with Sun in Leo or Aries, the native will become a successful physician or surgeon. He may be a politician, if other planets also favour.

If Sun is afflicted, due to association or aspect of malefic planets, there will be defamation, failure of undertakings, sinful deeds and professional reversals etc. However, a well fortified placement of Sun in the tenth house makes one quite successful person in the professional sphere.

Illustration : 2.1 (**Nusli Wadia**) *Horoscope No.: 2*

Date of birth : 15.02.1944 Time of birth : 13:30:00 hrs

Place of birth : Mumbai Lat 18:58:00 N Long 72:50:00E

Ayanamsa : 23:04:22 Sidereal Time : 21:28:03

Pln	Degree	Rasi	Nakshatra	Pad
Asc	8:25:36	Tau	Kritika	4
Sun	2:24:28	Aqu	Dhanistha	3
Mon	8:46:22	Lib	Swati	1
Mar	18:41:05	Tau	Rohini	3
Mer	10:40:37	Cap	Sravana	1
Jup (R)	28:33:40	Can	Aslesa	4
Ven	29:04:47	Sag	Uttarasadha	1
Sat (R)	26:38:01	Tau	Mrigshira	1
Rah (R)	13:29:51	Can	Pushya	4
Ket (R)	13:29:51	Cap	Sravana	2

Lagna Chart

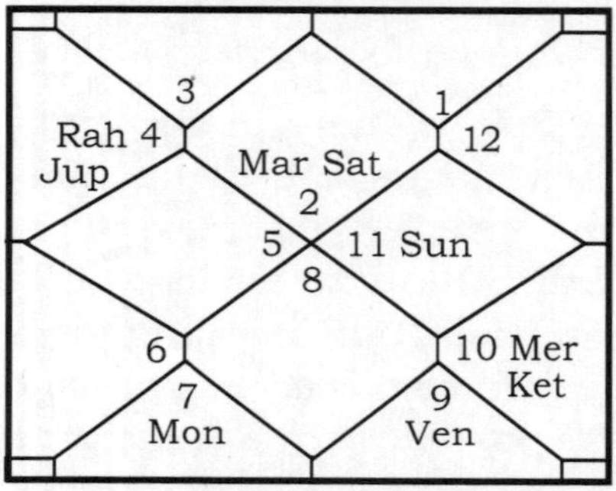

Navamsa Chart

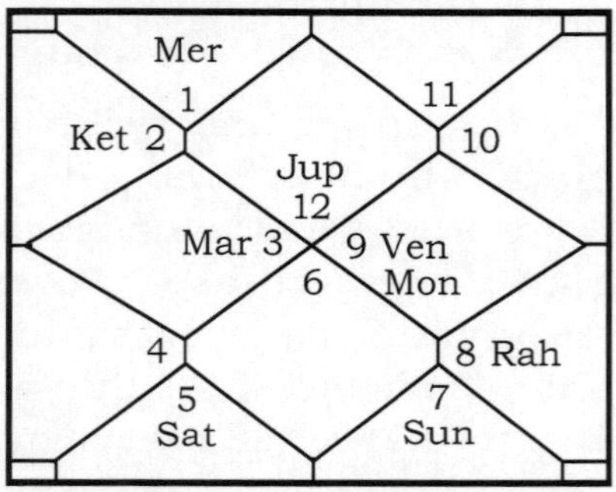

Balance of Vimshottari Dasa of **Rah 15Y 1M 26D**

Mr. Nusli Wadia's name comes in the top ranking industrialists of the country. He came from a very humble background and by his own endeavors rose to erect an empire of his own. He owned a number of industrial units manufacturing variety of things.

The placement of Sun in the tenth house blessed him with grand professional success. Lord of the 2nd and 5th, Mercury occupies the 9th house under the aspect of exalted 11th lord Jupiter. The second and eleventh lords, Mercury and Jupiter, mutually aspect each other. *Yogakaraka* Saturn occupies the ascendant and aspects the 10th house of its own. There is formation of *Gajkesari* and *vasumati* Yoga also. These factors contributed in his phenomenal rise.

SPECIFIC RESULTS:

If Sun falls in Aries, Cancer, Leo, Scorpio or Sagittarius in the 10th house, one will become a successful doctor, politician, police personnel or will work in the revenue department, CID or the forest department. The Sun in the 10th house makes one *Karmyogi* i.e. he has dignity of labour to his credit.

If Sun is placed in the tenth house in Taurus, Gemini, Virgo, Capricorn or Pisces, the individual becomes MLA, MP, minister, or Governor. He may also become a famous businessman.

If Sun falls in Libra, one becomes a judge, advocate or law personnel. In Scorpio, the Sun makes one a good surgeon or physician. He gets elevation by his own endeavors and earns fame. He, generally, does not have good relations with father or his father dies early. Mr. H. N. Ketve does not have a good opinion about the Sun in the 10th house, as it brings downfall in the end of one's life.

अष्टादशवर्षे विद्याधिकारेण प्रसिद्धो भवति द्रव्यार्जनसमर्थश्च।
दृष्टित्रितः राजप्रियः सत्कर्मरतः राजशूरः ख्यातिमान्।।
स्वोच्चे स्वक्षेत्रे बलपरः।। कीर्तिप्रसिद्धिः।।
तटाकक्षेत्रगोपुरादिब्राह्मण प्रतिष्ठासिद्धिः।।

पापक्षेत्रे पापयुते पापदृष्टिवशात् कर्मविघ्नकरः।।
दुष्टकृतिः।। अनाचारः दुष्कर्मकृत्पापी।।

(*Bhrigu Sutram,* Part II/Chap-I/Verse-88 to 95)

If Sun is in the tenth house, the native will make distinctive achievements in the educational sphere by his 18th year. He becomes famous and quite capable of learning well. If three planets aspect the Sun, the native will be liked by the king (Government), will do pious deeds, will be very brave and valorous and earns good reputation. If the Sun is exalted (that is, he is in Aries) or is in his own sign Leo, the native will become powerful and famous on account of his good qualities and achievements. He will construct ponds and temples and places for housing cows and Brahmins. If Sun is in the sign of a malefic, or is aspected by or associated with a malefic, there will be obstructions in his professional career. He will indulge in evil deeds; will be of undesirable conduct, immoral and sinful.

Kalyan Verma says in *Saravali*

अतिमतिरतिविभवबलो धनवाहनबन्धुपुत्रवान् सूर्ये।
सिद्धारम्भः शूरो दशमेऽधृष्यः प्रशस्यश्च।।

(*Saravali,* Chap-30/Verse-11)

It means that when the Sun is placed in the tenth house, the native is intelligent, has all amenities and material prosperity, strength, wealth, conveyances, relatives and sons. He succeeds in his undertakings. He is very courageous, unassailable and praiseworthy.

Phaldeepika mentions:

ससुतयानस्तुतिमतिश्रीबलयशाः खे क्षितिपतिः।

(*Phaldeepika,* Chap-8/Verse-4)

It means that if the Sun is placed in the tenth house, one is blessed with conveyances; he is praised by the people; he has good intelligence, wealth, strength and fame; he will live like a king.

Varahmihir says:

सुखशौर्यभाक् खे ।

(*Brihat Jatak*, Chap-20/Verse-3)

The person will lead a happy life and will be very courageous.

Vaidynath writes in *Jatak Parijat*:

मानस्थिते दिनकरे पितृवित्तशीलविद्यायशोबलयुतोऽवनिपालतुल्यः ।

(*Jatak Parijat*, Chap-8/Verse-89)

He gets the benefit by inheritance. He is educated, famous and strong, and gets recognition like a king.

All classical works have appreciated the presence of Sun in the tenth house as it makes one successful, famous, prosperous, popular, powerful, praiseworthy and great in his life. One is endowed with wealth, conveyances, comforts, wife and children. His undertakings and endeavors are successful.

2.2 Placement of Moon in the Tenth House

Placement of Moon in the tenth house makes one successful in his professional life. He will be religious, courageous and performer of good deeds. He will be wealthy and gets success in undertakings. He will be generous in giving and his influence will always be there over others, i.e. he will always have an upper hand. He has reliable and trustworthy friends and generally lives long. He will be industrious and will lead a comfortable life. He will command respect, fame and honour in the society and his profession will have a concern with the government.

Moon's placement in the tenth house is extremely good and he will acquire a high position in life. He will be well educated. If malefics are associated with Moon in the tenth house, he will indulge in sinful deeds and will face obstacles in various paths of life.

If Moon is placed in own sign Cancer or in the sign of Sun Leo, matters of the tenth house will be highly promoted.

One gets professional success in the 24th year. Moon in tenth gives success in business as well.

If Moon is placed in Aries, Cancer, Libra or Capricorn in the 10th house i.e. inmovable sign, one may lose either of his parents during childhood. One gets recognition of merits and success in election. The native will be successful in business of milk, medicine, spices, grains, hotel, bakery, commission agent, insurance agent and retail sales.

If Moon joins the tenth house identical to Taurus, Virgo or Scorpio, the native will have to pay the loans to others taken by his father. If Moon falls in Aries, Cancer or Capricorn, the native remains unsettled throughout his life. Many times, he faces defamation without his fault and he also undergoes many changes in his professional field. Even if parents are alive, relations with them will not be smooth. Moon in the tenth house can make the subject a minister, IAS, or administrator, if it is exalted (i.e. for Leo *lagna*).

Illustration : 2.2 (**RRS**) *Horoscope No.: 3*

Date of birth : 26.08.1940 Time of birth : 05:30:00 hrs
Place of birth : Allahabad Lat 25:27:00 N Long 81:50:00E
Ayanamsa : 23:01:45 Sidereal Time : 3:43:42

Pln	**Degree**	**Rasi**	**Nakshatra**	**Pad**
Asc	6:25:10	Leo	Magha	2
Sun	9:33:48	Leo	Magha	3
Mon	7:52:44	Tau	Kritika	4
Mar (D)	10:59:55	Leo	Magha	4
Mer (C)	0:08:34	Leo	Magha	1
Jup	22:29:52	Ari	Bharani	3
Ven	24:09:29	Gem	Punarvasu	2
Sat	21:45:05	Ari	Bharani	3
Rah (R)	18:41:15	Vir	Hasta	3
Ket (R)	18:41:15	Pis	Revati	1

Lagna Chart

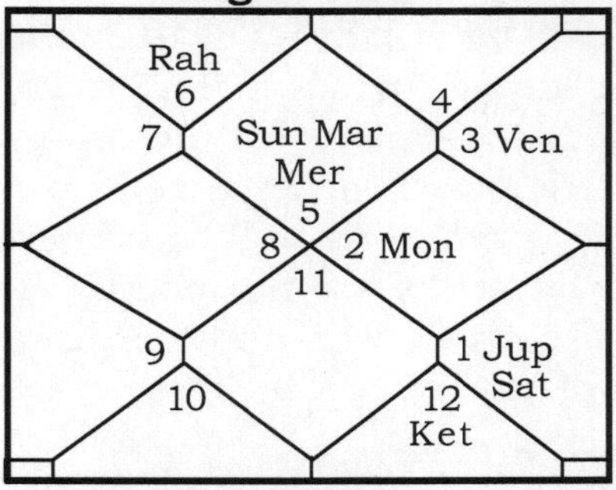

Navamsa Chart

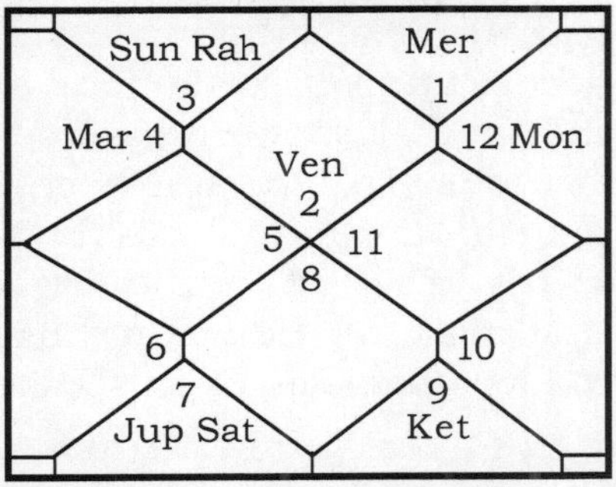

Balance of Vimshottari Dasa of **Sun 0Y 11M 13D**

This horoscope belongs to a famous politician who remained minister and leader of opposition a number of times. But he also faced false charges and defamation. Position of Sun and Mars in Leo *lagna* with exalted Moon in the 10th house is most encouraging factor for a successful politician.

Following combinations explain his present position:

1. *Yogakaraka* Mars is placed in the *lagna* with the *lagna* lord Sun and 11th and 2nd lord Mercury. Jupiter lends his favourable aspect over this combination.
2. Moon is exalted in the 10th house and there is no malefic aspect over the 10th house.

The exalted Moon in the tenth, the Sun in exaltation sign Aries in the ninth house and the 10th lord Venus in the 8th house in Pisces, the sign of its exaltation, make one successful in IAS. Being the fastest moving planet, Moon generally brings many changes in one's career.

विद्यावान् ।।
पापयुते सप्तविंशतिवर्षे विधवासंगमेन जनविरोधी ।।
अतिमेधावी ।। सत्यकर्मनिरतः कीर्तिमान् दयावान् ।।
भावाधिपे बलयुतेविशेसत्कर्मसिद्धिः ।।
पापनिरीक्षिते पापयुते वा दुष्कृतिः ।। कर्मविघ्नकरः ।।

(*Bhrigu Sutram*, Part-II/Chap-2/Verse-54 to 60)

If Moon is in the tenth house, the native will realize high academic attainments. He will be brilliant, will do pious deeds, and will be famous and kind hearted. If the lord of the ninth is powerfully disposed, the native will be highly virtuous. If Moon is in conjunction with or aspected by a malefic, the native will have illicit relations with a widow, in his 27th year, and will earn bitterness of the people on that account. He will indulge in sinful deeds and will have to face obstacles in all spheres of his life.

Kalyan Verma mentions in *Saravali*:

अविषादी कर्मपरः सिद्धारम्भश्च धनसमृद्धश्च।
शुचिरतिबलोऽथ दशमे शूरो दाता भवेच्छाशिनि।।

(*Saravali,* Chap-30/Verse-23)

Meaning, when the Moon is placed in the 10th house, one will be free from grief, ever devoted to his duties and work. He will be successful in his undertakings. He will be wealthy, pure, strong, cruel but generous.

Brihat Jatak says:

निष्पत्तिं समुपैति धर्मधनधीशौर्यैर्युतः कर्मगे।।

(*Brihat Jatak,* Chap-20/Verse-5)

That is, the job undertaken by the native succeeds; he is righteous and endowed with wealth, intellect and courage.

Jatak Parijat mentions:

चन्द्रो यदा दशमगो
धनधान्यवस्त्रभूषावधूजनविलासकलाविलोलाः।।

(*Jatak Parijat,* Chap-20/Verse-89)

It means, when the Moon is placed in the 10th house, one gets wealth, food, dress, and ornament; enjoys wife, luxury and arts.

Mantreshwara says in *Phaldeepika*:

जयी सिद्धारम्भो नभसि शुभकृत्सत्प्रियकरः।

(*Phaldeepika,* Chap-8/Verse-7)

That, the person meets with success in undertakings. He does good acts, is virtuous and helpful.

The Moon in the 10th house gives popularity in public, changes in career, and travels in professional life etc. One may deal in articles signified by Moon. He is much respected and popular in society due to his own deeds like Mahatma Gandhi, Swami Shivanand etc. He will be respected by relatives. He will be generous and kind and may be a trustee of religious institution. He will have many friends and will be successful easily. He will be active, smart, energetic and intelligent. Fluctuations in professional life are also expected, especially when Moon falls in a moving sign. One is engaged in profession like business of silver, rice, milk or milk products, water, canal, dam, bridge construction, rowing boats, fishing, pearl, cold drinks, oily substances, soaps, detergents, sugar and ghee etc. A strong and benefic Moon in the 10th house is very good for all professional aspects of the native.

Moon also indicates lime which is used in building work. Therefore, influence of Moon over the 10th house or its lord can make one a civil engineer i.e. the engineer of construction of building etc.

2.3 Placement of Mars in the Tenth House

Placement of Mars in the 10th house makes one learned, active and energetic. He becomes famous due to his deeds and activities. It is *Kuldeepak Yoga* i.e. the native becomes prosperous and famous and brings good name to his family. The progress and prosperity of the native is more than his father or grand father. Mars of the 10th house makes one successful in police service, defense, medical profession and engineering etc. He can enter in the trade of petroleum, cooking gas, copper, weapons, match box, crackers or may deal in landed property. Mars and Sun, if conjoined in the 10th house, make one a doctor, surgeon or physician. If the Sun falls in the 4th house, and Mars is placed in the 10th house, the native or his father may suffer from heart trouble.

If Mars is afflicted in the 10th house, one may become a criminal or a thief, provided the 10th lord is also under the influence of malefics. His career will be disturbed throughout and he may not be honest with anyone, though he will pretend to be like that.

Mars gains cent per cent directional strength in the 10th house, therefore the native will be strong in profession he undertakes.

If Mars joins the 10th house identical to own sign, Aries or Scorpio, or the sign of its exaltation Capricorn, it will give the results of *Ruchhak Mahapurush Rajyoga*. For Pisces or Leo ascendant, position of Mars in the 10th is an asset, as in both the cases Mars will own 9th and join 10th. For Leo and Cancer ascendants, Mars happens to be a *yogakaraka* and produces *Rajyoga* in the 10th house and promotes all matters related to the 10th house. If Mars and Jupiter occupy the 10th house, the native will have a good reputation in the society and will possess lands, houses, conveyances and glory. Well fortified Mars in the 10th house, if has a connection with 3rd or the 11th house, will cause prosperity and longevity to brothers. It will be just reverse if Mars is afflicted, as Mars signifies brothers. If Mars and Sun are conjoined in the 10th house, in Leo or Scorpio, one is likely to become a surgeon.

जनवल्लभः ।। भावाधिपे बलयुते भ्राता दीर्घायुः ।।
विशेष भाग्यवान, ध्यानशीलवान् गुरुभक्ति युतः ।।
पापयुते कर्मविघ्नवान् ।। शुभयुते शुभक्षेत्रे कर्मसिद्धि ।।
कीर्तिप्रतिष्ठावान् अष्टादशवर्षे द्रव्यार्जन समर्थः ।।
सर्वसमर्थः दृढ़गात्र चोरबुद्धिः पापयुते पापक्षेत्रे कर्मविघ्नकरः ।।
दुष्कृतिः ।। भाग्येश कर्मेशयुते महाराजयौवराज्ये पट्टाभिषेकवान् ।।
गुरुयुते गजान्तैश्वर्यवान् ।। भूसमृद्धिमान् ।।

(*Bhrigu Sutram,* Part-II/Chap-3/Verse-75 to 85)

If Mars is in the tenth house, the native will be acclaimed by the people. If the lord of the tenth is strong, the brothers will be long lived. The native will be particularly fortunate and prosperous; he will take interest in meditation, and will be devoted to his preceptor. If Mars is in conjunction with a malefic, there will be obstructions in the professional career. If he is associated with a benefic or is in the house of a benefic, the native will be successful in his undertakings. He will be famous and respected, and will commence earning from his 18th year. He will have a stout body and will be well off in every respect, but he may have mentality of a thief. If Mars is associated with a malefic, or is in the house of a malefic, the native's life will be full of obstructions and he will indulge in sinful deeds. If Mars is associated with lords of the 9th or 10th, the native will be installed as a king or heir apparent. If Mars is associated with Jupiter, the native will possess elephants (conveyances) and will be full of glory. He will also possess lands.

Saravali says:

कर्मोद्युक्तो दशमे शूरोऽधृष्यः प्रधानजनसेवी।
सुतसौख्ययुतो रुधिरे प्रतापबहुलः पुमान् भवति।।

(*Saravali,* Chap-30/Verse-35)

If Mars occupies the 10th *bhava*, the native will be proficient in the acts, be valorous, unconquerable, will serve important people, be endowed with sons and happiness, and be very courageous.

Mars is *Bhoomi putra,* therefore it has deep concern with lands and house. It can make one a dealer of landed property, building houses etc. A powerful Mars in the 10th house also makes one successful in police department and defense services. If Mars is afflicted in the 10th house, and 3rd house is also strong and afflicted, one may earn money through crime, killing, robbery, smuggling etc. Violence, assassination, bombing and terrorism are also ruled by Mars, in one or the other way. In that case, affliction of the 5th house is also essential, which wrongly diverts intelligence and actions of the native.

Mars indicates biology, geology and other such sciences. It makes one confident, proud, quarrelsome, faultfinding and a critic. Mars and Mercury can make one mechanical or product engineer. Mars makes one manufacturer of automobiles, engines and tools etc. Mars, in fiery sign, indicates inflammable items such as petrol, kerosene, cooking gas, sulphur etc.

Satyacharya suggests that building made of masonry bricks, discussions, arguments, dispute, bold ventures, fire, administration and murders are signified by Mars, depending upon various other factors as well.

If Mars is placed in the 10th house in Cancer, Scorpio, Pisces, Aries, Leo or Sagittarius, it gives good effects normally. But it gives adverse results in Taurus, Virgo, Capricorn, Gemini, Libra and Aquarius. Mars causes rise of fortune after 36th years of age.

Mr. H.N. Ketve opines that Mars in Scorpio, in the 10th, makes one a surgeon and famous doctor. Service persons have lot of fight with their officers due to such Mars. An advocate becomes a successful criminal lawyer, if Mars is placed in the 10th house, along with other combinations of becoming successful in the field of law.

2.4 Placement of Mercury in the Tenth House

Placement of Mercury in the 10th house provides immense intelligence, courage and general awareness of various fields of knowledge. The native will be very truthful, honest, sincere and sensitive to his work, if Mercury is unafflicted and well disposed. The native will have long and real happiness, concerning mother particularly. He will possess much mental strength and stamina. He will engage himself in any industry or undertaking successfully. According to a few writers, the native may get wealth at the age of 17 or 19 in any way. It is possible through legacy or sudden gain, provided other indications are also present.

If Mercury is posited in the 10th house, all alone, and is well disposed in a fiery sign i.e. Aries, Leo or Sagittarius, one will become a mathematician, computer specialist, typist, stenographer, engineer or clerk in any department of the above mentioned works.

Mercury provides mental ability to become a poet, writer, dancer, actor, musician, singer, editor, publisher, astrologer, palmist, *pandit*, orator, teacher, spiritualist, computer expert, accountant, CA, journalist, businessman, lawyer, psychologist, psychiatrist, or mathematician. He may work in communication, transportation, or postal services, or as travel agents etc. He gets benefits from friends and associates. He is witty and has lot of fun in his conversation. He is intelligent and knows what to talk and at which place. Mercury is the planet of wisdom and intelligence. Mercury also indicates speech. Therefore, one can earn money by his lectures, speeches, sermons, *pravachan* etc. Without favour of Mercury, one can not become an astrologer or fortuneteller.

It has been mentioned by classical astrologers that Mercury in Kendra and Jupiter in triangle, or vice versa, makes one a good astrologer. World famous astrologer Sri B. Suryanarainrao had Mercury and Jupiter in the 10th house in Aquarius. Strong Mercury in the 10th house, with a powerful 11th house, makes one an industrialist.

Illustration : 2.3 (**R.K. Dalmia**) *Horoscope No.: 4*

Date of birth : 07.04.1893 Time of birth : 10:42:00 hrs
Place of birth : Chirawa Lat 28:12:00 N Long 75:42:00E
Ayanamsa : 22:21:50 Sidereal Time : 23:44:54

Pln	**Degree**	**Rasi**	**Nakshatra**	**Pad**
Asc	16:21:11	Gem	Ardra	3
Sun	25:15:47	Pis	Revati	3
Mon	0:22:52	Sag	Moola	1
Mar	13:48:35	Tau	Rohini	2
Mer (R/C)	14:32:41	Pis	U. Bhadrapad	4
Jup	10:35:56	Ari	Ashwini	4
Ven (C)	18:42:27	Pis	Revati	1
Sat (R)	16:26:50	Vir	Hasta	2
Rah (C)	6:18:37	Ari	Ashwini	2
Ket	6:18:37	Lib	Chitra	4

Lagna Chart

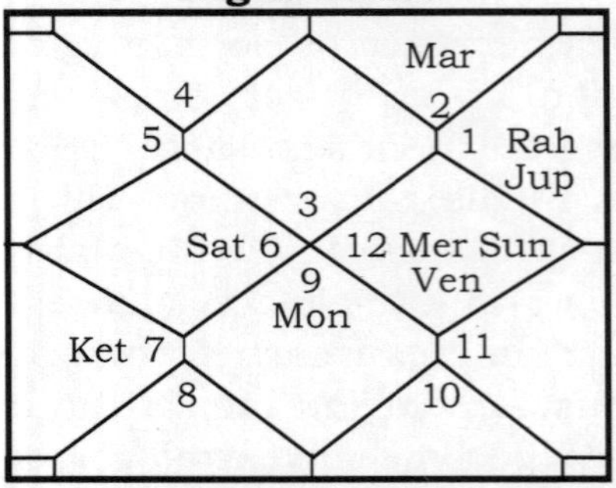

Navamsa Chart

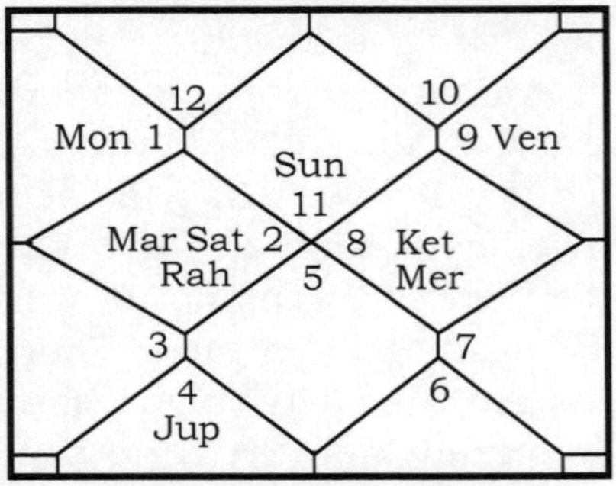

Balance of Vimshottari Dasa of **Ket 6Y 9M 18D**

The native was a world famous industrialist. *Lagna* lord Mercury is placed in the 10th house under *neech bhanga rajyoga.* The 5th lord Venus and 3rd lord Sun are associated with Mercury in the 10th house. The 11th house is also very powerful as Jupiter and Rahu are conjoined there. The 9th lord Saturn falls in 4th, and the 5th lord Venus falls in 10th. Both, Venus and Saturn, are opposite to each other. There is powerful *Kendra Trikona Rajyoga,* which has made the native a great man and an industrialist of worldwide fame.

There are innumerable examples to show that the placement of well-fortified Mercury in the 10th house, with a strong 11th house, has made the native business magnet. But ill-disposed Mercury in 10th can make one an ordinary clerk even.

Saravali mentions:

प्रवरमतिकर्मचेष्टः सफलारम्भो विशारदो दशमे ।
धीरः सत्वसमेतो विविधालंकारसत्त्वभाक सौम्ये ।।

(*Saravali,* Chap-30/Verse-47)

That means, if Mercury occupies the 10th house, the native will possess distinguished intelligence, will perform distinguished acts, will attain fruition in undertakings, be very learned, courageous, strong and will be endowed with various kinds of ornaments.

If only Mercury is placed in the 10th house and there is

no other planet with Mercury in fiery signs viz. Aries, Leo and Sagittarius, one will become a mathematician, computer specialist, teacher or the native will work in engineering, postal, telegraph or telephone department. If Mercury in 10th house is in airy signs viz. Gemini, Libra or Aquarius, the native will be employed in postal department, PWD, electricity or the like. In Taurus, Virgo or Capricorn Mercury will make one knowledgeable in literature, linguistics, commission agents, businessman etc. If Mercury falls in Cancer, Scorpio or Pisces, in the 10th house, it will engage the native in the job of editor, publisher, printer, travelling agent, or stationer. But the exact nature of job depends upon various other factors also. However, the strong Mercury in the 10th house gives lot of happiness from the side of mother.

Illustration: 2.4 (**Manmohan Singh**) *Horoscope No.: 5*

Date of birth : 26.09.1932 Time of birth : 14:00:00 hrs
Place of birth : Jhelum Lat 33:00:00 N Long 73:45:00E
Ayanamsa : 22:55:07 Sidereal Time : 13:44:44

Pln	**Degree**	**Rasi**	**Nakshatra**	**Pad**
Asc	16:20:47	Sag	Purvasadha	1
Sun	10:06:48	Vir	Hasta	1
Mon	19:07:15	Can	Aslesa	1
Mar (D)	10:24:55	Can	Pushya	3
Mer	7:37:50	Vir	U Phalguni	4
Jup	17:00:04	Leo	P Phalguni	2
Ven	25:07:14	Can	Aslesa	3
Sat (R)	5:13:51	Cap	Uttarasadha	3
Rah	24:16:01	Aqu	P Bhadrapad	2
Ket	24:16:01	Leo	P Phalguni	4

Lagna Chart

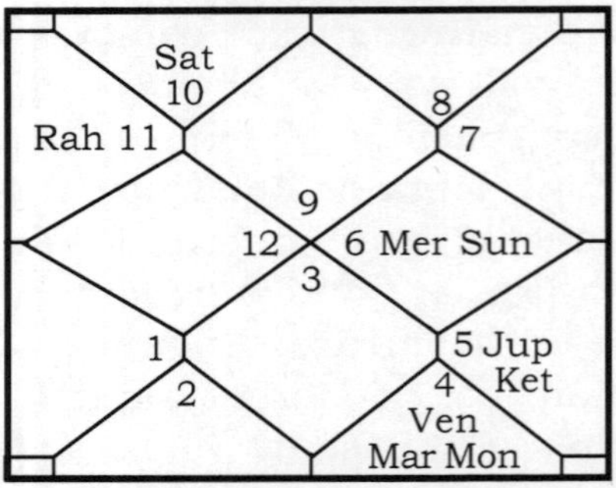

Navamsa Chart

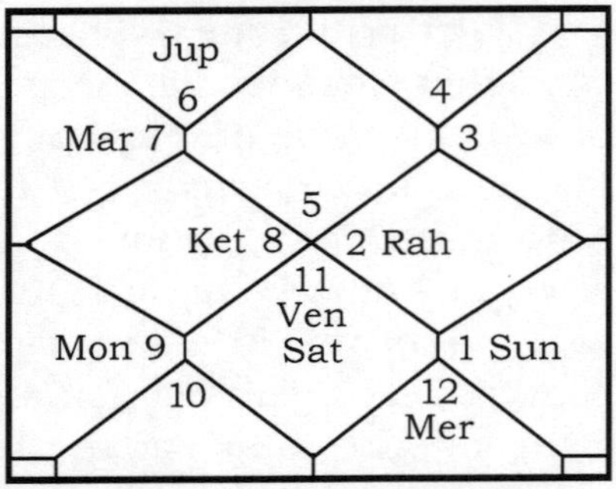

Balance of Vimshottari Dasa of **Mer 13Y 10M 13D**

Known as the Finance minister of India who was instrumental in bringing the liberalization in economy, Dr. Manmohan Singh rose to the level of Prime Minister of the country.

Exalted Mercury is placed in the 10th house in association with the 9th lord Sun. The *lagna* and 4th lord Jupiter in the 9th house has also given him a good fortune, high education and influential personality as *lagna* also receives the benefic aspect of Jupiter. Thus, Mercury can elevate one up to this level, if it is well disposed, as it is there in the present case. Economists, commerce specialists, business magnets, traders, manufacturers, industrialists, policy makers, planners business and hotel managers etc. come under the purview of Mercury.

Strong Mercury elevates one to a very high level but weak Mercury can make the native a clerk, typist, copyist, dispatcher, proofreader etc.

Bhrigusutra mentions:

सत्कर्मसिद्धिः धैर्यवान् बहुलकीर्तिमान् बहुचितवान्।।
अष्टाविंशतिवर्षे नेत्ररोगवान्।।
उच्चस्वक्षेत्रे गुरुयुतेऽग्निष्टोमादि बहुकर्मवान्।।
अरिपापयुते मूढकर्मविघ्नवान् दुष्कृतिः अनाचारः।।

(*Bhrigusutra,* Part-II/Chap-4/Vers-67 to 70)

If Mercury is placed in the 10th house, the native will be successful by performing virtuous deeds. He will be patient; will have wide spread reputation and will be a great thinker. He will suffer from eye trouble in the 24th year of his age.

If Mercury is in own sign or in his sign of exaltation or in conjunction with Jupiter, many kinds of religious rites are performed by him. If Mercury is placed in an inimical sign or is associated with malefics, the native will be stupid and indulge in sinful deeds and will be of bad conduct. In this *sloka,* the statement of eye trouble at the age of 24 is not relevant and has not been found correct in practice.

Brihat Jataka, Phaldeepika, Saravali, Chamatkar Chintamani and various other classical works have appreciated the position of Mercury in the 10th house for good professional prospects, name, honour, success, intelligence, knowledge and wisdom.

2.5 Placement of Jupiter in the Tenth House

Bhrigu has specified in *Bhrigusutram*:

धार्मिकः शुभकर्मकारी गीतापाठकः ।।
योग्यतावान् प्रौढ़कीर्तिः बहुजनपूज्यः ।।
भावाधिपे बलयुते विशेषक्रतुसिद्धिः ।।
पापयुते पापक्षेत्रे कर्मविघ्नः ।। दुष्कृतियात्रालाभहीनः ।।

(*Bhrigusutra,* Part-II/Chap-5/Vers-46 to 49)

The native will be religious minded and will perform righteous deeds, study Geeta, will be very able, will have wide spread reputation and will be respected by the masses. If the 10th lord is strong, the native will perform high-class religious sacrifices. If the lord of the 10th house is associated with a malefic or is situated in the house of a malefic planet, there will be obstacles in professional career or the native will indulge in evil deeds and will suffer financially.

Kalyan Verma states in *Saravali*:

सिद्धारम्भो मान्यः सर्वोपायः कुशलसमृद्धश्च ।
दशमस्थे त्रिदशगुरौ सुखधनजनवाहनयशोभाक् ।।

(*Saravali,* Chap-30/Vers-59)

One gets success in his undertakings, if Jupiter is placed in the 10th house. He is highly respected. He has all the amenities. He is clever and very prosperous. One gets much happiness, wealth, relatives, conveyances and fame. According to Varahmihira one becomes very wealthy if Jupiter is placed in the 10th house.

Mantreshwara has mentioned in his great classic *Phaldeepika*:

स्वाचारः सुयशा नभस्यतिधनी जीवे महीशप्रियः।

(*Phaldeepika,* Chap-8/Vers-16)

That is, the person follows the right course of conduct. He is famous and very wealthy. He is the friend of the king. Jupiter in the 10th house shows prosperous and happy life. The person rises in his life and gains wealth. Honour and success come to him.

Vaidyanath writes in *Jatak Parijat*:

सिद्धारम्भः साधुवृत्तः स्वधर्मी विद्वानाढयो मानगे चामरेज्ये।।

(*Jatak Parijat,* Chap-8/Vers-91)

It means that one succeeds in his undertakings. His conduct is noble. He is dutiful, learned and very rich.

Jupiter's placement in the 10th house is a very good disposition for a successful and prosperous career, provided Jupiter is well fortified. One becomes rich by his own endeavours. He has all kinds of comforts and luxury. This is quite an encouraging location of Jupiter for wealth, prosperity, conveyances, attendants, name, fame and honour etc. Such a native receives the favour of superiors, government and rulers. The native is wise, clever and successful in all his undertakings. Generally, such a person is religiously inclined and has good conduct. He may overcome most of the problems of his professional life. Jupiter in the 10th comes for rescue at the eleventh hour when one is put in trouble. If the lord of the 10th house is well associated with benefics, one will be extremely well placed and will be involved in good deeds, help others, will read Vedant, Darshan and religious books, and will perform *Havan*,

Yagnya and will arrange religious meetings, speeches, *pravachan* etc from time to time. If Jupiter is ill disposed and the 10th lord is associated with malefic planets, the native will be involved in unrighteous deeds. Jupiter in the 10th house may give wealth at 9th, 12th or 19th years of age, as has been mentioned in one script.

Jupiter's position in the 10th house is a great asset of the horoscope. One gets high position in the government and maintains high values and standards of decency. If Jupiter joins Venus in the 10th house, one reaches very high in govt. service. If Jupiter and Venus are placed in Pisces in the 10th house, it gives rise to *Hansa* and *Malvya Mahapurush Rajyoga*. If Jupiter is associated with Mars in the 10th house, one is involved in research work and becomes the head of any educational institute or he promotes his own research activities in the field of vedas, spiritualism, science, literature, astrology, and occult sciences etc. Rahu's conjunction with Jupiter in the 10th house makes one a trouble creator for others. He makes mischief and is a sadist i.e. he gets pleasure in troubling others. Persons working under such an individual experience lot of problems and disgrace.

Jupiter in the 10th house indicates professions connected with law and justice. Jupiter has a quality of healing, helping and cure, so Jupiter in 10th can also give a medical career, provided the Sun and Mars are also associated with the 10th house. This disposition of Jupiter makes one employed in banks or other financial organizations. If Jupiter is very strong and 2nd, 7th, 11th houses are also strong, one runs a finance company of his own. Such a person can earn through interest, rent or brokerage as well. If Jupiter is the lord of 9th house and falls in the 10th, and the 10th lord is also well disposed, one gets a high position in govt. service. One may become the head of any religious organization or institution. In the horoscopes of many astrologers, Jupiter is well positioned in the 10th house.

The world famous astrologer Dr. B.V. Raman had Jupiter

in the 10th house in Scorpio. If any planet, that owns the 2nd house & joins the 10th, it becomes the absolute representative of the means of his livelihood i.e. his profession. In Dr. Raman's chart, Jupiter is the lord of the 2nd house and is posited in the 10th that is why he entered into the sublime profession of advancement of astrology.

Illustration : 2.5 (**Dr. B.V. Raman**) *Horoscope No.: 6*

Date of birth : 08.08.1912 Time of birth : 19:42:44 hrs
Place of birth : Bangalore Lat 13:00:00 N Long 77:35:00E
Ayanamsa : 22:38:07 Sidereal Time : 16:29:56

Pln	**Degree**	**Rasi**	**Nakshatra**	**Pad**
Asc	10:29:17	Aqu	Satabhisha	2
Sun	22:59:14	Can	Aslesa	2
Mon	23:40:37	Tau	Mrigshira	1
Mar	21:21:50	Leo	P Phalguni	3
Mer (R)	13:57:17	Leo	P Phalguni	1
Jup	12:58:03	Sco	Anuradha	3
Ven (C)	2:14:50	Leo	Magha	1
Sat	10:09:33	Tau	Rohini	1
Rah (R)	21:41:55	Pis	Revati	2
Ket (R)	21:41:55	Vir	Hasta	4

Lagna Chart

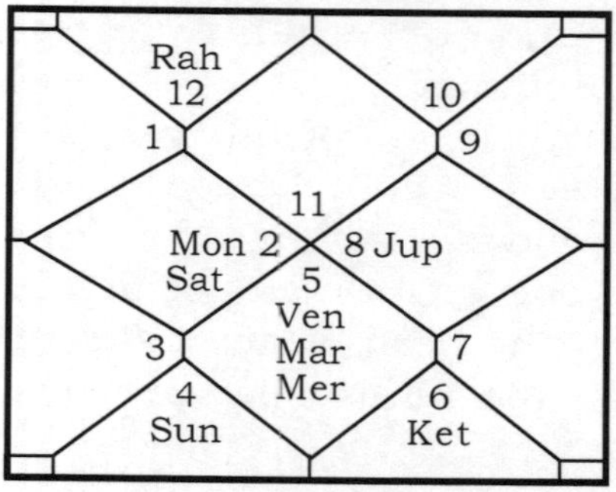

Navamsa Chart

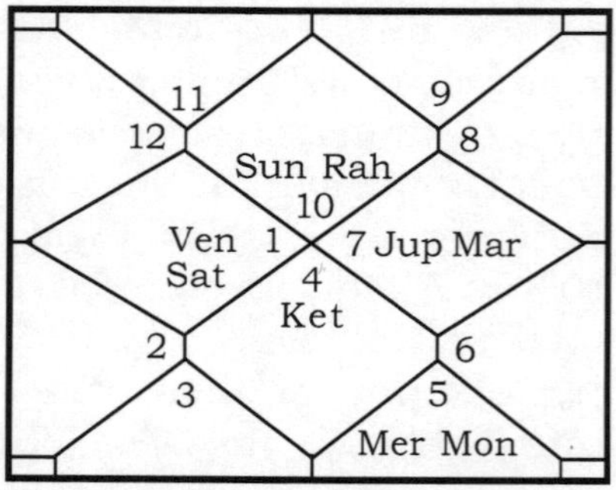

Balance of Vimshottari Dasa of **Mar 6Y 9M 25D**

Mr. H.N. Ketve, who was a great astrologer of his time, has written that Jupiter's placement in the 10th house causes the death of father around 16 or 24 years of age. Both, father and son, do not get elevation in life simultaneously. One is bound to take loan and debts increase. One is to borrow for his routine expenses, especially during Jupiter's major period. Mostly he gets defamation for deeds he is not responsible. These results will be more pronounced in Taurus, Virgo, Libra, Capricorn or Aquarius. This position of Jupiter is adverse for father and may even cause his death.

Jupiter gives auspicious results in other signs in the 10th house. If Jupiter falls in the 10th house in male sign then children are few, as against more children in female signs.

It is difficult to specify the exact profession by Jupiter in the 10th. Beggars, street hawkers, Judge, businessmen doing export-import etc., all may have Jupiter in the 10th house.

Other classics mention that Jupiter in 10th give profession of law. He may become a successful advocate or judge. He may become a minister, astrologer, teacher, priest, banker, and clothier and may run a restaurant, hotel or hospital etc. Strong Jupiter in the 10th house gives a high or prominent official position. But Jupiter should not be regarded good for many other aspects such as age, father's problems and debts and sorrows during Jupiter's *mahadasa*. Jupiter in Leo gives best results in the 10th house for children and money matters but that will also not give good results during its own *mahadasa*.

2.6 Placement of Venus in the Tenth House

Mantreshwara has specified in *Phaldeepika*:

नभस्यतियशः सुहृत्सुखिवृत्तियुक्तम् प्रभुम् ।।

(*Phaldeepika,* Chap-8/Vers-19)

This means that the placement of Venus in the 10th house gives rise to high degree of fame and honour. He will have many friends. He will be a lord and will have a pleasant profession.

Bhrigusutram states:

बहुप्रतापवान् पापयुते कर्मविघ्नकरः
गुरुबुधचन्द्रयुते अनेकवाहनारोहणवान्।।
अनेकक्रतुसिद्धिः।।
दिगन्तविश्रुतकीर्तिः अनेकराजयोगः बहुभाग्यवान् वाचालः।।

(*Bhrigusutram,* Part-II/Chap-6/Vers-59 to 61)

It means that the life of native will be glorious, if Venus joins the 10th house. If Venus is associated with or aspected by malefics, one will have obstacles and problems in his undertakings and professional aspects.

If Venus is associated with Mercury, Jupiter and Mars, the native will enjoy the comfort of many conveyances; he will perform religious ceremonies of various kinds and will enjoy worldwide reputation. He will enjoy various *Rajyogas* giving wealth, honour and fame. He will be quite fortunate and talkative.

For Capricorn, Aquarius and Virgo ascendants, Venus gives very auspicious results, especially if placed in the 10th house. For earlier two ascendants, Venus happens to be a *Yogakaraka* and promotes the house occupied by it. For Cancer and Virgo ascendants, Venus becomes the lord of 4th & 11th houses and 2nd & 9th houses respectively. The matters of the 10th house will be highly promoted. One will be a high official or may even be successful in civil services if other combinations also support, or the native may become an industrialist. This disposition of Venus gives rise to a powerful *Dhanyoga*. If Venus is present in the 10th house in own sign or the sign of its exaltation *Malvya Mahapurush Rajyoga* is created.

सौभाग्यसम्मानविराजमानः स्नानार्चनध्यानमनाधनाढयः।
कान्तासुतप्रीतिरतीव नित्यं भृगोः सुते राज्यगते नरस्य।।

(*Jatak Bharanam,* Chap-*Dasham Bhava Vichar*/Vers-10)

Such a native will be fortunate; he honours poor persons and is clean. He is particular about bath, worship and meditation. He is wealthy and very affectionate towards wife and children. Venus in 10th gives powers also.

Kalyan verma writes in *Saravali*:

उद्यानसुविभवा हितसुखरतिमानार्थकीर्तयो यस्य।
दशमस्थे भृगुतनये भवति पुमान् बहुमतिः ख्यातः ।।

(*Saravali,* Chap-30/Vers-71)

That is, if Venus is placed in the 10th house, one is very intelligent and famous. He has many friends, much happiness and respect, wealth and fame. He possesses gardens and all amenities.

Jataka Parijat says:

शुक्रे कर्मस्थानगे कर्षकाच्च स्त्रीमूलाद्वा लब्धवित्तो विभुः स्यात् ।।

(*Jatak Parijat,* Chap-8/Vers-91)

One is a lord getting wealth through women and agriculture, if Venus occupies the 10th house.

All the authors of classical works have appreciated the presence of Venus in the 10th house. It may be summarized thus that the native earns through houses and buildings. He will be very influential and may be working with many females either as colleague, superior or subordinate. He will be social, friendly and renowned. If Venus and Saturn are conjoined together, one will earn money by profits in cosmetics and articles used by ladies. He will have respect for divine persons, saints, astrologers and priests. Venus in the 10th house makes one a trader dealing in cosmetics, paints, distemper, flowers, perfumes, plastics, polyester, polythene, glass, adhesives, fabrics, textiles, garments, ornaments and paper etc. He may be an architect or be engaged in farming. Venus is the significator of vehicles; therefore, one may be dealer of automobiles. He may have a studio of his own for making films or photographs. He may own cinema hall, or a place of other kinds of entertainment. He may manufacture television, radio, music system, C.D. player, VCR or other musical instruments. He may deal in making films, staging dramas and presenting musicians, magicians, singers and dancers. The native may employ himself in various fields of entertainment, architecture, perfumes and art of acting, dancing, singing and painting etc.

Placement of Venus in the 10th house in male signs curtails marital happiness. Such a native is less interested in females. The native wants to marry only after his own earnings or after proper settlement in life. If the native, having Venus in the 10th house, is blessed with a good wife and decent children, the happiness of profession is curtailed. If Venus is afflicted or hemmed between malefics, one may have a strong relationship with a female, in addition to his wife. You may call her the second woman in the life of the native.

If Venus is placed in the female sign in the 10th house, it indicates rise of fortune and proper settlement only after marriage. Venus in fiery and airy signs viz. Aries, Leo, Sagittarius, Gemini, Libra and Aquarius gives good results in professional matters. One receives high education of science and becomes an administrative or executive officer.

We have observed Venus as the significator of IAS or equivalent services, where one gets both power and comfort. Venus owns Taurus and Libra, and Libra is indicated by a measuring balance. This may be compared with justice i.e. balanced judgement. Therefore, Venus has also produced many barristers, lawyers, judges and law professionals. The native is generally kind hearted, popular, decent, loving, caring and friendly but he often gets cheated by others. Such natives are addicted to something and that may be anything. The native earns lot of wealth by his own endeavor but spoils also due to his liberal attitude, overconfidence and much trust over others. The native enjoys wealth by various means in his professional life, by purchase of many vehicles, air conditioners, beautiful office and rich living, dressing and going to high class restaurants, hotels and spending lot over picnics, site seeing, enjoyments and entertainment. And as such his money is used and accumulation of wealth becomes difficult. One gets defamed due to female, if Venus is afflicted.

One tries various professions but does not get success

in any one of them generally, especially in those fields in which one gets engaged in the profession of which Venus is the *Karaka*. He hardly gets success in any such business. Subjects having Venus in the 10th house do not enter into politics, as they are not accustomed to hard work. They believe in life full of pleasure and comforts.

Let us see this in a practical case:

Illustration : 2.6 (**RS**) *Horoscope No.: 7*

Date of birth : 20.07.1952 Time of birth : 12:45:36 hrs
Place of birth : Jabalpur Lat 23:10:00 N Long 79:57:00E
Ayanamsa : 23:11:50 Sidereal Time : 8:27:27

Pln	**Degree**	**Rasi**	**Nakshatra**	**Pad**
Asc	10:21:44	Lib	Swati	2
Sun	4:18:02	Can	Pushya	1
Mon	15:55:18	Gem	Ardra	3
Mar	17:03:49	Lib	Swati	4
Mer	0:24:49	Leo	Magha	1
Jup	23:44:51	Ari	Bharani	4
Ven (C)	11:18:34	Can	Pushya	3
Sat	16:16:51	Vir	Hasta	2
Rah (R)	28:26:31	Cap	Dhanistha	2
Ket (R)	28:26:31	Can	Aslesa	4

Lagna Chart

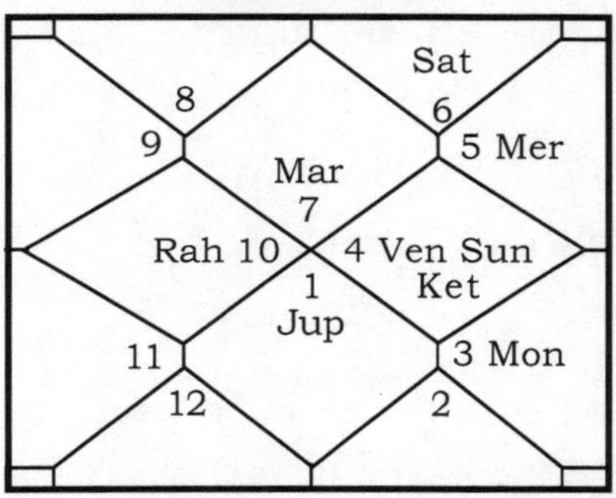

Navamsa Chart

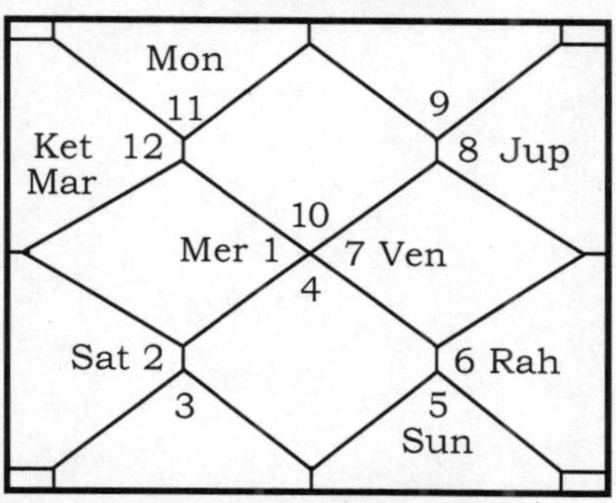

Balance of Vimshottari Dasa of **Rah 5Y 6M 2D**

This is the horoscope of an engineer who initially joined a service but after some time picked up the business of garments, plastic, polyester, polythene, lamination, and milk, and manufactured many articles as indicated by Venus. Slowly and slowly, by dint of his hard work and meticulous planning, he multiplied his business into having a turnover of around 50 crore rupees per annum, with in a span of about 8 years. But the sub period of Venus, in the major period of Mercury, brought the downfall of the native. He placed too much trust on his employees and was cheated by them. Many of his earlier employees are prospering in their own businesses, whereas he has been forced to serve in an organization to have his both ends met.

Illustration : 2.7 (**AG**) *Horoscope No.: 8*

Date of birth : 05.09.1963 Time of birth : 11:24:00 hrs

Place of birth : Kanpur Lat 26:27:00 N Long 80:19:00E

Ayanamsa : 23:20:42 Sidereal Time : 10:09:46

Pln	**Degree**	**Rasi**	**Nakshatra**	**Pad**
Asc	1:35:09	Sco	Vishakha	4
Sun	18:36:41	Leo	P Phalguni	2
Mon	7:52:44	Pis	U Bhadrapad	2
Mar	1:56:00	Lib	Chitra	3
Mer	11:38:50	Vir	Hasta	1
Jup (R)	24:59:14	Pis	Revati	3
Ven (D)	20:17:55	Leo	P Phalguni	3
Sat (R)	24:45:59	Cap	Dhanistha	1
Rah (R)	25:40:45	Gem	Punarvasu	2
Ket (R)	25:40:45	Sag	Purvasadha	4

Lagna Chart

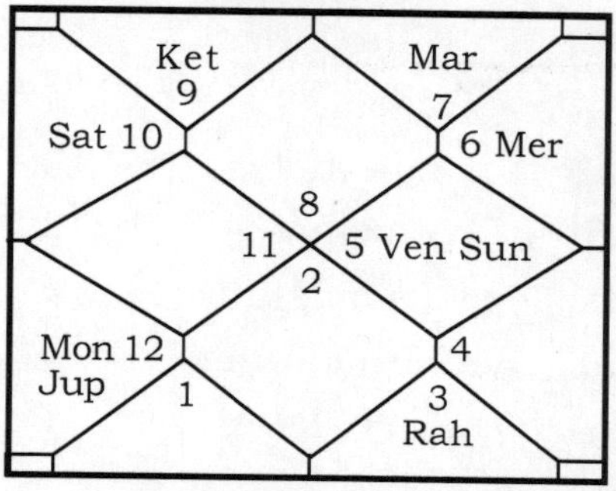

Navamsa Chart

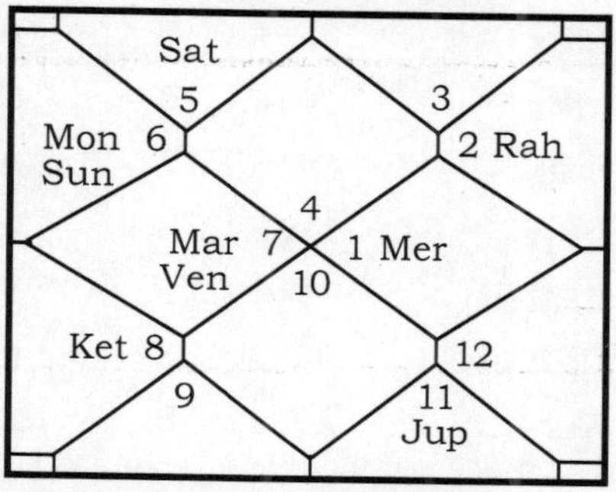

Balance of Vimshottari Dasa of **Sat 12Y 6M 8D**

The native entered into the business of a large printing press at the age of 18 years and earned millions. Thereafter, with the beginning of Ketu *Mahadasa*, he started a milk dairy. He worked very hard but could not get the desired success. Venus *Mahadasa* started from 14.3.2000. Venus is placed in the 10th house. Serious financial problems are still there. *Sade sati* of Saturn ended on 6.6.2000. Nearly 40% of Venus *dasa* has passed. But that is of no advantage to the native. Here, Venus is the lord of 7th and 12th houses and its presence in the 10th house is not congenial to high professional prospects during its major period.

Many such illustrations can be given that a strong Venus in the 10th house made the subject an IAS or PCS officer or an administrator, but in our experience, Venus in the 10th house, many times harms the stability of occupation, business or industrial growth.

Illustration : 2.8 **(EA)** *Horoscope No.: 9*

Date of birth : 18.01.1951 Time of birth : 13:13:00 hrs
Place of birth : Harda Khas Lat 22:22:00 N Long 77:08:00E
Ayanamsa : 23:10:27 Sidereal Time : 20:39:10

Pln	**Degree**	**Rasi**	**Nakshatra**	**Pad**
Asc	26:36:30	Ari	Bharani	4
Sun	4:13:56	Cap	Uttarasadha	3

Mon	10:19:49	Tau	Rohini	1
Mar	3:29:57	Aqu	Dhanistha	4
Mer	10:43:44	Sag	Moola	4
Jup	14:58:37	Aqu	Satabhisha	3
Ven	19:54:53	Cap	Sravana	3
Sat (R)	9:09:19	Vir	U Phalguni	4
Rah (R)	27:27:58	Aqu	P Bhadrapad	3
Ket (R)	27:27:58	Leo	U Phalguni	1

Lagna Chart

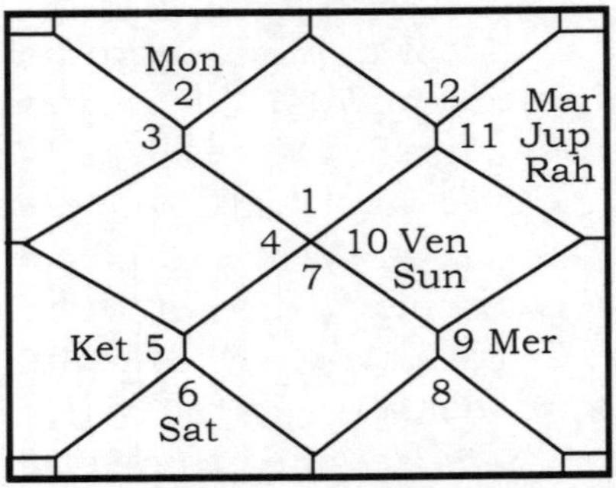

Navamsa Chart

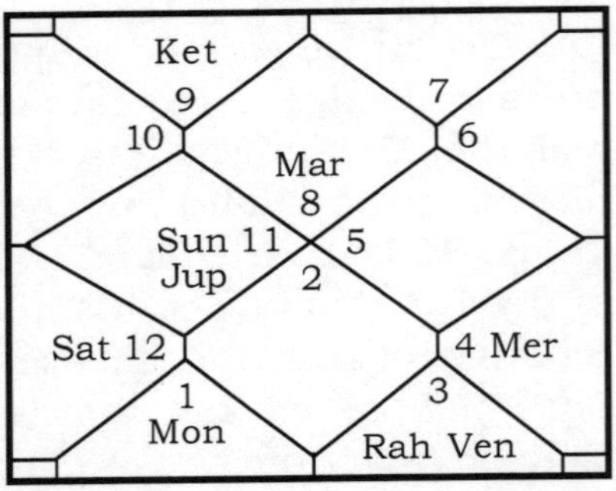

Balance of Vimshottari Dasa of **Mon 9Y 9M 0D**

The native is one of the biggest merchants of cotton in India. He is a multimillionaire. The lord of the 2nd and 7th house, Venus, is placed in the 10th house. The lord of 5th house, Sun, has also joined Venus in the 10th house. Venus falls in the constellation of Moon, which signifies the business of cotton. In our opinion, if the lord of 2nd house gets posited in the 10th house then it becomes the strong indicator of profession. In such a case, 10th lord and its placement should be judged to supplement the view. Here, the 10th lord Saturn is placed in the 6th house in Virgo. Thus, the planets involved- Saturn, Mercury and Mars- do not have any concern with the business of cotton. However, exalted Moon in the 2nd house, in earthy sign, indicates the business of cotton.

This is a tough job to decide a single means of livelihood, as there may be so many planets influencing the profession of the native.

Venus in the 10th house, in a watery sign, indicates a job related with navigation, perfumes, plastic, nylon, rubber, adhesives and also administration. In airy signs, Venus makes one a lawyer, consultant, architect or a beautician. In earthy signs, Venus gives TV, drama, success in the business of cotton, garments, textiles, musical instruments, decoration material, and management etc. In Fiery signs, Venus makes one ruler, minister, engineer, philosopher etc.

Illustration : 2.9 (**PA**) *Horoscope No.: 10*

Date of birth : 25.02.1962 Time of birth : 10:50:00 hrs

Place of birth : Lucknow Lat 26:50:00 N Long 80:54:00E

Ayanamsa : 23:19:30 Sidereal Time : 21:01:59

Pln	**Degree**	**Rasi**	**Nakshatra**	**Pad**
Asc	4:53:54	Tau	Kritika	3
Sun	12:48:07	Aqu	Satabhisha	2
Mon	14:38:36	Lib	Swati	3
Mar	24:49:16	Cap	Dhanistha	1
Mer	16:35:55	Cap	Sravana	2
Jup	0:06:49	Aqu	Dhanistha	3
Ven (C)	19:46:09	Aqu	Satabhisha	4
Sat	12:46:33	Cap	Sravana	1
Rah (R)	24:30:11	Can	Aslesa	3
Ket (R)	24:30:11	Cap	Dhanistha	1

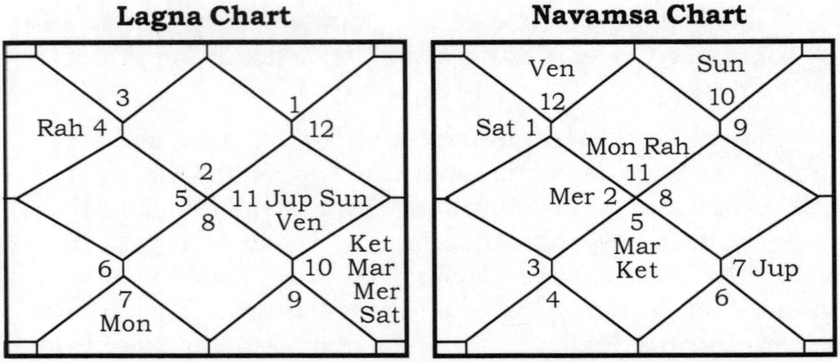

Balance of Vimshottari Dasa of **Rah 7Y 2M 23D**

The native is an IFS officer. *Lagna* and 6th lord Venus is placed in the 10th house, in association with Jupiter and Saturn. As we have said earlier, Venus has a prominent role in the charts of administrative officers, in relation to the 10th house. Here, the 9th and 10th lord Saturn is placed in the 9th house with exalted Mars. *Kemadrum Yoga* is also present, which created many obstacles in the early stage of profession. He succeeded in IFS only after serving in a bank for some time.

Illustration : 2.10 (**BB**) *Horoscope No.: 11*

Date of birth : 30.08.1961 Time of birth : 09:46:00 hrs

Place of birth : Lucknow Lat 26:50:00 N Long 80:54:00E

Ayanamsa : 23:19:08 Sidereal Time : 8:12:05

Pln	**Degree**	**Rasi**	**Nakshatra**	**Pad**
Asc	5:59:50	Lib	Chitra	4
Sun	13:13:59	Leo	Magha	4
Mon	8:48:02	Ari	Ashwini	3
Mar	15:05:44	Vir	Hasta	2
Mer	27:15:26	Leo	U Phalguni	1
Jup (R)	4:57:09	Cap	Uttarasadha	3
Ven	7:21:59	Can	Pushya	2
Sat (R)	0:34:07	Cap	Uttarasadha	2

Rah (R/C)	3:56:22	Leo	Magha	2
Ket (R)	3:56:22	Aqu	Dhanistha	4

Lagna Chart

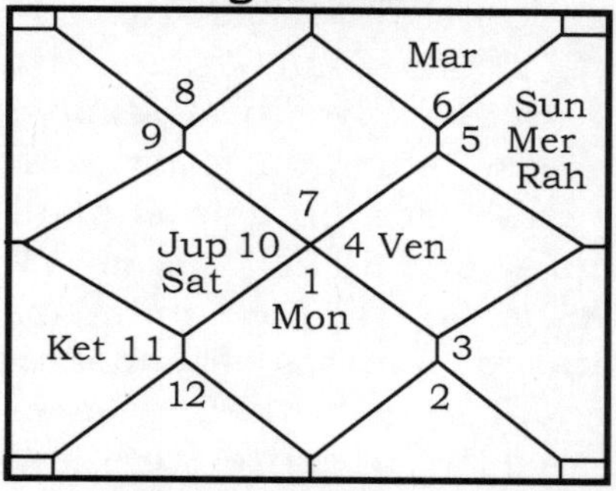

Navamsa Chart

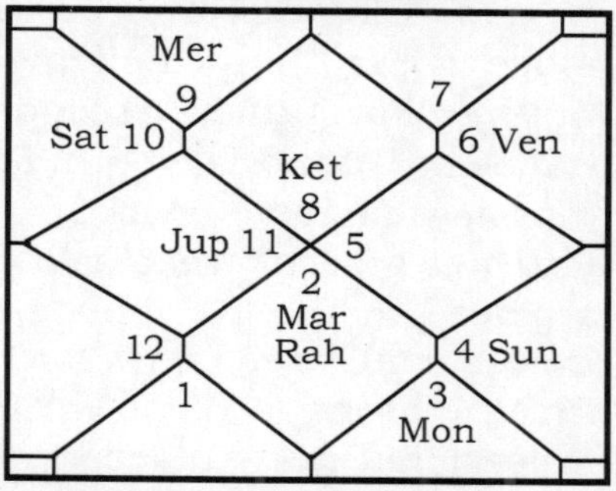

Balance of Vimshottari Dasa of **Ket 2Y 4M 16D**

Lagna lord Venus is placed in the 10th house and *Yogakaraka* Saturn is placed in the 4th house giving rise to *Sash Mahapurush Rajyoga*. Venus forms *Amla Yoga*. The native started his business of wax-coated wrappers at a very low scale. He worked hard in the field of lamination of pouches and earned a lot. Thereafter, he started making plastic films and got roaring success. In a short period of 10 years, when he was running under Moon *mahadasa* from 16.1.1990 to 16.1.2000, he came almost on the top in the field of plastic films, lamination and design work of pouches of different material. Thus Venus in the 10th house gave him all success in these fields. *Kemadrum Yoga* caused obstacles in the beginning. Mars *dasa* was not a good period for him.

2.7 Placement of Saturn in the Tenth House

Maharishi Bhrigu says:

पंचविशतिवर्षे गंगास्नायी अतिलुब्धः पित्तशरीरी ।।
पापयुते कर्मविघ्नकरः शुभयुते कर्मसिद्धिः ।।

(*Bhrigu Sutram*, Part-II/Chap-7/Vers-44 to 45)

That is, if Saturn is placed in the 10th house, the native will take bath in Ganges in 25th year. If Saturn is conjoined with a malefic, the native will have to face various obstacles in his professional career. The undertakings of the native will be successful, if Saturn is associated with a benefic in the 10th house.

For Aries and Taurus ascendants, Saturn in the 10th house will fall in own sign, giving rise to *Sash Mahapurush Rajyoga*. For Taurus ascendant, Saturn gives best results, as it owns 9th and 10th both. For Aries, Saturn will give wealth in profession, as it owns 10th and 11th. For Libra ascendant, Saturn is a *Yogakaraka* as it owns 4th and 5th houses and if it is placed in the 10th house, the native will have immense professional rise. Thus, for Libra and Taurus ascendants, Saturn being a *Yogakaraka* will give high degree of professional rise, unaccounted wealth, immense fame and honour and all-round success in life.

For Capricorn ascendant, Saturn is exalted in the 10th house and as Saturn owns 2nd house as well, it confers wealth prosperity and all kinds of professional success. Here, Saturn will indicate the profession for which it is a *Karaka*. For Aquarius ascendant, Saturn will be the owner of *lagna* and 12th house and its placement in the 10th is a favourable disposition for career. Saturn, for Taurus, Aries and Capricorn ascendants, will give rise to *Sash Mahapurush Rajyoga*, which makes one prosperous, successful, wealthy and happy like a king.

Kalyan Verma writes in *Saravali*:

धनवान् प्राज्ञः शूरो मन्त्री वा दण्डनायको वाऽपि ।
दशमस्थे रवितनये वृन्दपुरग्रामनेता च ।।

(*Saravali*, Chap-30/Vers-83)

It means that if Saturn joins the 10th house one will be rich and learned. He may become a minister or may have an authority to punish (like a judge). He will be courageous and will be a leader of a group, village or city.

Mantreshwar mentions:

मन्त्री वा नृपतिर्धनी कृषिपरः शूरः प्रसिद्धोऽम्बरे ।।

(*Phaldeepika*, Chap-8/Vers-24)

That is, the person, having Saturn in the 10th house, will become a minister or a king. He is much wealthy or he may be engaged in agriculture. He is quite brave and famous.

It has also been said:

मन्दे यदा दशमगे यदि दण्डकर्ता मानी धनी निजकुलप्रभवश्च शूरः।

(*Jatak Parijat,* Chap-8/Vers-92)

That, if Saturn is posited in the 10th house, one is a punishing officer. He is wealthy, courageous and important in his family.

These are the results of a strong and well-disposed Saturn such as for Aries, Taurus, Libra, Capricorn and Aquarius ascendants. A malefic Saturn, for Cancer, Leo, and Sagittarius ascendants etc., will bring disgrace, dishonour, failure of undertakings, defeat, despair, disappointment, dissatisfaction, humiliation, suspension, reversion or demotion etc.

For Libra ascendant, conjunction of Venus and Saturn in the 10h house is very auspicious for profession, prosperity, power and pelf. A strong and well-disposed Saturn in the 10th house makes the native reach the top but that is also followed by a steep fall from that position and status. This is a special characteristic of Saturn's placement in the 10th house. It is just like loosing an election after becoming a minister. If Saturn is conjoined with Venus and Jupiter, the professional aspects are very strong and highly pronounced, and demotion or suspension etc would not take place after attaining the top position, as said earlier. For Capricorn ascendant, Venus who is a *Yogakaraka,* if conjoined with *lagna* lord Saturn in the 10th house will promote the professional prospects very high in a dignified way. Even better results for Venus Saturn in the 10th house will come in evidence for Aquarius ascendant.

Causing high rise and then pulling down from a prestigious, high status or then sudden down fall is the characteristic of the placement of Saturn in the 10th house, if it is not supported by a benefic like Venus or Jupiter. The best example of such a Saturn is that of Hitler.

Illustration : 2.11 **(Hitler)** *Horoscope No.: 12*

Date of birth : 20.04.1889 Time of birth : 18:30:00 hrs
Place of birth : Brabhaw Lat 33:00:00 N Long 73:45:00E
Ayanamsa : 22:18:22 Sidereal Time : 8:25:20

Pln	**Degree**	**Rasi**	**Nakshatra**	**Pad**
Asc	8:24:07	Lib	Swati	1
Sun	8:20:08	Ari	Ashwini	3
Mon	11:54:24	Sag	Moola	4
Mar (C)	23:57:09	Ari	Bharani	4
Mer (C)	3:00:46	Ari	Ashwini	1
Jup	15:56:10	Sag	Purvasadha	1
Ven (R)	24:27:37	Ari	Bharani	4
Sat	21:09:04	Can	Aslesa	2
Rah (R)	22:45:03	Gem	Punarvasu	1
Ket (R)	22:45:03	Sag	Purvasadha	3

Lagna Chart

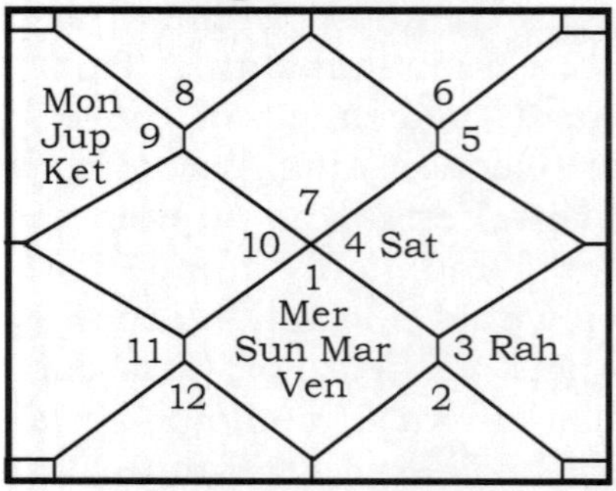

Navamsa Chart

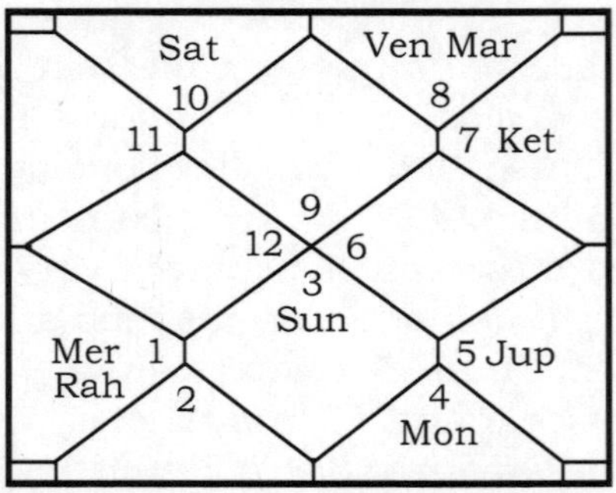

Balance of Vimshottari Dasa of **Ket 0Y 8M 30D**

It is a well known fact about Hitler that he was the son of a cobbler. His father died when Hitler was 13 and his mother when he was 15. Then for 8 years he learnt draftsmanship. He joined the army in 1914 and floated his own party under the sub-period of Mars. Gradually, he brought many countries under the German flag. Saturn in the 10th, which is also *Yogakaraka* for Libra ascendant, took Hitler to new heights of power, position, rights and fame. In his birth chart Saturn is aspected by Mars, and Saturn is aspecting Mars. Saturn is also powerful and *Yogakaraka* and therefore, entirely beneficial since it is also situated in its own *navamsa*. But Mars is *'Markesh'* (planet causing death) for Libra ascendant. During the major period of Rahu and sub-period of Mars, Hitler suffered setbacks and he had to flee from the battle field. In melodramatic and mysterious circumstances, he met his death in 1945.

If in the birth chart, Saturn is in the 10th and Mars, Ketu or Rahu influence it, then the rise to the highest point and then total decline of the native is inevitable. In Hitler's birth chart, this fact can be seen clearly. Napoleon Bonaparte was also born in Libra *lagna* where Saturn was in the 10th, and Moon was in the 4th house in the sign of Capricorn. There was *"Vinimaya parivartana yoga"* (mutual exchange position) between Saturn and Moon but Saturn was bereft of conjunction with or aspect by any auspicious planet. Therefore, Saturn acted similarly in his case as in that of Hitler. A rise to the pinnacle and then an ignoble downfall. Any Sutra or principle of astrology depends upon the situation of other planets and their strength. Saturn in the 10th causes high rise only when it is powerful, in its own house, exalted or a *Yogakaraka*. Conjoined with evil planets or even aspected by them, it causes a down fall. Conversely, conjoined with auspicious planets or aspected by them, Saturn loses much of its ferocity.

Illustration : 2.12 **(AKS)** *Horoscope No.: 13*

Date of birth : 05.05.1956 Time of birth : 02:10:00 hrs
Place of birth : Lucknow Lat 26:50:00 N Long 80:54:00E
Ayanamsa : 23:15:05 Sidereal Time : 16:54:23

Pln	Degree	Rasi	Nakshatra	Pad
Asc	14:09:48	Aqu	Satabhisha	3
Sun	21:04:55	Ari	Bharani	3

Mon	10:32:59	Aqu	Satabhisha	2
Mar	19:16:53	Cap	Sravana	3
Mer	11:42:43	Tau	Rohini	1
Jup	28:41:28	Can	Aslesa	4
Ven	4:28:20	Gem	Mrigshira	4
Sat (R)	7:25:11	Sco	Anuradha	2
Rah (R)	15:04:15	Sco	Anuradha	4
Ket (R)	15:04:15	Tau	Rohini	2

Lagna Chart

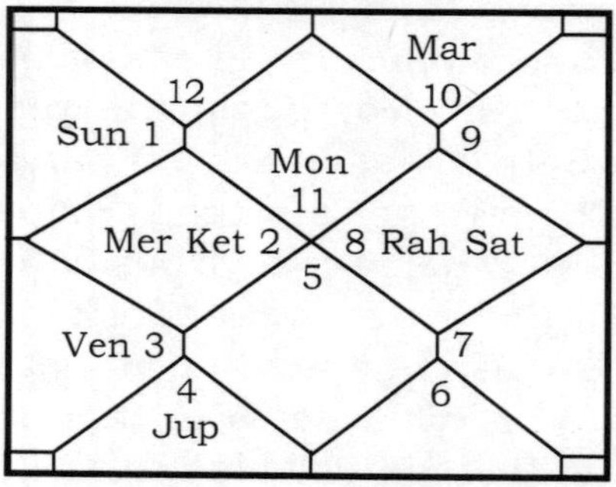

Navamsa Chart

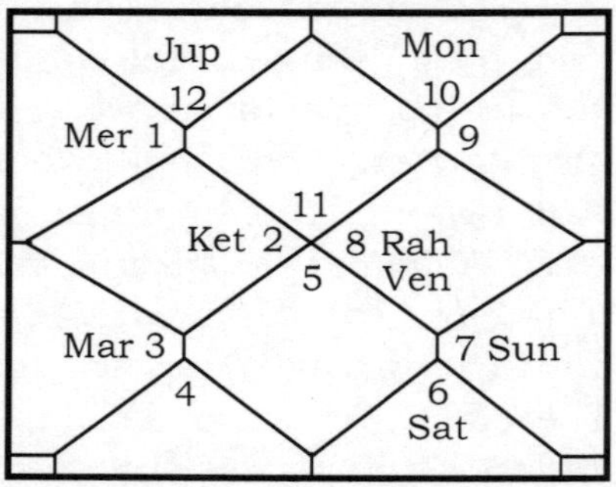

Balance of Vimshottari Dasa of **Rah 12Y 9M 2D**

This is the birth chart of a native who spent his childhood in extreme poverty. After facing many problems, he managed to earn a living through an ordinary job in the Secretariat. After some time he was promoted to the post of a clerk there. Time's wheel kept moving. Gradually, he became an important trade union leader. Name and success made him arrogant. It is then that Saturn started to show the effect of its power and he had to leave his job and leadership both, and run away.

As per the birth chart of this native, Saturn's major period (*Mahadasa*) started from (24-01-1985). A pleasant period of progress began in his life. He started a small scale industry. At present, this person is a multimillionaire and running big industries successfully. In the birth chart, Saturn is the lord of the ascendant and situated in the 10th house in the sign of Scorpio, which belongs to Mars. It is also beneficially aspected by an exalted Jupiter, and lord of the 5th Mercury. Jupiter's aspect mitigates Saturn's ferocity but here Saturn is conjoined with Rahu. Rahu, therefore, is enhancing its evil effects. At the same time, Jupiter and Mercury are diminishing these evil effects. To analyze Saturn and the 10th house, it is necessary to consider Mars, the lord of the 10th, as well. Lord of the 10th Mars is in the 12th house, in its own exaltation sign Capricorn, and also establishing *Vinimaya Parivartana Yoga* with Saturn. The aspect of Jupiter over the 10th house, lord of the 10th Mars and Saturn and Rahu in the 10th house is enhancing the auspicious results of the 10th house. Before reaching a conclusion, the *navamsa* of Saturn and Mars should also be considered. Saturn is situated in the *navamsa* of Mercury and aspected by Mars and Jupiter which is in its own *navamsa*. Therefore, in the *navamsa* chart also, lord of the ascendant Saturn is influenced by both Mars and Jupiter. A proper study reveals that Saturn will take this native to the top. Because of Mercury being in the *navamsa* of Mercury, the native would prosper only in business, not in a service. Because of Saturn's conjunction with Rahu in the 10th, there would always be ups and downs in the business. Lots of success may be followed by continuous losses. A favourable position is created by the aspect of own *navamsa*-placed Jupiter over Saturn. The native will keep moving towards progress. Even in an adverse situation, he will not lose his courage, strength, patience, discretion or intelligence. Soon, he will regain his original glory.

Saturn, most often, gives the profession, which requires hard work, struggle, toiling labour, and fatigue. Cutting of rocks, working with cement, construction of roads and related works come under the influence of Saturn. One earns livelihood through land, iron, steel, oil, mineral, coal, leather, wool or blankets etc. Saturn engages the native in the jobs of engineer, railway worker, engine driver, blacksmith, carpenter, mason, industrialist, telephone instrument maker, instructors, lawyers, judges, advocates, magistrates etc. It makes one a minister, ruler, farmer. He will be judicious and work in the capacity of a judge. He may be spiritually inclined, towards his old age. The profession of the native will be marked by sudden and unexpected elevations and depressions. If Saturn is associated with the 8th lord in a malefic *navamsa*, the native suffers damages and losses in his career by superiors. If the 10th lord joins Saturn, together with the lord of *navamsa* occupied by the 10th lord, and is influenced by aspects or conjunction with the 6th lord, the native will have more than one wife. If Saturn creates obstruction, the 36th year brings success by the blessings of Saturn.

Well placed Saturn in the 10th house may also make one a yogi, spiritualist, *peethadheesh* etc. Shankaracharya of Nasik Dr. Kurtkoti had Saturn in Pisces in the 10th house. Swami Vivekananda had Saturn in Virgo in the 10th house while Saturn in the 10th in Aries was present in the chart of Baba Saheb Khapde. Their Saturn gave inclination towards spiritualism. Many times, persons having Saturn in the 10th house have more than one wife. Saturn's affliction in the 10th house brings innumerable miseries, poverty, problems, tensions, failures, reversals, diseases, suspensions, setbacks, demotion, distress, theft, disappointment, dejection, losses, defamation, disrespect, insult, and daily wages job etc.

Let's discuss the results of a well-fortified Saturn in the 10th house with the help of practical illustration:

Illustration : 2.13 **(AS)** *Horoscope No.: 14*

Date of birth : 14.12.1964 Time of birth : 16:32:00 hrs
Place of birth : Delhi Lat 28:39:00 N Long 77:13:00E
Ayanamsa : 23:21:45 Sidereal Time : 21:43:28

Pln	**Degree**	**Rasi**	**Nakshatra**	**Pad**
Asc	16:52:17	Tau	Rohini	3
Sun	29:08:25	Sco	Jyestha	4

Mon	25:57:45	Pis	Revati	3
Mar	24:31:37	Leo	P Phalguni	4
Mer (R/C)	9:02:35	Sag	Moola	3
Jup (R)	23:58:13	Ari	Bharani	4
Ven	0:37:40	Sco	Vishakha	4
Sat	6:30:43	Aqu	Dhanistha	4
Rah (S)	29:39:03	Tau	Mrigshira	2
Ket (S)	29:39:03	Sco	Jyestha	4

Lagna Chart

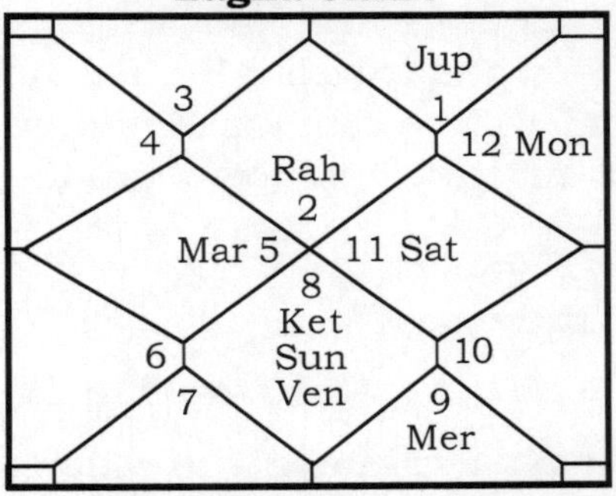

Navamsa Chart

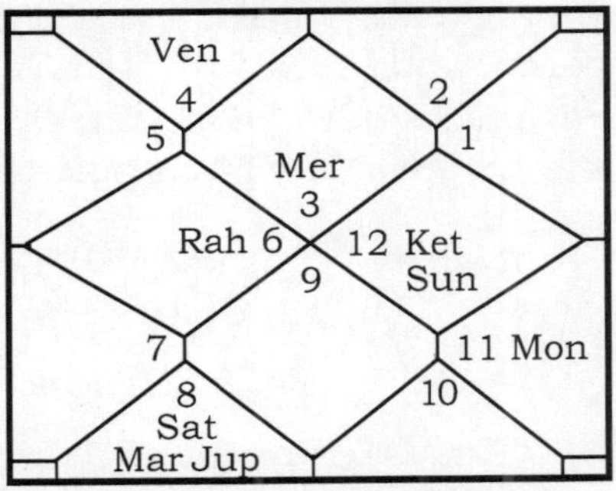

Balance of Vimshottari Dasa of **Mer 5Y 1M 23D**

This is the horoscope of a top ranking officer, presently working in one of the biggest organization of the country. The native started his career from a very low post but at the age of 37 he was among one of the top executives of the management. He is not only successful but also very learned, intelligent and deserving officer. He has been to almost every corner of the world in connection with his professional requirements.

For Taurus ascendant, Saturn is a *Yogakaraka* and it is placed here in the 10th house, in own sign Aquarius, which will further elevate the native. Saturn has formed *Sash Yoga*. (Various other auspicious *Yogas* are also present in the birth chart which is off the subject). Thus, a *Yogakaraka* Saturn elevates the native to the topmost position and the progress gets speedily pronounced after the age of 36. For Taurus and Libra ascendants, Saturn happens to be a *Yogakaraka* and if it occupies the 10th house, it gives the most favourable results to promote the native to the topmost position. It is also believed and experienced by the scholars that the downfall also comes while the native is at the pinnacle of his career, as in case of Hitler, Indira Gandhi, and Rajneesh etc.

2.8 Placement of Rahu in the Tenth House

Rahu's placement in the 10th house has not always been considered very auspicious. There is a tendency to run after females. He will be a skilled artist with the knowledge of poetry and literature. He is learned and travels a lot. He will engage himself in business and will be famous. Children will be few. He will be bold and adventurous. He is sinful.

वितन्तुसंगमः ।। दुर्ग्रामवासः ।।
शुभयुते न दोषः ।। काव्यव्यसनः ।।

(*Bhrigu Sutram,* Part-II/Chap-8/Vers-25 to 28)

That is, the native will have sexual contacts with widows and will live in slums. He will live in good places, if Rahu or Ketu is associated with a benefic. The native will also be interested in poetry.

Vaidyanath Says:

चोरक्रियानिपुणबुद्धिरतो विशीलो मीनं गते फणिपतौ तु रणोत्सुकः स्यात् ।

(*Jatak Parijat,* Chap-8/Vers-92)

That is, the native becomes clever in stealing. One is devoid of good conduct. One has liking for war and strife.

Bhavarth Ratnakar mentions that Rahu is good in the 10th house for professional aspect. In fact, the sign occupied by Rahu, the planets conjoined with it and the planets aspecting it will determine the exact results provided by Rahu.

Strong Rahu in the 10th house can make one an administrator. He may be cruel but famous and successful. Generally, such a native works for others, that is, he engages himself in service. According to Bhaskaracharya, Rahu in the 10th house makes the native sexy, clever, ill tempered, greedy and poor. Garg says that the native will be minister, head of army, officer, bold and wise. He is generally proud and interested in females and is troubled by others. In Taurus, Aries, Virgo and Scorpio Rahu ruins the enemies. Good results are more pronounced in male signs and adverse results come in evidence in female signs.

If Rahu is placed in odd sign, the native will be like insane, proud, talkative, indifferent and may be employed in Post, Railways, Insurance, Bank etc. but that depends on various other factors also. Financial condition is unstable. Parents have physical and financial problems. Either of the parents may die during the early age of the native. The rise of fortune takes place at the age of 21. Professional prosperity and ultimate progress comes in 36th year and he gets honour from the government at 42nd year.

Illustration: 2.14(**Mahatma Gandhi**) *Horoscope No.: 15*

Date of birth : 02.10.1869 Time of birth : 07:45:00 hrs
Place of birth : Porbandar Lat 21:40:00 N Long 69:40:00E
Ayanamsa : 22:02:03 Sidereal Time : 9:23:40

Pln	**Degree**	**Rasi**	**Nakshatra**	**Pad**
Asc	24:28:19	Lib	Vishakha	2
Sun	16:57:13	Vir	Hasta	3
Mon	28:49:06	Can	Aslesa	4
Mar	26:24:30	Lib	Vishakha	2
Mer	11:46:17	Lib	Swati	2
Jup (R)	28:08:03	Ari	Kritika	1
Ven	24:28:21	Lib	Vishakha	2
Sat	20:19:57	Sco	Jyestha	2
Rah (R)	13:39:43	Can	Pushya	4
Ket (R)	13:39:43	Cap	Sravana	2

Lagna Chart

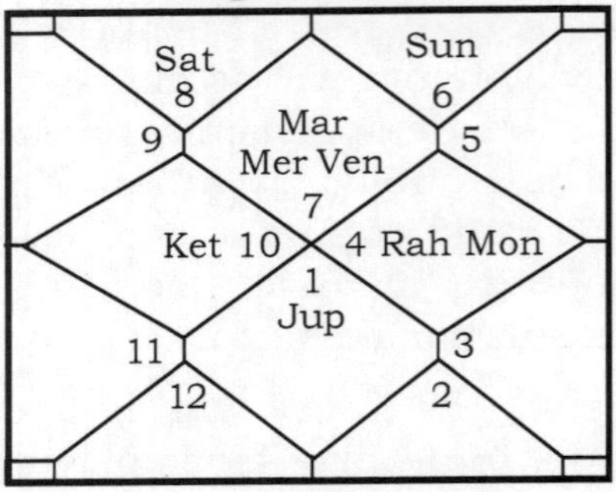

Navamsa Chart

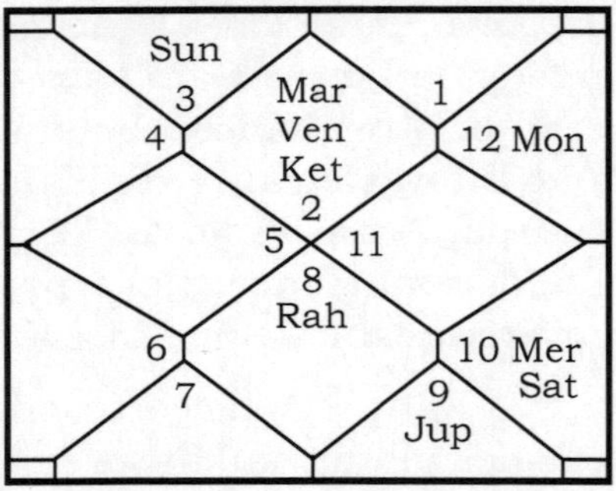

Balance of Vimshottari Dasa of **Mer 1Y 6M 2D**

This is the birth chart of our Father of the Nation, Mahatma Gandhi. Rahu is placed in the 10th house and its dispositor Moon joins Cancer in the 10th house. Rahu gives political success, provided Sun and Mars are also well disposed perfectly, in a *Kendra.* Here, the lord of the *lagna* Venus is conjoined with 9th lord Mercury, which made the Mahatma a leader of the masses. He was a fortunate and intelligent person that all his undertakings became successful. Mars happens to be a strong *Marak* for Libra ascendant and its placement in the *lagna* lends the aspect over 7th and 8th house. Saturn also lends aspect over the 8th house, which resulted in his cruel assassination. There are many peculiarities of this chart, which will be mentioned elsewhere, as this will be out of context here.

Illustration: 2.15(**Dr.Rajendra Prasad**) *Horoscope No.:16*

Date of birth : 03.12.1884 Time of birth : 08:45:00 hrs

Place of birth : Jirade Lat 25:33:00 N Long 77:29:00E

Ayanamsa : 22:15:02 Sidereal Time : 13:34:29

Pln	Degree	Rasi	Nakshatra	Pad
Asc	18:42:09	Sag	Purvasadha	2
Sun	19:11:08	Sco	Jyestha	1
Mon	24:19:03	Tau	Mrigshira	1

Mar (C)	5:57:30	Sag	Moola	2
Mer	4:28:58	Sag	Moola	2
Jup	13:04:22	Leo	Magha	4
Ven	12:58:30	Lib	Swati	2
Sat (R)	29:14:55	Tau	Mrigshira	2
Rah (R)	19:57:43	Vir	Hasta	3
Ket (R)	19:57:43	Pis	Revati	1

Lagna Chart

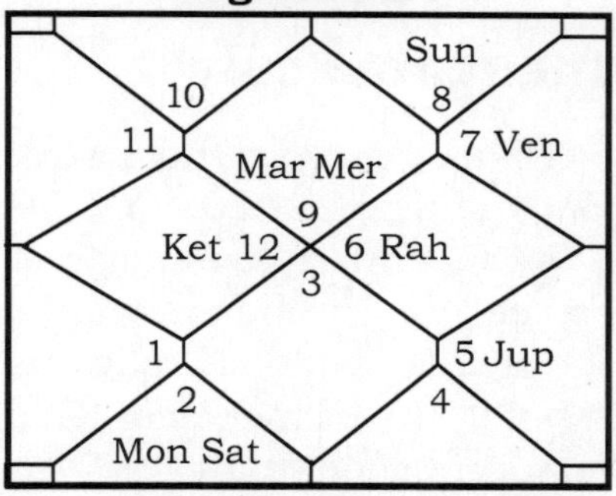

Navamsa Chart

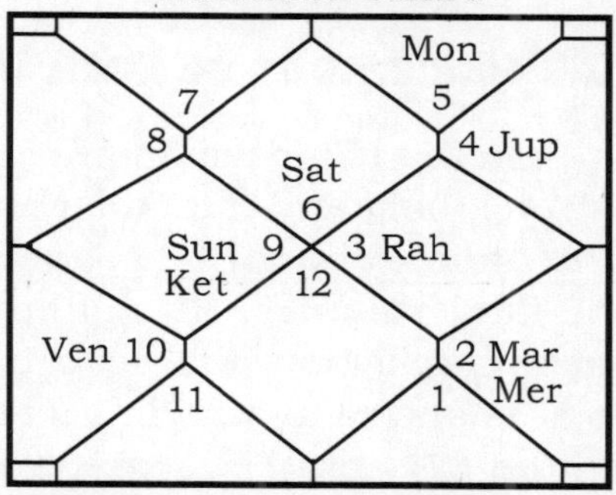

Balance of Vimshottari Dasa of **Mar 6Y 5M 24D**

This is the birth chart of the first President of India Dr. Rajendra Prasad. Rahu is placed in the 10th house in Virgo and the dispositor of Rahu, which is said to be the Karmic Control planet, Mercury, is placed in the *lagna* itself with the 5th lord Mars. What is there in this birth chart which made him so great? The ascendant is strong, as the lord of the ascendant who occupies the 9th house, in a friendly sign Leo, aspects the *lagna*, the 10th lord Mercury and the 5th lord Mars. Venus is the lord of 6th and 11th houses and joins its own sign Libra in the 11th house itself. Strong Rahu is placed in the 10th house. Venus and Jupiter, both aspect the 5th house, which gave him sharp intellect and unmatched brilliance.

Dispositors of Rahu and Ketu are called the Karmic Control planets. Theory of Karmic control planets is a great research work of Sri M. C. Jain, a famous scholar of astrology.

If Karmic control planets are conjoined together or are in mutual *Kendra* or are in triangle from each other, the native touches a very high position in his career depending upon the exact behaviour, nature, *Karakatwa* and the lordship of their Karmic control planets. In this birth chart, Jupiter and Mercury are Karmic control planets and are in mutual triangle from each other. Mercury falls in the sign of Jupiter, Sagittarius, which is a fiery sign, and Jupiter falls in Leo, which is also a fiery sign. Mercury and Jupiter are so well placed that the native became the first citizen of India.

2.9 Placement of Ketu in the Tenth House

Ketu, if placed in the 10th house, makes the native strong, bold and famous. He will commit vile deeds and his intentions will not be good. He will face many obstacles in his undertakings. He will be very clever. The native will be happy, religious, well read in scriptures, will visit religious places and take bath in sacred rivers. The influence of Ketu in the 10th house is, sometimes, a mix of good and bad. Even enemies appreciate him in the battlefield. He defeats his enemies. But he gets less paternal happiness; is worried on account of conveyances and suffers from gastric complaints. If Ketu is placed in Virgo, one gets happiness and sorrow both.

Ketu gives good results in the sign of Jupiter i.e. Sagittarius and Pisces. Native gets prosperity and fame. But it gives adverse results in Gemini, as one is forced to leave the job of eminence and importance. He is learned, intelligent, winner or victorious and generally lives in a foreign land. If Ketu falls in Virgo, Aquarius, Gemini and Taurus, the native is polite and decent. This is an adverse disposition for business and industries. If Ketu falls in a movable sign, the rise of fortune comes only after going away from the motherland.

Mantreshwar says:

सत्कर्मविघ्नमशुचित्वमवद्यकृत्यं तेजस्विनं नभसि शौर्यमतिप्रसिद्धम् ।।

(*Phaldeepika,* Chap-8/Vers-32)

This means, that he experiences obstacles in the performance of good acts. He does diplomatic and lowly acts. He is energetic, bold and widely renowned.

Vaidyanath Dixit says:

सुधीर्बली शिल्पविदात्मबोधी जनानुरागी च विरोधवृत्तिः।
कफात्मकः शूरजनाग्रगण्यः सदाटनः कर्मगते च केतौ।।

(*Jatak Parijat,* Chap-8/Vers-93)

Meaning, if Ketu is placed in the 10th house one is learned, strong, and proficient in sculpture and arts; has self realization; loves mankind: has inimical activities: is phlegmatic in nature; a leader among braves, and travels always.

The conjunctions, aspect and sign etc. are to be taken into vital consideration before reaching any conclusion.

One may change his job, if the 10th house is aspected by its own lord or benefics, and Jupiter, Venus, Mercury, Moon and lord of the 10th house are also well disposed in *Kendra* or *Trikona.* If 10th house and Ketu are hemmed between benefic planets, *Shubhkartari yoga* is formed and the matters of 10th house get promoted.

In our experience, Ketu is a planet which provides intuitional power. A well-placed Ketu gives high degree of intuition or insight, which is a very essential factor for becoming a successful astrologer. Ketu in the 10th house can make one a novelist, astrologer, interpreter of dreams and articles of law, and he may solve the complicated things easily. He may even become a minister.

Illustration : 2.16 (**Dev Anand**) *Horoscope No.: 17*

Date of birth : 26.09.1923 Time of birth : 21:30:00 hrs

Place of birth : Gurdaspur Lat 22:12:00 N Long 85:23:00E

Ayanamsa : 22:47:24 Sidereal Time : 21:59:16

Pln	**Degree**	**Rasi**	**Nakshatra**	**Pad**
Asc	18:08:15	Tau	Rohini	3
Sun	9:44:16	Vir	U Phalguni	4

Mon	27:34:54	Pis	Revati	4
Mar (C)	23:30:35	Leo	P Phalguni	4
Mer (R/C)	15:00:02	Vir	Hasta	2
Jup	24:47:52	Lib	Vishakha	2
Ven (R)	14:05:15	Vir	Hasta	2
Sat	27:45:10	Vir	Chitra	2
Rah (R)	18:43:33	Leo	P Phalguni	2
Ket (R)	18:43:33	Aqu	Satabhisha	4

Lagna Chart

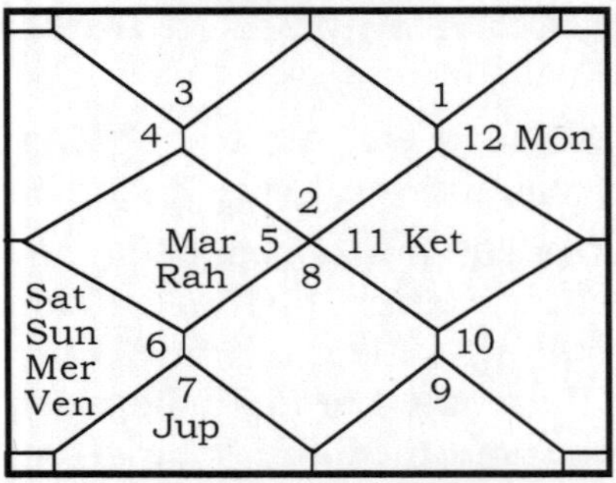

Navamsa Chart

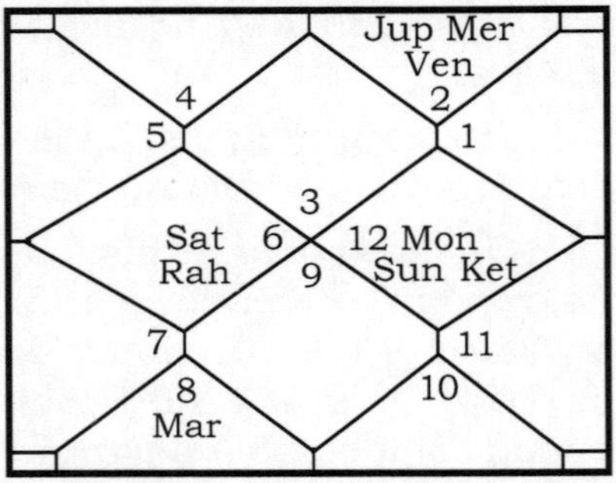

Balance of Vimshottari Dasa of **Mer 3Y 1M 0D**

The famous film actor Dev Anand was born in Taurus ascendant with Ketu in the 10th house. Ketu is aspected by Mars and Jupiter, which has made him one of the best and most successful, popular and famous actor of his times. Here, ketu will give the effects of Saturn as it is posited in Aquarius. Saturn is the dispositor of Ketu. Ketu is aspected by Mars and Jupiter, hence it will exhibit the results of these planets too. Thus, Ketu is here under the influence of Saturn, Mars and Jupiter. Therefore, Dev Anand has been a highly talented actor, producer, director and film maker. He has made a history of great success and name in the film industry. At the age of 85 years, he is quite active and energetic and keeps on working, in one or the other aspect of the film. Ketu has made him bold, courageous, fearless, innovative and full of skill and talent.

These are the general results of placement of various planets in the 10th house. These results are not specific and should not at all be applied verbatim. It is really a tough job to decide the profession of the native on the basis of his birth chart. It is not only the planet, which occupies the 10th house, but also various other factors, which determine the exact occupation of the subject. Lord of the 10th house, planets placed in the 10th house and their *navamsa* lords etc. should be taken into consideration. These points can be listed as below :

A. Significance of the planet placed in the 10th house.

B. Lord of the 10th house and *navamsa* lord thereof, and judge which has more influence on the 10th house.

C. Ownership of the planet or planets that join the 9th house, and relative results.

D. Planets lending their aspect over the 10th house, the 10th lord and the planets in the 10th house.

E. The dispositor of the 10th lord and its position in the natal chart.

F. The lord of the 2nd house, if placed in the 10th, becomes a strong representative of the profession of the native and vice versa.

G. If the 11th lord is placed in the 10th house or vice versa, one has a profession of high status, whether in service or business.

H. If the 9th and 10th lords have mutual exchange of houses, one will be very fortunate in respect of profession. He may become a class I officer, minister or PM or President provided the *lagna* is also quite strong and the 10th house is well disposed.

I. If there is mutual exchange between the lords of 5th and 10th, one will be highly placed viz. IAS or minister or a business magnate.

J. If the 5th and 9th lords are conjoined in the 10th house, with the 10th lord, or the 10th lord is placed in 5th or 9th, he native will be most successful, rise speedily and will be very rich.

K. Similarly, if the 10th lord is placed in the 5th house and 9th lord is placed in the 4th house with mutual exchange, it will give rise to *Maharaja Yoga*. One becomes very successful in his professional sphere. In all such cases, the *lagna* should be strong and well fortified. A weak *lagna* will reduce the benefic results of these *Yogas*.

L. The planets in the 10th, placed in their own sign or in exaltation, and the planets in the 9th house, in their own or exaltation sign, will also give a high-class career and professional progress.

These points should be taken into consideration, before reaching any conclusion, in respect of one's occupation and career.

2.10 Results of the Lord of the Tenth House being situated in Different Houses

In the First House: When the lord of the tenth house occupies the ascendant, the native rises in life by sheer dint of perseverance. He will be self-employed or pursue a profession of independence. When the *lagna* and the 10th lord combine in the first house, the native becomes very famous and a pioneer in the field of work. He founds a public institution and engages himself in social projects.

In the Second House: The 10th lord in the second house makes the native fortunate. He rises well in life and makes a lot of money. He may engage himself in the family trade and develop it. If malefics afflict the 10th house, he will suffer losses and be responsible for winding up the family business. He will prosper in catering and restaurant businesses.

In the Third House: The native may have to travel constantly on short-journeys. He will be a speaker or writer or celebrity, if the 10th lord is well-placed. His brothers may be instrumental, to some extent, in advancing his career. If

10th lord is in the 6th, 8th or 12th from *navamsa lagna* or in an unfriendly constellation in the 3rd house, the native's rise in life is slow and beset with obstacles. If the 3rd lord is also afflicted, rivalry between brothers may lead to reversals, obstacles, etc., in the native's career.

In the Fourth House: The native will be a lucky man and highly learned in various subjects. He will be famous, both for his learning and generosity. If the 10th lord is strong, the native is respected wherever he goes, and he receives royal favour. He may engage in agricultural pursuits or in dealings with immovable properties. If the 4th lord, the 9th lord and the 10th are beneficially disposed and related to one another, the native wields great political authority as a President or head of a government. If the 10th lord is depressed, eclipsed, in an inimical sign or afflicted by malefic planets, the native will lose his lands and be forced to take to a life of servitude. The same results are obtained, if the 10th lord conjoins the 8th lord in the 4th house, in a malefic *shashtyamsa*.

In the Fifth House: The native shines well as a broker and engages in speculation and similar business. If benefics join the lord of the 10th in the 5th house, the native leads a simple and pious life engaging himself in prayers and pious activities. He may become the head of an orphanage or remand home, if the 10th lord occupies the 6th, 8th or 12th *navamsa*.

In the Sixth House: The person will have an occupation bearing on judiciary, prisons or hospitals. If Saturn aspects the 10th lord, he may have to work all his life in a low-paying job with not much prospects. If benefics aspect the 10th lord, he holds a post of authority and will be held in high esteem for his character. If Rahu or afflicted malefics are with the 10th lord, he may suffer disgrace in his career. He may be exposed to criminal action and face imprisonment.

In the Seventh House: The 10th lord, placed in the 7th house, gives a mature wife who will assist the native in his work. He will travel abroad on diplomatic missions. He will be well known for his skill in talking and achieving objectives. He will make profits through partnerships and co-operative ventures. If malefics afflict the 10th lord, the native will be debased in his sexual habits and indulge in every kind of vice.

In the Eighth House: The native has many breaks in career. If the 10th lord is fortified, he will occupy a high office in his field but only for a short time. If a malefic planet afflicts the 10th lord, the person has criminal propensities and commits offences. If Jupiter influences the 10th lord, by aspect or association, in the 8th house, he will become a mystic or spiritual teacher. Saturn here makes the person an undertaker or otherwise employed in burning *ghats*, graveyards etc.

In the Ninth House: The 10th lord, in the 9th house, makes the native a spiritual stalwart. He will be a beacon light to spiritual seekers, if Jupiter aspects the 10th lord. If both, benefics and malefics, aspect the 10th lord, the native is generally fortunate and well-to-do. He follows a hereditary profession or that of a preacher, teacher or healer. The father of the native has a great influence on him. He will be a dutiful son and do many charitable deeds.

In the Tenth House: If the 10th lord is strongly disposed in the 10th, the native can be highly successful in his profession and command respect and honour. If the lord is weak and afflicted, he will have no self-respect, always cringing for favours. He will also be a dependent, all his life. He will be fickle-minded. If the 10th lord occupies the 6th, 8th or 12th houses from *navamsa,* the native's career will be routine and ordinary. If three other planets conjoin the 10th lord, in the 10th house, the native becomes an ascetic.

In the Eleventh House: The person earns immense riches. Fortunate in every respect, he will engage himself in meritorious deeds. He will give employment to hundreds of persons and will be endowed with a high sense of humour.

He will have many friends. If the eleventh house comes under affliction, his friends will turn enemies and cause him every sort of hardship and worry.

In the Twelfth House: If the 10th lord occupies the twelfth house, the native will have to work in a far-off place. He will lack comforts and face many difficulties in life. If beneficially disposed, the native becomes a spiritual seeker. He will be separated from his family and wander about without success, if malefics afflict the 10th lord. He will indulge in smuggling and other nefarious activities. Rahu, afflicting the 10th lord, makes the native a cheat and a criminal. He causes sorrow to his family and relatives.

2.11 Lord of 12 houses placed in the Tenth house

1. **Lord of 1st house in the 10th house:** In addition to the results of the 4th house, there will be professional success, honoured by eminent men, a research scholar or specialization in that branch of knowledge or profession, which is represented by the lord of *lagna* and the 10th.

2. **Lord of 2nd house in the 10th house:** Respect from elders and superiors, learned, wealthy and he earns by his own exertions.

   The native will take to a number of useful vocations. He will do business or take to agriculture and also engage himself in philosophical lectures and dissertations, and thereby benefit financially. Here again, the constellation and the sign held by the 2nd lord determine the exact nature and source of earnings. Powerful afflictions will cause loss from the very same sources.

3. **Lord of 3rd house in the 10th house:** The native's partner will be querulous and untrustworthy. The native will become rich. He will be happy and intelligent. He will gain from journeys connected with profession.

When the 3rd lord is in the 10th, all the brothers will shine well and they will be helpful to the native in all ways.

4. **Lord of 4th house in the 10th house:** The native will have political success. He will be an expert chemist. He will vanquish his enemies and make his personality felt by the world. Loss of reputation is possible, if the 4th lord is afflicted.

5. **Lord of 5th house in the 10th house:** If the lord is beneficially disposed, *Raja Yoga is* formed. Native acquires landed property; earns the goodwill of the rulers, constructs temples and performs religious sacrifices; one of the sons becomes a gem of the family. If aspected by the Sun, the native may join the intelligence department. If the lord is afflicted, he faces the wrath of the rulers and contrary results will happen.

6. **Lord of 6th house in the 10th house:** If fortified, sinful and destructive nature, poses as an orthodox and pious man but really unscrupulous in regard to religious matters. When the lord is weak, dismissal, formidable enemies, low life or begging.

7. **Lord of 7th house in the 10th house:** The native may flourish in a profession abroad or his career may involve constant travelling. One will get a devoted and faithful wife or husband. The wife may also be employed and contribute to the native's income. Or, she may help in the advancement of the native's career. If afflicted, wife will be avaricious and over-ambitious but without sufficient capacity. Consequently, native's career may suffer and deteriorate.

8. **Lord of 8th house in the 10th house:** If the lord of the 8th house is in the 10th house with the 10th lord, the native has slow advancement in career. He faces obstacles and impediments in his activities. In the appropriate period, he may be superseded by his subordinates and his merit may go unnoticed. He may resort to deceit and

unrighteous means to gain his ends. His thinking will be clouded and his actions will invite the wrath of the government or the law. He may have to put up with poverty. If the 2nd lord is also afflicted and joins the 8th lord, his reputation may suffer due to involvement in huge debts and inability to repay them. If the 8th lord is placed in the 6th, 8th or 12th from *navamsa lagna*, the intensity of the evil is greatly reduced. The 8th lord in the 10th may also confer unexpected gains due to the death of superiors or elders.

9. **Lord of 9th house in the 10th house:** If the ninth lord is in the tenth house, the native will become very famous and powerful. He will be generous and occupy posts of authority. He will earn much wealth and acquire every kind of comfort and luxury. His means of livelihood will be righteous and he will be a law abiding citizen.

10. **Lord of 10th house in the 10th house:** If the 10th lord is strongly disposed in the 10th, the native can be highly successful in his profession and command respect and honour. If the lord is weak and afflicted, he will have no self-respect, cringing for favours. He will also be a dependent all his life. He will be fickle-minded. If the 10th lord occupies the 6th, 8th or 12th houses from *navamsa*, the native's career will be routine and ordinary. If three other planets conjoin the 10th lord in the 10th house, the native becomes an ascetic.

11. **Lord of 11th house in the 10th house:** The native prospers very well in his business and makes good profits. His elder brother will also help him in his business. He will earn some prize-money for original contributions to the subject of his study or profession. Depending upon the benefic or malefic nature of the planet, he will earn through fair or foul means.

12. **Lord of 12th house in the 10th house:** Hard-working and having to undertake tedious journeys for his occupation, he will be a jailor, doctor or work in the cemetery and

such places. He spends money on agricultural pursuits in which he makes profits. The native will derive no happiness or physical comforts from his sons.

2.12 Lord of the Tenth house placed in various houses with the Tenth Lord

The following results can be generally expected to take place during the *Dasa* of the lord of the tenth house:-

1. Benefics with the tenth lord in the ascendant, with the ascendant lord, make the native renowned. He will occupy a top position in the Government and exercise much power and authority. He will be noble and engage himself in charitable deeds such as gifting away clothes, building hostels, orphanages, wells and hospitals.

   If the tenth lord is placed in the sixth, eighth or twelfth in the *navamsa*, the native will be a just and peace-loving man. He will be of a moderate means with neither fame nor power.

   If the tenth lord combines with malefics in the ascendant, his *Dasa* brings in disgrace and humiliation. The native may live on gifts obtained at death and similar inauspicious ceremonies.

2. If the lord of the tenth house is placed in the second with the second lord, the native earns riches in the *Dasa* of the tenth lord. His fame for his riches spreads widely. His family will look to him for everything and will hold his opinions in high esteem. He will work for the government, in an influential job, with many servants at his beck and call. He will have many dependents. He will feed innumerable people. He will be magnanimous and always help others. If *Rajayogas* obtain in the chart, the native's power and authority will have no limit.

3. If the lord of the tenth house occupies the third house with the third lord, the native's prosperity booms in the *Dasa* of the tenth lord. He becomes famous as a bold

writer during this period. He rises swiftly in his career with frequent promotions. His brothers will prosper. He acquires musical talent and becomes famous in this field.

4. If the lord of the tenth house occupies the fourth house with the fourth lord, the native enjoys mental happiness and gains fame through his immovable properties. His income will be through lands and buildings, if the fourth lord is Mars or Mars associates with the tenth lord. He will also undertake agricultural pursuits.

5. If Mercury or Jupiter is with the tenth lord, the native heads an educational or research organization. His family will come to be known for its respectability.

6. If malefics afflict the tenth lord, the native suffers mental vacillation and takes wrong decisions, which affect his reputation adversely.

7. If the tenth lord joins the fifth lord in the fifth house and benefics also aspect the combination, the native rises to the rank of a minister during this period. If powerful *Rajayogas* are present, the native may even become the ruler of a country.

8. If a beneficially disposed eighth lord joins the combination, the native may become a ruler or prime-minister following the death of his predecessor.

9. If Rahu or Saturn, in strength, is involved in the combination, the native is elected to office.

10. When the lord of the tenth house occupies the sixth house, the former's *Dasa* will make the native a court official. If powerful planets are involved, he becomes a High Court or Supreme Court Judge.

11. If Mars, the Sun, Leo, Scorpio, Aries are the planets and signs involved, the native becomes a skilled surgeon or physician.

12. If the lord of the tenth house occupies the seventh with

the seventh lord, the native works abroad where he gets distinction and recognition. He marries a wife from a good family. She will also work, or otherwise boost his earnings by helping him in his work.

13. If the lord of the tenth house is in the eighth with the eighth lord, the native may lose his job in humiliating circumstances, in the *Dasa* of the tenth lord. If the tenth lord is fortified, he will be only suspended and then reinstated. The native will hold low jobs or take to a career of crime, if Rahu afflicts the Moon and the tenth lord.

14. If the lord of the tenth house is in the ninth with the ninth lord, subject to beneficial aspects, the native leads a life of righteousness. He will earn through fair means and become well-known for his sense of fair play and justice. If Ketu joins the tenth lord, the person embarks on a life of spiritual *sadhana*. If the Sun influences powerfully the tenth lord, the native works for the government or takes up the medical profession. If the Moon be strong, he will work as an auditor or banker in the government or in some big undertaking. If Mars aspects the tenth lord or associates with him, he will acquire immovable property from his father. If Mercury is powerfully disposed, he goes abroad for education and research in the *Dasa* of the tenth lord. The native will prosper along with his father, if Jupiter associates with the tenth lord. Venus in the same position will confer on the native gold, precious stones, conveyances and all kinds of comforts in the tenth lord's *Dasa*. If Saturn is the influencing planet, the native will head an industrial or other concern employing labour. If Saturn and the tenth lord are both weakly disposed or if the tenth lord is in an inimical sign, eclipsed or debilitated or in the sixth, eighth or twelfth in *navamsa*, the native himself will be forced to work as a servant.

15. If the lord of the tenth house is placed in the tenth house

with benefics, the native will become wealthy and fortunate. He achieves distinction in his profession but after a hard struggle. If *Rajayogas* are present, the native acquires power, status and eminence in the *Dasa* of the tenth lord. There will be many people working under him who will respect his word as law. The native enjoys good health and does many charitable deeds. He founds institutions relating to his field of activity.

16. If the lord of the tenth house occupies the eleventh house with the eleventh lord, the native will become a rich and prosperous man. He will have many businesses and all his ventures will turn out successful. He will have powerful friends in the government and upper classes. His personality will acquire charm and he will be a popular figure in social circles. He will have many men at his command and get possession of many mansions.

17. If the Moon is with the tenth lord, he earns through vehicles, trade in sea-products, milk, restaurants.

18. If the Sun is with the tenth lord, his income comes from wooden factories, match industries, gold market and chemicals.

19. If Mercury is with the eleventh lord, he earns distinction as a great intellectual and thinker and gets some fabulous cash award.

20. If Jupiter, he will head many institutions of learning as a chairman or trustee. Or he may be a newspaper magnate or prosperous publisher.

21. If the ruler of the tenth house is placed in the twelfth house with the twelfth lord with benefics, the native may head a medical institution or a prison or a remand home in the tenth lord's *Dasa*. If the tenth lord is fortified, the native pursues his spiritual inclinations with zeal.

An examination of professional prospects would include the study of the second house also, as the source of income, which must necessarily be through one's occupation. The ninth house is also of relevance, since it rules luck or fortune, and indirectly all distinction, fame, success and sudden gains as attributed to *Bhagya*. The eleventh house rules gains and especially in professions that are in the nature of trade gives a clue to the calling in which the native would prosper.

If the tenth house is vacant, then the lord of the *navamsa* occupied by the tenth lord gives a clue to the nature of the profession the native may follow. In this case also, the reckoning is to be made from the *lagna*, the Moon or the Sun depending on whichever of the three is most powerful.

•

Chapter-3

Professions indicated by Constellations

Constellations do play very prominent role in the judgement of one's profession. There are various houses and their lords, which should be taken into consideration viz., the ascendant, the tenth, the second, the eleventh, the seventh and the ninth house. It is really a tough exercise to concentrate over the specific house, lord thereof and constellation occupied by the lord of that house, because all may be different from each other. Different planets will indicate different profession. We will discuss in length the art of reaching the final conclusion while determining the specific profession or one's career. Here, we will discuss the role of all the 27 constellations. This will help a lot in finding out most appropriate and suitable profession of the native. A constellation contains 13° 20' and each constellation has four divisions or *Padas*. Thus, total number of *padas* of all the constellation will be 27 x 4 = 108.

Each sign consists of 30° and it is divided in nine *navamsas*. Each *navamsa* consist of 3° 20'. Thus 9 x 3° 20' = and 30° and there are twelve signs so 12 x 9 x 3° 20' = 360°. Total number of *navamsa* are 12 x 9 = 108. Total number of padas of 27 constellations = 27 x 4 = 108. Thus, *navamsa* and constellations both are 108 that is the reason that a *Japmala* contains 108 points. However, if we concentrate on the *navamsa* and constellation occupied by the tenth lord and by the lords of the other concerning houses, we are likely to reach on the correct conclusion with regard to most suitable occupations. First of all, we will mention the professions indicated by all the 27 constellations. This will help in judgement of appropriate direction during selection of the suitable profession.

The professional indications for each of the 27 constellations are described below:

1. ASHVINI

Location: 00°:00' to 13°:20' Aries; **Sign Lord** : Mars
Constellation Lord: The South node(Ketu)

General characteristics : The native is clever, intelligent, lucky, honest, efficient, short tempered and popular.

Professions: The vocations falling under this constellation are related to defense, law (particularly criminal courts), transport, the heavy metal industry, surgery, Yoga, horse grooming and training.

2. BHARANI

Location: 13°:20' to 26°:40' Aries; **Sign Lord** : Mars
Constellation Lord : Venus

General characteristics : The native is pleasure seeking, aspiring, truthful, clever, determined, courageous, selfish and indulgent.

Professions: All vocations related to pleasurable pursuits, the entertainment industry, sports, agriculture, the tanning industry, the hospitality industry, advertising and the fine arts.

3. (A) KRITIKA (The first quarter falling in Aries sign)

Location : 26°:40' to 30°:00' Aries; **Sign Lord** : Mars
Constellation Lord : Sun

General characteristics : The native is enthusiastic, competitive, and has leadership qualities.

Professions: Professions related to national and civic defense, real estate, mining, astrology, pottery, surgery, the explosives and fireworks industry.

3. (B) KRITIKA (Remaining three quarters)

Location:0°:00' to 10°:00' Taurus; **Sign Lord**:Venus
Constellation Lord : Sun

General characteristics : The native likes the company of others and is sociable, generous, courteous and pleasure seeking.

Professions: All professions related to the fine arts, sculpting, photography, global trade, chartered accountancy, budgeting, tax collection, medicine, ephemeris making, and manufacture of stationery.

4. ROHINI

Location:10°:00' to 23°:20' Taurus; **Sign Lord** :Venus
Constellation Lord : Moon

General characteristics : The native is cordial, well-mannered, sympathetic, truthful and good looking.

Professions: Professions related to the hospitality industry, automobiles, milk and dairy products, perfumes, cosmetics, glass and plastic, shipping, sugar, aquatic animals, agriculture, yoga, aviation, travel agencies, readymade garments etc.

5. (A) MRIGSHIRA (First two quarters)

Location: 23°:20' to 30°:00' Taurus; **Sign Lord**: Venus
Constellation Lord : Mars

General characteristics : The native is alert and aware, witty, strong, enthusiastic, attractive, selfish and quarrelsome.

Professions: Professions related to real estate, fertilizers, automobile-engineering, entertainment, income and sales tax, tobacco and tobacco-products, tailoring, confectionary, fruit selling and tanning industries.

5. (B) MRIGSHIRA (Last two quarters)

Location:0°:00' to 6°:40' Gemini; **Sign Lord** : Mercury
Constellation Lord : Mars

General characteristics : The native is witty, sharp, quick to react, impulsive, easily excitable, timid and passionate.

Professions: Professions related to general and surgical instruments, wires and cables, textile engineering, research, construction, publishing, journalism, computers, astronomy, post and telegraph, machinery, company representation, brokerage, horticulture and radio.

6. ARDRA

Location:6°:40' to 20°:00' Gemini; **Sign Lord** :Mercury
Constellation Lord : The North node(Rahu)

General characteristics : The native is ingenious, perceptive, resourceful and mentally active.

Professions: All professions related to communication, post and telegraph, radio, advertising, writing, research and invention, exploration, skilled work, handwriting and finger print analysis, physics, dynamics and statistics, sale of books, tantra (the occult) and magic.

7.(A) PUNARVASU (First three quarters)

Location:20°:00' to 30°:00' Gemini; **Sign Lord** :Mercury
Constellation Lord : Jupiter

General characteristics : The native is intuitive, good looking and broadminded. He/She has a good memory, wisdom and a balanced mind.

Professions: Professions related to editing, publishing, journalism, poetry, insurance agencies, accounts, finance, civil engineering, teaching, astrology, mathematics, dealership, auditing, story-writing, literary-translations and interpreting.

7.(B) PUNARVASU (Fourth quarter)

Location: 0°:00' to 3°:20' Cancer; **Sign Lord**: Moon
Constellation Lord : Jupiter

General characteristics : The native has good imagination and judgment and is benevolent, compassionate and sympathetic.

Professions: Bankers, judges, travelers, principals of institutions and professors, statisticians, economists, heads of religious institutions, physicians, sailors, nurses, water suppliers, *purohits* all come under this constellation.

8. PUSHYA

Location: 3°:20' to 16°:40' Cancer; **Sign Lord**: Moon
Constellation Lord : Saturn

General characteristics : The native is mentally composed, careful, and patient and learned.

Professions: Professions related to submarines, petroleum products, coal, grave-digging, agriculture, plumbing, digging of wells, all underground works, construction.

9. ASLESA

Location: 16°:40' to 30°:00' Cancer; **Sign Lord**: Moon
Constellation Lord: Mercury

General characteristics : The native has an ingenious and sharp mind and likes traveling.

Professions: All professions related to global trade, writing, manufacturing, textile engineering, paper, writing instruments (pens), inks, astrology, traveling, water-diving (dowse), mathematics, nursing, clerical work, commerce, trading and brokerage.

10. MAGHA

Location:0°:00' to 13°:20' Leo; **Sign Lord** : Sun
Constellation Lord : The South node (Ketu)

General characteristics : The native is short tempered, impulsive, industrious, sensual and outspoken.

Professions: Professions related to defense, surgery and surgical instruments, chemicals and drugs manufacturing, government service, artificial jewellery, low-cost ornaments and electroplating.

11. POORVA PHALGUNI

Location:13°:20' to 26°:40' Leo; **Sign Lord** :Sun
Constellation Lord : Venus

General characteristics : The native is generous, affectionate, honest and soft-spoken person.

Professions: Professions related to radio, automobiles, entertainment, photography, tanning, revenue, transport, service in government departments, education, preservation of monuments, sports, optical work, institutions for women, cigarette manufacturing, restaurants and canteens, animal husbandry and their medical care.

12. (A). UTTARA PHALGUNI (first quarter)

Location:26°:40' to 30°:00' Leo; **Sign Lord** : Sun
Constellation Lord : Sun

General characteristics : The native is optimistic contented, happy, rich and likes to showoff.

Professions: Professions related to commerce, the stock-exchange, shipping, government service and medicine, particularly heart-care.

12. (B) UTTARA PHALGUNI (Last three quarters)

Location:0°:00' to 10°:00' Virgo; **Sign Lord**: Mercury
Constellation Lord : Sun

General characteristics : The native is tactful, intelligent, studious and industrious.

Professions: Professions related to astrology communications, education, tourism, public relations and health, contract work, hospitals, and registration of newspapers, births and deaths; Astronomers, manufacturers, agents, physicians, correspondents, lecturers and handwriting experts also come under this constellation.

13. HASTA

Location:10°:00' to 23°:20' Virgo; **Sign Lord** :Mercury
Constellation Lord : Moon

General characteristics : The native is industrious, full of energy, quarrelsome and courageous.

Professions: Professions related to mail order business, commerce, shipping, textile, engineering, building dams, bridges and tunnels, manufacture of printing inks, practice of law, sanitary engineering, import and export, related to art and painting, politics and messaging services.

14. (A). CHITRA (First two quarters)

Location:23°:20' to 30°:00' Virgo; **Sign Lord**: Mercury
Constellation Lord : Mars

General characteristics : The native is practical, courageous, and full of energy, active, restless and irritable.

Professions: Professions related to building, mechanical engineering; taxation, revenue, finance and defense departments; criminal law, electricity, police, traffic police, mining, fingerprint analysis, jewellery and perfume making and mathematics.

14. (B). CHITRA (Last two quarters)

Location:0°:00' to 6°:40' Libra; **Sign Lord**: Venus
Constellation Lord : Mars

General characteristics : The native is adventurous, perceptive, intuitive and loves science.

Professions: Professions related to law, surgery, defense, decoration, advertising, science, registration of marriages, radio and television, tailoring, cigarette trading, automobile parts.

15. SWATI

Location:6°:40' to 20°:00' Libra; **Sign Lord**: Venus
Constellation Lord : The North node (Rahu)

General characteristics : The native is adaptive, sensitive, peaceful, social and compassionate, and has initiative.

Professions: Professions related to transport, automobiles, manufacturing X-ray instruments, bakery products, fancy goods, perfumes, readymade dresses, and leather goods, confectionary bakery, plastic, mica and pasteurized milk.

16. (A). VISHAKHA (First three quarters)

Location:20°:00' to 30 °:00' Libra; **Sign Lord**: Venus
Constellation Lord : Jupiter

General characteristics : The native is well mannered, polite, an atheist, generous, truthful and just; a believer in universal brotherhood and love.

Professions: Professions related to traveling, shipping, foreign trade, auditing, expensive dresses, jewellery, air travel, partnership, tax and revenue, international trade, entertainment and publicity, and speculation.

16.(B). VISHAKHA (Fourth quarter)

Location:0°:00' to 3°:20' Scorpio; **Sign Lord** :Mars
Constellation Lord : Jupiter

General characteristics : The native is straightforward, sincere, independent, generous and wise.

Professions: Professions related to insurance, share market, defense department, criminal law, betting, ayurveda, cotton growing and chemical and drug manufacturing.

17. ANURADHA

Location:3°:20' to 16°:40' Scorpio; **Sign Lord** :Mars
Constellation Lord : Saturn

General characteristics : The native is self-centered, aggressive, courageous, intelligent, straightforward and hard working.

Professions: Professions related to surgery, medicine, tanning and leather goods, homeopathic medicines, plumbing and water diving (dowse), mechanical engineering, woolens, jail, mustard and groundnut.

18. JYESTHA

Location:16°:40'to 30°:00' Scorpio; **Sign Lord**: Mars
Constellation Lord : Mercury

General characteristics : The native is spontaneous, learned, practical, philosophical and witty.

Professions: Professions related to surgery, horse racing, press publication, publicity, manufacture of printing inks, calculators, generation and distribution of electric power, textile machinery, manufacture of cables and wires.

19. MOOLA

Location: 0°:00' to13°:20' Sagittarius; **Sign Lord**: Jupiter
Constellation Lord : The South node (Ketu)

General characteristics : The native is aggressive, grave looking, proud, generous, cordial, charitable, honest and law-abiding.

Professions: Professions related to global trade, legal practice, imports, teaching, religious scriptures, social work, ayurveda, jail, secret service, dealership of cotton, wheat and gur (jaggery), medical practice, horse racing, dealing in provision goods, fruits and seeds.

19. POORVASHADHA

Location: 13°:20'to26°:40' Sagittarius; **Sign Lord**: Jupiter
Constellation Lord : Venus

General characteristics : The native is broad-minded, polite, compassionate, hopeful, extravagant, sensitive to others' feelings and honest.

Professions: Professions related to astrology, the occult science, law, banking, accountancy, trade of diamonds and gold, revenue and finance departments, gardens, hotels and restaurants, nursing homes for women and children, foreign exchange, air-travel, welfare and transport.

20. (A). UTTARASHADHA (First quarter)

Location:26°:40'to30°:00' Sagittarius; **Sign Lord**: Jupiter
Constellation Lord : Sun

General characteristics : The native is righteous living, charitable, good-natured, joy loving and successful in religious activities.

Professions: Professions related to politics, financial institutions, ayurveda, nursing homes, hospitals, charitable institutions, export and embassies, education, interpretation, business representation, shipping, jails.

20. (B). UTTARASHADHA (Last three quarters)

Location:0°:00'to10°:00' Capricorn; **Sign Lord**: Saturn
Constellation Lord : Sun

General characteristics : The native is well organized, sincere, reliable, intelligent, fore-sighted and thrifty.

Professions: Professions related to underground work, mining, scientific research, engineering, wool, skins and bones, archaeology, antiques, coal mining, monuments, jail and ancient languages.

22. SHRAVANA

Location: 10°:00'to23°:20' Capricorn; **Sign Lord**: Saturn
Constellation Lord : Moon

General characteristics : The native is pessimistic, extra cautious, thrifty and timid.

Professions: Professions related to mining and mined products, coal and metals, oil, petrol, petroleum products, excavation, agriculture, cooling of air, submarines, cold drinks and ice cream, dairy products, plumbing, fish selling.

23. (A). DHANISHTHA (First two quarters)

Location:23°:20'to30°:00' Capricorn; **Sign Lord**: Saturn
Constellation Lord : Mars

General characteristics : The native is active, strong-willed, careful, selfish and greedy.

Professions: Professions related to labour and welfare, insurance, machines, making and selling of liquor, production of telephones and television, ayurveda, slaughter houses, rehabilitation, tools and spare parts and cement.

23. (B). DHANISHTHA (Last two quarters)

Location:0°:00' to 6°:40' Aquarius; **Sign Lord**: Saturn
Constellation Lord : Mars

General characteristics : The native is short-tempered reliable, social, charitable and logical.

Professions: Professions related to agriculture, exploration, mining, coal, engineering, defense, electricity, communication, archaeology, television, telephone, atomic energy, leather goods, tanning, recycling of waste, foundries.

24. SHATBHISHA

Location:6°:40' to 20°:00' Aquarius; **Sign Lord**: Saturn
Constellation Lord : The North node (Rahu)

General characteristics : The native is independent, patient, leisure loving and lazy.

Professions: Professions related to electricity, science, air-travel, astronomy, astrology, stock exchange, statistics, translation work, writing, the occult science, iron and lead, explosives.

25. (A). POORVA BHADRAPAD (First three quarters)

Location:20°:00' to 30°:00' Aquarius; **Sign Lord**: Saturn
Constellation Lord: Jupiter

General characteristics : The native is optimistic, honest, reliable and able to take work from others.

Professions: Professions related to astronomy and astrology, the stock exchange, planning, global trade, foreign exchange, overseas banking, education, temples, intelligence department, medicines, aeroplanes and research work.

25. (B). POORVA BHADRAPAD (The last quarter)

Location:0°:00' to 3°:20' Pisces; **Sign Lord**: Jupiter
Constellation Lord: Jupiter

General characteristics : The native is a music and art lover, polite, broad-minded and joyful.

Professions: Professions related to planning, foreign exchange, public limited companies, hospitals, criminal law, camps for refugees, tourism, exploration, expansion work, religious activities, investment, banking, law, education, ministers and ministries.

26. UTTARA BHADRAPAD

Location:3°:20' to 16°:40' Pisces; **Sign Lord**: Jupiter
Constellation Lord: Saturn

General characteristics : The native is philosophical, peace and seclusion loving, helpful and independent.

Professions: Professions related to prisons, sanatoriums, places of isolation, jails for political prisoners, engineering, mining, shipping, charitable institutions, education, import and export, manufacture of umbrellas and raincoats, construction of canals.

27. REVATI

Location:16°:40' to 30°:00' Pisces; **Sign Lord**: Jupiter
Constellation Lord: Mercury

General characteristics : The native is intuitive, sympathetic, clever, honest, studious and flexible.

Professions: Professions related to auditing, excise and customs, preaching, astrology, mathematics, banks, accountancy, publicity, editing, publishing, law, newspapers, administration of religious institution, civil engineering, advertising, politics and radio.

●

CHAPTER-4

Role of *Navamsa* in Profession

Navamsa chart is the most important divisional chart and must be taken into consideration during the judgement of each and every aspect of life along with the natal chart. We have a firm belief after the study of several lacks of birth charts during our 35 years experience in the field of practical astrology that without consideration of *navamsa* chart, the astrologer does a 'crime' with the native, whose horoscope he examines. The results will always be misleading and will give faulty predictions. Suppose, a planet is debilitated in natal chart but the same planet get exalted in *navamsa* chart, the native will certainly get the results of exaltation and not the results of debilitation of that planet. There are so many factors, which only *navamsa* chart can reveal. If one has Mars in his 10th house, he may get the result of Mars during the *Dasa Bhukti* of the planet, which obtains the navamsa of Mars, and so on.

One *navamsa* consists of 3° 20' and one *Pada* of single *nakshatra* contains 3° 20'. Therefore, *nakshatra* and *navamsa* should be taken into consideration along with each other. One sign contains 30°, which has been divided in nine *navamsas* and each *navamsa* runs for 3° 20'. One sign consists of 2¼ *nakshatras* and one *nakshatra* is made of 13° 20'. Thus, 2¼ *nakshatras* of one sign are made of 13° 20' + 13° 20' + 3° 20' = 30°. Thus, one sign contains nine *navamsas* of 3° 20' as well as nine charans of 2¼ *nakshatras*. Thus, *nakshatras* and *navamsas* are related to each other. In Krishnamurthi Paddhati, one *nakshatra* has been divided further into nine parts, whereas in traditional Hindu Astrology, one sign has been divided in nine *navamsas*. In this way only Krishnamurthi Paddhati is different from traditional Hindu

Astrology. *Nakshatras* and *navamsas* have further divisions too, which we will not be taking here.

For the detailed study of *navamsa* chart, we will have to write a separate book as all that can not be included in this treatise on professional aspects. We have written much about the *navamsa* chart at various places of this book, as and where it was essential. We will be giving some specific points on the basis of classical works and that of our experience here under.

4.1 Role of *Navamsa* in the assessment of the strength of the planets

Compare the sign wise position of the ascendant, the 10th house and all the natal planets with those of the *navamsa* chart.

If the ascendant of the birth chart has the same sign as the *navamsa* ascendant then the birth ascendant is called *vargottam* and it improves the overall condition of the birth ascendant and gives better results.

Similarly any planet, which is *vargottam* due to acquiring the same sign in the *navamsa* chart, becomes strong and auspicious for the native.

We would like to clarify that if a planet is debilitated in both the charts then it remains debilitated and does not gain any positive effect due to being *vargottam*.

If the position of any planet improves in the *navamsa* chart, over its position in the natal chart, then that planet gains strength and gives better results.

Suppose, a planet is debilitated in the birth chart but becomes exalted in the *navamsa* chart then, although it may not be right to say that it's debilitation is cancelled, yet it has been observed that the said planet becomes favourable in giving results. The reverse condition is also true, that is, if a planet is exalted in the birth chart and becomes debilitated in the *navamsa* chart then one can expect just average results of that planet.

4.2 Role of *Navamsa* in determining the profession

The *navamsa* lord of the 10th lord (of birth chart) may indicate the profession of the native. Various professions indicated by planets, as the *navamsa* lord of the 10th lord, are given below:

Sun: The professions indicated are trading of woolens, contractual work, medical practice, sale of medicines, practice of alternative system of medicine, work related to gold mines, shipping, jewellery, courts.

Executives in defence, ministers, managers or administrators and government servants are also governed by the Sun. It may also indicate independent business.

Moon: Milk and milk products, ice factory, cold storages, cold drinks, rice, salt, naval officers, hospital staff, liquid products, bar owners, poultry raisers, midwife, sales men.

Mars: Professions related to metals, buildings, weapons, Fire, fireworks, engineering, defence, police, circus, criminal courts. It also indicates surgeons, robbers, butchers and thieves.

Mercury: Professions related to mathematics, engineering, astrology, poetry, oratory, sculpting, journalism etc.

Jupiter: Jupiter indicates heads of religious organizations, judges, counselors, lawyers, bankers, teachers and religious preachers.

Venus: It indicates jewellers, precious stone dealers, and traders of dairy products, vehicle dealers, and hotelier, fruits and flower sellers.

Professions related to perfumes, cosmetics, cinema, dance bars, casinos etc. are also under Venus.

Saturn: Professions related to wooden goods, craft, foot wear, metals and oils. Saturn also indicates all types of workers, jailors, miners etc.

Each planet indicates innumerable professions, whereas many professions are the outcome of the positive and negative effect of the group of planets, which we have tried to discuss in length in this book. The *navamsa* lord of the 2nd, 11th and 9th houses must also be examined, in addition to the lord of the 10th house. These factors and *navamsa* position of the lords of the various houses will certainly help readers and astrologers to pin point the profession of the native.

The judgement of the exact occupation depends on various factors. The planets placed in the 10th house, *navamsa* lord of the 10th lord and the planet which falls in the *nakshatra* or the *navamsa* of the planet posited in the 10th house. Find out all of these planets from the ascendant or Moon, whichever is stronger. This will help a lot in the judgement of exact occupation of the native. If the Sun, Moon, Mars etc. influence the 10th house, either by occupation or by ownership of the 10th house, or these are the *navamsa* lord of the 10th lord or planet placed therein, the following occupations will become the source of earning money, and livelihood will depend on these vocations.

The following verses may be referred for the classification and judgement of occupation. These aphorisms of planetary combinations, with regard to *navamsa,* have been taken from various classical texts and are given below for the benefit of our readers.

क्लेशोदवसितेशेन कलिते कण्ठमन्दिरे ।
विक्रेता दृषदादीनां काष्ठानां जनितो जनः ।।

(*Jyotish Tattavam,* Chap-32/Vers-123)

If the lord of the 6th house falls in the third house, the native is sculptor of stone or seller of wood.

यद्गोलवे पदपतिः परिवर्त्ततेऽस्य तत्तुल्यकर्म्मवशतो जनितस्य वृत्तिः।
पौरेन्दुपाथपदगांशकपालवत्त्या किं मासहोत्थघनतो गगने बली यः।।

तत्खेटव त्त्या मनुजस्य जीवनं किं वीर्य्ययुक्ताद् गणपाद् द्युचारिणः।
दाये हृतौ तस्य खगस्य जीवनं भवेन्नराणां जनके जडद्यतौ।।

वृत्तिर्विलासैर्वचनस्य चोद्यमैः सर्वैः कलाकौशलसाहसादिभिः।
खे सस्वभेऽहौ भविदार वीक्षितयुक्ते क्षणस्वर्द्धिधनक्षयं भवेत्।।

कायेन्दुतः कपिमुखैः कुलगैर्धनाप्तिस्तातप्रसूरिपुसुहृत्सहजाङ्गनाभ्यः।
भृत्यात् क्रमेण कथिता तनुतारकेशतिग्मांशुतातपगगोलवपालवृत्त्या ।।

(*Jyotish Tattavam,* Chap-32/Vers 124-127)

Traits of occupation of native can be decided by the planet in whose *navamsa* the lord of the 10th house falls. Or money is gained as per the nature or characteristics of the planet who is the lord of the *navamsa* falling in the 10th, as reckoned from the stronger among the *lagna*, Moon or the Sun. Or the earning depends upon the nature of the strongest planet in the 10th, from the *lagna* or the Moon sign, whichever is stronger. The lord of sign occupied by the strongest planet fixes the occupation of a person in its *dasa* or *antar dasa*. If Moon occupies the 10th house, livelihood comes through enterprises, by use of his speech, arts and crafts and courageous acts. If Rahu falls in own sign in the 10th house and is aspected by or conjoined with Venus, Mercury, or Mars, money is gained, as well as lost, in no time. The native gains money from the relatives as indicated by the planets placed tenth to the *lagna* or Moon. For example, money is gained from father if Sun is placed in the 10th house, form mother if Moon, from enemies if Mars, from friends if Mercury, from brothers if Jupiter, from wife if Venus, and from servants if Saturn is placed 10th. Gain of money can be predicted according to the nature & characteristics of the planet owning the *navamsa* occupied by the lord of the sign falling tenth, from whichever is strongest among the Sun, Moon or the *lagna*.

We will discuss the results of various planets, which

are placed in the 10th house or the lords of the *navamsa* occupied by the 10th lord. Various classics have given amazing facts about the planets, which rule over the 10th house in anyway. We are quite confident that the study of following will certainly add a lot even in the knowledge of widely experienced astrologers.

अर्थाप्तिं कथयेद्विलग्न - शशिनोः प्राबल्यतः सेचरैः
कर्मस्थैः पितृ-मातृ-शात्रव-सुहृद्-भ्रात्रादिभिः स्त्री-धनात्।
भृत्याद्वा दिननाथ - लग्न -शशिनां मध्ये बलीयांस्ततः
कर्मेशस्य नवांश - राशिप - वशाद् वृत्तिं जगुस्तद्विदः।।

(*Phalit Martand,* Ch-11/Vers-1)

The lord of the 10th house from the *lagna* or Moon, whichever is stronger, reflects the source of income or gain of money according to its *'Karkatwa'* (signification). For example, money is gained from father if Sun is placed in the 10th house, from mother if Moon, from enemies if Mars, from friends if Mercury, from brothers if Jupiter, from wife if Venus, and from servants if Saturn is placed in the 10th house. Besides the family business, learned should predict the means of livelihood from the lord of the *navamsa* occupied by the 10th lord as reckoned from the Sun, Moon or the lagna, whichever is stronger.

भैषज्योर्ण-तृणाम्बु-धान्य-कनक-व्यापार-मुक्तादिभिः ।
अन्योऽन्यागम-दूत-वृत्तिभिरिनस्यांशे तु जीवत्यसौ ।।

(*Phalit Martand,* Ch-11/Vers-2)

If the lord of the 10th house, from the *lagna* or Moon, obtains the *navamsa* of Sun, means of livelihood may be predicted through the trading of medicines, wool, woolen clothes, water, cereals, gold, pearl, or through traveling or by being the emissary of rich persons.

Note: Means of livelihood have also been seen to be through trading of grass, fruit bearing tress, wood or cereals, or by reciting mantras or speaking lies, if 10th lord obtains the *navamsa* of Sun.

जलोद्भवानां क्रय-विक्रयेण कृषेश्च मृद्भाण्डविनोद-मार्गात्।
राजाङ्गना-संश्रय-वित्तरूपान्निशाकरांशे वसन-क्रयाद्वा।।

(*Phalit Martand,* Ch-11/Vers-3)

If the lord of the 10th house, from the *lagna* or Moon or Sun, obtains the *navamsa* of Moon, means of livelihood may be predicted through trading of the articles grown from water such as conch shell, Pearl, water chest nut, or through agriculture, or toys or utensils or instruments of entertainment made of clay, sale & purchase of cotton clothes or gain of money by taking shelter under some queen or rich lady.

Note: Means of livelihood have also been seen to be through trading of liquids like soda, soft drinks, *Khand,* sugar, agriculture, sale or purchase of animals or pilgrimage.

धातोर्विवादेन रण-प्रकारात् स्तब्धाग्नि-वादात् कलह-प्रवृत्त्याः।
जीवत्यसौ साहस-मार्ग-रूपाद् धरा सुतांशे यदि चौर-वृत्त्याः।।

(*Phalit Martand,* Ch-11/Vers-4)

If the lord of the 10th house, from the *lagna* or Sun, obtains the *navamsa* of Mars, means of livelihood may be predicted through metal-gold, silver, copper, brass or steel, tin; through dealing in conflicts and disputes (arbitrator, advocate etc.); service in army, coal, fire, by courageous and difficult acts, and watchman or security personnel; or by stealing things.

Note: Means of livelihood have also been seen to be through factories, arms, goldsmith, sculptor, electrical works, cookery, sweetmeat shop, butchery, vegetable vendor, soldier, dyeing, goat, sheep, shelter of unholy people, spying, engine driver etc, if the 10th lord obtains the *navamsa* of Mars.

काव्यागमादथ शास्त्र-मार्गाज्ज्योतिर्गण-ज्ञान-वशाद् बुधांशे।
परार्थ-वेदाध्ययनाज्जपाच्च पुरोहिताद्याज्य-वशात् प्रवृत्तिः।।

(*Phalit Martand,* Ch-11/Vers-5)

If the lord of the 10th house, from the *lagna,* Moon or

Sun, obtains the *navamsa* of Mercury, means of livelihood may be predicted through sculpting, crafting, essay writing, pictures, clothes manufacturing, poetry, knowledge of *Shastras*, astrology, reciting mantras or *Path* of Vedas for others (clients), priest, performing *Yagnya, havan* etc.

Note: Livelihood is earned by the occupation of clerk, assistant or through falsehood, in the *navamsa* of Mercury.

जीवांशके भूसुर-देवतानामुपासनाध्यापक-रूप-मार्गात् ।
पुराण-शास्त्रागम-नीति-मार्गाद्धर्मोपदेशेन कुसीदमाहुः ।।

(*Phalit Martand,* Ch-11/Vers-6)

If the lord of the 10th house, from the *lagna,* Moon or Sun, obtains the *navamsa* of Jupiter, means of livelihood may be predicted through Brahmins' or Devtas' Ashrams, priesthood, teaching, by following the righteous path of religion and religious books, worshipping or preaching etc.

Note: In the *navamsa* of Jupiter, livelihood may also be earned through trading in gold, salt, eye lotions; favour of king or the like; trading in products under the ground taken through mines, coal; occupation of advocate, lawyer, barrister, judge; donations, tailor, modes of transport, or income through interest.

सुवर्ण-माणिक्य-गजाश्वमूलाद् गवां क्रयाज्जीवनमाहुरार्याः ।
गुडौदन-क्षार-दधि-क्रयेण स्त्रियां प्रलोभेन भृगोः सुतांशे ।।

(*Phalit Martand,* Ch-11/Vers-7)

If the lord of the 10th house, from the *lagna,* Moon or Sun, obtains the *navamsa* of Venus, means of livelihood may be predicted through trading in gold, jewels, gems, elephant, horses, cow, buffalo; sale & purchase of Gur, rice, salt, curd, and also through the closeness of ladies.

Note: Earning of livelihood is also seen through iron, singing, cinema, trading in liquor or wine, milk, medicines, eye lotions, scented articles, brokerage or being assistant to some influential person, if Venus is the *navamsa* lord of the 10th lord.

शन्यंशके कुत्सित-मार्ग-वृत्त्या शिल्पादिभिर्दारु-मयैर्वधाद्यैः।
विन्यस्त-भाराज्जन-विप्रलंभादन्योऽन्य-वैरागम-मार्गमूलात् ।।

(*Phalit Martand,* Ch-11/Vers-8)

If the lord of the 10th house, from the *lagna,* Moon or Sun, obtains the *navamsa* of Saturn, means of livelihood may be predicted through some condemned acts (against the family tradition and pride) sculpturing in wood, murder, torturing the animals, coolie, cheating others, enmity, disputes and court cases

Note: If the lord of the 10th from Moon or the Sun, occupies the *navamsa* of Saturn, money is earned as peon, messenger, vegetables, betel nuts, cigattete, fruit vending, laborer, wood from orchards, printing press, employee in printing press or temple, traveling and working as an agent.

However, it should be kept in mind that the *navamsa* lord, which has been referred to, must also be considered for its auspiciousness or otherwise, and the benefic or malefic results should be modified accordingly. For example, if the malefic lord of *navamsa* occupies its friendly, auspicious or exalted divisions, even the inauspicious nature would turn to be benefic. And similarly, even the benefic lord of *navamsa,* if occupies debilitated or inimical divisions, its beneficence would be reduced. Above, a number of trades or occupations, for a particular lord of *navamsa,* have been mentioned. The native would go for which occupation, the learned should predict after careful consideration of the native's existing position, his family business, caste, class, customs and country. Favorable transit of the planet (lord of *navamsa*), indicating the occupation, would cause it to prosper. Also, if benefic planets transit or aspect the 10th house, the business or vocation flourishes.

अंशेशे बलवत्ययत्न - धन - संप्राप्ति बलोनांशपे
स्वल्पं प्रोक्त-फलं भवेदुदयतः कर्मर्क्ष-देशे फलम् ।

अंशस्योक्त-दिशं वदेत्पति-युते दृष्टे स्व-देशे फलं
सत्यन्यैः पर-देशजं तदधिपस्यांशे स्व-देशे स्थिरे ।।

(*Phalit Martand,* Ch-11/Vers-9)

If the lord of *navamsa* indicating the occupation is strong, the job is easily obtained without any struggle. More is gained without much labor. If the lord of the *navamsa* is weak, the profession involves much struggle and the gain is not significant. The result is obtained in the country/place according to the sign in the 10th house. The direction, where the profession would be, is determined by the direction of the planet who is the lord of the *navamsa*. If the lord of *navamsa* occupies or aspects his own sign, the native would take up the job in his own country or place. If other planets aspect or occupy that *navamsa* sign, livelihood would be earned in a foreign country. If the lord of *navamsa* occupies a fixed sign, native's own country/place should be predicted for his vocation.

Note: If the lord of the *navamsa* occupies a moveable sign, native may prosper in profession in a foreign country, and if it falls in a common sign, he may earn in own land as well as in a foreign land. However, a very careful examination of signs and planets placed in the 10th house, as reckoned both from the *Rashi* as well as the *navamsa* chart, should be made to decide the place and direction, where the profession would prosper.

चार-क्रमेणोदयतोऽन्वयाधिपो यस्मिन्नवांशे परिवर्तते यदा ।
या जीविका प्राक् कथिता तदीक्षितुर्विचक्षणस्तां प्रतिवासरं वदेत् ।।

(*Phalit Martand,* Ch-11/Vers-10)

The learned should predict the means of livelihood according to the nature of the planet who is the lord of the *navamsa* in which the 10th lord, as reckoned from the *Rashi* chart, transits.

Note: The lord of the 10th will continue transit in whatever *navamsa*, the lords of those *navamsas*, according to their nature and characteristics bring change in the profession and give benefits.

मित्रारि-स्वगृह-गतैर्ग्रहैस्ततोऽर्थ-स्तुङ्गस्थे, बलिनि च भास्करे स्व-वीर्यात् ।
आयस्थै रुदय-धनाश्रितैश्च सौम्यैःसंचिन्त्यं बलसहितैरनेकधा स्वम् ।।

(*Phalit Martand,* Ch-11/Vers-11)

As mentioned earlier, if the 10th lord, as reckoned from *lagna,* Moon or Sun, occupies a friendly sign, the gain of money can be predicted through a friend (or through the advice of a friend), in an inimical sign from an enemy (disputes, court cases) or in own sign by self endeavour. Accordingly, if the 10th lord Sun is exalted, the native earns money through his own undertakings. If in the birth chart, powerful benefic planets occupy the 11th, *lagna* or the 2nd house, he earns money though multifarious sources. Or to say, the native will earn money in whatever occupation he indulges in for profit.

Note: If in a birth chart malefics occupy the 11th, *lagna* or the 2nd, in inimical or debilitated sign, the native will face failures in all his undertakings.

Such natives should go for service or should depend upon others in a partnership. If in a birth chart, Moon is afflicted by Saturn, the native can not prosper in an independent enterprise. Even if he has a partnership, he should not take initiatives. This would be to his advantage.

Explanation: The native should choose the occupation, as per his choice, from amongst the occupations under the aegis of the lord of the *navamsa,* as mentioned earlier. This will work. If he is not able to do that particular work he may opt for the job of similar nature and characteristics. Some Acharyas decide the profession according to the occupations indicated by the lord of sign in which the strong ascendant lord is placed.

अर्थाप्तिः पितृजननीसपत्नमित्र-भ्रातृस्त्रीभृतकजनाद्दिवाकराद्यैः ।
होरेन्द्वोर्दशमगतैर्विकल्पनीयाभेन्द्वर्कास्पदपतिगांशनाथवृत्त्या ।।

(*Jatak Parijat,* Ch-15/Vers-43)

Now we describe how the means of livelihood would be. From *lagna* or the Moon, if the 10th place is occupied by

1. Sun, money is gained through father.
2. Moon, money is gained through mother.
3. Mars, money is gained through enemies.
4. Mercury, money is gained through friends.
5. Jupiter, money is gained through brothers.
6. Venus, money is gained through wife.
7. Saturn, money is gained through servants.

If 10th house, from Moon and *lagna* both, is occupied by planets, those will give the results in their periods. If many planets are there in the 10th house, they will benefit the native in their own periods.

This is one way. Not only from the *lagna* or Moon, but also from the Sun, find out the 10th house. Find the *navamsas* in which these lords of the 10th places fall in. Native earns money according to the lord of *navamsa.*

अर्थाप्तिं कथयेद्विलग्नशशिनोर्मध्ये बली यस्ततः ।
कर्मेशस्थनवांशराशिपवशाद् वृत्तिं जगुस्तद्विदः ।।

(*Jatak Parijat,* Ch-15/Vers-43)

Find out in which sign or the *navamsa* the 10th lord from the *lagna* or Moon (whichever is stronger) falls. That *navamsa* lord decides the occupation of the native according to its nature or signification. This is written that auspicious planets in the *lagna,* 11th and 2nd bestow accumulation of money through many sources.

4.3 Secrets of *Dasamsa* Chart

There are so many divisional charts, which are helpful in the judgement of various aspects of life. Divisional charts should be examined for the confirmation of our judgement with regard to various aspects of life. For the purpose of marriage, the examination of *navamsa* chart is essential, whereas for the study of progeny and children, *Saptamsa* chart should be taken into consideration. Similarly, for the confirmation of the judgement of occupation, it is always advisable to go through the *Dasamsa* chart, in addition to natal *Rasi* chart and *navamsa* chart. These divisional charts are the supporting tools in the judgement of predictions. Due importance must be attached to divisional charts, provided the time of birth is precise and accurate, otherwise the divisional charts may not be correct, which may lead to wrong information.

The divisional charts known as *Varga* Charts play an important role in Vedic predictive astrology.

4.4 What is a *Dasamsa* chart?

Dividing a sign in ten equal divisions, each one of 3°, give rise to *Dasamsa* chart. As we know that a sign is of 30° therefore its 10th part is equal to 30°/10 = 3°.

4.5 How to prepare a *Dasamsa* chart?

A *Dasamsa* chart can be easily prepared from the birth chart with the help of following table:

Conversion table for making a *Dasamsa* chart from a birth chart

Birth chart→ Signs Degrees↓	**1**	**2**	**3**	**4**	**5**	**6**	**7**	**8**	**9**	**10**	**11**	**12**
0° to 3°	1	10	3	12	5	2	7	4	9	6	11	8
3° to 6°	2	11	4	1	6	3	8	5	10	7	12	9
6° to 9°	3	12	5	2	7	4	9	6	11	8	1	10
9° to 12°	4	1	6	3	8	5	10	7	12	9	2	11
12° to 15°	5	2	7	4	9	6	11	8	1	10	3	12
15° to 18°	6	3	8	5	10	7	12	9	2	11	4	1
18° to 21°	7	4	9	6	11	8	1	10	3	12	5	2
21° to 24°	8	5	10	7	12	9	2	11	4	1	6	3
24° to 27°	9	6	11	8	1	10	3	12	5	2	7	4
27° to 30°	10	7	12	9	2	11	4	1	6	3	8	5

4.6 General indications of the *Dasamsa* chart

- The planet posited in the 10th house of the *Dasamsa* chart may decide the direction of profession depending upon its strength in the birth chart.
- The *Dasamsa* ascendant lord is very important planet. If this planet is well placed in the birth chart then the native gets success and prosperity in profession, particularly during the periods and favourable transits of this planet.
- If the ascendant lord of the birth chart is well placed in the *Dasamsa* chart then the native is lucky to have well suited profession along with success and name. Placement of the birth ascendant in the *Dasamsa* ascendant is considered very auspicious and bestows success and prosperity.

4.7 Planets in *Dasamsa* and their *Dasa Bhukti*

The main and sub periods (*dasa* and *antardasa*) of the following planets are favourable for success, gain, rise in status and overall betterment of one's profession

- The 10th lord of the *Dasamsa* chart.
- Planets associated with the 10th lord of the *Dasamsa* chart.
- Planets associated with the 10th house of the *Dasamsa* chart.
- Planets associated with the *Dasamsa* ascendant.
- Planets associated with the *Dasamsa* ascendant lord.
- Planets posited in the square and trine houses of the *Dasamsa* chart.

The 6th, 8th and 12th house lords of the *Dasamsa* chart, particularly when these are associated with the ascendant, 10th house or profession determining planets in the birth chart, give problems and obstacles related to profession and prosperity during their main and sub periods.

●

CHAPTER-5

Badhaka Grahas

Many complications and confusions are there in our system of astrological science like all other branches of knowledge. A few confusions and doubts need straight clarifications. *"Badhakas"* is one such subject for which specific clarification is essential.

Revered Babuji, Dr. B.V. Raman has invited the views, experiences and researches made by the scholars of astrology over the factor of *"Badhakas"*. Numbers of famous astrologers of India have in the past expressed their valuable views over *"Badhakas"* through the columns of esteemed journal, "The Astrological Magazine", from time to time.

Acharya Vaidyanath has specified in Jatak Parijat Vol. I chapter 2, shloka no. 48 about *"Badhakas"* :

क्रमाच्च रागद्वि शरीर भानामुपान्त्य धर्मस्मरगास्तदीशाः।
खरेशमान्दि स्थितराशिनाथा ह्यतीव बाधाकरखेचराः स्युः।।

(*Jatak Parijat,* Ch-2/Vers-48)

If any dispositor of *Mandi* or *Kharesa* also owns the 11th house or falls in the 11th house for moving *lagnas* like Aries, Cancer, Libra and Capricorn, that planet acts as *badhak.* Similarly, if the dispositor of *Mandi* or *Kharesa* also owns the 7th house or joins the 7th house, for dual sign ascendants like Gemini, Virgo, Sagittarius and Pisces, that planet will act as *badhak.*

If the dispositor of *Mandi* or *Kharesa* also owns the 9th house or falls in the 9th house, that creates obstacles and should be treated as *badhak* planet.

Generally, we miss to consider the dispositors of *Mandi*

and *Kharesa,* and treat the 7th, 9th and 11th house as *badhak* houses for dual, fixed and moving *lagnas* respectively. The lords of these houses are *Badhakas* and the planets placed therein are also Badhakas only if those are the dispositors of *Mandi* or *Kharesa.*

Mr. V. Subhramanya Shastri translated this shloka that the concerning planet will be a *badhak* only if it also owns the sign where *Mandi* or *Kharesa* is posited. The basis of *Badhakas* is taken as the position of planets or rulers from *lagna.* It is wrong in our humble opinion. Suppose, we have to consider the aspect of children. The 5th house should be analyzed. If the *lagna* is Gemini, the Libra sign will fall in the 5th house which is a moving sing. Suppose, *Mandi* is posited in the 8th house whose dispositor is Saturn and that falls in 3rd house in Leo. Here, Leo is 11th from the 5th house and Saturn will act as *"Badhak"* for the matters related to the 5th house.

If *Mandi* falls in the 3rd house in Leo, the Sun will act as *Badhak.* Similarly, for Scorpio *lagna,* for matters related to the 10th house (Leo) Mars will be *Badhak,* only if *Mandi* or *Kharesa* falls in Scorpio or Aries. Here, Aries will be 9th from Leo i.e. 10th house of Scorpio *lagna.* If the Leo is *lagna* and *Mandi* falls in the 5th house in Sagittarius, Jupiter will be the *Badhak* for the matters of the 3rd house (Libra), if it joins the ascendant, as in this case the ascendant will be 11th from 3rd house.

The *dasa bhukti* of *Badhak* planet causes adversities, pertaining to the house, for which that planet is a *Badhak.*

What does a *Badhak* planet do? It creates obstacles in undertakings, brings opposition and results into impediments in the way of enjoyment, peace of life, comforts and sucks the pleasure and happiness of life, in one way or the other, during its *dasa bhukti* particularly.

In our opinion, the modern theory of consideration of *Badhak* planets is not fully dependable. Better results may be obtained, if we altogether reject *"Badhakas"* in our judgement of the natal chart. The lords of the triangles, if placed in *Kendras,* give auspicious result and lords of quadrants are good in triangles particularly. Wherever the lords of quadrants or triangles are posited, the matters related to that house are promoted. Suppose, Scorpio is the ascendant. The 9th house i.e. Cancer is a *badhak sthana* and Moon, the lord thereof is the *badhak* lord. This means that Moon's period should be adverse, whereas Moon is considered best benefic planet for Scorpio *lagna.*

We have thus tried to show that *Badhakas* should not be attached with so much importance as it is in general practice. We will surely be able to get better results if we do not take *Badhakas* into consideration at all. If it is at all essential to consider *Badhakas,* it should be taken into consideration only if Badhakas become the dispositor of *Mandi* and *Kharesa,* otherwise those planets will not be *Badhak* for any of the *lagna.* There are various other views that the 7th, 9th and 11th *navamsas* are *Badhaka* or the 3rd house should be taken as *Badhaka* place instead of 11th house in a moving sign. There are various other views of research scholars.

However, we have obtained amazing success in our humble observations without consideration of *Badhakas* and combustion of planets, in addition to *Vedhas.* These create unnecessary confusion and are not of much avail. However, if there are obstacles in the birth chart due to various kinds of planetary affliction, obstacles and problems are bound to come. In that case we have experienced that recitation of following remedial measures do wonders and eliminate obstruction to a great degree.

These mantras are given hereunder, which may be recited, if serious obstacles appear in the path of progress, prosperity, popularity, property, power and pelf. If the subject is not able to recite these mantras, he or she should engage a learned, experienced and talented Acharya to recite these mantras on his or her behalf, after proper *Sankalp* etc.

9, 18, 27 or 36 *Samput Path* with these mantras of *Durga Saptashati* do miracles :

1. सर्वाबाधाविनिर्मुक्तो धनधान्यसुतान्वितः।
मनुष्यो मत्प्रसादेन भविष्यति न संशयः।।

(*Durga Saptashati,* Ch-12, Vers-13)

2. यं यं चिन्तयते कामं तं तं प्राप्नोति निश्चितम्।
परमैश्वर्यमतुलं प्राप्स्यते भूतले पुमान्।।

(*Durga Saptashati, Kavach,* Vers-44)

3. सर्वाबाधाप्रशमनं त्रैलोक्यस्याखिलेश्वरि।
एवमेव त्वया कार्यमस्मद्वैरि विनाशनम्।।

(*Durga Saptashati,* Ch-11, Vers-39)

4. सर्व बाधासु घोरासु वेदनाभ्यर्दितोऽपि वा।
स्मरन्ममैतच्चरितं नो मुच्यते संकटात्।।

(*Durga Saptashati,* Ch-12, Vers-28)

5. करोतु सा नः शुभहेतुरीश्वरी
शुभानि भद्राणिभिहन्तु चापदः।।

(*Durga Saptashati,* Ch-5, Vers-81)

6. शरणागत दीनार्त परित्राण परायणे।
सर्वस्यार्ति हरे देवि! नारायणि नमोऽस्तु ते।।

(*Durga Saptashati,* Ch-11, Vers-12)

All these above mantras, if recited for the requisite number of times everyday or *Samputit Path* of *Durga Saptashati* by applying the same mantras as Samput, all kinds of obstacles will be prevented. The progress of the native will be faster and higher, undoubtedly. It is always advisable to recite the Vedic Mantras of the planets who are creating obstacles, obstruction and problems in the path of progress, either in natal chart or transit.

●

CHAPTER-6

Profession through Second House

Deciding profession is decidedly not an easy exercise for an astrologer. More so, in modern times, when increasing competition and resultant specialization has opened up new and newer branches of career & vocation, not known or popular in the age of sages. It, therefore, requires intelligent interpretation of behavior of same planets & their combinations, as modified according to the present context. Generally, judgement of profession begins with the consideration of relevant house namely the 10th, its lord & *Karaka*. But this has been observed that consideration of the 10th house alone may lead to erroneous conclusions at times. Some more factors are equally relevant & among them examination of 2nd house is of equal importance, if not more. This observation, which forms the subject matter of the present chapter, needs more research & verification by the learned readers.

The second house is generally dealt for the judgement of financial aspect of the native. The source of income may also be known by the second house and its lord. {It is therefore, important to include 2nd house also while deciding profession}. It does not mean that 10th house has not much to do with the profession. The 10th house and its strength shows the status of one's placement in a particular career. The second house, for example, may show that the subject will decide whether one will become a teacher of a primary school or a degree college. He may be a Professor, Head or a Vice Chancellor of a University, depending upon the disposition of the 10th house, its lord and the strength of *lagna*, but that the individual will earn his livelihood by teaching may be correctly judged by the 2nd house.

6.1 Significators of Profession

According to *Jatak Parijat*, the Sun, Mercury, Jupiter and Saturn are *Karakas* of different occupations. The Sun may be the *Karaka* for politicians & kings; Mercury is the significator of business, trades and industries; Jupiter should be the *Karaka* of vocation related to agriculture, spiritualism, of service and begging. But how to find out the correct *Karaka* of a birth chart, if the subject is young and it is not known whether he will join service, will go in business or he will take up agriculture? The results of all the four *Karakas* can not be blended. This is a state of utter confusion. We would like to invite kind attention of the readers towards our humble observations in this regard.

The second house indicates wealth and the source of income because 11th house happens 10th from the 2nd house. In zodiac, the second sign is ruled by Venus. So, Venus is the main significator.

In zodiac, the ruler of the 10th and 11th house is Saturn who should also be recognized as significator of profession. Saturn indicates "*KARMA*". Saturn shows work. It is important to consider Saturn's location in a birth chart to find out the suitable profession. Conjunction of Saturn with Moon causes fluctuation of thoughts, tension and worries. Placement of Saturn in various signs gives rise to various vocations, depending upon the nature of the sign and behavior of the lord of the sign.

Thus, the 2nd and 10th house from *lagna* have a control over occupation of the native, whereas the lords of the 2nd and 10th signs of the natural zodiac i.e. Venus and Saturn, are causative or *Karaka* of career.

The second house provides us equipment to search out resources of livelihood and means to earn money. The second house is dealt for gains, acquisitions, profits and accumulation, whereas the 10th house is referred for post and position, rank and power, authority and status, dignity and honour, credit and conduct, success, recognition and reputation. The 10th house rules over the appointment, promotion and advancement in career.

Tenth house is the most important house in a birth chart and that should certainly be considered for the determination of vocation and means of livelihood but the second house should not be ignored. By making the proper analysis of the second house and its lord, we may be able to decide the vocation of the native more correctly and precisely.

Before determining the profession, the students are advised to acquire good working knowledge in the following spheres :

1. Vocation indicated by each planet, and sign and combinations for going into business, service or agriculture.

2. The strength of *Dhana Yoga* will decide the status of one's occupation. If Mars is placed in the 10th house, with weak *Dhana Yoga*, that can result into a profession of ordinary policeman or a soldier in the army or a fighter. But if a strong *Dhana Yoga* is there, one can become a General in army, Director General of Police or even a Minister or so. *Dhana Yoga* should be judged by the examination of the 2nd, 11th, 5th and the 9th houses; their lords, conjunctions, aspects and mutual exchange of houses. A planet with *Daridra Yoga* can make one a beggar, whereas with a very powerful *Dhana Yoga*, the same planet can make one a King or equivalent.

3. No vocation can be decided by any single planet or its placement. There is a group of planets whose influence over other planets, association or conjunction, may determine one's vocation. Concerning houses also play an important role. For example, Jupiter, Venus and Mercury should influence the concerning houses in the horoscope of an advocate or a law professional, because Mercury provides logic and argument. Venus is the lord of sign Libra, i.e. balance of wrong and right, fair and foul. Jupiter signifies truth and justice. The 5th

and 6th houses have also to play a role as 6th house rules over litigation and the 5th house shows ability to analyze and to make thought provoking arguments presented in an effective manner. The fifth house also gives ability, cleverness and cunnings to twist the fact and event in one's favour by making appropriate logical arguments. Libra, Sagittarius and Aquarius etc. are the signs to be taken into consideration while making the judgement of vocation.

At least this much knowledge is essential for the determination of profession connected with law. Similarly, a student should properly know the knowledge of planetary combinations, signs and houses involved.

All planets denote innumerable professions nowadays. Therefore, single planet will always create confusion. Having such knowledge, one should: -

4. Find out the rulers of the 2nd and 10th house and the signs and *navamsa* occupied by these planets.
5. Make correct judgment of Venus and Saturn considering as *Karaka*.
6. Look at the houses whose lords occupy or aspect the 10th and 2nd house. Also find out the houses and signs where the 2nd and 10th lords are placed. Try to analyze the results of all these factors together to determine one's exact occupation.

Illustration : 6.1 (**RS**) *Horoscope No.: 18*

Date of birth : 20.07.1952 Time of birth : 12:45:36 hrs

Place of birth : Jabalpur Lat 23:10:00 N Long 79:57:00E

Ayanamsa : 23:11:50 Sidereal Time : 8:27:27

Pln	**Degree**	**Rasi**	**Nakshatra**	**Pad**
Asc	10:21:44	Lib	Swati	2
Sun	4:18:02	Can	Pushya	1

Mon	15:55:18	Gem	Ardra	3
Mar	17:03:49	Lib	Swati	4
Mer	0:24:49	Leo	Magha	1
Jup	23:44:51	Ari	Bharani	4
Ven (C)	11:18:34	Can	Pushya	3
Sat	16:16:51	Vir	Hasta	2
Rah (R)	28:26:31	Cap	Dhanistha	2
Ket (R)	28:26:31	Can	Aslesa	4

Lagna Chart

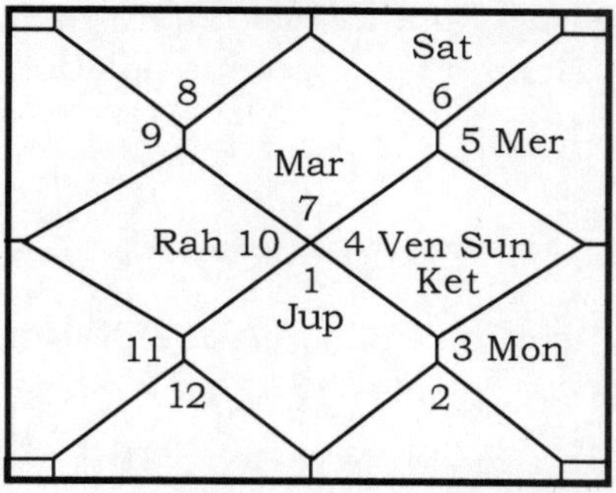

Navamsa Chart

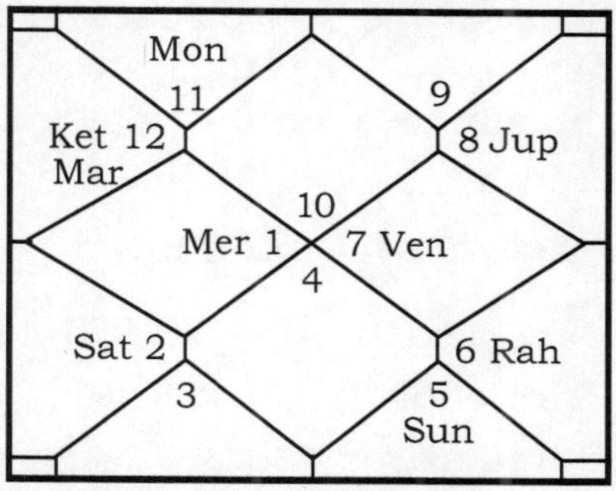

Balance of Vimshottari Dasa of **Rah 5Y 6M 2D**

This is the birth chart of a dynamic, energetic and bold businessman who is nearing an annual turnover of rupees one hundred crores. He is dealing in plastic films, polythene, lamination etc.

Let us analyze his horoscope to determine his vocation and status. The lord of the 2nd house is Mars who is placed in *lagna,* in the sign Libra i.e. a sign of Venus. The 10th house is occupied by the 11th lord Sun, *lagna* lord Venus and Ketu. The 10th lord Moon falls in the 9th house in Gemini i.e. the sign of Mercury. *Yogakaraka* Saturn falls in the 12th house in Virgo and obtains the *navamsa* of Venus. Involvement of Mercury shows that the native will be a successful businessman. Placement of 11th lord Sun in the 10th house, as the strongest planet (10.81 *Rupa Shada Balas*), ensures that he will become a successful and famous industrialist. The lord of the 2nd, Mars, falls in the sign of Venus and Venus joins the 10th house, in the sign of Moon. This shows that the native will be dealing in plastics, garments, manufacturing polythene films or he will be dealing in rubber, wax or glass work, plastic films or fabrics and PVC material or the like. The native is at present dealing in almost all such products. Venus obtains own *navamsa* of Libra and that too falls in the 10th house from *navamsa lagna*. Thus, Venus is placed in movable sign and *navamsa*. This indicates independent profession as the 10th lord Moon (7.65 *Rupa Shada Bala*) is also very strong in addition to the 11th lord Sun. The 11th house of this birth chart obtains 12.28 *Rupa Bhava Bala*, which has elevated the subject to a very rich and prosperous position though he is a son of a teacher.

Illustration : 6.2 (**PK**) *Horoscope No.: 19*

Date of birth : 19.12.1971 Time of birth : 20:12:00 hrs
Place of birth : Lucknow Lat 26:50:00 N Long 80:54:00E
Ayanamsa : 23:28:08 Sidereal Time : 1:55:46

Pln	**Degree**	**Rasi**	**Nakshatra**	**Pad**
Asc	12:56:00	Can	Pushya	3
Sun	3:34:18	Sag	Moola	2
Mon	25:06:53	Sag	Purvasadha	4
Mar	1:58:26	Pis	P Bhadrapad	4
Mer (R)	19:24:18	Sco	Jyestha	1
Jup (C)	26:06:16	Sco	Jyestha	3
Ven	1:59:40	Cap	Uttarasadha	2
Sat (R)	7:43:12	Tau	Kritika	4
Rah (R)	12:16:13	Cap	Sravna	1
Ket (R)	12:16:13	Can	Pushya	3

Lagna Chart

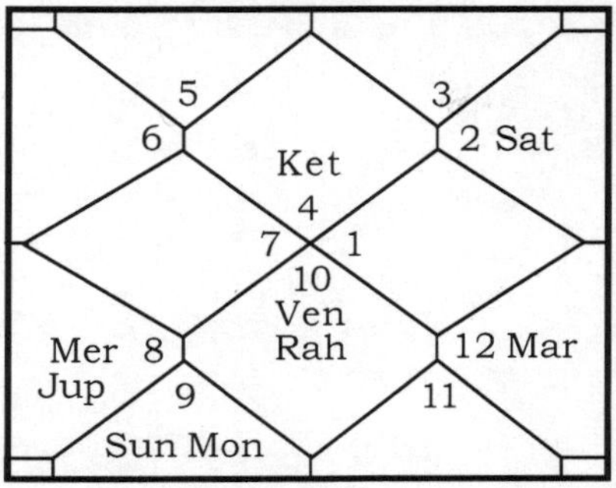

Navamsa Chart

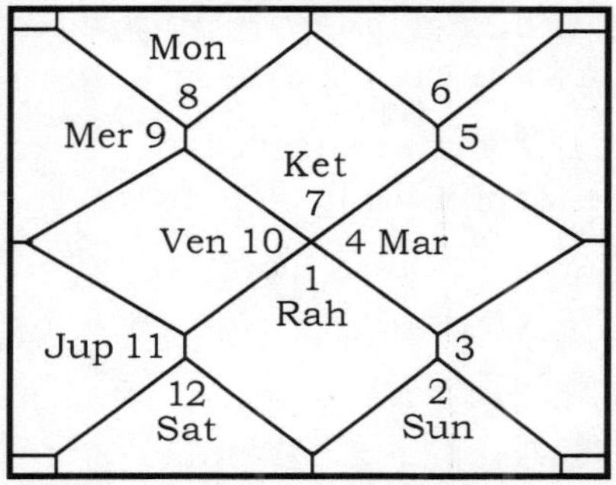

Balance of Vimshottari Dasa of **Ven 2Y 3M 28D**

This horoscope belongs to a charming girl who is looking after a business of lottery. She became an organizer only when she was 22 years of age. Nobody in the family ever expected her to be successful in this business but she proved her merits within a very short period.

Let us examine this chart to determine her profession:

The lord of the 2nd house, Sun, occupies the 6th house, in Jupiter's sign Sagittarius, in association with *lagna* lord Moon. The 10th lord Mars also falls in Jupiter's sign Pisces. Jupiter is well placed in the 5th house. There is also a mutual exchange between the 9th lord Jupiter and the 5th lord Mars. The 10th lord, Mars, is aspected by Jupiter. The 7th lord Saturn occupies the 11th house, in Taurus, and 11th lord Venus falls in the 7th house in Capricorn giving rise to mutual exchange of the lords of 7th and 11th houses. This indicates her success in business and not in service. Powerful influence of Jupiter over the 10th and 2nd lord indicates success in finance or educational work like banking, money lending, running any educational institution, to organize lottery or chit fund etc. The main planet, who is influencing her career, is Jupiter who falls in the 5th house. The 5th house shows lottery or speculation or unearned wealth in which she, in fact, is dealing. The second lord Sun obtains the *navamsa* of Venus. The 10th lord Mars obtains the *navamsa* of Moon. This shows success in plastic in plastic business, garments, nylon thread or cloth, lamination, wax, manufacturing paints, dealing in paper or pulp, polythene, plastic sheets etc. Venus falls in the sign of Saturn and Saturn in that of Venus.

To determine one's suitable vocation is an art of interpretation of planetary influence.

Illustration : 6.3 **(PKS)** *Horoscope No.: 20*

Date of birth : 08.01.1942 Time of birth : 19:50:00 hrs
Place of birth : Delhi Lat 28:39:00 N Long 77:13:00E
Ayanamsa : 23:02:46 Sidereal Time : 2:38:52

Pln	Degree	Rasi	Nakshatra	Pad
Asc	23:12:33	Can	Aslesa	2
Sun	24:38:26	Sag	Purvasadha	4
Mon	3:54:23	Vir	U Phalguni	3
Mar	5:19:55	Ari	Ashwini	2
Mer (C)	5:13:47	Cap	Uttarasadha	3
Jup (R)	19:37:34	Tau	Rohini	3
Ven	27:45:01	Cap	Dhanistha	2
Sat (R)	28:47:23	Ari	Kritika	1
Rah	22:05:44	Leo	P Phalguni	3
Ket	22:05:44	Aqu	P Bhadrapad	1

Lagna Chart **Navamsa Chart**

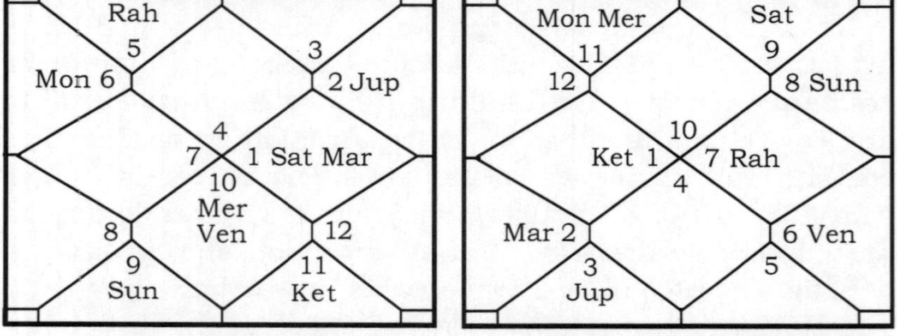

Balance of Vimshottari Dasa of **Sun 2Y 8M 27D**

This is the birth chart of a Commissioner of Police. The lord of the 2nd house Sun is placed in the 6th house, in Sagittarius and obtains *navamsa* of Mars. The 10th house is owned and occupied by Mars. Venus falls in the sign of Saturn, who is posited in the 10th house in Aries, in association with Mars. Saturn, the *Karaka* of profession, has joined Mars in a Martian and fiery sign Aries. Mars also happens to be a *Yogakaraka* for Cancer *lagna*. Thus, the profession should be connected mainly with Mars, Jupiter, Saturn and Sun, which shows Police Service. Involvement of the 6th and 8th house shows that the profession may be connected with sin, crimes, culprits and thieves etc.

There may be many other jobs, which may be indicated by these planets, but we can pin point that the native will be in police service because Police has to deal with culprits and criminals. Involvement of fiery sign has further strengthened the combination. Mars and Saturn alone can make one a criminal but Jupiter provides protection, defense and security. The Sun indicates the discipline, power and government. So, the joint influence of Mars, Sun and Jupiter, over the profession of the native made him successful in police service only.

Illustration : 6.4 **(MM)** *Horoscope No.: 21*

Date of birth : 28.11.1934 Time of birth : 07:05:00 hrs
Place of birth : Hegarwal Lat 26:29:00 N Long 74:40:00E
Ayanamsa : 22:57:05 Sidereal Time : 10:58:44

Pln	**Degree**	**Rasi**	**Nakshatra**	**Pad**
Asc	12:29:50	Sco	Anuradha	3
Sun	12:11:00	Sco	Anuradha	3
Mon	29:31:25	Can	Aslesa	4
Mar	0:09:04	Vir	U Phalguni	2
Mer	24:51:42	Lib	Vishakha	2
Jup	17:23:00	Lib	Swati	4

Ven (D)	14:24:40	Sco	Anuradha	4
Sat	29:26:03	Cap	Dhanistha	2
Rah	9:52:50	Cap	Uttarasadha	4
Ket	9:52:50	Can	Pushya	2

Lagna Chart

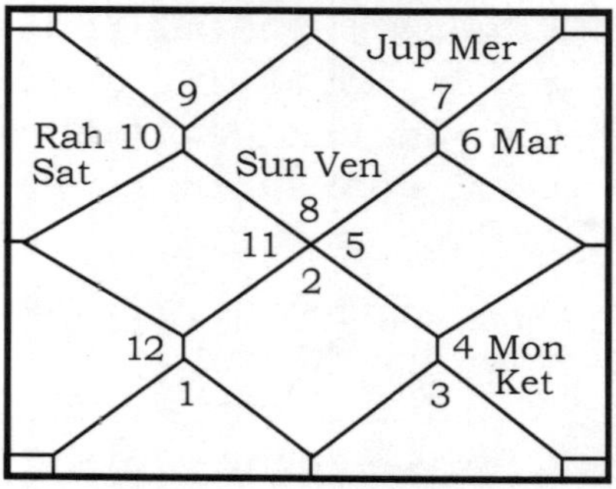

Navamsa Chart

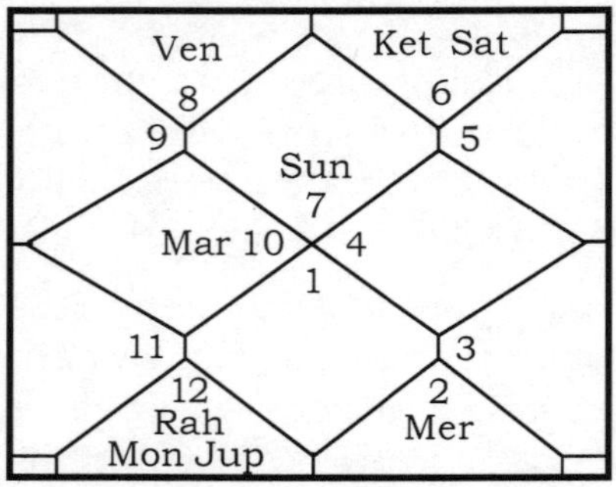

Balance of Vimshottari Dasa of **Mer 0Y 7M 8D**

The lord of the 2nd house Jupiter is placed in the 12th house, in Venus' sign Libra. Venus, who also happens to be the causative planet, obtains sign and *navamsa* of Mars. Venus is *vargottam* in Scorpio. The 10th lord Sun is posited in Scorpio *lagna* and obtains *navamsa* of Venus. Saturn, the *Karaka*, is posited in own sign Capricorn and obtains the *navamsa* of Mercury. Thus, Mars, Mercury, Saturn and Venus are the planets, who should justify the occupation of the native. Combined effect of Mars, Mercury and Venus makes one an engineer. If Saturn is involved, one becomes a Civil Engineer. The native is a Chief Engineer (Civil). Involvement of Mercury and Jupiter provided him the writing ability and he delivered thought-provoking lectures in civil engineering, in various foreign countries. The native is also running an institute of engineering after retirement. The placement of the Sun and Venus in the *lagna* has provided him a handsome and attractive personality. He is extremely dynamic, aggressive, bold and courageous. He is a hard worker and is famous for his honesty.

Illustration : 6.5 (**GDN**) *Horoscope No.: 22*

Date of birth : 05.01.1925 Time of birth : 02:15:00 hrs
Place of birth : Etawah Lat 26:46:00 N Long 79:02:00E
Ayanamsa : 22:48:23 Sidereal Time : 8:56:53

Pln	Degree	Rasi	Nakshatra	Pad
Asc	16:17:41	Lib	Swati	3
Sun	21:12:38	Sag	Purvasadha	3
Mon	24:06:39	Ari	Bharani	4
Mar	17:12:24	Pis	Revati	1
Mer (R)	4:18:00	Sag	Moola	2
Jup (C)	11:13:34	Sag	Moola	4
Ven	24:38:27	Sco	Jyestha	3
Sat	19:33:45	Lib	Swati	4
Rah (R)	21:19:10	Can	Aslesa	2
Ket (R)	21:19:10	Cap	Sravna	4

Lagna Chart

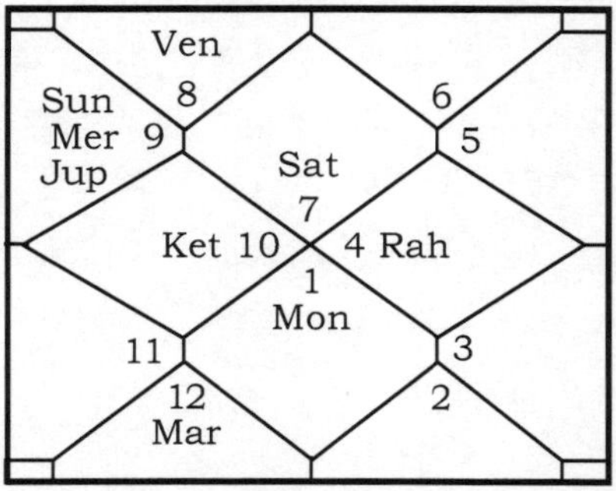

Navamsa Chart

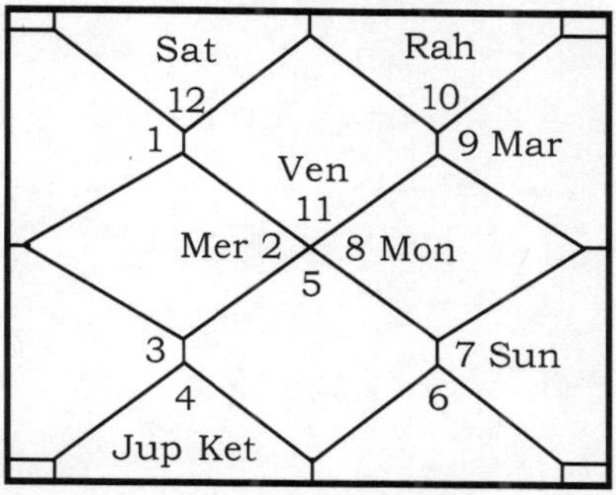

Balance of Vimshottari Dasa of **Ven 3Y 10M 0D**

This is the birth chart of Padma Shree Gopal Das Neeraj, the famous poet of India. He is a philosopher, as well as a scholar of Hindi poetry. He has been awarded various top awards and honours. He is still a very popular poet of India. He is also a good singer.

The lord of the 2nd house, Mars, falls in the 6th house in Pisces, the sign of Jupiter. Venus falls in the 2nd house in Scorpio, which has provided a sweet voice to him. Moon falls in the sign and *navamsa* of 10th lord Mars. Rahu is posited in the 10th. Except Saturn, no planet aspects the 10th house. One can not explain the profession of a poet, only by analysis of the 10th house. The influence of Mars is very prominent over the 10th and 2nd house. Mars is the worst planet for Libra *lagna*, as it owns the 2nd and the 7th house.

If we examine the 2nd house, we will find that Venus is placed there and the lord thereof falls in Jupiter's sign and *navamsa*. Significator Saturn is exalted in the *lagna*, in the sign of Venus. So Jupiter, Venus and Moon should shape out the profession in this case and that can be of a poet or a writer. Venus and Moon made him a good singer also. Placement of Venus in the sign of Mars and *navamsa* of Saturn, and the position of Saturn in the sign of Venus and *navamsa* of Mars has created immense and intense feeling of love and attraction, for beauty and poetry.

Illustration: 6.6 (**Amitabh Bachchan**) *Horoscope No.: 23*

Date of birth : 11.10.1942 Time of birth : 16:00:00 hrs
Place of birth : Allahabad Lat 25:27:00 N Long 81:50:00E
Ayanamsa : 23:03:18 Sidereal Time : 16:14:42

Pln	**Degree**	**Rasi**	**Nakshatra**	**Pad**
Asc	1:55:45	Aqu	Dhanishtha	3
Sun	24:22:51	Vir	Chitra	1
Mon	10:18:36	Lib	Swati	2
Mar (D)	22:36:12	Vir	Hasta	4
Mer (R/D)	23:39:28	Vir	Chitra	1
Jup	0:32:15	Can	Punarvasu	4
Ven (C)	15:11:20	Vir	Hasta	2
Sat (R)	19:13:52	Tau	Rohini	3
Rah (R)	10:22:03	Leo	Magha	4
Ket (R)	10:22:03	Aqu	Satabhisha	2

Lagna Chart

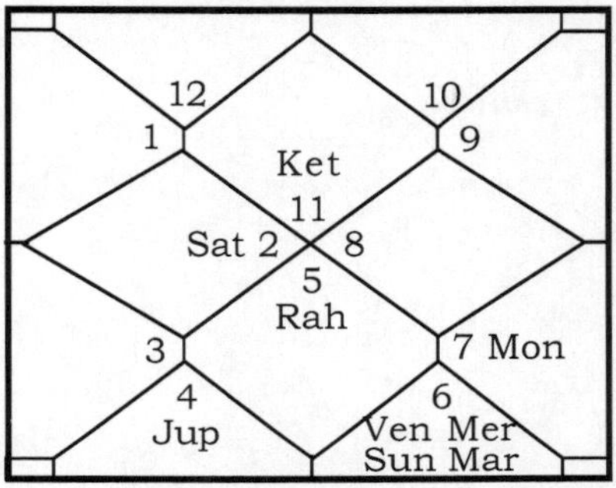

Navamsa Chart

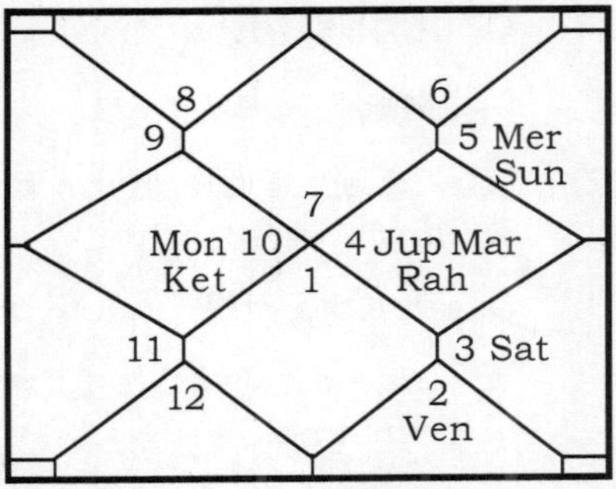

Balance of Vimshottari Dasa of **Rah 13Y 0M 29D**

Amitabh Bachhan, the famous film actor, was born in Aquarius ascendant. The 2nd lord, Jupiter, obtains the *Rashi* and *navamsa* of Moon. Lord of the 10th house Mars falls in 8th house, in Virgo, and obtains the *navamsa* of Moon i.e. its debilitation *navamsa*. *Yogakaraka* Venus obtains own *navamsa* and Mercury's sign due to its debilitation. The consideration of the 10th house alone can not justify his profession of an actor because the 10th lord Mars falls in Virgo and obtains the *navamsa* of its debilitation. The 10th house receives the aspects of Jupiter and retrograde Saturn. This alone does not justify the career of a super class actor.

Now, consider the 2nd house. Lord of the 2nd house Jupiter, is exalted in the 6th under *vargottam navamsa*. The second house is aspected by Venus, Moon, Mars, Mercury, the Sun and Jupiter, which shows income from various sources and multifarious activities.

We have earlier mentioned that Venus and Saturn should also be taken in the judgement of profession. Here, Venus obtains own *navamsa* and Saturn falls in the *navamsa* of Venus. Thus, the influence of Moon and Venus over his professional aspect of life made him a great actor off all times. The influence of Mercury over most of the planets brought him in business.

6.2 Important points for the Judgement of Occupation

1. Find out the lord of 2nd and 10th house.
2. The ruler of the signs and *navamsas*, occupied by the 2nd and 10th lord.
3. Occupants of 2nd and 10th houses.
4. The planets, which aspect the 10th and the 2nd houses, or their lord.
5. Judge the position of Venus and Saturn in the same way as above. These are the significators of profession for all.
6. The houses, which are related with the 10th or 2nd house, their lords or the respective *Karakas*.
7. Also note the nature and the behaviour of the sign and the planet, and the element of the sign, in which the concerning planet is placed.
8. *Dasamsa* chart will be of great use in case of compact analysis.
9. Running *Dasa Bhukti*, as the profession may be changed with running *Dasas*.

There may be many planets and houses that will be related to the profession of the native. It may be quite confusing and tough, at times, to pinpoint a single vocation. Now see, which group of planet and house is playing an influential role in deciding the profession and the income accruing thereby.

Note the *Dasa Bhukti* being faced by the native. What do that planet and its position, whose *dasa* is operative on the native, signify? These factors will help us to find out the most appropriate vocation of the subject.

6.3 Source of Livelihood through Second House

The second house stands for profits and gains, money,

bank balance, fixed deposits in banks, liquid cash, wealth, foods and drinks, speech and voice, family trade, jewellery, gold, silver, movable assets, precious stones and happy ending. It also shows inheritance of ancestral properties by its reflex action to the 8th house. It also represents 1. vision or power of observation, 2. memory 3. imagination 4. intellect 5. ready wit 6. power of expression 7. ability to express oneself, either in speech or in writing 8. tongue, teeth, mouth, cheeks, and chin. It gives the resources to earn money; it shows the ways and means to earn money; it indicates the tools and implements by which one can earn his livelihood; it reveals the directions and sources to earn money. It gives the necessary or requisite talent, ready wit, dexterity, intellect, and will-power to earn money. It is for this reason, the second house gives indications as to which vocation one will shine best in the life.

It shows rank and position, nature of foods and drinks, power and strength, profiles and gains, stamina and vitality. The most important point is that it rules over the speech or voice. Speech or voice is said to be the seat of all sorts of creative and spiritual activities.

Taurus is the second sign of the Zodiac and its ruler is Venus. As the Moon gets exalted here, so it is highly auspicious and fortunate house. The second house is a strong and powerful intellectual house. It determines earning power, profits and gains, ability to earn, capacity to save and will-power to accumulate.

6.4 Results of Planets posited in the 2nd house

The second house shows the ability to earn money, the capacity to save, the will-power to accumulate property. It shows the ways and means to earn money; it provides the necessary resources to earn money; it indicates the tools and implements to apply to earn money. Planets (sub-lords) posited in the second house will indicate the nature of labour and hardships to be employed to earn money.

Mars or Saturn, if posited in the second house demand

hard labour and challenging struggles, in early life, to earn money. By its aspect on the 8th house, it deprives one to own or inherit any ancestral properties. The native will be a self-made man and he will have to proceed alone. He will not get any outside help. Self-help will be his best help. Saturn purifies one by putting him into hard labour and testing struggles in early life, but it gives success and prosperity in later life. Conjunction of Mars and Saturn, or Mars and Rahu, or Saturn and Ketu, in the second house, has given, many a celebrities, this sort of hard labour and struggle, in their early life, but it gave success and prosperity in later life.

Jupiter, Venus, or Moon or Mercury, in the second house give very easy money or quick money. By its aspect on the 8th house, it gives enough of ancestral properties and liquid cash through inheritance. The native becomes rich just after birth.

Rahu is the lord of the *Asuras*. Its desires have no end. It does not remain satisfied with petty things of life. It is the chief controller of all sorts of underhand business, or secret incomes. It gives enough of secret money like bribes, black money etc. If we go through the horoscopes of bank officers, Export and Import Officer, Income Tax Officers, police officers, we will find that Rahu is posited either in 2nd house or in the 11th house. Rahu in the 2nd or 11th house gives enough of secret money, black money, bribes, speculation profits, income from gambling etc. It makes one very rich, wealthy and prosperous in life. The native may have seven or eight different source of income like 1. Salary income 2. Rental income 3. Dividend income 4. Interest income 5. Commission 7. Speculation profits 8. Share income from partnership firms etc.

The Sun in the second house gives enough of ancestral properties, through inheritance, by its reflex action to the 8th house. But it demands hard labour and struggles in early life, though it gives success in later life. The native gets a high Govt. post, or top business executive post.

The second house is a strong and powerful intellectual house. Conjunction of the Sun, Mercury and Venus; Ketu, the Moon and Venus; Ketu, Jupiter and the Sun; Jupiter and Venus; the Moon, Mercury and Jupiter etc., in the 2nd or the 5th house, and in airy sign like Gemini or Aquarius, makes one genius.

6.5 Signs & vocation corresponding to 2nd house

Aries : Political leaders, Debaters, Engineers, Scientist, Police and Army General, Top Business Executives, High Govt. officials, Sportsmen, Athletes, Cricketers, Mechanics, Machinists, Wrestlers, Departmental heads, Secretaries, Ministers, Prime Ministers, President etc.

Taurus: Financiers, Bankers, Stock-brokers, Musicians, Film-Actors, General artists, House Owners, Stage artists, Film directors, Singers, Football players, Cricketers, Athletes, High Govt. Officers, Top business executives, Capitalists, Conservatives.

Gemini: Debaters, Orators, Lawyers, Advocates, Lecturers, Professors, Teachers, Writers, Poets, Novelists, Dramatists, Scientists, Inventors, Singers, Musicians, Film Directors, High Govt. Officers, Top business executives, Astrologers, Palmists, Occultists, Accountants, Clerks, Intellectuals, Publishers, Editors, Journalists, Critics, Diplomats, Correspondents, Interpreters etc.

Cancer: Clerks, Traders, Naval Officers, Sailors, Nurses, Matrons, Wine-merchants, Petrol dealers, Navigators, Explorers, Mystics, Psychics, Saints, Doctors, Physicians, Chemists and Druggists, Caterers, Bar owners, Hotel owners, Restaurant owners, Brewery owners, Milkmen, Decorators, Dress-Makers, Tailors, Political leaders, Ministers etc.

Leo: Political leaders, Ministers, Prime Ministers, Presidents, High Govt. officials, Top business executives, Industrialists, Business magnets, Sportsmen, Athletes, Football Players, Financers, Stock Brokers, Capitalists.

Virgo: Critics, Editors, Journalists, Interpreters, Writers, poets, Novelists, Astrologers, Clerks, Accountants, Oculists, Doctors, Physicians, Nurses, Chemists, Druggists, Scientists, Inventors, Professors, Teachers, Orators, Debaters, Artists etc.

Libra: Musicians, Judges, Film-Stars, Film Directors, Sportsmen, Athletes, Diplomats, High Govt. Officers, Top business executives, Jewelers, Decorators, Dressmakers, Theatre owners, Cinema owners, Film Financiers, singers, clerks etc.

Scorpio: Engineers, Astrologers, Crime Detectives, Investigators, Police and Army officers, Physicians, Doctors, Chemists, Druggists, Dacoits, Criminals, Robbers, Thieves, Barbers, Butchers, Wrestlers, Sportsmen, Athletes, Football Players, Black-smiths etc.

Sagittarius: Philosophers, Teachers, Professors, Lecturers, Judges, Lawyers, Advocates, Tax-consultants, Accountants, Mystics, Saints, Publishers, Printers, Editors, Bankers, High Govt. Officials, Top business executives, Businessmen.

Capricorn: Political Leaders, Ministers, Prime Ministers, Presidents, Departmental Heads, Priests, Clergymen, Managers, Executives, Top Ranking Officers, Business Magnates, Industrialists, Trade union leaders, High Govt. Officers, Businessmen.

Aquarius: Scientists, Inventors, Poets, Novelists, Teachers, Professors, Lecturers, Lawyers, Advocates, Tax-

Advisors, Accountants, Writers, Intellectual men, Journalists, Editors, Correspondents, Diplomats, High Govt. Officers, Top business executives.

Pisces: Mystics, Saints, Spiritualists, Physicians, Doctors, Nurses, Nursing-home owners, Nurses, Matrons, Traders in Liquids, Wine-merchants, Petrol-dealers, Foot Wear dealers, Shoe-merchants, Services in Hospitals, Prisons, Jails, Dacoits, Robbers, Thieves, Smugglers.

6.6 The navamsa and nakshatra lord of Dhanadhipati (Lord of the Second House)

The Sun: Its keynotes are authority, command, power, dignity, rule, great executive ability, ability to control and demand.

Its vocations are; Bankers, Prime Ministers, Ministers, Secretaries, High Govt. Officers, Top business executives, Firemen, Departmental Heads, Capitalists, Industrialists, Business Magnates, Heart specialists, Surgeons, Lawyers, Advocates, Tax-Advisors, Physicians, Cricketers, Sportsmen, Football Players, Athletes.

The Moon: Its keynotes are change, inconstancy, fluctuation, fickle-mindedness, liquids, real estates, and the public.

Its vocations are: Sailors, Naval Officers, Hospital Staff, Wine merchants, Petrol dealers, Liquid merchants, Bar-owners, Bakery owners, Cheese Manufacturers, Brewery owners, Poultry Raisers, Obstetricians, Gynecologists, Midwives, Waiters, Watchmen, Dairy Farmers, Salesmen, Dealers in milk and milk products like Cheese, butter, ghee etc.

Mars: Its keynotes are dynamic energy, high push

and dash, great executive ability, to undertake risky adventures, initiative, quarrels, disputes etc.

Its vocations are: Army and Police Officers, Engineers, Surgeons, Dentists, Barbers, Butchers, Firemen, Guards, Hardware Merchants, Mechanics, Machinists, Foremen, Supervisors, Sportsmen, Athletes, Wrestlers, Body-builders, Cricketers, Football Players, Dacoits, Robbers, Smugglers, Thieves.

Mercury: Its keynotes are the Mind, mental stability, memory, concentration, intellect, transportation, documents, teaching, writing, debating etc.

Its vocations are : Clerks, Accountants, Book Keepers, Orators, Debaters, Writers, Poets, Novelists, Scientists, Inventers, Critics, Journalists, Editors, Correspondents, Secretaries, High Govt. Officers, Top business executives, Authors, Typists, Diplomats, Grocers, Stationers, Shop-Keepers, Printers, Doctors, Physicians, Lawyers, Advocates, Tax Advisors, Teachers, Lecturers, Professors.

Jupiter: Its keynotes are abundance, affluence, expansion, increase, spirituality, religion, law, prosperity, wealth, publication, long voyages etc.

Its vocations are: Philosophers, Lecturers, Teachers, Professors, Editors, Publishers, Printers, Writers, Poets, Judges, Physicians, Financiers, Bankers, Stock-Brokers, Sporting Good Leaders, Priests, Monks, Nuns, Mystics, and Spiritualists etc.

Venus: Its keynotes are love, romance, beauty, artistic taste, music, sports, amusements, money, profits and gains etc.

Its vocations are: Musicians, Film artists, Film directors, Stage Stars, Singers, Toilet Makers, Decorators, Dress-Tailors, Theater Owners, Cinema Owners, Export good dealers, Sportsmen, Athletes, Cricketers, Football Players, Throat Specialists, Photographers, Tellers, Cashiers, Money lenders, Furniture Makers etc.

Saturn: Its keynotes are hardship, delays, troubles, misfortunes, poverty, hard labor, hard struggle, real estates.

Its vocations are: Miners, Laborers, Workers, Coal merchants, Iron and Steel merchants, Real Estate Agents, Builders, Contractors, Shoe merchants, watch and Clock makers, Priests, Monks, Mystics, Spiritual Leaders, Night Workers, Repairers, Govt. servants, Office Workers, Menials, Inferiors etc.

6.7 Guidelines to point out exact vocation

1. See the position of the lord of the second house and Venus in a natal chart, which may give the important points to identify the appropriate vocation.
2. The position of the Moon in a natal chart is also important.
3. The position of the 4th lord in a natal chart gives the indications whether one will get proper education, in time and peacefully. If it is posited in angular or trine houses, it shows that the native will get proper education in time. If it is posited in evil house, it may deny the formal school education.
4. The third house should remain vacant. If it is afflicted by malefic, one may have disturbed mind. This may give much trouble.
5. If the second house is tenanted by malefics, then the

native will have to face hard labor and hard struggles in the life.

6. The first house should not remain vacant. If one or two creative planets are found posited in the first house, it shows that the native will surely rise to the top.

7. The position of 6th and 8th lords should be determined. If any one of these is found either in 2nd or 3rd house, it may hamper progress.

8. Ketu in Gemini, Saturn in Cancer, Mars in Libra are very harmful. It will give too much trouble, diseases and hardships and strife in life.

Thus, it has been observed that the second house gives indications towards the appropriate vocation. The position of Venus in a birth-chart will also indicate the vocation. Second house should be examined in addition to the 10th house and that should never be overlooked. If the 10th lord falls in 2nd house or vice versa or there is mutual exchange between the 2nd and 10th lords, one will decidedly earn his livelihood through the vocation indicated by both of these planets or the stronger planets of the two. We have observed that profession of native is guided by the nature of the lord of 2nd house, if that is posited in the 10th house. Most of above factors will be of immense use if implemented properly, carefully, methodically and intelligently and will help an astrologer truly.

●

Chapter-7

The Sixth House and Service

The sixth house is most neglected house and has not been given due importance, especially in consideration of the professional aspects, though in true sense it plays vital role in the judgment of the occupation of the subject.

The sixth house is ninth from the tenth house and tenth from the ninth house. Therefore, fortune, whether good or bad, should be examined from the sixth house. The relationship between the tenth and the sixth house or the ascendant lord and the sixth house is of great importance in reference to the vocation of the native.

1. If the tenth lord is posited in the sixth house, one will earn his livelihood through service and vice versa.
2. If the lord of ascendant occupies the sixth house the subject will enter service only and vice versa.
3. If there is mutual exchange between the lords of sixth and tenth or sixth and the first, there are strong indications of a career through service only and not by business as such.
4. If the Sun or Moon i.e. the luminaries are involved in the relationship of the tenth and the sixth or first and sixth or the other way, one is likely to get a govt. job.

Saturn is also the significator of service. If Saturn is involved with the 1st, 6th and the 10th house in any way, either by conjunction or by aspect or due to sign position of *navamsa* or due to placement in the concerning constellation, livelihood through service should be predicted.

Let us illustrate our point of view with the help of certain illustrations.

Illustration : 7.1 **(KP)** *Horoscope No.: 24*

Date of birth : 13.11.1942 Time of birth : 05:50:00 hrs
Place of birth : Nainital Lat 29:23:00 N Long 79:27:00E
Ayanamsa : 23:03:22 Sidereal Time : 8:03:36

Pln	**Degree**	**Rasi**	**Nakshatra**	**Pad**
Asc	3:52:03	Lib	Chitra	4
Sun	26:53:37	Lib	Vishakha	3
Mon	26:28:24	Sag	Purvasadha	4
Mar (C)	14:23:37	Lib	Swati	3
Mer (C)	16:22:13	Lib	Swati	3
Jup (R)	2:10:56	Can	Punarvasu	4
Ven (D)	26:00:50	Lib	Vishakha	2
Sat (R)	17:28:30	Tau	Rohini	3
Rah (R)	7:18:21	Leo	Magha	3
Ket (R)	7:18:21	Aqu	Satabhisha	1

Lagna Chart

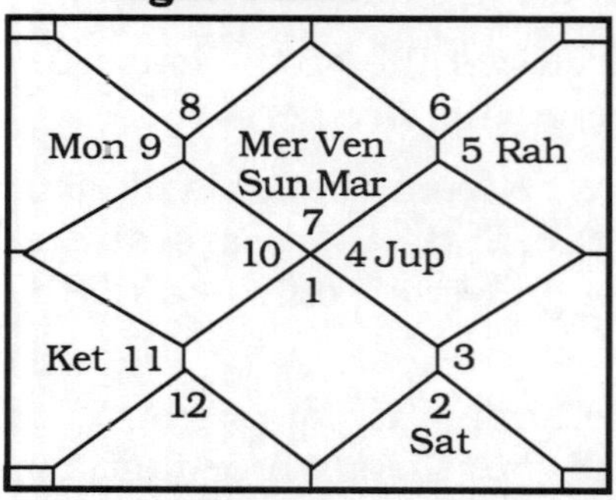

Navamsa Chart

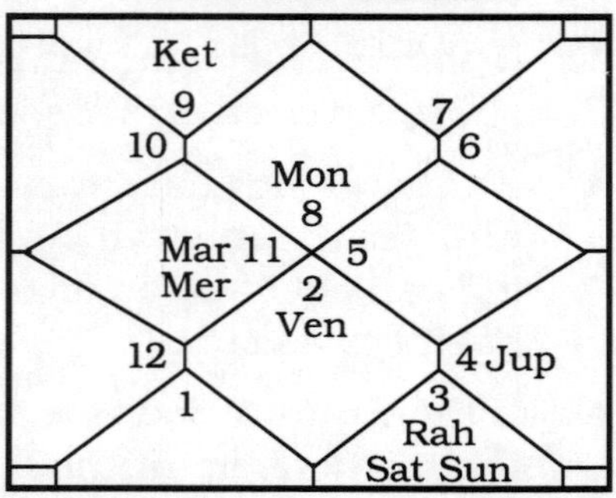

Balance of Vimshottari Dasa of **Ven 0Y 3M 14D**

The native held a top most position in the bureaucracy and commanded lot of power. He remained in the key position of various departments. He worked as chairman, Managing Director, chief commissioner etc from time to time. Following combinations of the birth chart of the native will prove our point of view with regard to service career through the sixth house. This will make our observation more distinct about the govt. job.

Planetary combination for service

The 6th lord Jupiter joins the tenth house in exaltation and the sixth house is also aspected by the 6th lord Jupiter from the tenth house.

GOVT. OCCUPATION :

The sixth lord Jupiter falls in Cancer, which is owned by one of the luminaries Moon. Involvement of the luminary, in one or the other way, with regard to the sixth house is indicative of Govt. service.

CIVIL SERVICE :

The 10th lord Moon aspects the 9th house and the 9th lord Mercury occupies the ascendant, in association with its lord Venus, the 11th lord Sun and the 2nd & 7th lord Mars. This is one of the most powerful combinations and makes the ascendant quite strong.

- There is mutual exchange between the 10th lord Moon and the 6th lord Jupiter.
- The lord of the 2nd house, Mars, and that of the 11th house, Sun, are well associated in the ascendant giving rise to *Dhan yoga.*
- Venus in Libra, in the ascendant, has formed *Malvya Mahapurush Rajyoga* and Venus is the *Karaka* of civil services.
- Karmic control planets are the Sun and Saturn. The Sun joins the ascendant and it is associated with the 9th lord Mercury and 2nd & 7th lord Mars, which has further strengthened the combination of high success in the civil services.
- The 6th lord Jupiter obtains the *vargottam navamsa* whereas the ascendant lord Venus falls in own *navamsa.* The 2nd & 7th lord Mars obtains the *navamsa* of its exaltation.

- There is mutual exchange of *navamsa* of the 9th lord Mercury with *Yogakaraka* Saturn. However, the 10th lord Moon occupies the *navamsa* of Mars and the sign of Jupiter. Therefore, the native entered into politics after retirement.

  Following *Rajyogas* are present in the birth chart:

  - *Malvya Mahapurush Rajyoga*
  - *Maha Bhagya Yoga*
  - *Hamsa Mahapurush Rajyoga*
  - *Rajlaksha Yoga*
  - *Akhand Samrajya Yoga*

All these factors of the birth chart of the native made him a successful top bureaucrat and politician after retirement.

Illustration : 7.2 (**AS**) *Horoscope No.: 25*

Date of birth : 30.04.1968 Time of birth : 03:25:00 hrs

Place of birth : Sitapur Lat 27:33:00 N Long 80:40:00E

Ayanamsa : 23:24:46 Sidereal Time : 17:49:19

Pln	**Degree**	**Rasi**	**Nakshatra**	**Pad**
Asc	2:49:41	Pis	P Bhadrapad	4
Sun	16:12:41	Ari	Bharani	1
Mon	10:52:35	Tau	Rohini	1
Mar (C)	0:26:37	Tau	Kritika	2
Mer (C)	22:02:25	Ari	Bharani	3
Jup	2:30:51	Leo	Magha	1
Ven	2:26:05	Ari	Ashwini	1
Sat	25:01:51	Pis	Revati	3
Rah (R)	25:09:43	Pis	Revati	3
Ket (R)	25:09:43	Vir	Chitra	1

Lagna Chart

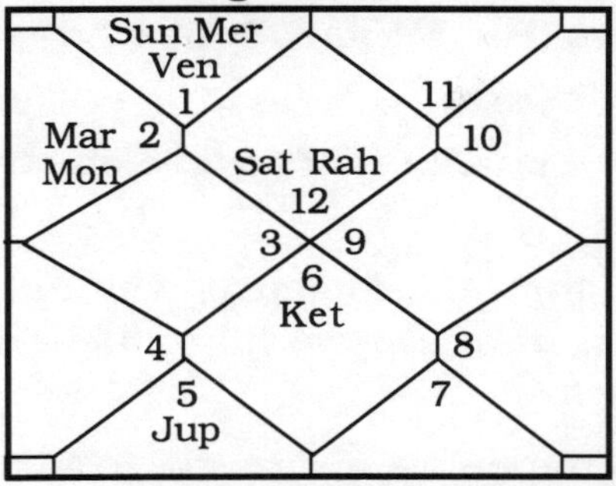

Navamsa Chart

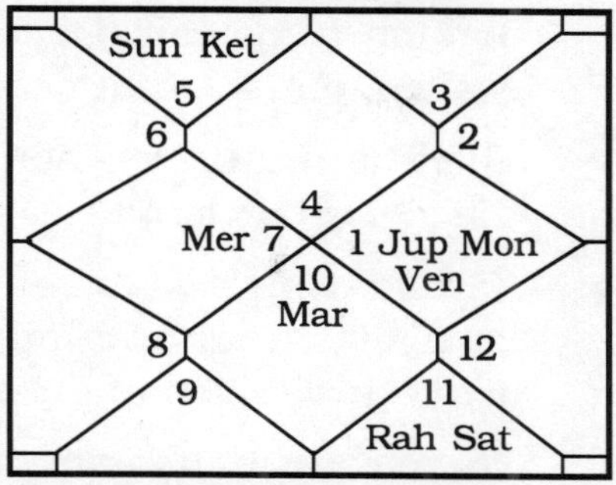

Balance of Vimshottari Dasa of **Mon 9Y 4M 3D**

The native had been a topper throughout and finally he was successful in IAS.

Planetary Combinations for service

The placement of the 10th lord Jupiter in the 6th house, who lends his favourable aspect over the 10th house, should be noted. Here, Jupiter is the *lagna* lord as well.

GOVT. SERVICE:

The lord of the 10th and the ascendant, Jupiter, falls in Leo i.e. the sign ruled by a luminary, Sun, and this confirms the govt. service, as per the rules and observations mentioned above. This resulted in high govt. service.

CIVIL SERVICE:

- The 9th lord Mars aspects the 9th house and the 10th lord Jupiter aspects the 10th house which is a powerful combination for class one service.
- The lords of both the triangles i.e. Moon and Mars, are placed together in the 3rd house.
- The 9th lord Mars aspects the 9th house and the 10th lord Jupiter.
- Both the luminaries, the Sun and Moon, are exalted.
- The 9th lord Mars obtains the *navamsa* of exaltation.

Jupiter obtains the *navamsa* of 9th lord Mars. Venus obtains *vargottam navamsa.* The 6th lord Sun, who is exalted, obtains own *navamsa.*

- There is mutual exchange between Mars and Venus, the 8th and 9th lords.
- Karmic control planets Jupiter and Mercury, who are triangular from each other, have a powerful influence on the profession of the native.

These combinations made the native successful in IAS proper.

Let us once again summarize the combinations for service and a govt. service

COMBINATIONS FOR SERVICE

1. The lord of the ascendant or the 6th house should have a concern with the 10th house.
2. The 6th lord may be placed in the ascendant or the 10th.
3. The lord of the ascendant or the 10th joins the 6th house.
4. The lord of the ascendant and the 6th are conjoined with each other.
5. Lords of the 10th and the 6th are conjoined with each other or aspect each other.
6. Lords of ascendant, 6th or the 10th fall in each others constellation.
7. Lords of ascendant, 6th or the 10th obtain *navamsa* of the relevant lords.

COMBINATION FOR GOVT. SERVICE

1. For a govt. service, influence of either of the luminaries must be there over the 6th, 10th or the ascendant.
2. If the combination of earning livelihood through service is present in the birth chart, identical to signs Cancer or Leo, govt. service will be there.

3. If the concerning planets obtain the *navamsa* of luminaries.
4. If the lords of relevant houses or the planets placed therein fall in the constellation of a luminary.

Illustration : 7.3 **(NKM)** *Horoscope No.: 26*

Date of birth : 12.04.1941 Time of birth : 07:50:20 hrs
Place of birth : Bareilly Lat 28:20:00 N Long 79:24:00E
Ayanamsa : 23:02:12 Sidereal Time : 20:57:32

Pln	Degree	Rasi	Nakshatra	Pad
Asc	4:43:29	Tau	Kritika	3
Sun	28:45:07	Pis	Revati	4
Mon	1:45:43	Lib	Chitra	3
Mar	13:36:03	Cap	Sravana	2
Mer	6:38:13	Pis	U Bhadrapad	1
Jup	26:37:51	Ari	Bharani	4
Ven (D)	26:52:51	Pis	Revati	4
Sat	21:34:38	Ari	Bharani	3
Rah (R)	8:41:53	Vir	U Phalguni	4
Ket (R)	8:41:53	Pis	U Bhadrapad	2

Lagna Chart

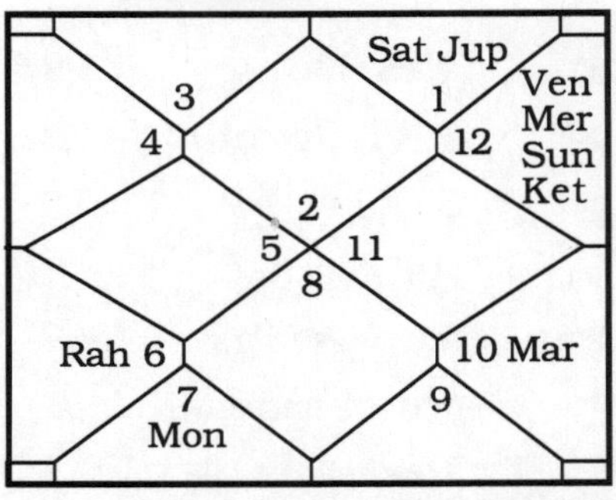

Navamsa Chart

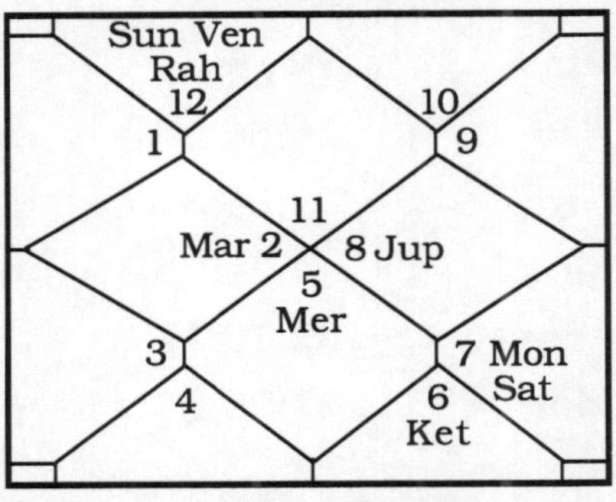

Balance of Vimshottari Dasa of **Mar 2Y 6M 27D**

The native at first joined the class one service IAS wherein he served as Legal Advisor to the Govt. Later, he was shifted to judiciary where he rose to the highest level and retired as Chief justice of a high court. He was blessed with three meritorious and talented daughters.

Let us find out whether our observations, regarding the govt. service and the 6th house and luminaries, hold any water, in his case, or not.

- The 6th lord, also the ascendant lord, falls in the 11th house, in association with a luminary Sun, while another luminary Moon occupies the 6th house.
- The 10th lord Saturn directly aspects the 6th house.
- Saturn and Moon are conjoined in *navamsa*, as also the Sun and Venus.
- Saturn, the 9th & the10th lord, falls in the constellation of Venus, the 6th lord.

These are the combinations which prove our observation regarding the 6th house, in confirming the native's job to be government one.

Illustration : 7.4 **(RG)** *Horoscope No.: 27*

Date of birth : 25.12.1963 Time of birth : 22:44:00 hrs
Place of birth : Jammu Lat 32:42:00 N Long 74:52:00E
Ayanamsa : 23:20:56 Sidereal Time : 04:27:28

Pln	**Degree**	**Rasi**	**Nakshatra**	**Pad**
Asc	16:58:50	Leo	P Phalguni	2
Sun	9:50:31	Sag	Moola	3
Mon	4:24:29	Ari	Ashwini	2
Mar (C)	22:13:17	Sag	Purvasadha	3
Mer	27:20:57	Sag	Uttarasadha	1
Jup	16:53:41	Pis	Revati	1
Ven	9:02:32	Cap	Uttarasadha	4

Sat	26:27:06	Cap	Dhanishtha	1
Rah (R)	17:53:22	Gem	Ardra	4
Ket (R/C)	17:53:22	Sag	Purvasadha	2

Lagna Chart

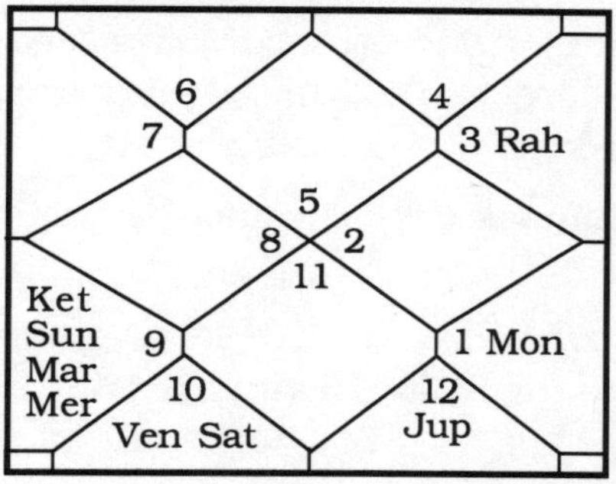

Navamsa Chart

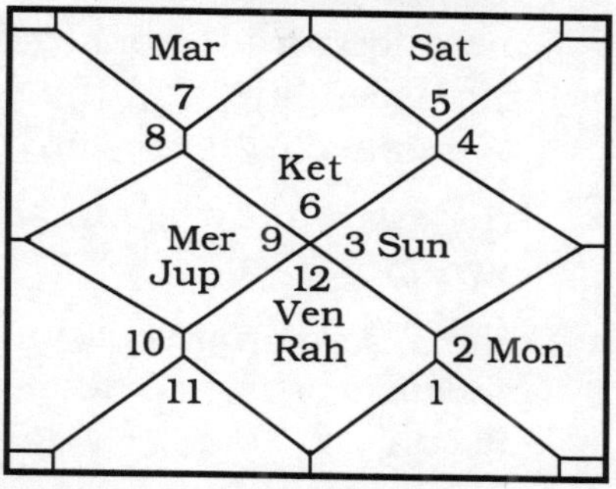

Balance of Vimshottari Dasa of **Ket 4Y 8M 6D**

The native of this horoscope got very senior position in his batch of civil services in the year 1990. Due to his virtues and forte he has always been conferred high profile and prized postings. He was Secretary (Home) before recently ascending to the post of Principal Secretary.

In this horoscope too, we wish to demonstrate our point that the involvement of the 6th house in relation to the ascendant or the 10th house tends one to earn his livelihood through service.

- The 10th lord Venus occupies the 6th house in association with the 6th lord Saturn.
- Venus, the 10th lord falls in the constellation of Sun and obtains the *navamsa* of its exaltation.

These are strong indicators for a govt. service. Other important combinations in addition to above, for civil service are:

- The 9th lord *Yogakaraka* Mars and ascendant lord Sun conjoin in another triangle, giving rise to *Kendra Trikona Rajyoga.*

- The 9th lord Mars aspects the 8th house as well as its lord.
- The 9th lord Mars falls in the constellation of Venus, the 10th lord and also obtains the *navamsa* of Venus as well
- Karmic control planets are Mercury and Jupiter who are in quadrant from each other. Mercury conjoins with the ascendant and the 9th lord while Jupiter joins the 8th house. Both are conjoined in the *navamsa* chart.
- The sixth and the eighth houses are occupied by their own lords.
- The 8th lord Jupiter obtains own *navamsa*, 10th lord Venus *navamsa* of its exaltation and the 6th lord Saturn *navamsa* of Sun.

At least one of the luminaries should influence the 10th or the 9th house. Here, Moon occupies the 9th house and obtains the *navamsa* of its exaltation i. e. Moon obtains the *navamsa* of 10th lord Venus.

These combinations signify civil services.

Illustration : 7.5 (**SKB**) *Horoscope No.: 28*

Date of birth : 17.01.1947 Time of birth : 04:30:00 hrs
Place of birth : Bijnor Lat 29:22:00 N Long 78:09:00E
Ayanamsa : 23:06:47 Sidereal Time : 11:54:44

Pln	Degree	Rasi	Nakshatra	Pad
Asc	23:07:14	Sco	Jyestha	2
Sun	2:52:32	Cap	Uttarasadha	2
Mon	4:23:17	Sco	Anuradha	1
Mar (D)	0:15:05	Cap	Uttarasadha	2
Mer (C)	28:45:36	Sag	Uttarasadha	1
Jup	29:52:02	Lib	Vishakha	3
Ven	16:33:15	Sco	Anuradha	4
Sat (R)	13:04:56	Can	Pushya	3

Rah	17:44:34	Tau	Rohini	3
Ket	17:44:34	Sco	Jyestha	1

Lagna Chart

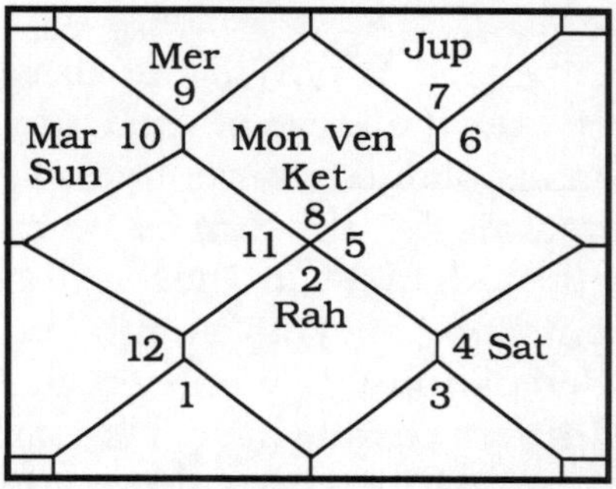

Navamsa Chart

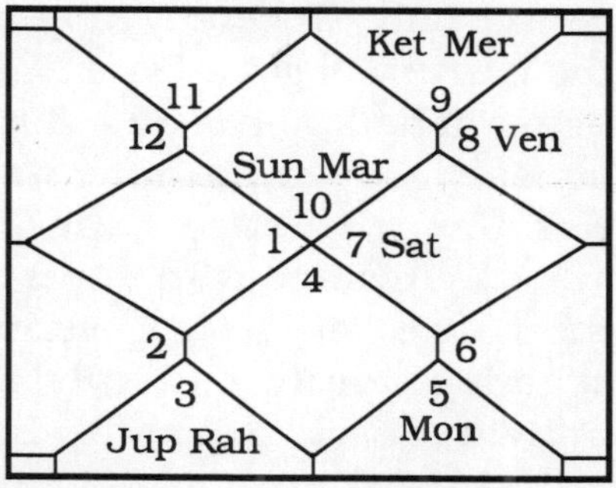

Balance of Vimshottari Dasa of **Sat 17Y 5M 29D**

The native of this birth chart retired as General Manager of Indian Potash Limited after serving the govt. departments for more than 35 years.

He was born in Scorpio ascendant. The lord of ascendant and the 6th, Mars conjoins with the 10th lord Sun in the 3rd house, where Mars is exalted. Both, Sun and Mars, obtain *vargottam navamsa*. Here, the 6th lord Mars has influenced the 10th lord, luminary Sun, which has resulted in a high class govt. service.

- **If the 10th lord is associated with the 6th or the ascendant lord, earning through service will be there.**
- **If either of the lords is a luminary i. e. Sun or Moon, the native will enter into a govt. service.**
- **Influence of Saturn on the 10th, 6th or the ascendant or their lords confirms livelihood through service, in addition to above.**

Those, who are scholars of Krishnamurthy Paddhati, they know that the sixth house is a positive house and it should not be considered adverse, if the tenth lord joins the sixth house or the sixth lord is tenanted in the tenth. If the lord of the ascendant falls in the sixth or anywhere, in association with the sixth lord, it shows the livelihood through service.

Similarly, if the tenth lord and the lord of the sixth house are placed together anywhere, one earns livelihood through service only. Generally, a question will always be there that the native will get a Government service or not? If the sixth house or its lord has an influence over the *lagna* or the tenth house, in one or the other way, as explained above, one will earn through service. If the luminaries i.e. the Sun or Moon are also involved with either of these houses or their lords, the native will get a government service. This should be examined quite carefully and cautiously, whether the individual will earn his livelihood through service or business. If strong planetary indications are there for entering into service, we should find out, if the involvement of luminaries is there and it is showing the livelihood through government service.

CHAPTER-8

Profession from the 8th House

We have penned many articles on the aspect of profession wherein we have emphasized the importance of the 8th house in the judgment of profession. On the face of it, it looks funny that occupations should be judged with the help of 8th house; the house that is treated as the worst, as it covers the adversities of life such as death, disease, tensions, failures, destruction, disappointments and disturbances. Mr. S. Kannan was a great research scholar, who wrote in the annual issue of 1963 of 'The Astrological Magazine' that the 8th and 10th houses, as reckoned from the *lagna* and Moon, indicate means of livelihood. He also suggests considering the lords of the signs, which fall in the 8th and the 10th house.

The *lagna* shows the aptitude of a person i.e. his interest towards a particular field, whereas the 10th house represents the kind of job, which will be taken up. The 8th house indicates nature of work to be done by the native.

It is believed that the 8th lord if placed in the 10th house or if the 10th lord joins the 8th house, the aspect of profession will be adversely tempered. The native will lose the job; he will be suspended or terminated, or he will suffer innumerable professional losses, and so on. Classics have the same opinion. But in reality it is not so. It has been observed, in number of cases, that the 10th lord joins the 8th house or 8th lord falls in the 10th house even in the birth charts of top administrative service personnel, top executives, GMs, MDs and CMDs etc.

The 8th house is the place of mysteries, secrets, complications, masses and legacy. One's profession is also a secret. The son of a millionaire may become a clerk and the son of a beggar can become a king. The secret is hidden in the depth of 8th house. Moreover, the 8th house is 11th from the 10th house and 10th from the 11th house. So, the 8th house governs the nature of job one will be doing to earn his livelihood. This is the principle of *'Bhavet Bhavam'*. If the 5th from the 5th reveals the prospects of children, the 9th from 9th can reveal prospects of fortune, why the 8th house can not reveal professional prospects as it is 10th and 11th as reckoned from 11th and 10th houses.

We do not want to say that the 10th house may be ignored. That is also equally important in finding out one's vocation. It is essential to remind that astrology is not a science of fatalism. It is a science of tendencies. It is an indicative science. One has to apply rules carefully by using his full intelligence, as well as art of interpretation. The application of rules in a nativity is not so simple. Many confusions and contradictions do create problems in the judgment of profession. For example, let us take up the significator of profession. There are different views of different authors and research scholars. *Jatak Parijat* suggests that the Sun, Jupiter, Mercury and Saturn are the *karaka* of profession. The Sun is the significator for politicians, Mercury for businessmen, Saturn for service class and Jupiter for various other professions. How can you find out the particular significator for one, so long his occupation is not known and when it is known, what is the use of application of significator. A few astrologers have established Venus and Moon as the *karaka* of profession. Mr. S. Kannan considers Moon in his one research article in the A.M. of January 63 and considers the Sun as significator in another article on the same subject of profession, in his article in A.M. of September 1971. Mr. N.N. Saha, a good research scholar has taken Venus as significator. Thus, only one planet Mars is left out who has not been considered as *karaka* of profession. For all other matters, there is only one significator. Then why should there be so many significators for profession. We suggest that one should leave the consideration of *karakas* as far as the judgment of professon is concerned, to avoid confusion on the subject of *karaka*.

One should be well conversant with the professions as indicated by various planets and signs. This we are not repeating here as all the scholars of astrology know it well. Let us apply these rules over the practical horoscopes :

Illustration: 8.1 (**Amitabh Bachchan**) *Horoscope No.: 29*

Date of birth : 11.10.1942 Time of birth : 16:00:00 hrs
Place of birth : Allahabad Lat 25:27:00 N Long 81:50:00E
Ayanamsa : 23:03:18 Sidereal Time : 16:14:42

Pln	Degree	Rasi	Nakshatra	Pad
Asc	1:55:45	Aqu	Dhanishtha	3
Sun	24:22:51	Vir	Chitra	1
Mon	10:18:36	Lib	Swati	2
Mar (D)	22:36:12	Vir	Hasta	4
Mer (R/D)	23:39:28	Vir	Chitra	1
Jup	0:32:15	Can	Punarvasu	4
Ven (C)	15:11:20	Vir	Hasta	2
Sat (R)	19:13:52	Tau	Rohini	3
Rah (R)	10:22:03	Leo	Magha	4
Ket (R)	10:22:03	Aqu	Satabhisha	2

Lagna Chart

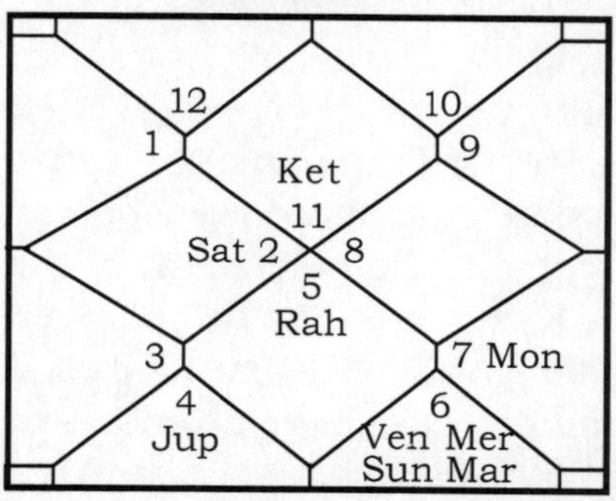

Navamsa Chart

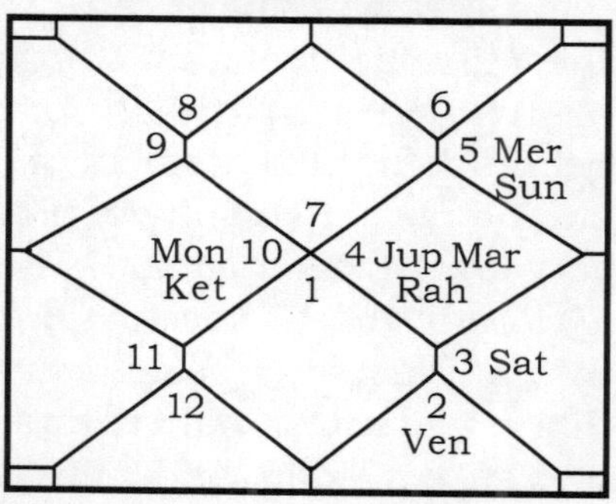

Balance of Vimshottari Dasa of **Rah 13Y 0M 29D**

This is the birth chart of world famous actor Amitabh Bachchan who is a legendary in the history of Indian films.

Venus, Mercury and Moon make one a good film actor, if these planets have a concern with the profession of the native. The signs involved are that of these planets i.e. Taurus, Gemini, Libra, Virgo and Cancer.

The 10th lord Mars falls in the 8th house in Virgo in *Hasta nakshatra* with *Yogakaraka* Venus placed there, under debilitation in *Hasta nakshatra*. Thus, Mars and Venus, fall in Virgo in the 8th house in *Hasta,* in association with Mercury and the 7th lord Sun. Mars obtains *navamsa* of Moon as the 10th lord. Moon falls in the sign of Venus. The 2nd and 11th lord, Jupiter, falls in the sign of exaltation in *vargottam navamsa* in the sign of Moon. Such Jupiter aspects the 10th house. The *lagna* lord Saturn is placed in the 4th house in Taurus sign i.e. the sign of Venus and obtains *navamsa* of Mercury and in the constellation Rohini i.e. that of Moon. Thus, most of the planets, the 10th lord, 2nd and 11th lord and planets placed in the 8th house are under the heavy influence of Venus, Moon and Mercury. Therefore, Amitabh Bachchan is a great film actor. Satrun and Sun are most powerful planets. Therefore, Saturn's *mahadasa* which was operative on him from 10-11-1971 to 10-11-1990 was best for him. Mercury is heavily afflicted by Mars and is also combust. Therefore, he faced various problems, losses, tensions and adversities during the major period of Mercury.

Here, we want or draw the attention of readers towards the placement of the 10th lord Mars in the 8th house, in association with the 8th lord Mercury. As per established belief about the placement of the 10th lord in *Trikas,* the native should have no dignity of profession. He should have been a very lowly placed person. This fact, i.e. the placement of the 8th lord in the 10th or 10th lord in 8th house, may be observed in many persons placed very high in life. However, a good film actor, singer, dancer and director must have prominence of Venus, Moon and Mercury in relation to the houses connected with occupation.

Illustration: 8.2 (**AKC**) *Horoscope No.: 30*

Date of birth : 15.10.1954 Time of birth : 07:16:00 hrs
Place of birth : Kanpur Lat 26:27:00 N Long 80:19:00E
Ayanamsa : 23:13:47 Sidereal Time : 8:39:30

Pln	**Degree**	**Rasi**	**Nakshatra**	**Pad**
Asc	12:10:30	Lib	Swati	2
Sun	27:56:35	Vir	Chitra	2
Mon	8:22:26	Tau	Kritika	4
Mar	2:41:02	Cap	Uttarasadha	2
Mer	20:53:45	Lib	Vishakha	1
Jup	4:59:24	Can	Pushya	1
Ven	4:46:48	Sco	Anuradha	1
Sat	16:21:41	Lib	Swati	3
Rah (R)	15:28:33	Sag	Purvasadha	1
Ket (R)	15:28:33	Gem	Ardra	3

Lagna Chart

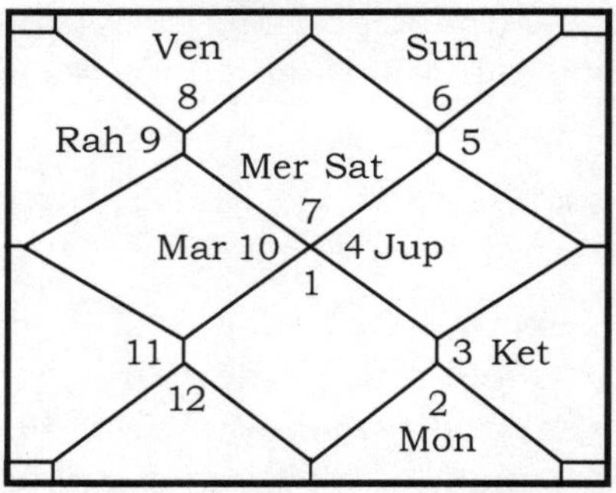

Navamsa Chart

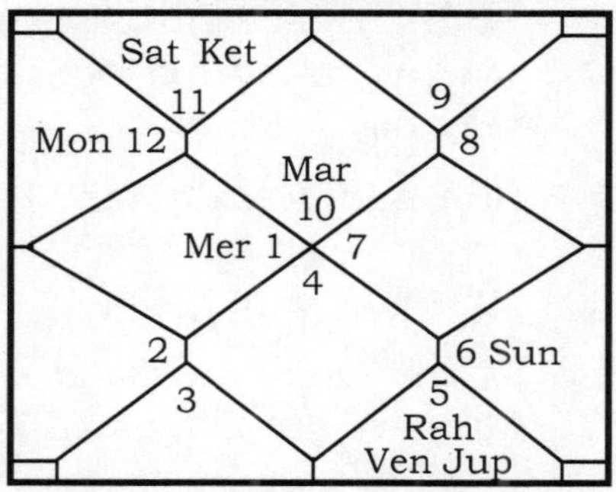

Balance of Vimshottari Dasa of **Sun 0Y 8M 23D**

This is the horoscope of a 54 years old industrialist who laid down an industry of various plastic materials and lamination, polyester and polythene etc. This is said to be the biggest industry of plastic in whole of Asia. The native started his career by selling plastic from shop to shop on bicycle.

In this birth chart, the 10th lord Moon falls in the 8th house in Taurus. Venus joins the 2nd house in Scorpio and aspects Moon and the 8th house. This represents the occupation connected with plastic material. However, such a placement of Moon and Venus only indicates the business of plastic but other *yogas* of the chart have made him so successful and world renowned. Following powerful combinations have blessed the native with the enormous height as an industrialist.

1. The ascendant Libra with *yogakaraka* Saturn in exaltation giving rise to *Sasa Mahapurusha Rajyoga.*

2. Conjunction of the lord of the 5th house, Saturn, and the lord of the 9th house, Mercury, in the ascendant, which is a powerful combination of *Kendra Trikona Rajyoga* blessing the native with fame, honor and recognition.

3. Four planets, Saturn, Mars, Jupiter and Moon are placed in their signs of exaltation, out of which three are in quadrants giving rise to *Ruchaka, Hansa, Sasa Mahapurusha Rajyogas.*

4. Both karmic control planets, Jupiter and Mercury, are in quadrants from *lagna* and each other, which shows a very high position.

5. Sun and Mars obtain *vargottam navamsa* and Saturn obtains own navamsa.

6. The 11th lord Sun, who occupies the 12th house, is shifted in the *lagna* in *bhava* chart, so Saturn, the Sun and Mercury are conjoined in the *lagna* itself showing the livelihood by business. The aspect of all these planets over the 7th house, in addition to Mars, is also to be noted.

7. The 2nd lord Mars and Venus, placed in the 2nd house, receive the aspect of exalted Jupiter, showing success in trades.

There are many other powerful combinations present in this horoscope, which have blessed the native with wealth, fame, ability, handsome personality and world wide trade.

In this birth chart, the wonderful results of placement of the 10th lord Moon in the 8th house can be seen. So, we again and again invite the attention of readers to verify this humble research finding.

Illustration: 8.3 *Horoscope No.: 31*

Pln	Degree	Rasi	Nakshatra	Pad
Asc	14:02:12	Lib	Swati	3
Sun	25:33:20	Tau	Mrigshira	1
Mon	7:52:15	Aqu	Satabhisha	1
Mar	21:54:21	Ari	Bharani	3
Mer	18:49:52	Gem	Ardra	4
Jup (R)	26:24:18	Lib	Vishakha	2
Ven	2:38:47	Tau	Kritika	2
Sat	12:35:31	Can	Pushya	3
Rah (R)	9:17:41	Tau	Kritika	4
Ket (R)	9:17:41	Sco	Anuradha	2

Lagna Chart

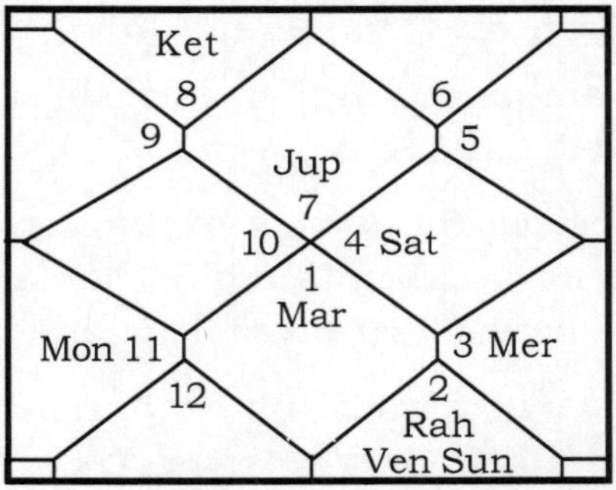

Navamsa Chart

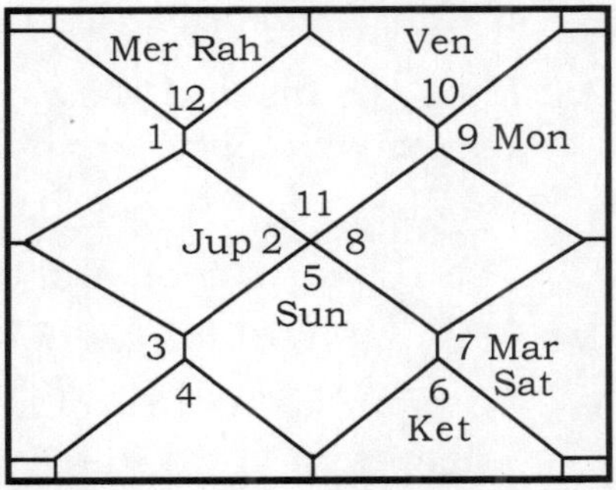

Balance of Vimshottari Dasa of **Rah 16Y 4M 14D**

The native is a multimillionaire and pays many thousand crore rupees as income tax. He is most successfully running a finance organization having various branches all over the world.

The mutual exchange between the lords of the 5th and 10th houses can be seen. *Yogakaraka* Saturn, the lord of the 4th and 5th, joins the 10th house, whereas the 10th lord Moon is posited in the 5th house. The lord of *lagna* Venus, the 11th lord Sun and Rahu are conjoined in the 8th house. Here, three vital planets join the 8th house which shows the life full of problems, tensions, stress, despairs and distress but the case is just reverse. The native is exceptionally rich and successful person in each and every sphere of life. The 10th lord Moon and 9th lord Mercury obtain the *navamsa* of Jupiter indicating profound success in finance company. Powerful Saturn in the 10th house will give rise to industries. Combination of the Sun, Venus and Rahu in the 8th house, in an earthy sign Taurus, shows making of big complexes like an independent city. Lord of *lagna* Venus and the 11th lord Sun are conjoined together in the 8th house. The native is successful in earning wealth in his own way. All his undertakings will be successful.

Following combinations of this birth chart may be observed :

1. Mutual exchange between the 10th lord Moon and the 5th lord *Yogakaraka* Saturn.
2. Mars, Venus and Mercury are placed in their own signs respectively fiery, earthy and airy signs.
3. *Bhagyadhipati* Mercury receives the aspect of Jupiter. The 10th lord Moon and the lord of the 2nd and 7th house Mars are also receiving the benefic aspect of Jupiter.
4. *Yogakaraka* Saturn obtains *navamsa* of its exaltation, whereas 11th lord, the Sun, falls in own *navamsa* Leo.
5. Mars aspects Saturn and Saturn aspects Mars, whereas both obtain the same *navamsa* of Libra, giving an inclination towards the beauty of nature, constructions and human being.
6. Moon, who is so well placed giving rise to *Kendra Trikona*

yoga, obtains *navamsa* of Jupiter but Moon is 12th in *navamsa* chart, from the *navamsa* position of the *lagna* lord Venus.

7. Mutual exchange of *navamsa* of Venus and Saturn, which results in deep attraction of persons towards him.

8. Jupiter's placement in Libra and in the *navamsa* of Venus has blessed him with very handsome, captivating and attractive personality.

9. The 2nd lord Mars aspects the 2nd house of its own, and the 4th lord *Yogakaraka* Saturn aspects 4th house of its own. Saturn and Mars, both aspect each other. They are conjoined in the *navamsa* of Venus.

Illustration: 8.4 **(JM)** *Horoscope No.: 32*

Date of birth : 21.02.1943 Time of birth : 02:31:00 hrs

Place of birth : Azamgarh Lat 28:20:00 N Long 79:24:00E

Ayanamsa : 23:03:37 Sidereal Time : 11:18:07

Pln	**Degree**	**Rasi**	**Nakshatra**	**Pad**
Asc	15:44:52	Sco	Anuradha	4
Sun	8:15:18	Aqu	Satabhisha	1
Mon	14:55:00	Leo	P Phalguni	1
Mar	25:16:47	Sag	Purvasadha	4
Mer	11:58:28	Cap	Sravna	1
Jup (R)	22:43:02	Gem	Punarvasu	1
Ven	1:09:30	Pis	P Bhadrapad	4
Sat	12:43:28	Tau	Rohini	1
Rah (R)	1:51:19	Leo	Magha	1
Ket (R/C)	1:51:19	Aqu	Dhanistha	3

Lagna Chart

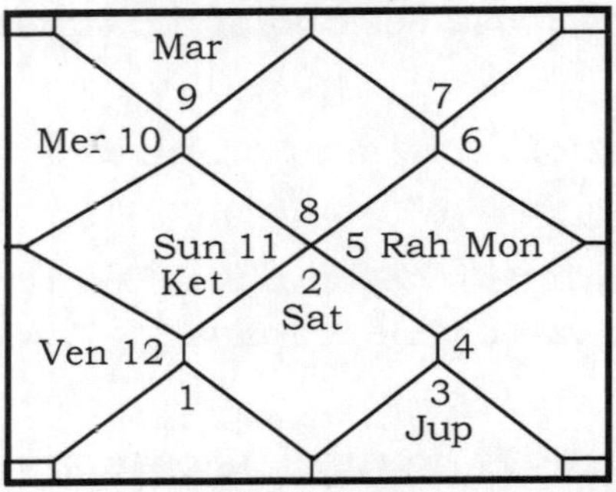

Navamsa Chart

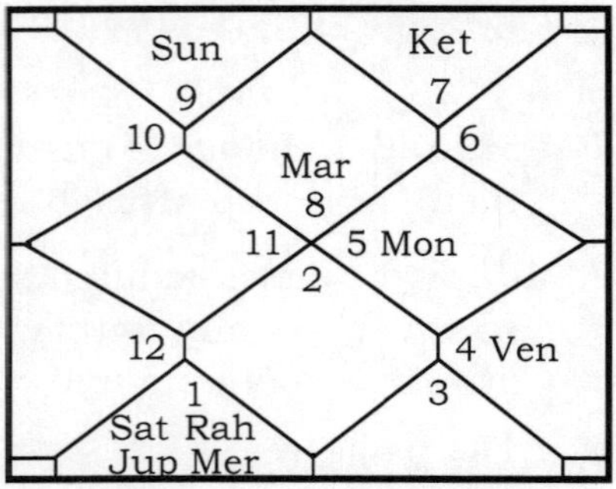

Balance of Vimshottari Dasa of **Ven 17Y 7M 15D**

The native is one of the best Homeopathic doctors in U.P. Let us look if the 10th house reveals his medical profession. He has his own Pharmaceutical Company too.

Rahu and Moon are associated in the 10th house and the 10th lord Sun aspects the 10th house. The 10th lord Sun obtains the *navamsa* of Jupiter. This indicates medical profession. However, 2nd and the 5th lord Jupiter falls in the 8th house in Mercurian sign Gemini and the *lagna* lord Mars aspects Jupiter. This also indicates medical career. In fact, the Sun, Mars and Jupiter govern medical career. The 8th lord Mercury falls in the 3rd house but obtains the *navamsa* of Mars in association with Jupiter. Thus, the 8th house is under the influence of Mars, Jupiter and Mercury. The Sun, Mars and Jupiter have prominent role here, so as to decide medical career.

Illustration: 8.5 **(EA)** *Horoscope No.: 33*

Date of birth : 18.01.1951 Time of birth : 13:13:00 hrs
Place of birth : Harda Khas Lat 22:22:00 N Long 77:08:00E
Ayanamsa : 23:10:27 Sidereal Time : 20:39:10

Pln	**Degree**	**Rasi**	**Nakshatra**	**Pad**
Asc	26:36:30	Ari	Bharani	4
Sun	4:13:56	Cap	Uttarasadha	3

Mon	10:19:49	Tau	Rohini	1
Mar	3:29:57	Aqu	Dhanistha	4
Mer	10:43:44	Sag	Moola	4
Jup	14:58:37	Aqu	Satabhisha	3
Ven	19:54:53	Cap	Sravna	3
Sat (R)	9:09:19	Vir	U Phalguni	4
Rah (R)	27:27:58	Aqu	P Bhadrapad	3
Ket (R)	27:27:58	Leo	U Phalguni	1

Lagna Chart

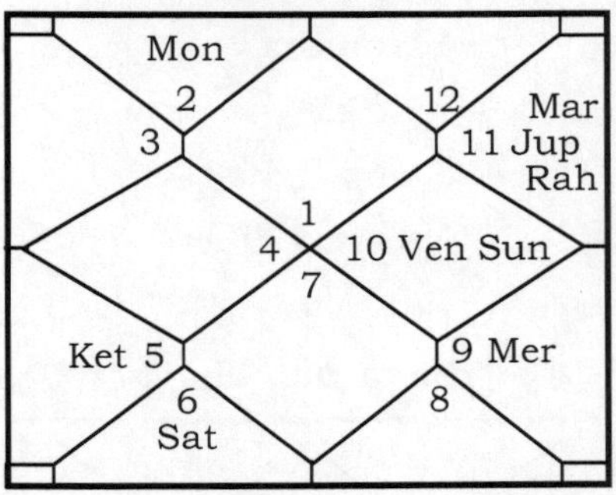

Navamsa Chart

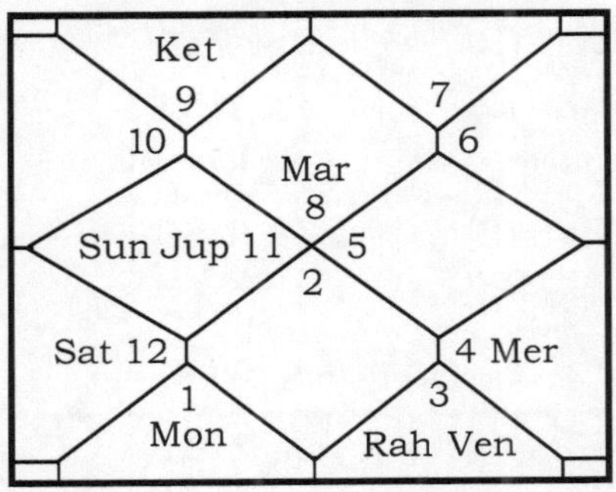

Balance of Vimshottari Dasa of **Mon 9Y 9M 0D**

The native is a very rich and successful businessman of Madhya Pradesh. At present he is dealing in the business of cotton, which is chiefly represented by Moon and Venus. Conjunction of the 2nd and 7th lord Venus with the 5th lord Sun indicates that the native will earn through business only. Moon falls in the 2nd house, in an earthy sign Taurus, in exaltation. Moon aspects the 8th house, representing the business of cotton, textiles, threads and fabrics. The 2nd and 7th lord Venus falls in the 10th house in Capricorn i.e. earthy sign and obtains *navamsa* of Moon. This is a powerful indication of the business of cotton. Thus, the judgment of the 8th house, in addition to the 10th house, will give more accurate results in deciding one's occupation.

Illustration: 8.6 (**LJT**) *Horoscope No.: 34*

Date of birth : 12.04.1935 Time of birth : 05:03:00 hrs
Place of birth : Lucknow Lat 26:50:00 N Long 80:54:00E
Ayanamsa : 22:57:25 Sidereal Time : 18:13:35

Pln	**Degree**	**Rasi**	**Nakshatra**	**Pad**
Asc	11:46:56	Pis	U Bhadrapad	3
Sun	28:11:18	Pis	Revati	4
Mon	11:49:58	Can	Pushya	3
Mar (R)	21:00:58	Vir	Hasta	4
Mer	12:38:24	Pis	U Bhadrapad	3
Jup (R)	28:43:13	Lib	Vishakha	3
Ven	1:51:54	Tau	Kritika	2
Sat	13:29:17	Aqu	Satabhisha	3
Rah (R)	4:19:55	Cap	Uttarasadha	3
Ket (R)	4:19:55	Can	Pushya	1

Lagna Chart

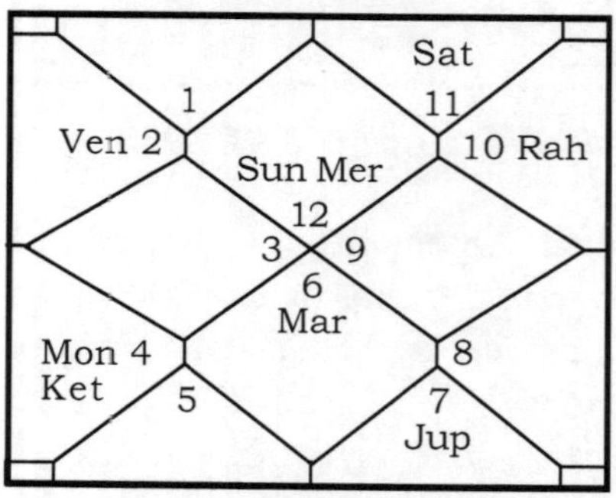

Navamsa Chart

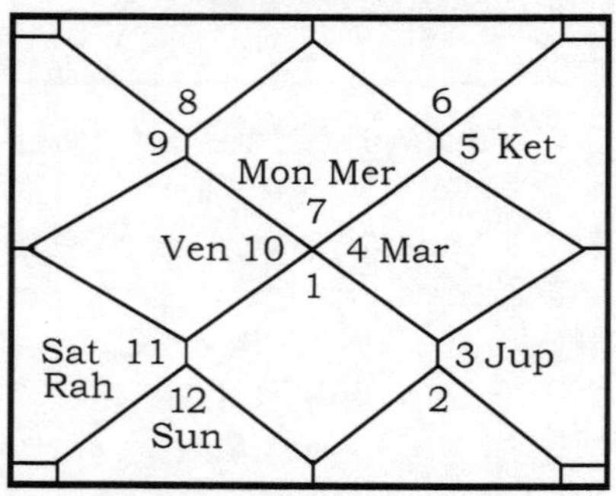

Balance of Vimshottari Dasa of **Sat 6Y 10M 19D**

This birth chart belongs to a very famous former minister of U.P. Govt. who has done lot of improvement of roads, parks, buildings, shops and markets in Lucknow.

The native is born in Pisces ascendant. The Sun and Mars join the *lagna* and the 7th house, respectively, which has developed an aptitude towards politics and he became a minister. Only the Sun and Mars, if so placed, can not make one a minister unless other strong combinations are also present. Here the Moon, Saturn and Venus are posited in their own signs. The Sun and Saturn obtain *vargottam navamsa*. The *lagna* and the 10th lord, Jupiter, falls in the 8th house in sign of Venus, Libra. Even then the native rose to such a high position. We, therefore, again and again say, that the 8th house is adverse for health but it is good for profession, if unafflicted. Here, Jupiter in the 8th falls in the sign of Venus and Venus falls in own sign in the 3rd house. This shows the business of fabrics. The native earlier had a vast business of chikan garments. Jupiter obtains *navamsa* of Mercury, which has resulted in the promotioin of educational institute. The second house is aspected by Mars, Jupiter and Saturn; therefore, the native has many sources of income. Placement of 6th lord, Sun and 7th lord Mercury in *lagna*, Jupiter in 8th as *lagna* lord and mutual aspect between the 2nd and 7th lords, Mars and Mercury, has given him bad health.

Illustration: 8.7 (**BSM**) *Horoscope No.: 35*

Date of birth : 15.10.1925 Time of birth : 16:46:00 hrs
Place of birth : Bulandshahar Lat 28:30:00 N Long 77:49:00E
Ayanamsa : 22:48:58 Sidereal Time : 18:01:10

Pln	**Degree**	**Rasi**	**Nakshatra**	**Pad**
Asc	7:35:52	Pis	U Bhadrapad	2
Sun	28:45:42	Vir	Chitra	2
Mon	1:32:57	Vir	U Phalguni	2
Mar (C)	18:00:43	Vir	Hasta	3
Mer (C)	4:25:31	Lib	Chitra	4
Jup	21:53:32	Sag	Purvasadha	3
Ven	11:40:47	Sco	Anuradha	3
Sat	21:11:39	Lib	Vishakha	1
Rah (R)	8:18:38	Can	Pushya	2
Ket (R)	8:18:38	Cap	Uttarasadha	4

Lagna Chart

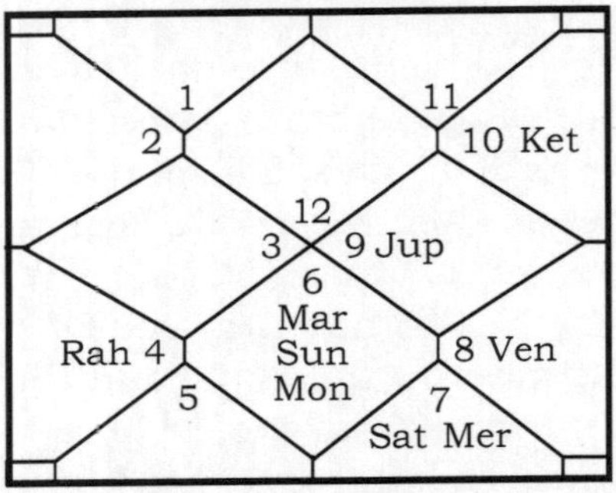

Navamsa Chart

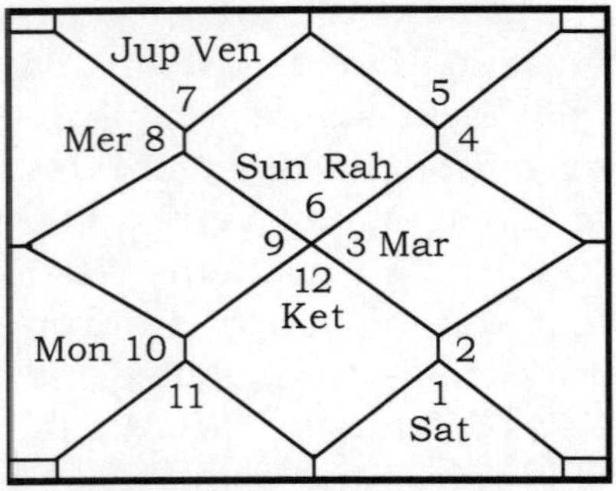

Balance of Vimshottari Dasa of **Sun 3Y 9M 19D**

This horoscope pertains to an engineer holding highest position in UPSEB. Mercury, Mars and Saturn make one an engineer, if these planets are related with the 10th and the 8th house.

In this nativity, Jupiter joins his own sign Sagittarius in the 10th house and obtains *navamsa* of Venus. Mars and Saturn lend their aspect over Jupiter in the 10th house. Thus, Jupiter is afflicted. Profession of an engineer can not be explained only on the basis of 10th house.

Now let us examine the 8th house, which contains Saturn and Mercury. The lord of 8th house, Venus, falls in the 9th house owned by Mars. Therefore, the 8th house is under the influence of Mars, Mercury and Saturn. This explains the profession of the native as an engineer.

Illustration: 8.8 (**GPM**) *Horoscope No.: 36*

Date of birth : 06.08.1961 Time of birth : 16:00:00 hrs

Place of birth : Jahanabad Lat 26:06:00 N Long 80:21:00E

Ayanamsa : 23:19:05 Sidereal Time : 12:50:18

Pln	**Degree**	**Rasi**	**Nakshatra**	**Pad**
Asc	6:57:52	Sag	Moola	3
Sun	20:23:26	Can	Aslesa	2

Mon	25:12:19	Tau	Mrigshira	1
Mar	0:00:52	Vir	U Phalguni	2
Mer (C)	11:27:35	Can	Pushya	3
Jup (R)	7:23:26	Cap	Uttarasadha	4
Ven	9:50:48	Gem	Ardra	1
Sat (R)	1:55:47	Cap	Uttarasadha	2
Rah (R/C)	3:57:19	Leo	Magha	2
Ket (R)	3:57:19	Aqu	Dhanistha	4

Lagna Chart

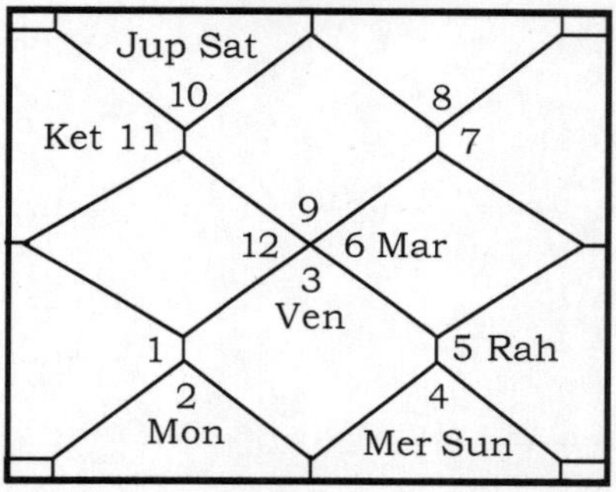

Navamsa Chart

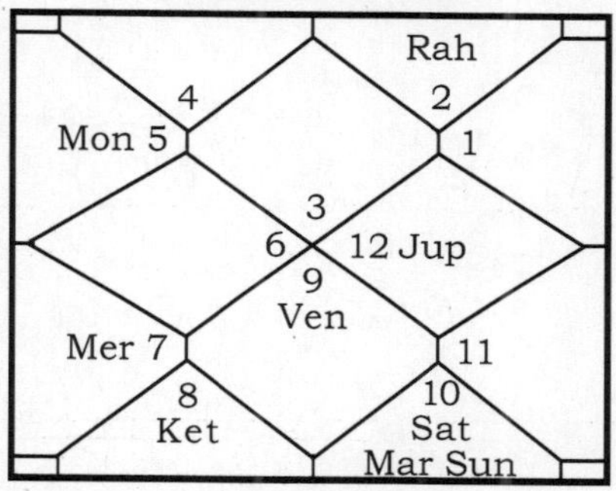

Balance of Vimshottari Dasa of **Mar 6Y 0M 6D**

The native is working as a Hindi Officer in the State Bank. The 10th lord Mercury is placed in the 8th house under the mutual aspect with Jupiter and Saturn. Mercury indicates translation and Jupiter shows teaching. This has made the native a Hindi Officer. The 5th lord Mars joins the 10th house under the aspect of Jupiter. This also confirms the livelihood by teaching. The 8th lord Moon, who is exalted in the 6th house, receives the aspect of the 4th and *lagna* lord Jupiter. Jupiter is debilitated but retrograde in *Rasi* chart and obtains own *navamsa*. Saturn obtains *vargottam navamsa*. The 10th lord Mercury obtains navamsa of Sun.

Thus, the 8th house plays quite important role in the judgment of profession but it never means that the 8th house is more important than the 10th house or the 10th house can at all be ignored. The 8th house decides the nature of actual work, one will do. An engineer can become a businessman or he may run an industry. A doctor may earn his livelihood by dealing in property matters. The 8th house will certainly assist in determining one's vocation, but the application and the judgment of the 8th house and planets placed therein should be carefully made in respect to the 10th house. Placement of the lord of 8th in the 10th and 10th lord in the 8th should not be considered adverse for occupation, if the planets are well fortified and are unafflicted by association or aspect of malefics.

●

CHAPTER-9

The Moon Myths and Facts

The sovereign queen of the nights, Moon, has been held in a very high esteem in Hindu Astrology. The cold and feminine Moon, regarded as the mother of heavens, is very close to the earth. It moves fastest among all the planets. The motion of Moon has a great significance in our lives.

Though very small, the Moon has very evident effects on all ailments and inanimate objects of the earth. Trees and plants grow faster in the bright lunar half than they grow in the dark lunar half. Thus, a Muhurat is fixed to sow the seeds, keeping the motion of the Moon. A western astrologer, Jeri has observed that the beard of men grows faster in *Shukla Paksha* than it happens in *Krishna Paksha*. It is well known that ebbs and tides of the oceans are caused by the influence of Moon on the earth. On a full Moon day, the sea remains tranquil. Fish lay eggs only in the bright lunar half. All such observations indicate the moon's powerful influence on the earth.

After the successful sojourn of man on the Moon, the scientists could know only abut its physical structure, constituents of its soil, density, reactions and the gravitational force. The Astrologers know, though a very little, about the actual influence of Moon on different events of human life. In fact, it is true about all other planets.

9.1 Moon : A Planet of Paramount Importance

The Moon, no doubt, is a planet of great importance, though some astrologers may not readily accept this fact. The cycle of human lives is largely governed by the Moon.

The degrees travelled by the Moon, in a particular sign, at a particular time, decide the condition of our body and mind. The position of the Moon, at birth, decides the time of various events of our lives. Longitudes of the Moon fix the *"dasha bhukti"* one has to undergo in his life. This ultimately reflects the period of any happenings in our life, good or bad. To denote the Moon's position easily, we even used Rasi name which indicates the Moon's position in particular *Nakshatra* and *Pada*. The Moon's movement controls our day to day routine, our mood, behaviour, nature and temperament. Moon largely controls the span of life of children, menstruation cycle of women. All auspicious celebrations, such as marriage, important undertakings, long journeys, festivals, vratas and religious rites, are observed during the stay of Moon in an auspicious star.

There has been great significance of the full Moon and the new Moon. The Moon, if placed suitably, can make one a king or equal to him. Mantreshwar has described it in the Chapter-VII, Shloka-VII, as given below:

गुणोत्तमे लग्न नवांशकोद्‌गमे निशाकरश्चापि गणोत्तमेऽपिवा।
चतुर्ग'हैश्चन्द'विवर्नितैस्तदा निरीक्षितः स्याद धमोङ्वो नृपः।।

(*Phaldeepika,* Ch-7, Vers-5)

If the full Moon is being aspected by a planet that occupies its own house or exaltation sign, one becomes a king even if he is born with a humble background.

In another shloka of *Phaldeepika*, author expresses his view about the Moon, as under :

सुधा मृणालोपम बिम्ब शोभितः शशी नवांशे नलिनीर्पियस्य।
यदि क्षितिशो बहुहस्तिपूर्णः शुभाश्च केन्द्रेषु न पापायुक्ताः।।

(*Phaldeepika,* Ch-7, Vers-11)

The author means to say that the full Moon, if falls in the *Navamsa* of the Sun, benefics are unafflicted and they join *Kendras,* the native becomes a king who has many elephants (a very prosperous, famous and rich person).

जलचर शशि नवांशक इन्दुस्तनुभवने शुभदस्वक वर्गे।
अशुभकरः खलु कण्टकहीनो भवति नृपो बहुवारण नाथः।।

(*Phaldeepika,* Ch-7, Vers-19)

If Moon falls in a watery sign and *Navamsa* in the *lagna,* own *Vargas* or in a benefic *Vargas,* one becomes a king with many elephants, provided no malefic occupies a Kendra.

Thus, Moon is a planet of great importance. *Phaldeepika* states that the strength of the Moon is a basic foundation of the strength of a person.

Many more such verses may be quoted expressing the importance of Moon under particular planetary setup of planets.

The fourth sign of the zodiac, Cancer, is ruled by Moon, which gets exalted in Taurus, a sign ruled by its enemy, Venus, while it is debilitated in Scorpio, owned by Mars, its friend. Likewise, Mars gets debilitated in its friends house, Cancer. Thus, both friends get weakened in each other's place. Suppose, Moon joins the 7th house in Venus sign Taurus, auspicious results regarding 7th house will be predicted as a general rule, while its presence in the 7th, in Scorpio, though in its friends sign, will be regarded to forestall evils. Does it not look absolutely impractical?

9.2 When to consider the Moon Chart ?

A very popular and widely practised aphorism is that predictions should be made with the help of *lagna Kundali* or the *Chandra Kundali,* whichever is stronger. It implies that all the judgments are required to be done by Moon chart only if Moon chart is stronger than the *lagna* chart. Here, an important question arises as how to judge which one is stronger? It is not so easy so long as *Shadabala* of planets and *Bhava Balas* are not worked out correctly. We do not know if the strength of the *Bhava* occupied by Moon, should be taken as the strength of the Moon chart. If it is not so, the strength of the Moon should be taken into account. How will we compare the strength of Moon with the strength of the first house. Obviously, Moon and *lagna* are the two different things, while one is a planet, other is a house and these can not be compared to judge their relative strength. If it is so, the stronger chart, should be taken into consideration for judgment. Also, one should consider the house owned by Moon and *lagna* together.

The other possibility of comparing the relative strength is to consider the strength of the Moon and lagnadhipati together. Suppose, the *lagnadhipati* occupies the 12th house, one will say that *lagna* is weak. Now, see the Moon chart. The dispositor of Moon is situated in the 8th or 12th house from Moon, which will be treated as stronger? Merely by placement of *lagnadhipati* in 12th, 6th or 8th house, the *lagna* does not become weak. And if the *lagna* is weak, why should Moon chart be considered for judgment of horoscope? as lord of the Moon's house, too, is placed in a similar position. If the *lagna* is weak, overall strength of the horoscope gets reduced. The native concerned will have to face adversities in his life. If it is so, why should the Moon chart be considered? In our view, predictions should always be made on the basis of *lagna* and not on the basis of Moon.

Moon has vital importance in our lives and governs one's will, desires, emotions, thoughts, mind, wishes, sentiments, ambitions, decisions and temperament. If the Moon is strong, one is controlled by his mind. He has a strong will. He has a good decision making power. He acts as per his analytical mind and makes all kinds of judgments, after thoroughly weighing the pros and cons of everything. Such a native is ruled by mind, while others are ruled by circumstances.

If a strong Moon is there, with a weak ascendant and vocation is to be judged, one should try to find it out from the Moon and from *lagna*. If the Moon chart indicates any particular profession and *lagna* chart supports it, the native concerned will certainly be engaged in that occupation. Similarly, if the *lagna* is very strong and signifies any particular field of means of livelihood which is also supported by weak Moon chart, that field of business or service will favour the native. If the *lagna* is strong and Moon is weak, and one joins the profession indicated by *lagna*, which is not supported by the Moon chart, it will not give job satisfaction to the native. The nature of one's occupation depends also on the strong determination and will. For obtaining main object, one should not be guided only be moods but should work in a particular and specific way to achieve his objectives. Strong Moon chart makes one act with strong determination and will, positively, but he can get complete success only if the *lagna* chart also supports him, otherwise he may start with a bang but abandon the work, as soon as he starts meeting adversities.

Suppose, the judgment about progeny is required, one should never judge it from Moon chart. This aspect of life, like various others, should be judged from *lagna* and Jupiter. Sickness, accidents, longevity, should be judged from the *lagna* chart. Readers are very intelligent and they can easily decide what aspects of life should be judged from the Moon chart and that, too, if the Moon chart is stronger than the *lagna* chart.

Strong Moon chart should be considered only when certain specific aspects of life involve element of one's strong determination and will power positively. It will be the biggest error, if a strong Moon chart is taken into account for the judgment of all the events of life, without taking actual *lagna,* into consideration.

The query on how to judge the *lagna* and the Moon chart, remains unanswered. Sketch the Moon chart and work out the strength of the Moon *lagna*. Compare both and use the *lagna* chart for all purposes and see if it is stronger. If the Moon chart is stronger than the *lagna* chart, use it for certain specific aspects only and not for all purposes, but also take the *lagna* into consideration. The actual *lagna* should never be ignored and must be taken into consideration, side by side.

9.3 Why to consider transit from Natal Moon?

An important aspect of Hindu Astrology is consideration of relative movements of planets in relation to natal horoscope, Gochar or transit. Whatever may be the ascendant, the transits of different planets are taken into consideration in respect of position of the natal Moon only. On this point, views of modern scholars are different. Some of them maintain that transit of planets should be taken into consideration, in relation to the *lagna*. However, we do think our sages were absolutely right to consider transit results in relation to the position of radical Moon.

We have just seen above that only the fastest moving Moon decides the *Dasha Bhukti,* we have to undergo in our life time. The timing of various events, good or bad, is thus under the control of Moon, whereas the nature and shape of events that would take place in our lives, is governed by *lagna*. Can *lagna* chart alone, without taking Moon into consideration, decide the time of different events in one's life? It is simply the position of Moon in the horoscope, which decides the future happening in our lives. Our view in this regard is that the strength of the *lagna* and the lord of the *lagna* should be kept together, at one place, and that of the Moon at another.

Similarly, the consideraion of transit is done to fix the timing of events that will take place in future, more precisely and minutely. Moon rules over timing. Why should we not consider transits in relation to Moon? There is every logic to support the views of our sages that movement of different planets should be counted with the help of Moon sign, as the Moon rules over timing of events of our lives. It should not be done with the help of *lagna,* which decides the nature of events.

9.4 The combination of the Sun and Moon

The association of the Sun with the Moon occurs around new Moonday during *Amavasya,* which is regarded as adverse to commence all kinds of auspicious works. This combination has been named as *Kohoo Yoga,* which is an adverse *yoga.* In fact, this yoga should not be treated as an adverse *yoga* for all occasions. Moon owns the 9th and the Sun rules the 10th, for Scorpio ascendant. If both, the Sun and Moon, combine in the 9th, 10th, 4th or 5th or even 11th, results will be quite auspicious and this will be a powerful *Raj Yoga.* For Aries ascendant, being the lord of the 4th and 5th, the association of the Sun and Moon, forms a *Kendra Trikona Raj Yoga* in the 9th, 10th, 4th, 5th, or 11th house. For Libra ascendant, the combination of the Sun, Moon and Mercury, the lords of 9th, 10th and 11th, gives rise to prosperity and wealth. This combination is very adverse for Taurus, Virgo and Capricorn ascendants. Generally, if they are associated with the 6th, 8th or 3rd house, except for Libra, the combination produces very adverse results. The adverse results may cause death of any of the parents before 7 years of age and sickness. Chronic diseases may be full of miseries and sickness, which may cause worries. If the combination has an influence over marriage or marital life, one may have two marriages. If the 5th house is involved and remains weak, along with a weak *Santan Karaka* Jupiter, this combination deprives a native of children. This forms a *Daridra Yoga* if unfavourably placed, as mentioned above. One will have to serve others for whole of life and face various kinds of troubles. Old age is very bad.

9.5 Moon and Saturn

Saturn has been regarded as worst malefic. There is no other planet which is as kind as Saturn is. Saturn creates a feeling of detachment from the worldly affairs and creates interest in spiritualism. Saturn has always produced real saints like Ram Krishna Paramhansa. Saturn creates miseries so that the native may be detached from the peripheral pleasures and glamour of life and may proceed towards the path of real attainment. Any planet, associated with Saturn, will either make him a king or beggar, depending on their positions in the horoscope.

If Moon and Saturn are conjoined, one runs under the adversities of the *Saadhe Saati* of Saturn, right from the birth. This is named as *Udarastha Saadhe Saati* of Saturn. This combination keeps one worried and devoid of happiness. At least the real happiness is absent. One faces innumerable miseries throughout and remains disturbed even in the best days of his life.

The combination of the Moon with Saturn is always adverse but the adversities will not be more pronounced, if conjunction takes place in Libra or Capricorn or is aspected by Jupiter. Even if the combination of Moon-Saturn is auspicious in any horoscope, it will give mental gloom, melancholy and worry, unless strongly aspected by Jupiter. However, if mutual exchange of Moon and Saturn takes place, in respect to an angle and triangle, the *Raja yoga* is formed and may promote the native to the level of sky. For Libra ascendant, the lord of 4th and 5th house Saturn, if occupies the 10th house and the 10th lord Moon, if falls in the 5th house, there will be mutual exchange of the lords of the 10th and 5th house i.e. an angle and triangle, and that will result into a very high professional and financial elevation of the native and he may lead a kingly life. Similarly, for Scorpio ascendant, the mutual exchange of the 4th lord Saturn and the 9th lord Moon will make the native very prosperous and happy.

9.6 Moon-Saturn Association : Relations with Mother

The Moon Saturn association indicates that the native had harmed some woman or a girl in his previous life. The harm was so unbearable that the woman has given birth to the native and became his mother. It may be otherwise also, that any woman harmed the native in such a way that he has taken the birth as her son. In any case, the native does not have smooth relations with his mother. The native becomes poor and leads a miserable life. If son's enemity towards mother is greater, Saturn is stronger than Moon. In this case, mother may expire soon after the birth of the native or she lives a very long life to face the enemity of her son, till old age, as a revenge of the previous birth. This yoga is more effective till 14 years of age of the native. One gets inclined towards spiritualism, after facing endless worries and leading a life full of sins and curses, crime and greed. A time comes when Saturn gives sense of detachment to the native, from all worldly involvements, deceits, greediness, false glamour and sins. He becomes a sage or a real preceptor in old age.

In fact, the combination of the Moon and Saturn should be carefully judged. It needs expertise to reach any conclusion in this regard. Readers should never speak out the effect of this combination, even if they are sure of it.

9.7 Saturn's transit over the combination of the Sun and Moon

Saturn's transit over the radical location of the combination of the Sun and Moon, produces many worrries caused due to serious adversities to self and closely related persons like parents, children, wife and husband etc. There is always a fear of death. One suffers from chronic disease and gets depressed very much. At times, the native receives serious setbacks in his profession, gets suspended, charge sheeted or looses service. He may be required to leave the job or place of residence. He suffers from humiliation and dishonours, defamations and disrespect. He wanders here and there aimlessly. His qualities and abilities are overlooked and he is insulted. All ambitions and desires and expectations are spoiled. He is also distressed, unhappy with his wife and children. False charges may cause even imprisonment or any kind of prosecution to the native. The effects of the transit of Saturn are so powerful that they affect the native throughout his life. It has been said that one suffers from such miseries due to the ill behaviour with the parents in the previous life. This is always the worst transit of the Saturn which adversely influences the native, if at all, it comes between 30 to 60 years of age. After 60th year and before 30th year, it is not so an effective transit.

The combination of Moon, with other planets, has a great significance. The results are modified according to the influence of different planets over Moon, their nature and lordships. The association of Moon, with the pious Jupiter, is regarded to be an ever auspicious combination, but there are circumstances when this produces extremely adverse and distressful results. There is need to scrutinize, properly and deeply, various astrological factors before pronouncing good results of this or any other such combination, as those may not be always realized. The peculiar and strange behaviour of Jupiter, with respect of *Kuja Dosha,* has been dealt with in a separate articulation.

9.8 The Moon : Neo Classical Observation

The fastest moving planet, Moon, does play the most important and significant role in shaping the human life. Writing on Moon is a subject of a complete book. We will make an honest endeavor to cover the importance of Moon, as much as possible, in this small article.

Likewise ascendant and 9th house, the supreme importance of Moon cannot be neglected. It plays significant role in shaping, as well as in building the blocks of one's future. Acharya Kalyan Verma in the 11th chapter of his classical work *"Saravali"* quotes that evils of Moon get reduced or nullify to a large extent, if the Moon is full at birth time, especially those concerning with health. *Balarishta Yoga* loses its intensity if Moon is full. *Yogas* like *Gajkesari, Shakata, Chandra Mangal, Kemdrum, Anapha, Sunapha, Durdhara* and *Chandradhi Yogas* etc. involve Moon. Moon is a pivot for astrological judgement of the effects of transiting planets. To understand the effects of Moon one is required to study the exact influence of the combination of different planets with Moon.

9.9 The Sun and Moon jointly placed in Quadrant

(a) The Moon and Sun in the Ascendent

Conjuction or association of the Sun and Moon forms *"Koohoo Yoga"* that causes adversities. If the Moon is conjoined with the Sun in the ascendant, one will suffer in respect of his or her father and mother. The native may be separated from parents during childhood or may not get their affection and love. He may command respect in the society but may not accumulate wealth. Such a native suffers in respect of children, in one or the ther way. Humuliation or fear may be one of the causes of suffering due to own children.

However, such a native will be successful in mechanics and may earn money by manufacturing machines, spare parts and articles made of stone. The native will be expert in dealing in fermented drugs, spirits and liquids. He will be diplomatic in dealing resulting into a rich personality. However, females will influence such a native.

(b) Moon and the Sun in the 4th House

If the Moon is conjoined with the Sun in the 4th house, the native will be deprived of good relations and sons. The native is not intelligent and suffers financilly.

(c) Moon and the Sun in the 7th House

If these two luminaries are conjoined in the 7th house, the native is bereft of the sons and friends. He is always humuliated by females and remains frustrated due to desire for females.

(d) Moon and the Sun in the 10th House

The native will be blessed with an attractive physique

and will be head of many people. He will vanquish his opponents and rivals. He will be harsh and cruel and will be of uneven temperament. He will acquire large paraphernalia.

If these two occupy the 9th house, one will be rich. If they are in the 12th house, one may suffer eyesight or may even lose the sight of his eyes. The combination of the Sun and Moon is not generally good for promotion or financial aspect, except in the 9th house.

If the Sun and Moon occupy the same sidereal sign, they will be treated as conjoined with each other. Exact conjuctions will be there when both planets will have same longitudes and same sign.

Moon gives wealth if it is associated with Venus or Jupiter, more so with Jupiter. If Moon is associated with Mars, one will be prosperous but mental satisfaction may not be there, as Mars creates the desire always to have some thing more and new.

9.10 Moon and Jupiter

The combination of the Moon with Jupiter is a very positive factor for any horoscope. One will be laborious, knowledgeable, intelligent, optimistic, decent, honest, truthful, loyal, faithful and generous. If Jupiter falls in the ascendant and Moon falls in the 10th house, one may become a saint like man. He will be free from sins, lies, dishonesty, deception, distrust and negative approach. He will be pious and prosperous with a positive thinking and optimistic attitude. Mutual exchange of Moon and Jupiter, for Aries ascendant, will be the exchange of 4th lord Moon and 9th lord Jupiter, which will confer the same results but greater fortune, promotion of prosperity and financial aspect.

However, we believe that the combination will pronounce the best results only when full, strong and well aspected Moon is there. Moon, if placed favourably, as mentioned above at 180 degree from Jupiter, best results would come in evidence.

The ascendant denotes life and Moon denotes body and mind. In female nativity, Moon chart certainly plays a prominent role. For Libra *lagna,* the 9th lord Mercury, the 10th lord Moon and 11th lord the Sun, if conjoined together, will be quite beneficial and auspicious and the combination will result into high prosperity and immense professional and financial success.

Conjunction of Moon with nodes is very adverse, unless aspected by Jupiter. *Chandradhi yoga* is always advantageous and auspicious provided there is full Moon. Moon is a benefic for Aries, Cancer, Libra, Scorpio and Pisces ascendant. It gives wealth to Virgo ascendant. *Vasumati yoga* also gives immense wealth, if natural benefics occupy *upchayas,* either from ascendant or Moon. If benefic planets occupy 12th and 2nd houses, as reckoned from Moon, the *Durdhara Yoga* is formed, which is a combination of *Sunapha* and *Anapha Yoga.* This *Yoga* nullifies all adversities and gives wealth and prosperity.

Moon and Mercury are good for culture and generalism, information technology and computer science. Moon Venus are good for artistic talents, dance, fine arts and prosperity. The combination of the Sun and Moon does play a negative role, as explained above, and same happens with Moon and Saturn combination. But Moon Jupiter are best and bestow strong and noble aptitude.

•

CHAPTER-10

Business : The Best Occupation

Here we will make exclusive observations whether one will earn his or her livelihood through service or business. This is most important query in connection to profession, which almost every parent or guardian wants to know about their children.

Almost all classical works suggest that the judgement of vocation should be made from the 10th and other houses, from the ascendant or Moon, whichever is stronger. In this connection, we would like to quote following verses of great classic *'Jyotish Tatwam'* of Daivegya Mukund, in which the principles for the judgement of profession have been propounded very clearly and distinctly.

10.1 Independent Business

Following planetary position in the horoscope of the native result into independent occupation i.e. means of livelihood through business:-

व्यापारी खे मृगधरजनौ वाथ राज्ये शुभानां
दृष्ट्याधिक्येऽथ दिवि तनुपेऽथोदयाभ्रेशयोगे।
किं कृत्येशे मतिगुरुफले कण्टके चारुदृष्टे
तद्वत्खेशे नभसि सशुभे मानशीलस्तथा स्यात्।।

(*Jyotish Tattvam,* Ch-32, Vers-149)

If ascendant lord Mercury falls in the 10th house, the native is a trader. If the 10th house is aspected by several benefic planets, OR if ascendant lord occupies the 10th, OR lords of 10th and 1st are conjoined, OR fifth and ninth lords occupy the 11th house and 10th lord a quadrant, aspected by benefics, the native is a trader. If the 10th lord, conjoined with auspicious planets, occupies the 10th itself, the native is a recognized and respected businessman

खे ज्ञे व्यापारी।।
राज्येशुभदृष्ट्याधिक्ये व्यापारी।।
खाङ्गेशयोगे व्यापारी।।
खेऽङ्गेशे व्यापारी।।
खेशे केन्द्रायकोणे शुभदृष्टे व्यापारी।।

(*Jatak Tattvam,* Ch-3, Part-X, Vers-2 to 6)

- If Mercury occupies the 10th house the native is a trader.
- If several benefic planets aspect the 10th house, the person is a businessman.
- Native is engaged in a business, if the 10th and the ascendant lords conjoin in the birth chart.
- Lord of ascendant joining the 10th causes business to be the vocation of the native.
- If the lord of the 10th house occupies a quadrant, trine or the 11th house and is aspected by the benefic planets, the native is a tarder.

These are the specific rules for an individual to choose business as the means of livelihood. However, certain important observations are given below, which will help the readers to find out whether the business as an occupation will be suitable and appropriate for the native :

1. The Sun or Moon, or both must be strong for an independent business, laying industry and involving in consultation business.
2. Mercury is the main significator of business but the 2nd and 11th lords, or the planets placed therein, must also be taken into consideration.
3. The 7th house is 10th from the 10th and it indicates earning through business provided it has some concern with the 10th, 11th, 2nd or the 9th house. If the lords of the

7th and 10th are placed together, either in 2nd, 7th, 10th or 11th, the native will adopt business for his livelihood. If the 7th lord is connected, either by aspect or by conjunction or by mutual exchange of signs, *navamsa* or *nakshatras*, one will earn money through business.

4. If Mercury is strongly disposed in the 10th or 11th house, with *lagna* lord, or receives the aspect of the ascendant lord, one will be doing business.

5. Three or four planets, if well disposed in the 10th or 11th house, one is likely to do business, provided one of the planets owns the 2nd or the 7th house.

6. If Mercury joins the 10th house, identical to Gemini or Virgo, there is a strong possibility of doing business.

7. If 11th and 2nd lords are associated, in either of these houses, or in the 10th or 7th, one undertakes business as vocation of life.

8. If the lords of 2nd & 11th or both are associated with the 10th lord, one will be engaged in business, provided one of the lords aspects either of these houses.

9. If the 10th and 11th lords, or the 10th and 2nd lords, occupy 11th or 2nd house or exchange their houses, the means of livelihood will be business and not service.

10. If the lords of the 2nd or 9th, or both, occupy the 7th house, with the 7th lord, one will earn money through business.

11. If the 5th and 11th lords are placed with each other in the 11th or 10th house, one will undertake business.

12. If the 7th and the 10th lords are placed in either of these houses or aspect each other or if both lend aspect over the 10th or 11th house, one earns through business.

13. Combination of the lords of the 10th and 11th or 1st and 11th or 1st and 10th or 7th and 10th or 7th and 11th or 11th and 2nd or 7th and 11th lords, by way of conjunction or aspect or exchange of houses, makes one a business-

man. Mercury does play a prominent role along with strong Sun.

14. Thus, if the lord of the 2nd house joins the 10th house, with 11th lord, one will earn through business. If Mercury is also involved, by conjunction or aspect, or due to exchange of sign or *navamsa*, that will strengthen the combination of a business person.

15. If the 9th and the 10th lords are associated in the 7th house and Mercury has an influence over the 7th or the 10th, the subject will earn money through business.

16. It has been found that one can become a successful businessman only if the Sun is strong and well disposed.

It is not sufficient to find out whether one will be engaged in service or business. It is essential to find out whether one will become an Engineer, Doctor, I.A.S., I.P.S., Journalist, Advocate, Industrialist, Bank Employee, Clerk, Gazetted Officer or Manager. These all points with regard to professional aspect have been dealt exhaustively in our book 'Astro-equations for specific professions'. Now, if the business is indicated, one must know in what kind of business he will be successful? Which business will suit him? He should deal in automobile or should invest in a rolling mill for his own business or the native should lay down a factory. Should he deal in Gold, Ornaments, Gems, Petrol Pump, Glass, Textile, Rubber, Iron, Wood, Fertilizer, Medicines, Hotels or the like?

The following verse of '*Jaatak Parijaat*' has made it clear that what kind of business will be appropriate for the native.

10.2 How the planets affect the vocation

भैषज्योर्णतृणाम्बुधान्यकनकव्यापारमुक्तादिकै -
रन्योन्यागमदूतवृत्तिभिरिनस्यांशे तु जीवत्यसौ ।।

जलोद्भवानां क्रयविक्रयेण कृषेश्च मृद्धाद्यविनोदमार्गात् ।
राजाङ्गनासंश्रयवित्तरूपान्निशाकरांशे वसनक्रयाद्वा ।।

धातोर्विवादेन रणप्रकारात् स्तब्धाग्निवादात् कलहप्रवृत्त्या ।
जीवत्यसौ साहसमार्गरूपाद् धरासुतांशे यदि चौरवृत्त्या ।।

शिल्पादिकाव्यागमशास्त्रमार्गाज्ज्योतिर्गणज्ञानवशाद् बुधांशे ।
परार्थवेदाध्ययनाज्जपाच्च पुरोहिताद्याज्यवशात् प्रवृत्तिः ।।

जीवांशके भूसुरदेवतानामुपासनाध्यापकरूपमार्गात् ।
पुराणशास्त्रागमनीतिमार्गाद्धर्मोपदेशैरकुसीदमाहुः ।।

सुवर्णमाणिक्यगजाश्वमूलाद् गवां क्रयाज्जीवनमाहुरार्याः ।
गुडौदनक्षारदधिक्रयेण स्त्रियाः प्रलोभेन भृगोः सुतांशे ।।

शन्यंशके कुत्सितमार्गवृत्त्या शिल्पादिभिर्दारुमयैर्वधाद्यैः ।
विन्यस्तभाराज्जनविप्रलम्भादन्योन्यवैरागममार्गमूलात् ।।

(*Jatak Parijat,* Ch-15, Vers-44 to 50)

Seven combinations have been enumerated:

1. If the 10th lord, from the Moon or the ascendant, obtains the *navamsa* of Sun, the native earns his livelihood through medicines, wool, woolen clothes, grass, cereals growing in water, trading in gold, pearl, or as an emissary.

2. If the 10th lord, from the Moon or the ascendant, obtains the *navamsa* of Moon, the native earns his livelihood through trading in pearls, water chest nut, and fish etc. Such native earns money from agriculture, earthen pots and toys, instrument of music and entertainment, manufacture of clothes or the favour of queen.

3. If the 10th lord, from the Moon or the ascendant, obtains the *navamsa* of Mars, the native earns money by dealing or trading in gold, through conflict, war, coal, art, acts of courage or by stealing things.

4. If the 10th lord, from the Moon or the ascendant, obtains the *navamsa* of Mercury, the native earns his livelihood through craft and sculpture, art, writing books, manufacturing clothes, poetry, knowledge of *shastras,*

astrology, performing worship for others (*Pandit*), study of Vedas and chanting of Mantras.

5. If the 10th lord, from the Moon or the ascendant, obtains the *navamsa* of Jupiter, the native earns his livelihood through worship of *Devtas* or Brahmins, teaching, *Shastras* and *Puranas*, preaching of religion and interest on money.
6. If the 10th lord, from the Moon or the ascendant, obtains the *navamsa* of Venus, the native earns his livelihood through dealing in gold, pearl or gems, jaggery, sugar, curd, cows, entertainment means like cinema and favour of ladies.
7. If the 10th lord, from the Moon or the ascendant, obtains the *navamsa* of Saturn, the native earns his livelihood through condemned acts, wood work, murder, torturing others, carrying loads, cheating others and by provoking conflicts.

These results have been envisaged only on the basis of *navamsa* of the 10th lord, as reckoned from the Moon or the ascendant. However *navamsa* of the 10th lord from the Sun would also give the same result.

10.3 Horoscopes of Businessmen

Illustration : 10.1 *Horoscope No.: 37*

Date of birth : 27.07.1987 Time of birth : 10:32:00 hrs
Place of birth : Lucknow Lat 26:50:00 N Long 80:54:00E
Ayanamsa : 23:40:59 Sidereal Time : 6:43:00

Pln	Degree	Rasi	Nakshatra	Pad
Asc	15:55:06	Vir	Hasta	2
Sun	9:58:32	Can	Pushya	2
Mon	24:41:36	Can	Aslesa	3
Mar (C)	19:23:19	Can	Aslesa	1

Mer	20:13:04	Gem	Punarvasu	1
Jup	5:08:33	Ari	Ashwini	2
Ven (C)	2:31:58	Can	Punarvasu	4
Sat (R)	21:16:27	Sco	Jyestha	2
Rah (R)	10:23:24	Pis	U Bhadrapad	3
Ket (R)	10:23:24	Vir	Hasta	1

Lagna Chart

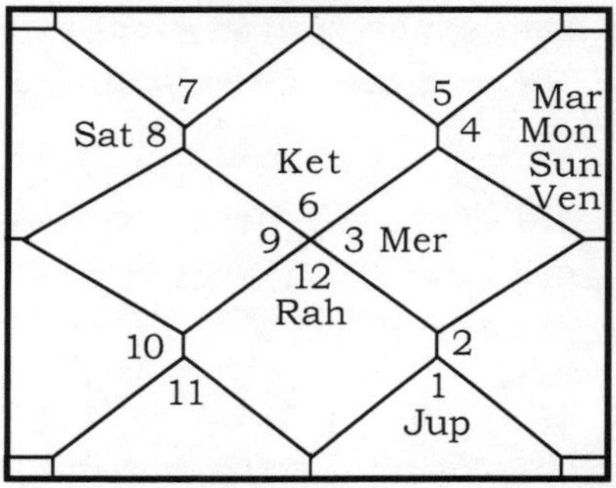

Navamsa Chart

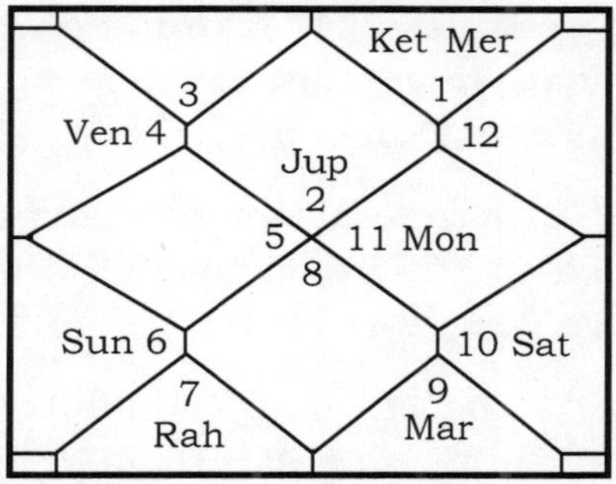

Balance of Vimshottari Dasa of **Mer 6Y 9M 5D**

The native is elder son of an industrialist, who is running a biscuit factory along with many other businesses. The business of biscuit factory was continuously running in loss. We advised him to transfer the proprietorship to his son as soon as he was 21 years of age and to withdraw himself completely. He followed our advice. The son, whose horoscope we are dealing, worked very hard and started earning profit of Rs. 25 to 50 lacks per month. It was unbelievable for his father, as the factory was facing losses continuously and he wanted to dispose it off.

The planetary position in the birth chart of this young man of 21 years of age is extremely encouraging.

He was born in Virgo ascendant, which obtains Taurus *navamsa*. The ascendant lord Mercury occupies its own sign Gemini in the 10th house, giving rise to *Bhadrika Mahapurusha Rajyoga* justifying business as his occupation.

Rule - If Mercury joins the 10th house, identical to Gemini or Virgo, there is a strong possibility of doing business.

The 11th house is very well disposed as it is occupied by four planets, the Sun, Mars, Moon and Venus and that too without any malefic aspect. A well disposed 11th house shows that the native will be very rich person by earning money through business.

Rule – If 11th and 2nd lords are associated, in either of these houses, or in the 10th or 7th, one undertakes business as vocation of life.

In this chart, the 2nd and 9th lord Venus is placed together with 11th lord Moon, 3rd lord Mars and the 12th lord Sun. This is a very strong *Vasumati* and *Dhana Yoga*.

The 11th lord Moon falls in *Aslesa* and obtains Saturn's *navamsa* and Saturn falls in Scorpio in *Jyestha* ruled by Mercury. This also shows business as occupation.

The 2nd lord Venus obtains *navamsa* of Moon and 7th lord Jupiter obtains *navamsa* of Venus, which tend him towards the business of Milk Dairy and products of milk like Ghee, Dry milk powder etc. Moon is *Atmakaraka* planet and obtains Saturn's *navamsa*. Therefore, the native is likely to undertake the business signified by Saturn as well, like contractor ship, dealing in real estate business, making roads, rolling mill of steel, oil manufacturing, woolen blanket manufacturing etc. Lord of the ascendant and 10th house, Mercury, falls in *Punarvasu* and obtains *navamsa* of Mars and this is an indication of the extremely bright future of this 21 year old boy, who is very confident of himself. This signifies the business of biscuits, lands, property as well as dealership of automobiles, petrol pumps etc.

Illustration : 10.2 *Horoscope No.: 38*

Date of birth : 02.06.1944 Time of birth : 02:15:00 hrs
Place of birth : Peshawar Lat 34:02:00 N Long 71:37:00E
Ayanamsa : 23:04:34 Sidereal Time : 17:12:08

Pln	**Degree**	**Rasi**	**Nakshatra**	**Pad**
Asc	18:40:23	Aqu	Satabhisha	4
Sun	18:04:39	Tau	Rohini	3
Mon	19:02:32	Vir	Hasta	3
Mar	12:51:01	Can	Pushya	3
Mer	23:49:51	Ari	Bharani	4
Jup	27:29:07	Can	Aslesa	4
Ven (C)	11:10:17	Tau	Rohini	1
Sat	4:32:19	Gem	Mrigshira	4
Rah (R)	5:43:04	Can	Pushya	1
Ket (R)	5:43:04	Cap	Uttarasadha	3

Lagna Chart

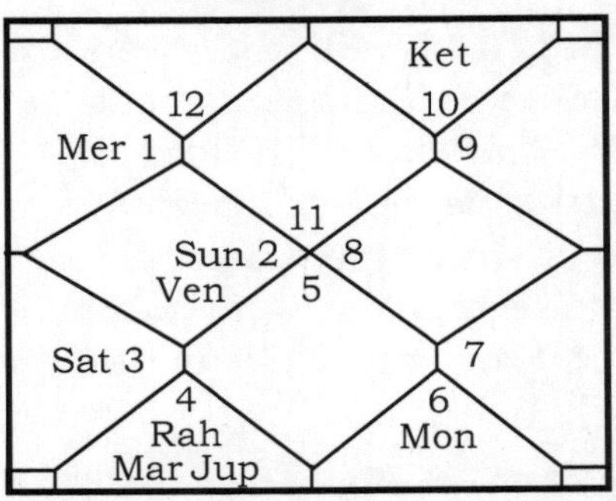

Navamsa Chart

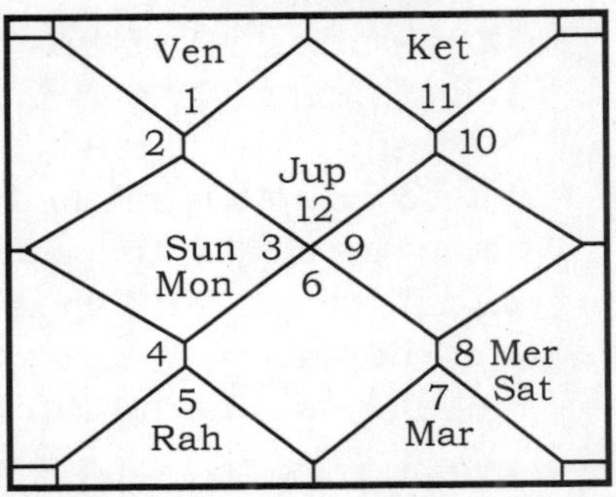

Balance of Vimshottari Dasa of **Mon 3Y 2M 18D**

The native is running a pharmaceutical company and has earned enormous money. He owns lot of immovable property and is a self made man too.

The native was born in Aquarius ascendant, whose lord

Saturn is posited in the 5th house in Gemini and lends its aspect over the 7th, 11th and 2nd house having their own important role in earning money through business.

1. The 7th house has a great importance in the birth chart of businessmen. It's lord, the Sun, is conjoined with 4th and 9th lord *yogakaraka* Venus, in the 4th house itself and both lend their aspect over the 10th house. The Sun is the significator of medicines whereas Venus represents chemicals.

2. The lord of the 10th house Mars, and 11th and 2nd lord Jupiter are placed together in the 6th house in Cancer. The 10th house receives the aspect of Jupiter, Sun and Venus and is owned by Mars. This is a strong combination of manufacturing medicines. Jupiter signifies herbs, recovery, healing etc. whereas the Sun and Mars indicate medicines, treatment, illness, fever, cold, injury, operation etc. including life force, energy, strength, actions and alertness. Venus shows chemical, which are used in manufacturing medicines. Thus, the combination of business of manufacturing medicines is strongly present in this birth chart.

3. Luminaries must be strong and well disposed for independent work and business etc. The Sun obtains 1.58 and Moon obtains 1.25 *Shadabalas*. The lord of 11th and 2nd Jupiter is *Atmakaraka* planet and obtains own *navamsa* Pisces and also lends its aspect over the 10th and 2nd house. Jupiter is the second strongest planet in this horoscope and its position very well justifies a business of Pharmaceuticals.

   Rule – If the lords of 2nd& 11th or both are associated with the 10th lord, one will be engaged in business provided one of the lord aspects either of these houses.

   If the 10th and 11th lords, or the 10th and 2nd lords, occupy 11th or 2nd house or exchange their houses, the means of livelihood will be business and not service.

4. Here the 10th lord Mars and 11th and 2nd lord Jupiter are placed together in the 6th house and Jupiter aspects both these houses justifying business as occupation.

Illustration : 10.3 *Horoscope No.: 39*

Date of birth : 18.09.1961 Time of birth : 18:54:00 hrs
Place of birth : Lucknow Lat 26:50:00 N Long 80:54:00E
Ayanamsa : 23:19:10 Sidereal Time : 18:36:30

Pln	**Degree**	**Rasi**	**Nakshatra**	**Pad**
Asc	19:21:59	Pis	Revati	1
Sun	2:03:54	Vir	U Phalguni	2
Mon	11:06:01	Sag	Moola	4
Mar	27:47:14	Vir	Chitra	2
Mer	26:16:07	Vir	Chitra	1
Jup (R)	4:02:25	Cap	Uttarasadha	3
Ven	0:30:44	Leo	Magha	1
Sat (R)	29:59:12	Sag	Uttarasadha	1
Rah	3:38:53	Leo	Magha	2
Ket	3:38:53	Aqu	Dhanistha	4

Lagna Chart **Navamsa Chart**

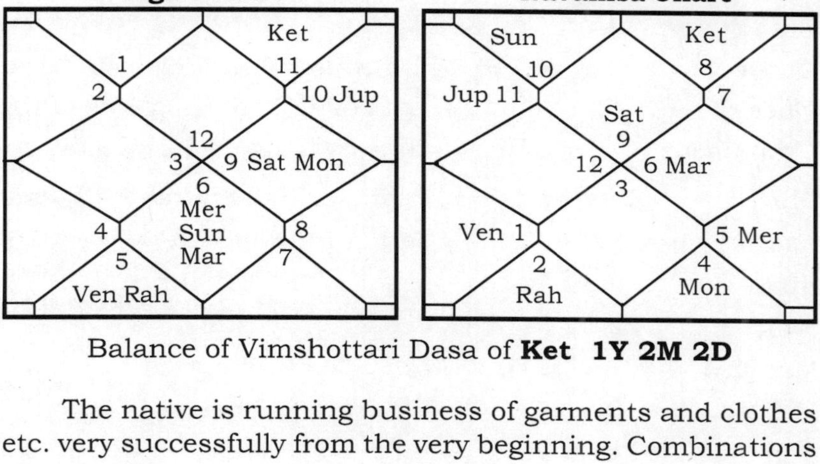

Balance of Vimshottari Dasa of **Ket 1Y 2M 2D**

The native is running business of garments and clothes etc. very successfully from the very beginning. Combinations of earning money through business are very clear in this horoscope.

There is mutual exchange between the lords of the 10th Jupiter and 11th Saturn, which shows that the native will adopt business, which is an important and positive planetary position for business.

The 7th house should be examined along with the 10th, 11th and 2nd house for success in business.

The Sun, Mercury and Mars are placed together in the 7th house, where Mercury is exalted. Here, Mars is the lord of 2nd and 9th house, and joins the 7th house with the 7th lord, directing the native to undertake business as means of livelihood.

Rule – If the lords of the 2nd or 9th or both occupy the 7th house with the 7th lord, one will earn money through business.

The Sun and Moon are strong but Moon is the strongest planet and obtains 1.39 *Shadabalas* and joins *Atmakaraka* Saturn, which is the 2nd strongest planet, in the 10th house.

Rule – Thus, the 5th and 11th lords, if placed with each other in the 11th or 10th house, one will undertake business.

Illustration : 10.4 *Horoscope No.: 40*

Date of birth : 01.09.1957 Time of birth : 22:47:00 hrs

Place of birth : Lucknow Lat 26:50:00 N Long 80:54:00E

Ayanamsa : 23:16:09 Sidereal Time : 21:22:59

Pln	Degree	Rasi	Nakshatra	Pad
Asc	10:38:20	Tau	Rohini	1
Sun	15:42:54	Leo	P Phalguni	1
Mon	22:02:31	Sco	Jyestha	2
Mar (C)	22:17:34	Leo	P Phalguni	3
Mer (R)	0:31:45	Vir	U Phalguni	2
Jup	11:40:06	Vir	Hasta	1

Ven	21:52:52	Vir	Hasta	4
Sat	14:45:33	Sco	Anuradha	4
Rah	19:28:00	Lib	Swati	4
Ket	19:28:00	Ari	Bharani	2

Lagna Chart

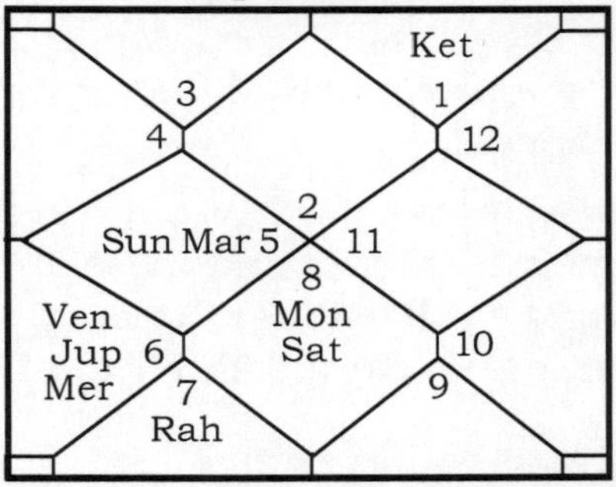

Navamsa Chart

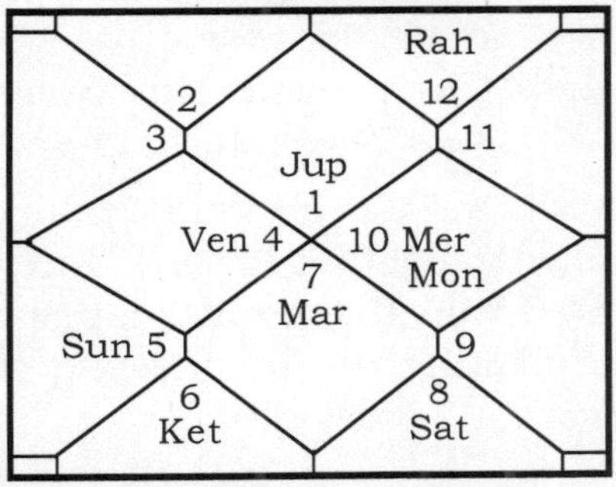

Balance of Vimshottari Dasa of **Mer 10Y 1M 23D**

The native is extremely polite, highly generous and very noble businessman, who is running a huge printing press and has recently started his own publication. He is God fearing, bright, sharp and highly intelligent, handsome young man and his press is well equipped with most modern equipments and machines.

The native was born in Taurus ascendant falling in Aries *navamsa*. The 2nd and 5th lord Mercury is closely associated with ascendant lord Venus and 11th lord Jupiter in the 5th house, corresponding with Virgo sign. This is a strong combination of earning money through business or by entering into independent work. The Sun must be well disposed and strong, for choosing business as vocation. In the birth chart, the Sun occupies his own sign Leo in the 4th house and obtains 1.66 *Shadabalas*. The 9th and the 10th lord Saturn occupies the 7th house, identical to Scorpio sign. In fact, Saturn obtains *vargottam navamsa* and falls in own constellation *Anuradha*. Saturn, in Scorpio, aspects the 9th house, the ascendant, the 4th house, the Sun and the 7th lord Mars. This indicates printing and publication.

Rule – If the 7th and the 10th lords are placed in either of these houses or aspect each other or if both lend aspect over the 10th or 11th house, one earns through business.

In this chart, 7th lord Mars and the 10th lord Saturn aspect each other, corresponding to the 7th and 4th house. The 7th lord Mars aspects the 7th, 10th and 11th, whereas the 9th and 10th lord Saturn aspects the 9th, the ascendant and the 4th house with Mars. Thus, the profession of the native will be entrepreneurship or business.

The ascendant lord Venus and 11th lord Jupiter are placed together in Virgo with exalted Mercury and these are 5th from ascendant aspecting the 11th house, strongly indicating the business of Printing Press and Publication work.

Rule – Combination of the lords of the 10th and 11th, or 1st and 11th, or 1st and 10th, or 7th and 10th, or 7th and 11th, or 11th and 2nd, or 7th and 11th, by way of conjunction or aspect or exchange of house, makes one a businessman. Mercury does play a prominent role along with strong Sun.

Illustration : 10.5 *Horoscope No.: 41*

Date of birth : 29.07.1981 Time of birth : 15:49:00 hrs
Place of birth : Lucknow Lat 26:50:00 N Long 80:54:00E
Ayanamsa : 23:35:44 Sidereal Time : 12:10:32

Pln	Degree	Rasi	Nakshatra	Pad
Asc	27:21:24	Sco	Jyestha	4
Sun	12:36:03	Can	Pushya	3
Mon	19:53:05	Gem	Ardra	4
Mar	13:49:44	Gem	Ardra	3
Mer (C)	29:45:48	Gem	Punarvasu	3
Jup	12:07:11	Vir	Hasta	1
Ven	12:14:47	Leo	Magha	4
Sat	11:45:00	Vir	Hasta	1

Rah (C)	8:08:41	Can	Pushya	2
Ket	8:08:41	Cap	Uttarasadha	4

Lagna Chart

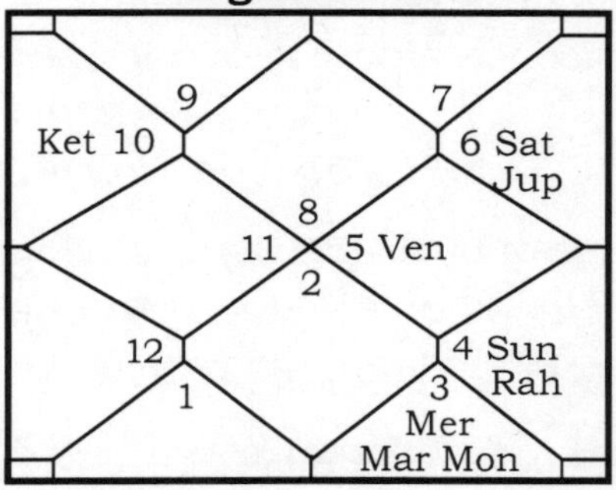

Navamsa Chart

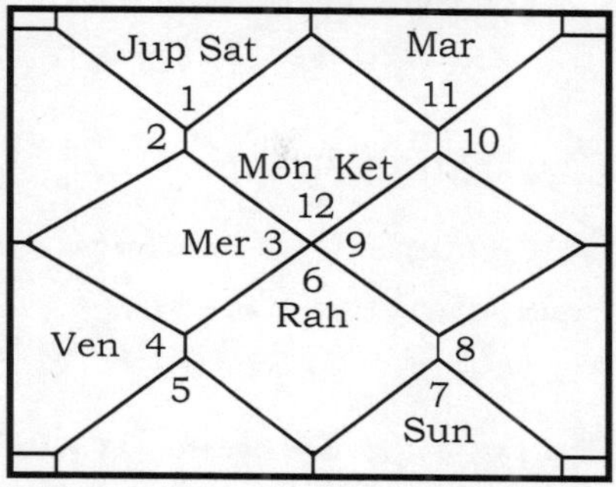

Balance of Vimshottari Dasa of **Rah 0Y 1M 26D**

The native is a dealer of many four wheelers. He has many branches in U.P. Mainly he deals with all cars of Maruti Motors. Following planetary combinations may be noted:

1. The native was born in Scorpio ascendant. The 7th lord Venus is posited in the 10th house and 10th lord Sun joins the 9th house. 11th house, Mercury and Jupiter indicate means of livelihood through business.

2. In this horoscope, Jupiter and Saturn join the 11th house, identical to Virgo ruled by Mercury. Venus obtains Moon's *navamsa* and the 11th lord Mercury obtains own *navamsa* and is *vargottam* as well. This shows that the native will earn his livelihood through business.

3. The 7th house is aspected by 2nd lord Jupiter. Thus, the 10th house is under the influence of significator of vehicles and 11th house is under the influence of 10th lord, 2nd lord Jupiter, 4th lord Saturn and *lagna* lord Mars, whereas 11th lord Mercury is quite strong and obtains *vargottam navamsa*.

4. The 10th lord Sun obtains the *navamsa* of Venus and falls in *Pushya nakshatra*. Moreover, the Sun is the strongest planet in this birth chart. Thus, the 10th lord

Sun is strongest, falls in Saturn's constellation *Pushya* and obtains *navamsa* of Venus, Libra. This strongly justifies that the native will be dealing in automobiles. He will be a successful, prosperous, famous, reputed trader dealing in Cars and concerning accessories etc.

Illustration : 10.6 *Horoscope No.: 42*

Date of birth : 04.05.1960 Time of birth : 12:00:00 hrs
Place of birth : Lucknow Lat 26:50:00 N Long 80:54:00E
Ayanamsa : 23:18:07 Sidereal Time : 02:42:11

Pln	**Degree**	**Rasi**	**Nakshatra**	**Pad**
Asc	23:05:18	Can	Aslesa	2
Sun	20:29:30	Ari	Bharani	3
Mon	23:03:07	Can	Aslesa	2
Mar	1:19:26	Pis	P Bhadrapad	4
Mer	5:53:28	Ari	Ashwini	2
Jup (R)	10:00:14	Sag	Moola	4
Ven	7:14:18	Ari	Ashwini	3
Sat (R)	25:05:27	Sag	Purvasadha	4
Rah	0:06:22	Vir	U Phalguni	2
Ket	0:06:22	Pis	P Bhadrapad	4

Lagna Chart

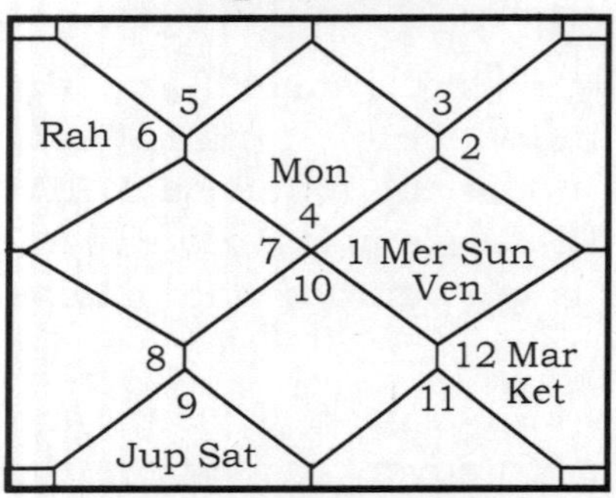

Navamsa Chart

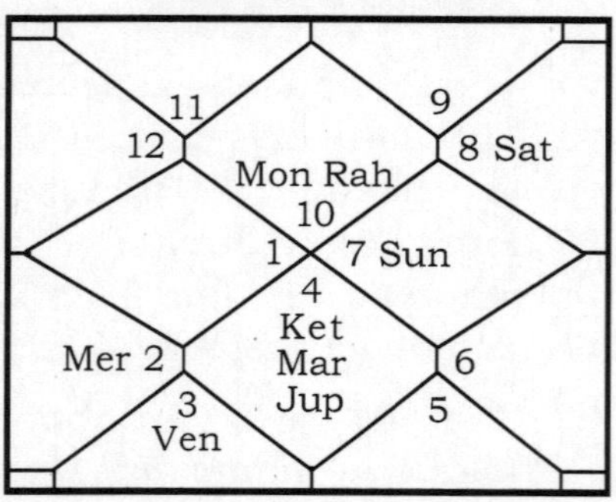

Balance of Vimshottari Dasa of **Mer 8Y 10M 9D**

The native is a young smart and bright businessman. After completing his education up to M.Sc. he entered in the parental business of gold ornaments and touched the apex within a short period.

He was born in Cancer ascendant with the placement of Moon therein. Mercury, the Sun and Venus occupy the 10th house. The Sun is the lord of the 2nd house and is conjoined with the 11th lord Venus in the 10th house. This represents that the native will undertake the business of jewels, gems and ornaments and he will earn good reputation, fame and honour because the Sun in the 10th house is not only exalted but it is unusually strong and obtains 2.15 *Shadabalas*. The Sun falls in the constellation *Bharani,* ruled by Venus, and obtains *navamsa* of Venus as well, and Venus is the main significator of ornaments and gems.

The Sun signifies gold and its conjunction with Mercury in the 10th house justifies the occupation of a gold merchant. The 9th lord Jupiter is associated with the *Atmakaraka* Saturn in the 6th house, in Sagittarius. Here, the 9th lord Jupiter aspects the 10th and the 2nd house, in addition to the 2nd lord Sun, 11th lord Venus and the 3rd lord Mercury, which is a powerful indication of becoming a successful and famous business man.

Atmakaraka Saturn occupies the constellation of Venus i.e. *Purvashadha* and sign of Jupiter and obtains *navamsa* of the 10th lord Mars. This represents educational institute and construction business as well. The native is in fact running a Computer College and is also involved in property dealing. The 10th and the 5th lord Mars is tenanted in the 9th house, in Pisces in *Purvabhadrapada* constellation i.e. sign and constellation ruled by the 9th lord Jupiter, which points out business having a concern with education. The lord of the 9th Jupiter and that of the 10th house Mars are in quadrant from each other and both obtain *navamsa* of Moon, where Jupiter is exalted. Mercury's placement in the 10th house, if well fortified, tends one to earn his livelihood through business. Here, Mercury which is placed in the 10th house, obtains *navamsa* of Venus, which again shows tendency of the business of ornaments and gem stone etc.

Rule - Thus, if the lord of the 2nd house joins the 10th house with 11th lord, one will earn through business. If Mercury is also involved, by conjunction or aspect or due to exchange of sign or navamsa, that will strengthen the combination of a business person.

Illustration : 10.7 *Horoscope No.: 43*

Date of birth : 01.07.1970 Time of birth : 19:19:00 hrs

Place of birth : Allahabad Lat 25:17:00 N Long 81:50:00E

Ayanamsa : 23:26:48 Sidereal Time : 13:53:08

Pln	**Degree**	**Rasi**	**Nakshatra**	**Pad**
Asc	22:07:23	Sag	Purvasadha	3
Sun	15:51:19	Gem	Ardra	3
Mon	22:10:44	Tau	Rohini	4
Mar (C)	25:44:57	Gem	Punarvasu	2
Mer (C)	9:20:38	Gem	Ardra	1
Jup	2:43:25	Lib	Chitra	3
Ven	23:55:58	Can	Aslesa	3
Sat	25:43:12	Ari	Bharani	4
Rah (R)	10:53:04	Aqu	Satabhisha	2
Ket (R)	10:53:04	Leo	Magha	4

Lagna Chart

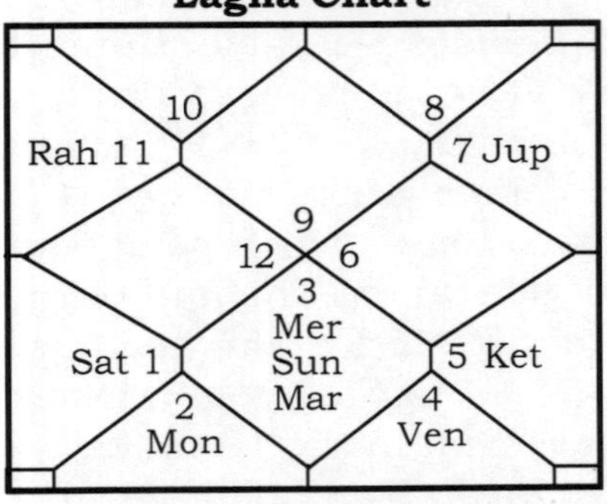

Navamsa Chart

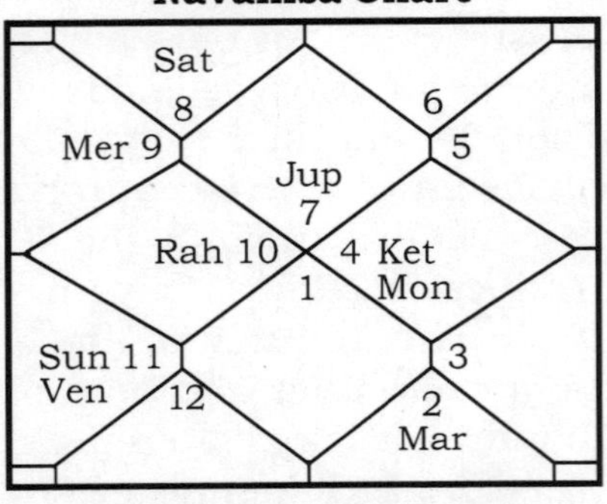

Balance of Vimshottari Dasa of **Mon 0Y 10M 11D**

The native is a highly skilled photographer of U.P. He struggled a lot on various fronts of life such as livelihood, marriage, health and family disputes etc. He is absolutely a self made man and has earned very good reputation of a highly skilled photographer.

1. The lord of the 7th and the 10th, Mercury, occupies the 7th house of its own, in association with the 9th lord Sun and the 5th lord, Mars. This is a very encouraging combination with regard to success in business. This is also an important planetary position for love marriage with a skilled and intelligent girl.
2. The planetary combination of the 7th house is aspected by the ascendant lord Jupiter, who obtains *vargottam navamsa* in Libra i.e. a sign of Venus, the significator of the art of photography.

Rule: If the 9th and the 10th lords are associated in the 7th house and Mercury has an influence over the 7th or the 10th, the subject will earn money through business.

Rule: It has been found that one can become a successful businessman only if the Sun is strong and well disposed.

In this birth chart, the Sun is very strong and obtains 1.58 *Shadabalas* beside the ownership of the 9th house and aspect of the ascendant lord Jupiter. This has given a great success to the native and made him a rich businessman dealing in art of photography.

Illustration : 10.8 *Horoscope No.: 44*

Date of birth : 19.01.1957 Time of birth : 00:00:00 hrs
Place of birth : Lucknow Lat 26:50:00 N Long 80:54:00E
Ayanamsa : 23:15:41 Sidereal Time : 7:45:10

Pln	Degree	Rasi	Nakshatra	Pad
Asc	0:08:03	Lib	Chitra	3
Sun	5:09:47	Cap	Uttarasadha	3

Mon	10:46:14	Leo	Magha	4
Mar	0:48:57	Ari	Ashwini	1
Mer (R)	18:40:29	Sag	Purvasadha	2
Jup (R)	8:31:46	Vir	U Phalguni	4
Ven	14:08:16	Sag	Purvasadha	1
Sat	17:49:34	Sco	Jyestha	1
Rah (R)	3:36:05	Sco	Anuradha	1
Ket (R)	3:36:05	Tau	Kritika	3

Lagna Chart

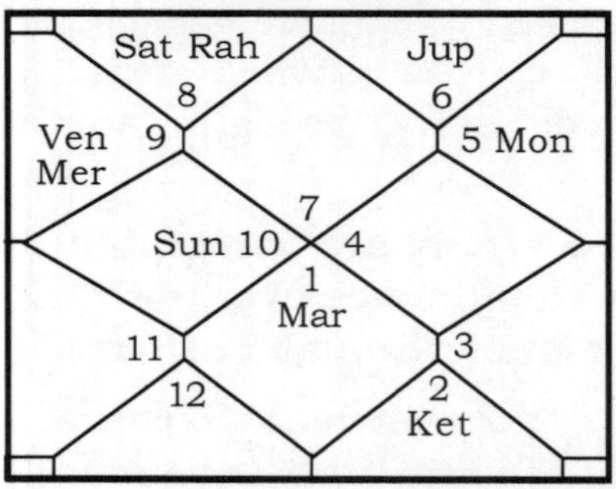

Navamsa Chart

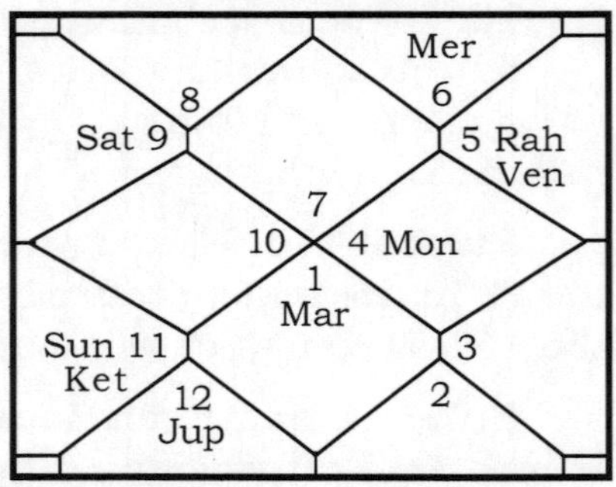

Balance of Vimshottari Dasa of **Ket 1Y 4M 4D**

The native is one of the richest and most successful businessman of U.P. dealing in gold and gem stones. Following planetary combinations may be noted:

1. The 7th house is 10th from the 10th house and 9th from the 11th house. Therefore, the 7th and 11th house play a prominent role in the birth charts of businessmen.
2. In this horoscope, 7th lord Mars is placed in the 7th house, in own sign, and obtains *vargottam navamsa*. Mars aspects the 10th house and the ascendant.
3. 10th lord Moon joins the 11th house in Leo and obtains own *navamsa*. Moon signifies silver.
4. In *navamsa* chart, Moon is aspected by Mars and Jupiter both. Mars is the strongest planet in this birth chart and

its placement in the 7th house in own *navamsa* shows that the native will be a very successful businessman. Mars obtain 1.3 *Shadabalas*, which is unusually strong. Mercury is also very strong, who is associated with Venus in the 3rd in Sagittarius. Mercury indicates business and Venus indicates the business of Gems, Jewels, Jewellery and ornaments etc. Both Venus and Mercury fall in the *Poorvashada* constellation ruled by Venus. The 10th house is aspected by Mars and the Sun. Thus, the lords of the 11th and the 7th house have an aspect over the 10th house, which confirms that the native will be a famous and successful Gold merchant.

5. *Yogakaraka* Saturn is posited in the 2nd house, in Scorpio, and aspects 10th lord Moon. Saturn falls in *Jyestha nakshatra* of Mercury and obtains Jupiter's *navamsa*, whereas Jupiter joins the sign of Mercury, Virgo, and obtains own *navamsa*. Jupiter and Saturn both aspect the 11th lord Sun. Thus, 11th house is under the influence of Saturn and Jupiter both, and the 10th house is under the influence of Sun, Mars and Moon, who are the lords of 11th, 7th and 10th. This is a combination of successful businessman dealing in Gold and Gem stones.

Illustration : 10.9 *Horoscope No.: 45*

Date of birth : 06.08.1957 Time of birth : 02:30:00 hrs
Place of birth : Muzaffarpur Lat 26:07:00 N Long 85:23:00E
Ayanamsa : 23:16:06 Sidereal Time : 23:38:05

Pln	**Degree**	**Rasi**	**Nakshatra**	**Pad**
Asc	12:53:36	Gem	Ardra	2
Sun	19:52:24	Can	Aslesa	1
Mon	27:06:54	Sco	Jyestha	4
Mar (C)	5:14:40	Leo	Magha	2
Mer	16:03:41	Leo	P Phalguni	1

Jup	6:30:54	Vir	U Phalguni	3
Ven	19:42:58	Leo	P Phalguni	2
Sat (R)	14:26:37	Sco	Anuradha	4
Rah (R)	22:14:28	Lib	Vishakha	1
Ket (R)	22:14:28	Ari	Bharani	3

Lagna Chart

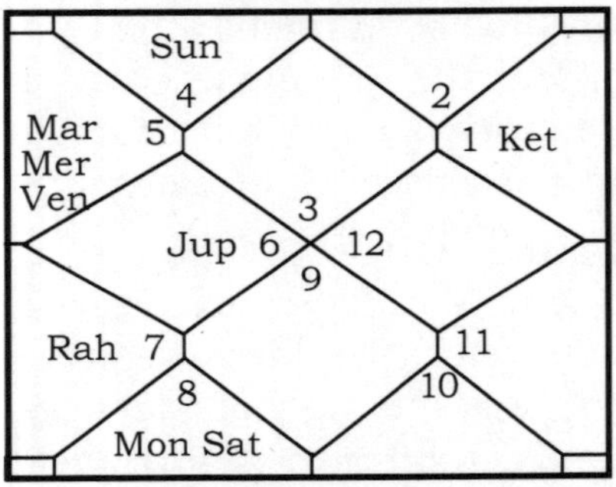

Navamsa Chart

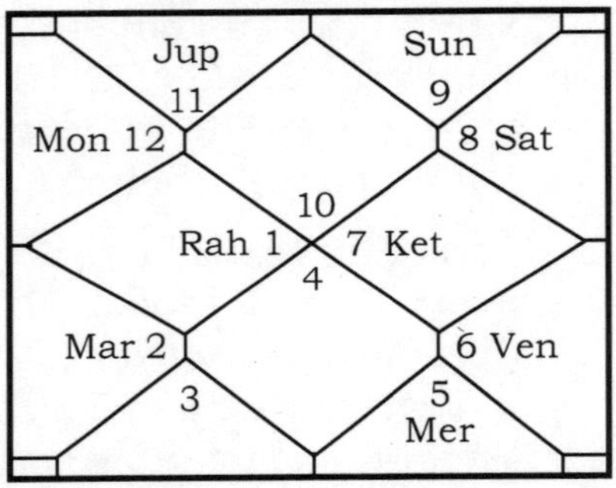

Balance of Vimshottari Dasa of **Mer 3Y 8M 4D**

The native was a dealer of automobiles. He had a steep rise and achieved the aim soon after entering into dealership of MARUTI. It was unfortunate that Cancer was diagnosed to him in the year 2004 and he could not be saved in spite of best kind of treatment.

1. The native was born in Gemini ascendant, which obtains Capricorn *navamsa*. The lord of 11th house Mars is associated with the ascendant lord Mercury and the 5th lord Venus, in the 3rd house, giving rise to a powerful *Vasumati Yoga*.

2. Lord of the 7th and 10th house, Jupiter, aspects the 10th house of its own.

3. The lord of the 2nd house Moon and 9th lord Saturn are placed together in the 6th house in Scorpio.

4. The Sun and Moon are the strongest planets in the birth chart as these obtain 1.36 and 1.55 *Shadabalas* respectively, and both fall in the constellations of

Mercury, *Aslesa* and *Jyestha* respectively. Mercury plays a prominent role in the birth charts of businessmen.

5. Here, the Moon is strongest and *Atmakaraka* and owns the 2nd house, falls in Scorpio in *Jyestha* constellation. Moon obtains *navamsa* of Jupiter. This should decide the nature of business, the native should undertake. Jupiter occupies the 4th house, identical to Virgo, and rules and aspects the 10th house. Jupiter obtains *navamsa* of Saturn and falls in the *Uttaraphalguni* constellation ruled by the Sun.

6. Mercury and Jupiter are the significators of business. Saturn, Venus and the Sun or Saturn, Venus and Mars are the significators of automobile business. The 10th lord Jupiter, placed in Virgo in *Uttraphalguni* and Saturn's *navamsa,* directs the native towards automobile business. The 4th house should also be involved there, as far as automobile business is concerned. Here, the lord of the ascendant and 4th house Mercury, and that of the 5th house Venus, are closely associated with the 6th and 11th lord Mars, in the 3rd house, and join the sign Leo of the significator Sun, and are aspected by the significator Saturn. This strongly denotes automobile business.

Illustration : 10.10 *Horoscope No.: 46*

Date of birth : 10.09.1963 Time of birth : 23:25:00 hrs
Place of birth: Kanpur Lat 26:27:00 N Long 80:19:00E
Ayanamsa : 23:20:43 Sidereal Time : 22:34:47

Pln	**Degree**	**Rasi**	**Nakshatra**	**Pad**
Asc	28:35:21	Tau	Mrigshira	2
Sun	23:56:59	Leo	P Phalguni	4
Mon	27:17:56	Tau	Mrigshira	2
Mar	5:33:58	Lib	Chitra	4
Mer (R)	11:02:27	Vir	Hasta	1

Jup (R)	24:29:07	Pis	Revati	3
Ven (C)	27:07:50	Leo	U Phalguni	1
Sat (R)	24:25:22	Cap	Dhanistha	1
Rah (R)	25:09:42	Gem	Punarvasu	2
Ket (R)	25:09:42	Sag	Purvasadha	4

Lagna Chart

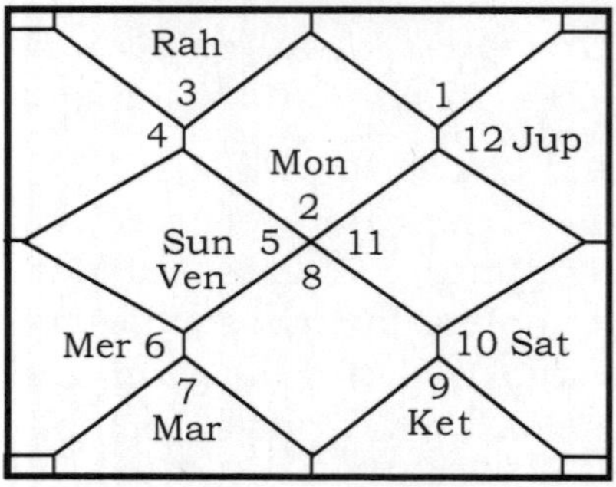

Navamsa Chart

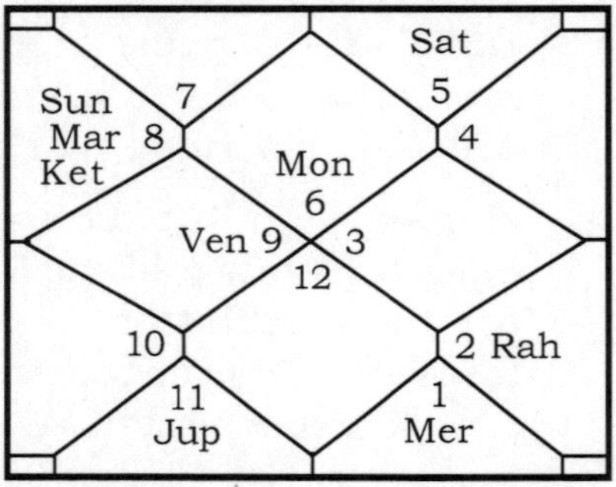

Balance of Vimshottari Dasa of **Mar 4Y 11M 0D**

The native started his career from an office contractor. He started his own independent business of the hardware at a very small scale and reached to apex within a period of 20 years. He is a multimillionaire businessman of Kanpur.

The native was born in Taurus ascendant, which obtains Scorpio *navamsa*. The Sun or Moon or both must be strong for a successful businessman and it is so in this birth chart. The lord of the 9th and 10th i.e. *Yogakaraka* Saturn occupies the 9th house of its own indicating the business of iron, steel, hardware etc.

The lord of the 11th house Jupiter joins the 11th house, whereas the lord of the 2nd and 5th house and significator Mercury occupies the 5th house. There is mutual aspect between 11th lord Jupiter and 2nd lord Mercury, corresponding with the 11th and 5th house and own signs. This confirms that the native will earn lot of wealth through business.

The ascendant lord Venus joins the 4th house in conjunction with the 4th lord Sun. Both, the Sun and Venus, aspect the 10th house. Moreover, the Sun obtains *navamsa* of Mars and falls in the constellation of Venus. Moon is *Atmakaraka* planet and falls in the constellation *Mrigshira,* ruled by Mars. Mars is the strongest planet in this birth chart. Therefore, the native's occupation must have an influence of Mars, Saturn, Mercury and Venus. The 10th lord, too, falls in *Dhanishtha* and obtains the *navamsa* of the Sun. This shows that apart from the business of Hardware, Steel, Glazed Tiles, Sanitary goods, he will also be dealing in automobile business. In fact, he is trying for the dealership of a well known and highly reputed two wheeler. He is also involved in various political activities, side by side.

•

CHAPTER-11
Profession of the Prospective Spouse

The most common question that an astrologer has to face every day is regarding the profession of the prospective partner. What will her husband do? Will he be in service or business? What kind of employment will he have? Will he be an IAS, Engineer or Doctor or he will be engaged in Defence Services or be an Advocate, Teacher, Musician, Writer or he will be an Industrialist etc. So many questions regarding the occupation of the husband are a matter of every day astrology. Let us analyze this very important aspect of astrology.

The 7th house, its lord, sign and *Navamsa* occupied by the 7th lord will decide the profession of the husband. The 4th house is 10th from the 7th house. Therefore, proper examination of the 4th house, its lord, the sign, *navamsa* and *nakshatra* occupied by the 4th lord and planets placed therein should be carefully examined, for the judgement of the profession of the husband. Jupiter is the significator or *Karaka* of husband. Therefore, much emphasis should be given to Jupiter while working out the occupation of the life companion. Profession of the husband may be examined as under.

11.1 Profession of the Husband

1st STEP

Planet or planets placed in the 7th house and the lord of the 7th house are quite important. Their sign, *navamsa* and *nakshatra* do play a vital role.

2nd STEP

Planet or planets placed in the 4th house, their sign, *navamsa* and *nakshatra* lord should be taken into consideration.

3rd STEP

Jupiter is the significator of the husband. Therefore, position of Jupiter is equally important and must be given due importance. The sign, *navamsa* and *nakshatra* occupied by Jupiter should also be analyzed properly.

Profession of the husband should be judged by the group of planets so arrived. Strong planets having an influence over the 7th house, 4th house and Jupiter should be considered and remaining places should not be taken into account while making the judgment of the occupation of the husband. This requires sufficient astrological knowledge and skill in the judgement of occupation of the life partner of a lady. So, proper skill and care must be applied before reaching any conclusion. The profession of the husband should be verified with the help of planetary combinations, so arrived at. Any profession or business is ruled by a group of planets which may be two, three or even four. The third or fourth planet will decide the exact branch of any particular profession. That does the sharp tuning and enables us to reach the final conclusion of the occupation of the husband.

Following illustrations will make the subject quite clear and distinct.

Illustration : 11.1 *Horoscope No.: 47*

Date of birth : 25.12.1970 Time of birth : 12:50:00 hrs
Place of birth : Bombay Lat 18:58:00 N Long 72:50:00E
Ayanamsa : 23:27:15 Sidereal Time : 18:24:54

Pln	Degree	Rasi	Nakshatra	Pad
Asc	14:30:31	Pis	U Bhadrapad	4
Sun	9:37:59	Sag	Moola	3
Mon	29:51:57	Lib	Vishakha	3

Mar	18:21:38	Lib	Swati	4
Mer (R/C)	17:10:05	Sag	Purvasadha	2
Jup	2:49:51	Sco	Vishakha	4
Ven	26:10:22	Lib	Vishakha	2
Sat (R)	22:44:25	Ari	Bharani	3
Rah (R)	1:35:10	Aqu	Dhanistha	3
Ket (R)	1:35:10	Leo	Magha	1

Lagna Chart

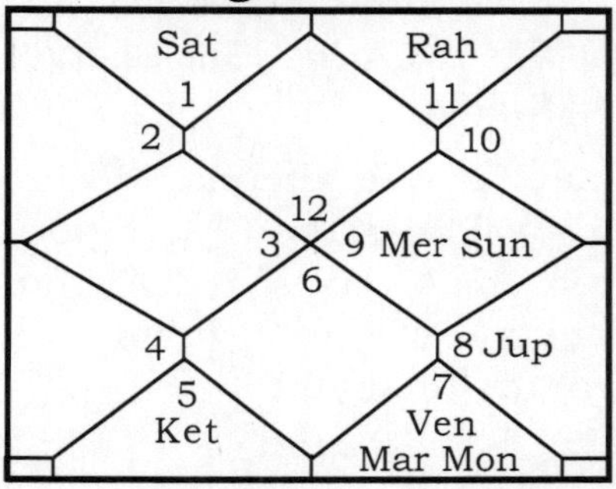

Navamsa Chart

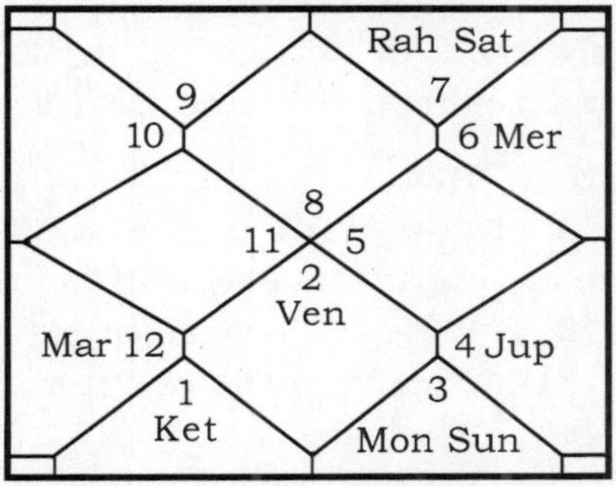

Balance of Vimshottari Dasa of **Jup 4Y 1M 28D**

She is an extremely charming, very fair, tall, slim and attractive girl and possesses an overall impressive personality. She is highly educated, largely travelled in various countries and is daughter of an IAS officer. She was married with a professional but was compelled to seek divorce within two years of her marriage. She was remarried in the latter half of 1997.

Placement of 2nd and 9th lord Mars in the 8th house with 8th lord Venus, in association with Moon, is mainly responsible for such a severe suffering in her life. Opposition of Mars and Saturn, identical to 8th and 2nd house, is always adverse for conjugal life.

The girl came to us in the year 1997 and asked, 'when will she be married'? After examining her horoscope, we told her that she was hiding the truth. She might have already been married and she would suffer separation and thereafter, could be married again during the sub-period of Venus in the major period of Mercury. She felt guilty as she concealed the truth and again asked that what would her husband do?

The lord of the 7th house Mercury joins the 10th house in Sagittarius and obtains own *navamsa* Virgo. Thus, Mercury is prominent in deciding profession of her husband. It was told to her that her husband would be in Accounts Services. He could either be in the Indian Audit and Accounts Service or a Chartered Accountant. She was again shocked as her earlier husband was a CA in USA. She got married second time with an IAAS officer.

Thus, the 7th lord, or planets placed therein, decide profession of the husband. *Navamsa* lord of the 7th lord does also play a vital role in this matter. The 4th house is 10th from the 7th house. Therefore, examination of the 4th house will further confirm the occupation of the husband.

Illustration : 11.2 *Horoscope No.: 48*

Date of birth : 29.02.1964 Time of birth : 11:30:00 hrs
Place of birth : Delhi Lat 28:39:00 N Long 77:13:00E
Ayanamsa : 23:21:06 Sidereal Time : 21:41:14

Pln	Degree	Rasi	Nakshatra	Pad
Asc	16:18:23	Tau	Rohini	2
Sun	16:19:54	Aqu	Satabhisha	3
Mon	7:18:10	Vir	U Phalguni	4
Mar (D)	13:42:19	Aqu	Satabhisha	3
Mer (C)	5:26:19	Aqu	Dhanistha	4
Jup	26:47:55	Pis	Revati	4
Ven	28:17:23	Pis	Revati	4
Sat (C)	3:54:59	Aqu	Dhanistha	4
Rah (R)	15:56:58	Gem	Ardra	3
Ket (R)	15:56:58	Sag	Purvasadha	1

Lagna Chart

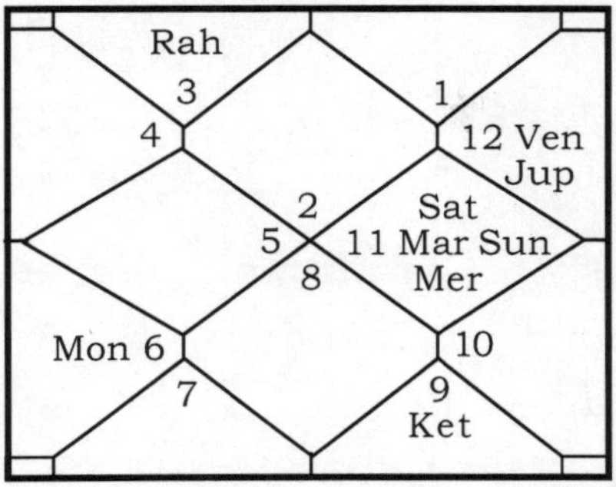

Navamsa Chart

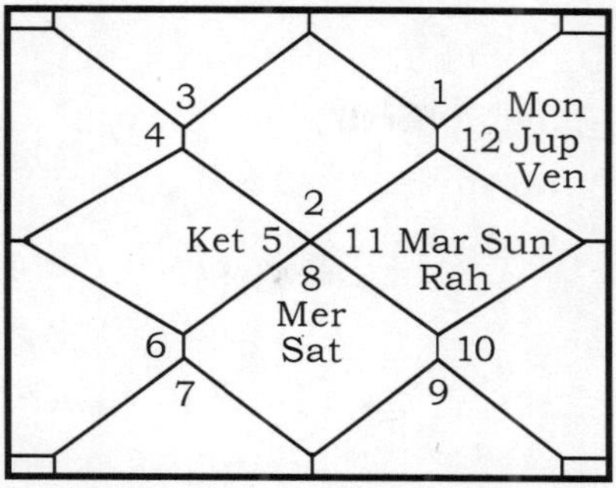

Balance of Vimshottari Dasa of **Sun 1Y 2M 17D**

She was born in the Taurus ascendant. She was married on 16.11.1983 with an Advocate and has been blessed with two sons born on 16.1.1985 and 4.1.1992. Lord of the 7th house, Mars, joins the 10th house in Aquarius and obtains *vargottam navamsa*. Mars falls in *Satbhisha nakshatra* which is ruled by Rahu and it is associated with Mercury, Saturn and the Sun. Moreover, the 7th house is aspected by Jupiter and Saturn simultaneously. Joint influence of Jupiter, Saturn and Mars on the 7th house indicates that her husband will be a law professional.

The 4th house is 10th from the 7th house, which should also be taken into consideration for the judgement of occupation of the husband. Here, 4th house is owned by the Sun, who falls in Saturn's sign Aquarius in *Satbhisha nakshatra* of Rahu and obtains *vargottam navamsa* as well. The Sun is under the influence of Saturn, Mercury and Mars. This confirms that her husband will be a dynamic law professional. In fact, her life partner is a lawyer and President of the Bar Council and is going to become a Judge soon.

Jupiter is the significator of the husband, who joins Jupiter's sign Pisces, with exalted Venus. Both are under *vargottam navamsa*, which further confirms the law profession of her spouse.

Illustration : 11.3 *Horoscope No.: 49*

Date of birth : 29.05.1951 Time of birth : 06:33:00 hrs
Place of birth : Shahjahanpur Lat 27:53:00 N Long 79:55:00E
Ayanamsa : 23:10:45 Sidereal Time : 22:43:37

Pln	Degree	Rasi	Nakshatra	Pad
Asc	1:38:47	Gem	Mrigshira	3
Sun	13:41:39	Tau	Rohini	2
Mon	28:19:25	Aqu	P Bhadrapad	3
Mar (D)	12:02:48	Tau	Rohini	1
Mer	19:32:10	Ari	Bharani	2
Jup	14:25:50	Pis	U Bhadrapad	4
Ven	26:56:28	Gem	Punarvasu	3
Sat (S)	2:21:38	Vir	U Phalguni	2
Rah (S)	22:09:11	Aqu	P Bhadrapad	1
Ket (S)	22:09:11	Leo	P Phalguni	3

Lagna Chart

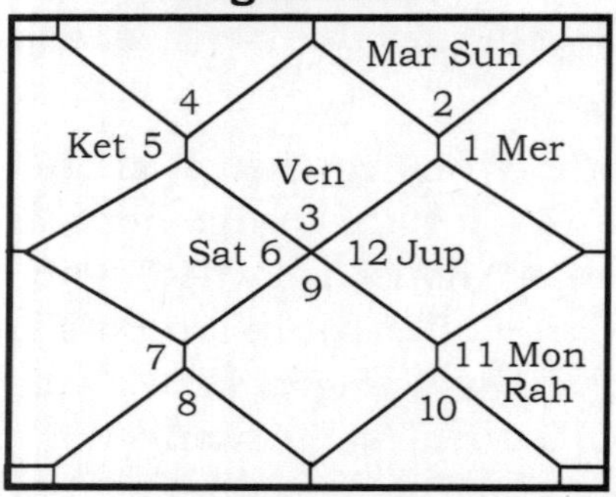

Navamsa Chart

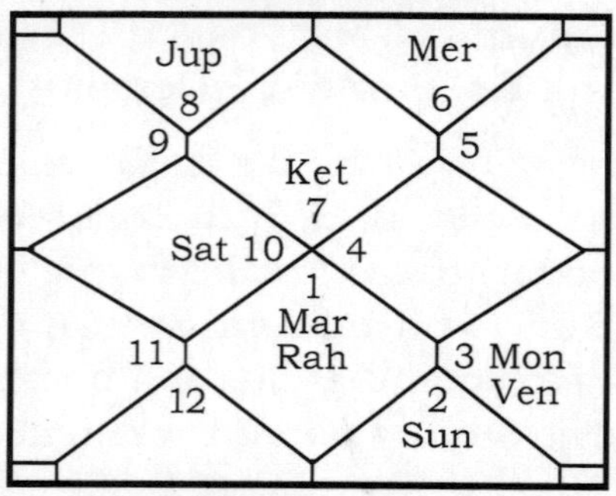

Balance of Vimshottari Dasa of **Jup 6Y 0M 4D**

She is the wife of a Regional Manager of Central Bank of India. Her marriage took place on 15.12.1974. She has been blessed with one son born on 27.9.1975 and two daughters born on 4.12.1976 and 20.9.1990 respectively.

The lord of the 7th house, Jupiter, falls in the 10th house

of its own i.e. in Pisces. The 7th lord Jupiter, who obtains *navamsa* of Mars, is aspected by 9th lord Saturn. Jupiter indicates Bank service or the teaching profession. Mars and Mercury indicate mathematics and accounts. The 4th lord Mercury falls in Aries i.e. in the sign of Mars. Thus, the profession of her husband is indicated by Jupiter, Mercury and Mars, which confirm bank service. Anyway, placement of Saturn in the 4th, in Virgo, under the aspect of Jupiter, could have also given her a law professional. Now, it should be compared as to which indication of the profession of her husband is stronger.

Here, it is certainly the service of bank or of a finance company is stronger. Involvement of the aspect of 8th lord Saturn signifies that her life partner will do government service. Jupiter is the significator of husband, who joins own sign Pisces and obtains *navamsa* of Mars which further justifies the law profession of her husband.

Illustration : 11.4 *Horoscope No.: 50*

Date of birth : 03.03.1976 Time of birth : 10:30:00 hrs
Place of birth : Lucknow Lat 26:50:00 N Long 80:54:00E
Ayanamsa : 23:31:40 Sidereal Time : 21:07:59

Pln	**Degree**	**Rasi**	**Nakshatra**	**Pad**
Asc	6:20:27	Tau	Kritika	3
Sun	19:13:28	Aqu	Satabhisha	4
Mon	13:42:01	Pis	U Bhadrapad	4
Mar	0:14:09	Gem	Mrigshira	3
Mer	26:55:46	Cap	Dhanistha	2
Jup	1:21:43	Ari	Ashwini	1
Ven	21:52:52	Cap	Sravana	4
Sat (R)	3:02:47	Can	Punarvasu	4
Rah (R)	20:52:35	Lib	Vishakha	1
Ket (R)	20:52:35	Ari	Bharani	3

Lagna Chart

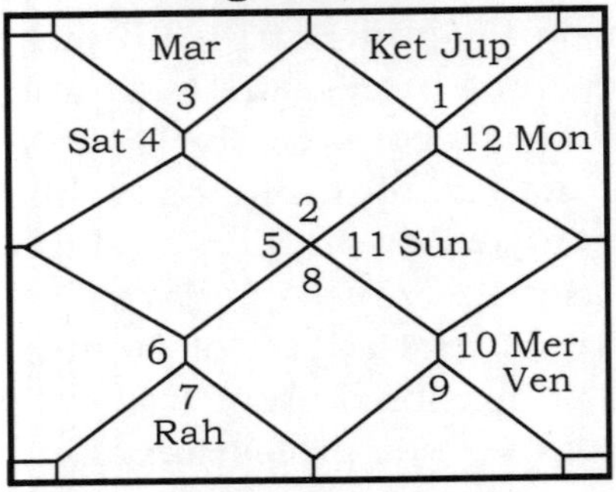

Navamsa Chart

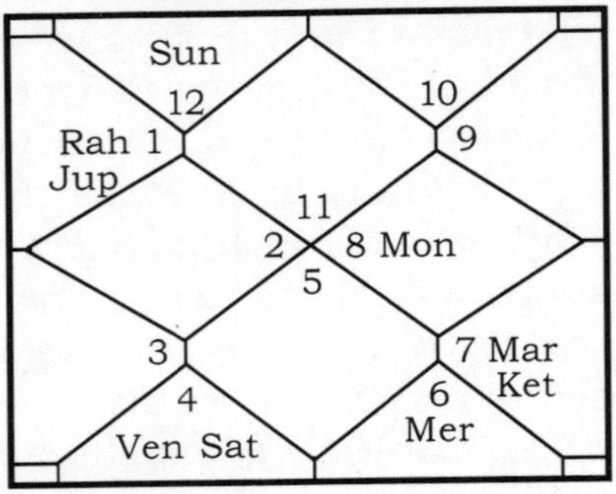

Balance of Vimshottari Dasa of **Sat 4Y 2M 21D**

She is a beautiful and charming girl. She had a deep love affair with a businessman and had gone a long way with him. She could not be married to that man as there is a clear indication that her husband will come from the Army. Ultimately, she was married on 27.11.1997 with a Major who is working in the Indian Army.

The lord of the 7th house, Mars, occupies the 2nd house, which indicates service of Police or the Army. Mars obtains *navamsa* of Venus and falls in its own constellation *Mrigshira.* This also confirms that her spouse will be an Army personnel. Placement of Mars, in Venusian sign Libra, shows authority and comfort. Therefore, her husband is an officer and not in force. The 4th house is owned by the Sun who occupies the 10th house and obtains Jupiter's *navamsa.* Here, Jupiter falls in Martian sign, Aries, under *vargottam navamsa.* Thus, the profession of her husband is governed jointly by Mars, Sun and Jupiter. Therefore, her husband could either be an Army officer or a Surgoen Doctor. Here, Saturn's involvement is also there as the 4th lord Sun falls in Aquarius. This shows the higher possibility of service because Saturn happens to be a *Yogakaraka* here. Jupiter is a *Karaka* of the husband, who falls in the sign of Mars, Aries, under *vargottam navamsa.* This is further verification that her husband will be an Army man.

Illustration : 11.5 *Horoscope No.: 51*

Date of birth : 11.02.1945 Time of birth : 22:15:00 hrs
Place of birth : Delhi Lat 28:39:00 N Long 77:13:00E
Ayanamsa : 23:05:10 Sidereal Time : 6:19:14

Pln	**Degree**	**Rasi**	**Nakshatra**	**Pad**
Asc	11:09:03	Vir	Hasta	1
Sun	29:29:07	Cap	Dhanistha	2
Mon	14:56:32	Cap	Sravna	2
Mar	4:47:43	Cap	Uttarasadha	3
Mer (C)	16:46:55	Cap	Sravna	3
Jup (R)	2:58:09	Vir	U Phalguni	2
Ven	16:03:38	Pis	U Bhadrapad	4
Sat (R)	11:12:10	Gem	Ardra	2
Rah (R)	24:58:09	Gem	Punarvasu	2
Ket (R)	24:58:09	Sag	Purvasadha	4

Lagna Chart

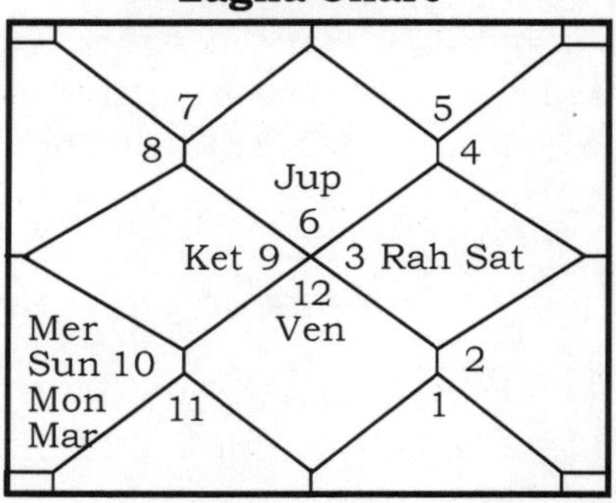

Navamsa Chart

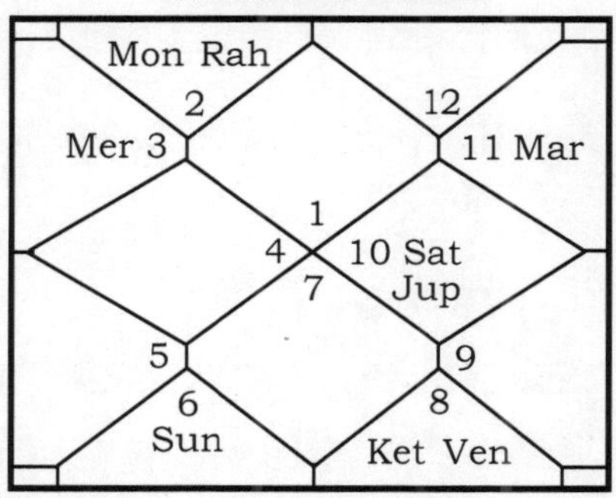

Balance of Vimshottari Dasa of **Mon 6Y 3M 15D**

Please see this horoscope of a most unfortunate lady. She was married after a small affair of liking, at 19 years of age, with a handsome person who was working as a Lecturer. The married life was extremely miserable. Her husband was always looking for various other females. She got divorce after long and torturous court case on 2.2.1990 but she got remarried with a Muslim IAS officer, on 19.12.1990, who loved her very much for 7 years. Both were separated from each other in early 1997.

Let us judge the profession of her husband. The 7th lord Jupiter aspects 7th house from *lagna* and exalted Venus is placed there in the 7th house. There is mutual aspect between Jupiter and Venus. The 4th house should also be analyzed for the judgement of job of the life partner. Here, the 4th house is owned by Jupiter and is aspected by Saturn. The 7th house and Venus also receive the aspect of Saturn. It means that the job of her husband will be governed mainly by Jupiter, which will also have the influence of Saturn and Venus. Main planet indicating profession of the husband obtains *navamsa* of Saturn. Thus, the husband should be a teacher of law or should be a lawyer. Jupiter, Venus and Saturn jointly indicate law. Here, Jupiter is playing a very prominent role as Jupiter is the significator and *Karaka* of profession. Jupiter falls in the sign of Mercury. The profession of the native, therefore, should be related with teaching. The involvement of Saturn indicates that he should be a government servant. The husband of the female was working as lecturer in a government college. This rules out the possibility of a lawyer and indicates that her life partner will be a teacher.

Illustration : 11.6 *Horoscope No.: 52*

Date of birth : 09.11.1924 Time of birth : 05:35:00 hrs
Place of birth : Chandausi Lat 28:06:00 N Long 77:50:00E
Ayanamsa : 22:48:14 Sidereal Time : 8:27:54

Pln	**Degree**	**Rasi**	**Nakshatra**	**Pad**
Asc	9:39:47	Lib	Swati	1
Sun	23:31:04	Lib	Vishakha	2
Mon	24:52:34	Pis	Revati	3
Mar	15:13:46	Aqu	Satabhisha	3

Mer (C)	1:47:44	Sco	Vishakha	4
Jup	28:32:30	Sco	Jyestha	4
Ven	14:48:24	Vir	Hasta	2
Sat (C)	13:41:22	Lib	Swati	3
Rah (R)	25:56:12	Can	Aslesa	3
Ket (R)	25:56:12	Cap	Dhanistha	1

Lagna Chart

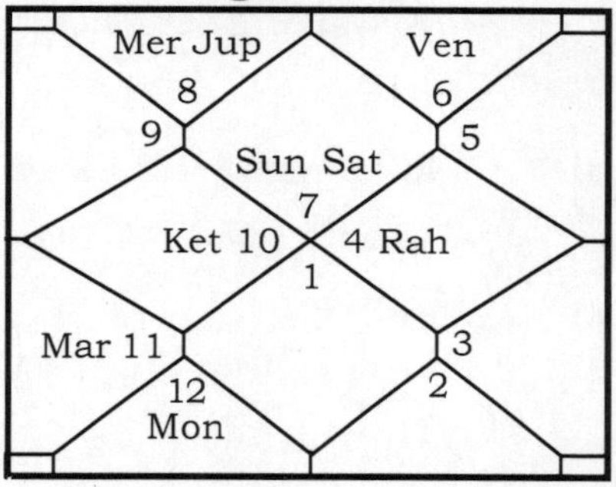

Navamsa Chart

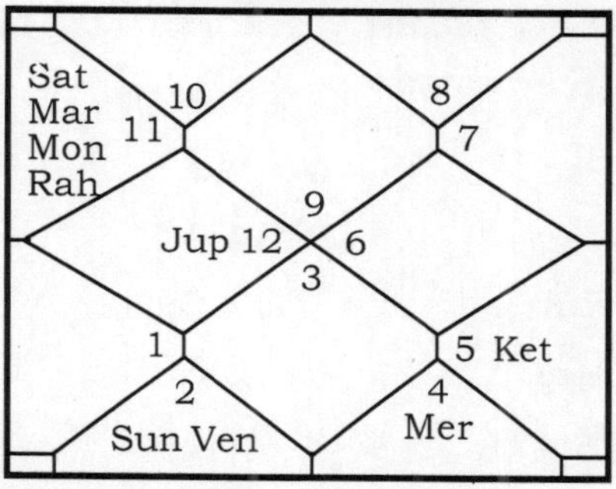

Balance of Vimshottari Dasa of **Mer 6Y 6M 12D**

She has Libra ascendent. Mars owns 7th house and joins Saturn's sign Aquarius. Saturn, who happens a *Yogakaraka* for Libra, falls in the *lagna,* in the sign of its exaltation, and lends aspect over the 7th house. Saturn also obtains own *navamsa*. The 7th lord Mars also obtains *navamsa* of Saturn. Thus, Saturn is quite prominent as regards the profession of her husband.

Now, let us analyze the 4th house which is equally important in determination of the profession of the husband. In this birth chart, Saturn is the ruler of the 4th house and aspets the 7th house, from its exalted position. Saturn indicates Engineering and involvement of Mars makes one a Civil Engineer. Here, Mars is the 7th lord and obtains Saturn's *navamsa* and Saturn is very powerful in reference to the 7th and 4th house. This indicates that her husband should be a civil engineer. In fact, the husband was a very famous and successful Civil Engineer in PWD. He lived like a king and established many economical designs of various structures. Jupiter, who is the significator of husband, joins the 2nd house in Scorpio whose lord Mars obtains the *navamsa* of Saturn. That further indicates that her husband would be a Civil Engineer.

Illustration : 11.7 *Horoscope No.: 53*

Date of birth : 21.04.1957 Time of birth : 03:52:03 hrs
Place of birth : Kanpur Lat 26:27:00 N Long 80:19:00E
Ayanamsa : 23:15:51 Sidereal Time : 17:38:14

Pln	**Degree**	**Rasi**	**Nakshatra**	**Pad**
Asc	29:11:10	Aqu	P Bhadrapad	3
Sun	7:17:29	Ari	Ashwini	3
Mon	25:53:50	Sag	Purvasadha	4
Mar	28:07:35	Tau	Mrigshira	2
Mer	25:17:21	Ari	Bharani	4
Jup (R)	29:45:16	Leo	U Phalguni	1
Ven (D)	8:56:41	Ari	Ashwini	3
Sat (R)	20:25:02	Sco	Jyestha	2
Rah	26:28:29	Lib	Vishakha	2
Ket	26:28:29	Ari	Bharani	4

Lagna Chart

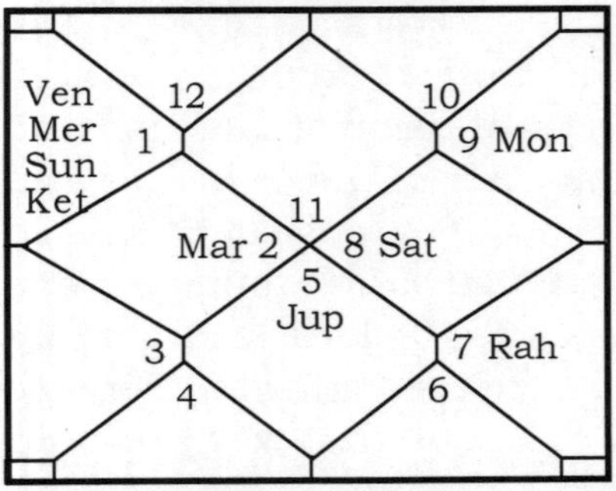

Navamsa Chart

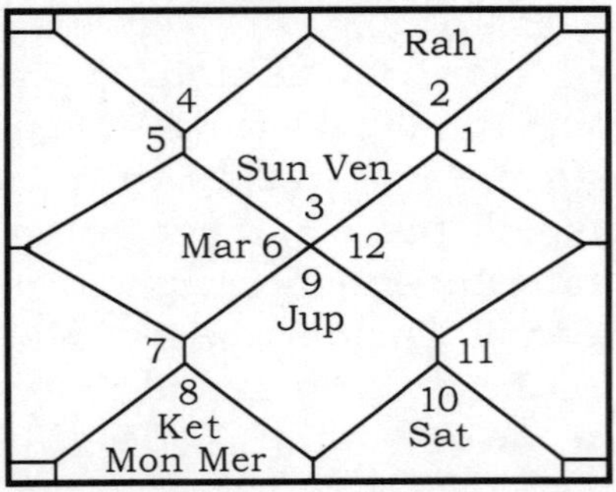

Balance of Vimshottari Dasa of **Ven 1Y 1M 25D**

This horoscope belongs to a beautiful lady, the wife of an Electrical Engineer, who worked as Chief Engineer in J.K. Later on, the husband began an industry of his own. He entered the plastic industry.

The 7th house is owned by Sun, who is exalted in the 3rd house. This indicates independent work of the husband and exaltation of the Sun will make the husband successful, famous, bold, engergetic and dynamic. Mars is posited in the 4th house and has mutual aspect with Saturn. Saturn and Mars, both, have an aspect over the 7th house. Thus, the influence of Mars, Saturn and Jupiter over the 7th house indicates that her husband will be learned and successful in various fields. Influence of Saturn, Mars, Sun and Jupiter over the 7th house indicates that her husband will be an Engineer and will become an industrialist after marriage. Jupiter, who is the *Karaka* of husband obtains own *navamsa.* 7th lord Sun joins the *navamsa* of Mercury. 4th lord Venus also obtains the *navamsa* of Mercury. When the involvement of Mercury is there, one tends towards the business and if Sun is also involved, he certainly takes up an independent profession. The involvement of Mars and Saturn over the profession of her husband made him industrialist. 7th lord Sun gives clue for independent work. The Sun and Mars, both, obtain *navamsa* of Mercury, owned by Venus, which confirms the business of plastic.

Illustration : 11.8 *Horoscope No.: 54*

Date of birth : 02.07.1963 Time of birth : 01:55:00 hrs

Place of birth : Delhi Lat 28:39:00 N Long 77:13:00E

Ayanamsa : 23:20:33 Sidereal Time : 20:10:33

Pln	**Degree**	**Rasi**	**Nakshatra**	**Pad**
Asc	20:49:28	Ari	Bharani	3
Sun	15:55:48	Gem	Ardra	3
Mon	18:50:11	Lib	Swati	4

Mar	21:53:03	Leo	P Phalguni	3
Mer (C)	2:09:01	Gem	Mrigshira	3
Jup	23:47:16	Pis	Revati	3
Ven	29:47:54	Tau	Mrigshira	2
Sat (R)	29:07:46	Cap	Dhanistha	2
Rah (R/C)	27:05:31	Gem	Punarvasu	3
Ket (R)	27:05:31	Sag	Uttarasadha	1

Lagna Chart

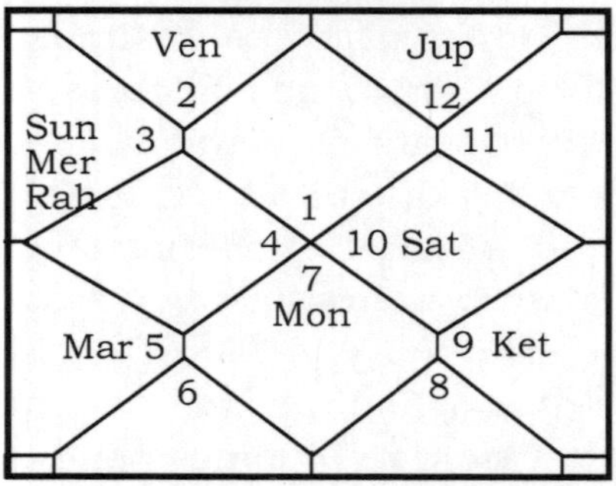

Navamsa Chart

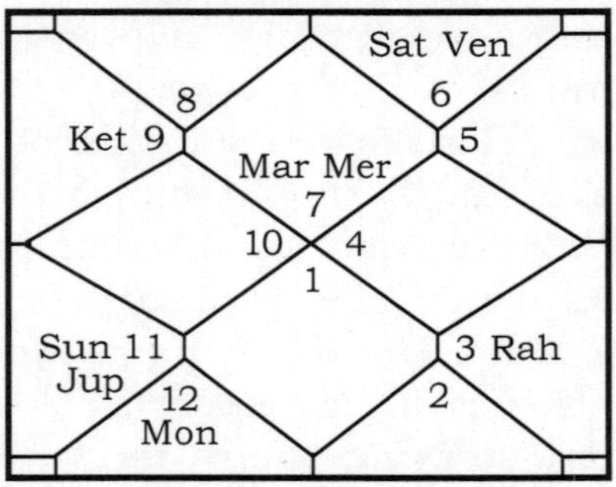

Balance of Vimshottari Dasa of **Rah 1Y 6M 25D**

She was born in Aries ascendant. She is successful IAS officer and has been married to an IAS officer as well. Here, the 4th lord Moon occupies the 7th house, in Libra. The 7th lord, Venus, joins the 2nd house, in its own sign. This is an indication that the husband will be in the IAS. Venus is the *Karaka* of IAS services and it may be noted that the 7th lord if placed in the 2nd house, indicates profession of the native. Here, 7th lord Venus has conjoined with the 2nd house, in own sign Taurus, therefore, IAS services is indicated to her husband. Royal planet Moon occupies the 7th house and Saturn aspects the 7th house as 10th lord. This indicates government service. The 7th lord Venus obtains the *navamsa* of debilitation and 4th lord Moon joins Jupiter's *navamsa*. Therefore, her husband had been connected with finance, education and the home departments.

Illustration : 11.9 *Horoscope No.: 55*

Date of birth : 08.03.1957 Time of birth : 02:59:00 hrs
Place of birth : Lucknow Lat 26:50:00 N Long 80:54:00E
Ayanamsa : 23:15:46 Sidereal Time : 13:53:54

Pln	**Degree**	**Rasi**	**Nakshatra**	**Pad**
Asc	21:46:29	Sag	Purvasadha	3
Sun	23:47:34	Aqu	P Bhadrapad	2
Mon	4:15:15	Tau	Kritika	3
Mar	0:27:39	Tau	Kritika	2
Mer (C)	12:35:11	Aqu	Satabhisha	2
Jup (R)	4:53:06	Vir	U Phalguni	3
Ven (C)	14:15:48	Aqu	Satabhisha	3
Sat	20:49:42	Sco	Jyestha	2
Rah	28:47:10	Lib	Vishakha	3
Ket	28:47:10	Ari	Kritika	1

Lagna Chart

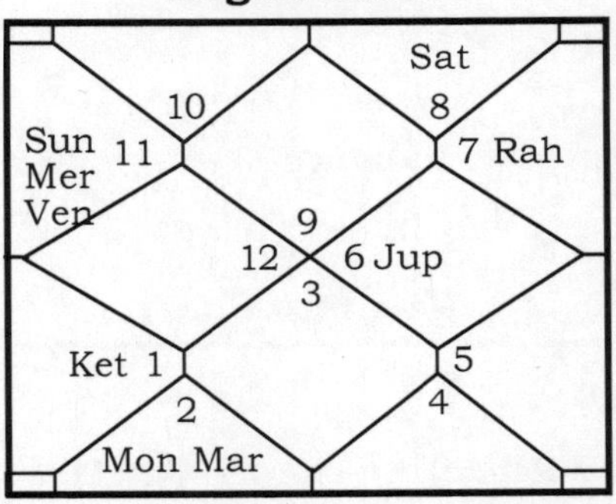

Navamsa Chart

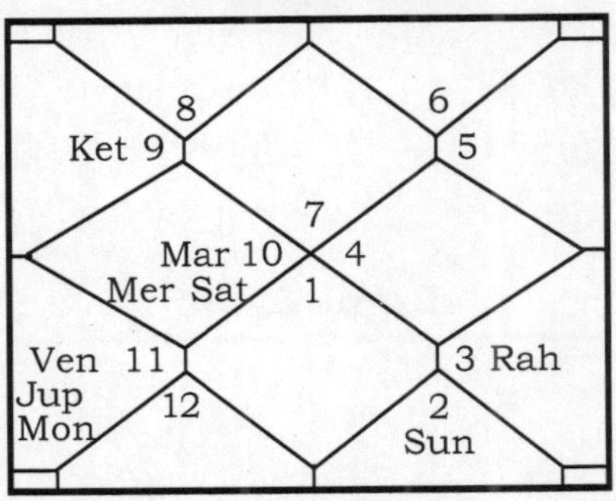

Balance of Vimshottari Dasa of **Sun 2Y 7M 0D**

She was born in Sagittarius ascendant and had a love marriage with a Bank Officer who was her colleague in the State Bank of India. Here, the lord of the 7th house, Mercury, joins the 3rd house, in Aquarius, and obtains the *navamsa* of Saturn. 4th lord Jupiter aspects the 4th house and is placed in Virgo in the 10th house. Thus, the influence of Jupiter and Mercury is found present in regard to the profession of her husband, which indicates bank services or service in any financial organization. Jupiter and Mercury, both, obtain the *navamsa* of Saturn, which indicates a government job.

Illustration : 11.10 *Horoscope No.: 56*

Date of birth : 25.11.1967 Time of birth : 22:55:00 hrs
Place of birth : Lucknow Lat 26:50:00 N Long 80:54:00E
Ayanamsa : 23:24:22 Sidereal Time : 3:04:28

Pln	**Degree**	**Rasi**	**Nakshatra**	**Pad**
Asc	27:48:23	Can	Aslesa	4
Sun	9:20:44	Sco	Anuradha	2
Mon	18:17:18	Leo	P Phalguni	2
Mar	1:53:16	Cap	Uttarasadha	2
Mer	21:55:08	Lib	Vishakha	1
Jup	11:18:54	Leo	Magha	4
Ven	23:32:01	Vir	Chitra	1
Sat (R)	12:24:34	Pis	U Bhadrapad	3
Rah	4:01:53	Ari	Ashwini	2
Ket	4:01:53	Lib	Chitra	4

Lagna Chart

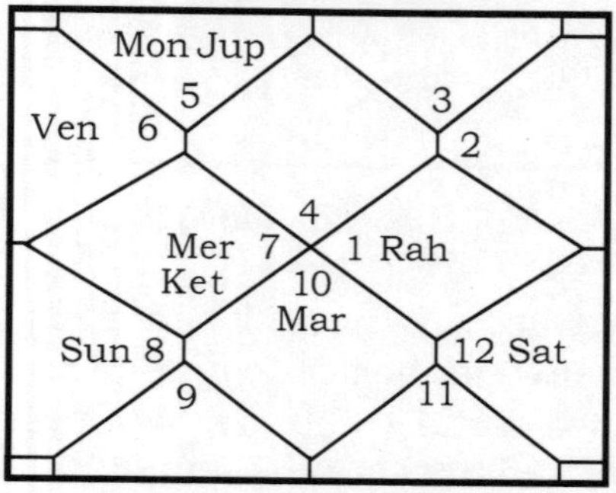

Navamsa Chart

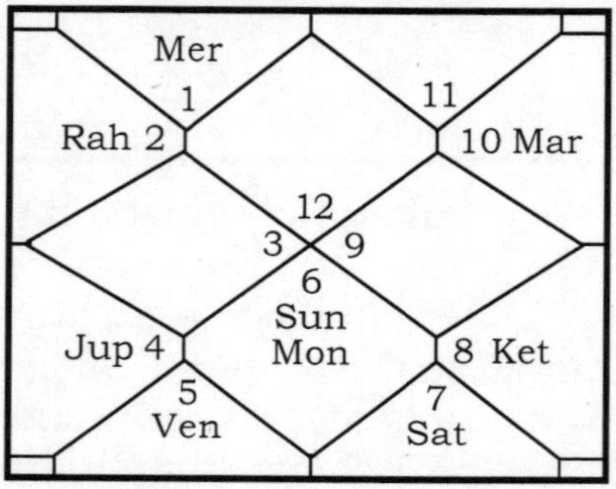

Balance of Vimshottari Dasa of **Ven 12Y 6M 24D**

She was employed in a private organization at a very low scale and cadre but rose to a very high position as the Managing Director of the organization. Many people liked her in various ways. She was promoted very frequently and reached to the top within a span of 15 years. Therefore, she was very proud and that could not be appreciated by the Managing Director. She was kept aside of important duties and responsibilities. She got deeply depressed and ultimately died in early January 2004 at the age of 36 years.

Mars is exalted in the 7th house in her horoscope and the 7th lord Saturn falls in the 9th house under retrograde motion in Pisces. Mercury and Ketu occupy the 4th house in Libra and the lord of the 4th house, Venus, is debilitated in the 3rd house. Thus, Mars, Saturn, Mercury and Venus will decide the profession of her husband. There is mutual exchange between Mercury and Venus. Therefore, husband is an MBA. 7th lord Saturn is exalted and Mars obtains vargottam *navamsa*. Therefore, the influence of Saturn is very much there over the profession of her husband. The husband got innumerable promotions due to her close and powerful impression over the Managing Director. Venus, Mercury and Sun made him Head of the Section within a span of 5 years and he commanded a lot of power, respect and position there. Mercury, Venus, Mars and Saturn made her husband successful in various jobs though he was an MBA and became Manager soon. The joint effect of Mercury, Mars and Venus shows the lady will work in a managerial capacity. Saturn's role signifies that her husband will be connected with services and will not do independent work or business.

Illustration : 11.11 *Horoscope No.: 57*

Date of birth : 05.09.1955 Time of birth : 17:45:00 hrs
Place of birth : Moradabad Lat 28:50:00 N Long 78:45:00E
Ayanamsa : 23:14:34 Sidereal Time : 16:25:18

Pln	Degree	Rasi	Nakshatra	Pad
Asc	3:52:46	Aqu	Dhanistha	4
Sun	18:54:57	Leo	P Phalguni	2

Mon	29:00:28	Pis	Revati	4
Mar (C)	12:32:14	Leo	Magha	4
Mer	12:27:15	Vir	Hasta	1
Jup	24:50:12	Can	Aslesa	3
Ven (C)	20:03:18	Leo	P Phalguni	3
Sat	23:04:31	Lib	Vishakha	1
Rah (R)	29:24:07	Sco	Jyestha	4
Ket (R)	29:24:07	Tau	Mrigshira	2

Lagna Chart

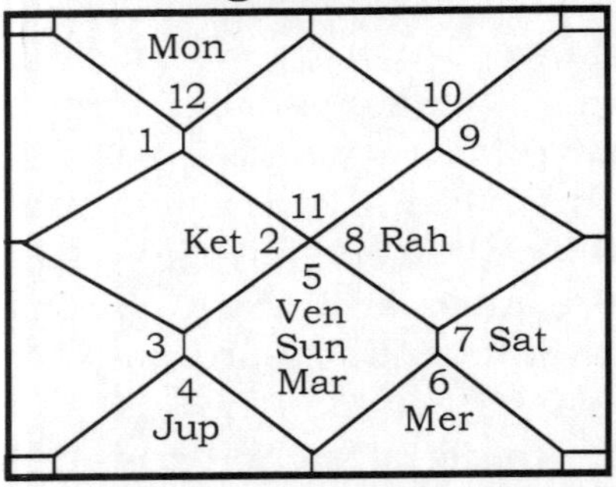

Navamsa Chart

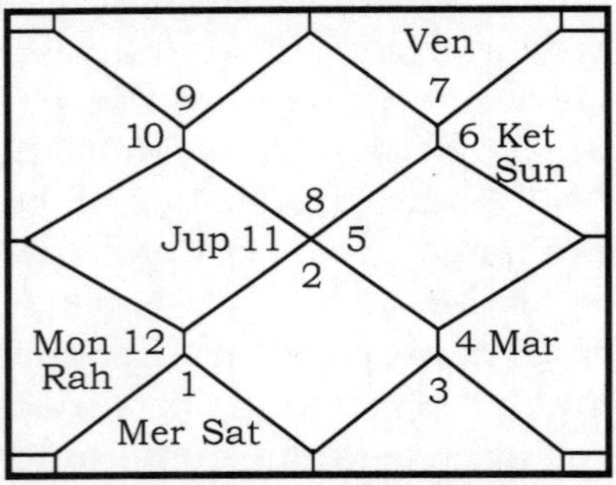

Balance of Vimshottari Dasa of **Mer 1Y 3M 5D**

She was born in Aquarius ascendant with Venus, Mars and Sun in the 7th house. She had a love marriage in the year 1979 with a handsome and smart boy. Here, the 7th house is occupied by Sun and Mars. The Sun indicates independent work and medicines. Mars also joins the Sun that governs manufacturing of medicines. The 4th lord Venus joins the 7th house in Leo. Thus, the 4th lord Venus, 7th lord Sun and 10th lord Mars occupy the 7th house and the combination of Venus, Sun and Mars shows native will come from medical field. In fact, the native has his own pharmaceutical company of country-wide fame.

Thus, the profession of the husband can be correctly judged on the basis, as mentioned above. The 7th and 4th houses should be properly examined. The 7th house covers everything about husband, his appearance, profession, education, manners, family, behaviour, married life, character etc. So, the 7th house and its lord are very important for the examination of the occupation of life partner. 4th house is 10th from 7th and that should also be examined in the same way.

Jupiter happens to be the significator of husband and its placement in the sign, *navamsa* and *nakshatra* plays a prominent role for the judgement of livelihood of the husband. If the 7th lord is placed in the 2nd house, it should be treated as the most important planet for the treatment of the profession. If 7th lord is placed in the 7th house, that has also to do a lot with her husband. If 4th lord occupies the 7th house or 7th lord joins the 4th house, the lord thereof will decide the profession of the native. However, involvement of many planets often creates confusion for the judgement of the profession of the husband. One must have a deep knowledge of the subject of the profession of the planets such as Saturn, Mercury and Mars may govern engineering services; Mars, Sun and Jupiter may have a concern with medical services; Venus and luminaries are the significator of IAS; Saturn, Jupiter and Mercury signify law profession; Jupiter and Mercury govern bank services and the services of teaching; industries are ruled by Saturn, Mars and Mercury, and political future comes under Sun, Mars and Jupiter, and so on. These principles should be carefully applied. Generally, the 3rd and 4th planet will help in making sharp tuning of the profession i.e. if the husband of the native is governed by Mars and Sun, that may indicate the medical profession but if Moon is also involved, the husband will be a Pediatrician, and she may be a Gyaneacologist. If Saturn is involved, the husband may have a concern with urology or neurology etc. Involvement of Sun and Moon may indicate that the husband will be an eye surgeon or a cardiologist or so on.

Generally, the involvement of Saturn over the 7th house or its lord shows that the native will be in the services. The prominent influence of Mercury shows that the husband will be a businessman and the influence of the Sun indicates that he will be doing independent work of industries or manufacturing goods. The rold of the Sun in the judgment of profession of the life partner may also decide that the husband will come from the political sphere. If the horoscope indicates more than one profession of the native, the *dasha* should be taken into consideration. The *dasha,* which will be operative at the time of marriage, may indicate the profession of the husband. If major period of Venus is operative and the Venus is quite strong in the birth chart of the girl and the chances of civil services and medical sevices are found present in the birth chart of the woman, which will be the actual profession of the husband? The running of *dasha* of Venus will show that the husband will be an IAS and will not be a Doctor. However, after becoming an IAS, medical services may come under him. Similarly, the other professions may be judged from the horoscope of a lady in regard to her husband. Final conclusion of the profession of the husband should be drawn only after a thorough analysis of the birth chart of the native.

11.2 Examination of Education and Profession of the Wife

Education of person is judged from his 2nd, 4th, 5th and the 10th houses and also from the planets in airy signs at the birth. 2nd house rules writing qualities of a person, 4th house his academic knowledge, 5th house governs intellect and memory and 10th house shows success and reputation. Jupiter and Mercury signify our intellect, memory and wisdom and the Sun is the significator of our success and reputation.

So, the combined strength of all these houses and planets, rules the education and knowledge of a person.

The 7th house from the *lagna,* the Moon, Venus and the Sun rule the wife of a person and therefore, the education and knowledge of the wife of the person is to be judged from the houses ruling the education etc., taking 7th house as *lagna.* When these houses are conjoined with benefics and with lords of *Kendra* and *kona* houses, one will marry an educated girl. When these houses and their lords are influenced by both malefics and benefics or by both good and evil houses, the result will be mixed i.e. the wife will be neither highly educated nor uneducated. When malefic influences are more, and lords of the houses are also weak and ill situated, the person is likely to marry an illiterate woman with very little education.

It is seen, sometimes, that a person possesses high intellect and high knowledge, but he has no educational qualification. Such peculiarities are found in horoscope where 5th house is very strong but 4th is weak. The 10th house rules success and reputation. A person having a strong 10th house or a strong 10th lord, guarded by benefics and lords of benefic houses, will have educational success and reputation. 2nd house rules writing capacity. When 2nd house and its lord are strong, one may be proficient in writing. Nature of education whether Science, Arts, Medicine or Engineering etc. will depend on the nature of the planets influencing concerning houses and their lords.

The combination of Jupiter and Moon, by conjunction or by their mutual aspect or one being in other's house aspected by each other, develops the cultural instinct and thirst for knowledge. When these are lords of *Kendra* and *kona* houses from the 7th house and have made a combination in *Kendra* or *kona* house, one is likely to have a cultured wife, educated and proficient in some branch of learning. Similarly, when the Moon and Venus make a combination in a similar manner, they make a wife skilled in some branch of arts and make proficient in subjects, which specially interest the woman. Mercury-Venus combination also makes one learned and skilled in many branches. Planets ruling the education and knowledge, when posited in airy signs or *Rashis,* make a person educated and learned.

Now-a-days, women are having education in schools and colleges in different branches. These should be judged from the nature of the planets influencing the houses concerning education. As social laws, family environments and time factor also work, with planetary influences to build up the career of a human being, these also should be considered.

Women have also taken up various professions. Women are working almost in every office. They are working also independently in various professions and are engaged in teaching and medical practice and some have even achieved a very high position in life. The 10th house rules profession and 9th and 5th houses are said to be the houses of fortune, of which the 9th is strongest. When the lords of the above houses are strong, well situated and well aspected or have mutual exchange of houses etc., these place a person in a good position in life. Afflicted and disturbed houses, affect the profession and fortune, by providing a disturbed career. The 11th house rules earnings and the 2nd house rules the wealth, in general. So, the strength and position of these two houses and their lords are also to be considered.

When a man has a very strong 10th house, he may be very well placed in life and may be endowed with fame and position, but his income and earning will depend on the strength of the houses ruling income and fortune. When these houses and their lords are strong, a person may have a good income even though placed in a very ordinary profession.

Therefore, the profession of the wife is to be judged from the 10th house from the 7th, from *lagna,* Sun, Moon and Venus, and also from the 5th lord and 10th house there from. The income and wealth of the wife depend on the 11th and 2nd houses, from the 7th house.

Whether the wife will have a long active life or work for only a short period, is to be judged from the houses and planets ruling her profession and income. When these are afflicted, weak, disturbed and related with evil houses and evil lords, there will be a break in profession and irregular income. When the lords of the above houses are retrograde or retrograde planets join any of the above houses, similar results may be witnessed. During the *Dashas* and *Anter-Dashas* of the planets afflicting the houses and planets ruling profession and income, one is likely to witness a break in profession, disturbed work and irregular and low income.

Chapter-12

Secrets of Saturn

Saturn's placement in "*Upchaya*" in a birth chart is considered beneficial. In any case, all malefic planets give beneficial results when placed in the third, the sixth or the eleventh house. Within these houses, which native Saturn would affect better will depend on his *lagna* (ascendant) and the position of other planets. Being placed in the 10th house, Saturn predominantly affects the occupation of the native. If the situation is good, the native can reach the pinnacle of progress. But an inauspicious situation brings downfall, ill fame, insults and deprivations. One may not get timely promotions and may even have to face humiliation of demotion or suspension.

For the Capricorn ascendant, Saturn in the 10th is exalted and very beneficial. In the sign of Libra, if Saturn in the 10th is conjoined with Venus, the results get a further boost. In Aquarius ascendant, such Saturn is even better, although here it is placed in a sign governed by its adversary, Mars. For Aries ascendant, Saturn in the 10th house falls in the sign of Capricorn, its own, and obviously provides superior results. Saturn in the 10th house makes the native reach the top, but it is followed by a steep fall from position and status. This is a fundamental characteristic of Saturn.

It is like a Prime Minister losing an election, even for an MP's seat. Ex-PM of India, late Indira Gandhi became world famous due to Saturn but later she couldn't even win an MP's election. If Saturn in the 10th is placed beneficially, aspects or conjoins an exalted Venus, or is under the influence of an auspicious Jupiter, then such demotion will not occur. For Gemini ascendant, Saturn as lord of the 8th or 9th, will give similar results for the 10th house. But, if Saturn in the 10th is conjoined with Venus or Jupiter, then it will not give an inauspicious result. In the same way, for Capricorn ascendant, Saturn and Venus in the 10th house would give very good results. The ferocity of Saturn is surely mitigated by the influence of Jupiter.

For Taurus ascendant, Saturn in the 10th is good almost as much as for Aries ascendant. In both these *lagnas,* Saturn in the 10th is *Swa-grahi* (in his own house), hence it creates "*Shash Mahapurush Raj Yoga*". But for Aries ascendant, sometimes Saturn is considered a '*Badhaka*' (obstacle or deterrent) since it is lord of the 11th house. Consequently, some scholars have stated the results of Saturn in the 10th, for Taurus ascendant, to be better than that for the Aries ascendant. Reference may be made of 48th couplet in the 2nd chapter of "*Jataka Parijat*", where '*Badhaka*' planets have been explained i.e.:

क्रमाच्चराग द्विशरीर भानामुपान्त्यधर्मस्मरगास्तरीशाः।
खरेशमान्दिस्थित राशिनाथा ह्यतीव बाधकरस्वेचराः स्युः।।

(*Jatak Parijat,* Ch-2, Vers-48)

That is, for movable, fixed and common ascendants, 11th, 9th and 7th houses respectively are *Badhaka* places. Planets situated in these houses or those possessing their lordship, are *Badhakas* and give unpleasant results, provided in the signs controlled by them "*Mandi* or *Khara*" are also present. This means that firstly it should be found out as to "*Mandi*" or "*Khara*" are situated in which sign. If the lord of that sign is situated in *Badhaka* place, or is the lord of a *Badhaka* house, then only it causes problems.

Mandi : It is sub-planet, which is the son of Saturn. It is the most harmful among the evil planets. Cause of greater suffering than that caused by Saturn, enhancer of distress and losses, this sub-planet becomes even more malefic, if conjoined with or aspected by Saturn. If *Mandi* is placed in the 8th house, the native dies at a young age. Even when several planetary positions, giving longevity, are there in the birth chart but *Mandi* falls in the 8th house, the person has a short life span. It is, therefore, necessary to be informed about *Mandi's* position when predicting from the birth chart.

Khara: The 56th couplet from the 5th chapter of *'Jataka Parijat'* is quoted below which talks about *Khara* :

विलग्न जन्म द्रेक्काणद्यस्तु द्वविंशति खरः।
सुधाकरोपगांशर्क्षाच्चतुः षष्ट्यंशको भवेत।।

(*Jatak Parijat,* Ch-5, Vers-56)

(That is, the planet which owns the 22nd 'Dreshkana' from the ascendant is called *Khara*).

The misconceptions prevalent about *Badhaka* planets are responsible for the belief that for Aries ascendant, Saturn owning the 11th house is considered *Badhaka.* But for both, Taurus and Aries ascendant, even when Saturn is the lord of the *Badhaka* houses, it should not be considered as *Badhaka*, unless *Mandi* or *Khara* also are not situated in the sign of Capricorn or Aquarius. For Aries ascendant, Saturn in the 7th house is exalted in Libra and gives remarkable rise in business. But sometimes Saturn in the 7th house is also fatal. Whenever such a Saturn influences the native, business would prosper but health would cause concern, due to diseases connected with Saturn.

Causing high rise and then pulling down, a prestigious high status and then sudden downfall- this is the characteristic of Saturn in the 10th, unless here Saturn is the lord of the ascendant, in his own house, is exalted, or *yogakaraka.* If Saturn in the 10th, is under the influence of Jupiter or Venus, its ferocity is sufficiently diminished. On the contrary, if such a Saturn is conjoined with other evil planets or aspected by them, then it spells absolute decline.

Illustration : 12.1 (**Hitler**) *Horoscope No.: 58*

Date of birth : 20.04.1889 Time of birth : 18:30:00 hrs

Place of birth: Brabhaw Lat 33:00:00 N Long 73:45:00E

Ayanamsa : 22:18:22 Sidereal Time : 8:25:20

Pln	Degree	Rasi	Nakshatra	Pad
Asc	8:24:07	Lib	Swati	1
Sun	8:20:08	Ari	Ashwini	3
Mon	11:54:24	Sag	Moola	4
Mar (C)	23:57:09	Ari	Bharani	4
Mer (C)	3:00:46	Ari	Ashwini	1
Jup	15:56:10	Sag	Purvasadha	1
Ven (R)	24:27:37	Ari	Bharani	4
Sat	21:09:04	Can	Aslesa	2
Rah (R)	22:45:03	Gem	Punarvasu	1
Ket (R)	22:45:03	Sag	Purvasadha	3

Lagna Chart

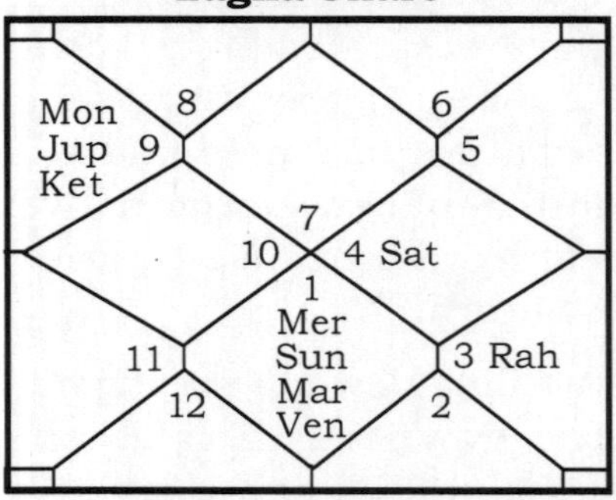

Navamsa Chart

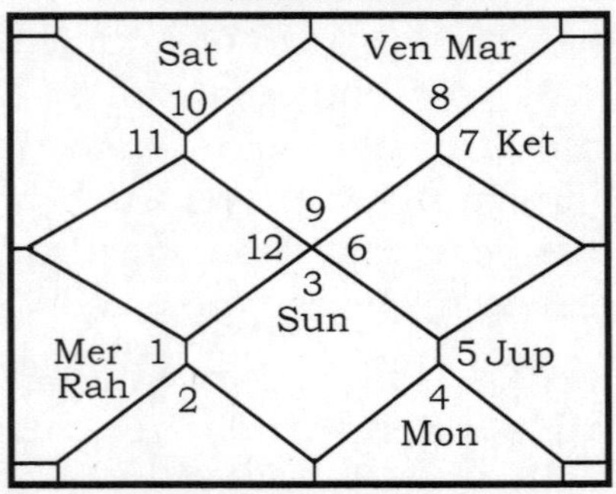

Balance of Vimshottari Dasa of **Ket 0Y 8M 30D**

It is a well known fact about Hitler that he was the son of a cobbler. His father died when Hitler was 13 and his mother when he was 15. Then for 8 years he learnt draftsmanship. He joined the army in 1914 and floated his own party under the sub-period of Mars. Gradually, he brought many countries under the German flag. Saturn in the 10th, which is also *yogakaraka* for Libra ascendant, took Hitler to new heights of power, position, rights and fame. In his birth chart, Saturn is aspected by Mars, and Saturn is aspecting Mars. Saturn is also powerful and *yogaKaraka* and therefore, entirely beneficial, since it is also situated in its own *navamsa*. But Mars is '*Markesh*' (planet causing death) for Libra ascendant. During the major period of Rahu and sub-period of Mars, Hitler suffered setbacks and he had to flee from the battle field. In melodramatic and mysterious circumstances he met his death in 1945.

If in a birth chart, Saturn is in the 10th and Mars, Ketu or Rahu influence it, then the ascent to the peak and then complete downfall of the native is inevitable. In Hitler's birth chart, this fact can be seen clearly. Napoleon Bonaparte was also born in Libra *lagna* where Saturn was in the 10th, and Moon was in the 4th house in the sign of Capricorn. There was "*Vinimaya parivartana yoga*" (mutual exchange position) between Saturn and Moon but Saturn was bereft of conjunction with or aspect by any auspicious planet. Therefore, Saturn acted similarly in his case, as in that of Hitler. A rise to the pinnacle and then an ignoble downfall. Any Sutra or principle of astrology depends upon the situation of other planets and their strength. Saturn in the 10th causes high rise only when it is powerful, in its own house, exalted or a *yogakaraka*. Conjoined with evil planets or even aspected by them it causes a downfall. Conversely, conjoined with auspicious planets or aspected by them, Saturn looses much of its ferocity.

Illustration : 12.2 **(AKS)** *Horoscope No.: 59*

Date of birth : 05.05.1956 Time of birth : 02:10:00 hrs
Place of birth : Lucknow Lat 26:50:00 N Long 80:54:00E
Ayanamsa : 23:15:05 Sidereal Time : 16:54:23

Pln	Degree	Rasi	Nakshatra	Pad
Asc	14:09:48	Aqu	Satabhisha	3
Sun	21:04:55	Ari	Bharani	3
Mon	10:32:59	Aqu	Satabhisha	2

Mar	19:16:53	Cap	Sravna	3
Mer	11:42:43	Tau	Rohini	1
Jup	28:41:28	Can	Aslesa	4
Ven	4:28:20	Gem	Mrigshira	4
Sat (R)	7:25:11	Sco	Anuradha	2
Rah (R)	15:04:15	Sco	Anuradha	4
Ket (R)	15:04:15	Tau	Rohini	2

Lagna Chart

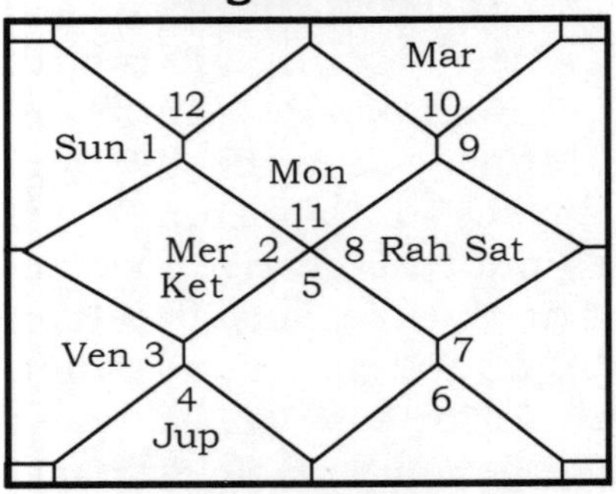

Navamsa Chart

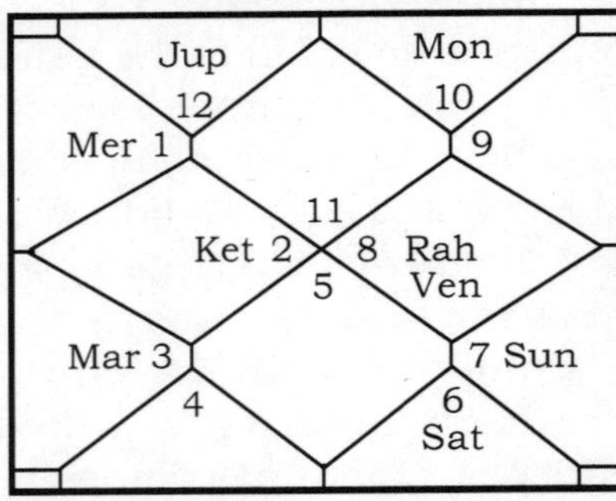

Balance of Vimshottari Dasa of **Rah 12Y 9M 2D**

This is the birth chart of a native who spent his childhood in extreme poverty. After facing many problems he managed to earn a living through an ordinary job in the secretariat. After some time he was promoted to the post of a clerk there. Time's wheel kept moving. Gradually he became an important trade union leader. Newly acquired name and success made him arrogant. It is then that Saturn started to show the effect of its power and he had to leave his job and leadership both, and run away.

As per the birth chart of this native, Saturn's major period (*Mahadasa*) started from 06-02-1985. A pleasant period of progress began in his life. He started a small scale industry. At present, this person is a multimillionaire running big industries successfully. In the birth chart, Saturn is the lord of the ascendant and situated in the 10th house, in the sign of Scorpio, which belongs to Mars. It is also beneficially aspected by an exalted Jupiter, and lord of the 5th Mercury. Jupiter's aspect mitigates Saturn's ferocity but here Saturn is conjoined with Rahu. Rahu, therefore, is enhancing its evil effects. At the same time, Jupiter and Mercury are diminishing these evil effects. To analyze Saturn and the 10th house, it is necessary to consider Mars, the lord of the 10th, as well. Lord of the 10th, Mars, is in the 12th house, in its own exaltation sign Capricorn, and also establishing *Vinimaya Parivartana Yoga* with Saturn. The aspect of Jupiter on the 10th house, lord of the 10th Mars, and Saturn and Rahu in the 10th house is enhancing the auspicious results of 10th house. Before reaching a conclusion, the *navamsa* of Saturn and Mars should also be considered. Saturn is situated in the *navamsa* of Mercury and aspected by Mars, and also Jupiter, which is in its own *navamsa*. Therefore, in the *navamsa* chart also, lord of the ascendant Saturn is influenced by both, Mars and Jupiter. A proper study reveals that Saturn will take this native to the top. Because of Mars being in the *navamsa* of Mercury, the native would prosper only in business, not in a service. Because of Saturn's conjunction with Rahu in the 10th, there would always be ups and downs in the business. Lots of success may be followed by continuous losses. A favourable position is created by the aspect of own *navamsa*-placed Jupiter over Saturn. The native will keep moving towards progress. Even in an adverse situation, he will not lose his courage, strength, patience, discretion or intelligence. Soon, he will regain his original glory.

We have mentioned earlier that the beneficial effect of Saturn begins in the 36th year of life. The major period of Saturn for this native began in the 29th year-when he started a small scale industry of making telephone parts. At the commencement of the 36th year, the sub-period of Mercury began within the major period of Saturn. He came into contact with some important persons. He moved to Delhi (North-West, direction of Mercury) and set up huge industry of making "Pagers" with an investment of billions. The Saturn in the 10th established him amongst the front ranking industrialists of India, from the humble position of an assistant clerk, where he has success, fame, wealth, in short everything. It is therefore, imperative that the position of Saturn should be analyzed very carefully.

The late PM and popular leader of Bangladesh Shri Mujeeburrahman was born in Scorpio ascendant. In his birth chart, Saturn was in the 10th house while being retrograde, which caused his murder while in office. It was this Saturn in the 10th house which gave him immense popularity despite such a humble start. Pakistan got divided and he became the PM of Bangladesh. Later, it was the same Saturn that caused his terrible end.

Everybody is conversant with the name of Albert Einstein. A scientist like him takes birth once in centuries. He was born with Gemini in the ascendance. The lord of the 8th and 9th, Saturn is in the 10th, conjoined with Mercury and Venus, and the lord of the 10th house Jupiter is in the 9th house. Here, Venus is in its exalted sign, which is a highly favourable planet for Gemini ascendant. Lord of the 9th, Saturn, and lord of the 10th, Jupiter, are forming *Vinimaya Yoga*, while Mercury also in the 10th house is creating *Neech Bhanga Raj Yoga.* Lord of the ascendant Mercury, lord of the 5th Venus and lord of the 9th Saturn have joined together in the 10th house creating *Ishtabala Yoga.* Apart from this, because of the mutual exchange of lords of the 9th and 10th another yoga called *'Dharma Karmadhipa'* has been established. Apart from these extraordinary *yogas*, it is Saturn in the 10th which gave him worldwide fame.

Hence, if Saturn is in the 10th and in a favourable situation, i.e. because of its situation it is gaining beneficence, then the native achieves a very high position in life, in terms of place and designation or becomes highly successful in business or reaches a high, popular level in politics. When such a Saturn is lord of the ascendant, in its own house or in an exalted sign, or being lord of the ascendant is located in the 7th house-then only such a result would obtain and a prediction may be made to this effect. If

Jupiter, Venus or Mercury influence the Saturn placed in the 10th house, by aspect or conjunction, downfall would not be there. But if a cruel planet like Mars or Rahu influences such Saturn, downfall after rise is certain. These features of 10th placed Saturn are worth remembering. While assessing results given by Saturn, its auspiciousness or inauspiciousness should be taken note of carefully.

Acharya Kalyan Varma has stated in *Saravali* that if Saturn and Jupiter are together in the 10th house then the native becomes very rich, famous and is highly talented. He may become the head of the city. If Saturn is in the sign of Jupiter and Jupiter is aspecting Saturn then the native becomes the chief or chief commander or commander of the army. In this case, Saturn does not cause a downfall but if the lord of the sixth or eighth house is in the 10th house and it is not even aspected by Jupiter, then downfall takes place

Illustration : 12.3 (**NB**) *Horoscope No.: 60*

Date of birth : 19.03.1947 Time of birth : 21:30:00 hrs
Place of birth : Sitapur Lat 25:11:00 N Long 80:52:00E
Ayanamsa : 23:06:55 Sidereal Time : 9:08:54

Pln	**Degree**	**Rasi**	**Nakshatra**	**Pad**
Asc	19:03:46	Lib	Swati	4
Sun	5:05:41	Pis	U Bhadrapad	1
Mon	29:02:32	Cap	Dhanistha	2
Mar (C)	18:39:48	Aqu	Satabhisha	4
Mer (R)	16:26:34	Aqu	Satabhisha	3
Jup (R)	4:24:19	Sco	Anuradha	1
Ven	23:38:26	Cap	Dhanistha	1
Sat (R)	9:02:33	Can	Pushya	2
Rah (R)	12:00:57	Tau	Rohini	1
Ket (R)	12:00:57	Sco	Anuradha	3

Lagna Chart

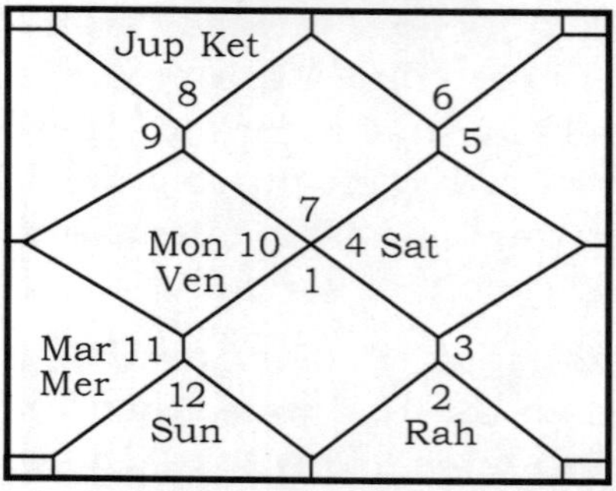

Navamsa Chart

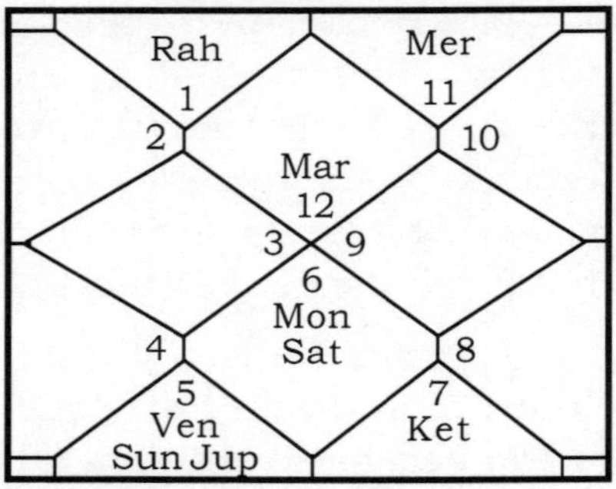

Balance of Vimshottari Dasa of **Mar 4Y 0M 1D**

This is the birth chart of Mr. Nimai Banerjee, who is an astrologer of great repute and countrywide fame. He is the Chief Editor and founder of the famous Journals of Astrology "Planets and Forecast", and *"Bhagya Lipi"*, which come out from Cuttack, Orissa.

He was born under extremely humble circumstances, when Libra was rising. *Yogakaraka* Saturn falls in the eighth in Cancer, in own constellation *Pushya.* Major period of Saturn was running over the native from 20.03.1985 to 20.03.2004. There was enormous rise and elevation of Dr. Nimai Banerjee during Saturn *Mahadasa* due to his very accurate political, professional and personal forecasts. Saturn has also bestowed upon him wealth, prosperity and property along with meritorious learned, talented, handsome and obedient children.

Jupiter is posited in the second house in Saturn's constellation *Anuradha* and Saturn, who joins the tenth house, receives the favourable aspect of Jupiter. Thus, the joint influence of Jupiter and Saturn is there on the tenth house.

Mars and Mercury are associated with each other in the fifth house, which has provided him retentive memory, immense intelligence, creativity of mind, independent thinking and views along with knowledge, study and experience in the field of astrology. Lord of the ascendant,

Venus occupies the fourth house, in association with the tenth lord Moon. There is mutual exchange of the lord of the tenth and fourth houses, Moon and Saturn. Opposition of Venus and Saturn, with mutual aspect between them, made him so great, successful and famous. A *Yogakaraka* Saturn in the tenth house, elevates one to extra ordinary high position, like Dr. Nimai Banerjee and others.

Illustration : 12.4 (**DPS**) *Horoscope No.: 61*

Date of birth : 30.01.1966 Time of birth : 14:05:00 hrs
Place of birth : Fatehpur Lat 25:56:00 N Long 80:55:00E
Ayanamsa : 23:22:45 Sidereal Time : 22:35:12

Pln	**Degree**	**Rasi**	**Nakshatra**	**Pad**
Asc	28:11:05	Tau	Mrigshira	2
Sun	16:37:48	Cap	Sravna	2
Mon	22:53:11	Ari	Bharani	3
Mar	6:40:17	Aqu	Satabhisha	1
Mer (C)	11:53:38	Cap	Sravna	1
Jup (R)	28:17:40	Tau	Mrigshira	2
Ven (R/C)	10:08:58	Cap	Sravna	1
Sat	21:48:51	Aqu	P Bhadrapad	1
Rah	8:44:32	Tau	Kritika	4
Ket	8:44:32	Sco	Anuradha	2

Lagna Chart

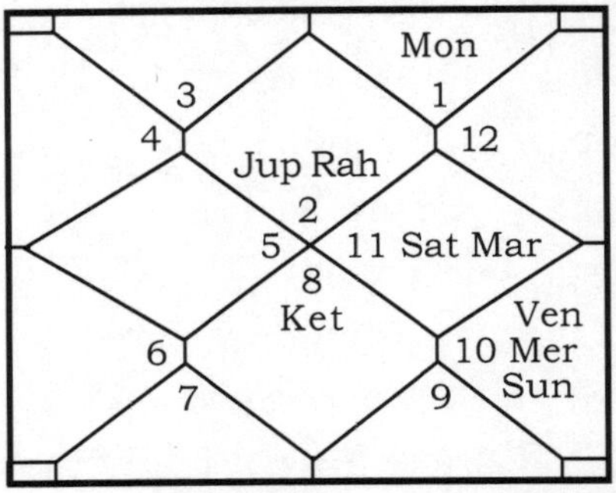

Navamsa Chart

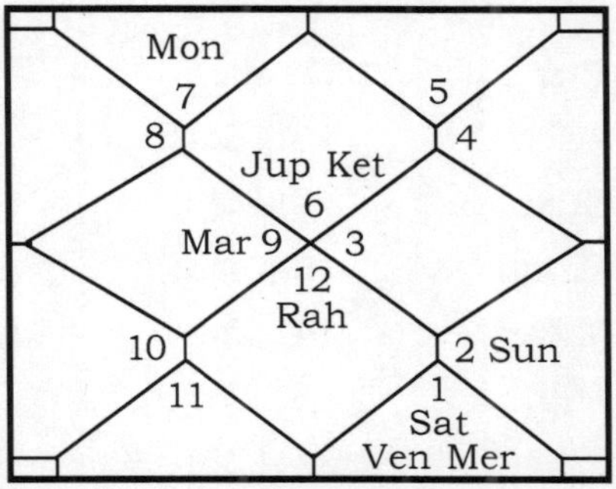

Balance of Vimshottari Dasa of **Ven 5Y 8M 1D**

The native is a young industrialist, who reached at a very glorious and glamorous position within a short span of few years. He was engaged in a very small business of Iron at Fatehpur. Fortunately, he got the agency of a few Motorcycles, Scooters and Tractors, one by one. He also started to deal in real property matters and became quite a big and rich colonizer. He got the success gradually. At present, he is a big business magnet. He has built a few multiplexes as well.

He was born in Taurus Ascendant with *Yogakaraka* Saturn in the tenth house in Aquarius. Here, Saturn has given rise to *Sasa Mahapurush Rayjoga*. All credit should be given to strongly placed Saturn in the tenth house in Aquarius, in the constellation of eleventh lord Jupiter. Saturn's position has elevated him to extra ordinarily high and wealthy disposition, within a short period. Conjunction of Mars with Saturn in the tenth house cannot be appreciated, as both of these planets are opposite each other in nature. But both are malefics. Mars owns the seventh house. The conjunction of seventh lord Mars with tenth lord Saturn is a powerful combination of enormous success in business.

Illustration : 12.5 **(PA)** *Horoscope No.: 62*

Date of birth : 25.06.1965 Time of birth : 03:43:35 hrs

Place of birth : Sitapur Lat 25:11:00 N Long 80:52:00E

Ayanamsa : 23:22:12 Sidereal Time : 21:48:28

Pln	**Degree**	**Rasi**	**Nakshatra**	**Pad**
Asc	16:18:18	Tau	Rohini	2
Sun	9:46:52	Gem	Ardra	1
Mon	12:11:59	Ari	Ashwini	4
Mar	4:36:07	Vir	U Phalguni	3
Mer	24:39:10	Gem	Punarvasu	2
Jup	21:12:40	Tau	Rohini	4
Ven	29:19:25	Gem	Punarvasu	3

Sat	23:50:29	Aqu	P Bhadrapad	2
Rah	20:23:21	Tau	Rohini	4
Ket	20:23:21	Sco	Jyestha	2

Lagna Chart

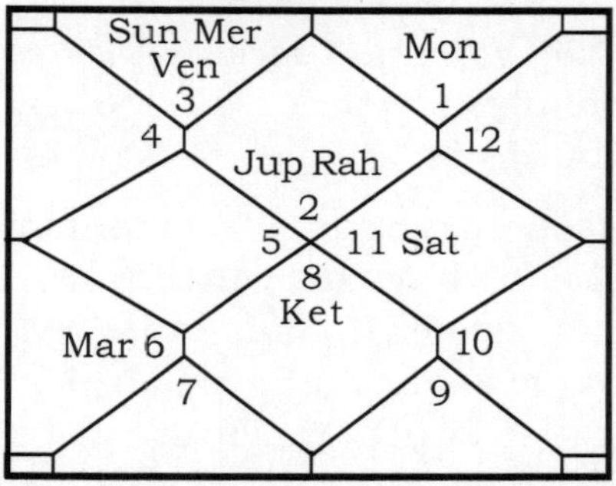

Navamsa Chart

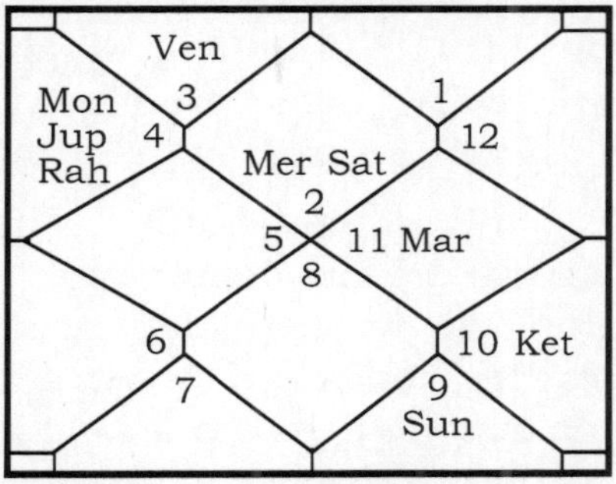

Balance of Vimshottari Dasa of **Ket 0Y 7M 4D**

The native was born in Taurus ascendant with *Yogakaraka* Saturn in the 10th house, in own sign Aquarius. This has given rise to *Sasa Mahapurush Rajayoga*. The father of the native was a sugar manufacturer. He had big Crashers and earned handsome profit. However, the native could not be successful in manufacturing of sugar and decided to venture into other business.

In fact, when the native contacted us, he was running under the major period of Mars from 28.01.2002 to 28.01.2009. Mars is the lord of 7th and 12th house and is posited in the 5th house, in inimical sign Virgo. Generally, major period of Mars was quite struggling for the native. During the sub-period of Saturn, in the major period of Mars, native decided to enter into the business of mild steel Bars. It was absolutely new business for him, but he is earning quite handsomely thereafter and has regained lost reputation. Saturn in the 10th house, for Taurus ascendant, is certainly extremely auspicious because, it is *Yogakaraka* as well as the 10th lord. Saturn obtains a friendly *navamsa* of Venus and falls in the constellation of Jupiter *Poorva Bhadrapada*. Saturn and Jupiter, who are 10th and 11th lords respectively, are placed in quadrant from each other, and from *lagna* as well. This is also an auspicious combination and has given rise to *Lakshmi Yoga*.

The native became a multimillionaire after taking up the business of M.S. Bars (i.e. Iron business). He will certainly be able to run Rolling Mill during the major period of Rahu and will become prominent business magnet due to the position of *Yogakaraka* Saturn in the 10th house of its own.

If a native is subjected to such type of placement of Saturn, he must enter into profession having a concern with iron, oil, wool, woolen garments, cement, coal, buffaloes, leather, shoes and sleepers etc. It is said that Saturn in 10th makes one equal to a king but also brings downfall, when the native reaches at the top. This does not hold good, when the native is born in Taurus or Libra ascendant, where Saturn is a *yogakaraka*. It is also not so, for the natives of Capricorn and Aquarius ascendants. In case of Capricorn, Saturn will be exalted in the 10th and in case of Aquarius, Saturn will be in Scorpio, in the 10th house. Both these positions will elevate the native to the top most position. Anyway, Saturn in Cancer, for Libra ascendant, if afflicted or aspected by malefic or Mars, does bring a severe downfall when the native reaches at the highest position of fame, honour and professional prosperity etc.

Illustration : 12.6 **(MR)** *Horoscope No.: 63*

Date of birth : 17.11.1962 Time of birth : 16:05:00 hrs
Place of birth : Moradabad Lat 28:39:00 N Long 77:13:00E
Ayanamsa : 23:20:02 Sidereal Time : 19:27:54

Pln	Degree	Rasi	Nakshatra	Pad
Asc	7:14:28	Ari	Ashwini	3
Sun	1:15:45	Sco	Vishakha	4
Mon	12:27:57	Can	Pushya	3
Mar	23:25:21	Can	Aslesa	3

Mer (C)	26:39:27	Lib	Vishakha	2
Jup	10:05:31	Aqu	Satabhisha	2
Ven (R/C)	23:53:03	Lib	Vishakha	2
Sat	12:39:41	Cap	Sravna	1
Rah (R)	8:40:51	Can	Pushya	2
Ket (R)	8:40:51	Cap	Uttarasadha	4

Lagna Chart

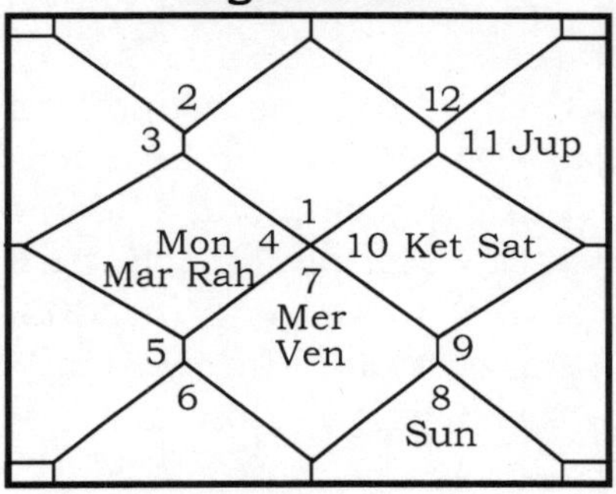

Navamsa Chart

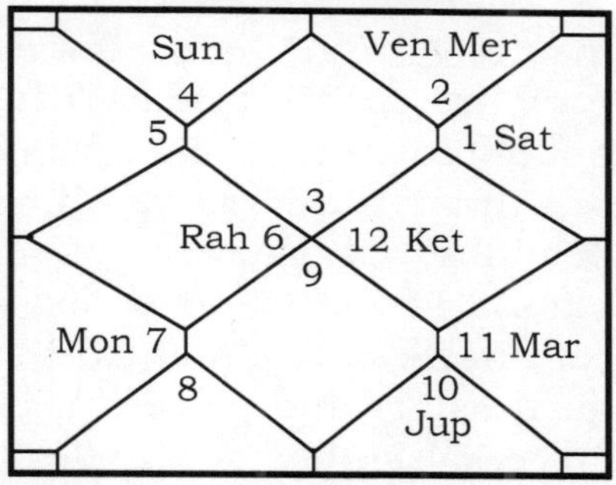

Balance of Vimshottari Dasa of **Sat 5Y 11M 25D**

The native was born in Aries Ascendant, with Saturn in the tenth house in Capricorn. Saturn's position has given rise to *Sasa Mahapurush Rajayoga*. This is splendid. Venus and Mercury are posited in the seventh house, where Venus has given rise to *Malavya Mahapurush Rajyoga*. Moon falls in own sign in Cancer, in the fourth house. Mars obtains *Neechbhanga Rajyoga*. The ninth lord Jupiter joins the eleventh house and receives the aspect of Mars. This is quite an encouraging horoscope for brilliant business prospects. The native was running a Rolling Mill near Moradabad. The native made sincere, serious and systematic endeavors and put in hard labour to reach an income of million of rupees per month, while he had started from the scratch. He had number of luxury cars, bungalows, Jewels, ornaments and all kinds of comforts. He has also been blessed with a beautiful wife and two charming and pretty daughters.

The native visited us during Venus-Jupiter period

sometime in 2004. We categorically and clearly invited his attention towards the sub-period of Saturn in the major period of Venus (12.09.2005 to 12.11.2008). We specified that this period will be extremely adverse and will bring a sudden downfall. We made a forecast that he would loose his everything during Venus-Saturn *dasa bhukti*.

In *Uttrakalamrita*, it is clearly stated that Venus-Saturn or Saturn-Venus period brings a heavy downfall during its period, provided both Saturn and Venus are exalted or placed in own sign in *Kendras*. In this horoscope, Venus and Saturn both are posited in *Kendras* in their own signs, Capricorn and Libra respectively. The native was shocked to hear this and did not believe it at all. He went away with some degree of annoyance. However, as soon as the sub-period of Saturn started in the major period of Venus, in the end of 2005, certain inevitable problems started worrying him. He made all possible and sincere efforts to check the downfall but failed miserably.

That is a long story of his downfall, which we do not feel essential to lay down. However, the native lost his 'kingdom' fully during the sub-period of Saturn, so much so that his meritorious children have been compelled to study in very ordinary schools. In fact, native is not able to afford the high fees of children. He left Moradabad and is residing at a small place in one room house on rent. We just want to specify that lord of tenth house brings downfall only during the sub-period of Venus or Saturn, provided planets are exalted in the birth charts. We have not seen the downfall, if Saturn is a *yogakaraka* or *lagna* lord or exalted in the tenth house.

We would like to invite the attention of readers towards certain special characteristics and results of Saturn in different positions, which will be of immense benefit for readers.

This is a wrong conception that Saturn in the tenth surely brings downfall when one reaches at the top of his career. At least we can not say so, even after having an experience of 35 years in the field of astrology.

12.1 Saturn's presence in other houses

Saturn in the 2nd and 12th house is always bad. Loss of wealth, danger from enemies, theft, eye ailments, failure and hopelessness are its results. Saturn in the 8th house confers longevity but in several ways it is inauspicious. Then it creates difficulties in marital life and worries regarding offspring. Wastage of money, repeated losses, theft or robbery, as well as trouble from adversaries also occur. If the ascendant is Leo or Cancer, Saturn's placement in the 8th house is not inauspicious, because then Saturn is lord of the 6th or 8th house as well. Similarly, if Saturn is the lord of the 8th house and situated in the 12th, then because of the formation of *Vipreeta Rajyoga,* its ferocity is considerably reduced. For Aries ascendant, Saturn in the 12th house is under the sign of Pisces. If such a Saturn is aspected by Jupiter, then Saturn's inauspiciousness disappears. Saturn in the 12th house, aspecting the 2nd house, is harmful for money matters.

12.2 Auspiciousness of Saturn and Saturn in the Ascendant

In the first, fourth, fifth and ninth house, Saturn gives bad results and harms the interests of the house where it is located. But, if this fact is accepted on its face value, then one would predict wrongly. If Saturn is also lord of the *lagna* when in these positions, while also being their lord, then it gives beneficial results. It is a common principle, enunciated by *Laghu Parashari* that even evil planets do not harm their own houses, rather they enhance its good effects. Saturn in ascendant is bad. It gives the native long-term diseases, body ache, gastric problems, spondylitis, hair loss, physical deformity, boils and soars, pimples or other factors diminishing the glow of the face, pessimistic outlook and a disease like arthritis. Saturn in the *lagna* causes diseases of old age, even in youth, and the person concerned looks older than his or her age. In the same way, if Mars is placed in the ascendant, then the native looks younger than his actual age. The very nature of Saturn is inclined towards diseases of old age, pains and aches etc. Before explaining these facts, a proper and thorough analysis of Saturn should be done. If Saturn is in an exalted sign, like Libra or in its own sign Capricorn or is placed in the ascendant in Aquarius, then the above mentioned ill effects are considerably reduced. Similarly, if Saturn is conjoined with Jupiter or aspected by it, then also, its ferocity is diminished and good effects are enhanced.

Several sages have considered positioning of Saturn in Jupiter's sign Pisces or Sagittarius as beneficial. Rishi Garga has written that if Saturn is in its exalted sign of Libra, Pisces or Sagittarius, in the ascendant, then the individual has an immensely attractive personality and physique both. He is like a king. It is stated in *Shondahora* that Saturn in Libra, Sagittarius or Pisces, in the ascendant, gives wealth and prosperity. Saturn in Sagittarius appeals better than Saturn in Pisces.

Illustration : 12.7 (**GDN**) *Horoscope No.: 64*

Date of birth : 05.01.1925 Time of birth : 02:15:00 hrs
Place of birth : Etawah Lat 26:46:00 N Long 79:02:00E
Ayanamsa : 22:48:23 Sidereal Time : 8:56:53

Pln	**Degree**	**Rasi**	**Nakshatra**	**Pad**
Asc	16:17:41	Lib	Swati	3
Sun	21:12:38	Sag	Purvasadha	3
Mon	24:06:39	Ari	Bharani	4
Mar	17:12:24	Pis	Revati	1
Mer (R)	4:18:00	Sag	Moola	2
Jup (C)	11:13:34	Sag	Moola	4
Ven	24:38:27	Sco	Jyestha	3
Sat	19:33:45	Lib	Swati	4
Rah (R)	21:19:10	Can	Aslesa	2
Ket (R)	21:19:10	Cap	Sravana	4

Lagna Chart

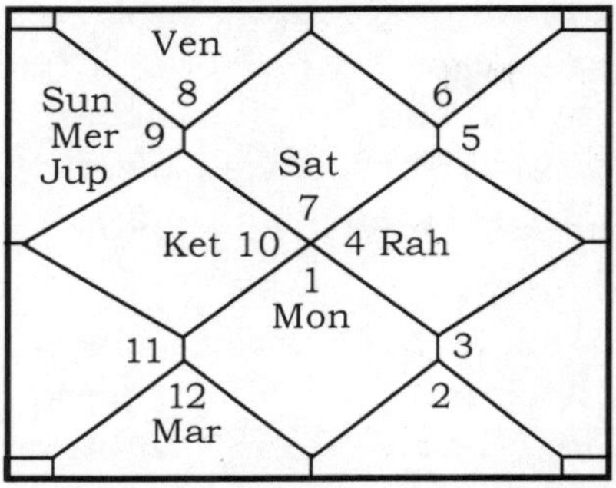

Navamsa Chart

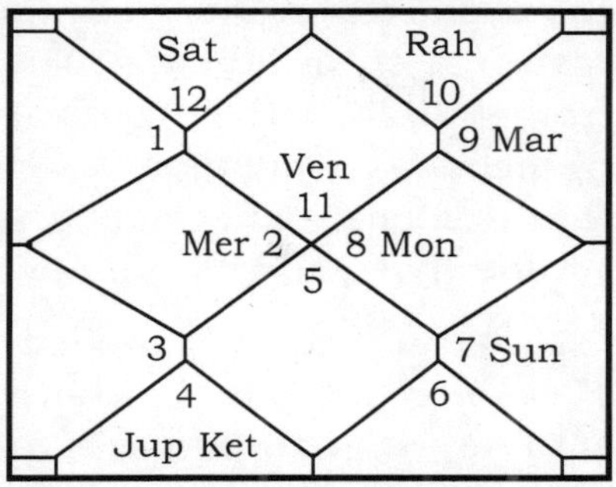

Balance of Vimshottari Dasa of **Ven 3Y 10M 0D**

This is the birth chart of a famous and popular poet of India. Here, as a *Yogakaraka*, Saturn is retrograde and is situated in an exalted sign Libra, in the ascendant, which resulted in the native attaining extensive fame and a top position among contemporary poets. He has received scores of national and international awards. Here, Saturn is the lord of the 4th and 5th and situated in the ascendant. The native is handsome and possesses an impressive personality. Lord of the *lagna* Venus is in the 2nd house, in the sign of Scorpio; hence he also has a melodious voice. He charms his audience with his enthralling poetry recital. Saturn's major period operated from 5.11.1985 to 5.11.2004. During this period only, he has attained maximum accolades and awards. Because of the influence of Saturn, he received Padmashree as well. This positioning of Saturn, in exaltation in Libra, is creating *Sasa Mahapurush Rajyoga*. Here, the position of Moon, as the lord of 10th, in the 7th house is also worth considering. Moon is in the sign of Mars as well as in its *navamsa*. Lord of the *lagna* Venus is in Mars' sign Scorpio and is also aspected by Mars. Moon is also aspected by Jupiter besides Saturn, and is situated in the fourth division of Venus-controlled "Bharani" constellation. The early life of the native was spent in extreme poverty. Collecting money by diving in the rivers was his means of earning. Then starting from a typist's job, today he is a world renowned poet. For this, Saturn in Libra, situated in the ascendant, is the main reason. Normally Saturn starts giving its beneficial results after the 36th year. The rise of this native also occurred from 1962-1963 when he wrote a song which became tremendously popular. Readers would be pleased to know that this poet is not only a serious scholar of astrology but very well versed in it too.

The native got married on 18.11.1946 on the day of "*Devathani Ekadashi*", when he was under the major period of Mars with sub-period of Jupiter. Here, Mars is lord of the 2nd and 7th house and is situated in Jupiter's sign Pisces, in the 6th house. Jupiter, placed in its own sign Sagittarius, is aspecting the 7th house. At the time of the marriage, transiting Saturn was passing through the ascendant Libra. The father of the native died when he was six and sub-period of Rahu was running in the major period of Sun. Birth of his son took place on 01.06.1951, when the sub-period of Moon was continuing under the major period of Mars. Here, Moon is lord of the 5th from Mars, being situated in Mars' sign only, and is being aspected by the significator of children Jupiter. From 09.02.1960 to 1965, the native wrote songs for films. His mother died on 07.12.1977 when Venus' sub-period was continuing, within the major period of Jupiter. The native went to U.S.A. for the first time during the sub-period of Rahu, within the major period of Jupiter, on 13.09.1984 and was conferred Padmashree on 26.11.1991, during the sub-period of Mercury within the major period of Saturn.

12.3 Combination of Saturn & Venus

Saturn and Venus have a complementary relationship. Both these planets are friends and show their results during each other's periods and sub-periods. Kalidasa has mentioned in his book *'Uttarakalamrita'*, that when Venus' sub-period is running during Saturn's major period then Saturn's influence is seen and vice-versa. These influences are according to their planetary positioning. Their relationship is beneficial. The effects of the house, where they are together, are enhanced. Their conjunction in the 7th house is inauspicious for the marital happiness and the person concerned suffers from low moral values in his character. Saturn's aspect on, or conjunction with Venus, lords of the 7th and 2nd, or planets in the 7th and 2nd houses, causes delay in marriage. Saturn and Venus situated in each other's *navamsa* give good results, in matters relevant to the concerned houses, because in Pisces Venus is exalted and Saturn also is favourable.

Saturn and Mercury are also friends, and their mutual relationship also gives good results. If Jupiter is in an inauspicious position with Saturn then the native's life is full of struggles. Financial condition sees ups and downs. If Saturn and Venus are conjoined, they make the native a skilled painter, artist or calligraphist. They are often expert cartoonists too. The money position of the native improves with the help of some female. According to *Jataka Parijat*, the combination of Saturn and Venus makes a person skilled in sports, swimming etc. and an animal lover. He loves travelling. He may be a good surgeon, or a successful businessman in timber. When Saturn and Venus are placed in the ascendant, the native possesses an attractive personality and has interest in several women. This usually leads to an immoral life style. Despite having several, he is unhappy.

If Saturn and Venus are conjoined in the 4th house, then the individual receives money from women and friends. He is respected by his relatives. In the 7th house, conjunction of these two planets gives birth to character depravity. In the 10th house, they together make one glorified and prosperous, like a king. In the birth chart of people with Capricorn or Aquarius as ascendant, this *yoga* gives the best results. For them, Venus is *Yogakaraka* and Saturn being lord of the *lagna*, together with Venus, enhances the effects of the concerned houses and gives good results. For Libra and Taurus ascendants also, the conjunction of Saturn and Venus is auspicious. For these ascendants, Saturn is

Yogakaraka and Venus is benefic, being the lord of ascendant. Combination of such a Saturn and Venus enhances the effects of the concerned houses and lends them auspiciousness.

According to *Hora Sara*, if the conjunction of Saturn & Venus is in the 1st, 4th, 5th, 9th or 10th house, then the native is under the influence of a woman and works in a high position. In other houses, the same combination spells poverty and depletes physical strength and energy. If the *lagna* is Taurus, Libra, Capricorn or Aquarius, and Saturn-Venus conjunction is also in one of these signs, then the results are very satisfying.

If Saturn is conjoined with Jupiter, then its ferocity and evil is diminished. Saturn attains some auspiciousness, but the auspiciousness of Jupiter is destroyed owing to Saturn's malevolence. That means, Saturn-Jupiter combination makes the Saturn's inauspiciousness and Jupiter's auspiciousness a little less. Experience proves that if these two are situated at *"Samasaptaka"* from each other i.e. facing each other, they exchange their effects. Saturn gives Jupiter's results and vice-versa.

12.4 Saturn–Sun relationship

Saturn and Sun are ideal enemies. In qualities and shortcomings, both are opposite to each other. Such animosity is not seen in any other two planets. Saturn rules the West while Sun rules the East. Sun is an indicator of fame, prosperity, and state positions, while Saturn indicates poverty, notoriety and servile work. The planets, friendly to Saturn, are inimical to Sun, excepting Mercury. Likewise, planets friendly with Sun, are inimical to Saturn. The combination of Saturn and Sun spells trouble. The house, where they are together, loses its effects. Father and son are against each other. Even if they are not against each other, one or the other suffers misfortune. The renowned scholar of astrology Acharya H.N. Katve has disclosed a well researched fact regarding Sun and Saturn in his book, which has proved true in our experience also. It is, that when Saturn and Sun are conjoined in the birth chart of a native then he and his father, or he and his son had been enemies in their previous birth. They are born as father and son in this birth, so as to take revenge from the other's fortune. Nature regulated by planets, itself arranges this rigmarole. Often the Son's luck is gained by the father. The Son is poor, he can not progress, faces numerous hurdles, problems, and difficulties. While after his birth the father constantly prospers, progresses and becomes luckier. This usually happens when the vanquished enemy of the previous birth is father in this birth and by depleting the luck of his former victorious enemy, now his son, avenges himself. If the defeated enemy is the son in this birth then father's downfall starts after the birth of son. Father may die or face imprisonment or suspension. Theft, robbery or accident can also happen.

In short, the father faces calamities after the birth of his son. If the combination of Saturn and Sun is in the birth chart of the child then it would be injurious to the father or the son, this can be known from experience, test and analysis.

12.5 Saturn–Moon relationship

Just as Saturn and Sun create adverse relationship between father and son, likewise Moon and Saturn also create clashing relationship between mother-son or mother-daughter. Ill fame, mental illness, suffering, loss of intelligence, mental defects or problems, loss of memory, troubles to the mother, antagonistic mentally etc. are caused by it. But the Saturn-Sun combination is worse than the Saturn-Moon one.

Saturn in the signs of Leo and Cancer is harmful. In Taurus, Libra, Gemini and Virgo, Saturn gives beneficial results. Saturn situated in Scorpio or Aries is also inauspicious. If Saturn in the Aries possesses *Neech Bhang Raj yoga*, then it gives pleasant results. In its own signs, Capricorn and Aquarius, Saturn is beneficial. Once again it can be mentioned that Saturn for Libra is the best since it creates great *Yogas*. Period and sub-period of Jupiter and Saturn are good for those with Libra ascendant. For such a native, even in the 6th, 8th and 12th houses, Saturn gives favourable results.

Illustration : 12.8 (**RS**) *Horoscope No.: 65*

Date of birth : 20.07.1952 Time of birth : 12:45:36 hrs
Place of birth : Jabalpur Lat 23:10:00 N Long 79:57:00E
Ayanamsa : 23:11:50 Sidereal Time : 8:27:27

Pln	**Degree**	**Rasi**	**Nakshatra**	**Pad**
Asc	10:21:44	Lib	Swati	2
Sun	4:18:02	Can	Pushya	1
Mon	15:55:18	Gem	Ardra	3
Mar	17:03:49	Lib	Swati	4
Mer	0:24:49	Leo	Magha	1
Jup	23:44:51	Ari	Bharani	4
Ven (C)	11:18:34	Can	Pushya	3
Sat	16:16:51	Vir	Hasta	2
Rah (R)	28:26:31	Cap	Dhanistha	2
Ket (R)	28:26:31	Can	Aslesa	4

Lagna Chart

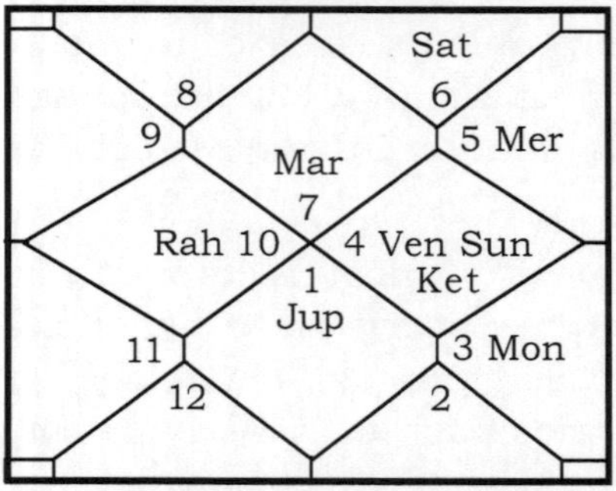

Navamsa Chart

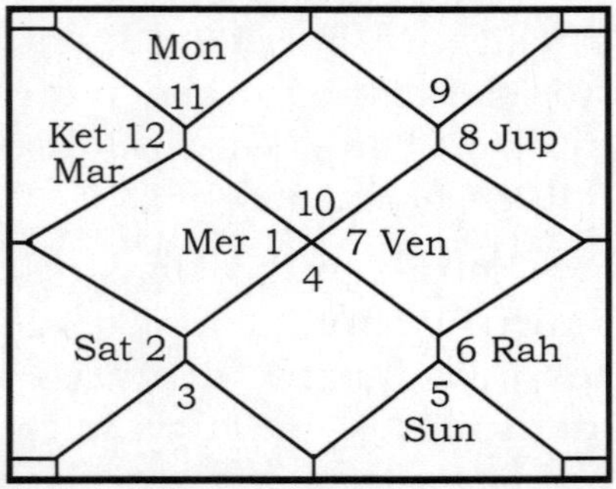

Balance of Vimshottari Dasa of **Rah 5Y 6M 2D**

The native was born in an ordinary family of a teacher. After studying electrical engineering, from 1972 to the beginning of 1986, he served in various concerns. On 13.05.1986 he started his own industry. Despite initial setbacks, he did not lose heart or patience. He had faith in his intelligence and fate both. Ultimately, when sub-period of Jupiter began within the major period of Saturn, on 13.07.1990, his industrial position stabilized and profitable situation commenced. In his birth chart, Saturn as the lord of the 4th and 5th houses is situated in the friendly sign of Virgo and in Venus' *navamsa* Taurus. Jupiter is forming the *Khadashtaka* yoga (6/8) with Saturn. In the period-sub-period of Saturn-Jupiter, the native suffered the first heart attack on 19.02.1991. Later in the *Dasa Bhukti* of Mercury, on 12.09.1994 he underwent heart surgery. It is notable that Mercury is situated in the *navamsa* of Mars.

The native completed his 36th year in July 1988. Only after that Saturn made him an industrialist. If Saturn is in an auspicious position and its period also starts near about the 36th year, then the results are highly beneficial and fortune also improves. This native started his industry with merely Rs. 5000/- in 1986. In 1988, the industry was established and 1991 saw it being stabilized. At present the native owns five industrial units. His 11th house has 12.28 *Bhavabala,* which is unusual. Venus is in the 10th house as lord of the *lagna* and is placed in 10th house from *navamsa lagna*, in its own *navamsa*. Venus is placed 10th in the *Dasamsa* chart also. It is due to this, that he was successful and famous in plastic industry.

For Aries ascendant, combination of Saturn and Jupiter in the 9th house is auspicious and creates *Rajyoga*. Some books of astrology contradict it but our experience supports it. For Gemini ascendant, Jupiter and Saturn are lords of the 10th and 9th respectively. Both the planets, if situated in the 10th and 9th houses, help in the progress of the native. He attains some prestigious position.

One misconception, which is prevalent is, that if Saturn's

main period is fourth from the period continuing at the time of birth then it may cause the native's death. He faces severe problems, wife or child may die suddenly, impoverishment may happen. Our experience is contrary to this. In the birth chart of one very close, Saturn's main period is fourth from the period at the time of birth, but he has achieved the best results during this period only, in his life so far.

Illustration : 12.9 (**Indira Gandhi**) *Horoscope No.: 66*

Date of birth : 19.11.1917 Time of birth : 23:33:55 hrs
Place of birth : Allahabad Lat 25:27:00 N Long 81:50:00E
Ayanamsa : 22:42:52 Sidereal Time : 3:24:00

Pln	**Degree**	**Rasi**	**Nakshatra**	**Pad**
Asc	2:23:37	Leo	Magha	1
Sun	4:08:27	Sco	Anuradha	1
Mon	5:48:06	Cap	Uttarasadha	3
Mar	16:22:58	Leo	P Phalguni	1
Mer (C)	13:15:12	Sco	Anuradha	3
Jup (R)	14:60:00	Tau	Rohini	2
Ven	21:01:19	Sag	Purvasadha	3
Sat	21:47:15	Can	Aslesa	2
Rah	9:18:39	Sag	Moola	3
Ket	9:18:39	Gem	Ardra	1

Lagna Chart **Navamsa Chart**

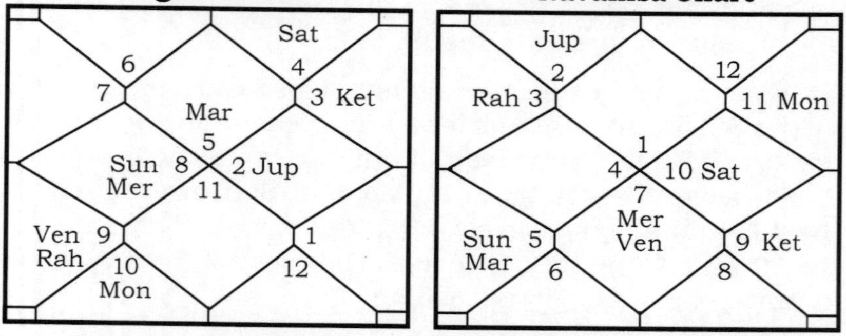

Balance of Vimshottari Dasa of **Sun 1Y 10M 20D**

It is believed that our late PM Mrs. Indira Gandhi, who was born in the Cancer ascendant, was one of the ablest in the world. Whatever predictions were made during her lifetime proved entirely untrue. That is not to say that all those astrologers were ignorant or incompetent, but that owing to faulty birth time in the birth chart, it was full of errors.

A number of scholars in India had expressed their doubts regarding it. In the English journal of astrology "Planets & Forecasts" published from Orissa, I wrote in December 1983 an article entitled 'Indira Gandhi – An Astrological Profile', in which I mentioned the correct time of her birth as 11:33 hours. According to this time, Leo was in ascendant at 2° 23'. In this article all the major events of her life were astrologically analyzed and her end in 1984 was also predicted. Due to *Vinimaya Parivartana* (Mutual Exchange) *Yoga* between lords of the 5th and 10th houses, her son Rajiv Gandhi becoming the Prime Minister, was also predicted in the very same article. Saturn's *Mahadasa* started for Mrs. Gandhi in 1970.

In its early part, she got the victory in Indo-Pak war. From 1970 to 1984 she carried India to remarkable new heights. Of course, being lord of the 7th, Saturn is also the *Markesh*– lord of death or the planet causing death. But at the same time there is "*Khadashtak*" *yoga* between Rahu and Saturn, which renders Rahu also as fatal. On 17.05.1984 Rahu's sub-period, within Saturn, commenced. During this period only, she was cruelly murdered on 31.10.1984. Saturn only, brought her among the front rankers of world politics.

In her birth chart Saturn is making "*Vipreet RajYoga*' and is situated in its own *navamsa*. Saturn is in the *nakshatra* of Mercury and vice-versa. Lord of *lagna*, Sun is also in *Anuradha*, the *nakshatra* of Saturn. In a way Indira Gandhi's personality was controlled by Saturn. Her Moon sign was Capricorn, whose lord is also Saturn. Moon and Saturn share *Vinimaya Parivartana Rajyoga*. To conclude, for persons with Leo ascendant, Saturn, despite being the fatal planet, by virtue of its situational auspiciousness gives prestige, fame, popularity and power.

In the following couplet, Sage Garga has clearly expressed his views regarding Saturn:

तुला कोदण्ड मीनानं लग्नं संस्थेपि चेत शनि।
करोति करोति भूपतेर्जन्म महापुष्यां नु भावत।।

(*Garga Hora*)

That is, Saturn if in Libra, Pisces or Sagittarius ascendant, makes the native like a king

Skandha Hora says:

इत्यासि धरो पापेषु लक्ष्मीप्रदः

(*Skandh Hora*)

In the above mentioned *lagna*s Saturn gives wealth, luxury and prosperity.

If Saturn is in its own sign, Aquarius or Capricorn, then it gives enough wealth, but being in a Jupiter sign, it overwhelms with immeasurable wealth, worthy progeny and a good wife. It also confers headship of some city or village. This is obvious from the *Shloka* given below:

स्वन्तः प्रत्ययितो नरेन्द्र भवने सत्पुत्रजायाधनो,
जीव क्षेत्रज्ञ तेऽर्कजः पुरवल ग्रामाग्रनेताथबा।।

In the 4th and 5th house, Saturn is inauspicious. Aspected by Jupiter, Saturn loses some of its evilness. If Saturn is in the 7th house, the wife of the native is dark complexioned but trustworthy and faithful. If Saturn is afflicted by evil effects, then only it indicates dark complexion, otherwise in Sagittarius, Pisces and Libra, if Saturn is in the 7th house, the spouse is not dark complexioned.

For Cancer and Leo ascendants, Saturn in the 7th is injurious. For Scorpio ascendant, Saturn being lord of the 3rd or 4th is beneficial. If in the 11th or 3rd house, it causes very good '*Dhanyoga*' (special money position). For Capricorn *lagna*, Saturn is better than in Aquarius *lagna*. In *Saravali*,

Kalyan Varma has stated:

शुरो वित्तसमृद्धौ नगराधिपतिर्यशस्वीच ।
शनि जीवयोः प्रधानः श्रेणि सभाग्रामसंघमाः ।।

(*Saravali*)

Combination of Saturn and Jupiter makes the native brave and courageous. He begets enough wealth and heads some village or town. In another *shloka* it has been stated that if Saturn is situated in the sign of Jupiter and is aspected by it, then the native becomes a king or commander of an army.

Saturn is also a planet causing renunciation. It possesses unlimited patience, tolerance and diligence. An ability to control all sensual powers and a capacity for concentration, loyalty and devotion are also present in Saturn, if it influences the 9th house.

Illustration: 12.10 (**RKP**) *Horoscope No.: 67*

Date of birth : 18.02.1836 Time of birth : 06:21:00 hrs
Place of birth : Kamarhati Lat 22:40:00 N Long 88:22:00E
Ayanamsa : 21:33:56 Sidereal Time : 16:09:05

Pln	Degree	Rasi	Nakshatra	Pad
Asc	2:39:37	Aqu	Dhanishtha	3
Sun	6:52:22	Aqu	Satabhisha	1
Mon	22:00:18	Aqu	P Bhadrapad	1
Mar (C)	22:15:00	Cap	Sravana	4
Mer (R/C)	15:07:37	Aqu	Satabhisha	3
Jup (R)	14:33:12	Gem	Ardra	3
Ven	9:03:53	Pis	U Bhadrapad	2
Sat (R)	13:41:27	Lib	Swati	3
Rah (R)	2:36:33	Tau	Kritika	2
Ket (R)	2:36:33	Sco	Vishakha	4

Lagna Chart

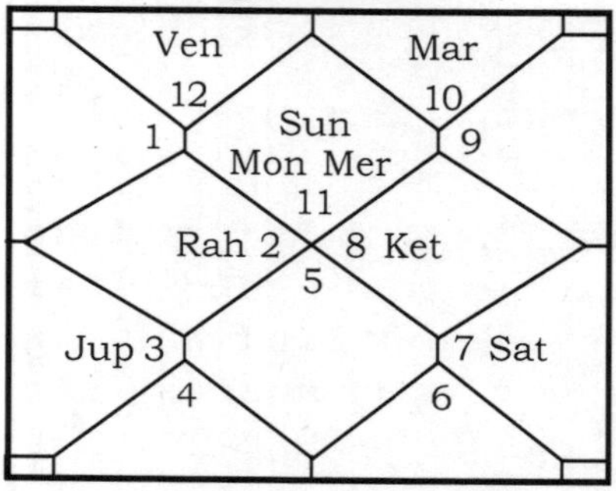

Navamsa Chart

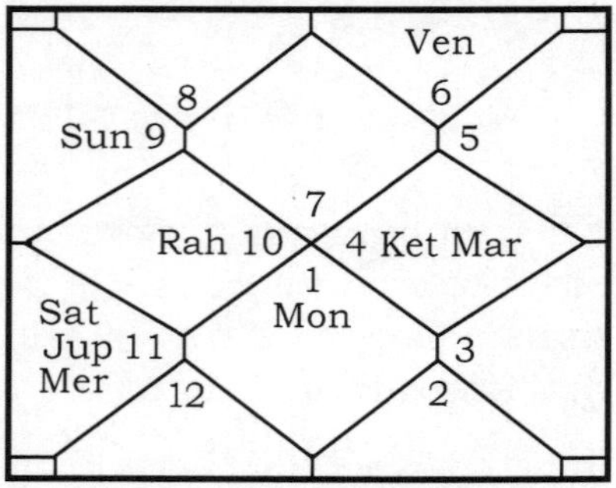

Balance of Vimshottari Dasa of **Jup 13Y 7M 3D**

In Swami Ram Krishna Paramhansa's birth chart, Saturn, lord of *lagna* and the 12th house, is situated in the 9th house, in exalted sign of Libra, and is aspected by Jupiter, whose benefic aspect is on both the ascendant and its lord Saturn, which gave the native unfathomable devotion to God and spiritual power.

Lord of the 9th and 4th Venus, is *Yogakaraka* and is situated in its exalted sign Pisces. Lord of the 10th and 3rd Mars, is also in the 12th house, in the exalted sign of Capricorn. Saturn, therefore, along with Mars and Venus in their respective exalted signs, made the native the world's greatest yogi and conferred various *Siddhis* on him.

If Saturn, being the lord of the 4th, is placed in the 9th, then also it produces devotion to God and faith and belief in him. This is possible for the natives of Scorpio and Libra ascendant.

When ascendant is Libra, lord of the 9th Mercury is in 4th, and lord of the 4th Saturn is in the 9th, then also the native is devoted to good. If such a Saturn is being aspected by Jupiter, then feeling of renunciation is very strong. Saturn in the 9th house lessens materialistic desires and worldly concerns. It inspires religious and pious feelings in the native's heart. If Saturn also receives the benefit of Jupiter's aspect, then the devotee also achieves the five fruits of his devotion.

Rule: For Libra ascendant, Saturn is *Yogakaraka* and if it is placed in the 10th house, it gives immense professional rise. If there is mutual exchange between Moon and Saturn i.e. lord of 10th and 5th, this forms a *Maharaja Yoga* and makes one equal to a King, P.M., Minister or equivalent. One reaches the topmost position and thereafter suffers a steep downfall.

Illustration: 12.11 *Horoscope No.: 68*

Pln	Degree	Rasi	Nakshatra	Pad
Asc	14:02:12	Lib	Swati	3
Sun	25:33:20	Tau	Mrigshira	1
Mon	7:52:15	Aqu	Satabhisha	1
Mar	21:54:21	Ari	Bharani	3
Mer	18:49:52	Gem	Ardra	4
Jup (R)	26:24:18	Lib	Vishakha	2
Ven	2:38:47	Tau	Kritika	2
Sat	12:35:31	Can	Pushya	3
Rah (R)	9:17:41	Tau	Kritika	4
Ket (R)	9:17:41	Sco	Anuradha	2

Lagna Chart

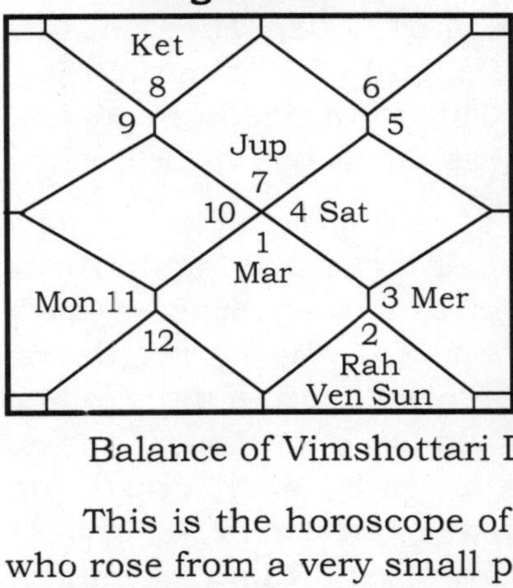

Navamsa Chart

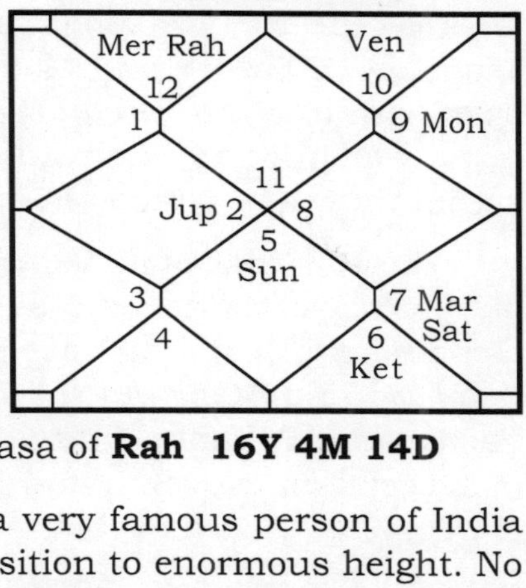

Balance of Vimshottari Dasa of **Rah 16Y 4M 14D**

This is the horoscope of a very famous person of India who rose from a very small position to enormous height. No planet is exalted in the birth chart but 3 planets i.e. Mars,

Venus and Mercury are placed in their own signs in 7th, 8th & 9th house, respectively.

The native is an extremely handsome, fair and attractive person with magnificent physique. He is a person of charming and pleasing manners coupled with an extremely perspicacious mind. A man of humble beginning, the native has risen to create his own empire in the world of finance and aviation. He also owns a television channel. Such heights have been achieved by dint of hard work and good fortune.

The native has his own demesne comprising several well appointed bungalows of latest architecture, garden, fountains, picnic spot and big halls for holding private and public functions. The mansion, in which he resides, is comparable to the best anywhere in the world. The native's love for his motherland is immeasurable. Thus, the native is blessed with exceptionally bright fortune along with innumerable qualities like sharp intelligence, courage, patriotism and organizational ability of highest order. He is meritorious, rich, industrious and energetic.

Let us judge the planetary position of his birth chart:

Saturn is *Yogakaraka* as it is the lord of 4th and 5th house and is placed in the house of profession i.e. the 10th house, whereas the 10th lord Moon falls in 5th house. Thus, mutual exchange of Saturn and Moon i.e. lord of 10th and 5th, has given rise to a *Maharaja yoga.* This is the main important *yoga,* which is responsible for his steep rise in profession within the major period of Saturn.

The 10th lord Moon, 9th lord Mercury and 2nd and 7th lord Mars receive the benefic aspect of Jupiter. The 9th lord, *Mercury,* is placed in 9th itself. Similarly, the 7th lord, Mars, is placed in own sign in the 7th house, aspecting the *lagna.* The *lagna* lord, Venus, falls in 8th house, in own sign Taurus, in association with Sun and Rahu. Thus, Mars, Venus and Mercury are placed in their own signs in the 7th, 8th and 9th house, respectively. But it is Saturn, which is mainly responsible for the rise of the native, during Saturn's

Mahadasa. Saturn obtains *navamsa* of its exaltation. The lord of 11th house, Sun also obtains own *navamsa*, which has given him lasting fame.

Here, we see that Saturn is a king maker, if it is well placed in the birth chart. Generally, people always have some apprehension regarding this vital planet Saturn, but how wrong this belief is, can be very well seen in the present birth chart. As far as *Sade Saati* of Saturn is concerned, it was auspicious for the native, at least for his professional prosperity, except the last phase when the native underwent minor health problems. So, Saturn can give more to a person if it is *Yogakaraka* and is placed in the 10th house.

The native is endowed with outstanding nobility manifested through his innumerable philanthropic activities. Almighty has blessed him with an extremely courteous and beautiful wife, loving and decent children, cooperating brothers and sisters.

He is a great patriot as well. He spends crores of rupees towards any national cause. He is a true son of the nation. He is not only a multi billionaire but also a thinker, philosopher, singer, artist, planner and visionary. He started an organization with a meager capital, which has developed into a multi thousand crore rupees entity.

Illustration:12.12(**AB**) *Horoscope No.: 69*

Date of birth : 11.10.1942 Time of birth : 16:00:00 hrs
Place of birth : Allahabad Lat 25:27:00 N Long 81:50:00E
Ayanamsa : 23:03:18 Sidereal Time : 16:14:42

Pln	**Degree**	**Rasi**	**Nakshatra**	**Pad**
Asc	1:55:45	Aqu	Dhanishtha	3
Sun	24:22:51	Vir	Chitra	1
Mon	10:18:36	Lib	Swati	2
Mar (D)	22:36:12	Vir	Hasta	4
Mer (R/D)	23:39:28	Vir	Chitra	1

Jup	0:32:15	Can	Punarvasu	4
Ven (C)	15:11:20	Vir	Hasta	2
Sat (R)	19:13:52	Tau	Rohini	3
Rah (R)	10:22:03	Leo	Magha	4
Ket (R)	10:22:03	Aqu	Satabhisha	2

Lagna Chart

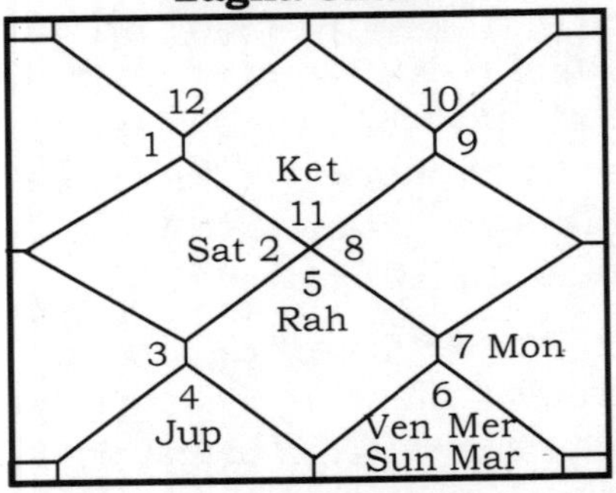

Navamsa Chart

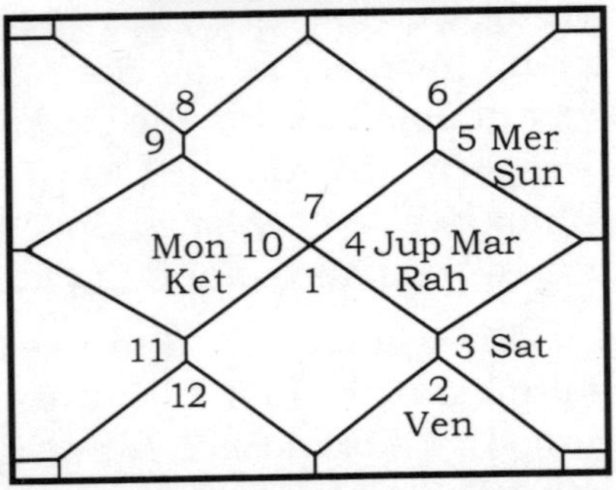

Balance of Vimshottari Dasa of **Rah 13Y 0M 29D**

Amitabh Bachchan is a great celebrity and has earned world wide fame for his outstanding performances in films. He was born in Aquarius ascendant, whose lord Saturn is well placed in the 4th house, in a friendly sign Taurus. Major period of Saturn lasted from 22.10.1971 to 22.10.1990. Saturn's period of 19 years, and that of his full youth, was the best period of his life, which made him practically equal to a king of film industry and of the heart of the people. He suffered severe setbacks in almost all of his undertakings, after Saturn's major period.

Now, a question arises whether Saturn in 4th, for Aquarius ascendant, will give such enormous height and rise to everybody. No, it is not so. There are various other factors to be judged in birth charts. In this horoscope, Saturn is not only lord of *lagna* but it contains a very high degree of strength, as much as 6.30 *Rupas* in *Shadabala*. Secondly, Saturn is retrograde and is unaspected by any malefic planet. Saturn obtains friendly *navamsa* of Mercury, in the house of fortune. Let us judge the other factors, which are responsible for the rise of this great actor of all times.

1. The *lagna* is strong, as the *lagna* lord Saturn aspects *lagna*.
2. The 10th house is strong, because the 10th house is aspected by Saturn and Jupiter both.
3. The 11th and 2nd lord *Dhankaraka* Jupiter is not only exalted but it also obtains *Vargottam navamsa* and joins the 10th lord Mars in *navamsa* chart. Jupiter aspects the 10th and 2nd house and promotes the prospects of these houses.
4. The *lagna* lord Saturn is 9th from the 10th lord Mars, 9th from the 7th lord Sun, and most of all Saturn is 9th from 9th and 4th lord i.e. the *Yogakaraka* Venus. The Saturn is also 9th from the 5th and 8th lord Mercury. Thus, Saturn is placed in the 9th house from 3rd, 4th, 5th, 7th, 8th, 9th and 10th lords. This is a unique and rare combination of this great man's chart.
5. Saturn is 11th from 11th and 2nd lord Jupiter, which made him so wealthy during Saturn's period of 19 years.

Every birth chart has unique combinations and learning the art of judgement of such combinations, makes one an expert astrologer. One can make blunders if one misses to check that Saturn, which gives very good results for Aquarius borns, is posited 9th from 9th lord, 11th from 11th lord and lends its aspect over the 10th house in association with exalted Jupiter. One should also see that *Yogakaraka* Venus, the 7th lord Sun, 11th and 2nd lord Jupiter are in own signs and in the sign of exaltation in *navamsa* chart, and planet responsible for wealth, Jupiter, falls in own constellation and obtains *Vargottam navamsa*.

This unique planetary setup made this native Amitabh Bachchan the strongest pillar of the film world.

Illustration: 12.13 (**AKC**) *Horoscope No.: 70*

Date of birth : 15.10.1954 Time of birth : 07:16:00 hrs
Place of birth : Kanpur Lat 26:27:00 N Long 80:19:00E
Ayanamsa : 23:13:47 Sidereal Time : 8:39:30

Pln	**Degree**	**Rasi**	**Nakshatra**	**Pad**
Asc	12:10:30	Lib	Swati	2
Sun	27:56:35	Vir	Chitra	2
Mon	8:22:26	Tau	Kritika	4
Mar	2:41:02	Cap	Uttarasadha	2
Mer	20:53:45	Lib	Vishakha	1
Jup	4:59:24	Can	Pushya	1
Ven	4:46:48	Sco	Anuradha	1
Sat	16:21:41	Lib	Swati	3
Rah (R)	15:28:33	Sag	Purvasadha	1
Ket (R)	15:28:33	Gem	Ardra	3

Lagna Chart

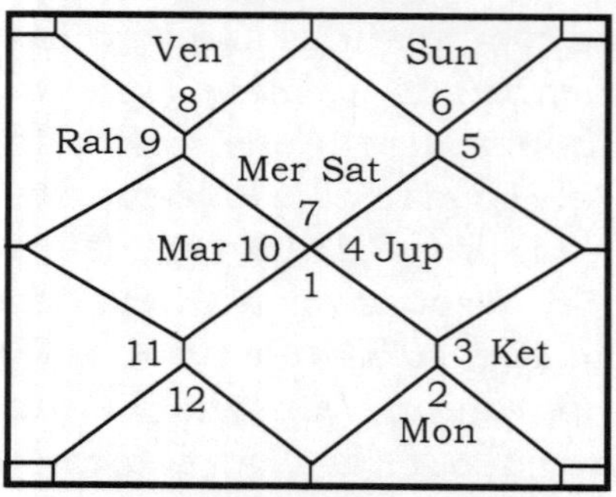

Navamsa Chart

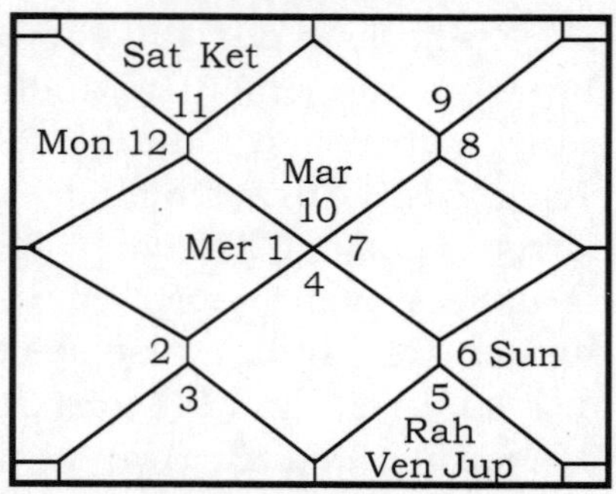

Balance of Vimshottari Dasa of **Sun 0Y 8M 23D**

The native is a great Industrialist of Asia dealing in plastic, lamination and packaging material. He started his career from a very low position and had to do a lot of cycling in the early young age, to make both ends meet. Now he is the owner of unlimited wealth, a number of industries, farms, lands and houses etc.

The native was born in Libra ascendant with exalted Saturn therein. Saturn happens to be a *Yogakaraka* for Libra borns and that has given rise to *Sasa Maha Purusha Rajyoga*. It is not only Saturn, which has done the miracle in such a short period. The following planetary setup is strong enough to elevate the native to the present height.

1. Saturn exalted in *lagna*, Mars exalted in the 4th, Jupiter exalted in the 10th and Moon exalted in the 8th house i.e. vital planets are exalted and three out of them are exalted in the angles only.
2. The combination of '*Bhagyadhipati*' (lord of luck) Mercury with *Yogakaraka* Saturn, in the ascendant, is the best. Lords of both the triangles are associated in the *lagna* itself. This combination can elevate any one to a very strong and high position.
3. Saturn obtains own *navamsa*, Mars obtains *vargottam navamsa*, in exaltation in *navamsa lagna*, which has given lot of youth, charm, energy, activeness, dynamism and dashing qualities to the native.
4. The Sun, who is the 11th lord, obtains *vargottam navamsa*. This provided fame, honour, reputation, recognition, prosperity, power and popularity to the native.

Mercury is the strongest planet as far as *shadabala* of planets is concerned. Mercury obtains 11.03 *Rupa Shadabala*, which is an extraordinary high strength. Thereafter, Jupiter and Saturn are strong. All the three planets are placed in *Kendras*. Rahu is also best placed in the 3rd house. These splendid and powerful combinations have given a steep and exceptional professional rise to the native.

12.6 Saturn : The Timer

To predict the exact spell of time, for any event to happen, is one of the most arduous tasks in astrology. There are innumerable systems, which help in timing the events in various ways. *Vimshottari dasa* system and transits are the most customary procedures, which are considered one of the vital tools of an astrologer. Apart from various kinds of *dasa* systems such as *Vimshottari, Asttottari, Yogini, Kalchakra* and *Jaimini,* solar return charts and transits of planets also help us in precise predictions as far as the timing of an event is concerned.

Transit of Saturn is a supporting tool in pin pointing the period of occurrence of important events, and more so the turning points of one's life. The study of the role of Saturn in any horoscope is quite complicated and tough exercise, which may be correctly and successfully worked out only after a thorough study and wide experience of the subject. In fact, generally, we know very little about predictions on the basis of transiting planets and more so about the transit of Saturn. There are a few veteran scholars, who are able to predict all important, good or bad, events and their periods, only on the basis of transiting planets, without taking any help of *dasa-bhukti* etc.

Whenever Saturn transits over the natal Sun, many adversities take place, especially with regard to the matters of the house owned by the Sun. Suppose, Scorpio is the ascendant and the 10th lord Saturn is posited in Cancer in the 9th house. Whenever Saturn will transit over the 10th lord Sun, in Cancer, serious problems are bound to arise in professional matters.

Saturn is a planet of paramount importance. Saturn covers one's career and moulds it according to its placement in the birth chart. Saturn indicates the accumulated power of *Karmas* of past life and the outcome of the *Karmas* of the past life comes in evidence in the present life. From Saturn's transit, in relation to the natal position in the chart, one can find out the changes, promotions and demotions in the career, or which may cause recognition, or otherwise affect the native.

Saturn's transit is quite important with regard to the 10th house, or professional matters, that may cause promotion, appreciation, recognition, expansion, extension and all-round professional success. Contrary effects may also be experienced. What will be the exact result depends on the 10th lord and the position of the 10th lord, both from ascendant and Moon. In case of mutual exchange of the 10th lord with any other planet, transit of Saturn over the other planet will bring prosperity and popularity in all professional matters. If the 10th lord, or the planet of mutual exchange, is inimical to Saturn, negative results appear, as soon as Saturn transits over that particular planet.

Saturn stays two and a half years in one sign. An expert and experienced astrologer may foresee whether that two and a half year period is favourable or unfavourable. The life of a person may be covered in three or four circles of Saturn's transit. Each cycle of thirty years may be divided into twelve segments of two and a half years each. Saturn will transit for two and a half years in each sign. One zodiacal sign contains two and a quarter constellations, nine *navamsa* signs and thirty degrees. There will be different dates or time periods when Saturn transits in different asterisms and *navamsa*s. Saturn transits in one constellation for 13 months and 10 days and in one *navamsa* for 3 months and 10 days approximately, and these segments of time span are of great significance and use, with regard to determination of correct events. But it requires expert experience and practice with regard to transiting planets. A few important points should be kept in view quite distinctly.

1. Transiting planets do not create events. If any event is not indicated in the birth chart i. e. the event, which is not promised by natal chart, will not take place. Transiting planets help in precise timing of any event.

2. Saturn indicates losses, sickness, obstacles, restriction, worries and pains. If Saturn is in a negative transit, its occupation, aspect or conjunction with any house or lord thereof, will certainly cause problems. However, if Saturn's transit is positive, quite encouraging results will be experienced with regard to the concerning house.

3. The exact result of the transit of Saturn depends on the nature of sign through which it is passing. If Saturn is a *Yogakaraka* and transits over the sign of exaltation, or own sign, the benefic results will be the outcome. If Saturn transits in its sign of debilitation or inimical sign, the negative results will come up.

4. Whenever Saturn transits over the natal Mars, the life takes a prominent turn. When Saturn transits 4th, 7th, and 11th as reckoned from natal Mars, vital changes with prominence are experienced. These are the turning points of life. One should be quite cautious at the time of change of sign during the transit of Saturn. This turning point may either be favourable or unfavourable, which depends on the position and ownership of natal Mars.

Illustration : 12.8 (**RS**) *Horoscope No.: 71*

Date of birth : 20.07.1952 Time of birth : 12:45:36 hrs

Place of birth : Jabalpur Lat 23:10:00 N Long 79:57:00E

Ayanamsa : 23:11:50 Sidereal Time : 8:27:27

Pln	**Degree**	**Rasi**	**Nakshatra**	**Pad**
Asc	10:21:44	Lib	Swati	2
Sun	4:18:02	Can	Pushya	1
Mon	15:55:18	Gem	Ardra	3
Mar	17:03:49	Lib	Swati	4
Mer	0:24:49	Leo	Magha	1
Jup	23:44:51	Ari	Bharani	4
Ven (C)	11:18:34	Can	Pushya	3
Sat	16:16:51	Vir	Hasta	2
Rah (R)	28:26:31	Cap	Dhanistha	2
Ket (R)	28:26:31	Can	Aslesa	4

Lagna Chart

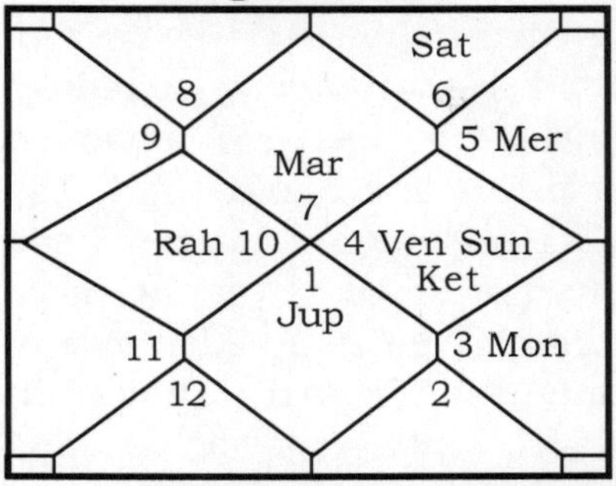

Navamsa Chart

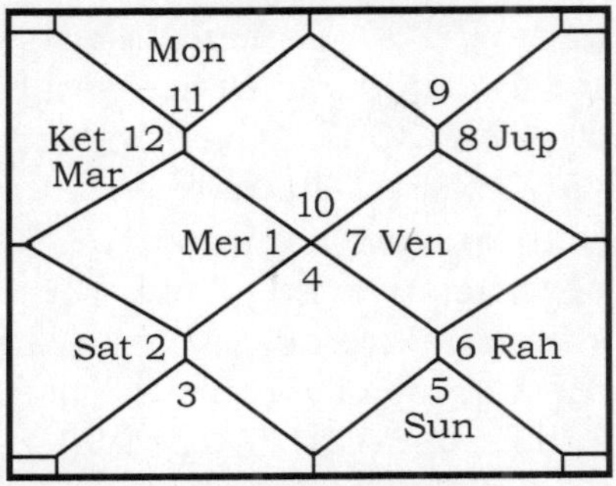

Balance of Vimshottari Dasa of **Rah 5Y 6M 2D**

In the case of illustration no. 12.8, the native was a famous, very well established and well-known business magnet. He was running many large units of Plastic industry. Everything was quite fine and bright. There were at least two cars for each member of the family. The native had a turn over of approximately one billion rupees per annum. Suddenly, an abrupt & steep descent came in his business w. e. f. May 1998, when Saturn was transiting in Aries. Saturn transited in Aries from 17.4.1998 to 7.6.2000. The native was born in Libra ascendant with Mars. Saturn's transit in Aries should be properly studied.

Transit of Saturn was 11th from radical Moon. With that reason, auspicious and benefic results should have come but it was just the opposite. Saturn's transit in Aries was 7th from natal Mars and that changed the course of life of the native by bringing a heavy downfall. The transit of Saturn in Aries wrecked the empire of the native. All factories were locked out, cars and land were sold. The native was compelled to dispose off his valuable gems, ornaments, machines and the like. Here, the transit of Saturn through Aries changed the life of the native in a most unprecedented manner. This downward trend has not yet stopped, even after nearly 10 years. We humbly opine that the transit of Saturn, just opposite natal Mars in a birth chart, brings negative U-turn in one's life, if Mars is a negative planet for that particular ascendant.

The native had to undergo imprisonment from 5-3-2003 to 14-3-2003, when Saturn was transiting over the lord of the 10th house i. e. the natal Moon. He was again locked up on 29-7-2007, when Saturn entered in Leo and aspected natal Mars. The native has reached to the bankruptcy. His relations with almost all his friends and relatives have become strained. Thus, the transit of Saturn over the natal Mars is extremely adverse. Let us derive the positive side of the transit of Saturn in the same case. Saturn transited in Libra from 7.10.1982 to 30.12.1984. The native was working as the Chief Engineer in a private firm. He resigned there and came to Lucknow with bag and baggage. He started independent Plastic business during the transit of Saturn through Libra and got astonishing success in a short span of time. From Rs. 5000/- he started earning billions of rupees. The growth, expansion and regular flow of income continued all through the transit of Saturn from Libra to Pisces and downfall started w.e.f. transit of Saturn through Aries as discussed above.

Mars is a negative planet for Libra ascendant but it gives positive results in the 11th, 3rd and 10th house, in spite of the lordship of the 2nd and 7th house. The transit of Saturn, in the 4th, 7th and 11th house, as reckoned from natal Mars, brings prominent changes and turnings in life. These are not the events but the change of course of events. These are the prominent turning points, which are over and above the *dasa-bhukti.* All those who know astrology will find our observation very useful when sudden positive or negative changes are not explained by *dasa- bhukti.*

Illustration: 12.15 (**AG**) *Horoscope No.: 72*

Date of birth : 05.09.1963 Time of birth : 11:24:00 hrs

Place of birth : Kanpur Lat 26:27:00 N Long 80:19:00E

Ayanamsa : 23:20:42 Sidereal Time : 10:09:46

Pln	**Degree**	**Rasi**	**Nakshatra**	**Pad**
Asc	1:35:09	Sco	Vishakha	4
Sun	18:36:41	Leo	P Phalguni	2

Mon	7:52:44	Pis	U Bhadrapad	2
Mar	1:56:00	Lib	Chitra	3
Mer	11:38:50	Vir	Hasta	1
Jup (R)	24:59:14	Pis	Revati	3
Ven (D)	20:17:55	Leo	P Phalguni	3
Sat (R)	24:45:59	Cap	Dhanistha	1
Rah (R)	25:40:45	Gem	Punarvasu	2
Ket (R)	25:40:45	Sag	Purvasadha	4

Lagna Chart

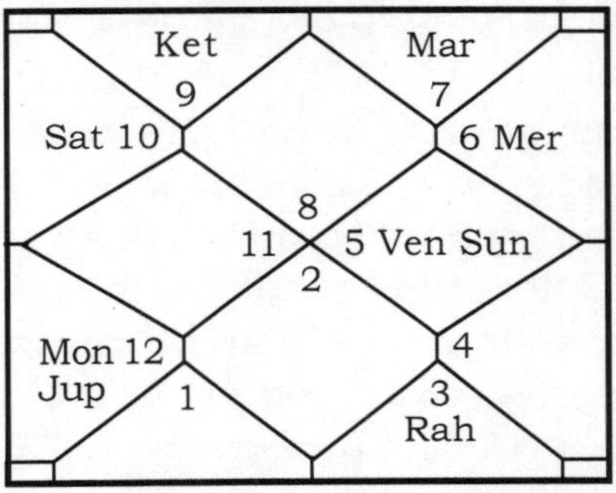

Navamsa Chart

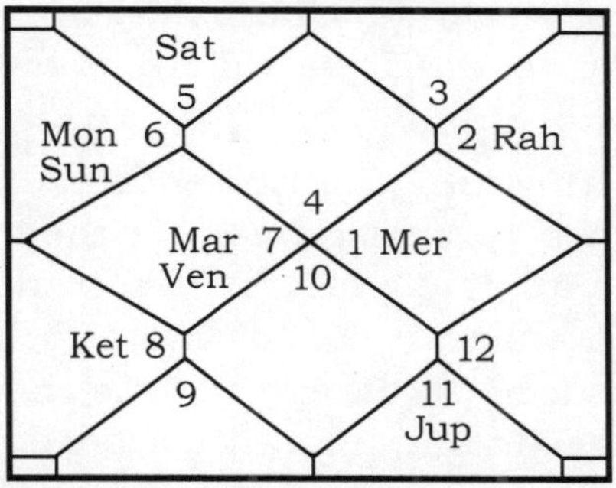

Balance of Vimshottari Dasa of **Sat 12Y 6M 8D**

The native entered in business only at the age of 16 years and became one of the leading businessmen within 15 years. The native was running a very large security printing press and was earning millions of rupees per month. He decided to enter into dairy business at a large scale during the year 1991. He implemented his idea and soon a large dairy was commissioned in the beginning of 1993, when Saturn was transiting in Capricorn from 5.1.1991 to 30.3.1993.

The native was born in Scorpio ascendant. Mars occupies the 12th house in Libra. Saturn's transit in Capricorn was a turning point of his career because natal Mars was aspected by transiting Saturn from Capricorn. The transiting Saturn completely changed the course of the life of the native. It was a positive change. It was so, because Saturn was transiting in own sign, Capricorn, where Mars gets exalted. Dairy started functioning very nicely, which was beyond the expectation of the native. Dairy was running round the clock. The native made many expansions and extensions in the dairy. He started producing dry milk, ghee and other products as well. Each and every thing of the business was running perfectly well in all aspects as long as transiting Saturn did not lend its aspect over the natal Mars. Saturn entered in Aries on 17.4.1998 and stayed there till 7.6.2000. Aries is the sign of debilitation of Saturn. Innumerable problems started creeping up in his industry. Incredible losses and obstacles were there in place of heavy profits and success. These sufferings have no end as yet.

Thus, as per our humble observations, whenever transiting Saturn lends its aspect over the natal Mars, it becomes a landmark or the turning phase of one's life. Also, transit of Saturn over radical location of Mars, brings prominent change in one's life and gives a sharp turn, in one or the other way. This change may be positive or negative, depending upon the ascendant, sign occupied by the natal Mars, and the sign in which Saturn transits. This is our view based on the study of these two and many other horoscopes. Our research on this point can be said to be in a nascent stage. Learned readers may verify these findings in their own studies as well. We are sure that similar results will be obtained.

12.7 Saturn's *Saadhe Saati*

Common belief among general people is that the *Saadhe Saati* of Saturn is a very adverse period of seven and a half year and it stops prosperity, happiness, progress, popularity and on the other hand brings miseries, mourns, losses, thefts, defamation, destruction, dishonour, despairs, disappointments, dejections, disruptions, and discontinuation of regular growth in various spheres of life. Here, we would like to say that for all this *Saadhe Saati* of Saturn can be held responsible. First of all let us explain all about *Saadhe Saati* of Saturn.

12.8 Evil effects of seven and a half year of Saturn's *Saadhe Saati* :

The very term strikes terror and extreme apprehension in the mind of the listener. It has been so from times immemorial. Several astrologers use it as an infailiable weapon to demoralize an individual. But there are a lot of misconceptions about "*Saadhe Saati*". In folklore it is always depicted as a devastating misfortune. Saturn's natural cruelty, when coupled with *Saadhe Saati*, sends shivering down one's spine. It is, therefore, imperative that this seven and a half year period of Saturn be properly analyzed.

When Saturn is situated in the 12-1-2 houses from Moon sign, then it is "*Saadhe Saati*".

In the 12th house, Saturn has 2½ years influence over eyes or sight. If in the 1st house then it is called 2½ years "bhog". In the 2nd house, it is called his "feet", which means that Saturn stays in the eyes, stomach and feet respectively during this period. This is also called the *"brihatkalyani"* period of seven and a half years.

Usually Saturn completes its cycle of passage through various signs in 30 years. Thus, it stays for 2½ year in each sign. The *Saadhe Saati* starts when transiting Saturn enters the twelfth house from the birth sign. Then from twelfth through first till after second house, the *Saadhe Saati* cycle lasts a total of seven and half years.

An individual who has suffered one *Saadhe Saati* will only be afflicted again by it after thirty years. If we discount the exceptions then an individual usually faces *Saadhe Saati* thrice in his lifetime.

Saadhe Saati is a fearsome term in itself. But the whole period of the seven and a half years is not necessarily devastating. Saturn affects the individual according to the situation in the birth chart. As per some astrologers, Saturn gives the following results in the *Saadhe Saati* according to the birth sign :

1.	Aries	The middle part is bad.
2.	Taurus	The beginning is dangerous.
3.	Gemini	The end is dangerous.
4.	Cancer	The middle and end is dangerous.
5.	Leo	The beginning and the middle are dangerous.
6.	Virgo	The beginning is dangerous.
7.	Libra	The end is dangerous.
8.	Scorpio	The middle and the end are dangerous.
9.	Sagittarius	The beginning and middle is dangerous.
10.	Capricorn	The first and last periods are dangerous.
11.	Aquarius	The whole period is good.
12.	Pisces	The end is dangerous.

Apart from the above, the overall effects of three stages of this period are as follows :

1. The first stage : The individual is financially in dire straits. Since expenditure outweighs the income all plans flop. Sudden financial loss catches one unawares. Physical comforts and health are afflicted. The individual turns into a nomad, roaming aimlessly. Father's mother suffers fatal pain. There may be some eye disease and one may have to use spectacles. The individual's mind is under terrible tension, frustation and dissatisfaction. Guardians and relatives suffer. Income and profits are adversely affected. Separation from family occurs. Father has to face problems.

2. The second stage : There are constant financial worries. Physical ability, status and movement are afflicted. There are terrible mental upheavals. Useless expenses cause worry. Nothing happens according to one's wishes. There are lots of hurdles. Incomplete work causes unhappiness. The personality is under cloud. Familial, marital and professional lives are in disarray. Some relative suffers fatal agony. Long journeys, trouble from enemies, separation from loved ones, even imprisonment, diseases, loss of property, social disgrace, lack of friends and blockage in work are the results of this stage. All attempts prove futile.

3. The third stage : Pointless disputes occur. There are useless clashes with relatives and friends. They suffer from serious illness, which may prove fatal in some case. The health and happiness from children and their longevity is affected. Power from position vanishes. There is excessive expenditure. One feels lethargic, inactive and weak physically. Enjoyment and happiness are disturbed. Money comes but goes just as fast. Some low-minded persons cheat the individual.

12.9 Repetition or Reoccurrence of *Saadhe Saati*

Usually a person suffers these seven and a half years of Saturn's period thrice in his or her lifetime. A fourth occurrence is a rare exception.

In every occurrence the power or strength of the *Saadhe Saati* differs. The first occurrence is very strong. The affected person is badly afflicted by problems, obstacles and losses. The second occurrence is comparatively more controlled. Its fatal influence is much less powerful. The person feels some relief too.

The third occurrence is full of the most gruesome effects. The person is afflicted by all round calamities. It seems as if Saturn is bent on destroying his or her life. Very lucky individuals come out unhurt from this period.

It is already well known that every planet gives good or bad results depending on its being exalted or debilitated. When Saturn is exalted in the birth chart, in its own sign or in a friendly sign or in "mooltrikona" then the results are relatively better. When Saturn in the birth chart is strong, and transiting Saturn is weak, then the results are mediocre. When it is weak both ways, the results are highly undesirable.

In this context the experts of astrology have mentioned some special conditions :

1. If a transiting Saturn is giving undesirable and bad results then the effects of other auspicious planets are also reduced.
2. If a transiting Saturn is giving inauspicious results and Jupiter is favourable then the inauspicious results gain in power.
3. In the period when Saturn is giving good results and Jupiter is unfavourable, then overall the results are good.
4. If Jupiter and Rahu are indicating bad results but Saturn is favourable then good results happen in a greater number.

12.10 Saturn's *Saadhe Saati* - Special Analysis

It is natural that *Saadhe Saati* of Saturn affects different signs differently, since Saturn in transit would produce results according to its relation with lord of each sign. The sign, through which Saturn is passing, would either be its exalted, debilitated, own, friendly or inimical sign. What is the relationship of Saturn with that sign, Saturn is owner of which house, what is the effect of Saturn's location in the birth chart—all these factors are to be considered. If the *Saadhe Saati* begins at a time when the period of some auspicious or a *Yogakaraka* planet is running, then the evil incluence of the *Saadhe Saati* will appear less powerful on its own. Whenever one has to predict or study the effects, good or evil, of Saturn's *Saadhe Saati*, it is advisable to do it after thorough analysis. Following points are worth keeping in mind in this respect.

1. Acharya H.N. Ketve, a very research oriented astrologer of Maharashtra, had a theory. Deduct forty-five degrees from the birth Moon and add forty-five degrees to birth Moon. This arc of ninety degrees is the actual *Saadhe Saati.*
2. It is our observation that Saturn in direct motion is more

malefic than when in retrograde motion. This needs more in-depth testing.

3. First two and a half years of *Saadhe Saati* are malefic for the parents, if the *dasha* and transit are also bad. Second 2½ years of *Saadhe Saati* are malefic for self. Saturn's *dasha* and transit on natal Moon give deep depression.

4. Transit of Saturn in the sign occupied by Moon in the natal chart, gives malefic results, if Saturn is a bad house lord and bad *dasha* and transit are also there.

5. Transit of Saturn in *Saadhe Saati* does not cause much harm, if the *dasha* running at that time is favourable.

6. Effects of *Saadhe Saati* are checked heavily, if strong Jupiter and *Maha dasha* lord in transit, protect the Moon, by aspect or conjunction.

7. Effects are also minimized, if the Saturn is transiting in its exaltation sign, own houses or friend's house.

8. *Saadhe Saati* of Saturn is not always harmful. It's ill effects are controlled by number of other factors such as operating *dasha*, transit of other major planets and conste-llations in which Saturn is transiting, position of natal Saturn from Moon and ascendant.

9. It may be seen that the *dasha* of a debilitated planet, placed in a malefic house, can give good results.

10. While delineating *Saadhe Saati*, to see the direction of events of the *Saadhe Saati*, the lordship/placement of Saturn from *lagna*/Moon and from its natal position need to be seen. The intensity would be felt when Saturn also afflicts the other luminary, the Sun.

11. *Saadhe Saati* can only supplement or modify, whatever has been dictated by the *dasha*.

12. The functional *karakatwas* of Saturn by lordship/ placement from Moon and *lagna* should not be overlooked. It gives the direction.

13. The trnasit of Saturn should also be seen with reference to natal Saturn and Sun.

14. In addition to the *Sarvashtaka Varga,* the points in the *Bhinnashtaka Varga* of Saturn and Moon may also be seen to see the intensity of *Saadhe Saati.*

15. *Saadhe Saati*, most of the times, proves dangerous to parents.

16. The concept that the *Yogakaraka* planet Saturn, for Libra and Taurus *lagna,* may not cause much harm during transit, is subject to exceptions.

17. If Saturn, during its transit, also afflicts other planets in their radical position, the damage could be more.

18. The concept, that the transit of Saturn through its exaltation, own house or friendly signs may not be harmful, is not universal.

19. The placement of Moon in the respective charts of the spouses has to be seen to see the intensity and duration of the effect of *Saadhe Saati.* If they are in 3/10 or 4/10 from each other and the *dashas* are also not favourable, it can spell disaster.

20. Saturn's transit through *Janma Nakshatra* and other remaining *nakshatras* in Saturn's *asthtanvarga* has to be watched with caution, in spite of fortification by *sarvashtaka varga.*

21. The transit of Saturn within 5 degrees behind or ahead of natal Moon's degree has to be watched. It is potent to cause alarm.

22. Saturn is the dispenser of justice. It is bound by duty to fructify the results as ordained by the promise in the horoscope. It is not absolute that the misfortunes confine to the period of *Saadhe Saati* only. Other good houses can also spell disaster if the *dasha* is not favourable and Saturn touches sensitive points.

23. *Saadhe Saati* in bad *dasha* compounds evil effects.

24. Generally *Saadhe Saati* gives rise to mental agony, which may or may not be related to other activities of life. It may be so.

25. The connection of *dasha* lords with *lagna* and tenth house in *rashi* and *dashamsha* charts and involvement in *Raja* and *dhana yogas*, is a green signal for his professional advancement.

26. Affliction to *dasha* lords by malefic, lord of 6th house, lord of 64th *navamsa*, lord of 22nd *dreshkana* and weakness in transit, is an important factor for bad health.

27. If the *dasha* lords are favourable along with transit of Saturn, Jupiter, Rahu and Mars, on *Sarvashtaka varga* and house-wise, they give good results during *Saadhe Saati.*

28. The aspect of transiting Jupiter on natal Moon is the most potent protector during *Saadhe Saati.*

29. Significations of lordship of Moon and Saturn activate during *Saadhe Saati.*

30. The transit of Saturn over the natal Sun, as well as 9th house, may give distress and illness to father in the bad *dasha.*

12.11 *Saadhe Saati* of Saturn : A Few Amazing Findings

The period of Saturn's *Saadhe Saati* is approximately seven and a half years. During this period a number of problems, afflictions occur which have been described earlier. The transitory period of Saturn through the sign fourth from the natal Moon is called *"Kantaka Shani"*. Our experience proves that this is the most afflicted period. *Ashtam Shani* (the eighth Saturn) i.e. Saturn transiting through the eighth sign (from the Moon sign), is also extremely inauspicious and produces evil results.

On the contrary when transitory Saturn passes through signs of third, sixth and eleventh houses (from the sign of birth Moon) then it produces very beneficial results. This fact is well recognized and well known; still our belief is based on in-depth analysis of the subject.

It we deduct 45 degrees from the natal Moon's sign, degree, minutes and seconds, then the resultant number indicates the sign which when transited by Saturn marks the beginning of the *Saadhe Saati* period. Accordingly, if we add 45 degrees to the birth Moon's sign, degrees etc., then the resultant sign is the one which when transited by Saturn, marks the end of the *Saadhe Saati.*

12.12 Propitiating Shani *Saadhe Sati*

When placed in undesirable positions during his Saadhe Saati, Saturn produces terrible results. Apart from the rituals, there are some special practices and experiments, which are recommended chiefly to propitiate Saturn during *Saadhe Saati.*

1. Every Saturday if one bathes with water to which saunf, khirenti, lodh khas, lobaan, surma, dhamani, black sesame, Gond, shat kusum, and khilla have been added, then the ill effects of Saturn are calmed.

2. Shani mandal yantra should be engraved on a sheet of iron or lead on a Saturday. A blue sapphire should be studded in the centre of the yantra.

   Then it should be enlivened (*prana pratishtha*) with the beejmantra. Then a lighted lamp (*deep*) should be offered to it in the afternoon. Afterwards the yantra should be given away as alms along with the following things :

   Iron, mustard oil, shoes, buffalo, black cloth, black cow, black flower, wool, blanket, umbrella, kulthi, musk and some money. These things may be reduced in number but the making of the yantra and the prana pratishtha must be flawless.

3. The yantra of Shani, which has 3 rows and 3 columns in which 4,9,2 in 1st row, 3,5,7 in 2nd row and 8,1,6 in 3rd row are written horizontally, should be engraved on

a sheet of iron and after being fortified with mantras should be worn. It removes the problems brought about by the *Saadhe Saati.*

4. One should observe fast on Saturday. After sunset lord Hanuman should be worshipped and then the fast broken. Vermillion, oil of black sesame and lamp of the same oil, along with red flowers, should be used for worshiping.

5. On a Saturday untwined cotton thread should be 7 times wound round a peepal tree while reciting some mantra of Saturn. Then the tree should be worshipped and offered a lighted lamp. On this day one should take salt less meal only once.

6. The story of "Shani Vrata" - people suffering from ill effects of the *Saadhe Saati* can obtain great relief by doing this fruitful experiment. The Vrata should preferably start on a flawless Saturday in the month of Shravana, otherwise it can begin on any Saturday.

7. One of the most useful and beneficial preventive measures to nullify the adversities caused by Saturn is named as "Shani Ki Patal Yatra". This should be done only by any experienced Acharya otherwise even the demise of Acharya is possible. It has been tested by us number of times that "Shani Ki Patal Yatra" can prevent maximum evils caused by malefic Saturn during its *Saadhe Saati*, Kantak Shani, Laghu Kalyani Dhaiya or its dasa bhukti. This is a strong measure to eliminate all adversities caused by Satury to burry those evils in patal lok. If these measures are properly followed by the sufferers of Saturn, all kinds of ailments, problems, losses, tensions, frustations, failure of undertaking, death of family member, loss of property etc. can be minimized to a very great extent.

8. It is most essential to recite Vadic, Pauranik and Tantrik mantras of Saturn everyday during the *Saadhe Saati* of Saturn. The mantras should be recited for atleast 108

times everyday. The number of mantras should be enhanced at equivalent intervals. However, dashansha havan, tarpan, maarjan should be performed as per rituals.

<u>वैदिक मंत्र-</u> **ॐ खां खीं खौं सः ॐ भूर्भुवः स्वः ॐ शन्नोदेवीरभिष्टय आपो भवन्तु पीतये। शंय्योरभिस्रवन्तु नः। ॐ स्वः भुवः भूः ॐ सः खौं खीं खां ॐ शनैश्चराय नमः।**

<u>तांत्रिक मंत्र-</u> **ॐ प्रां प्रीं प्रौं सः शनये नमः।**

अथवा

ॐ खां खीं खौं सः शनये नमः।

<u>पौराणिक मंत्र-</u> **ॐ नीलांजनसमाभासं रविपुत्रं यमाग्रजम्।**
छायामार्तण्डसम्भूतं तं नमामि शनैश्चरम्।।

9. "Dashrath krit Shani Strota" should also be read with absolute devotion, dedication and concentration correctly. Shani Strota is easily available everywhere.

We have mentioned innumerable preventive measures for the prevention and rectification of the *Saadhe Saati* of Saturn in our famous work "Shani Shaman".

12.13 Secrets of the son of the Sun : Saturn

1. Yogakaraka Saturn in the 10th house :

For Libra ascendant, Saturn is a *Yogakaraka* planet and its placement in the 10th house gives enormous professional rise.

Any person having such placement of Saturn, in the 10th house, will become a king, ruler, administrator, minister, Governor, chairman, or the like, even if he is born in a very poor family. Hitler was born in Libra ascendant, having Saturn in the 10th house, and that made a history.

2. Mutual exchange of 10th and 5th lords, for Libra ascendant :

Moon becomes the lord of the 10th house and Saturn is the 5th lord. If there is mutual exchange between Moon and Saturn, or both are conjoined in the 10th or 5th house, one becomes equal to a King, P.M. or Chief Minister or head of a very big organisation.

This has also been observed that Saturn snatches a lot and brings a heavy downfall when the period is over.

3. Saturn in the 7th house :

Saturn's placement in the 7th house causes delay in marriage, especially if it is retrograde. If Sun is placed in the ascendant and Saturn in the 7th house, and both of these planets are almost at same degrees, marriage will be completely denied.

Conjunction of Saturn and Rahu in the 7th house is extremely adverse and causes separation after marriage.

If Saturn is placed in the ascendant and it has direct motion, the rivals and opponents are destroyed by the grace of God, automatically.

If Saturn is retrograde in the ascendant and is aspected by malefics and unaspected by benefics, one becomes a murderer and is not caught. However, the benefic aspect of Jupiter or Venus will prevent him to become a killer.

If Saturn becomes a *"Markesh"* and it is placed in an airy sign i.e. Gemini, Libra or Aquarius, one dies due to poison. If Saturn falls in fiery sign i.e. Aries, Leo or Sagittarious, one dies due to poison but placement of Saturn in earthy sign such as Taurus, Virgo or Capricorn will cause death due to war, quarrel or murder. If *"Markesh"* Saturn falls in watery sign such as Cancer, Scorpio, or Pisces, one dies due to adverse or negative effects of medicines. However, 22nd *dreshkaan* should also be taken into consideration before arriving at any conclusion for the cause of death.

4. Saturn in the 8th house :

Saturn's placement in the 8th house gives a good longevity i.e. a long span of life. However, the diagnosis of the disease is always deceptive in such case and old age is tough, as far as health is concerned.

Placement of Saturn in the ascendant, in Capricorn or Aquarius, will eliminate all opponents and rivals automatically. However, if retrograde Saturn occupies the ascendant and ascendant lord Saturn is affected by malefics, the person will be removed or he will be hanged to death.

5. Saturn's Transit in 8th gives enormous wealth :

When Saturn transits in the 8th house, one receives appreciable amount of wealth from any old person, male or female. This is not our finding but we found this observation correct in a few cases. However, this rule should be used only for timing this event, provided such indication of getting money or property, through legacy or so, is there. Such a property, wealth or job can be received, when Saturn transits at 1st degree of the sign falling in the 8th house.

6. Paralysis and Saturn :

If Saturn and Rahu afflict the 8th house, or these have concern with the 8th house, in one or other way, or both Rahu and Saturn are placed in the constellation of each other and one of these is positioned in the 8th house, one will suffer from paralysis. If Venus is also involved, the combination becomes harmful.

If Saturn becomes a killer and falls in airy sign i.e. Gemini, Libra or Aquarius, one may die due to poison.

7. Saturn in the 6th and chronic ailments :

One suffers from various ailments such as gout, rheumatism, gastric disorder, spondylitis, arthritis, asthma, troubles connected with veins, polio, disorders of limbs, trouble in legs, respiratory complaints, early decay of hair and teeth etc., if Saturn is placed in the 6th house, especially in airy signs such as Gemini, Libra or Aquarius.

8. Saturn *Mahadasha* at 4th in sequence :

If Saturn *Mahadasha* is the 4th reckoned from the balance *Mahadasha* of birth, one will suffer a lot. He will become poor, diseased and sicky. He may lose all his money and be prosecuted. He will be charge-sheeted and face lot of defamation, humiliation, frustation, tension and failure in undertakings, and deaths of near and dear ones. However, though this is an important rule of astrology but we have not found it applicable in all cases. But in our case Saturn's *Mahadasha* the 4th one, and this has been the best *Mahadasha* of our life so far, certainly superior to previous 3 *Mahadashas*.

9. Saturn in 6th House in Cancer :

For Aquarius ascendant, Saturn's placement in the 6th house in Cancer, gives innumerable diseases but if it is posited in the 8th house, in Virgo, it gives a long span of life but problems in lower extremities and waist etc. are there.

10. Saturn in the 11th house :

Saturn's placement in the eleventh house gives wealth through illegal means. This is further multiplied if Saturn is debilitated in the eleventh house. However, it is a great dissociation for wealth and enhancement of income. Placement of Mercury in the 11th house also gives illegitimate income.

In number of cases, Mercury of 11th house has made the native a successful businessman. The *Mahadasha* of Mercury causes a lot of income through unrighteous means and by manipulation. Conjunction or mutual aspect or exchange of signs between Saturn and Mercury, identical to 11th house, multiplies illegal income and through manipulations.

11. Saturn and Venus combination :

Combination of Saturn and Venus is extremely adverse for maintaining moral values. This causes tendency towards physical relations with persons of advance age or with the person of same sex. We have explained this in length in the chapter "Pointers to Carnality" in our book "Predicting Marriage".

12. Saturn in 4th house :

Saturn obstructs fortune, especially if it is posited in the 4th house. Though the fortune has no concern with the 4th house, even then Saturn's placement in the 4th house is one of the worst combinations for proper rise of fortune, at proper age and time. Such a Saturn also gives rise to diseases connected with lungs such as asthma, T.B., bronchitis and pleurisy etc. One does not tell his secrets to anyone.

Nobody can understand such expression easily. This also causes imprisonment to the native but other combination should also be judged before reaching to any conclusion. This is worst position as regards the placement of Saturn (in the 4th house).

13. Saturn in the 12th house :

Saturn's placement in the 12th house gives huge wealth to the native but a powerful downfall of post, position, rank, wealth and prosperity definitely comes one day.

It Saturn is afflicted and indicates income, the native will earn money by unrighteous means such as theft, smuggling, deceit, misplaced confidence, dacoity, illegal love and evil deeds.

Conjunction of the Sun and Saturn, or their opposition, is very adverse for marriage especially if the longitudes are nearly the same. We have discussed a lot about the combination earlier.

Placement of Saturn in the 12th house is extremely

damaging. Even a prosperous and rich person may have to face imprisonment, poverty, funerals and prosecution etc. A rich will lose his everything gradually, if Saturn falls in the 12th house and is weak and afflicted. Adversities will be more prominent if the ascendant is weak. First 6 year and 4 month will be adverse; another 6 years and 4 month will be prosperous, full of gains, acquistions, elevation, name, fame, honour etc. but last 6 year and 4 month will snatch everything given by Saturn during its *Mahadasha.*

14. Favorable signs for *Saadhe Saati* Saturn :

For persons born in Capricorn or Aquarius, *Saadhe Saati* of Saturn does not cause much adversities. Similarly, persons born in Libra and Taurus also do not suffer during the *Saadhe Saati* of Saturn.

15. Saturn in Sagittarius or Pisces :

Jupiter and Saturn have a peculiar relationship, which we have explained earlier. However, Saturn bestows very good and auspicious results during the major or sub-period of Saturn, if it is placed in Sagittarius or Pisces. The native gets power, authority, position, prosperity and happiness on that account. It has been observed that Saturn gives result like that of exaltation if falls in any sign of Jupiter. However, well placed Saturn is beneficial for persons born in Taurus, Libra, Sagittarius, Capricorn, Aquarius and Pisces.

16. Saturn in the 9th house :

If a well fortified Saturn is placed in the 9th house, one will be blessed with powers and respect in the society. He will not believe in superstitions. It has been found that Saturn in the 9th house makes the native religious. One is deeply involved in spritualism. However, if there is mutual exchange between 4th and 9th lord, a *Raja Yoga* is formed and in that case one enjoys wealth, power, prosperity and happiness but that native is fully dedicated to Almighty.

17. Conjuction of Saturn and Moon :

If Saturn conjoins with Moon, one will suffer from headache and if the combinations is death inflicting, one will die in water as Moon is the significator of water. The combination causes T.B. or pleurisy, if occurs in the 4th house or affects the 4th house.

18. Combination of Saturn and Sun :

If Saturn is conjoined with the Sun, the native will suffer from heart trouble, especially if the 4th house is involved in one or the other way.

19. Saturn Signifies :

Saturn governs strike, labour problems, tensions, impotency, humiliation, worries, frustations, pain, falling of hair and teeth, untraditional things, intercaste and illegitimate marriage. It destroys balance of mind and one treats enemy as friend, and friends and well wishers as rivals.

20. Saturn and Mercury :

Both these planets are enunch. If these are placed in the 8th house, impotency and nervous disorder will be there. One may suffer nervous breakdown if Rahu is also involved. Combination of Mercury and Saturn causes all kinds of illegitimacy. In the 5th house, this combination will give illegitimate birth of children. Similarly, in the 7th house, it may cause illegitimate relationship with women, and so on.

21. Saturn at same degree of *Lagna* :

If Saturn has same degree as that of *lagna,* it is extremely bad. The native will have bad health throughout his life.

22. Saturn in the 5th house :

Saturn in the 5th house causes delay in birth of children. Many times the birth may be completely denied, if Saturn and Rahu are there and the combination is afflicted. In watery signs, Saturn gives birth to male children, where as Jupiter gives daughter in watery signs, in the 5th house, i.e. in Cancer, Scorpio or Pisces. Saturn in fiery signs gives birth to female children i.e. if Saturn is placed in Aries, Leo or Sagittarius, female children will be born unless other strong combinations of male children are present. Jupiter in fiery signs in 5th gives male children.

23. Saturn in the 6th house in Airy signs :

If Saturn is placed in the 6th house in Gemini, Libra or Aquarius, one will suffer from one or the other trouble throughout life, especially from chronic ailments. If Moon is also there with Saturn, it is impossible that the native would be cured.

●

CHAPTER-13

Houses and Significators of Education

Education is the basic need for the prosperity and elevation of the society. The education develops new ways to understand the intricacies of the world around us. The education provides knowledge of various aspects of life. It is one of the most important essentials of a person. The education is nothing but the procedure of learning different subjects by nature, teaching, books and experience.

The progress of the native will certainly be better and quicker if he obtains the education, according to planetary vibrations and indications for him. Education in the suitable field gives rise to speedy and steep progress of the native and he can do outstanding work in that field. On the contrary, the native will not progress if he gets education of opposite subjects, which is reverse to planetary tendencies.

Many persons, who do not get the right guidance for suitable education or are not able to select the appropriate subjects, can not exhibit their talents. Their merits are not used in the proper direction. Only the science of astrology can help them select those subjects, which will take them to right direction, where they will shine and rise. Their knowledge and intelligence will be used in the most suitable and appropriate jobs. Many persons, who have chosen the right education, have always progressed speedily and steeply. An artist can not do much if he becomes a mechanical engineer. A person, who can become a very successful surgeon, if enters into the study of mathematics or geology, will certainly not be able to do much in his professional career. So, education is as important as the selection of appropriate subject according to one's talent and mental tendencies. Let us see here, how much help we can obtain by making the best use of astrology in deciding the course of education of a child from the very beginning.

Education is directly proportional to occupation. Most professions require specific studies of a particular field based on concerned subjects. One should find out the nature of his prospective profession. Thereafter, it becomes easy to find out the relevant subjects for study. In the present and modern era of twenty first century, there are unlimited occupations and hundreds of subjects and various kinds of education. There are mainly nine planets that rule all subjects and services. As such, it is quite a tough work to single out one occupation and one subject. In previous times there were very few vocations, few jobs and few subjects only. It was relatively easy to find out the influence of a particular planet over the concerning houses of profession and education. But now days it is a tough exercise to suggest proper brand of education to the native.

There are more than one house, which are required to be analyzed for the education of the native. Similarly, there are more than one house for the proper judgment of profession. Similarly, the study of a single planet is not sufficient to point out the suitable subjects. The influence of more than one planet over concerning houses will reveal the nature of appropriate subject.

The judgment of one's education is not possible until unless we correctly know the various significators of education. The education is governed by which house or houses, is also essential to be clarified. Let us make a sincere effort to know about the judgment of educational aspect of one's life. What will be the actual qualification of the native? How many subjects will he study? In what kind of education will he be able to exhibit his talent? In what field the native will progress speedily? What kind of education is required for the native to enter into a particular occupation, as indicated by his horoscope?

It is the 4th house that should be dealt with properly for the judgment of educational qualification. The 4th house shows basic and advanced education, which is obtained in schools, colleges or universities- the education for which a certificate is issued in writing. Thus, the 4th house is the base or platform, which provides a place where we get education year after year. The education is provided and we pay fee for that. The subject's level of qualification, standard of education, getting through to the next class, all is to be judged from the 4th house.

The *karaka* of the 4th house is Moon, which is also to be studied properly. A well placed and strong Moon will provide high educational qualification, merits in studies and certificates of educational ability.

A few astrologers have lot of confusions about house of education. Parashar has specified the 5th house for *Vidya.* Therefore, they are restricted to the 5th house only, for the judgment of all aspects of education, intelligence, qualification, specialization, professional studies and writing ability. At the time of Maharishi Parashar, there were no educational institutes or colleges. Education was possible only for the children of very high persons, families of kings, ministers etc. and only intelligent boys used to secure education. Rest of the children were not getting any formal education. That is why the 5th house has been paid all importance for study and education.

In modern contexts, modification of rules is quite essential. There has been so much advancement and expansion of humanity and generation, the principles need to be modified accordingly. As per present structure of the society, the 5th house should be dealt with for intelligence, capacity and fertility of brain, logic, memory, retention of thoughts, imagination and emotional feelings etc. Structure of thoughts, manipulations, constructive or destructive ideas, dull or active mind, all come under the domain of the 5th house.

The *karaka* of the 5th house is Mercury. If the 5th house is well disposed along with Mercury, one will be quite intelligent and have a good capacity of brain, lasting memory and logical thinking. If Mercury is weak, with strong 5th house, one will have limitations of intelligence and constructive thoughts. But the native will be excellent in studies, will have good grasp of new subjects and will possess high degree of analytical power, if the 5th house and Mercury, both, are strong.

The 2nd house is the most forgotten house, as far as the field of education and studies is concerned. The 2nd house is the 5th from the 10th and 10th from the 5th house. The 2nd house indicates the source of income or earning and the nature of job. Any occupation requires some knowledge of a particular aspect. All professions need specific education and knowledge, and this knowledge, study and merit should be judged from the 2nd house. If one has educational qualification in history and he is working as a Priest or *Pandit*, or he is running a religious organization, Jupiter must have an influence over the 2nd house, in one or the other way. The 2nd house, in that case, may be occupied or owned by Jupiter. **There is a golden observation, that if the 2nd lord occupies the 10th house or the 10th lord falls in the 2nd house, it becomes a very strong indicator of the means of livelihood.**

The significator or the *karaka* of the 2nd house is Jupiter and that should also be properly judged. Affliction of Jupiter, or a weak Jupiter, will bring reversals in education. One may not obtain required professional education or qualification, if Jupiter and 2nd house are under the influence of malefics, in any manner.

The 3rd house is also not given much importance in the matters regarding education. A strong 3rd house, or well fortified 3rd house, adds creativity to knowledge. One may become a writer, if a strong Jupiter occupies the 3rd house. In fact, the 3rd house is as good as the 5th. The 3rd house indicates the mental ability and desire for creation. This house rules over the mental balance, direction of desires, new thoughts and inclination towards study, and the subject of choice. Mercury is also the *karaka* of the 3rd house.

Thus,

- the 4th house and Moon, indicate the regular study, pre or post graduation, certificates and qualification of the native.
- The 3rd house shows specialization, creation and inclination of any branch of knowledge.
- The 9th house indicates higher education, taste, interest and chances of further study.
- The 5th house governs concentration, intelligence, memory, emotions, thoughts, mental aptitude, framework of brain, destructive or constructive bent of mind etc.

Thus the 4th, 3rd, 2nd and 5th houses indicate all aspects of education, knowledge, intelligence, aptitude, qualification, professional studies, constructive or destructive thinking, memory, specialization etc. The 9th house governs interest and inclination of mind and higher education, including education in foreign countries or visit abroad for specialization etc.

13.1 Important observations about various combinations regarding education

- The lord of the 2nd house and Jupiter, if occupy a quadrangle or a triangle, one will get suitable education, which will also be used in profession, for the purpose of earning wealth.
- Jupiter, Venus and Mercury are important planets for education. One of these planets should occupy a triangle or an angle, in association with or under the aspect of the 2nd lord.
- The 2nd house should also be examined for the judgement of knowledge by inheritance i.e. the knowledge through ancestors (Forefathers), knowledge or talent transferred by family traditions.

- If the 2nd house and/or its lord come under the influence of Venus, the native will have a love for music, dance, singing or fine arts etc. If strong and well fortified Mercury has an influence over the 2nd house or its lord, the native will be a good mathematician, accountant, chartered accountant, a computer specialist or an information technologist etc. The Sun will provide interest in politics and medicines. Saturn will tend one towards the study of engineering, technology, mechanisms etc. Jupiter will do well to study Sanskrit, literature, Science, philosophy, law, banking etc., whereas Mars will incline one towards surgery, medicines, construction work etc.

- The occupants of the 4th house indicate the level of qualification. Venus and Saturn will make one an expert in engineering and computers. If the combination falls in the sign of Mercury or Jupiter, one may be a good lecturer in engineering college, and if the combination falls in the sign of Mars, one will work in the field after obtaining the same education.

- If the 5th house is occupied by Mercury, and is also aspected or associated, either by Jupiter or Venus, one will have very high degree of intelligence and acquire good education. Similarly, if the lord of 5th house joins the 5th house itself, and is associated or aspected by Jupiter, one is sure to get high intellect and education along with retentive memory.

- The influence of Saturn on the 5th house provides poor education, dull mind and low intelligence. If Saturn occupies the 5th house, it is so. Similar results of poor academic career, disinterest in studies will be there, if Saturn occupies the ascendant, and the 5th house or its lord is associated with malefics.

  If the 5th lord is debilitated and aspected by malefics, one may adopt mean methods. Saturn, Rahu, Ketu, Mars, the Sun, waning Moon are bad, if these are in adverse position and are under affliction, by one way or the other, or if these are afflicted identical to the 5th house.

- If the lord of the ascendant, and the ascendant itself, are strong, one obtains education till the age of 25 years. If the 3rd lord Mars is associated or influenced by *lagna,* its lord and the Sun, the native is sincere towards education. If the 5th house and Jupiter are not well fortified, one can not secure high percentage of marks. For high education, Mercury must be strong and well placed. The subjects should be decided by the examination of 3rd, 4th, 5th houses, and Moon and Mercury. Technical education is obtained by Saturn, Rahu, Ketu and Mars. Vaidyanath has specified education to 2nd house along with the 4th and 10th.
- One may be a good mathematician, if Jupiter is posited in an angle or triangle, Venus or 2nd lord Mercury is exalted, Mars joins the 2nd house with benefics and Mercury either aspects Mars or is posited in a quadrant.
- One will become expert in knowledge, if the 4th house and its lord are well fortified and Mercury is powerful. If the 4th lord, Mercury & Jupiter are exalted, *Swagrahi,* or are placed in angle or triangle, one will be inquisitive or will have love for learning.

13.2 Combinations for Lack of Knowledge and Intelligence

- He becomes void of knowledge if the 4th lord be in the 6th, 8th or 12th, in company with or aspected by malefics or be in evil signs.
- If Mercury, 2nd lord and Jupiter occupy the 8th house jointly, one will be devoid of education, in general.
- One will be illiterate, if Jupiter and Mercury occupy the 8th house, with 4th and 5th lords.
- The 2nd house, from Mercury, should also be examined along with that from *lagna.* If 2nd from Mercury is afflicted

by malefics, there will be obstacles in education. Weak Jupiter and Moon will also indicate this.

- If the 5th house is afflicted by Rahu without any other benefic aspect over the 5th house, the 5th lord or its *karaka* Mercury is also placed in the 5th house, one will have a weak memory and lack of intelligence.

If the 9th, 10th, 7th, 5th and the ascendant are occupied and aspected by malefics and their lords are powerful, then the person becomes a philosopher.

Vaidyanath says about the 5th house, that if Jupiter, Rahu and Saturn be together aspected by Venus and Mercury, the man becomes well versed in all sorts of knowledge. If Jupiter is posited in 2nd, 4th, 5th or 9th, the native will acquire vast knowledge, provided Jupiter is strong or well aspected or associated with *yogakaraka*. If Saturn aspects *lagna,* Jupiter and Moon, the native will have no interest in worldly affairs but will be dedicated to acquire more and more knowledge. If medical studies are indicated and the combinations are influenced by Moon, Mercury and Venus one will be an expert *Vaidya* (Ayurvedic physician). One will be an expert philosopher, if Jupiter and Mercury occupy the 2nd house. The study of philosophy is also indicated, if Venus or Jupiter were the 2nd lord, aspected by Sun and Mars. If Jupiter is in trine from Moon, and Mars is in trine from Mercury, one will be well versed in acquiring various kinds of knowledge.

Let us point out a few combinations for the study of mathematics and science:

1. One will study mathematics, if strong Jupiter is placed in angle or trine and Mercury is posited in the 2nd house and Venus is also exalted or strong.

2. If Mars is placed in the 2nd house, in the sign of Mercury, and is well fortified, one may be good in Maths and may study Physics as well.

3. In Sagittarius ascendant, if the Sun and Mercury join

the 10th house, Venus in 4th, one will study nuclear Physics.

4. If one of the planets among Mercury, Venus and Moon is placed in *lagna* and remaining two occupy *Kendra* or *Trikona* with a strong Sun, one will study medical science. If Mars also has an influence over the combination, he will be expert in surgery.

5. With Mercury and Venus in the 2nd and 3rd house respectively, one becomes and astronomer, if-

(a) The 2nd lord is strong enough and Mercury is placed in *Kendra* or *Trikona* or in the 11th, one becomes an astronomer.

(b) The ascendant is Gemini and if Jupiter resides in exaltation, one becomes an astrologer or astronomer.

(c) If in the 10th from Moon, there reside the Sun and strong Mercury, and if Jupiter aspects this 10th house, one becomes a famous astrologer or astronomer.

6. If the 2nd house and its lord are under the influence of Jupiter, the native will take interest in Philosophy, religious study, astrology or occult sciences etc.

7. If the 4th lord is strong, and well fortified by benefics, one will acquire knowledge from various branches of education.

8. If the Sun and Mercury are well placed in the 5th house, either from *lagna* or Moon, in a benefic sign or in the sign of a *Yogakaraka* planet, one will possess high degree of intelligence. Relationship of Sun and Mercury anywhere in the horoscope, if related to the 5th house, in any way by ownership, aspect or conjunction, will make one witty, sharp, brilliant, intelligent and knowledgeable.

9. If Moon falls in *Aswini* or *Satabhisha,* or if ascendant be in either of these two constellations, one will be likely to study about medical science.

10. Mars, occupying Leo, makes one a strong and successful physician, who has a zeal to cure or save his patients. Saturn plays very important role in determining medical education.

11. Homeopathy:

(a) The ascendant or Moon should either be in Taurus or Scorpio.

(b) Mars should be in 1st, 6th, 7th or 10th.

(c) Lord of 1st or 6th should fall in a watery sign.

(d) Jupiter should aspect the *lagna* or the 10th house, or it should be strong.

Placement of Mercury or Jupiter in the 4th house, without affliction, is a great asset for educational progress. If Mercury has a prominent influence over the 2nd, 3rd, 4th or the 5th house, the native will acquire good education. If Jupiter, Mercury and Venus are placed in an angle or triangle, as reckoned from the lord of the 5th house, one will be very intelligent. Same results will be obtained, if Mercury and Jupiter aspect each other, or they are conjoined or have mutual exchange of signs. Such a native will be known for his intelligence, knowledge and education in the society.

If Jupiter joins the 9th house, and Mercury and Venus are under the influence of each other, one will have high education. Jupiter in triangle and Mercury in angle give astrological knowledge. Involvement of Ketu, either by constellation or by its disposition, will give intuition and inner vision.

If the lord of the 4th joins the ascendant, and ascendant lord falls in the 4th house, the native will have suitable education and appropriate knowledge of the subject, as indicated by the concerning setup of planets.

If Jupiter is exalted in the 4th house and the 4th lord is in own sign, or the sign of exaltation, the native will acquire high degree of qualification of law.

If 4th, 5th and 2nd houses are well disposed or are occupied by benefics including Mercury and Jupiter, one will have no break in his educational career. If these houses are not well fortified or their lords are adversely placed, unaspected by benefics and aspected or associated with malefics, and the lord of 4th and 2nd are placed in evil houses, there will be break in education and one will not be able to get proper and suitable education that will be useful in the profession of the native.

We will now explain our view points with the help of a few practical illustrations showing the educational prospects, specific qualification with corresponding occupation.

Illustration: 13.1 (**CA**) *Horoscope No.: 73*

Date of birth : 15.08.1954 Time of birth : 22:13:00 hrs

Place of birth : Lucknow Lat 26:50:00 N Long 80:54:00E

Ayanamsa : 23:13:41 Sidereal Time : 19:40:48

Pln	**Degree**	**Rasi**	**Nakshatra**	**Pad**
Asc	10:52:19	Ari	Ashwini	4
Sun	29:04:36	Can	Aslesa	4
Mon	15:16:49	Aqu	Satabhisha	3
Mar	4:20:56	Sag	Moola	2
Mer (C)	22:34:27	Can	Aslesa	2
Jup	25:14:53	Gem	Punarvasu	2
Ven	13:59:38	Vir	Hasta	2
Sat	10:41:38	Lib	Swati	2
Rah (R)	21:03:52	Sag	Purvasadha	3
Ket (R)	21:03:52	Gem	Punarvasu	1

Lagna Chart

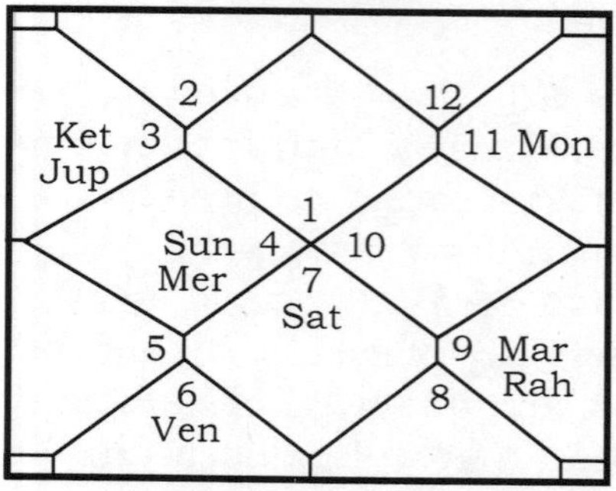

Navamsa Chart

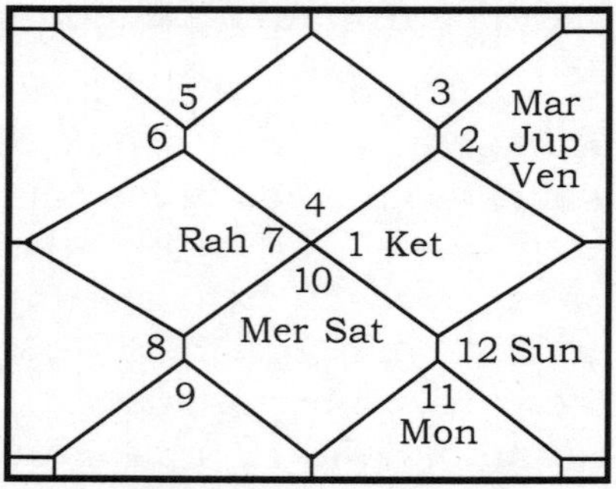

Balance of Vimshottari Dasa of **Rah 6Y 4M 13D**

The native is quite smart, young and intelligent Director and head of the finance in a multinational company. He enjoyed the top most position at the age of 35 years only due to his extra ordinary merits.

He did C. A. with highest marks and had a very bright career throughout. Let us study the horoscope of this genius CA.

The 4th House: The lords of the 3rd and 5th, Mercury and Sun, are conjoined in the 4th house. This is a clear significance of a very bright academic career. Mercury provides knowledge of accounts, computer, mathematics etc. This is unique and rare single combination, which has strengthened the 4th, 5th and 3rd houses simultaneously.

The 3rd House: Jupiter is the 9th and 12th lord and falls in the 3rd house of Mercury and aspects the 9th house of its own. This signifies high education and love towards the solution of the complexities of accounts. Jupiter lends its favourable aspect over the 10th and 11th lord, exalted Saturn, the 7th house, *lagna* lord Mars, the 9th house, 4th lord Moon and the 11th house. This has further strengthened the matters of educational achievements. As we have stated above, Mercury and Jupiter, give the qualification and knowledge of accounts and make one CA or the like. This can very well be seen in this birth chart.

The 5th House: The lord of the 5th house, Sun joins the 4th house with Mercury and 4th lord Moon aspects the 5th house. This combination of the influence of the *karaka* of 4th house Moon over the 5th house, and that of the *karaka* of the 5th house Mercury over the 4th house, is splendid and unique to provide extreme intelligence, sharpness of mind and high power of brain to work out solutions of complicated problems. Such combinations do not only provide high education, intelligence, and occupation but also make one a research oriented thinker. The native has also established many of his observations in the field of accounts and finance.

The 2nd House: The lord of the 2nd house, Venus is placed in Virgo, with *Neech Bhanga Rajyoga*. Venus obtains own *navamsa* with Mars and Jupiter shows scholarship to the native. The *karaka* of the 2nd house, Jupiter, is the 9th lord and aspects the 9th house and *lagna* lord Mars that gives extreme nobility and kindheartedness to the native. He has given service to more than 380 persons under him.

Illustration: 13.2 **(CA)** *Horoscope No.: 74*

Date of birth : 16.11.1945 Time of birth : 01:17:34 hrs
Place of birth : Saharanpur Lat 29:58:00 N Long 77:33:00E
Ayanamsa : 23:05:45 Sidereal Time : 4:35:54

Pln	Degree	Rasi	Nakshatra	Pad
Asc	18:37:06	Leo	P Phalguni	2
Sun	0:00:13	Sco	Vishakha	4
Mon	6:31:33	Pis	U Bhadrapad	1
Mar	7:51:54	Can	Pushya	2
Mer	22:09:16	Sco	Jyestha	2
Jup	24:15:57	Vir	Chitra	1
Ven	11:19:03	Lib	Swati	2
Sat (R)	1:43:32	Can	Punarvasu	4
Rah (R)	7:31:20	Gem	Ardra	1
Ket (R)	7:31:20	Sag	Moola	3

Lagna Chart

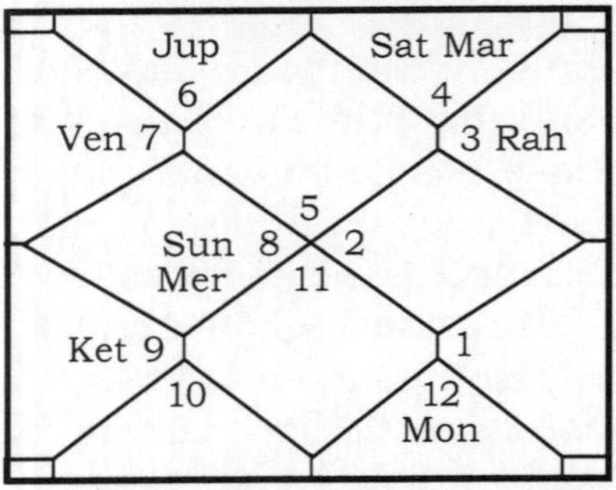

Navamsa Chart

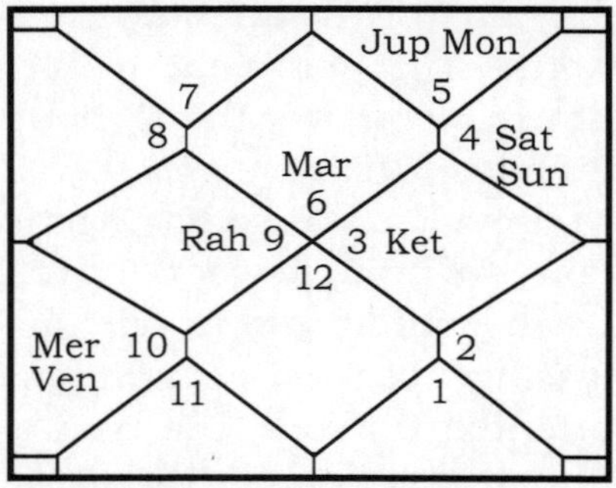

Balance of Vimshottari Dasa of **Sat 14Y 5M 12D**

The native is a most successful and meritorious Chartered Accountant having a roaring practice.

The 4th House: We have mentioned again and again that placement of Mercury or Jupiter in the 4th house is very encouraging asset for high professional career, meritorious qualification and knowledge. In this chart, the lord of 2nd house, Mercury, joins the 4th house in Scorpio. The influence of Mercury and Mars gives rise to mathematics and accounts etc., as important subjects of study.

The 5th House: The lord of the 5th house, Jupiter, joins the 2nd house in Virgo. It has been observed that Jupiter placed in Virgo, or Mercury placed in Sagittarius, give high educational qualification, provided these planets have influence over 2nd, 3rd, 4th and 5th houses.

The 3rd House: The lord of the 3rd house, Venus occupies the 3rd house itself. The 3rd house and its lord Venus are hemmed between Mercury and Jupiter. Here, Sun is the lord of *lagna* and Venus owns the 10th and 3rd. Both, 3rd house and Venus are placed under *Shubhkartari Yoga*, which provided immense success in the profession, prosperity, education, knowledge, brightness and fertility of brain. The native did CA and law as well. The aspect of Jupiter and Mercury over the 10th house made him practice law and accounts.

The 2nd House: Nothing could have been better than the placement of 5th lord Jupiter in the 2nd house and 2nd lord Mercury in the 4th house. This gives knowledge and qualifications of high level to the native that is appropriate for the profession of the native.

***Karakas*:** Mercury, Moon and Jupiter are the *karakas* of education, who are well placed and unafflicted. Moon is *karaka* of the 4th house, who occupies the 8th house, in Jupiter's sign Pisces, under the benefic aspect of Jupiter as well. The *karaka* of 2nd house, Jupiter, joins the 2nd and *karaka* of the 5th falls in the 4th house. This we believe is one of the best combinations for high level qualification of CA and law.

Illustration: 13.3 (**Prof. of History**) *Horoscope No.: 75*

Date of birth : 12.06.1942 Time of birth : 20:00:00 hrs

Place of birth : Lucknow Lat 26:50:00 N Long 80:54:00E

Ayanamsa : 23:03:04 Sidereal Time : 13:14:44

Pln	Degree	Rasi	Nakshatra	Pad
Asc	12:32:00	Sag	Moola	4
Sun	27:55:28	Tau	Mrigshira	2
Mon	14:02:12	Tau	Rohini	2
Mar	5:59:08	Can	Pushya	1
Mer (R/D)	28:19:29	Tau	Mrigshira	2
Jup (C)	7:26:22	Gem	Ardra	1
Ven	19:06:24	Ari	Bharani	2
Sat	11:25:13	Tau	Rohini	1
Rah (R)	14:33:04	Leo	P Phalguni	1
Ket (R)	14:33:04	Aqu	Satabhisha	3

Lagna Chart **Navamsa Chart**

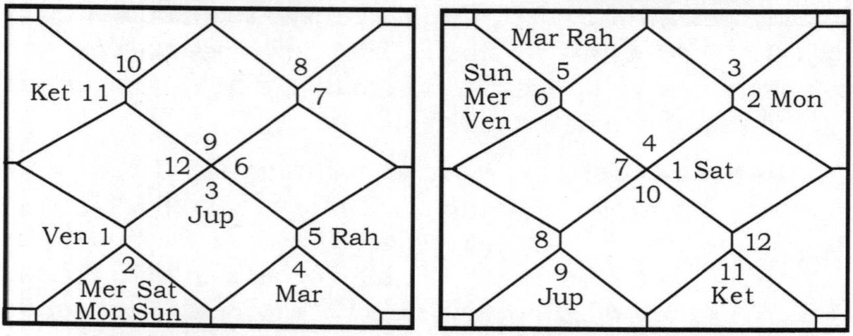

Balance of Vimshottari Dasa of **Mon 6Y 11M 20D**

The native is head of the department of History in a University.

The lord of the 4th house Jupiter is posited in the 7th house, in Gemini aspecting the ascendant and 3rd house. Placement of Jupiter in the sign of Mercury, obtaining own *navamsa* indicates high educational qualification.

The lord of the 2nd and 3rd house, Saturn occupies the 6th house, with 8th lord Moon, 9th lord Sun and 10th lord Mercury. This is a good combination of four planets in the 6th house, containing lords of 7th, 8th, 9th, 10th, 2nd and 3rd houses, placed under *shubhkartari Yoga* formed by benefic Jupiter and Venus. The 6th and 9th houses indicate scholarships. There is *Ashtagraha malika Rajyoga* as eight planets are placed in continuation from 5th to 9th house. Involvement of 6th house is also essential for the study of history.

The 5th house is not well disposed, as the lord of 5th house Mars, falls in the 8th house under debilitation and aspects 2nd and 3rd house. The 6th and 11th lord, Venus, joins the 5th house. This has reduced the strength of the 5th house. The 5th house also indicates children. The native had not been blessed with children till the age of 43. He consulted us and thereafter God was kind enough on him to bless him with a fortunate child. *Santakaraka* Jupiter is also placed under *papakartari yoga* though it obtains own *navamsa*.

Combination of Sun and Mercury provides sharp mind and quick understanding. *Karaka* of the 5th house, Mercury, is placed in Taurus, in the 6th house and obtains *navamsa* of its exaltation. *Karaka* of the 4th house, Moon, also obtains the *navamsa* of its exaltation, while *Karaka* of 2nd house, Jupiter, obtains own *navamsa*. All these *Karakas* of concerning houses are quite strong.

Illustration:13.4(**Computer Engineer**) *Horoscope No.: 76*

Date of birth : 20.04.1957 Time of birth : 03:10:00 hrs

Place of birth : Lucknow Lat 26:50:00 N Long 80:54:00E

Ayanamsa : 23:15:48 Sidereal Time : 15:43:30

Pln	Degree	Rasi	Nakshatra	Pad
Asc	21:35:33	Cap	Sravna	4
Sun	18:37:45	Pis	Revati	1
Mon	5:56:04	Ari	Ashwini	2
Mar	16:09:53	Tau	Rohini	2
Mer (C)	0:59:22	Ari	Ashwini	1
Jup (R)	1:42:19	Vir	U Phalguni	2
Ven (C)	15:22:27	Pis	U Bhadrapad	4
Sat (R)	20:58:45	Sco	Jyestha	2
Rah (R)	26:49:41	Lib	Vishakha	3
Ket (R)	26:49:41	Ari	Kritika	1

Lagna Chart

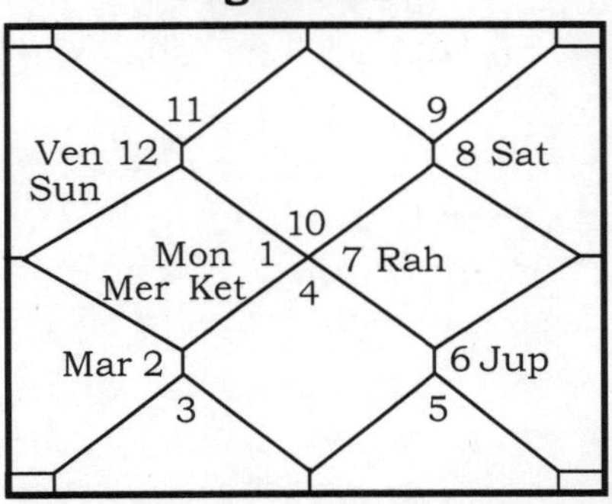

Navamsa Chart

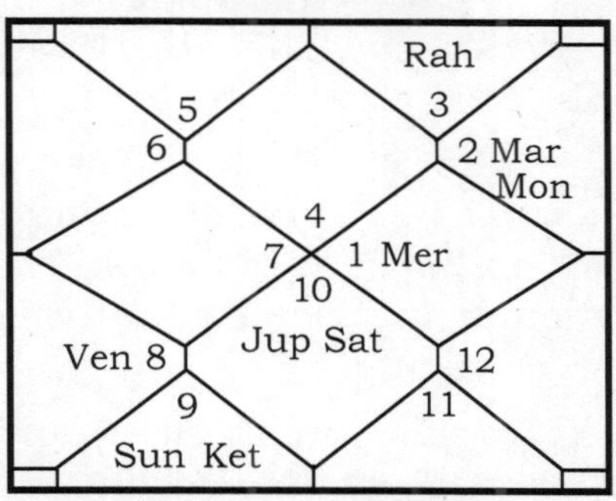

Balance of Vimshottari Dasa of **Ket 3Y 10M 18D**

The native has done engineering in computers from IIT, Kanpur. He ran a big computer institute at Lucknow for quite sometime and later shifted to U. S. A. He is at one of the top positions in that company.

The 4th House: The 9th lord Mercury is placed in the 4th house, along with Moon and Ketu. Mercury obtains *vargottam navamsa.* The lord of 4th house, Mars falls in Taurus, in the 5th house, which indicates good strength of the 4th house. Jupiter also lends its favourable aspect over the 4th lord Mars. Here Mercury, Mars and Venus indicate qualification of computer engineering.

The 5th House: The 5th lord Venus is exalted in the 3rd house and has mutual aspect with 3rd lord Jupiter. Thus, the lords of the 5th and 3rd houses, Venus and Jupiter, aspect each other, identical to 3rd and 9th house. This also signifies high education. The native later did M. Tech. also.

The 3rd House: The lord of 3rd house, Jupiter occupies the 9th house in the sign of Mercury, giving the native high degree of specialization and writing power in computers. Jupiter aspects the 3rd house, the 5th house, 5th lord Venus, the 4th lord Mars and ascendant itself. The native is a genius in the field of computers.

The placement of Mercury in *Kendra,* with Ketu and Jupiter in the 9th house i.e. in a triangle, has also blessed the native with intense knowledge of astrology. He has programmed many softwares of astrological calculations, that too in early eighties, when computer horoscopes were not very popular. This ability comes only when 3rd house is well disposed and strong.

The 2nd House: The lord of the 2nd house, Saturn occupies 11th in Scorpio, and here Saturn is aspected by the 4th and 11th lord Mars. This has given qualification of engineering. Usually, Saturn & Mercury incline one to study engineering.

In this horoscope, 9th lord Mercury, who is placed in the 4th house, obtain *vargottam navamsa. Karaka* of the 4th house, Moon obtains *navamsa* of its exaltation. The *karaka* of 2nd

house Jupiter, who is placed in inimical sign in the 9th house, obtains *navamsa* of its debilitation. Thus, the *karaka* of 2nd house and wealth, Jupiter, is weak and that has kept the native devoid of enormous wealth that should have come to the native due to his excellent knowledge and capacity of earning wealth. Mutual aspect of 2nd lord Saturn and 4th lord Mars is also adverse, which has resulted in too many ups and downs in the professional and financial career of the native.

Illustration: 13.5 (**Physics Lecturer**) *Horoscope No.: 77*

Date of birth : 19.11.1973 Time of birth : 22:35:00 hrs
Place of birth : Allahabad Lat 25:27:00 N Long 81:50:00E
Ayanamsa : 23:29:47 Sidereal Time : 2:26:39

Pln	Degree	Rasi	Nakshatra	Pad
Asc	19:05:05	Can	Aslesa	1
Sun	3:43:56	Sco	Anuradha	1
Mon	4:11:54	Vir	U Phalguni	3
Mar (R)	2:04:38	Ari	Ashwini	1
Mer	17:03:37	Lib	Swati	4
Jup	12:57:41	Cap	Sravna	1
Ven	20:41:41	Sag	Purvasadha	3
Sat (R)	10:15:01	Gem	Ardra	2
Rah (R)	5:34:57	Sag	Moola	2
Ket (R)	5:34:57	Gem	Mrigshira	4

Lagna Chart

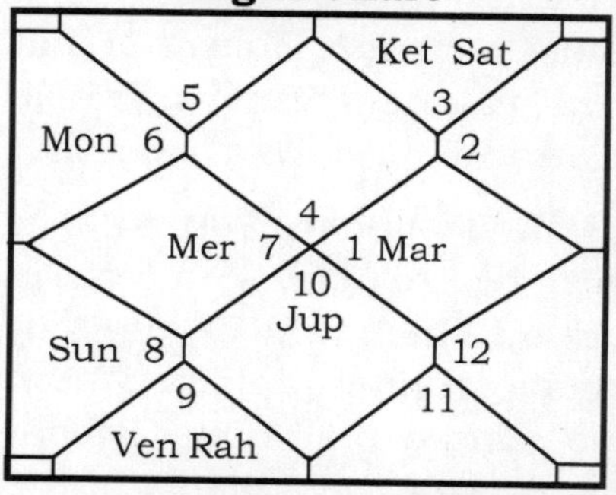

Navamsa Chart

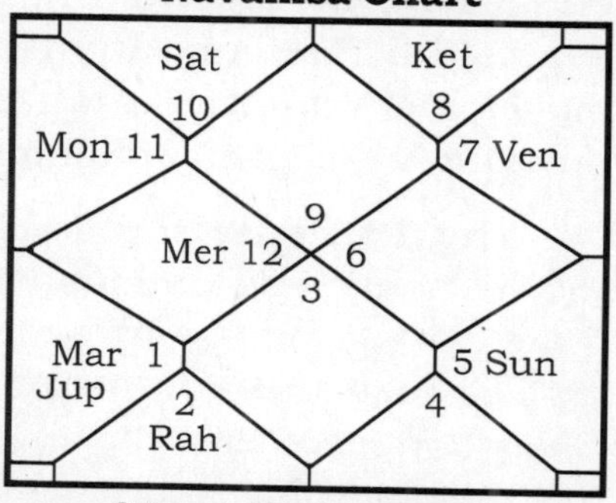

Balance of Vimshottari Dasa of **Sun 2Y 7M 10D**

The native of this chart has done M.Sc. in Physics and Ph.D. has also been conferred on him in 2001. The whole family of the native had always been toppers in Physics, at Agra College. The native had been a bright student since his childhood. He had also taken admission in MBA where his merits established him but he had to leave MBA due to sudden, shocking and untimely death of his father. Let us analyze the combinations of education in his birth chart.

The 4th House: Mercury is present in the 4th house, as an owner of the 3rd house. Physics is indicated by Jupiter, Mercury and Venus. Here, Mercury is placed in the sign of Venus and obtains *navamsa* of Jupiter. The 4th lord, Venus, falls in the 6th house, in the sign of Jupiter and obtains own *navamsa*. This shows the study, knowledge and qualification of Physics. The *karaka* of the 4th house, Moon, joins the 3rd house in Virgo, and is aspected by Jupiter. Thus, the effect of Jupiter, Mercury and Venus is predominant over the 4th house, which tends one towards the study of Science and Physics.

The 5th house: The lord of 5th house is Mars, who is also a *Yogakaraka* for cancer ascendant. Mars is retrograde in the 10th house, in own sign Aries, and lends its aspect over the 4th house, 3rd lord Mercury posited in the 4th house, the 5th house itself, and the Sun, occupying the 5th house as the lord of 2nd. The *karaka* of the 5th house, Mercury joins the 4th in Libra, the sign of Venus, indicating high-level intelligence and good mental power and capacity. The 5th lord Mars is aspected by Mercury and obtains *vargottam navamsa* that makes him impulsive and fast in making decisions. It also provides the capacity of administration and management.

The 2nd House: The lord of the 2nd house, Sun, falls in the 5th house and obtains own *navamsa*. The 2nd house is quite strong for useful education, which will be used in profession. *Karaka* of the 2nd house, Jupiter, obtains *Neech Bhanga Rajyoga* and aspects the *Karaka* of 4th house Moon, the *lagna* and *lagna* lord. This makes the personality of the native very influential and impressive.

The 9th House: The 9th house indicates higher education, whose lord Jupiter occupies the 7th house, aspecting the *lagna, lagna* lord and *Karaka* Moon. This has resulted in his doing Ph.D., and the native is also likely to further obtain degree of D.Sc. or the like.

Illustration: 13.6 (**Hindi Lecturer**) *Horoscope No.: 78*

Date of birth : 10.09.1956 Time of birth : 07:54:00 hrs

Place of birth : Jaipur Lat 26:53:00 N Long 75:50:00E

Ayanamsa : 23:15:23 Sidereal Time : 06:43:43

Pln	**Degree**	**Rasi**	**Nakshatra**	**Pad**
Asc	16:30:06	Vir	Hasta	2
Sun	24:05:42	Leo	P Phalguni	4
Mon	2:20:16	Sco	Vishakha	4
Mar (R)	25:06:57	Aqu	P Bhadrapad	2
Mer	18:19:40	Vir	Hasta	3
Jup (C)	20:00:21	Leo	P Phalguni	3
Ven	8:29:06	Can	Pushya	2
Sat	4:15:29	Sco	Anuradha	1
Rah (R)	8:40:07	Sco	Anuradha	2
Ket (R)	8:40:07	Tau	Kritika	4

Lagna Chart **Navamsa Chart**

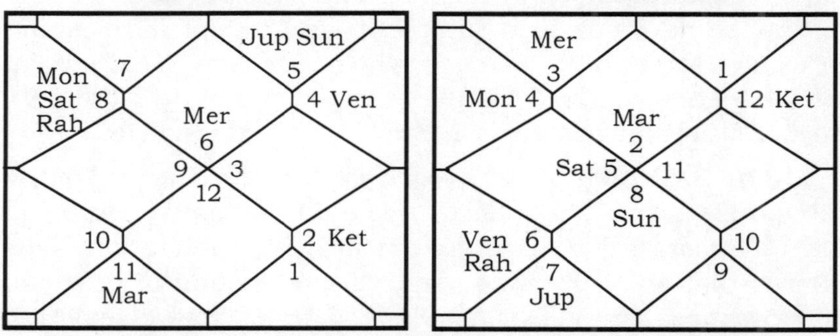

Balance of Vimshottari Dasa of **Jup 1Y 2M 10D**

The native is a lecturer in Hindi. She has done MA, M. Phil and Ph.D. in Hindi and has an extraordinary flair of acquisition of more and more knowledge of her field.

The ascendant is quite strong, as it is occupied by its own lord Mercury, in exaltation. Placement of Mercury in *lagna* provides high degree of sobriety, decency, politeness, intelligent way of conversation and impressive behaviour. It makes overall personality attractive, as far as intellectual merits are concerned.

The 4th house and its *karaka* Moon: The lord of the 4th house, Jupiter falls in the 12th house, in Leo with the 12th lord Sun. Thus, the 4th lord Jupiter is under heavy influence of Sun, which indicates Hindi. The aspect of Jupiter on its own 4th house has blessed her with high degree of educational qualification, such as M.Phil and Ph.D. in Hindi. The significator of 4th house, Moon falls in the 3rd house, in the sign of its debilitation, with malefics Saturn and Rahu. Moon is afflicted. She is a bold and courageous lady. But affliction of Moon caused some break in her education. She did M.A., M.Ed., M.Phil. and Ph.D. after her marriage. At present she is a lecturer in a prestigious college of Jaipur.

The 5th House and its *Karaka* Mercury: The 5th lord Saturn is posited in the 3rd house with Moon, over the axis of nodes. The 3rd lord Mars occupies the 6th house in Aquarius. Thus, there is mutual exchange between 6th lord Saturn and 3rd lord Mars. This is not an encouraging placement of 5th lord. She is very hard working and diligent but merits of the 5th house have not been so pronounced except the position of exalted Mercury in the *lagna,* who happens to be the *karaka* of the 5th house. The 5th house is aspected by the 2nd and 9th lord Venus that has given her talent in artistic field.

The 2nd House and its *karaka* Jupiter: The lord of the 2nd house, Venus, is placed in the 11th house, in inimical sign Cancer and obtains *navamsa* of its debilitation. This shows that she will make use of her education or talent in earning wealth. Venus is 9th lord too. That gives high education and qualification. The *karaka* of the 2nd house,

Jupiter, is placed in the 12th house, in a friendly sign and in the *navamsa* of 2nd lord Venus. Jupiter aspects the 4th house, the 6th house and the lord of the 3rd house. This is a good indication for high educational qualification

The weak 3rd house and 5th house has not provided enough creative ability and has reduced the interest and ability of research and original observations.

Illustration : 13.7 (**Cardiologist**) *Horoscope No.: 79*

Date of birth : 25.12.1958 Time of birth : 16:00:00 hrs
Place of birth : Kanpur Lat 26:27:00 N Long 80:19:00E
Ayanamsa : 23:17:08 Sidereal Time : 22:04:59

Pln	**Degree**	**Rasi**	**Nakshatra**	**Pad**
Asc	21:11:56	Tau	Rohini	4
Sun	9:50:49	Sag	Moola	3
Mon	1:27:06	Gem	Mrigshira	3
Mar	23:27:50	Ari	Bharani	4
Mer	18:09:36	Sco	Jyestha	1
Jup	29:27:13	Lib	Vishakha	3
Ven	20:30:42	Sag	Purvasadha	3
Sat (C)	5:24:48	Sag	Moola	2
Rah (R)	26:01:23	Vir	Chitra	1
Ket (R)	26:01:23	Pis	Revati	3

Lagna Chart

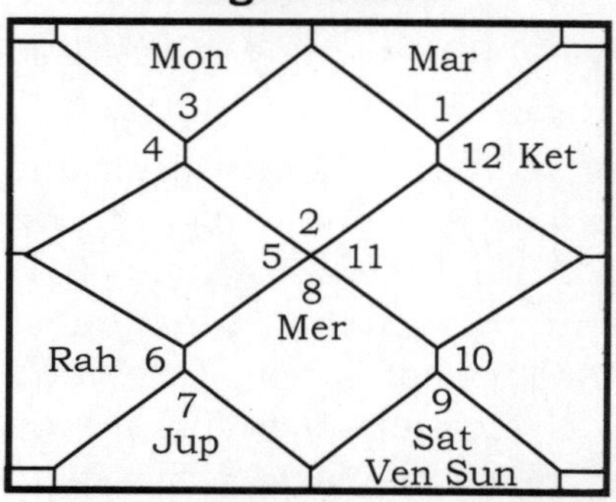

Navamsa Chart

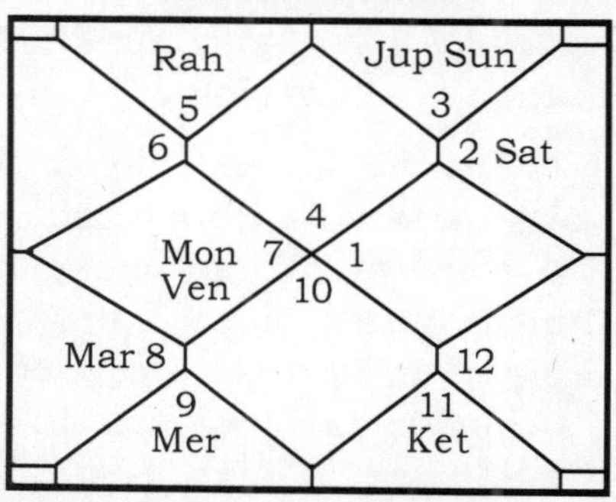

Balance of Vimshottari Dasa of **Mar 2Y 8M 25D**

The native is working in U.S.A. as a Cardiologist. He is highly qualified in Cardiology. He has done D.M. from four boards in different branches of Cardiology which is called Triple Board. The native is a very successful and famous Cardiologist of U.S.A. He has earned enormous wealth by way of his special skill in surgery of hearts. Let us examine his horoscope, as far as high degree of academic qualification is concerned.

The 5th house and its *Karaka* Mercury: The lord of 5th house, Mercury, is posited in the 7th house, in Scorpio and it is also aspected by Mars. This tends native to study medical science and gain expertise in surgery. Mercury obtains *navamsa* of Jupiter. Jupiter, Sun and Mars are the vital planets for a heart surgeon. However, Jupiter has mutual exchange with Venus and is aspected by Mars i.e. Mars and Jupiter, both have mutual aspect with each other. The 5th lord Mercury is also under the influence of Mars and Jupiter, which shows inclination, wisdom, intellect, research and invention in the field of Cardiology and talent of sharp and successful surgery.

The 4th house and its *Karaka* Moon: The lord of 4th house, Sun, falls in 8th house in Jupiter's sign Sagittarius. The Sun is associated with Saturn and Venus, and is aspected by 3rd lord Moon, who is also the significator of 4th house. Thus, the lord of 4th house Sun is under the influence of Venus, Saturn, Jupiter, Moon and Mercury, which has given such a high merit to the native in the field of medical science. He is highly qualified as he has 4 D. Ms. in various branches of Cardiology.

The 8th house: The 8th house is the most mysterious house and this house indicates professional heights and achievements. We have explained it in different articles that the 8th house plays a prominent role in the judgment of profession. In this horoscope, the lords of *lagna,* 4th, 9th and 10th houses are conjoined in the 8th house, which has placed the native very high in life. The 8th house is 11th from 10th house and 10th from 11th house. Therefore, the 8th house governs professional prosperity, professional status and achievements. The 8th house is also 5th from 4th and 4th from 5th house. Therefore, for the educational career, if essential, the 8th house should be taken into consideration. For medical profession, *Trik* houses, which indicate different kinds of diseases, do play a role in the judgment of profession and education.

13.3 Study of Medical Science

In this birth chart, Jupiter, Mars, Sun and Saturn are placed in *Trik* houses and this denotes medical career. The placement of 9th and 10th lord Saturn in the 8th house, with 4th lord i.e. Sun, and conjunction of the 9th lord Saturn, in the 8th house, with *lagna* lord Venus, indicates very high education of medical science in foreign countries.

The 2nd house and its *Karaka* Jupiter: The lord of 2nd house, Mercury, joins the 7th house in Martian sign Scorpio, which obtains *navamsa* of Jupiter and is aspected by Mars. Thus, the 2nd lord Mercury is also under the influence of Jupiter and Mars, which show talent and study of medical science, in Cardiology and heart surgery etc. The 2nd house and *karaka* of 4th house and 3rd lord Moon are aspected by Jupiter, Venus, the Sun and Saturn. This shows high education of the native in various fields of knowledge, which will help in professional prosperity.

The 3rd house and its *Karaka* Mercury: The 3rd house shows specialization. Here, the 3rd house is aspected by Mars. The 3rd lord Moon falls in *Mrigshira nakshatra*, whose ruler is Mars. Jupiter also lends its aspect over the 3rd lord Moon along with the aspect of the Sun, Saturn and Venus. Thus, the 3rd house is under the influence of Mars, Jupiter, Sun, Saturn and Venus. The *karaka* Mercury is also under the influence of Mars and Jupiter. That strongly indicates specialization in Cardiology and surgery.

The horoscopes should be analyzed properly in this way for the correct judgment of educational aspects of ones life.

Conclusion- For Cardiologist :

Significators - The Sun, Mars and Jupiter.

Houses – These planets should also either own, influence or be placed in one or all *Trik* houses.

13.4 Study of Law and Logics

Airy signs provide intelligence, imaginations, creations and research oriented work. The native will have wonderful planning and will implicate the schemes seriously and successfully, during the *dasa bhukti* of planets placed in Cancer or Capricorn. The native will possess real art of criticism, if Gemini or Sagittarius is occupied by the *karaka*.

Jupiter provides knowledge of law as it is applied to justice and true judgement. Mercury gives eloquence and fluency. Mars governs quick wit, logic, arguments, analysis, penetration, operation and authoritative working and debate and discussion.

The 6th house indicates litigation, court case, enmity, opponents, rivals etc. The 6th house must have an influence over the 10th house or its lord. The 5th house, Mercury and Mars should have influence over one's profession. That will provide the education of law. Mars and Jupiter show sufficient knowledge of law, and common sense and courage to threat the opponents and making arguments and cross examinations in the court, to find out the truth and reality.

Following combinations have been specified in texts for the study or education of law, LLB, LLM etc.

1. If the lord of 2nd house, Jupiter and Venus, occupy *Kendras*, in their own sign, sign of exaltation or *Mool trikona*, and if these are aspected by Sun and / or Mars, one becomes and expert in law and acquires education of law.
2. If the 3rd and 6th lords, the 10th house and Jupiter are strong in any birth chart, one studies law and allied subjects.
3. If Jupiter is the lord of the 5th house, or it is placed there,

and Saturn lends an aspect over that, one will study law.

4. If Jupiter and Mercury are conjoined together, or Mercury and Rahu are placed together, having an influence over the 2nd, 4th and 5th house, one will be qualified in law. If Mercury and Jupiter own these houses and are placed together or with Rahu, in the 10th house, education of law will be acquired by the native.

5. If Saturn occupies Capricorn or Scorpio, and falls in *lagna*, 2nd, 3rd , 9th or 11th house, or in quadrant, and 9th house is occupied or aspected by Jupiter and Moon, one will study law.

6. If Jupiter and Saturn are placed together, or opposite to each other, in the houses connected with education, one will acquire qualification of law. If Jupiter and Saturn are placed in triangle from each other and have a concern with the houses of education, one studies the law after graduation. If Saturn and Jupiter occupy Libra, Gemini, Aquarius or Leo, the same results come in evidence, regarding education of law. If Jupiter and Saturn occupy 1st and 7th, or 2nd and 8th, or 3rd and 9th, or 5th and 11th houses, the education of law is obtained.

Summarizing, we can say that the combinations for some of the subjects of study are as below:

Chartered Accountants: 1. Mercury- Jupiter
2. Mars, Mercury & Jupiter

History: Saturn and 6th house

Computer Engineer: Mercury, Venus and Ketu

Physics: Jupiter, Venus and Mercury

Hindi: The Sun and Jupiter

So, these are the few combinations, which indicate the course of education in a particular direction. We have not gone into the study of many other subjects lest the chapter becomes too lengthy, as this would, in fact, be a part of our forthcoming book on Education. Sometimes our study and profession are wholly distinct. One takes a degree in a particular subject but ultimately works in a different field. Acquiring a degree in engineering and venturing into business of garments or joining a service with a degree of law is definitely a possibility. This study would give us an insight into the subject of our studies, and whether or not our profession would be related with that. Or if we can say it otherwise, it can direct the native to take up the subject in studies, which are related with the occupation at a later stage, so that it gives better chances of success and interest.

CHAPTER-14

Fate and Finance

"भाग्यं फलति सर्वत्र
न च विद्या न च पौरुषम् ।।"

i.e. Merits and Wisdom matter the least. It is only the fortune which brings fruits, everywhere.

Money comes due to good luck and not merely due to hard work, wisdom and merits. The ninth house, if very well and strongly disposed, brings wealth. There is a strong relationship between *karma* and *bhagya*. Therefore, the relationship, conjunction or exchange of lords of the 9th and 10th house is considered most auspicious and highly beneficial, with regard to career and financial status. A strong and well disposed ascendant gives a concrete platform to rise more and more. A strong ascendant, with strong 9th house, will make the subject successful in various ways and will open sources for huge wealth. The intensity and strength of these houses, will decide the amount of wealth, whereas the 2nd house shows the resources of income.

The 9th house is the most important and auspicious house in the birth chart, if well disposed. However, one can enjoy wealth, only when the ascendant is strong and its lord is well disposed. The ascendant is strong if occupied by benefics and aspected by own lord, or occupied by own lord and aspected by benefics like Jupiter, Venus or well associated Mercury, provided the benefics do not own any of the *Trik* houses.

The 2nd, 11th and 9th houses determine the intensity of riches. The 5th and 9th are the houses of *'Poorva Punya'*. Therefore, these houses, and lords thereof, must be studied properly for the judgment of one's financial status. The exchange or conjunction of the 5th and 10th lords, or 9th and 10th lords, or their association in quadrant or triangle, gives high official position and strong favor of government through which one earns enormous wealth, fame, success and prosperity.

If the 9th lord is weak and ill disposed or falls in the sign of debilitation, one will suffer in respect of financial gains and success, in spite of well disposed 11th and 2nd house. Placement of the lord of the 9th house in the 9th house, well aspected or associated with benefics, blesses the native with immense wealth, prosperity, fortune, success, elevation and success in undertakings. A world renowned and extremely successful capitalist having roaring business in almost all countries of the globe has 9th lord Mercury in the 9th house in Gemini, under the aspect of Jupiter from the ascendant. This has bestowed immeasurable fortune to the native. He started from Rs. Two thousand only a few years back and within a span of twenty years, more than eleven lakhs employees are looking after his business of billions and billions. The 9th house signifies *'Poorva Punya'* i.e. the native is blessed with fortune and wealth etc. due to his *Punya* earned by him out of good deeds in the previous birth.

Bhartruhari, a famous Sanskrit poet, whose *shlokas* may breathe cynicism but reflect realism, says:

नवाकृति फलति नैवकुलं न शीलम्
विद्यपि न वा न च यत्नकृतापि सेवा।
भाग्यानि पूर्व तपसा खलु सञ्चितानि
काले फलन्ति पुरुषस्य यथैव वृक्षाः।।

One's personality, one being the scion of a great family, one's high character, not even one's educational attainments and learning, not even one's persistent, perseverance-these do not avail the native as much as *'Poorva Punya'* acquired due to good acts in the previous life which yields fruits in season, like fruit bearing trees. In the next *shloka*, the poet says that only *'Poorya Punya'* protects a person in a forest (infested by wild animals and venomous reptiles), in a battle field, in the midst of enemies, from a flood or swollen river, from a fire, in an ocean, when accidentally falling from the top of a hill (on a luscious grassy meadow), while asleep, when administered poison (by accidentally allowing the vessel to slip and spill or by taking another vessel without the poisoned drink).

God's grace is mightiest than the mighty and it protects one against all severe and terrific odds. Thus, the role of **fate or fortune** is accepted all over the world by all human beings.

Hindu astrology specifies that the ninth house is stronger trine than the fifth. The fifth house is also a strong *'Poorva Punya Sthana'*. For Scorpio ascendant, the fifth lord Jupiter is even more important than the ninth lord Moon, who is a *Badhakadhipati* as well. If Jupiter is well placed from Moon, in a quadrant, there is *Akhand Samrajya Yoga*. This can be correctly applied to Scorpio and Aquarius ascendants. For Scorpio, Jupiter is the lord of the 2nd and 5th, whereas for Aquarius, Jupiter is lord of the 2nd and 11th, as well as Jupiter is *Dhanakaraka*. Therefore, the placement of Moon and Jupiter in angle, for both these ascendants, makes one rich. For Gemini ascendant, Mercury, the lord of the ascendant and the fourth house, and Venus the lord of the fifth house, give rise to *Rajyoga*, if well placed and well disposed. For Gemini ascendant, Jupiter and Saturn, who own the tenth and the ninth house, do not make one so fortunate as Mercury and Venus. Mutual exchange of Jupiter and Saturn i.e. Jupiter in the 9th house in Aquarius and Saturn in the 10th house in Pisces, forms a *Rajyoga* but is less auspicious than the *Rajyoga* formed by Mercury and Venus under the mutual exchange, for Gemini ascendant.

The lord of the ascendant, if placed in the 9th house with the 9th lord, benefic or malefic, gives rise to good luck. Even if the 9th lord joins the 3rd house, it will promote one's fortune due to its aspect. However, the 9th lord should not be eclipsed or combust. In any birth chart, first of all, the 9th house should be examined properly. If the 9th house is strong, or occupied by its own lord, benefics or by the lords of angles, the intensity of malefic *yogas* will be minimized.

A well disposed ninth *bhava* and a strong ascendant make one rich and successful. If the tenth house or its lord also plays its role in it, one will be famous and rich due to his *karma* supported by fate.

Saravali says:

सर्वमपहाय चिन्त्यम् भाग्यम् ।
प्राणिनाम् विशेषेण भाग्यनविते नैव न जन्तुः ।

(*Saravali,* Ch-32; Vers-1)

"Life without luck is not worthwhile! So, examine the ninth house to the exclusion of all else."

Jatak Chandrika mentions :

भाग्यम् विना सर्वम् अधन्येमेव भाग्यं विथेन
एव नरेव भाव्यम् .....अथास्तु यं मुख्य थमोहि भावाहे ।

"Without luck or fortune, all will be fruitless. One with luck or fortune, does a native enjoy the fruits. So, the 9th is considered to be the most important *bhava.*"

A strong benefic, if well placed in the ninth house, makes the married life full of conjugal bliss, even if the 7th house is ill disposed. A natural malefic is good, provided that is the lord of the ascendant or the ninth house.

भाग्यस्थानस्थितैः सौम्येः सपापेस्तषतमेपिवा ।
भर्त्तुः पुत्र सुखैः स्वार्थम् दीर्घकालम् च जीवन्ति ।।

For Aries ascendant, placement of Jupiter in the 9th in Sagittarius, is certainly superior to Saturn in the 9th in Aquarius, for Gemini natives. Similarly, for Sagittarius ascendant, Jupiter in the 9th is better than Saturn in the 9th house in Virgo, for Capricorn native. Placement of Jupiter or Venus in the 5th shows keen intellect and high degree of wisdom, provided Jupiter or Venus do not own malefic houses. Jupiter in the 5th house in Pisces, for Scorpio, and Venus in the fifth in Taurus, for Capricorn, is excellent. Mercury in the fifth, especially in Virgo or Gemini, bestows native with piercing intellect, sharp brain and retentive memory and art of planning and analyzing the things logically.

For Taurus ascendant, Mercury owns the 2nd and the 5th, and it is splendid if placed in the fifth or fourth house with Sun. This kind of planetary combinations must be studied in **'How to Judge a Horoscope'** of **'Dr. B.V. Raman' Vol. I and II**, which will enable the students to make accurate judgement.

The 5th house indicates a feeling of power and pride and influential state of mind. The 9th house occupied by a benefic and its lord placed in a quadrant, triangle or 11th house, brings good luck, wealth and success. Jupiter in ascendant, in own sign, aspecting the 5th and the 9th lord, the Sun in the 5th under the aspect of Jupiter, for Sagittarius, makes the native fortunate. The concerning verse is given here:

जीवे लग्नेति सम्पूर्ण पुत्र मित्र सुतैर्युता।

Bhavarth Ratnakar says that Mercury is auspicious for Capricorn ascendant. Mercury in Virgo, in the 9th house, brings good fortune, as Virgo is *Mool trikona* sign of Mercury too. For Libra ascendant, Saturn is *Yogakaraka*, as it owns 4th and 5th house. But Saturn gives better results in Capricorn though Aquarius is its *Mooltrikona* sign. There is a dictum-

मृग सुख भावस्थ भानुपुत्रो नरेशः

It means, that if Saturn is placed in Capricorn, in the 4th house, it makes one a king. However, it has been experienced in many top Libra natives that mutual exchange of the 10th lord Moon and *Yogakaraka* Saturn, in the 10th, has made the native very powerful and placed at a very high position, which is equal to a king, Cabinet Minister, topmost Industrialist, chief secretary and the like. However, Saturn in the 10th house, for Libra and Taurus ascendants, gives a rise to dizzy heights and then throws down.

The lords of the 5th and the 9th signify *'Poorva Punya'*. If both the lords are placed together in any house, the matters of that house are largely promoted. However, it should be ensured that any one planet, out of two, has not shifted in *bhava* chart. We also have an experience of Karmic control planets that do play vital role in our lives. The dispositors of Rahu and Ketu are called Karmic control planets, and if both of them are placed together, it gives rise to great fortune and promotes the matter of that house. However, we would try to discuss about the role of Karmic control planets elsewhere. The strength and position of the lord of the ascendant can not be ignored. If the ascendant lord also joins the triangle lord or lords, in a benefic position, the matters indicated by that house are further advanced and elevated.

Brihat Parashar Hora Shastra specifies this fact as under:

सुतेश्वरो धर्मसंयुतश्चेत् लग्नेश्वराणि युतौ चेत्
लग्ने सुखेथवा मातगृहे स्यात् राज्याभिषिक्तो यदि
राजवंश राजाधिराजः

(*Brihat Parashar Hora Shastra,* Chap-36, Vers-11)

"If the lord of the 5th and the lord of the 9th are with the lord of *lagna,* in *lagna,* in the 4th or in the 10th, the native becomes a king of kings."

Eminent classic *Jatak Tatwa* written by Acharya Mahadev states:

धर्मापत्त्यपौ गुणो न केन्द्रे लग्नष्युतो राजाधिराजः

(*Jatak Tatwa,* Chap-3, Part-X, Vers-86)

"If the lords of the 9th and the 5th join in a *Kendra,* other than the 7th, with the lord of the *lagna,* the native becomes an emperor or king of kings."

However, if the combination occurs in the 7th house, the native will be fortunate in respect of spouse or his prosperity through spouse will be realized.

Bhava Kautuhalam also agrees to the same principle.

14.1 The Eleventh House

The eleventh house is always regarded the most auspicious house and all scholars have advocated this fact. What is far less known, or the least known, is the worst potential of the 11th house, in addition to its being one of the best house, the house of gain and progress. Even most of the classical texts do not refer to this worst potential of the 11th house. On the contrary, only praises are showered on the 11th.

Till some years back, we were also a staunch supporter of the 11th house and its lord. Later experiences and studies with test and horoscopes rather put us on the right path.

Thus, our understanding, as of date is, that the 11th lord or the planets, who occupy the 11th house or planets associated with the lord of the 11th house, promote the level of the native by gain and acquisitions. Here, the 11th house is the 10th from the 2nd house and 2nd from the 10th house. Therefore, the 11th house is a central point for gains through *karma* of present birth. This point of 11th house has been emphasized in all classics and texts. It is said that Ravan had a control over the movement of planets. He tried to place all the nine planets in the 11th house of the horoscope of his son Meghnaad.

The worst part of the 11th house is that it is the 6th from the 6th house and the 6th is the 8th from there. The 11th house, therefore, gives rise to difficulties, serious diseases, litigation and loans etc. which are originally indicated by the 6th house. This tendency applies to the main *dasa bhukti* of the concerning planets. This is the worst of the 11th house. So, one should not surprise, if the problems of this kind arise during the period of the 11th lord, or occupants thereof. Their *nakshatra* and *navamsa* lord should also be examined carefully.

Brihat Parashara states:

त्रिशडयाधिपः सर्वैग्रहाः पाप फलाः स्मृताः

(*Brihat Parashara*)

"Whoever owns the 3rd, 6th or 11th will produce sinful effects, such a planet is inauspicious and a trouble maker."

The term "*Sarve*" includes all the seven planets without any exception, be it Venus, Jupiter or anyone.

This view is not to be confused with *Upchaya*. That reference applies to a planet in *Upchaya* being auspicious and not the lord of *Upchaya* being auspicious. Even the concept, of the occupant of the three of the four *Upchaya* signs viz. 3rd, 6th or 11th being flatly auspicious, will be demolished, once we carefully understand the horoscope based on the current discussions and keep the misguided notions about these houses aside.

Thus, out of the 6 houses, Parashara removed three houses from the list of so called good ones and put them as evil. The other three houses 2nd, 8th and 12th are not so bad as 3rd, 6th and 11th but their lords will modify their effects and results on the basis of conjunctions, placement and aspect of other planets.

व्ययद्वितिय रन्ध्रेशाः साहचर्यात् फलप्रदाः।

"The lords of the 12th, 2nd and 8th will prove favorable, if they are related to angular or trinal lords. They are extremely adverse, if related to 3rd, 6th or 11th house.

Thus, the 9th and 5th house play a vital role in making one fortunate and wealthy. Many combinations involving these houses may be marked in the horoscopes of wealthy and fortunate persons. We have keenly observed the horoscopes of many natives who have a few of the above mentioned combinations but have suffered a lot in regard to their financial status. So, we strongly believe that something is there, in addition to the above beneficial and fortunate combinations, that make one exceptionally rich, famous, prosperous and fortunate. This needs lot of research in this sphere.

We have some of our humble observations, which we will try to explain and prove in this chapter. The role of nodes should also be carefully examined in all charts. First of all, we will try to explain these combinations on various practical cases of recognized rich and wealthy persons of the world. Thereafter, we will try to summarize and comment on the peculiar and specific role of Rahu and Ketu, their dispositions and role of planets placed in their constellations. Scholars are requested to please make a wide judgment of these findings, which are not covered in texts.

Illustration : 14.1 (**Bill Gates**) *Horoscope No.: 80*

Date of birth : 28.10.1955 Time of birth : 20:58:00 hrs
Place of birth : Seattle Lat 47:36:00 N Long 112:19:00E
Ayanamsa : 23:14:39 Sidereal Time : 23:55:44

Pln	**Degree**	**Rasi**	**Nakshatra**	**Pad**
Asc	29:28:37	Gem	Punarvasu	3
Sun	11:45:07	Lib	Swati	2
Mon	14:23:20	Pis	U Bhadrapad	4
Mar	16:50:47	Vir	Hasta	3
Mer	23:18:52	Vir	Hasta	4
Jup	4:32:04	Leo	Magha	2
Ven	26:55:57	Lib	Vishakha	3
Sat	28:20:33	Lib	Vishakha	3
Rah (R)	24:53:21	Sco	Jyestha	3
Ket (R)	24:53:21	Tau	Mrigshira	1

Lagna Chart

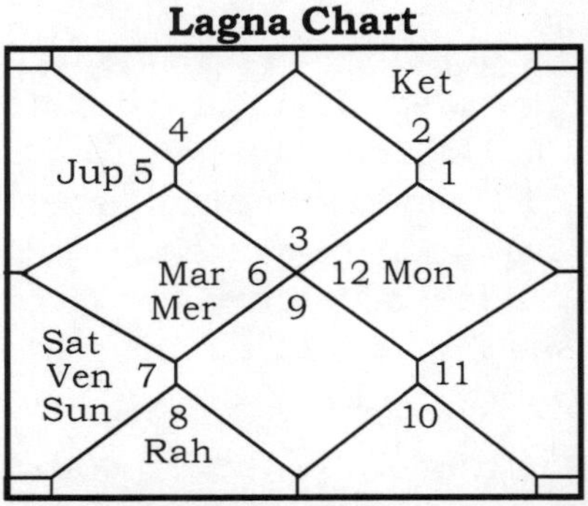

Navamsa Chart

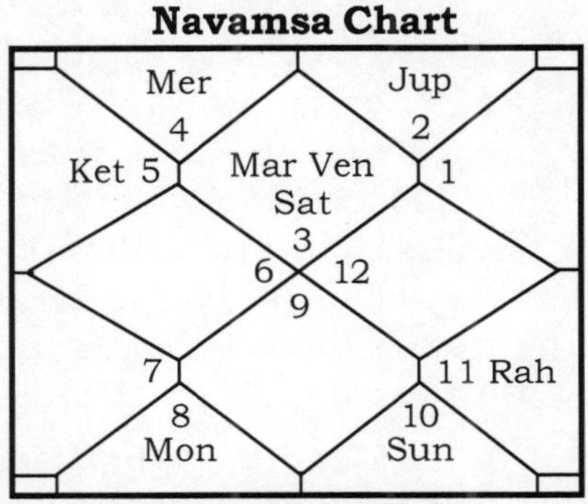

Balance of Vimshottari Dasa of **Sat 3Y 2M 28D**

Gates is one of the richest persons of the world. He is a self made person and would never have imagined his present status of life, fate and finance.

Planetary set up of the horoscope of Mr. Bill Gates clearly indicates that he has extraordinary merits, talents, ability as well as fortune. Bill Gates was born when Gemini ascendant was rising under *vargottam navamsa*. Following planetary combinations blessed him to be one of the very few top business tycoons of the present century.

1. Lords of both the triangles i.e. 5th and 9th are associated in the 5th house in Libra. The 5th lord Venus in own sign Libra, and the 9th lord Saturn, in its sign of exaltation,are excellent in the 5th house in conjunction. Both, Saturn and Venus, are closely associated, in the constellation of 7th and 10th lord Jupiter. Both, Saturn and Venus, obtain the *navamsa* of the lord of the ascendant Mercury i.e. Gemini, which is a friendly sign of these two planets. Saturn and Venus, both, are very strong in *shadabala* as well, as these obtain 1.3 and 1.63 *shadabalas* respectively. Conjunction of both the triangle lords, in a triangle, and that too in their own or exaltation sign, is a powerful *Rajyoga*, which should be held responsible for his becoming exceptionally wealthy person. In fact, the 5th house indicates *'Poorva Punya'* and if it is well disposed it shows that the native will become wealthy, famous and successful due to his past *karmas*.

2. The lord of the ascendant, Mercury, is exalted in the 4th house, and it is under the strong influence of the lord of the 2nd house Moon, as Mercury falls in the constellation *Hasta*, ruled by Moon, and obtains *navamsa* of Moon as well. Mercury and Moon lend mutual aspect over each other. Mercury is quite strong in *shadabala* as well as it obtains 1.16 *shadabala*. Mercury also gives rise to *Bhadrika Mahapurusha Raj Yoga*. This has given an extraordinary talent, brilliance and wisdom.

3. It may be noted that Moon is the lord of the 2nd house and falls in the 10th house, in the constellation of the 9th

lord Saturn. Mars is the lord of the 11th and 6th houses and it is tenanted in the 4th house, in the sign Virgo, and falls in the *Hasta* constellation of Moon, who is the 2nd lord. Thus, the 11th lord Mars and the 2nd lord Moon occupy the 4th and the 10th house respectively and aspect each other. The lord of the ascendant, Mercury, also joins the 4th house and that also falls in Moon's asterism *Hasta*. However, here the lord of the ascendant Mercury, lord of the 2nd house Moon and the lord of the 11th Mars are placed in quadrants and influence each other by conjunction or aspect. This is also a quite strong *Dhana Yoga,* which must be appreciated, for his enormous wealth.

4. The 2nd house is called ***Dhan bhava***, that is, the house of wealth. Triangular houses from the 2nd house are the 6th & 10th houses from the ascendant. Here, the lord of the 2nd Moon is posited in the friendly sign Pisces. However, the 6th house is occupied by Rahu under no benefic aspect. This is a combination of obstacles & problems. Gates had to face a lot of problems & obstacles in his career. Many enemies and jealous people attempted to drag him down. Except the 6th house, all other concerning houses are very well disposed. Placement of Mercury and Mars in the 4th house, Venus and Saturn in the 5th house made him expert in computer science

5. *Dhanakaraka*, the 7th and 8th lord Jupiter, falls in Leo in *Magha* and aspects the 7th house of its own, in addition to the 9th and 11th houses. Jupiter obtains *navamsa* of the 5th lord Venus, whereas Venus falls in the asterism of Jupiter. Thus, both first rate benefics, who own the 5th and 10th house respectively, influence each other, in one or the other way, which has promoted profession and finance largely. Jupiter is quite strong in *shadabala* as well, as it obtains 1.21 *shadabala*. We believe that Jupiter gives best results in Leo, for Gemini ascendant.

6. Best kind of ***Adhi Yoga*** has also been formed as Jupiter, Mercury and Venus occupy the 6th, 7th and the 8th house

respectively, as reckoned from natal Moon, giving rise to classical *Adhi Yoga*. Here, all the three benefics are quite strong in *shadabala* and obtain *navamsa* of Venus, Moon and Mercury respectively, who play a vital role in the augmentation of financial position of the native through his *karma* and fortune. *Adhi Yoga* is one of the rarest *Rajyoga* and makes one equal to a King. This yoga is generally found in the horoscopes of Prime Ministers, Presidents, Secretaries, top industrialists, CEOs of large companies etc.

7. The **9th house** governs the fortune of the native and if it has a concern with the 10th lord, it will bless the native with high status, position and power. Here, Jupiter, lord of the 10th house is aspecting the 9th house. Jupiter is also 11th from the 9th lord Saturn and 11th house rules over riches. This is a powerful combination to make him one of the wealthiest persons of the world.

8. The 11th house is ***Labh Bhava*** i. e. the house of income. One should examine the triangular positions from the 11th house to verify whether the 11th house is strong. In this chart, the 5th house from the 11th i.e. the 3rd house is strong enough as Jupiter is posited there and it is aspecting the 7th house, which is the next triangular from the 11th. Thus, the 3rd & 7th house from the ascendant are the 5th & 9th from the 11th and both are well disposed.

9. *Navamsa lagna* is occupied by 11th lord Mars, the 5th lord Venus and the 9th lord Saturn, which has added strength to the *navamsa* chart. This made the native world famous, rich and successful business tycoon.

Rahu and Ketu do play peculiar role in adding strength to the combinations. The nodes are somehow concerned with the good or bad deeds of the past birth i.e. *'Poorva Punya'*. Dispositors of Rahu and Ketu are called Karmic control planets and must be taken into consideration for the accurate judgment of fate and finance.

The 7th and 10th lord, Jupiter, falls in *Magha nakshatra*. Jupiter occupies Leo, whose lord Sun falls in *Swati nakshatra*. Thus, *Dhanakaraka* Jupiter falls in Ketu's *nakshatra* and the Sun, who is a planet of success, prosperity, name, fame, honor, merits, recognition etc. also joins Rahu's constellation. Karmic control planets are Mars and Venus. Venus, who is the 5th lord, has become much stronger to bless the native with countless wealth and that has added strength to Sun and Saturn as well. Similarly, Mars occupies the 4th house with exalted Mercury and strengthens the combinations good for financial status.

Illustration : 14.2 (**Dorab ji Tata**) *Horoscope No.: 81*

Date of birth : 27.08.1859 Time of birth : 12:00:00 hrs
Place of birth : Bombay Lat 18:58:00 N Long 72:50:00E
Ayanamsa : 21:54:02 Sidereal Time : 10:19:58

Pln	**Degree**	**Rasi**	**Nakshatra**	**Pad**
Asc	8:02:03	Sco	Anuradha	2
Sun	11:33:03	Leo	Magha	4
Mon	28:32:25	Can	Aslesa	4
Mar (C)	29:49:40	Can	Aslesa	4
Mer (R/C)	14:32:34	Leo	P Phalguni	1
Jup	25:04:44	Gem	Punarvasu	2
Ven (C)	3:01:12	Leo	Magha	1
Sat (C)	26:17:56	Can	Aslesa	3
Rah	28:33:35	Cap	Dhanistha	2
Ket (C)	28:33:35	Can	Aslesa	4

Lagna Chart

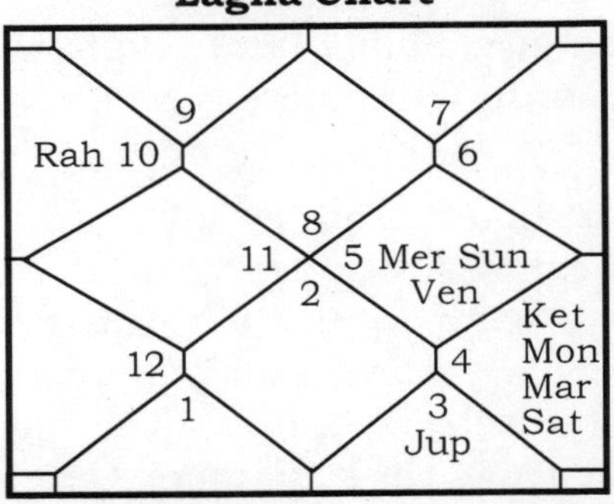

Navamsa Chart

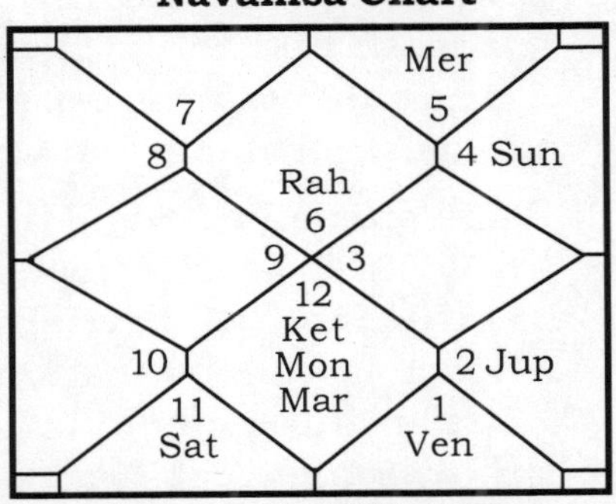

Balance of Vimshottari Dasa of **Mer 1Y 10M 10D**

The very name of Tata is a symbol of exceptionally rich person. Tata Estate is the name of the world renowned organization which has been formed and whose foundation has been laid by Tatas. He made Engines, Trucks, Electricity, Textiles, Chemicals, Cement, Cosmetics, Cars, Vehicles, all kinds of steel and iron, and almost everything has been world famous.

The important combinations of this world famous and best known name, in the sphere of wealth, around the globe, are as under:

1. The lord of the 10th house, the Sun, is exceptionally strong as it obtains 2.14 *shadabalas*. The 10th lord Sun occupies its own sign Leo in the 10th house and obtains *navamsa* of the 9th lord Moon. This falls in the constellation *Magha*. We will try to explain the role of *Magha nakshatra*, at the end of this chapter, as far as our humble observations are concerned.

2. The 9th lord, Moon, falls in own sign Cancer, in the 9th house itself. Moon obtains the *navamsa* of the 2nd and the 5th lord Jupiter. In fact, Moon is very strong in the 9th house and has bestowed immense luck and wealth to the native. The Moon obtains 1.33 *shadabala*, falls in the constellation of the 11th lord Mercury, obtains *navamsa* of Jupiter, is placed in own sign Cancer in the 9th house and is associated with the ascendant lord Mars and the 4th lord Saturn. Thus, the 9th lord Moon is under the strong influence of *dhanakaraka*, *dhanesh* (2nd lord), *labhesh* (11th lord), *lagnesh* (ascendant lord), *sukhesh* (4th lord) and *bhagyesh* (9th lord). What more is required to be so fortunate and wealthy, as the native was.

3. The lord of the 2nd and the 5th house, Jupiter, falls in the 8th house, which is considered as a house of mystery and secrets. We have always appreciated the role of 8th house in various matters such as profession, finance, foreign travel etc. in our research papers published in the Astrological Magazine from time to time. Here, *dhanakaraka* and *dhanesh* Jupiter joins the 8th house

in own constellation *Punarvasu* and obtains 1.17 *shadabala* as well. Jupiter lends its favorable and strong aspect over the 2nd, 4th and 12th house and adds much strength to the concerning houses of trade, finance, prosperity, power and property.

4. The 9th house, i.e. house of fortune and its lord Moon are hemmed between first rate benefic planets Jupiter on one side and Venus, Mercury on the other, giving rise to *Shubhakartari Yoga*, which is adding strength to the 9th house and ascendant. A strong *Durdhara Yoga* has also been formed.
5. The lord of the 11th house, Mercury, occupies the 10th house with the 10th lord Sun and the 7th lord Venus. Mercury obtains *vargottam navamsa*. Venus and the Sun both fall in *Magha nakshatra*. Mercury is tenanted in the constellation of Venus i.e. *Poorvaphalguni*. The combination of Sun, Mercury and Venus in the 10th house and the conjunction of the Moon, Mars, Saturn and Ketu in the 9th house, with Jupiter in the 8th house, blessed the native with immeasurable wealth, fortune, fame and success in almost all walks of life.
6. Role of Karmic control planets can also be judged in this birth chart. Saturn and Moon are Karmic control planets here and they are conjoined in the 9th house, with the ascendant lord Mars. This is the most powerful *Rajyoga* in this birth chart.

These combinations made Sir Dorab Ji Tata the richest industrialist of India.

Illustration : 14.3 (**JRD Tata**) *Horoscope No.: 82*

Date of birth : 29.07.1904 Time of birth : 12:39:00 hrs
Place of birth : Paris Lat 48:50:00 N Long 02:20:00E
Ayanamsa : 22:31:26 Sidereal Time : 09:15:16

Pln	Degree	Rasi	Nakshatra	Pad
Asc	12:52:20	Lib	Swati	2
Sun	13:23:58	Can	Pushya	4

Mon	6:49:34	Aqu	Satabhisha	1
Mar (C)	26:40:28	Gem	Punarvasu	3
Mer	2:33:51	Leo	Magha	1
Jup	6:55:25	Ari	Ashwini	3
Ven (C)	19:15:54	Can	Aslesa	1
Sat (R)	26:02:12	Cap	Dhanistha	1
Rah (R)	26:32:41	Leo	P Phalguni	4
Ket (R)	26:32:41	Aqu	P Bhadrapad	2

Lagna Chart

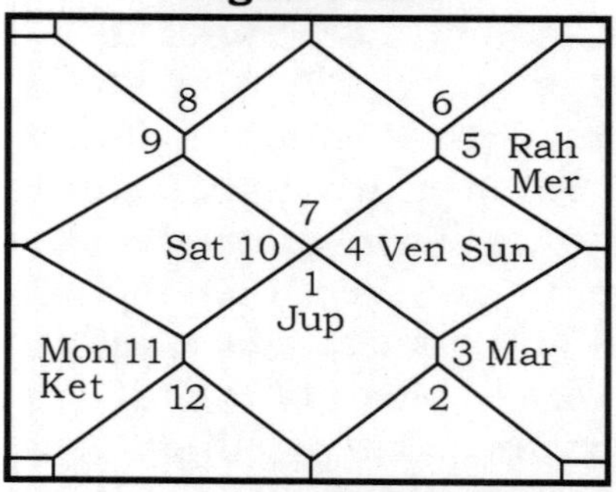

Navamsa Chart

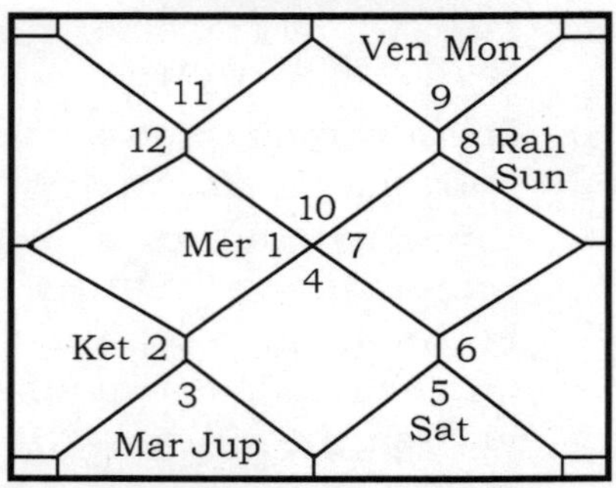

Balance of Vimshottari Dasa of **Rah 17Y 9M 12D**

This horoscope belongs to Bharat Ratna J.R.D. Tata, who earned worldwide recognition as steel king. He was one of the richest people of the present era. He entered in the industry business at 18 years of age in 1922. He became Director at 22 years of age in 1926. He became Chairman of Tata group in 1938. He was President of Air India during 1946 and became Chairman of Iron Steel. Padma Bhushan was conferred on him in the year 1955. He remained unmarried for whole of his life. He was honored as the wealthiest industrialist of India, as long as he survived. Following planetary set up made him such an organized top most and richest business tycoon.

1. The 9th lord Mercury occupies the 11th house, in association with Rahu, and falls in *Magha nakshatra*. Mercury receives the aspect of Jupiter and Moon.

2. The lord of the ascendant, Venus, occupies the 10th house in association with the 11th lord Sun. The Sun obtains 2.0 *shadabala* and Venus obtains 1.34 *shadabala*. This is a strong *Lakshmi, Mahalakshmi* or *dhana yoga*. The Sun falls in *Pushya nakshatra* and obtains *navamsa* of Mars.

3. *Yogakaraka* Saturn occupies the 4th house in Capricorn giving rise to *Sasa Mahapurusha Rajyoga*. The Sun and Venus are shifted in the 9th house and Moon is shifted in the 4th house. Thus, the *lagna* lord Venus, 11th lord Sun and the 2nd lord Mars are very well associated in the 9th house. The 10th lord Moon is conjoined with *Yogakaraka* Saturn in the 4th house. The 9th lord Mercury is shifted in the 10th house. This shows high degree of great fortune and finance.

4. Both Karmic control planets, Saturn and the Sun, are also placed opposite to each other, which is a great *Rajyoga*.

5. The lord of the 2nd house, Mars, joins the 9th house and falls in Jupiter's constellation *Punarvasu*. Mars also obtains *vargottam navamsa*. *Dhanakaraka* Jupiter also obtains *navamsa* of Mercury, and aspects Mercury as well, along with the 11th house, ascendant and the 3rd house.

6. Mercury, Jupiter and Venus are the strongest planets in this birth chart as these obtain 1.33, 1.27 and 1.34 *shadabalas* and are well placed.

7. The 10th lord Moon falls in the 5th house in *Satabhisha nakshatra* and obtains *navamsa* of Jupiter. *Nakshatra* lord Rahu is the best placed in the 11th house and is aspected by Jupiter. Moon's *nakshatra* and *navamsa* regularized his professional sphere and Mercury, Mars, Sun and Venus raised him to the level of sky.

8. Rahu and 9th lord Mercury occupy the 11th house, where Mercury falls in *Magha nakshatra*.

9. The 5th house is occupied by Moon and Ketu. Moon falls in *Satabhisha nakshatra.*

Thus, the 5th and 9th houses are under the influence of Rahu and Ketu. Karmic control planets, Sun and Saturn, occupy the 10th and 4th house, opposite to each other.

This has added strength to the *lagna* lord Venus and has further strengthened Saturn, who is not only a *Yogakaraka* but also forms *Sasa Mahapurusha Rajyoga. Dhanakaraka* Jupiter, who joins the 7th house, falls in *Aswani nakshatra* ruled by Ketu. Jupiter's aspect on the 11th house, Rahu and Mercury enhanced the good effects of the 11th house. Various combinations for wealth and fortune must be studied identical to the auspicious role of the constellation and dispositors of nodes, which add strength to the combinations.

Illustration : 14.4 (**Nizam Hyderabad**) *Horoscope No.: 83*

Date of birth : 06.04.1886 Time of birth : 18:36:00 hrs

Place of birth : Hyderabad Lat 17:22:00 N Long 78:26:00E

Ayanamsa : 22:16:02 Sidereal Time : 07:35:01

Pln	Degree	Rasi	Nakshatra	Pad
Asc	0:24:31	Lib	Chitra	3
Sun	24:23:44	Pis	Revati	3
Mon	17:28:39	Ari	Bharani	2
Mar (R)	14:17:48	Leo	P Phalguni	1
Mer (R/C)	28:53:11	Pis	Revati	4
Jup (R)	6:50:40	Vir	U Phalguni	4
Ven	10:51:16	Aqu	Satabhisha	2
Sat	10:14:42	Gem	Ardra	2
Rah (R)	23:39:08	Leo	P Phalguni	4
Ket (R)	23:39:08	Aqu	P Bhadrapad	2

Lagna Chart

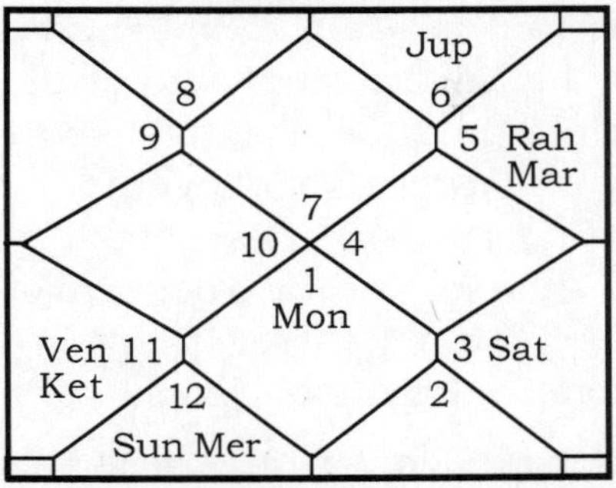

Navamsa Chart

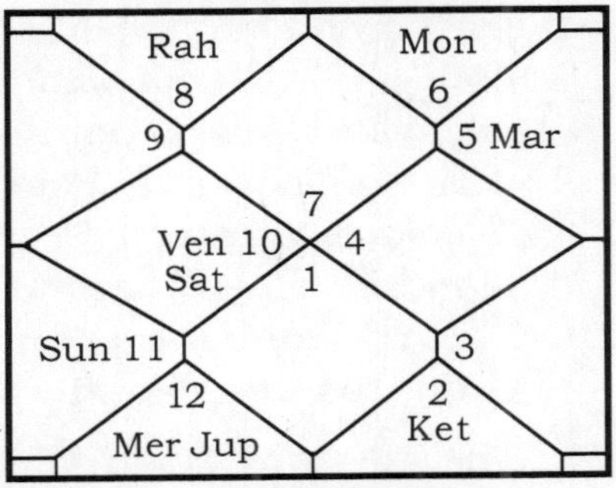

Balance of Vimshottari Dasa of **Ven 13Y 9M 12D**

Nizam Hyderabad had been a very famous, prosperous and wealthy person. He was said to be another name of Kuber. He himself was unaware of the amount of wealth he had. He was married in 1906 with Pasha. Thereafter, he had hundreds of wives and concubines and innumerable children with them. Identity cards were issued to children, to avoid any confusion by Nizam. He enjoyed the wealth and wasted a lot of it in all affairs for the fulfillment of his ambitions, right or wrong. What planetary positions made him so wealthy?

1. *Yogakaraka* Saturn is posited in the 9th house and obtains own *navamsa*. The lord of the 9th house, Mercury, falls in own constellation *Revati* with *Neechabhanga Rajyoga*. The lords of both the triangles i.e. Saturn and Mercury are posited in quadrant from each other, which shows good fortune and immense professional prosperity.

2. Lord of the ascendant, Venus, joins the 5th house and the 4th and 5th lord, *Yogakaraka* Saturn is in triangle from Venus. Here, Venus falls in *Satabhisha nakshatra* and is associated with Ketu. This confirms innumerable relationships and involvement with opposite sex.

3. Lord of the 2nd house, Mars, is best placed in the 11th house, with Rahu in Leo, in *Poorvaphalguni* constellation ruled by *lagna* lord Venus. Mars obtains *varogottam navamsa* and is the strongest planet in this birth chart

as it obtains 1.59 *shadabala*. Mars and Rahu are best placed and very well associated in the 11th house and both fall in *Poorvaphalguni* i.e. in the *nakshatra* of the *lagna* lord Venus. Both are placed under mutual aspect with *lagnadhipati* Venus and are also aspected by *Yogakaraka* Saturn. Thus, *Dhanesh* Mars is aspected by *lagnesh* Venus from the 5th house, and by *Yogakaraka* Saturn from the 9th house. This has given rise to countless wealth and women in the life of Nizam.

4. The 10th lord Moon joins the 7th house, in Aries, and falls in *Bharani nakshatra*. The Moon is the second strongest planet as it obtains 1.5 *shadabala*. Placement of Moon in the 7th house must be appreciated because its dispositor Mars occupies the 11th house.

5. Jupiter is the lord of 3rd and 6th houses and is posited in the 12th house, giving rise to *Vipreet Rajyoga*. Jupiter aspects the 9th lord Mercury and the 11th lord Sun. There is *Vinimai Parivartan Yoga* between Jupiter and Mercury, who are retrograde and join 12th and 6th house respectively. This is a strong benefic exchange of Mercury and Jupiter. However, Mercury is shifted in the 7th house, where it is the combination of the 9th and 10th lords.

These planetary combinations made him unparallel, as far as financial level is concerned.

Lord of the 2nd house, Mars, is posited in Leo and *Poorvaphalguni nakshatra*. Mars is associated with Rahu closely in same *nakshatra*. *Lagna* lord Venus is placed in Rahu's *nakshatra Satabhisha* and is associated with Ketu.

Thus, the lord of the *lagna* and 2nd house are under the influence of Rahu and Ketu. The 9th house is occupied by Saturn, who falls in Rahu's *nakshatra Ardra*.

Karmic control planets are Sun and Saturn, who are placed in the 6th and 9th house, respectively. The Sun and Mercury receive the aspect of *Yogakaraka* Saturn and both are in quadrant from each other. These combinations have made this horoscope as one of the most powerful and strong horoscope in regard to power, fortune and wealth.

Illustration : 14.5 (**Ratan Tata**) *Horoscope No.: 84*

Date of birth : 28.12.1937 Time of birth : 06:30:00 hrs
Place of birth : Bombay Lat 18:58:00 N Long 72:50:00E
Ayanamsa : 22:59:43 Sidereal Time : 12:15:40

Pln	**Degree**	**Rasi**	**Nakshatra**	**Pad**
Asc	2:45:24	Sag	Moola	1
Sun	12:53:25	Sag	Moola	4
Mon	21:37:02	Lib	Vishakha	1
Mar	11:46:27	Aqu	Satabhisha	2
Mer (R/C)	17:45:47	Sag	Purvasadha	2
Jup	8:44:48	Cap	Uttarasadha	4
Ven (C)	3:46:09	Sag	Moola	2
Sat	5:57:49	Pis	U Bhadrapad	1
Rah	12:50:43	Sco	Anuradha	3
Ket	12:50:43	Tau	Rohini	1

Lagna Chart

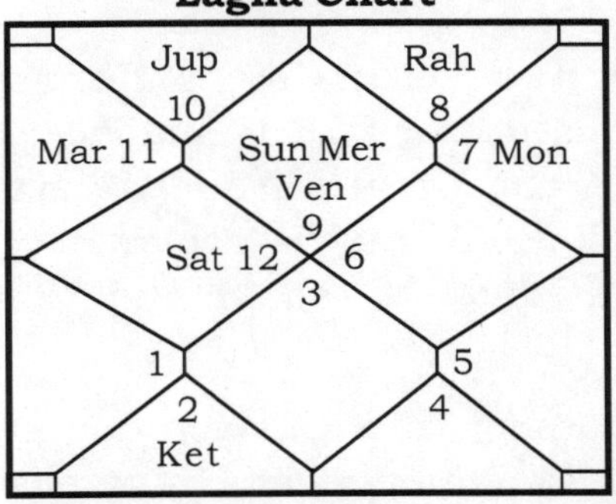

Navamsa Chart

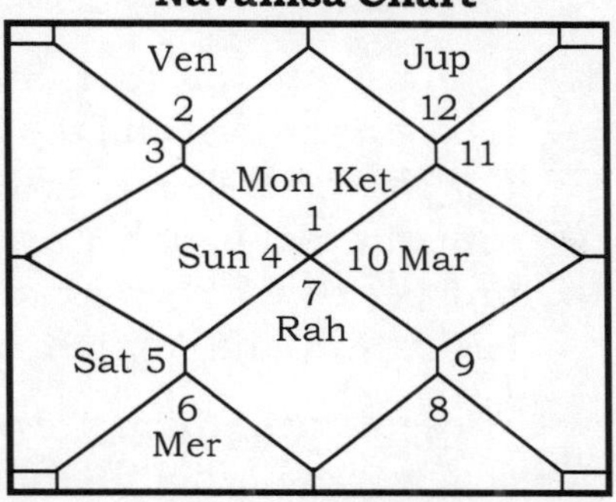

Balance of Vimshottari Dasa of **Jup 14Y 0M 21D**

The owner of Tata group of Industries, Ratan Tata is one of the greatest industrialists of India. He has countless wealth, prosperity and innumerable industries.

1. The 9th lord Sun, 10th lord Mercury and 11th lord Venus are associated in the ascendant.

2. The lord of the 5th house joins the 3rd house in Aquarius in *Satabhisha nakshatra.*

3. Lord of the 2nd house, Saturn, is placed in the 4th house, and 4th lord Jupiter joins the 2nd house. Thus, there is mutual exchange of the lords of the 2nd house Saturn and the 4th house, Jupiter. In other words, the exchange of Saturn and Jupiter has a concern with the ascendant and the 2nd house. However, Jupiter obtains own *navamsa.*

4. 11th lord Venus joins the ascendant with the 9th lord Sun. Venus obtains own *navamsa.* Mercury, who joins the 11th lord Venus and the 9th lord Sun, obtains own *navamsa.* The 5th lord, Mars, obtain the *navamsa* of its exaltation. Thus, Jupiter, Mercury, Venus obtain own *navamsa* and Mars obtains *navamsa* of exaltation and all are interrelated with 5th, 9th, 10th, 1st, 11th, 2nd and 4th house, in one or the other way.

5. All eight planets join 11th to 4th house in continuation like a garland. This is *Ekavali* and *Grahamalika Rajyoga.*

6. The ascendant, the Sun and Venus fall in Ketu's *nakshatra Moola* and the 5th lord Mars falls in *Satabhisha nakshatra* of Rahu. Thus, the 5th and 9th lords are influenced by Rahu and Ketu. Venus is a planet of prosperity who joins the ascendant, and 9th and 10th lords, Sun and Mercury.

These points which are not taken into consideration in classical works need a thorough examination over hundreds of birth chart.

Illustration : 14.6 (**DB Ambani**) *Horoscope No.: 85*

Date of birth : 28.12.1932 Time of birth : 07:37:00 hrs
Place of birth : Veraval Lat 20:53:00 N Long 70:28:00E
Ayanamsa : 22:55:22 Sidereal Time : 13:14:12

Pln	**Degree**	**Rasi**	**Nakshatra**	**Pad**
Asc	15:28:58	Sag	Purvasadha	1
Sun	13:13:47	Sag	Moola	4
Mon (C)	21:43:20	Sag	Purvasadha	3
Mar	24:09:34	Leo	P Phalguni	4
Mer	21:46:49	Sco	Jyestha	2
Jup	0:09:04	Vir	U Phalguni	2
Ven	15:29:14	Sco	Anuradha	4
Sat	10:40:37	Cap	Sravna	1
Rah (R)	16:58:02	Aqu	Satabhisha	4
Ket (R)	16:58:02	Leo	P Phalguni	2

Lagna Chart

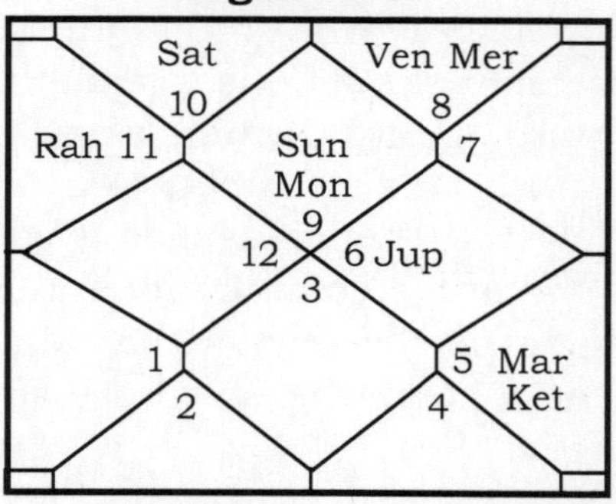

Navamsa Chart

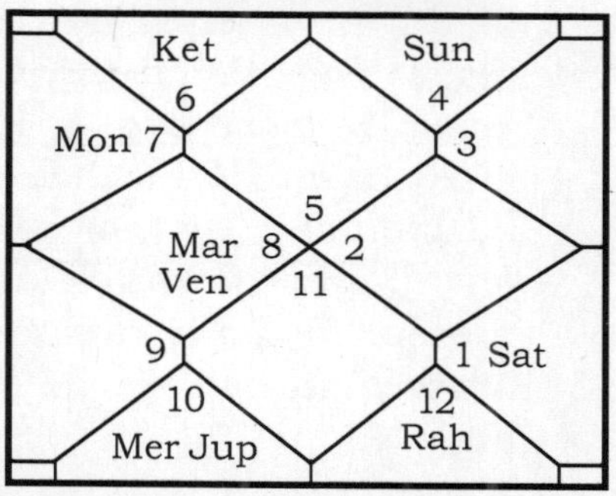

Balance of Vimshottari Dasa of **Ven 7Y 4M 30D**

Dheeru Bhai Ambani was a self made, great industrialist. He started from nothing and established Reliance group of industries at a small age of thirty years only. He had an unbelievable progress in the field of textiles. Thereafter, he entered in so many ventures including power and various projects connected with generation of energy etc. Dheeru

Bhai Ambani is the name of an institution now, which does not need any description. Let us study the planetary dispositions of his horoscope, which elevated him from ground to sky. The fortune certainly plays a vital role in the lives of such people who create history.

1. The 9th lord, Sun, joins the ascendant with Moon. Thus, both the luminaries occupy the ascendant. The Sun and Moon, both, are equally strong and obtain 1.33 *shadabalas*.

2. Jupiter occupies the 10th house but it is shifted in the 9th house. Thus, there is mutual exchange of lords of the ascendant and the 9th house i.e. Jupiter and the Sun. This is *Mahabhagya yoga* which made Mr. Ambani so fortunate and prosperous in a short span of time.

3. The lord of the 5th house, Mars, joins the 9th house in association with Ketu. This is also adding fortune to the native.

4. Lord of the 2nd house, Saturn, occupies the 2nd house itself. The 10th and 11th lords, Mercury and Venus, are placed together in the 12th house. It will not be out of place to mention that involvement of *trik* houses in such *yogas*, or *lagna* lord, or 10th lord, makes the native a self made man. He reaches to a very high position from a position of poverty or so. However, this rule holds good only if other favorable and fortunate combinations are present in the horoscope. That is the reason that Mr. Ambani started his career as a petrol boy and rose so high.

5. Rahu and Ketu are somehow connected with *Karma* and need vast research. Dispositors of Rahu and Ketu are called Karmic control planets. Rahu or Ketu do play an important role in making one exceptionally famous, rich and prosperous.

6. The ascendant, the 5th, the 9th house or their lords have influence of nodes in one or the other way. Here, the 9th lord occupies the ascendant and falls in Moola

nakshatra. The 5th lord, Mars, joins the 9th house in association with Ketu. Saturn and the Sun are Karmic control planets, who occupy the 2nd and 1st house respectively. Thus, the ascendant, and the 5th and the 9th houses are under the influence of Ketu or Rahu. This proves that the rise of the native took place due to *"Poorva Punya"* i.e. good deeds of the past birth).

Illustration : 14.7 (**M Arvind**) *Horoscope No.: 86*

Date of birth	: 27.10.1923	Time of birth :	17:00:00 hrs
Place of birth	: Bombay	Lat 18:58:00 N	Long 72:50:00E
Ayanamsa	: 22:47:27	Sidereal Time :	18:40:33

Pln	**Degree**	**Rasi**	**Nakshatra**	**Pad**
Asc	20:08:34	Pis	Revati	2
Sun	10:13:36	Lib	Swati	2
Mon	9:41:25	Tau	Kritika	4
Mar	13:08:24	Vir	Hasta	1
Mer (C)	27:51:56	Vir	Chitra	2
Jup	0:59:50	Sco	Vishakha	4
Ven	22:32:22	Lib	Vishakha	1
Sat (C)	1:28:34	Lib	Chitra	3
Rah (R)	17:11:08	Leo	P Phalguni	2
Ket (R)	17:11:08	Aqu	Satabhisha	4

Lagna Chart

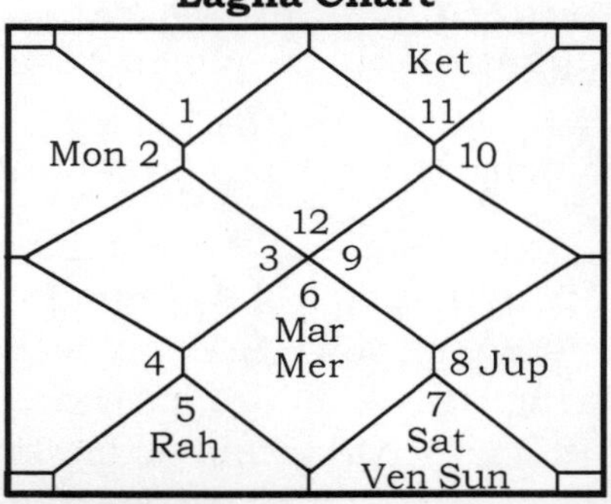

Navamsa Chart

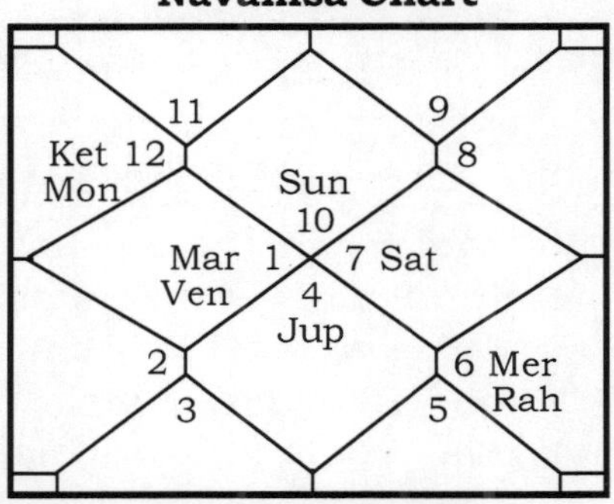

Balance of Vimshottari Dasa of **Sun 0Y 1M 20D**

The native established a world reputed textile industry. He had been one of the most dynamic, dashing and bold multimillionaire. He donated lot of wealth for various religious activities in different ways. Placement of the *lagna* lord Jupiter in the 9th house, with an aspect of Jupiter and the 9th lord Mars over the ascendant, made him so religious and spiritually inclined.

1. The lord of the 2nd and 9th house, Mars, is posited in the 7th house, with 7th lord Mercury. Thus, lord of the 2nd and 9th is placed together with the lord of 4th and 7th Mercury, in a quadrant, having an aspect over the ascendant. Here, the 2nd and 9th lord Mars also aspects the 2nd and the 10th houses.

2. Lord of the ascendant and the 10th house, Jupiter, occupies the 9th house and lends its favorable aspect over the ascendant, the 5th lord Moon and on the 5th house as well. This combination is very strong for financial upliftment because of the formation of the *Kendratrikona yoga, Gajakesari yoga, Dhanalakshmi yoga, Kahal yoga* etc.

3. The Sun and Venus, both, are shifted in the 7th house and the Sun falls in *Swati nakshatra* ruled by Rahu.

4. The 11th and 12th lord, Saturn, is exalted in the 8th house in Libra, and aspects the 10th, 2nd and the 5th house. Saturn is the strongest planet in this birth chart as it obtains 1.47 *shadabala*. Saturn has formed *Vipreet Rajyoga*. The joint aspect of the 2nd and 11th lords, Mars and Saturn, over the 10th and 2nd houses, is of course splendid for enormous wealth and prosperity.

5. Karmic control planets, Saturn and the Sun, are placed together in the 8th house, which shows the earning through his own *karmas*. The 8th house is 11th from the 10th and the 10th from 11th. So, a powerful and well fortified 8th house makes one multimillionaire, provided other conditions are also fulfilled. In the horoscope of Superstar Amitabh Bachchan, the 8th house is occupied

by five planets, which have made him the richest film star so far.

Illustration : 14.8 (**Jamshed ji Tata**) *Horoscope No.: 87*

Date of birth : 03.03.1839 Time of birth : 15:08:00 hrs
Place of birth : Navsari Lat 20:58:00 N Long 73:01:00E
Ayanamsa : 21:36:43 Sidereal Time : 1:50:02

Pln	Degree	Rasi	Nakshatra	Pad
Asc	11:23:59	Can	Pushya	3
Sun	20:34:42	Aqu	P Bhadrapad	1
Mon	24:14:06	Vir	Chitra	1
Mar (R)	2:46:41	Vir	U Phalguni	2
Mer (C)	11:47:10	Aqu	Satabhisha	2
Jup (R)	25:50:09	Vir	Chitra	1
Ven	8:26:59	Pis	U Bhadrapad	2
Sat	18:28:46	Sco	Jyestha	1
Rah (C)	3:14:14	Pis	P Bhadrapad	4
Ket	3:14:14	Vir	U Phalguni	2

Lagna Chart

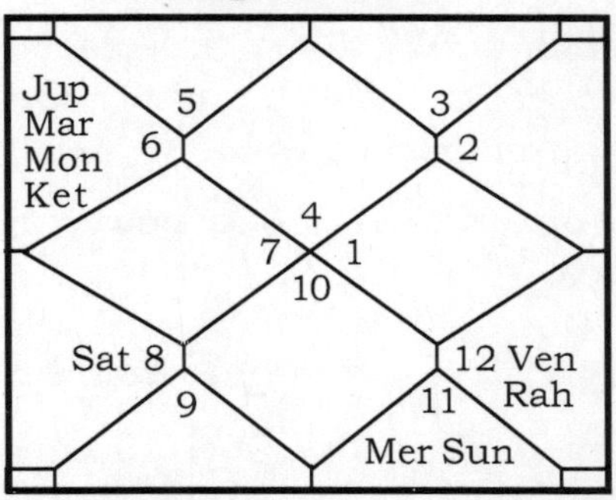

Navamsa Chart

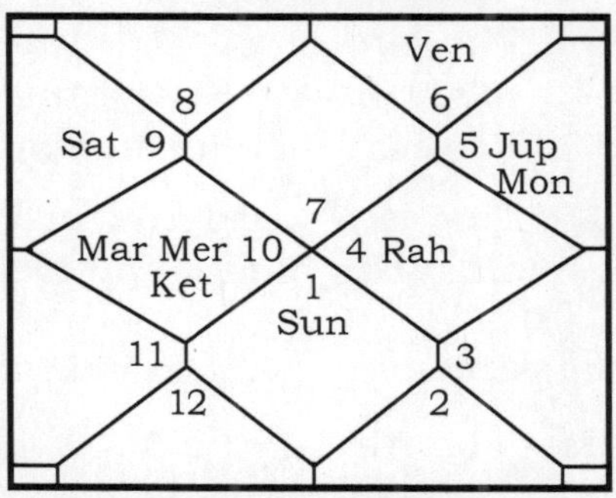

Balance of Vimshottari Dasa of **Mar 6Y 6M 9D**

Mr. Jamshed Ji Tata was the founder of Tata group of Industries. He was the iron king and made trucks, heavy vehicles etc. There is a city Jamshedpur Tata Nagar on his name. This proves his high stature of a multimillionaire and one of the biggest industrialists of the country. He was pride of India.

1. The lord of the ascendant Moon, the 9th lord Jupiter and the 5th lord Mars are very well placed together in the 3rd house with Ketu.
2. The 11th and 4th lord, Venus, is exalted in the 9th house and is associated with Rahu.
3. These combinations are strong enough to make him the richest person of his time, as the lords of 1st, 5th and 9th house are conjoined together in the 3rd house, which provided him courage and vision. The lord of the 11th house, Venus, has strengthened the fortune of the native to the maximum degree, as the 9th house also receives the aspect of its own lord Jupiter.
4. The lords of the 9th house, 11th house, ascendant and 5th house fall over the axis of Rahu and Ketu, which we believe, has further strengthened the power of these planets and combinations to make him richer and richer gradually.
5. The lords of the 2nd house, Sun, and the 7th and 8th house, Saturn, lend their aspect over the 2nd house.
6. The lord of the 9th, Jupiter and 10th, Mars are placed together with the mutual aspect of the 11th and 4th lord Venus, which made him a *karmayogi* as well.

This is a wonderful horoscope, which shows powerful combinations of fate and finance.

Illustration : 14.9 (**Rahul Bajaj**) *Horoscope No.: 88*

Date of birth : 10.06.1938 Time of birth : 05:10:00 hrs
Place of birth : Calcutta Lat 22:30:00 N Long 88:20:00E
Ayanamsa : 23:00:03 Sidereal Time : 22:20:38

Pln	**Degree**	**Rasi**	**Nakshatra**	**Pad**
Asc	23:20:05	Tau	Mrigshira	1
Sun	25:25:53	Tau	Mrigshira	1

Mon	22:00:48	Lib	Vishakha	1
Mar (C)	8:55:43	Gem	Ardra	1
Mer	10:38:22	Tau	Rohini	1
Jup	9:01:59	Aqu	Satabhisha	1
Ven	26:36:07	Gem	Punarvasu	2
Sat	22:55:32	Pis	Revati	2
Rah	3:51:06	Sco	Anuradha	1
Ket	3:51:06	Tau	Kritika	3

Lagna Chart

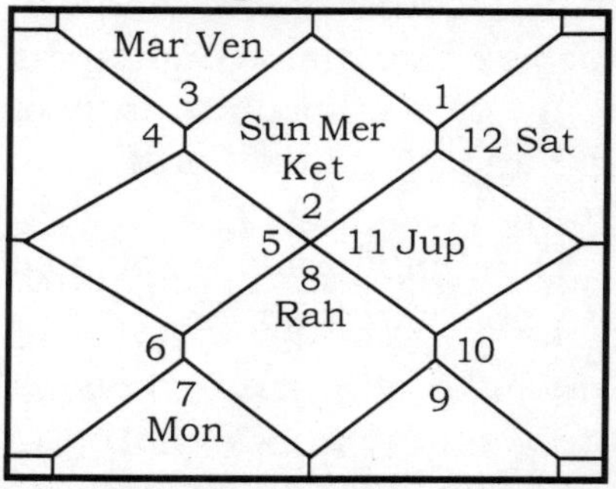

Navamsa Chart

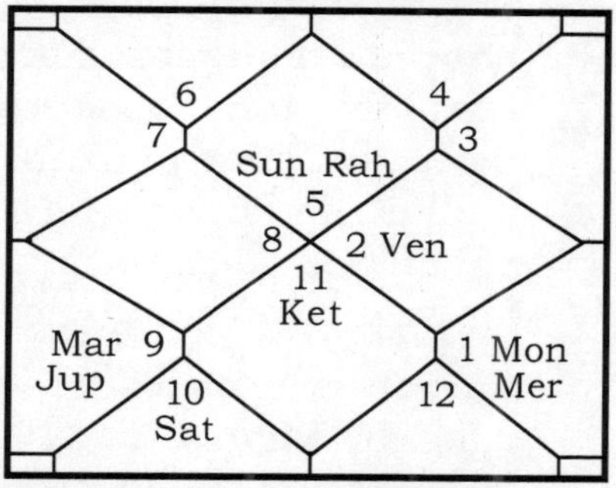

Balance of Vimshottari Dasa of **Jup 13Y 7M 0D**

Rahul Bajaj is one of the most successful and richest people in the field of automobiles. Many famous makes of scooters and motorcycles have been introduced by him from time to time. Here is something extraordinary in his birth chart, which made his efforts and endeavors so fruitful and rewarding.

1. *Yogakaraka* Saturn joins the 11th house and the 11th lord Jupiter occupies the 10th house. Such a strong mutual exchange of the 10th and 11th lords, Saturn and Jupiter, is an outstanding combination to elevate him to the present status.

2. The lord of the ascendant, Venus, joins the 2nd house, whereas the lord of the 2nd and 5th house, Mercury, is very well placed in the ascendant. Thus, there is mutual exchange of the *lagna* lord Venus and the 2nd lord

Mercury. Also, there is *Vinimai Parivartan Yoga* between 1st and 2nd lords and the 10th and 11th lords. This indicates that the native will earn unlimited wealth due to his hard work and fate.

3. Karmic control planets, Mars and Venus, are placed together in the 2nd house under the favorable aspect of the 11th lord Jupiter. The strength and auspiciousness of the 2nd house has been largely enhanced owing to combination of karmic control planets receiving Jupiter's aspect.

4. The 11th lord Jupiter and the 7th lord Mars obtain *navamsa* of Jupiter. Here, Jupiter occupies Sagittarius *navamsa* and *Yogakaraka* Saturn also obtains own *navamsa* Capricorn. Thus, 10th and 11th lords, Saturn and Jupiter, do not only have mutual exchange of signs but obtain own *navamsa* as well. The combination is splendid for wealth, prosperity, power, popularity and fortune.

5. Karmic control planet, Mars, falls in *Ardra nakshatra* ruled by Rahu. The 11th lord Jupiter, who is placed in the 10th house, in own *navamsa* falls in *Satabhisha nakshatra* ruled by Rahu. Thus, the role of nodes is quite evident that the strength of the planets and combinations gets largely multiplied if the planets fall in the constellation of Rahu or Ketu. The planets, who are the dispositor of Rahu and Ketu, give results of the deeds of the past life, good or bad, as the case may be. Conjunction of Rahu or Ketu with any planet enhances the strength of that planet. Ketu in the 2nd house, generally, makes one a multimillionaire.

6. Here, in this birth chart, the lord of the 5th and 2nd house, Mercury, is associated with the 4th lord Sun, in the ascendant itself, with Ketu. This has strengthened the *lagna* and shows the rise of Mr. Rahul Bajaj due to *Poorva Punya*. The fate, good or bad, depends on our *Karmas* of the previous birth.

   So the joint study of the 9th, 5th and 1st house is essential, for the proper judgment of the financial elevation and actual level of the native. This is a separate issue whether the good fortune will promote a particular sphere of one's life or will help in all matters of the life. Many multimillionaires suffered childlessness or conjugal bliss etc.

Illustration : 14.10 (**KMB**) *Horoscope No.: 89*

Date of birth : 14.06.1967 Time of birth : 08:45:00 hrs
Place of birth : Calcutta Lat 22:30:00 N Long 88:20:00E
Ayanamsa : 23:23:58 Sidereal Time : 2:35:17

Pln	**Degree**	**Rasi**	**Nakshatra**	**Pad**
Asc	20:07:30	Can	Aslesa	2
Sun	28:59:53	Tau	Mrigshira	2
Mon	11:41:02	Leo	Magha	4
Mar	23:42:10	Vir	Chitra	1
Mer	23:08:55	Gem	Punarvasu	1
Jup	10:26:02	Can	Pushya	3
Ven	14:12:07	Can	Pushya	4
Sat	17:40:23	Pis	Revati	1
Rah (R)	12:28:05	Ari	Ashwini	4
Ket (R)	12:28:05	Lib	Swati	2

Lagna Chart

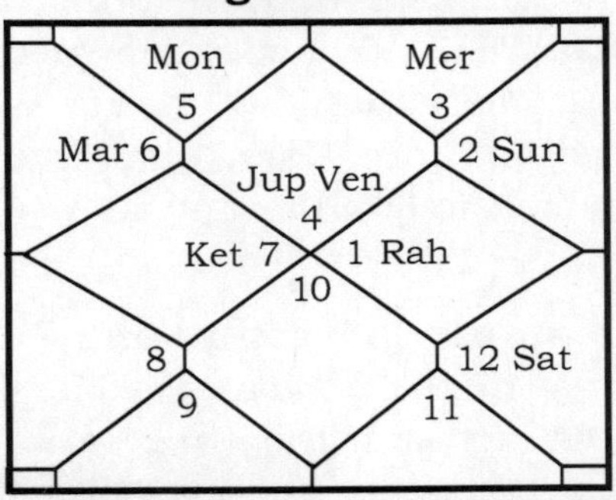

Navamsa Chart

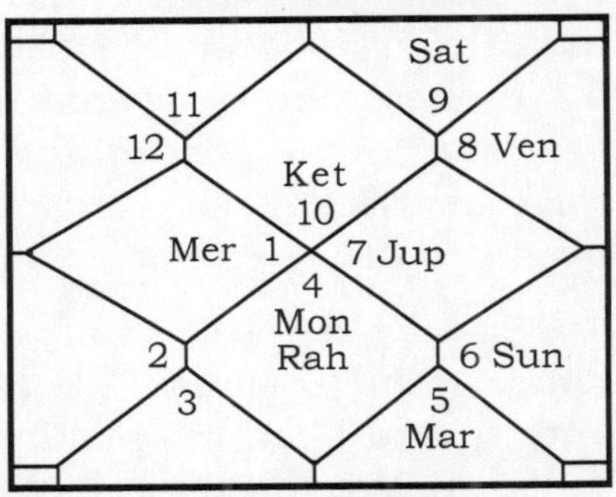

Balance of Vimshottari Dasa of **Ket 0Y 10M 11D**

Mr. Kumar Mangalam Birla is among the richest persons in India and the 8th youngest billionaire outside India, according to the Fortune Magazine. As of 6th October 2007, his net worth was estimated at $12.5 billion, making him the 7th richest Indian. Born on 14th June 1967, Mr. Birla has the following peculiar combinations in his birth chart.

The 9th lord Jupiter is exalted in the ascendant and is associated with the 11th lord Venus. The 9th house is aspected by the 10th lord and *Yogakaraka* Mars, as well as its own lord Jupiter. Jupiter obtains the *navamsa* of 11th lord Venus. The 9th lord Jupiter is the strongest planet, as it obtains 1.61 *shadabalas*. Thus, the 9th house is very well disposed.

The ascendant lord Moon occupies the 2nd house and obtains own *navamsa* Cancer. The ascendant is occupied by the exalted 9th lord Jupiter and the 11th lord Venus.

The 2nd lord Sun is placed in the 11th house and falls in the constellation of 10th lord Mars. Sun is *Atmakaraka* planet as well. Saturn, from the 9th house, aspects the Sun, in the 11th house. The 2nd house is occupied by ascendant lord Moon.

The 10th house is aspected by its own lord Mars. Mars falls in own constellation Chitra. Tenth lord Mars acquires the *navamsa* of 2nd lord Sun. Rahu occupies the 10th house.

Triangular lords from the 2nd and 11th should also be considered as we have shown earlier that these houses indicate *'Poorva Punya'*. Fifth from 2nd i. e. 6th house is owned by Jupiter, who is exalted in the ascendant. 6th house is aspected by the *Yogakaraka* and 10th lord Mars. Similarly, the other triangle i.e. 10th house is also quite strong, as has been discussed earlier.

The 5th & the 9th houses from the 11th are 3rd and 7th houses. The 3rd house is occupied by the *Yogakaraka* Mars and its lord Mercury falls in own sign and the *navamsa* of 10th lord Mars. The 7th house is aspected by the exalted Jupiter and its lord falls in the 9th house.

Dhankaraka Jupiter is exalted in the ascendant and is the strongest planet obtaining 1.61 *shadbalas*, associated with 11th lord Venus and acquires the *navasma* of Venus, the 11th lord, as well.

These splendid combinations are responsible for the wealthy status of Mr. Kumar Mangalam Birla.

Illustration : 14.11 (**Mukesh Ambani**) *Horoscope No.: 90*

Date of birth : 19.04.1957 Time of birth : 15:00:00 hrs
Place of birth : Aden Lat 12:45:00 N Long 45:00:00E
Ayanamsa : 23:15:50 Sidereal Time : 04:49:16

Pln	Degree	Rasi	Nakshatra	Pad
Asc	19:15:02	Leo	P Phalguni	2
Sun	5:53:38	Ari	Ashwini	2
Mon	8:13:40	Sag	Moola	3
Mar	27:13:37	Tau	Mrigshira	2
Mer	24:35:08	Ari	Bharani	4
Jup (R)	29:52:26	Leo	U Phalguni	1
Ven (C)	7:10:27	Ari	Ashwini	3
Sat (R)	20:28:41	Sco	Jyestha	2
Rah	26:26:35	Lib	Vishakha	2
Ket	26:26:35	Ari	Bharani	4

Lagna Chart

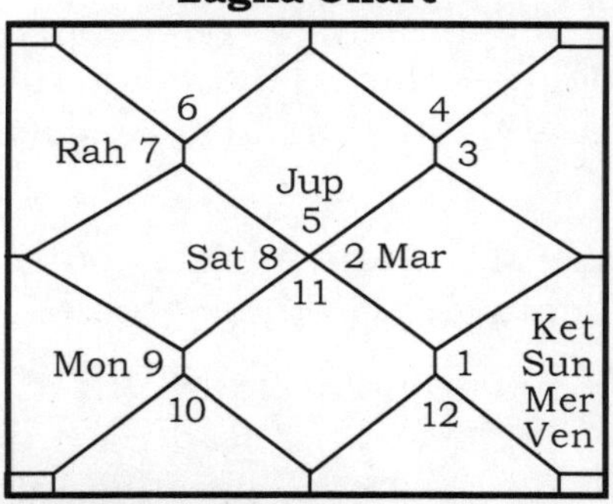

Navamsa Chart

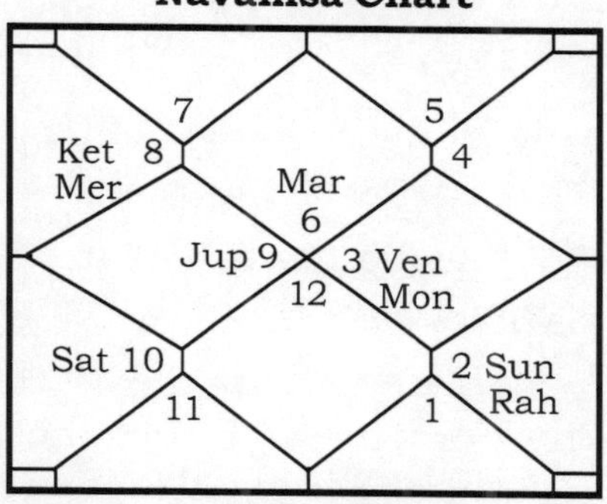

Balance of Vimshottari Dasa of **Ket 2Y 8M 5D**

This is the birth chart of the chairman of Reliance Industries, India's largest private sector enterprise. His wealth is estimated at $ 49 billion, according to Forbes India's 40 richest list of November 2007. He gifted his wife Nita a jet plane worth Rs. 242 crore recently on her birthday. Let us study his birth chart.

The 9th lord Mars is placed in the 10th house and the 10th lord Venus occupies the 9th house. This is a very strong '*Kendra Trikona Rajyoga*'.

The10th lord Venus, ascendant lord Sun and the 11th lord Mercury are conjoined in the 9th house, which is aspected by *Dhankaraka* Jupiter from the *lagna*. The 9th lord Mars occupies the sign of Venus and obtains the *navamsa* of 11th lord Mercury, whereas the 10th lord Venus occupies the sign of Mars and obtains the *navamsa* of 11th lord Mercury.

The ascendant lord Sun occupies the 9th house in conjunction with 10th & 11th lord, Venus and Mercury. Sun is also the strongest planet of the birth chart acquiring 1.54 *shadabalas*. *Dhankaraka* Jupiter occupies the *lagna*. The 9th lord Mars aspects the *lagna*. The ascendant is thus quite strong. Sun falls in the 9th house and obtains the *navamsa* of lord of the 10th house.

The 2nd lord Mercury occupies the 9th house in conjunction with *lagna* lord and the 10th lord. Mercury obtains the *navamsa* of the 9th lord, Mars, and falls in the constellation of the 10th lord, Venus.

The 5th lord, *Dhankaraka* Jupiter, occupies the *lagna* and aspects the 5th house of its own. 9th lord Mars also aspects the 5th house.

Karmic control Planets are Mars and Venus. Mars occupies the 10th house while Venus falls in the 9th house.

Let us also see the 5th & 9th houses from the 2nd & 11th. The 6th house (5th from the 2nd) is vacant. Its lord Saturn aspects it. Saturn also aspects the 10th house and obtains own *navamsa*. So, this is quite strong. The 10th house (9th from the 2nd) is occupied by the 9th lord Mars and its lord Venus falls in the 9th house. Saturn aspects the 10th house. Lords of the 5th & the 9th houses from the 2nd i.e. Saturn and Mars mutually aspect each other.

These splendid combinations are responsible for extraordinary wealth which Mr. Mukesh Ambani possesses.

Illustration : 14.12 (**Anil Ambani**) *Horoscope No.: 91*

Date of birth : 04.06.1959 Time of birth : 22:27:00 hrs
Place of birth : Mumbai Lat 18:58:00 N Long 72:50:00E
Ayanamsa : 23:17:26 Sidereal Time : 14:37:52

Pln	Degree	Rasi	Nakshatra	Pad
Asc	6:44:59	Cap	Uttarasadha	4
Sun	20:01:50	Tau	Rohini	4
Mon	0:28:00	Tau	Kritika	2
Mar	8:51:39	Can	Pushya	2
Mer (C)	22:55:06	Tau	Rohini	4
Jup (R)	1:45:07	Sco	Vishakha	4
Ven	4:20:38	Can	Pushya	1
Sat (R)	11:59:52	Sag	Moola	4
Rah (R)	17:59:40	Vir	Hasta	3
Ket (R)	17:59:40	Pis	Revati	1

Lagna Chart

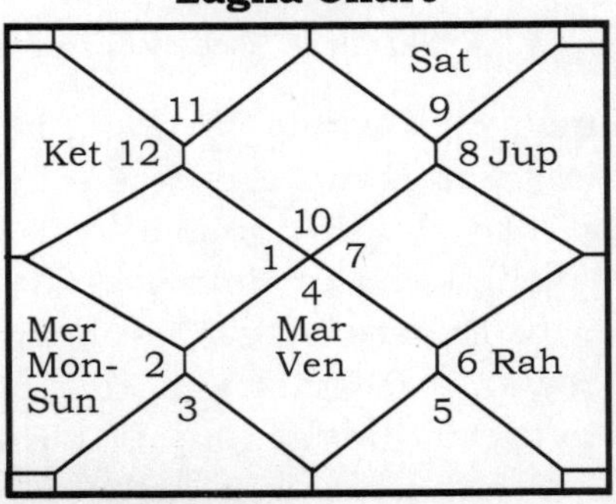

Navamsa Chart

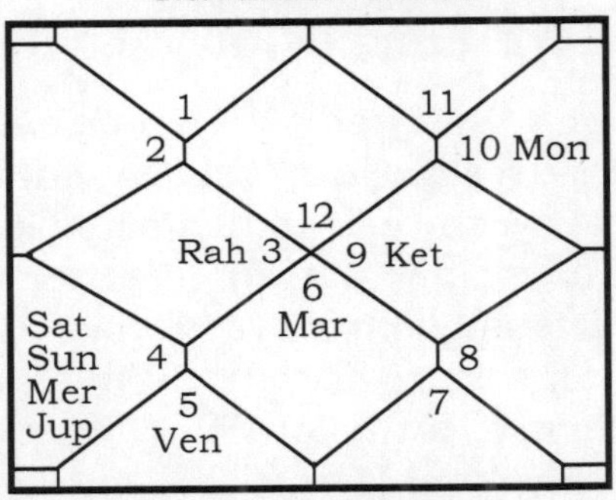

Balance of Vimshottari Dasa of **Sun 4Y 3M 14D**

Mr. Anil Ambani was born in Capricorn ascendant and Taurus Moon sign. There is mutual exchange of the 7th lord Moon and 5th lord Venus. The 9th lord Mercury joins the 5th house, in conjunction with the 7th lord Moon. This strongly indicates love marriage. Association of Mars and Venus in the 7th house has added fuel to the fire. This shows a strong inclination towards making love with a number of beautiful and charming females. However, aspect of Jupiter over the 5th and the 7th house and their lords, Venus and Moon, is splendid for a high degree of conjugal bliss.

Yogakaraka Venus is associated with the 11th lord Mars, in the 7th house and the conjunction of Mars and Venus is aspected by lord of the 3rd house Jupiter. Thus, there is a unique relation among the lords of 11th, 3rd and 7th house who are triangular from each other. This has strongly strengthened the 11th house, which has made Mr. Anil Ambani a business tycoon.

The lord of the 9th house, Mercury, who is *Atmakaraka* planet as well, occupies the 5th house, in conjunction with Sun and Moon. This indicates *'Poorva Punya'* of Mr. Anil Ambani due to which he obtained present position among the top business moguls. Both Karmic Control Planets, Jupiter and Mercury, are 7th from each other, identical to 11th & 5th houses. Both these houses indicate enormous wealth, immense prosperity and unaccountable series of industries etc.

14.2 Conclusion

One becomes rich or extremely rich when 2nd and 11th houses are inter-related, such as, there is mutual exchange between their lordships or if the lord of 11th house and 2nd house are placed together in either of the houses. The intensity of this yoga will further be enhanced, if 5th and 9th houses are also involved, as these are the houses of *Poorva Punya*. If the lord of 2nd occupies the 5th house and 5th lord joins the 11th or 2nd, one gets wealth through unearned sources such as lottery or speculation, provided the *lagna* is also strong. Mutual exchange of the lords of 5th and 9th houses is not as auspicious as that of 5th and 2nd, 9th and 2nd, 11th and 5th or 11th and 9th.

The conjunction of the lords of the 9th, 5th and ascendant, in either of these houses, is most auspicious to bless the native with unaccountable wealth. These combinations are mentioned in various classics and are mostly found present in the birth charts of eminent rich persons. The native will become exceptionally rich or his richness will be greatly multiplied, if nodes also play their role in the combinations of *Dhanayoga*. If the concerning planets occupy constellations of Rahu or Ketu, their strength to do well will be enhanced. Similarly, if the dispositors of Rahu and Ketu are placed together or in quadrant from each other, the native will be extremely fortunate to become very wealthy person. It may be noted that the strength of the planets gets heavily increased if they are combined with Rahu or Ketu, provided the planet is well placed in the birth chart and has a concern with the houses in question. It is essential that the 9th house and *lagna* must be strong, well disposed and well fortified along with all other combinations of becoming an extremely wealthy person. To understand the secrets of Rahu and Ketu, which are really very less known to us, needs much wider research as to how Rahu and Ketu play role in promoting the native in certain spheres of life?

•

CHAPTER-15

Pointers to Prosperity and Poverty

Prosperity is a general connotation, which has a wide coverage of finance, profession, property, children and the like. Here we will confine to the financial prosperity only. It is not only the judgement of 2nd and 11th houses and significator Jupiter, which may point out the prosperity of any native. Various other factors should also be taken into consideration, such as

(1) The 2nd and 11th houses, which are mainly connected with finance.

(2) The significator of wealth, Jupiter.

(3) The houses, which promote or assist in financial prosperity.

(4) Houses, who apply a negative or retarding force in one's financial prospects.

First of all we will look into the combinations responsible for the financial prosperity of a native.

15.1 Financial Prosperity

1. Placement of 2nd lord in the 11th house with 11th lord, or vice-versa i.e. 11th lord in the 2nd house with the 2nd lord, ensures wealth. Mutual exchange of the lords of the 2nd and 11th houses also makes the native wealthy. The position of Jupiter should also not be ignored.

2. If the lord of the 9th house falls in the 11th house and is associated or aspected by benefics and *Dhankaraka* Jupiter, one born even in humble circumstances, will become a recognized rich person and the luck of the

native will play a vital role, as the lords of 11th and 9th houses also make one rich. Similarly, if the 11th lord is posited in the 9th house with the 9th lord, or 9th lord joins the 11th house with 11th lord, financial prosperity is ensured. Involvement of Jupiter in this combination adds further strength to the combination.

3. If the lords of 5th and 9th houses are placed in a *Kendra,* in association with 2nd or 11th lord, the financial prosperity must be assured. Similarly, if the lords of 2nd and 11th houses combine with 5th and 9th lords in a *kendra,* richness of the native gets recognition.

4. The 9th lord in the 9th house and the 5th lord in 5th house ensure wealth.

5. If the lord of the 2nd house combines with the lord of the 5th or 9th house, in 2nd, 5th, 9th or 11th house, financial boost is assured.

6. The 9th, 10th and 11th houses are the most vital houses for prosperity. If these houses are occupied by natural benefics like Jupiter, Venus or Mercury or powerful Moon, influx of wealth will be there.

7. One will get immense professional success resulting into financial prosperity, if the lords of 10th and 11th exchange their signs, or 11th lord joins the 10th house with the 10th lord and vice versa.

8. The lords of 2nd and 11th houses combine with lords other than those of 5th and 9th, one will become wealthy but to a lesser degree.

9. *Dhana Yoga* is formed, if Jupiter conjoins with the lord of 2nd house and Mercury.

10. If the lords of 1st, 2nd and 11th houses are placed in their respective houses, *Dhana Yoga* arises.

11. If the lords of 2nd and 11th houses are associated with each other in the ascendant, the *Dhana Yoga* will be there.

12. If the lord of the 10th house occupies the 11th house with 11th and 9th lord, one becomes very rich and earns wealth by his own endeavours.

Observations regarding financial prosperity must be made only after the examination of the strength of the 11th house and its lord. The source of acquisition of wealth depends upon the planets placed in the 11th house. If there is no planet in the 11th house, examine the planets that are associated with the 11th lord. If Mercury joins the 11th house, gains will be through business. The Sun is a great asset in the 11th house, if it is unafflicted. One gains by little efforts. There may be many sources of income. The native will grow, but the prosperity will also give rise to various enemies. Moon in 11th will result into charity and gains through lands and journeys. Venus in the 11th may result into gains through TV, films, articles of entertainment, artistic activities, acting, cosmetics, vehicles, wine or other intoxicating material, women, decoration, or architecture etc.

Mars may give wealth through unfair means and also by dealing in weapons, petroleum, inflammable items, cooking gas, brick kilns, builders, or plotting. Jupiter may give money through eatables, scientific dealings, and religious activities. Fair dealing and fair money will also be indicated. One may earn by coaching institutes run on heavy donation, publication or by spiritual sermons, agriculture, farming, or manure etc. Saturn results into gains through politics, landed property, iron factories etc. It is a long range of articles through which one can gain wealth, which can not be covered in this small chapter.

We would like to illustrate a few cases of those persons who were born in humble circumstances or in a poor family but they became recognized rich person on account of their good fortune in respect of financial aspect.

Illustration : 15.1 (**RS**) *Horoscope No.: 92*

Date of birth : 20.07.1952 Time of birth : 12:45:36 hrs
Place of birth : Jabalpur Lat 23:10:00 N Long 79:57:00E
Ayanamsa : 23:11:50 Sidereal Time : 8:27:27

Pln	**Degree**	**Rasi**	**Nakshatra**	**Pad**
Asc	10:21:44	Lib	Swati	2
Sun	4:18:02	Can	Pushya	1
Mon	15:55:18	Gem	Ardra	3
Mar	17:03:49	Lib	Swati	4
Mer	0:24:49	Leo	Magha	1
Jup	23:44:51	Ari	Bharani	4
Ven (C)	11:18:34	Can	Pushya	3
Sat	16:16:51	Vir	Hasta	2
Rah (R)	28:26:31	Cap	Dhanistha	2
Ket (R)	28:26:31	Can	Aslesa	4

Lagna Chart

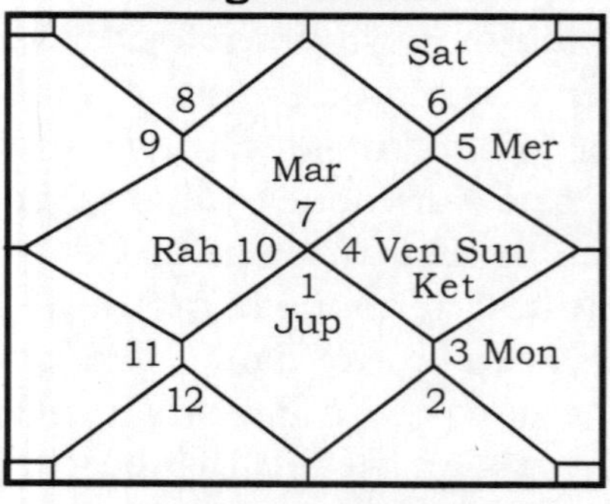

Navamsa Chart

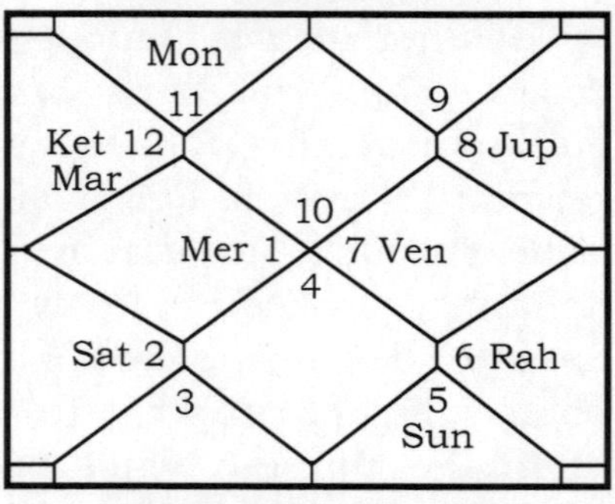

Balance of Vimshottari Dasa of **Rah 5Y 6M 2D**

The native is the son of a teacher who lived only on his salary. The native is handsome, smart and intelligent engineering graduate.

i) The lord of the 9th house, Mercury, is well placed in the 11th house under the aspect of benefic *Dhankaraka* Jupiter.

ii) The 11th house is the strongest house in this birth chart as it obtains 12.28 *rupa bhava bala.*

iii) The lord of the *lagna* Venus is conjoined with the 11th lord Sun, in the 10th house, which is a powerful *Dhana Yoga.*

iv) The 9th, 10th and 11th houses are occupied by the Sun, Moon, Venus, Ketu and Mercury. This it self is an auspicious combination for prosperity of the native. The intensity of the *Yoga* has been further multiplied due to the aspect of Jupiter over the 11th house, and 9th and 2nd lords, Mercury and Mars.

v) The 10th house is occupied by the Sun, Venus and Ketu and it is owned by Moon. 10th lord Moon obtains the *navamsa* of Saturn. Venus and Moon govern plastic work; Saturn shows iron machines involved in the business of the native. The native has many industries for the manufacturing of polythene films of different layers and that of lamination work.

These planetary combinations are responsible for his financial prosperity. The native is an industrialist having regular growth.

Illustration : 15.2 (**SCG**) *Horoscope No.: 93*

Date of birth : 20.04.1944 Time of birth : 17:28:00 hrs

Place of birth : Banda Lat 25:28:00 N Long 80:20:00E

Ayanamsa : 23:04:28 Sidereal Time : 6:12:58

Pln	**Degree**	**Rasi**	**Nakshatra**	**Pad**
Asc	9:51:14	Vir	U Phalguni	4
Sun	7:09:19	Ari	Ashwini	3
Mon	4:04:09	Pis	U Bhadrapad	1
Mar	18:57:01	Gem	Ardra	4
Mer	23:13:15	Ari	Bharani	3
Jup	24:02:35	Can	Aslesa	3

Ven	19:09:26	Pis	Revati	1
Sat	29:42:49	Tau	Mrigshira	2
Rah (R)	9:37:11	Can	Pushya	2
Ket (R)	9:37:11	Cap	Uttarasadha	4

Lagna Chart

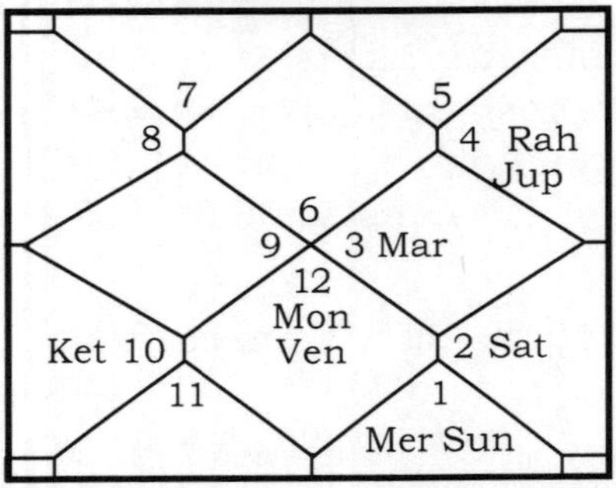

Navamsa Chart

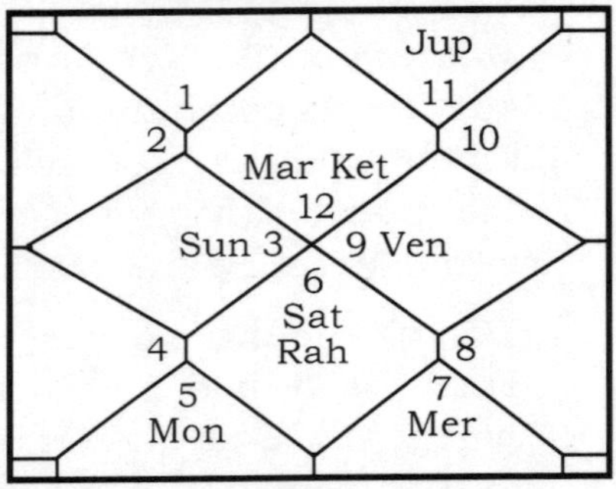

Balance of Vimshottari Dasa of **Sat 17Y 11M 12D**

The native was born in a poor family. Having attained youth, he had to seek his livelihood. He started making "bidi" with his own hands just like a labour. He used to sell the *bidi* in the evening to get a few chips for bread. Gradually, he started employing labour for the same work. Now, he is a multimillionaire in *bidi* trade. He has hundreds of trucks just to meet out the cartage work involved in his own business. He is running a few other industries too. Lately, he also entered into politics and fought elections for the Member of Parliament. He has been Mayor of one important city.

Let us examine the combinations, which made him so rich in a short period.

i) The lord of the 11th house, Moon, and the lord of the 2nd house, Venus, are conjoined in 7th house. The lord of 4th and 7th, Jupiter, is exalted in the 11th house. This is most powerful *Dhana Yoga*.

ii) There is mutual exchange between the lord of the 7th house, Jupiter, and the lord of 11th house, Moon.

iii) The 5th and 9th house and their lords do play a vital role in one's financial prosperity. The 5th lord Saturn falls in the 9th house, in a friendly sign Taurus and the lord of the 9th house Venus is exalted in the 7th house.

iv) There is mutual exchange between the 10th lord Mercury & 8th lord Mars, which is splendid for a commanding position.

v) The Sun, Venus and Jupiter are exalted.

vi) All houses starting form 7th house to the 11th house are well occupied giving rise to *Graha Malika Rajyoga.*

vii) *Kendradhipati* Jupiter is exalted in the 11th house in association with Rahu.

viii) The 10th house is owned by Mercury, occupied by Mars and 10th lord Mercury obtains the *navamsa* of Venus. Mercury indicates leaf, Venus indicates tobacco and Mars indicates use of fire. Blending of these explains the business of *bidi.*

Illustration : 15.3 (**AG**) *Horoscope No.: 94*

Date of birth : 05.09.1963 Time of birth : 11:24:00 hrs
Place of birth : Kanpur Lat 26:27:00 N Long 80:19:00E
Ayanamsa : 23:20:42 Sidereal Time : 10:06:06

Pln	**Degree**	**Rasi**	**Nakshatra**	**Pad**
Asc	0:05:36	Sco	Vishakha	4
Sun	18:36:41	Leo	P Phalguni	2
Mon	7:52:44	Pis	U Bhadrapad	2
Mar	1:56:00	Lib	Chitra	3
Mer	11:38:50	Vir	Hasta	1
Jup (R)	24:59:14	Pis	Revati	3
Ven (D)	20:17:55	Leo	P Phalguni	3
Sat (R)	24:45:59	Cap	Dhanistha	1
Rah (R)	25:40:45	Gem	Punarvasu	2
Ket (R)	25:40:45	Sag	Purvasadha	4

Lagna Chart

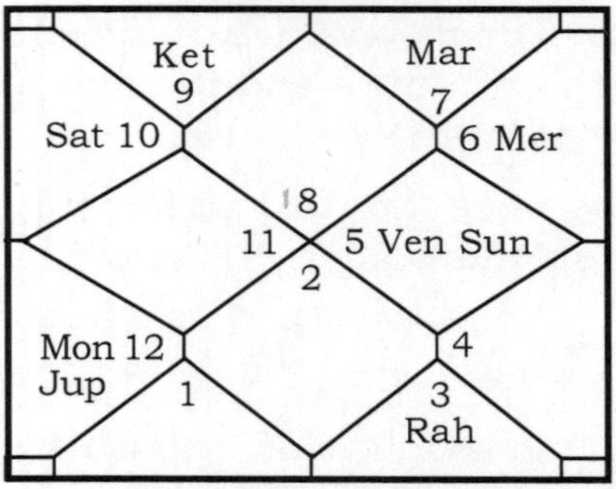

Navamsa Chart

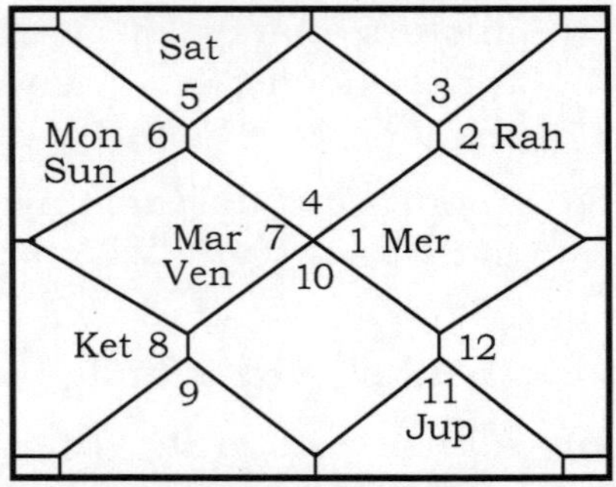

Balance of Vimshottari Dasa of **Sat 12Y 6M 8D**

The subject is a multimillionaire. He started his professional career from an ordinary printing press. In a small period of few years, the expansion of printing press was so fast that the native also started a milk industry. Following planetary combinations have made the native an extremely wealthy person:

i) The lord of the 2nd and 5th house, Jupiter, joins the 5th house, in association with the 9th lord Moon.

ii) The 11th lord Mercury is exalted in the 11th house and has a mutual aspect with 2nd lord and *Dhankaraka* Jupiter.

iii) The lords of 2nd, 5th, and 11th houses Jupiter, Moon and Mercury are placed in 5th and 11th houses and influence each other, either by association or aspect. This is a splendid combination for prosperity with regard to wealth.

iv) The lord of the 10th house, Sun, falls in own sign Leo in the 10th house, in association with 7th lord Venus.

v) Strong *vasumati Yoga* is present due to Saturn's placement in the 3rd house, in own sign Capricorn, and Mercury's placement in the 11th house in own sign Virgo.

vi) The lord of the 10th house, Sun, obtains the *navamsa* of Mercury, which explains the work of printing press. The Sun and Moon are associated in *navamsa* chart. Venus occupies the 10th house, which justifies the work connected with milk and its products.

Illustration : 15.4 **(BB)** *Horoscope No.: 95*

Date of birth : 30.08.1961 Time of birth : 09:45:00 hrs
Place of birth : Lucknow Lat 26:50:00 N Long 80:54:00E
Ayanamsa : 23:19:08 Sidereal Time : 8:11:05

Pln	**Degree**	**Rasi**	**Nakshatra**	**Pad**
Asc	5:46:39	Lib	Chitra	4
Sun	13:13:56	Leo	Magha	4
Mon	8:47:27	Ari	Ashwini	3
Mar	15:05:43	Vir	Hasta	2
Mer	27:15:22	Leo	U Phalguni	1
Jup (R)	4:57:09	Cap	Uttarasadha	3
Ven	7:21:56	Can	Pushya	2
Sat (R)	0:34:07	Cap	Uttarasadha	2
Rah (R/C)	3:56:23	Leo	Magha	2
Ket (R)	3:56:23	Aqu	Dhanistha	4

Lagna Chart

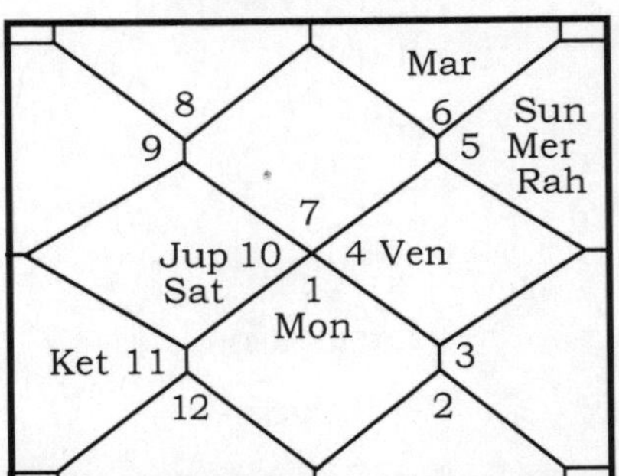

Navamsa Chart

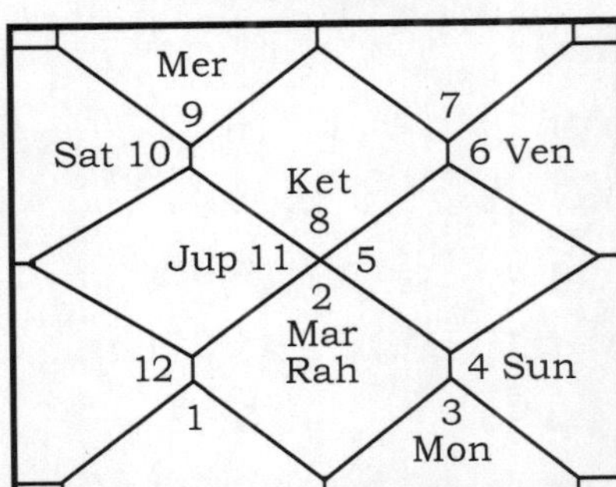

Balance of Vimshottari Dasa of **Ket 2Y 4M 18D**

The native was born and lived in very humble surroundings, but he always thought of becoming a very rich businessman. He started the work of wax-coated wrappers approximately 18 years before. He is a multimillionaire at present by dealing in lamination of plastic pouches. The 11th house is occupied by the 11th lord Sun, in conjunction with the 9th lord Mercury and Rahu. *Yogakaraka* Saturn under *vargottam navamsa* joins the 4th house, in own sign, in association with *Dhanakaraka* Jupiter. This position of planets made him rich. Placement of 2nd lord Mars in the 12th house is adverse, in spite of aspect of Jupiter. The native, therefore, suffers from sudden losses, raids, deceits, thefts etc from time to time. The position of Mars has always created scarcity of funds due to unwise planning. The 10th lord Moon is under *Kemadrum Yoga*, which has also reduced the intensity of auspicious *Dhanayoga*. Involvement of Venus in 10th house, in Moon sign resulted into success in lamination, waxing, plastic printing etc.

Illustration : 15.5 **(PCG)** *Horoscope No.: 96*

Date of birth : 25.01.1933 Time of birth : 12:19:13 hrs
Place of birth : Ghaziabad Lat 28:40:00 N Long 77:26:00E
Ayanamsa : 22:55:27 Sidereal Time : 20:15:27

Pln	**Degree**	**Rasi**	**Nakshatra**	**Pad**
Asc	22:45:07	Ari	Bharani	3
Sun	11:56:53	Cap	Sravna	1
Mon (C)	2:48:47	Cap	Uttarasadha	2
Mar (R)	27:14:42	Leo	U Phalguni	1
Mer (C)	2:45:57	Cap	Uttarasadha	2
Jup (R)	29:52:18	Leo	U Phalguni	1
Ven	20:38:50	Sag	Purvasadha	3
Sat (D)	13:57:14	Cap	Sravna	2
Rah (R)	15:10:49	Aqu	Satabhisha	3
Ket (R)	15:10:49	Leo	P Phalguni	1

Lagna Chart

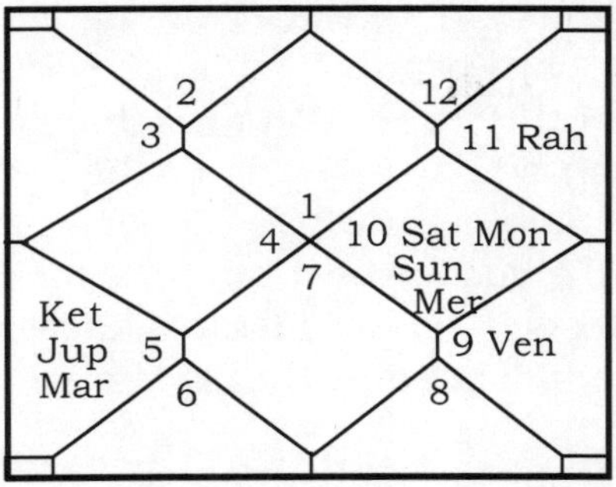

Navamsa Chart

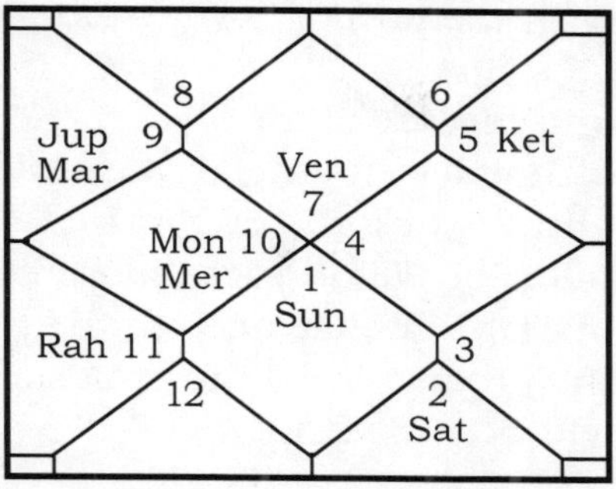

Balance of Vimshottari Dasa of **Sun 3Y 2M 24D**

The subject was quite poor person. It was difficult for him to retain his bicycle when he entered for the struggle to earn his livelihood. He started some business without much money and got eminent success in a short time. He later established a number of industries in different cities of India, which are running in quite a prosperous manner.

The 10th house is very strong in this birth chart as it contains Sun, Moon, Saturn and Mercury.

i) The lord of the 2nd and 7th house, Venus, is placed in the 9th house, whereas 9th lord Jupiter is placed in the 5th house, in association with *lagna* lord Mars. This is a conjunction of *lagna* lord and the 9th house in the 5th house. The *lagna* and the 9th house, both, are aspected by *Dhanakaraka* Jupiter.

ii) The 10th and 11th lord Saturn is conjoined with the 5th lord Sun in the 10th house. There is no malefic aspect over any of the concerning houses.

iii) The *lagna* is quite strong along with the 9th house. Thus, the *lagna,* the 9th house, 11th house 2nd house and the 5th house are strong and well disposed, which made the native rich and prosperous.

If the lords of the 9th and 5th are together, with the lords of 2nd and 11th in a *Kendra*, increase in the richness of a person is assured. Similarly, if the 2nd and 11th lords combine with the lord of the 5th and 9th house in a *kendra*, the native gets financial boost. Even if the lord of the 5th is in the 5th, and the lord of the 9th in the 9th, or they have mutual exchange of houses, financial gain is assured. If the lords of the 2nd and 9th, or lords of 2nd and 5th, combine in 2nd, 5th, 9th or 11th houses, *Dhana* yoga is formed. If a good aspect from the lord of the 2nd house or from the planets of the 2nd house is there, the prosperity by the profession, indicated by the 10th house, will come automatically.

15.2 Combinations for Poverty

A few fortunate persons are born in poverty but they become rich and prosperous by their own efforts. On the contrary, certain rich people become poor due to repeated failure of their undertakings and suffer regular losses on that account. Let us examine those combinations, which make a native poor.

i) If the lord of the ascendant is weak or placed in the 8th house; the 9th lord is also adversely placed in the association with the 4th lord, the native will be poor from birth to death.

ii) Mutual exchange of lords of the 2nd and 12th houses makes one deprived. If the lord of the 2nd house occupies the 12th house with the 12th lord, the native will become poor, even if he is born in a very rich family.

iii) If the 2nd lord falls in the 12th house and the 12th lord falls in the ascendant, one will become poor. The intensity will be more, if the 12th lord is aspected or associated with *marakas* or malefics.

iv) The lords of 2nd and 11th houses, if placed in the 12th house, with the 12th lord, either in the end or 11th, the subject will be bereft of wealth.

v) The 5th and 9th houses do play a vital role in one's prosperity. If the lords of the 5th and 9th houses are posited in the 6th and 8th house or even vice-versa, the person will have to struggle hard for money. The intensity will be higher, if the combination is under the influence of malefics.

vi) Jupiter, who is the significator of wealth, does play a vital role in the judgement of financial aspect of one's life. For persons born in Aquarius ascendant, Jupiter has a lot to do with the financial aspect of one's life, as Jupiter is not only the significator of wealth but it also owns the 2nd & 11th houses. If Jupiter is adversely placed in the birth chart of an Aquarius native, one will have to struggle hard. The position of Jupiter in the 12th house, in the sign of its debilitation, is the worst. The adversity will be further multiplied, if such a Jupiter is aspected or associated with malefic planets like Saturn or Rahu. However, if the 9th and 5th lords are well placed, the adversities related to financial aspects will be appreciably reduced.

Illustration : 15.6 (**PKG**) *Horoscope No.: 97*

Date of birth : 23.05.1961 Time of birth : 00:40:00 hrs
Place of birth : Meerut Lat 29:00:00 N Long 77:42:00E
Ayanamsa : 23:18:54 Sidereal Time : 16:21:29

Pln	**Degree**	**Rasi**	**Nakshatra**	**Pad**
Asc	2:29:39	Aqu	Dhanistha	3
Sun	8:07:06	Tau	Kritika	4
Mon	9:24:38	Leo	Magha	3
Mar	15:34:10	Can	Pushya	4
Mer	28:41:45	Tau	Mrigshira	2
Jup	13:49:30	Cap	Sravna	2
Ven	26:28:02	Pis	Revati	3
Sat (R)	6:24:04	Cap	Uttarasadha	3
Rah (S)	8:29:36	Leo	Magha	3
Ket (S)	8:29:36	Aqu	Satabhisha	1

Lagna Chart

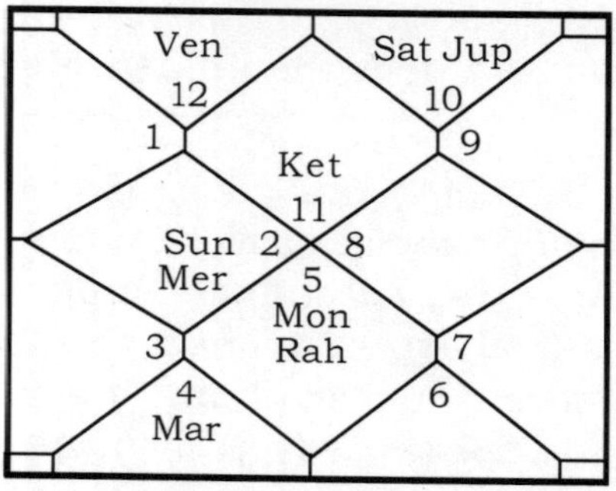

Navamsa Chart

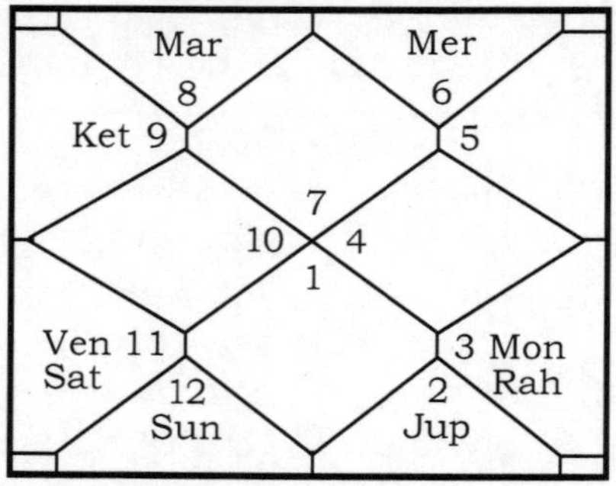

Balance of Vimshottari Dasa of **Ket 2Y 0M 21D**

The native was born when Aquarius ascendant was rising. The lord of the 2nd & 11th and *Dhanakaraka* Jupiter falls in the 12th house, in the sign of its debilitation, Capricorn. Lord of the *lagna*, Saturn, is also associated with Jupiter of the 12th house, which further harmed the native. The conjunction of Jupiter and Saturn in the 12th house is under the mutual aspect with debilitated Mars, which is posited in the 6th house. This is overall a very adverse combination for financial aspect of one's life. Further, we should examine the 9th lord and the 5th house also. *Yogakaraka* Venus, who happens to be the 4th and 9th lord, for Aquarius ascendant, joins the 2nd house under exaltation. The 5th lord Mercury occupies the 4th house. The lords of 5th and 9th, Mercury and Venus, are 3rd and 11th from each other. The lords of the 9th, 2nd and 11th are also 3rd and 11th from each other. The native is running a biscuit factory but he suffered heavy losses regularly for 10 or 11 years due to various reasons. The native is a good scholar of astrology and does understand this problem of his birth chart. He suffered a very heavy loss of rupees twenty lakhs, during the sub period of Jupiter in the major period of Moon, who are 6th and 8th from each other.

One of the important points, which we want to mention is, that the operation of favourable *dasa bhukti* over the native at the appropriate age is also quite essential, for becoming a rich person. One may be having good placement of planets but may not enjoy their *dasa bhukti*. That will be his bad luck.

Illustration : 15.7 **(RA)** *Horoscope No.: 98*

Date of birth : 27.04.1952 Time of birth : 07:45:00 hrs
Place of birth : Malwa Lat 26:02:00 N Long 80:42:00E
Ayanamsa : 23:11:35 Sidereal Time : 21:57:51

Pln	**Degree**	**Rasi**	**Nakshatra**	**Pad**
Asc	19:17:28	Tau	Rohini	3
Sun	13:34:20	Ari	Bharani	1
Mon	17:12:55	Tau	Rohini	3
Mar (R)	18:52:10	Lib	Swati	4
Mer	18:03:15	Pis	Revati	1
Jup (C)	6:22:54	Ari	Ashwini	2
Ven	27:51:49	Pis	Revati	4
Sat (R)	16:33:08	Vir	Hasta	2
Rah (R)	4:46:12	Aqu	Dhanistha	4
Ket (R)	4:46:12	Leo	Magha	2

Lagna Chart

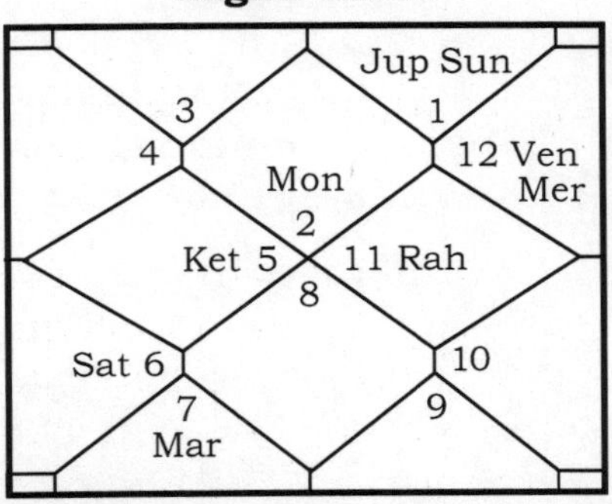

Navamsa Chart

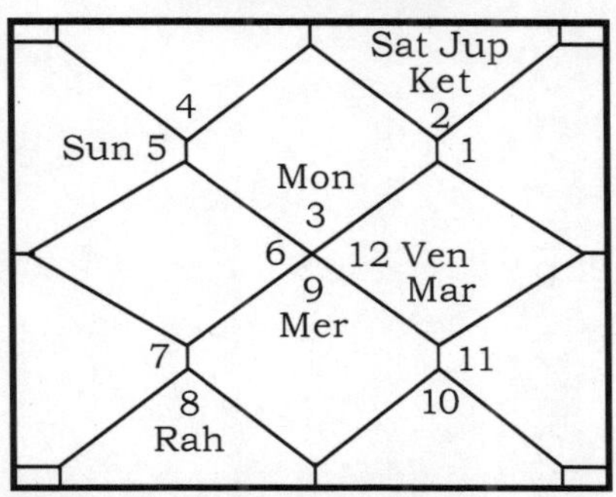

Balance of Vimshottari Dasa of **Mon 4Y 7M 1D**

The native was born in Taurus ascendant with exalted

Moon. Eleventh house contains Mercury and exalted Venus, who are the lords of the lagna , 2nd and 5th houses . This is a powerful combination of becoming rich but it did not happen so. The Sun is exalted in the 12th house, in association with 8th and 11th lord Jupiter that has spoiled the prosperity of the native, at least at his appropriate age. Jupiter's major period was running over the native from the age of 29 to 45 years. In spite of good income at times, the native is living in poverty. *Yogakaraka* Saturn is well placed in the 5th house. The lords of the 12th and 8th, Mars and Jupiter, are placed in the houses depicting heavy losses, cheating, deceits, failure of undertaking and unwise planning of the professional career. In spite of high-class educational career, the native faces great difficulty in making both ends meet.

Illustration : 15.8 (**SA**) *Horoscope No.: 99*

Date of birth : 02.07.1958 Time of birth : 16:28:00 hrs
Place of birth : Sitapur Lat 25:11:00 N Long 80:52:00E
Ayanamsa : 23:16:47 Sidereal Time : 11:01:22

Pln	**Degree**	**Rasi**	**Nakshatra**	**Pad**
Asc	13:17:29	Sco	Anuradha	3
Sun	16:46:18	Gem	Ardra	4
Mon	1:51:55	Cap	Uttarasadha	2
Mar	24:19:35	Pis	Revati	3
Mer	2:05:41	Can	Punarvasu	4
Jup	28:44:34	Vir	Chitra	2
Ven	13:11:38	Tau	Rohini	1
Sat (R)	27:48:55	Sco	Jyestha	4
Rah (R)	5:15:29	Lib	Chitra	4
Ket (R)	5:15:29	Ari	Ashwini	2

Lagna Chart

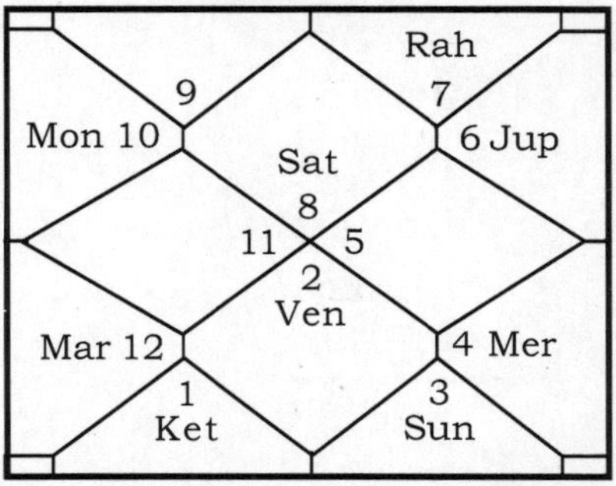

Navamsa Chart

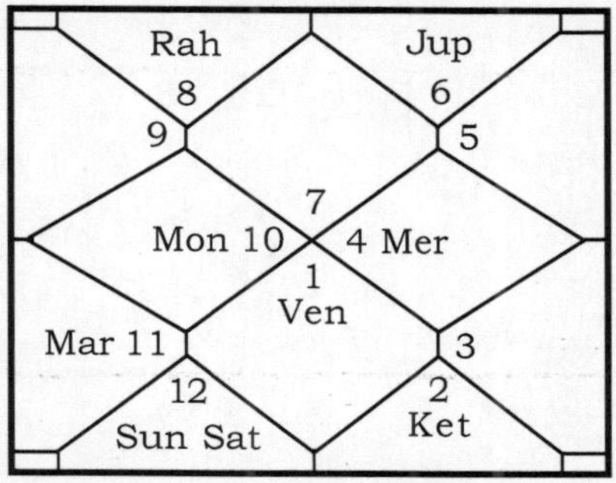

Balance of Vimshottari Dasa of **Sun 3Y 7M 28D**

The native is a highly qualified and talented person. The 2nd and 5th lord Jupiter falls in the 11th house, the 11th lord Mercury joins the 9th house, the 9th lord Moon falls in the 3rd house under *Kemadrum Yoga*. The *lagna* lord Mars is posited in the 5th house under the favourable aspect of Jupiter. Even then the native is poor. He has to work very hard to run his family. One will hardly be able to judge, by the examination of this horoscope, that the native will be suffering from poverty. The 10th lord Sun falls in the 8th house under the aspect of Mars. The 8th lord Mercury falls in inimical sign Cancer, in the 9th house. The 12th house is occupied by Rahu, and *Dhankaraka* Jupiter is receiving the aspect of Mars. Thus, all the benefic planets are afflicted by one another; Venus is afflicted by Saturn, Jupiter is afflicted by 6th lord Mars, and 10th lord is ill-disposed, again being aspected by the 6th lord Saturn.

Illustration : 15.9 (**SKB**) *Horoscope No.: 100*

Date of birth : 28.12.1952 Time of birth : 10:14:00 hrs

Place of birth : Sitapur Lat 25:11:00 N Long 80:52:00E

Ayanamsa : 23:12:13 Sidereal Time : 16:33:51

Pln	**Degree**	**Rasi**	**Nakshatra**	**Pad**
Asc	7:56:40	Aqu	Satabhisha	1
Sun	13:12:22	Sag	Moola	4

Mon	7:50:31	Tau	Kritika	4
Mar	4:42:43	Aqu	Dhanistha	4
Mer	23:29:25	Sco	Jyestha	3
Jup (R)	17:53:11	Ari	Bharani	2
Ven	27:17:54	Cap	Dhanistha	2
Sat	2:47:23	Lib	Chitra	3
Rah (R)	19:45:30	Cap	Sravna	3
Ket (R)	19:45:30	Can	Aslesa	1

Lagna Chart

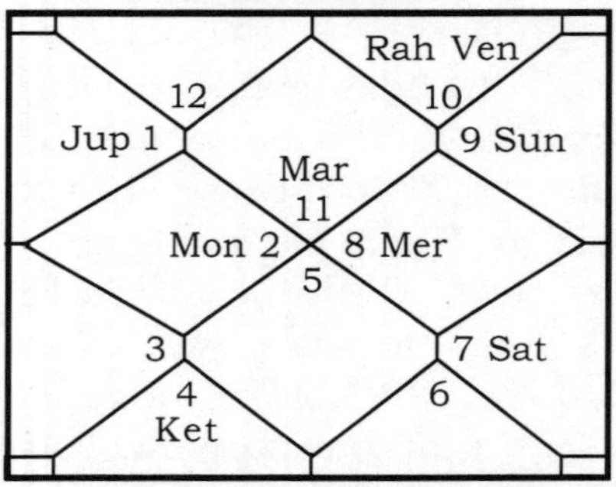

Navamsa Chart

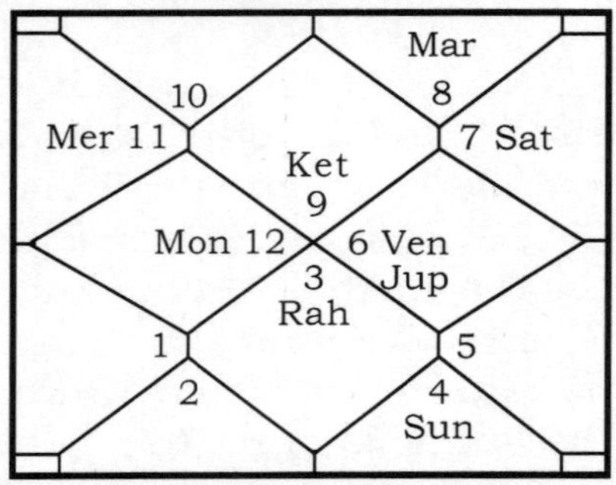

Balance of Vimshottari Dasa of **Sun 0Y 11M 19D**

The native has a bright professional career and has a prosperous background of his family. He is still unsettled and is struggling hard for his maintenance. He was born in Aquarius ascendant where 3rd lord Mars is placed. *Yogakaraka* Venus, who happens to be the 9th and 4th lord, joins the 12th house in association with Rahu. The 2nd and 11th lord Jupiter is retrograde in the 3rd house under the mutual aspect of Saturn. The 10th house is hemmed between malefics like Sun and Saturn resulting into formation of *Papakartari Yoga.* Mercury is also involved in *Papakartari Yoga.* Mutual exchange between 9th and 12th lords, Venus and Saturn, is present. All the concerning houses and their lords are afflicted.

If the lord of the 11th house is unfavourably placed in the 6th, 8th or 12th from the *Dhankaraka* Jupiter, the individual may get wealth but may loose later on. When Rahu or Ketu are involved, the individual may squander away riches. If the 2nd house is weak and afflicted, the bank account will be very little i.e. the native may not be able to accumulate much wealth. Moreover, when the lord of the 2nd and Jupiter are not well disposed, wealth may be there but it can not be enjoyed.

15.3 Source of Wealth

To determine the source of wealth, the joint influence of the lords of the 2nd and 11th houses, focused on a house or houses, should be examined properly. The planets placed in the 2nd house, the *navamsa*, the lords of the 10th and the 2nd house, and the planets occupied by the 10th house are to be analyzed. If the influence is focused on 1st and 2nd house, wealth comes with ease through successful efforts and paternal sources. On the 3rd house – through toil and brother; on the 4th house – in one's own country, through inheritance; on the 5th house – through children, occupation; on the 6th house – through maternal uncle, enemies; on the 7th house – through his life partner or business partner; on the 9th house – through father or uncle or religious institution; on the 10th house – through state or semi govt. organization and on the 11th house – through friends or elder brother.

If Rahu or Venus is also connected with it, the source may be foreigners.

To determine the source of wealth, the combined influence of lords of 2nd and 11th houses, on a house or houses, should be specified and then the characteristics of the houses thus influenced, will reveal the source of financial gains.

15.4 Sudden Gains

Sudden gains are possible through speculation, lottery, race, buried treasure and prizes and awards. We give below some of the combinations of sudden gains: -

1) If lord of 10th and 2nd combine in a *Kendra* (angle) or *Trikona* (trine).

2) If lords of 2nd and 1st, reckoned from the lord of 2nd, are in *Kendra* (angle).

3) If lords of 2nd and 11th are in a *Kendra*.

4) If benefics occupy 3rd, 6th, 10th, 11th houses from Moon.

5) If *Yogakaraka* planet is connected with the 5th house, success in speculation is assured, provided the 5th house is strong.

6) If Jupiter is strong and connected with the 5th house, as well as the 2nd house, success in speculation or gambling is achieved.

7) If lord of *lagna* is in the 11th, combined with the lord of 9th, and lord of 11th is in the 2nd, lottery *yoga* is formed.

8) If benefics are in 3rd, 5th, 7th and 11th houses.

9) If lords of 2nd, 9th, 11th are strong and free from the evil aspects of 6th and 8th lords. If lord of 1st or 2nd is in 10th, wealth from state is indicated.

In short, combinations between lords of the ascendant, the 11th, the 2nd, the 5th and 9th and 10th, generally, bring in sudden gains. If *Yogakaraka* or *Dhankaraka* (Jupiter) is combined with the lord of the 2nd and they occupy a favourable sign, a definite *Dhana yoga* is formed. The extent of wealth, however, depends on the strength of the *Yogakaraka* or *Dhankaraka*.

15.5 Windfall and Hidden Wealth

The 5th house is the house of speculation. Mars in the 5th house stimulates love for taking risk. If 5th house or its lord is weak and Jupiter is not strong, losses are in store for the native. Jupiter's association with the 5th brings in success. If lords of 9th and 11th combine in an angle or a trine, windfall is indicated.

For racing, 5th house and Jupiter should be strong. 2nd and 5th, and 1st and 11th houses should be exceptionally strong for sudden gains. Exchanges between lords of 1st and

2nd houses or between lords of 2nd and 11th houses give a sudden lift to the native's financial condition.

If the 4th house is occupied by the lord of the 11th and lord of 2nd and 4th are posited in the 9th, with strong benefic connection, hidden wealth buried in a house is indicated.

15.6 Economic Equations

Financial elevation, professional prosperity and progress, and enhancement and expansion of economical sphere are the foremost desires of individual natives, as well as all countries of the world. Therefore, financial aspect must be examined properly in the horoscopes. Apart from the judgment of the 11th and 2nd house, an extensive study of the horoscope, has to be done to evaluate the financial status of prosperity or poverty of a native.

The native is prosperous, only if the horoscope is strong. A strong ascendant, or the well fortified 11th or 2nd house, is not sufficient to produce enormous and everlasting wealth for the native. The 9th and 5th houses also play a vital role in making one exceptionally strong economically. It is an universal statement that the concerning houses must be well fortified and strong.

How is this examined; whether a particular house is well disposed and strong, or not? The house is strong, if it is well occupied by benefics, who are the lords of a quadrant or triangle. It becomes further strong, if the lord of the house is strongly placed in a quadrant or triangle. *Badhaka* elements and retrograde movements should also be taken into consideration for the judgment of the strength of the planets and houses.

The mutual exchange between the lords of the 2nd and 11th house makes one extremely rich. It is equally beneficial if the lord of the 2nd house joins the 11th lord, in either of the houses or the ascendant or the combination or exchange of the lords of the 2nd and 11th house is associated with the ascendant lord.

The strength of the 9th house is one of the important factors, not only for prosperity but also for power, property and pleasure. A well disposed and sufficiently strong 9th house elevates all the nativities accordingly.

The 5th house is 9th from the 9th and signifies unexpected gains through speculation, lottery, gambling, race course etc.

The 5th lord, if well disposed, with the 5th and ascendant lord, either in the 2nd or 11th house, one will gain much through speculation, shares, lottery etc. Mutual exchange of the lords of the 2nd and 5th house also signifies unearned wealth. If the concerning lords are adversely placed and ill disposed, the native is bound to lose wealth through speculation. Placement of a malefic in the 5th house, particularly Rahu, is very bad for share business.

Illustration : 15.10 (**DPS**) *Horoscope No.: 101*

Date of birth : 25.12.1958 Time of birth : 16:00:00 hrs
Place of birth : Kanpur Lat 26:27:00 N Long 80:19:00E
Ayanamsa : 23:17:08 Sidereal Time : 22:04:59

Pln	**Degree**	**Rasi**	**Nakshatra**	**Pad**
Asc	21:11:56	Tau	Rohini	4
Sun	9:50:49	Sag	Moola	3
Mon	1:27:06	Gem	Mrigshira	3
Mar	23:27:50	Ari	Bharani	4
Mer	18:09:36	Sco	Jyestha	1
Jup	29:27:13	Lib	Vishakha	3
Ven	20:30:42	Sag	Purvasadha	3
Sat (C)	5:24:48	Sag	Moola	2
Rah (R)	26:01:23	Vir	Chitra	1
Ket (R)	26:01:23	Pis	Revati	3

Lagna Chart

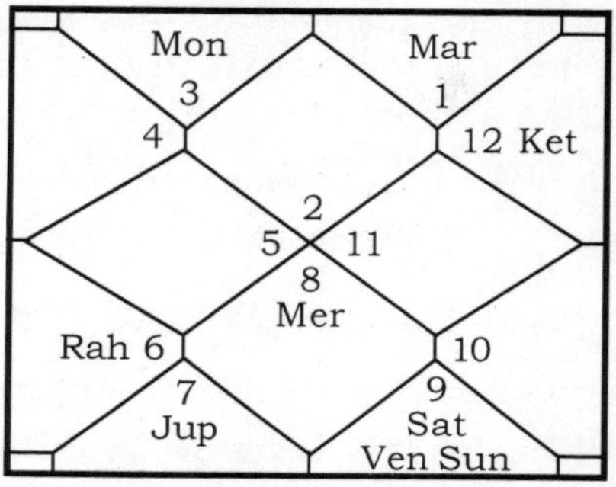

Navamsa Chart

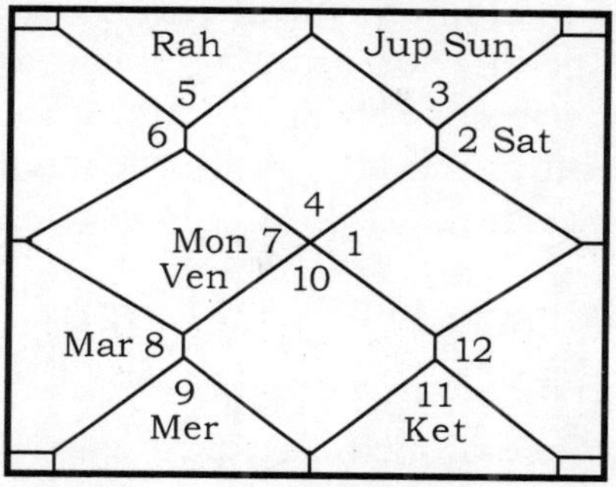

Balance of Vimshottari Dasa of **Mar 2Y 8M 25D**

The native is a highly qualified doctor of international fame. He works in U.S.A. In 2003 he lost 500 crore rupees (about 10 crore dollars) in shares. He lost everything in shares. He is able to meet both his ends with difficulty and has a very heavy loan to pay off.

He was born in Taurus ascendant with Rahu in the 5th house, under the adverse aspect of *Yogakaraka* Saturn from the 8th house. The lord of the 2nd and 5th house, Mercury, joins the 7th house, in sign Scorpio. Mercury is aspected by the 12th and 7th lord Mars. Thus, the 2nd and 5th lord Mercury, who falls in the sign of Mars, is aspected by Mars as well, which is an undoubtedly adverse combination indicating heavy loss of money owing to speculative dealings. Mercury obtains *navamsa* of Jupiter with mutual aspect of Jupiter. In fact, the 5th lord Mercury and the 11th lord Jupiter suffer mutual exchange of *navamsa* with mutual aspect. This combination can not be appreciated for speculative gains. The 9th house should also be examined for such matters as well as professional and financial prosperity. 9th and 10th lord *Yogakaraka* Saturn joins the 8th house and it is joined by inimical Sun. Both the luminaries, the Sun and the Moon, are under the aspect of inimical Saturn and Venus, identical to the 8th house. Saturn and Mars, both, have mutual aspect in *navamsa* as well. Moon is also adversely placed in inimical sign Gemini and Libra *navamsa*, with the formation of malefic

Kemadruma Yoga, identical to *Dhana bhava*. That is the astrological justification of loss of huge money through speculation, during the major period of Saturn and sub period of Venus and sub-sub period of Sun, Moon, Mars and Rahu; in spite of the presence of *Lagnadhi Yoga* in the birth chart.

Illustration : 15.11 (**HCG**) *Horoscope No.: 102*

Date of birth : 01.11.1945 Time of birth : 14:06:00 hrs
Place of birth : Lucknow Lat 26:50:00 N Long 80:54:00E
Ayanamsa : 23:05:43 Sidereal Time : 16:40:42

Pln	**Degree**	**Rasi**	**Nakshatra**	**Pad**
Asc	9:46:08	Aqu	Satabhisha	1
Sun	15:28:13	Lib	Swati	3
Mon	6:07:50	Vir	U Phalguni	3
Mar	3:40:36	Can	Pushya	1
Mer	3:12:59	Sco	Vishakha	4
Jup	21:21:28	Vir	Hasta	4
Ven	23:15:33	Vir	Hasta	4
Sat	1:46:54	Can	Punarvasu	4
Rah (R)	8:21:25	Gem	Ardra	1
Ket (R)	8:21:25	Sag	Moola	3

Lagna Chart

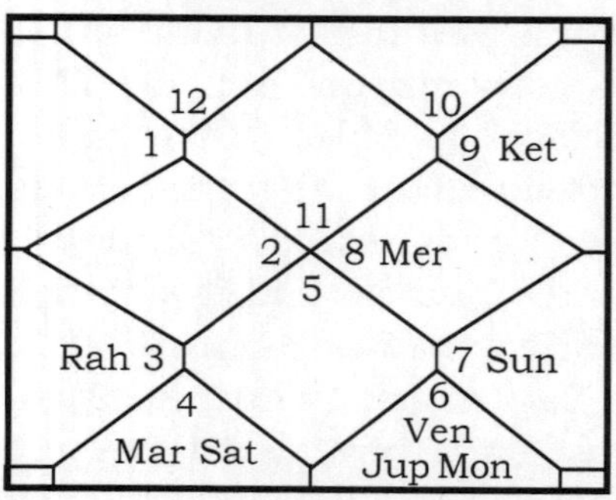

Navamsa Chart

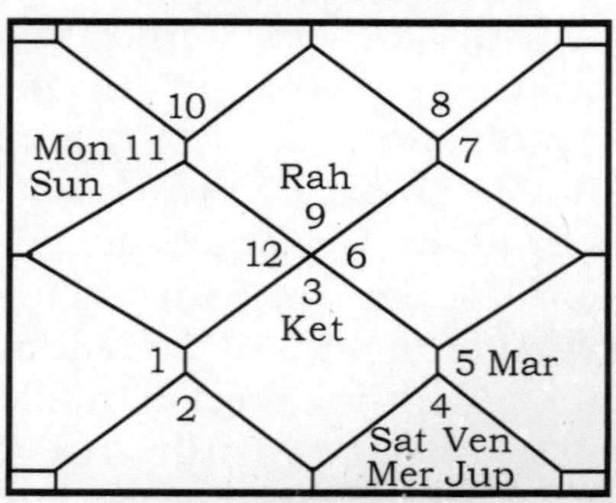

Balance of Vimshottari Dasa of **Sun 1Y 8M 27D**

The native did M. Sc. in physics and he was involved in various businesses from time to time. The presence of Rahu in the 5th house provoked him to do speculative activities and share marketing. Rahu in Gemini, in the 5th house, is adverse. With all other planets being placed on one side of Rahu-Ketu axis *'Kalsarpa Yoga'* in the horoscope is constituted.

The lord of the 5th house, Mercury, joins Scorpio in the 10th house and is placed under *Papakartari Yoga*. The 9th lord *Yogakaraka* Venus is placed in the 8th house, in debilitation. Here, Venus is associated with inimical Moon, and Jupiter, and it is also aspected by Saturn. Debilitated Sun in the 9th house is aspected by debilitated Mars. Ascendant lord Saturn is heavily afflicted due to inimical conjunction with Mars. *Dhanakaraka*, *Dhanadhipati* and *Labhadhipati* Jupiter is also afflicted due to inimical conjunction, as it occupies the inimical sign Virgo. Jupiter obtains the *navamsa* of exaltation but it is again associated with inimical Venus and Mercury. Thus, the ascendant and Saturn, the 9th lord Venus and 5th lord Mercury are all afflicted.

The native had a passion to deal in shares. At times he gained a lot, which inspired him to gradually invest all his wealth in share market. He lost his everything in share business. He, thereafter, faced a very difficult time. He was compelled by circumstances to leave Lucknow, which he loved most. Now at the age of sixty, he has no way out except indulging share business but his over confidence and passion did not allow him to follow astrological advice.

If the 5th and 2nd houses are well disposed and their lords occupy *Dhana bhava* or *Labha bhava*, there is sudden gain of money.

Illustration : 15.12 *Horoscope No.: 103*

Date of birth : 11.01.1964 Time of birth : 06:20:00 hrs

Place of birth : Lucknow Lat 26:50:00 N Long 80:54:00E

Ayanamsa : 23:20:59 Sidereal Time : 13:31:55

Pln	Degree	Rasi	Nakshatra	Pad
Asc	16:19:28	Sag	Purvasadha	1
Sun	26:28:04	Sag	Purvasadha	4
Mon	14:02:37	Sco	Anuradha	4
Mar (C)	4:54:30	Cap	Uttarasadha	3
Mer (R)	12:40:27	Sag	Moola	4
Jup	18:24:59	Pis	Revati	1
Ven	29:10:44	Cap	Dhanistha	2
Sat	28:07:13	Cap	Dhanistha	2
Rah	17:50:40	Gem	Ardra	4
Ket (C)	17:50:40	Sag	Purvasadha	2

Lagna Chart

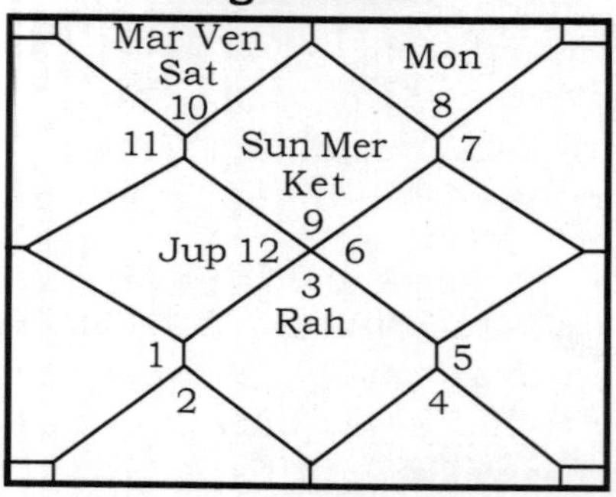

Navamsa Chart

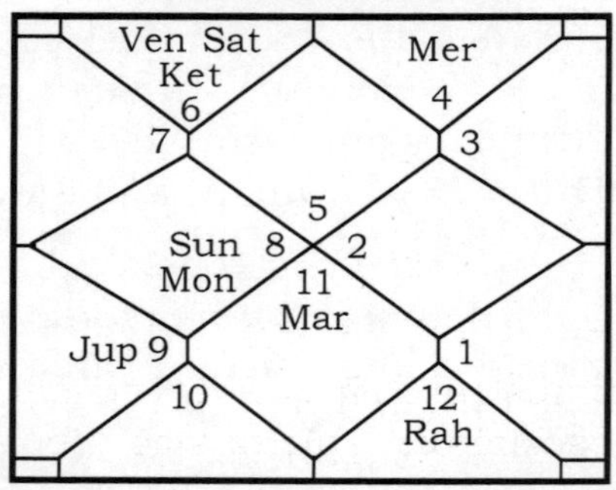

Balance of Vimshottari Dasa of **Sat 3Y 8M 25D**

The native is the wife of a car dealer and is quite prosperous. She won a car in lottery by spending nothing.

She was born in Sagittarius ascendant with the 9th lord Sun and 7th and 10th lord Mercury. This is a very encouraging combination of sudden gains. The lord of the 2nd house Saturn is conjoined with the 5th lord Mars and the 11th lord Venus, in the 2nd house itself. Thus, the lords of 11th, 2nd and 5th houses are placed together in the 2nd house, which is a powerful combination of unearned wealth. A strong 9th house is also very important, as in this case where 9th lord Sun occupies the ascendant, in a friendly sign Sagittarius. The ascendant lord Jupiter occupies the 4th house, identical to own sign Pisces, giving rise to *Hamsa Mahapurusha Rajyoga*, Jupiter obtains own *navamsa*. In *navamsa* chart, the lords of the 2nd Saturn, and that of 11th, Venus, are associated in a friendly *navamsa* of Virgo, in the 2nd house from *navamsa* ascendant. This is also a powerful combination for sudden gains through lottery, shares and gambling etc.

Thus, we can conclude that for the financial prosperity and a good income, not only the 11th & 2nd houses but the 5th & the 9th houses should also be examined, in addition to the 10th for profession. Mutual exchange between the lords of the 5th & the 9th houses, as also between 11th & 2nd, their conjunction in angle or trine, mutual aspect etc., as detailed earlier, are favourable for prosperity. *Dhankaraka* Jupiter should also be examined as also the strength of ascendant. Placement of 2nd & 11th lords in 6th, 8th or 12th, and similar inauspicious placement of 5th & 9th lords, along with the weak ascendant and Jupiter are not good for financial gains, accumulation or prosperity.

•

Chapter-16

Timing Promotions in Service

Dr. B.V. Raman clearly states, in his article on "Timing Events" in June 1981 issue of Astrological Magazine that it is very simple to find out the nature of events with the help of a horoscope but the toughest work in astrology is to time an event accurately and precisely. Practical utility of astrology is based on correct time of occurrence of events.

Promotion or an elevation is a very important aspect of life, for service class people. One always looks forward for improvement in professional career but this depends on the nature of job one is holding. Promotions are quite regular and timely in some cases but in certain cases it is delayed to the extent that the person is even superceded in the process.

If the effective *Kalsarpa Yoga* or *Kemadrum Yoga* is present and that has anything to do with the 10th, 9th, 6th house or the *lagna*, one has to face many obstacles in his progress, and the promotions also get delayed. Similarly, Saturn and Sun's combination or mutual aspect or exchange of houses, creates hurdles in promotion. This, in addition to the general principles for the delay or denial of promotions such as placement of lord of 10th in eighth or twelfth, or vice versa, combustion of the 10th lord, or conjunction of the 10th lord with evil planets and presence of malefic *yogas*, is of vital importance.

However, let us not go in for causes of delay and denial of promotion but confine us to the methods or principles to judge the time of promotions in service.

First, the *lagna* should be judged carefully. A strong *lagna* is a healthy sign for minimizing obstructions present in the horoscope, in the way of promotions. Afflictions of the 6th, 9th, and 10th houses and their lords cause delay and obstruction and also supercession.

In addition to the 10th and 9th houses, 6th house must also be referred for promotion, because it is 9th from the 10th and 10th from the 9th, which means one's fortune concerning his profession, which is shaped as promotion. Sixth house, in such cases, should be referred for professional elevation of the persons of salaried class.

In addition to the general principles of astrology, following rules should be applied for correct judgment of horoscope regarding the time of promotion:

1. Promotion takes place during the *Dasa-bhukti* of the lord of the tenth house or the planet occupying the tenth house or the one which aspects the tenth house. *Dasa bhukti* of the lord of the tenth house will surely promote the results of the tenth house, even if the lord is strongly placed in the eighth house or vice-versa.
2. Promotion may come in evidence during the *Dasa bhukti* of the lord of the ninth house or the planet occupying the ninth house or the one which aspects the ninth house.
3. Promotion may result in the *Dasa bhukti* of a *Yogakaraka* planet e.g. Mars for Cancer and Leo ascendants, and Saturn for Taurus and Libra ascendants. If a strong *Yogakaraka* planet is in evil house and benefic planets aspect him, then even that *Yogakaraka* planet can give promotion.
4. Promotion may also result in the *Dasa bhukti* of the lord of the sixth house or the planet occupying the sixth house or that aspect the sixth house, particularly when the sixth house has any connection with the ninth or the tenth house.
5. Promotion also takes place during the *Dasa bhukti* of malefic planets, favorably placed in the third or the eleventh house, receiving benefic aspects.

6. *Karaka* or significator of the tenth house is Mercury. Therefore, Mercury's *Dasa bhukti* also causes promotion, if any of the above conditions are satisfied.

More emphasis must be given to the *bhukti* lord. With the help of the above principles correct *Dasa bhukti* responsible for promotion may be known. To make the results more precise, transit details must also be kept handy for consideration.

However, at the moment, we will deal only with the *Dasa bhukti* that will cause promotion in services. The transiting planets improve or reduce the *dasa* results and help to make the time of event precise.

We will now explain the above principles with the help of certain examples.

Illustration : 16.1 (**BKS**) *Horoscope No.: 104*

Date of birth	: 20.10.1942	Time of birth :	07:30:00 hrs
Place of birth	: Kota	Lat 25:11:00 N	Long 75:58:00E
Ayanamsa	: 23:03:19	Sidereal Time :	7:55:10

Pln	**Degree**	**Rasi**	**Nakshatra**	**Pad**
Asc	2:53:49	Lib	Chitra	3
Sun	2:57:16	Lib	Chitra	3
Mon	12:33:36	Aqu	Satabhisha	2
Mar (C)	28:19:35	Vir	Chitra	2
Mer	17:32:32	Vir	Hasta	3
Jup	1:17:08	Can	Punarvasu	4
Ven (C)	26:00:01	Vir	Chitra	1
Sat (R)	18:54:56	Tau	Rohini	3
Rah	9:52:58	Leo	Magha	3
Ket	9:52:58	Aqu	Satabhisha	1

Lagna Chart

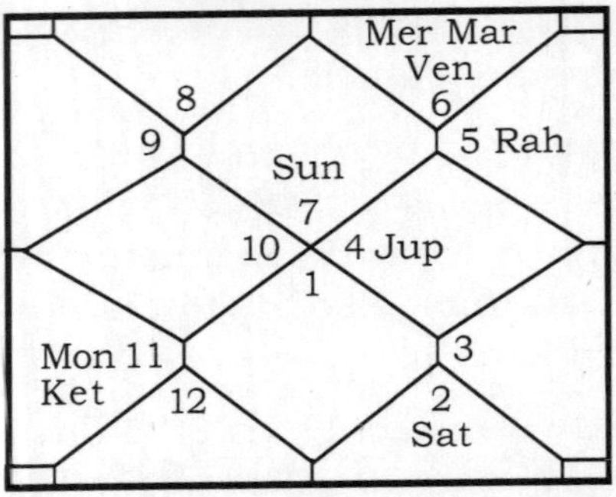

Navamsa Chart

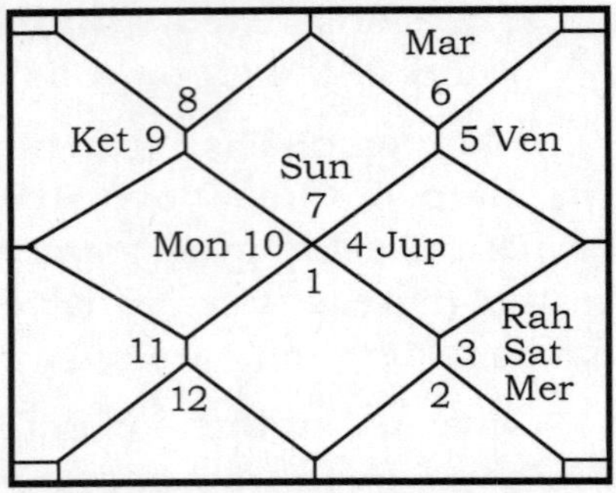

Balance of Vimshottari Dasa of **Rah 10Y 0M 16D**

Saturn is a *Yogakaraka* planet for Libra ascendant. Major period of Saturn lasted from 30.01.1968 to 30.01.1987. Mercury's *bhukti* was running from 30.02.1971 to 12.10.1973. Here, Mercury is the lord of the ninth house, is exalted and aspects the sixth. Therefore, Saturn's major period and Mercury's *bhukti* should cause promotion according to above rules. The promotion actually took place on 26.04.1973 as an Executive Engineer with change of place, because ninth lord Mercury is placed in the 12th. Another promotion took place in the month of September '86 in Jupiter's *bhukti*, which ran from 18.07.1984 to 30.01.1987, because Jupiter owns sixth and occupies tenth in the sign of its exaltation.

Presence of *Kemadrum yoga* and Saturn's aspect on the 10th house and on the lord of the 10th, Moon, caused some delay and disappointment in his progress.

Illustration : 16.2 (**RP**) *Horoscope No.: 105*

Date of birth : 25.09.1931 Time of birth : 09:44:00 hrs
Place of birth : Meerut Lat 29:00:00 N Long 77:42:00E
Ayanamsa : 22:54:11 Sidereal Time : 9:36:54

Pln	Degree	Rasi	Nakshatra	Pad
Asc	24:05:04	Lib	Vishakha	2
Sun	8:13:57	Vir	U Phalguni	4

Mon	20:22:42	Aqu	P Bhadrapad	1
Mar	12:22:16	Lib	Swati	2
Mer	21:19:12	Leo	P Phalguni	3
Jup	21:49:55	Can	Aslesa	2
Ven (C)	12:48:13	Vir	Hasta	1
Sat	23:45:10	Sag	Purvasadha	4
Rah (S)	12:34:48	Pis	U Bhadrapad	3
Ket (S)	12:34:48	Vir	Hasta	1

Lagna Chart

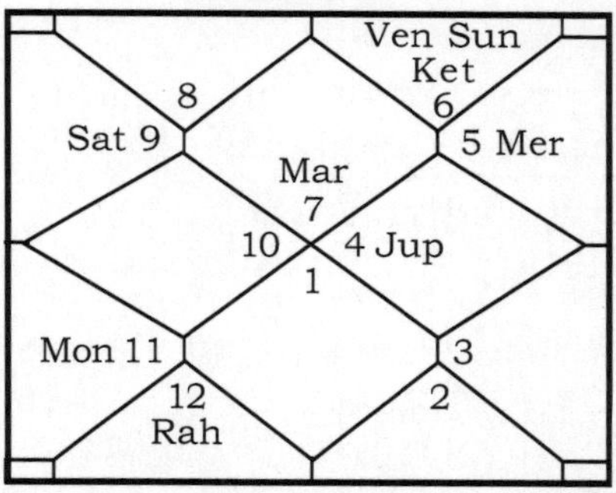

Navamsa Chart

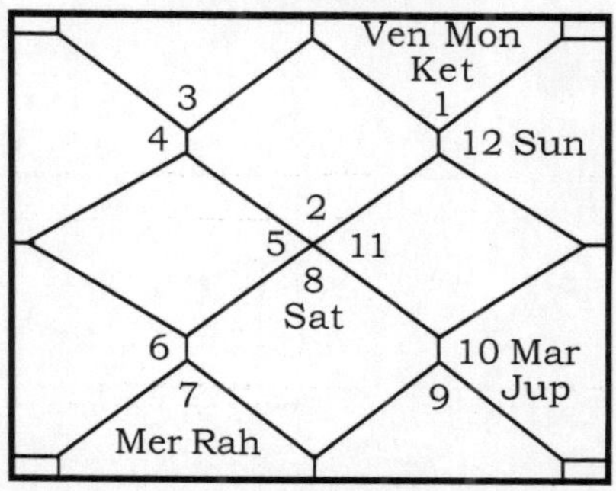

Balance of Vimshottari Dasa of **Jup 15Y 6M 16D**

The native was an engineer in the irrigation department of U.P. govt. Sub-period (*bhukti*) of Jupiter in the major period of Saturn lasted from 29.09.1963 to 11.04.1966. Major *dasa* lord Saturn happens to be a *Yogakaraka* for Libra ascendant. Jupiter, here, is the lord of 6th house and is placed in the 10th, in the sign of its exaltation. This was a splendid period for promotion, which had actually taken place on 14.11.1963.

Rahu's sub-period, in the major period of Mercury, ran from 08.10.1975 to 26.04.1978. Mercury is the lord of the 9th house and is placed in the 11th. *Bhukti* (sub-period) lord Rahu occupies the sixth house. Rahu is the dispositor of Jupiter and also receives the aspect of Jupiter. This again was a very good period for his elevation. His second promotion actually took place on 18.10.1975.

Here lord of the 10th house, Moon, receives the aspect of Saturn, which shows troubles in career.

Illustration : 16.3 (**VNM**) *Horoscope No.: 106*

Date of birth : 10.08.1937 Time of birth : 14:14:00 hrs
Place of birth : Muzaffarnagar Lat 29:28:00 N Long 77:42:00E
Ayanamsa : 22:59:25 Sidereal Time : 11:08:26

Pln	**Degree**	**Rasi**	**Nakshatra**	**Pad**
Asc	13:13:53	Sco	Anuradha	3
Sun	24:17:59	Can	Aslesa	3
Mon	12:13:06	Vir	Hasta	1
Mar	7:39:01	Sco	Anuradha	2
Mer	20:24:22	Leo	P Phalguni	3
Jup (R)	26:19:25	Sag	Purvasadha	4
Ven	13:13:01	Gem	Ardra	2
Sat (R)	11:39:41	Pis	U Bhadrapad	3
Rah (R)	19:47:47	Sco	Jyestha	1
Ket (R)	19:47:47	Tau	Rohini	3

Lagna Chart

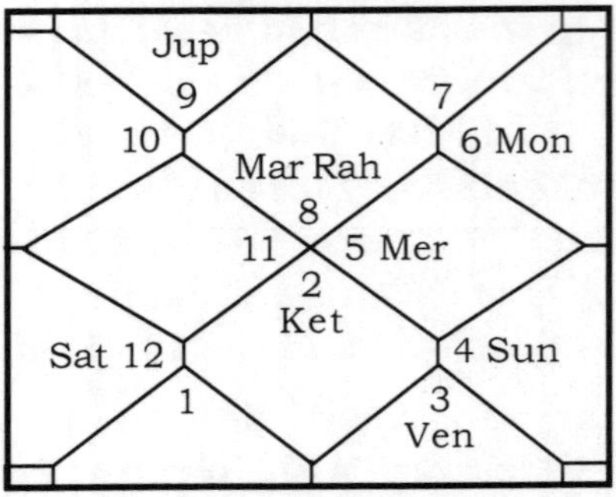

Navamsa Chart

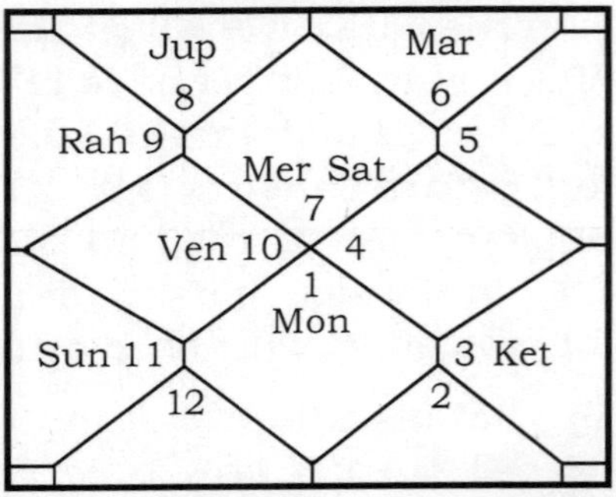

Balance of Vimshottari Dasa of **Mon 8Y 4M 1D**

The native retired as a chief engineer. He was running through Mercury's *bhukti* in the major period of Jupiter from 08.04.1975 to 14.11.1977. Maha*dasa* lord Jupiter is a benefic here and aspects the 6th and the 10th houses both. *Bhukti* lord Mercury is placed in the 10th house. Therefore, Mercury's *bhukti* caused promotion on 14.02.1977. Mercury is also a *Karaka* for tenth house.

Illustration : 16.4 (**GDA**) *Horoscope No.: 107*

Date of birth : 20.03.1930 Time of birth : 09:33:00 hrs
Place of birth : Etawah Lat 26:46:00 N Long 79:02:00E
Ayanamsa : 22:52:46 Sidereal Time : 21:07:00

Pln	**Degree**	**Rasi**	**Nakshatra**	**Pad**
Asc	6:41:26	Tau	Kritika	4
Sun	5:56:34	Pis	U Bhadrapad	1
Mon	13:46:34	Sco	Anuradha	4
Mar	9:24:25	Aqu	Satabhisha	1
Mer (C)	24:24:04	Aqu	P Bhadrapad	2
Jup	17:02:37	Tau	Rohini	3
Ven	16:06:38	Pis	U Bhadrapad	4
Sat	18:09:06	Sag	Purvasadha	2
Rah	10:19:26	Ari	Ashwini	4
Ket	10:19:26	Lib	Swati	2

Lagna Chart

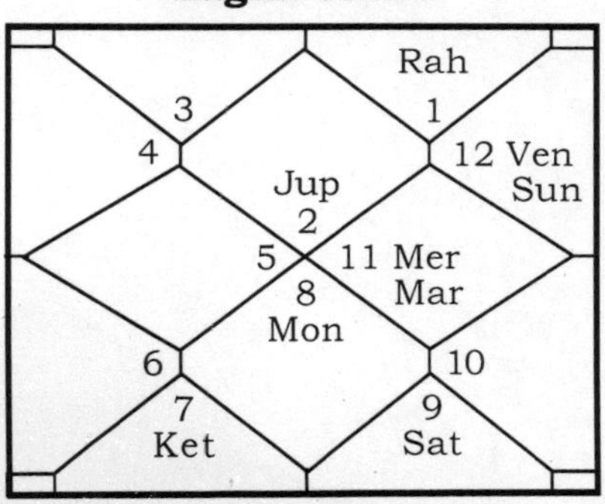

Navamsa Chart

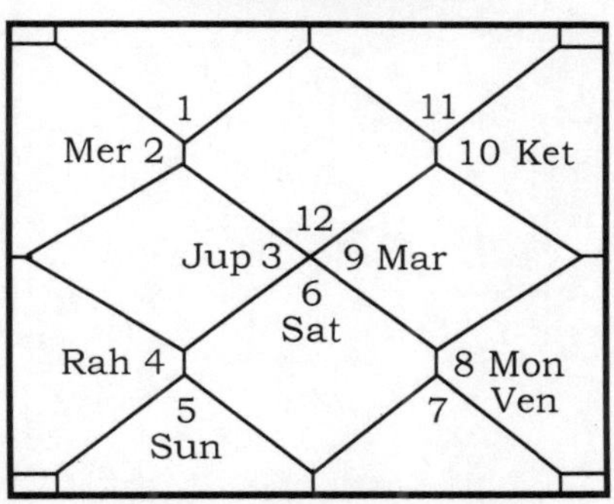

Balance of Vimshottari Dasa of **Sat 4Y 1M 13D**

The native was running through the *bhukti* of Saturn, in the major period of Venus, from 30.02.1964 to 30.04.1967. Maha*dasa* lord Venus owns sixth and occupies the sign of its exaltation in the 11th house. *Bhukti* lord Saturn is *Yogakaraka* for Taurus ascendant and Saturn also aspects the 10th house. The promotion of the native actually took place on 15th July 1966.

Illustration : 16.5 (**BBS**) *Horoscope No.: 108*

Date of birth : 29.01.1930 Time of birth : 12:35:00 hrs

Place of birth : Raibareilly Lat 26:46:00 N Long 79:02:00E

Ayanamsa : 22:52:41 Sidereal Time : 20:52:23

Pln	**Degree**	**Rasi**	**Nakshatra**	**Pad**
Asc	2:38:30	Tau	Kritika	2
Sun	15:47:14	Cap	Sravna	2
Mon (C)	10:19:49	Cap	Sravna	1
Mar (C)	0:35:02	Cap	Uttarasadha	2
Mer (R)	0:44:53	Cap	Uttarasadha	2
Jup (R)	13:28:47	Tau	Rohini	2
Ven (D)	13:45:19	Cap	Sravna	2
Sat	14:02:39	Sag	Purvasadha	1
Rah (R)	14:32:18	Ari	Bharani	1
Ket (R)	14:32:18	Lib	Swati	3

Lagna Chart

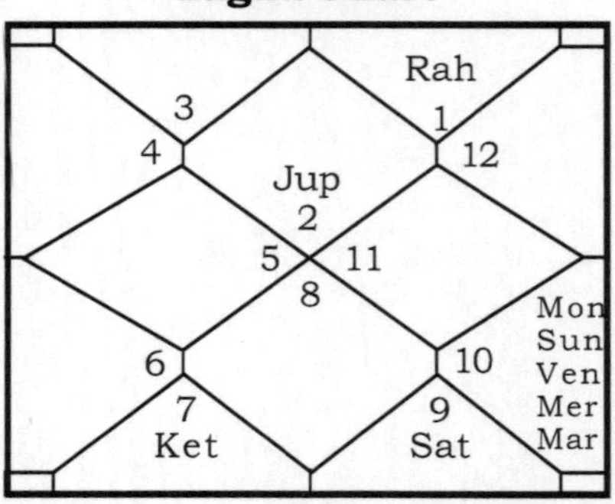

Navamsa Chart

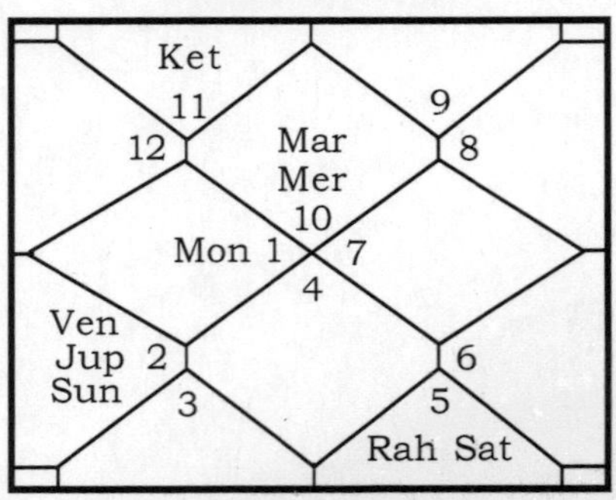

Balance of Vimshottari Dasa of **Mon 9Y 9M 0D**

Saturn's major period started from 30.10.1980 and Saturn's sub-period ran till 03.11.1983. Saturn is a *Yogakaraka* planet for Taurus lagna, therefore Saturn's *dasa bhukti* should give promotion, which in fact took place on 05.04.1982 when the native was elevated as Chief Engineer. His previous promotion had taken place in Venus sub-period of Jupiter's major period. Here, Venus is the lord of sixth house and occupies the ninth house.

Illustration : 16.6 (**MKG**) *Horoscope No.: 109*

Date of birth : 20.09.1938 Time of birth : 10:35:00 hrs
Place of birth : Allahabad Lat 25:27:00 N Long 81:50:00E
Ayanamsa : 23:00:17 Sidereal Time : 10:26:04

Pln	**Degree**	**Rasi**	**Nakshatra**	**Pad**
Asc	5:49:04	Sco	Anuradha	1
Sun	3:34:23	Vir	U Phalguni	3
Mon	14:37:48	Can	Pushya	4
Mar	14:50:11	Leo	P Phalguni	1
Mer	17:47:39	Leo	P Phalguni	2
Jup (R)	0:44:57	Aqu	Dhanistha	3
Ven	19:27:16	Lib	Swati	4
Sat (R)	22:59:48	Pis	Revati	2
Rah (R)	26:15:13	Lib	Vishakha	2
Ket (R)	26:15:13	Ari	Bharani	4

Lagna Chart

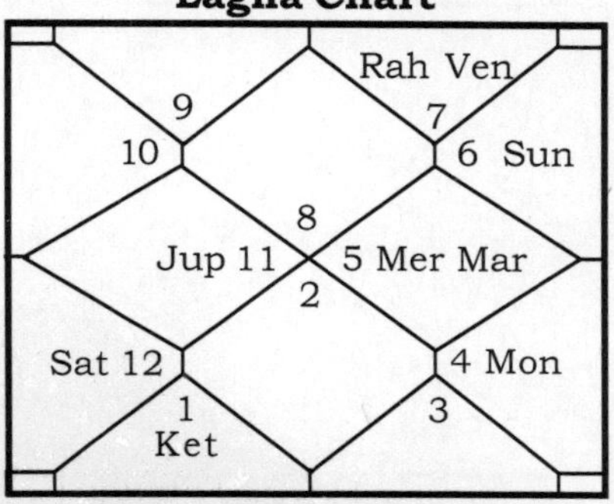

Navamsa Chart

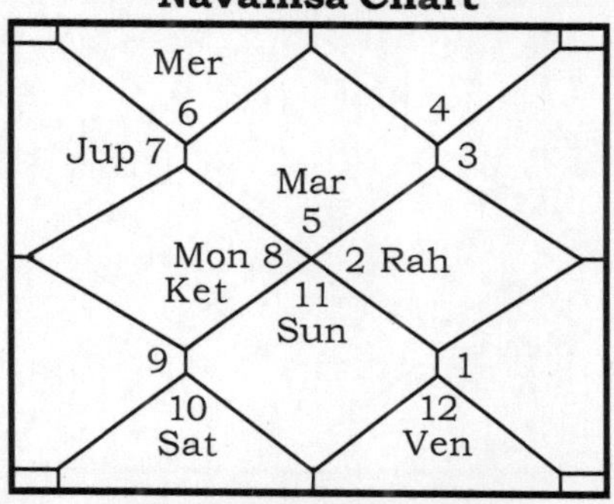

Balance of Vimshottari Dasa of **Sat 2Y 10M 25D**

Major period of Venus and Mercury's *bhukti* runs from 11.08.1981 to 11.06.1984. Major *dasa* lord Venus aspects the sixth house and *bhukti* lord Mercury is placed in the tenth. Both *Dasa* and *Bhukti* lords receive the aspect of Jupiter. This period of Mercury's *bhukti* in Venus is, therefore, a good period for promotion. The native was promoted as an Executive Engineer on 26.05.1982.

Illustration : 16.7 *Horoscope No.: 110*

Date of birth : 26.08.1941 Time of birth : 22:03:00 hrs
Place of birth : Bulandshahar Lat 28:30:00 N Long 77:49:00E
Ayanamsa : 23:02:30 Sidereal Time : 20:02:23

Pln	Degree	Rasi	Nakshatra	Pad
Asc	18:32:30	Ari	Bharani	2
Sun	9:59:04	Leo	Magha	3
Mon	1:25:40	Lib	Chitra	3
Mar	29:48:54	Pis	Revati	4
Mer (C)	17:23:31	Leo	P Phalguni	2
Jup	25:18:50	Tau	Mrigshira	1
Ven	13:45:36	Vir	Hasta	2
Sat	5:18:21	Tau	Kritika	3
Rah	29:47:59	Leo	U Phalguni	1
Ket	29:47:59	Aqu	P Bhadrapad	3

Lagna Chart

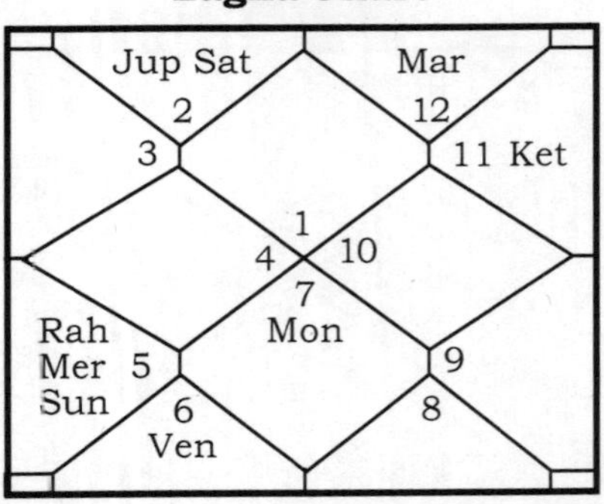

Navamsa Chart

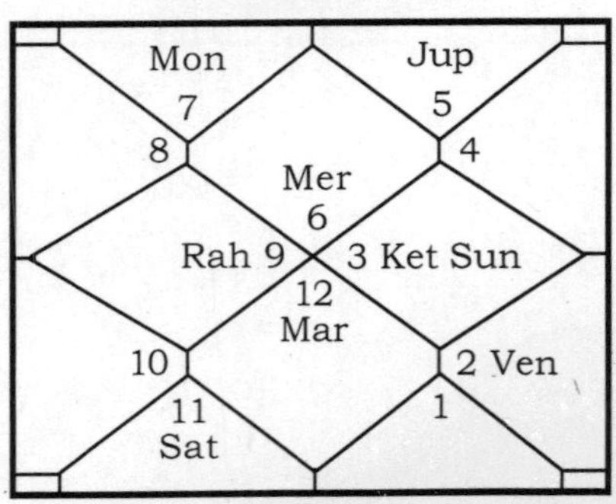

Balance of Vimshottari Dasa of **Mar 2Y 9M 0D**

This is the birth chart of a senior faculty member of Geology department of Lucknow University.

He was running through Jupiter's *Mahadasa* and Rahu's *bhukti* from 01.01.1976 to 25.05.1978. Jupiter is the lord of 9th house and is favorably placed in the 11th house receiving the benefic aspect of *Karaka* and sixth lord Mercury. *Bhukti* lord Rahu, who is placed inn the 6th house, is also a dispositor of *Karaka* Mercury. Thus, Rahu's *bhukti* in Jupiter's *Mahadasa* resulted in his promotion in December 1977, as reader in the department.

Illustration : 16.8 (**SKM**) *Horoscope No.: 111*

Date of birth : 02.05.1948 Time of birth : 00:27:00 hrs
Place of birth : Lucknow Lat 26:50:00 N Long 80:54:00E
Ayanamsa : 23:07:54 Sidereal Time : 14:59:02

Pln	**Degree**	**Rasi**	**Nakshatra**	**Pad**
Asc	8:55:37	Cap	Uttarasadha	4
Sun	18:09:19	Ari	Bharani	2
Mon	24:35:13	Cap	Dhanistha	1
Mar	0:41:34	Leo	Magha	1
Mer (C)	21:11:12	Ari	Bharani	3
Jup (R)	5:23:29	Sag	Moola	2
Ven	2:35:12	Gem	Mrigshira	3
Sat	22:48:55	Can	Aslesa	2
Rah (R/D)	20:51:45	Ari	Bharani	3
Ket (R)	20:51:45	Lib	Vishakha	1

Lagna Chart

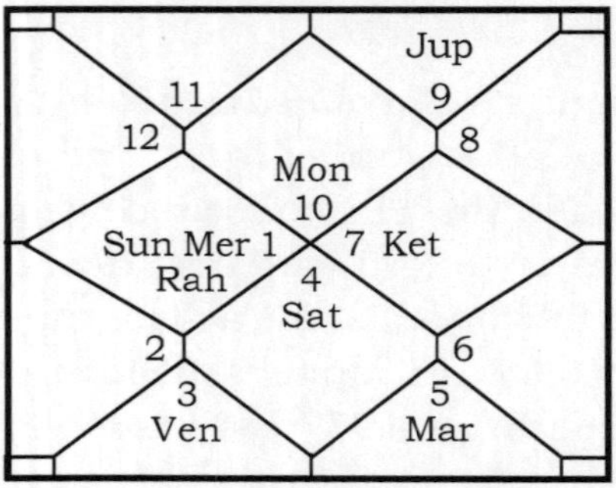

Navamsa Chart

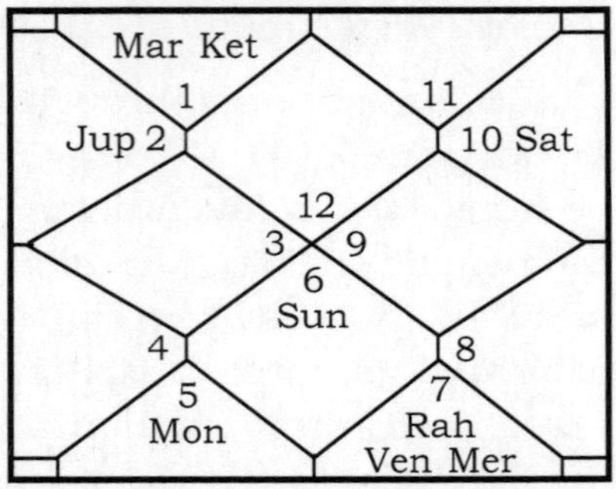

Balance of Vimshottari Dasa of **Mar 6Y 4M 3D**

The native was passing through sub-period of Venus in the major period of Jupiter from 17.07.1980 to 17.03.1983. Major period lord, Jupiter, aspects the 6th house. Sub-period lord, Venus, is *Yogakaraka* for Capricorn ascendant and is placed in the 6th house, as an owner of the 10th house. This caused his promotion on 31.08.1981.

Illustration : 16.9 *Horoscope No.: 112*

Date of birth : 10.04.1920 Time of birth : 06:44:00 hrs

Place of birth : Ajmer Lat 26:29:00 N Long 74:40:00E

Ayanamsa : 22:44:49 Sidereal Time : 19:24:32

Pln	**Degree**	**Rasi**	**Nakshatra**	**Pad**
Asc	5:59:41	Ari	Ashwini	2
Sun	27:07:23	Pis	Revati	4
Mon	10:36:52	Sag	Moola	4
Mar (R)	12:09:10	Lib	Swati	2
Mer	1:02:44	Pis	P Bhadrapad	4
Jup	15:24:45	Can	Pushya	4
Ven	4:45:08	Pis	U Bhadrapad	1
Sat (R)	12:41:27	Leo	Magha	4
Rah	23:03:09	Lib	Vishakha	1
Ket	23:03:09	Ari	Bharani	3

Lagna Chart

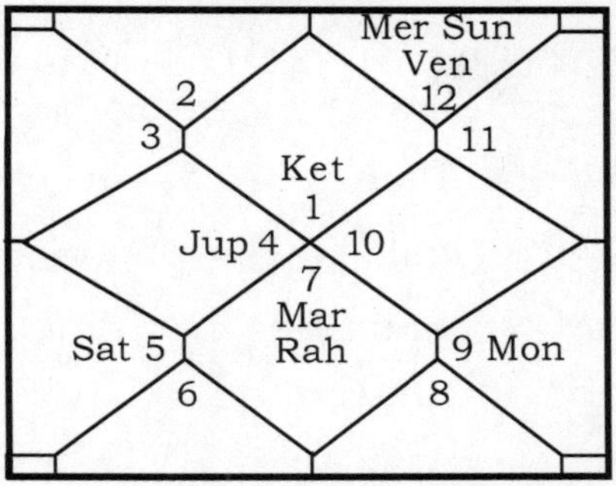

Navamsa Chart

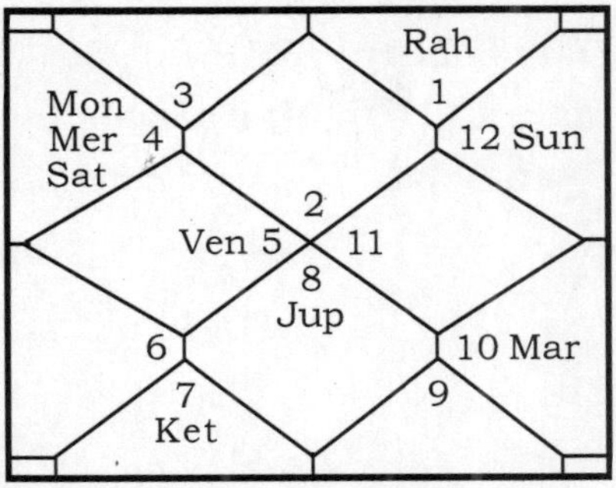

Balance of Vimshottari Dasa of **Ket 1Y 5M 3D**

He was promoted as Executive Engineer on 05.02.1944 during the sub-period of Saturn, in the major period of Venus. Major *Dasa* lord Venus is exalted and aspects the 6th house, whereas the sub-period lord Saturn owns the tenth.

His promotion as Superintending Engineer took place on 23.07.1962 during the major period of Moon and sub-period of Saturn. Moon, here, is creating a splendid *Bhagya Yoga,* as the lord of 4th, Moon, is placed in the 9th house. Jupiter is exalted in 4th. Sub-period lord Saturn owns tenth and is placed in a triangle.

Promotion to Deputy Chief Engineer happened on 01.06.1988 during Mars-Jupiter *Dasa bhukti.* Mars aspects the 10th house. Exalted 9th lord Jupiter also aspects the 10th.

Promotion to post of Chief Engineer occurred on 27.05.1973 during *Dasa bhukti* of Mars-Moon, which ran from 13.05.1973 to 13.12.1973. Mars aspects the 10th house and Moon is placed in the 9th.

Rahu's *Mahadasa* and Jupiter's *bhukti* elevated him to top most post in UPSEB on 01.02.1978 as its Chairman. Jupiter is the lord of the 9th house, occupies the 4th house in the sign of its exaltation and aspects the 10th house.

All these promotions of the native have taken place according to the principles mentioned above.

Illustration : 16.10 (**MM**) *Horoscope No.: 113*

Date of birth : 28.11.1934 Time of birth : 07:05:00 hrs
Place of birth : Hegarwal Lat 26:29:00 N Long 74:40:00E
Ayanamsa : 22:57:05 Sidereal Time : 10:58:44

Pln	**Degree**	**Rasi**	**Nakshatra**	**Pad**
Asc	12:29:50	Sco	Anuradha	3
Sun	12:11:00	Sco	Anuradha	3
Mon	29:31:25	Can	Aslesa	4
Mar	0:09:04	Vir	U Phalguni	2
Mer	24:51:42	Lib	Vishakha	2
Jup	17:23:00	Lib	Swati	4
Ven (D)	14:24:40	Sco	Anuradha	4
Sat	29:26:03	Cap	Dhanistha	2
Rah	9:52:50	Cap	Uttarasadha	4
Ket	9:52:50	Can	Pushya	2

Lagna Chart

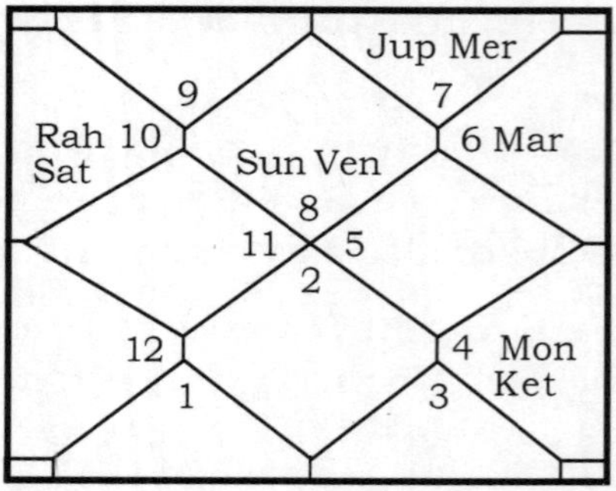

Navamsa Chart

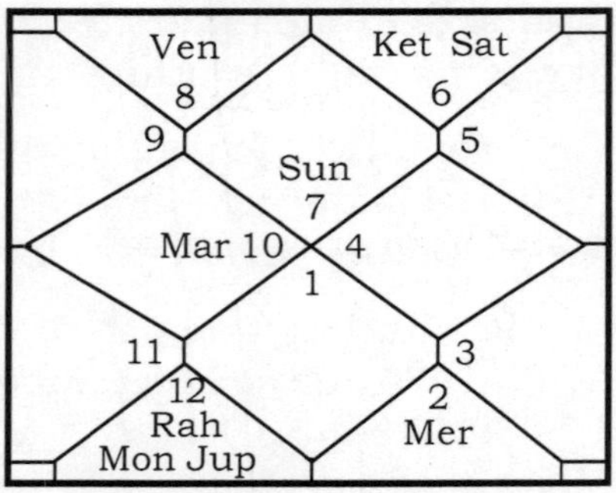

Balance of Vimshottari Dasa of **Mer 0Y 7M 8D**

The native was promoted as Superintending Engineer during the sub-period of Mercury (*Karaka*), in the major period of Moon. Sub-period lord aspects the 6th house, while major period lord Moon owns the 9th and occupies the 10th house. The promotion came in evidence on 25.08.1975.

Illustration : 16.11 (**GPS**) *Horoscope No.: 114*

Date of birth : 27.12.1927 Time of birth : 22:10:00 hrs
Place of birth : Varanasi Lat 26:50:00 N Long 80:54:00E
Ayanamsa : 22:50:48 Sidereal Time : 4:24:17

Pln	**Degree**	**Rasi**	**Nakshatra**	**Pad**
Asc	15:50:39	Leo	P Phalguni	1
Sun	12:05:40	Sag	Moola	4
Mon	24:04:12	Cap	Dhanistha	1
Mar	20:52:04	Sco	Jyestha	2
Mer (C)	4:59:35	Sag	Moola	2
Jup	3:08:26	Pis	P Bhadrapad	4
Ven	28:34:43	Lib	Vishakha	3
Sat	20:10:08	Sco	Jyestha	2
Rah (R)	25:47:16	Tau	Mrigshira	1
Ket (R)	25:47:16	Sco	Jyestha	3

Lagna Chart

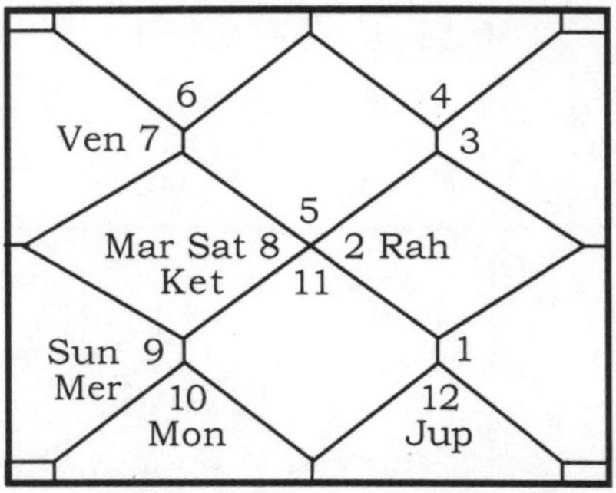

Navamsa Chart

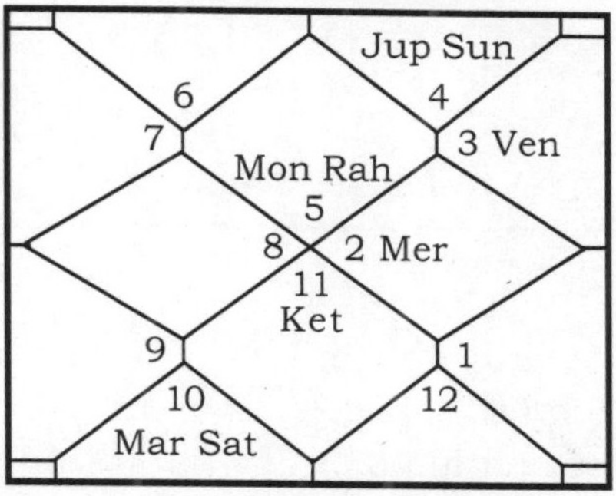

Balance of Vimshottari Dasa of **Mar 6Y 7M 10D**

Mars' sub-period, in Saturn's major period, lasts from 11.02.1981 to 20.03.1982. Mars is a *Yogakaraka* and aspects the 10th house but is severely afflicted due to conjunction with Saturn. His promotion was very much expected from the very beginning of the sub-period of Mars but, due to affliction, it was delayed and ultimately took place in Rahu's sub-period in Saturn's major period, which ran from 20.03.1982 to 26.01.1985. Sub-period lord Rahu is placed in the 10th house. Major period lord, Saturn, owns 6th and aspects the 10th house.

Illustration : 16.12 **(VPK)** *Horoscope No.: 115*

Date of birth : 29.02.1936 Time of birth : 02:05:40 hrs
Place of birth : Hoshiarpur Lat 31:30:00 N Long 75:59:00E
Ayanamsa : 22:58:13 Sidereal Time : 12:09:33

Pln	**Degree**	**Rasi**	**Nakshatra**	**Pad**
Asc	25:24:06	Sco	Jyestha	3
Sun	16:07:51	Aqu	Satabhisha	3
Mon	9:22:05	Tau	Kritika	4
Mar	12:09:21	Pis	U Bhadrapad	3
Mer	19:25:27	Cap	Sravna	3
Jup	28:51:13	Sco	Jyestha	4
Ven	15:13:10	Cap	Sravna	2
Sat (C)	19:23:33	Aqu	Satabhisha	4
Rah (R)	17:54:24	Sag	Purvasadha	2
Ket (R)	17:54:24	Gem	Ardra	4

Lagna Chart

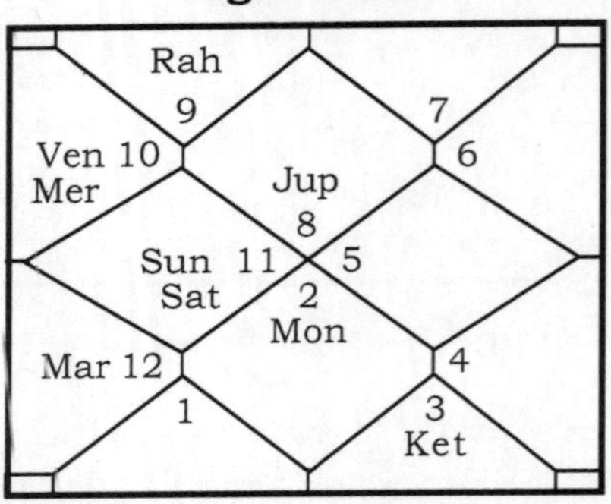

Navamsa Chart

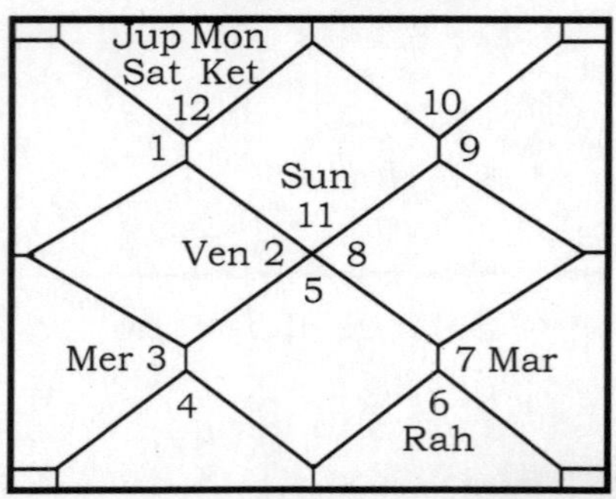

Balance of Vimshottari Dasa of **Sun 0Y 3M 12D**

Sun's sub-period in the major period of Rahu operated from 27.12.1967 to 21.11.1968. Here, Rahu aspects the 6th house and the 10th lord Sun, who is also the *bhukti* lord, aspects the 10th house. This resulted in his promotion to the post of Executive Engineer on 07.11.1968.

Venus *bhukti* in Jupiter runs from 21.04.1978 to 21.11.1980. Jupiter aspects the 9th house, while *bhukti* lord Venus is posited in 3rd house. Therefore, his promotion to superintending engineer came on 15.07.1978 during *Dasa bhukti* of Jupiter Venus. Due to conjunction of Sun and Saturn here the native had to face several difficulties in his promotion.

These examples confirm that apart from ninth and tenth house, sixth house is also equally important for finding out the time of promotion. *Karaka* of the tenth house, Mercury, should also be given due weightage, especially if Mercury has anything to do with the 6th, 9th or 10th house. Aspect of strong Mercury on the 6th house from 12th usually results into promotion, but this factor should be judged very carefully. In this way, we can find out the probable *Dasa bhukti* in which promotion should take place. Thereafter, we can proceed further to find out the time more precisely with the help of transits on the basis of principles given by Dr. B. V. Raman from time to time.

●

CHAPTER-17

Timing Occupation and Results of the Tenth House

Timing is most valuable aspect of any event of life. It is not enough to foresee the happening, until unless the time of the event or happening is known to the native. The tenth house is mainly dealt for one's occupation. It is important to know, when one will be able to secure the suitable occupation. One must have thorough knowledge of the timing events. The events with regard to occupation, such as securing job, professional prosperity, promotion, demotion, change of job, transfer from one place to another, suspension, extension or reversion etc. depend on the nature of major period and sub-period lords. Transiting planets should also be taken into consideration for the precise observation and prediction. We do not intend to deal with *Dasa-Bhukti* and transit results here, as it is quite a long and separate subject, which certainly needs a separate volume of the same size.

Dr. B.V. Raman has spelt out some valuable rules, for the examination of the birth-chart, for the judgement of occupation and its various aspects. According to him one should consider the following:

(a) Lord of the tenth house

(b) planet or planets aspecting the tenth house,

(c) planet or planets posited in the tenth house,

(d) planets aspecting the lord of the tenth house,

(e) planet or planets in association with the lord of the tenth house,

(f) the tenth lord from the Moon.

These factors may influence the tenth house, either as lords of the main periods or as lords of the sub-periods.

(1) The sub-periods of planets capable of influencing the tenth house in the major periods of planets, which are also capable of influencing the tenth house, produce results par excellence, pertaining to the tenth house.

(2) The sub-periods of planets, associated with the tenth house, in the major periods of planets, which are not related to the tenth house, produce results pertaining to the tenth house only to a limited extent.

(3) Similarly, the sub-periods of planets, that are not related to the tenth house, in the major periods of planets associated with the tenth house, will produce effects, pertaining to the tenth house, only to a small extent.

17.1 Events regarding occupation during the *Dasa Bhukti* of all Nine Planets

The lordship, aspects, location and the general strength of a planet capable of influencing the tenth house, determine the nature of results the planet produces in its *Dasa*. In general, the following results, relating to the tenth house, are likely in the *Dasas* and *Bhuktis* of different planets.

The Sun: Acquisition of wealth and learning; Health gains, vitality; founds institutions and gets a high position; Domestic happiness and prosperity of sons; succeeds in military career and political ambitions.

The Moon: Becomes passionate and adulterous; suffers mental unrest; a trustee of some religious or social institution; Gives away money in charity; Gets many friends; acquires health, wealth and comforts; if in unfriendly sign, death or illness to mother and danger from swindlers.

Mars: Acquires wealth and fame; Prospers in agriculture and gets good profits in business; Gets adoration of relations; Gains energy and clarity of thinking; If a *Yogakaraka*, happiness and success during the entire period; Gains through fine arts and increased income from lands.

Mercury: Gains academic distinction and recognition; Enjoys fortune of a high order; Eye-sight deteriorates; Indulges in charity and noble deeds; Succeeds in trade; religious activity and spiritual evolution.

Jupiter: Becomes virtuous; Acquires wealth and conveyances; Birth of issues; Prospers in agriculture.

Venus: Earns name, money and fame through law; Enjoys social life; Education suffers; acts in accordance with scriptures; doing his duty.

Saturn: Goes on pilgrimages; Suffers from gastric complaints; Meets with success in a sensational way; Goes to foreign countries; If a malefic by lordship and occupation, a very bad period in life.

Rahu: Involvement with undesirable women; Becomes a creative writer or artist; General prosperity; if Rahu is ill-disposed, mental derangement and affection.

Ketu: Does highly intelligent work; becomes spiritual and works for the poorer classes; Travels widely; Destruction of dear lives; properties and self-respect.

17.2 *Dasa Bhukti* Principles

Dasa Bhukti results may require a voluminous book, if explained fully and properly. We will deal with the prominent principles of *Dasa Bhukti* with regard to the matters of the tenth house, as mentioned in various classical works. We will also try to illustrate a few important principles of other concerning houses with regard to professional income i.e. source of income.

यद्यस्येक्षणयोगसंभवफलं भावेशयोगोरवं ।
भावेशैरपि भावगैरपि फलं वाच्यं दशायमिह ।।

Meaning, consider planets placed in the tenth house, the lord of the tenth house, planets associated with these, aspecting these and consider their *Dasa-Bhukthi* periods.

यत्कार्यमारब्धमुपैत्यनेन तस्यैव सिद्धिं सुखजीवनञ्च।
कीर्तिं प्रतिष्ठां कुशलप्रवृत्तिं मानोन्नतिं कर्मपतेर्दशायाम्।।

Meaning, during the *Dasa* of the lord of the tenth house, the person concerned will successfully complete any undertaking commenced by him. He will lead a happy life. He becomes famous and gets a permanent position. He commands great respect. All the good results are to be understood, when the planet is strong and has benefic aspects and influence of benefics. Otherwise, results will be different.

The lord of the second house, the planets placed in the second house, planets associated with the lord of second house, have also to be considered. Also, we should consider planets aspecting these. All these, in their periods and sub-periods, can give wealth.

लाभेशानतर्दशाकाले योगहीनो भवेद्ध्रुवम्।।

Meaning, in the sub-period of the lord of the eleventh house, one will not get any *yoga's* result. This is certain.

कर्मलग्नाधिनेतारावनयोन्याश्रयसंस्थितौ ।
राजयोगाविति प्रोक्तं विख्यातो विजयी भवेत्।।

Meaning, if the lords of the tenth and first house exchange houses, it causes *Rajayoga*. One becomes famous and attains much success.

स्वदशायां त्रिकोणेशभुक्तौ केन्द्रपतिः शुभम्।
दिशेत् सोऽपि तथा नोचेदसम्बन्धेन पापकृत्।।

Meaning, in the *dasa* of the lord of a *kendra*, the sub-period of the lord of a *trikona*, produces good results. If the *kendra* lord is not a malefic, the sub-period of the *kendra* lord, in the *dasa* of a *trikona* lord, produces good results.

राज्यलाभाधिपत्योश्च सम्बन्धो यदि विद्यते।
राज्येशदाये सम्प्राप्ते समयोग उदीरितः।।

तथा शुभस्थानगमानपस्य दशा हि मानार्थ सुखप्रदा स्यात्।
दशा नृणां सौख्यकरी सदैव सुखेशयुक्तस्य च मानपस्य।।

Meaning, the period of the lord of the tenth house, placed in the ninth house, will give honours, wealth and happiness. The *dasa* of the lord of the tenth house, associated with the lord of the fourth, produces happiness to people.

सपञ्चमेश लग्नेश दशा राज्यप्रदायिनी।
तथा धर्मपयुक्तस्य लग्नपस्य दशा मता।।

Meaning, the *dasa* of the lord of the *lagna*, associated with the lord of the fifth house, gives kingdom (good profession etc.). Similarly, the period of the lord of ascendant, combined with the lord of the ninth house, is also good.

सुखेशो मानभावस्थो मानेशः सुखराशिगः।
तयोर्दशां शुपामाहु ज्यौतिश्शास्त्रविदो जनाः।।

Meaning, if the lord of the fourth house is placed in the tenth house or if the lord of the tenth house is placed in the fourth house, their periods will be good, so the people learned in astrology say.

ताभ्यां युक्तस्य खेटस्य दृष्टियुक्तस्य चैतयोः।
राज्यप्रदां दशाम्प्राहुर्विद्वांसो दैवचिन्तकाः।।

Meaning, the *dasa* of the planet associated with the lord of the fifth house and the tenth house, or aspected by these, can also give a kingdom (good profession), so say the learned astrologers.

पञ्चमेशेन युक्तस्य मानेशस्य दशा शुभा।
सुखेशसहितस्यापि धर्मेशस्य दशा शुभा।।

Meaning, the *dasa* of the lord of tenth house, associated with the lord of the fifth house is good. The period of the lord of the ninth house, associated with the lord of the fourth house, will be very happy.

वाहनस्थानसंयुक्तमन्त्रनाथदशा शुभा।
सुखराशिस्थकर्मेशदशा राज्यप्रदायिनी।

Meaning, the *dasa* of the lord of the fifth house, placed in the fourth house, will be good. The *dasa* of the lord of the tenth house, placed in the fourth house will give a kingdom (good profession) and income.

17.3 Yogas proclaimed by Parasara

Sage *Parasara* is considered to be the father of Hindu Astrology. Principles propounded by him are mostly infallible and have stood the test of time.

सर्वे त्रिकोणनेतारो ग्रहाः शुभफलाः स्मृताः।

(*Brihat Parashara Horashasta*)

1. All the lords of *trikonas*, whether malefic or benefic, do well in respect of wealth.
2. If the lord of *lagna* is strong, in its period it gives much prosperity.

उपर्युपर्यभ्युदयाभिवृद्धिः प्राप्नोति बालेन्दुवदेष जातः।

(*Brihat Parashara Horashasta*)

This is because the ascendant lord is very auspicious. The ascendant can be reckoned as a *Trikona* and a *Kendra*.

3. Lords of third, sixth and eleventh give evil results.
4. Planets owning a *kendra* and a *trikona* become *Yogakarakas*. Their periods and sub-periods are very auspicious.

लक्ष्मीस्थानं त्रिकोणाख्यं विष्णुस्थानं तु केन्द्रकम्।
तयोस्सम्बन्धमात्रेण चक्रवर्ती भवेन्नरः।।

(*Brihat Parashara Horashasta*)

5. The *trikona* is a house of *Lakshmi* (wealth). The *kendra* is a house of Vishnu (lordship). A connection between